TWICE~TOLD TALES

TWICE~TOLD TALES

AN ANTHOLOGY OF SHORT FICTION

GERARD A. BARKER

Queens College of the
City University of New York

HOUGHTON MIFFLIN COMPANY BOSTON
Dallas Geneva, Ill. Hopewell, N.J. Palo Alto London

Cover photograph by Michael Malysko

Cover photograph Furnishings and Location by Roche-Bobois, 133 Lewis Wharf, Boston, Massachusetts

Printed in the U.S.A.

Library of Congress Catalog Card Number: 78–69561

ISBN: 0–395–26635–1

For Ann, Madeleine, and Derek

CONTENTS

STORIES FOR COMPARISON

STORIES FOR INDIVIDUAL STUDY

PREFACE

The first part of this anthology, "Twice-Told Tales," consists of either two versions of a story by the same author or pairs of stories by different authors that show striking similarities because one tale is a deliberate or coincidental variation of the other. Such an arrangement seems pedagogically valuable for several reasons: (1) If exposed to two versions, the inexperienced reader who does not know what to look for in a story will be likely to notice similarities and seek explanations for differences; (2) the more advanced student will find challenge and pleasure in a close comparison of style and technique. Indeed, just as a painter may benefit from comparing two portraits of the same subject or a musician may learn from analyzing sets of variations on the same musical theme, so the student of literature and composition will find value in the kind of comparison encouraged by this anthology. In each set of stories, obvious resemblances call attention to differences and thus throw light on the writer's craft. Hence comes the realization that a work of fiction is a deliberately shaped artifact rather than a mere record of experience; that, unlike life, relatively little in fiction is ruled by chance or closed to critical scrutiny.

Another advantage of such an approach to short fiction is that it leads to evaluation, for if there are two methods of handling a story, one is likely to be more effective than the other. Comparing two versions of a work by such writers as Frank O'Connor, Jack London, or Flannery O'Connor helps us develop a more objective standard for judging fiction. Moreover, this anthology of analogous tales will prove especially useful for courses that combine composition and literary analysis. The very act of comparing two versions of D. H. Lawrence's "Odour of Chrysanthemums" (printed here on facing pages) demands careful reading—an attention to individual words and phrases that few textbooks require. And just as two versions of the same story show the artist's freedom of choice, so two forms of the same sentence demonstrate the writer's freedom of expression.

The comparative method established in the first part is continued in the second, "Stories for Comparison." However, since the reader has by now increased his or her proficiency in analyzing short stories, particularly in comparing them, parallels are no longer as obvious or as extensive. The eleven "Stories for Individual Study" that make up the third part, on the other hand, are designed to give *Twice-Told Tales* the variety in scope that the exclusive use of analogous stories would preclude. Here are to be found familiar works as well as lesser known contemporary stories, ranging from traditional modes of fiction to examples of the absurd and experimental. This part may be read last in order to exercise and test the reader's new critical skills or, depending on the instructor's approach and purpose, may be read in conjunction with earlier selections.

Throughout this anthology, I have sought to choose stories that not only stimulate intellectually and engage emotionally but also offer a wide array of approaches to the art of fiction. Believing, moreover, that nothing should come between the reader and an initial experience with a story, I have avoided any prefatory remarks, but have assisted only by means of the discussion questions that follow the stories. These questions are designed to encourage close analysis by familiarizing the student with the elements of fiction and by offering a variety of critical choices and approaches to the interpretation of literature. And just as these questions aim to increase the students' sensitivity as readers, so those entitled Analysis and Application strive to widen their sensitivity as writers by confronting them with specific problems in style and rhetoric.

Twice-Told Tales is thus not only suitable for use in introductory courses in fiction but offers a natural means for teaching composition through literature. It can also be used in more advanced classes dealing with the techniques and aesthetics of the short story. Indeed, any course concerned with the craft of fiction, particularly one in creative writing, may be enriched by an anthology that illuminates the creative process through versions of stories never before readily accessible.

Annotation is provided for allusions, foreign expressions, and obscure terms—for most words, in fact, not listed in standard college desk dictionaries. In addition to the biographical notes, which briefly summarize each author's literary career, the end of the book also contains a concise Glossary of Literary Terms. To facilitate its use, words defined in the glossary are italicized whenever they appear in the questions.

While many persons have provided me with helpful suggestions and ideas during the preparation of this book, I am particularly indebted to my colleagues Professor Stanley Friedman for his constructive and invaluable criticism of the manuscript and Professor Donald A. McQuade for his generous advice and assistance. I appreciate as well the valuable suggestions offered by the following readers of the complete manuscript: Thomas Doulis, Leon Gatlin, Michael Jay Kalter, and Joanne McCarthy. I am also grateful to the library staffs of Queens College, State University of New York at Stony Brook, and the New York Public Library for many kindnesses shown to me during the compilation of this anthology. Finally, I would like to thank my wife for her conscientious and indefatigable help in preparing *Twice-Told Tales* for publication.

G.B.

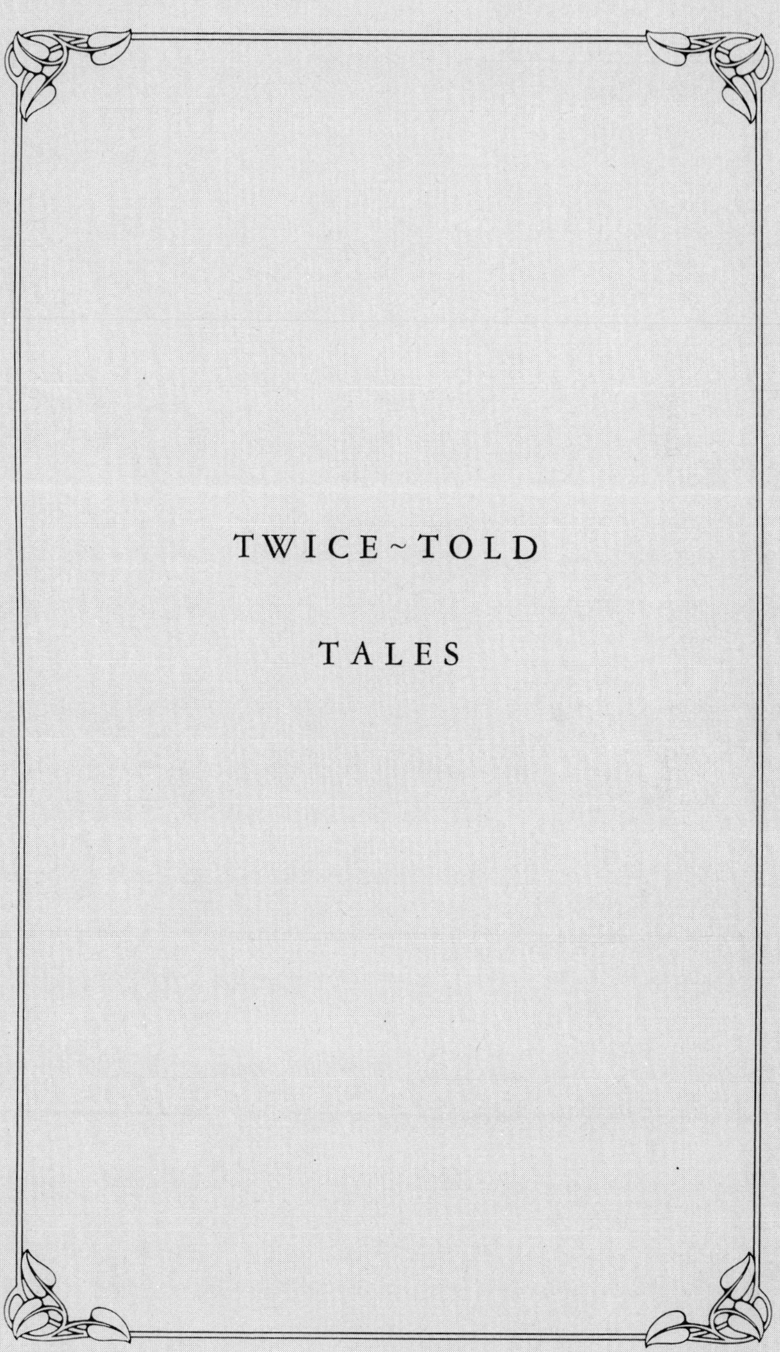

TWICE~TOLD

TALES

TO BUILD A FIRE

Version 1

JACK LONDON

FOR LAND travel or seafaring, the world over, a companion is usually considered desirable. In the Klondike, as Tom Vincent found out, such a companion is absolutely essential. But he found it out, not by precept, but through bitter experience.

"Never travel alone," is a precept of the North. He had heard it many times and laughed; for he was a strapping young fellow, big-boned and big-muscled, with faith in himself and in the strength of his head and hands.

It was on a bleak January day when the experience came that taught him respect for the frost, and for the wisdom of the men who had battled with it.

Originally appeared in *Youth's Companion,* 29 May 1902.

He had left Calumet Camp on the Yukon with a light pack on his back, to go up Paul Creek to the divide between it and Cherry Creek, where his party was prospecting and hunting moose.

The frost was sixty-degrees below zero, and he had thirty miles of lonely trail to cover, but he did not mind. In fact, he enjoyed it, swinging along through the silence, his blood pounding warmly through veins, and his mind carefree and happy. For he and his comrades were certain they had struck "pay" up there on the Cherry Creek Divide; and, further, he was returning to them from Dawson with cheery home letters from the States.

At seven o'clock, when he turned the heels of his moccasins toward Calumet Camp, it was still black night. And when day broke at half past nine he had made the four-mile cut-off across the flats and was six miles up Paul Creek. The trail, which had seen little travel, followed the bed of the creek, and there was no possibility of his getting lost. He had gone to Dawson by way of Cherry Creek and Indian River, so Paul Creek was new and strange. By half past eleven he was at the forks, which had been described to him, and he knew he had covered fifteen miles, half the distance. He knew that in the nature of things the trail was bound to grow worse from there on, and thought that, considering the good time he had made, he merited lunch. Casting off his pack and taking a seat on a fallen tree, he unmittened his right hand, reached inside his shirt next to the skin, and fished out a couple of biscuits sandwiched with sliced bacon and wrapped in a handkerchief—the only way they could be carried without freezing solid.

He had barely chewed the first mouthful when his numbing fingers warned him to put his mitten on again. This he did, not without surprise at the bitter swiftness with which the frost bit in. Undoubtedly it was the coldest snap he had ever experienced, he thought.

He spat upon the snow,—a favorite northland trick,—and the sharp crackle of the instantly congealed spittle startled him. The spirit thermometer at Calumet had registered sixty below when he left, but he was certain it had grown much colder, how much colder he could not imagine.

Half of the first biscuit was yet untouched, but he could feel himself beginning to chill—a thing most unusual for him. This would never do, he decided, and slipping the packstraps across his shoulders, he leaped to his feet and ran briskly up the trail.

A few minutes of this made him warm again, and he settled down to a steady stride, munching the biscuits as he went along. The moisture that exhaled with his breath crusted his lips and mustache with pendent ice and formed a miniature glacier on his chin. Now and again sensation forsook his nose and cheeks, and he rubbed them till they burned with the returning blood.

Most men wore nose-straps; his partners did, but he had scorned such "feminine contraptions," and till now had never felt the need of them. Now he did feel the need, for he was rubbing constantly.

Nevertheless he was aware of a thrill of joy, of exultation. He was doing something, achieving something, mastering the elements. Once he laughed aloud in sheer strength of life, and with his clenched fist defied the frost. He was its master. What he did he did in spite of it. It could not stop him. He was going on to the Cherry Creek Divide.

Strong as were the elements, he was stronger. At such times animals crawled away into their holes and remained in hiding. But he did not hide. He was out in it, facing it, fighting it. He was a man, a master of things.

In such fashion, rejoicing proudly, he tramped on. After an hour he rounded a bend, where the creek ran close to the mountainside, and came upon one of the most insignificant-appearing but most formidable dangers in northern travel.

The creek itself was frozen solid to its rocky bottom, but from the mountain came the outflow of several springs. These springs never froze, and the only effect of the severest cold snaps was to lessen their discharge. Protected from the frost by the blanket of snow, the water of these springs seeped down into the creek and, on top of the creek ice, formed shallow pools.

The surface of these pools, in turn, took on a skin of ice which grew thicker and thicker, until the water overran, and so formed a second ice-skinned pool above the first.

Thus at the bottom was the solid creek ice, then probably six to eight inches of water, then the thin ice-skin, then another six inches of water and another ice-skin. And on top of this last skin was about an inch of recent snow to make the trap complete.

To Tom Vincent's eye the unbroken snow surface gave no warning of the lurking danger. As the crust was thicker at the edge, he was well toward the middle before he broke through.

In itself it was a very insignificant mishap,—a man does not drown in twelve inches of water,—but in its consequences as serious an accident as could possibly befall him.

At the instant he broke through he felt the cold water strike his feet and ankles, and with half a dozen lunges he made the bank. He was quite cool and collected. The thing to do, and the only thing to do, was to build a fire. For another precept of the north runs: *Travel with wet socks down to twenty below zero; after that build a fire.* And it was three times twenty below and colder, and he knew it.

He knew, further, that great care must be exercised; that with failure at the first attempt, the chance was made greater for failure at the second attempt. In short, he knew that there must be no failure. The moment before a strong, exulting man, boastful of his mastery of the elements, he was now fighting for his life against those same elements—such was the difference caused by the injection of a quart of water into a northland traveller's calculations.

In a clump of pines on the rim of the bank the spring high-water had lodged many twigs and small branches. Thoroughly dried by the summer sun, they now waited the match.

It is impossible to build a fire with heavy Alaskan mittens on one's hands, so Vincent bared his, gathered a sufficient number of twigs, and knocking the snow from them, knelt down to kindle his fire. From an inside pocket he drew out his matches and a strip of thin birch bark. The matches were of the Klondike kind, sulphur matches, one hundred in a bunch.

He noticed how quickly his fingers had chilled as he separated one match from the bunch and scratched it on his trousers. The birch bark, like the dryest of paper, burst into bright flame. This he carefully fed with the smallest twigs and finest debris, cherishing the flame with the utmost care. It did not do to hurry things, as he well knew, and although his fingers were now quite stiff, he did not hurry.

After the first quick, biting sensation of cold, his feet had ached with a heavy, dull ache and were rapidly growing numb. But the fire, although a very young one, was now a success; he knew that a little snow, briskly rubbed, would speedily cure his feet.

But at the moment he was adding the first thick twigs to the fire a grievous thing happened. The pine boughs above his head were burdened with a four months' snowfall, and so finely adjusted were the burdens that his slight movement in collecting the twigs had been sufficient to disturb the balance.

The snow from the topmost bough was the first to fall, striking and dislodging the snow on the boughs beneath. And all this snow, accumulating as it fell, smote Tom Vincent's head and shoulders and blotted out his fire.

He still kept his presence of mind, for he knew how great his danger was. He started at once to rebuild the fire, but his fingers were now so numb that he could not bend them, and he was forced to pick up each twig and splinter between the tips of the fingers of either hand.

When he came to the match he encountered great difficulty in separating one from the bunch. This he succeeded in managing, however, and also, by great effort, in clutching the match between his thumb and forefinger. But in scratching it, he dropped it in the snow and could not pick it up again.

He stood up, desperate. He could not feel even his weight on his feet, although the ankles were aching painfully. Putting on his mittens, he stepped to one side, so that the snow would not fall upon the new fire he was to build, and beat his hands violently against a tree-trunk.

This enabled him to separate and strike a second match and to set fire to the remaining fragment of birch bark. But his body had now begun to chill and he was shivering, so that when he tried to add the first twigs his hand shook and the tiny flame was quenched.

The frost had beaten him. His hands were worthless. But he had the foresight to drop the bunch of matches into his wide-mouthed outside pocket before he slipped on his mittens in despair, and started to run up the trail. One cannot run the frost out of wet feet at sixty below and colder, however, as he quickly discovered.

He came round a sharp turn of the creek to where he could look ahead for a mile. But there was no help, no sign of help, only the white trees and the white hills, and the quiet cold and the brazen silence! If only he had a comrade whose feet were not freezing, he thought, only such a comrade to start the fire that could save him!

Then his eyes chanced upon another high-water lodgment of twigs and branches. If he could strike a match, all might yet be well. With stiff fingers which he could not bend, he got out a bunch of matches, but found it impossible to separate them.

He sat down and awkwardly shuffled the bunch about on his knees, until he got it resting on his palm with the sulphur ends projecting, somewhat in the manner the blade of a hunting-knife would project when clutched in the fist.

But his fingers stood straight out. They could not clutch. This he overcame by pressing the wrist of the other hand against them, and so forcing them down upon the bunch. Time and again, holding thus by both hands, he scratched the bunch on his leg and finally ignited it. But the flame burned into the flesh of his hand, and he involuntarily relaxed his hold. The bunch fell into the snow, and while he tried vainly to pick it up, sizzled and went out.

Again he ran, by this time badly frightened. His feet were utterly devoid of sensation. He stubbed his toes once on a buried log, but beyond pitching him into the snow and wrenching his back, it gave him no feelings.

His fingers were helpless and his wrists were beginning to grow numb. His nose and cheeks he knew were frozen, but they did not count. It was his feet and hands that were to save him, if he was to be saved.

He recollected being told of a camp of moose-hunters somewhere above the forks of Paul Creek. He must be somewhere near it, he thought, and if he could find it he yet might be saved. Five minutes later he came upon it, lone and deserted, with drifted snow sprinkled inside the pine-bough shelter in which the hunters had slept. He sank down, sobbing. All was over, and in an hour at best, in that terrific temperature, he would be an icy corpse.

But the love of life was strong in him, and he sprang again to his feet. He was thinking quickly. What if the matches did burn his hands? Burned hands were better than dead hands. No hands at all were better than death. He floundered along the trail until he came upon another high-water lodgment. There were twigs and branches, leaves and grasses, all dry and waiting the fire.

Again he sat down and shuffled the bunch of matches on his knees, got it into place on his palm, with the wrist of his other hand forced the nerveless fingers down against the bunch, and with the wrist kept them there. At the second scratch the bunch caught fire, and he knew that if he could stand the pain he was saved. He choked with the sulphur fumes, and the blue flame licked the flesh of his hands.

At first he could not feel it, but it burned quickly in through the frosted surface. The odor of the burning flesh—his flesh—was strong in his nostrils. He writhed about in his torment, yet held on. He set his teeth and swayed back and forth, until the clear white flame of the burning match shot up, and he had applied that flame to the leaves and grasses.

An anxious five minutes followed, but the fire gained steadily. Then he set to work to save himself. Heroic measures were necessary, such was his extremity, and he took them.

Alternately rubbing his hands with snow and thrusting them into the flames, and now and again beating them against the hard trees, he restored their circulation sufficiently for them to be of use to him. With his hunting-knife he slashed the straps from his pack, unrolled his blanket, and got out dry socks and footgear.

Then he cut away his moccasins and bared his feet. But while he had taken liberties with his hands, he kept his feet fairly away from the fire and rubbed them with snow. He rubbed till his hands grew numb, when he would cover his feet with the blanket, warm his hands by the fire, and return to the rubbing.

For three hours he worked, till the worst effects of the freezing had been counteracted. All that night he stayed by the fire, and it was late the next day when he limped pitifully into the camp on the Cherry Creek Divide.

In a month's time he was able to be about on his feet, although the toes were destined always after that to be very sensitive to frost. But the scars on his hands he knows he will carry to the grave. And—"*Never travel alone!*" he now lays down the precept of the North.

1902

TO BUILD A FIRE

Version 2

JACK LONDON

DAY HAD broken cold and grey, exceedingly cold and grey, when the man turned aside from the main Yukon trail and climbed the high earth-bank, where a dim and little-travelled trail led eastward through the fat spruce timberland. It was a steep bank, and he paused for breath at the top, excusing the act to himself by looking at his watch. It was nine o'clock. There was no sun nor hint of sun, though there was not a cloud in the sky. It was a clear day, and yet there seemed an intangible pall over the face of things, a subtle gloom that made the day dark, and that was due to the absence of sun. This fact did not worry the man. He was used to the lack of sun. It had been days since he had seen the sun, and he knew that a few more days must pass before that cheerful orb, due south, would just peep above the skyline and dip immediately from view.

The man flung a look back along the way he had come. The Yukon lay a mile wide and hidden under three feet of ice. On top of this ice were as many feet of snow. It was all pure white, rolling in gentle undulations where the ice jams of the freeze-up had formed. North and south, as far as his eye could see, it was unbroken white, save for a dark hairline that curved and twisted from around the spruce-covered island to the south, and that curved and twisted away into the north, where it disappeared behind another spruce-covered island. This dark hairline was the trail—the main trail—that led south five hundred miles to the Chilcoot Pass, Dyea, and salt water; and that led north seventy miles to Dawson, and still on to the north a thousand miles to Nulato, and finally to St. Michael, on Bering Sea, a thousand miles and half a thousand more.

But all this—the mysterious, far-reaching hairline trail, the absence of sun from the sky, the tremendous cold, and the strangeness and weirdness of it all—made no impression on the man. It was not because he was long used to it. He was a newcomer in the land, a *chechaquo,* and this was his first winter. The trouble with him was that he was without imagination. He was quick and alert in the things of life, but only in the things, and not in the significances. Fifty degrees below zero meant eighty-odd degrees of frost. Such fact impressed him as being cold and uncomfortable, and that was all. It did not lead him to meditate upon his frailty as a creature of temperature, and upon man's frailty in general, able only to live within certain narrow limits of heat and cold; and from there on it did not lead him to the conjectural field of immortality and man's place in the universe. Fifty degrees below zero stood for a bite of frost that hurt and that must be guarded against by the use of mittens, ear flaps, warm moccasins, and thick socks. Fifty degrees below zero. That there should be anything more to it than that was a thought that never entered his head.

As he turned to go on, he spat speculatively. There was a sharp explosive crackle that startled him. He spat again. And again, in the air, before it could fall to the snow, the spittle crackled. He knew that at fifty below spittle crackled on the snow, but this spittle had crackled in the air. Undoubtedly it was colder than fifty below—how much colder he did not know. But the temperature did not matter. He was bound for the old claim on the left fork of Henderson Creek, where the boys were already. They had come over across the divide from the

Indian Creek country, while he had come the roundabout way to take a look at the possibilities of getting out logs in the spring from the islands in the Yukon. He would be in to camp by six o'clock; a bit after dark, it was true, but the boys would be there, a fire would be going, and a hot supper would be ready. As for lunch, he pressed his hand against the protruding bundle under his jacket. It was also under his shirt, wrapped up in a handkerchief and lying against the naked skin. It was the only way to keep the biscuits from freezing. He smiled agreeably to himself as he thought of those biscuits, each cut open and sopped in bacon grease, and each enclosing a generous slice of fried bacon.

He plunged in among the big spruce trees. The trail was faint. A foot of snow had fallen since the last sled had passed over, and he was glad he was without a sled, travelling light. In fact, he carried nothing but the lunch wrapped in the handkerchief. He was surprised, however, at the cold. It certainly was cold, he concluded, as he rubbed his numb nose and cheekbones with his mittened hand. He was a warm-whiskered man, but the hair on his face did not protect the high cheekbones and the eager nose that thrust itself aggressively into the frosty air.

At the man's heels trotted a dog, a big native husky, the proper wolf-dog, grey-coated and without any visible or temperamental difference from its brother, the wild wolf. The animal was depressed by the tremendous cold. It knew that it was no time for travelling. Its instinct told it a truer tale than was told to the man by the man's judgment. In reality, it was not merely colder than fifty below zero; it was colder than sixty below, than seventy below. It was seventy-five below zero. Since the freezing point is thirty-two above zero, it meant that one hundred and seven degrees of frost obtained. The dog did not know anything about thermometers. Possibly in its brain there was no sharp consciousness of a condition of very cold such as was in the man's brain. But the brute had its instinct. It experienced a vague but menacing apprehension that subdued it and made it slink along at the man's heels, and that made it question eagerly every unwonted movement of the man as if expecting him to go into camp or to seek shelter somewhere and build a fire. The dog had learned fire, and it wanted fire, or else to burrow under the snow and cuddle its warmth away from the air.

The frozen moisture of its breathing had settled on its fur in a fine powder of frost, and especially were its jowls, muzzle, and eyelashes whitened by its crystal breath. The man's red beard and moustache were likewise frosted, but more solidly, the deposit taking the form of ice and increasing with every warm, moist breath he exhaled. Also, the man was chewing tobacco, and the muzzle of ice held his lips so rigidly that he was unable to clear his chin when he expelled the juice. The result was a crystal beard of the colour and solidity of amber was increasing its length on his chin. If he fell down it would shatter itself, like glass, into brittle fragments. But he did not mind the appendage. It was the penalty all tobacco chewers paid in that country, and he had been out before in two cold snaps. They had not been so cold as this, he knew, but by the spirit thermometer at Sixty Mile he knew they had been registered at fifty below and at fifty-five.

He held on through the level stretch of woods for several miles, crossed a wide flat of nigger heads,[1] and dropped down a bank to the frozen bed of a small stream. This was Henderson Creek, and he knew he was ten miles from the forks. He looked at his watch. It was ten o'clock. He was making four miles an hour, and he calculated that he would arrive at the forks at half-past twelve. He decided to celebrate that event by eating his lunch there.

The dog dropped in again at his heels, with a tail drooping discouragement, as the man swung along the creek bed. The furrow of the old sled trail was plainly visible, but a dozen inches of snow covered up the marks of the last runners. In a month no man had come up or down that silent creek. The man held steadily on. He was not much given to thinking, and just then particularly he had nothing to think about save that he would eat lunch at the forks and that at six o'clock he would be in camp with the boys. There was nobody to talk to; and, had there been, speech would have been impossible because of the ice muzzle on his mouth. So he continued monotonously to chew tobacco and to increase the length of his amber beard.

Once in a while the thought reiterated itself that it was very cold and that he had never experienced such cold. As he walked along he rubbed his cheekbones and nose with the back of his mittened hand. He did this automatically, now and again changing hands. But, rub as he would, the instant he stopped his cheekbones went numb, and the following instant the end of his nose went numb. He was sure to frost his cheeks; he knew that, and experienced a pang of regret that he had not devised a nose strap of the sort Bud wore in cold snaps. Such a strap passed across the cheeks, as well, and saved them. But it didn't matter much, after all. What were frosted cheeks? A bit painful, that was all; they were never serious.

[1] Dark-colored clumps of vegetation.

Empty as the man's mind was of thoughts, he was keenly observant, and he noticed the changes in the creeks, the curves and bends and timber jams, and always he sharply noted where he placed his feet. Once, coming round a bend, he shied abruptly, like a startled horse, curved away from the place where he had been walking, and retreated several paces back along the trail. The creek he knew was frozen clear to the bottom—no creek could contain water in that arctic winter—but he knew also that there were springs that bubbled out from the hillsides and ran along under the snow and on top of the ice of the creek. He knew that the coldest snaps never froze these springs, and he knew likewise their danger. They were traps. They hid pools of water under the snow that might be three inches deep, or three feet. Sometimes a skin of ice half an inch thick covered them, and in turn was covered by the snow. Sometimes there were alternate layers of water and ice skin, so that when one broke through he kept on breaking through for a while, sometimes wetting himself to the waist.

That was why he had shied in such a panic. He had felt the give under his feet and heard the crackle of a snow-hidden ice skin. And to get his feet wet in such a temperature meant trouble and danger. At the very least it meant delay, for he would be forced to stop and build a fire, and under its protection to bare his feet while he dried his socks and moccasins. He stood and studied the creek bed and its banks, and decided that the flow of water came from the right. He reflected awhile, rubbing his nose and cheeks, then skirted to the left, stepping gingerly and testing the footing for each step. Once clear of the danger, he took a fresh chew of tobacco and swung along at his four-mile gait.

In the course of the next two hours he came upon several similar traps. Usually the snow above the hidden pools had a sunken, candied appearance that advertised the danger. Once again, however, he had a close call; and once, suspecting danger, he compelled the dog to go on in front. The dog did not want to go. It hung back until the man shoved it forward, and then it went quickly across the white, unbroken surface. Suddenly it broke through, floundered to one side, and got away to firmer footing. It had wet its forefeet and legs, and almost immediately the water that clung to it turned to ice. It made quick efforts to lick the ice off its legs, then dropped down in the snow and began to bite out the ice that had formed between the toes. This was a matter of instinct. To permit the ice to remain would mean sore feet. It did not know this. It merely obeyed the mysterious prompting that arose from the deep crypts of its being. But the man knew, having achieved a judgment on the subject, and he removed the mitten from his right hand and helped to tear out the ice particles. He did not expose his fingers more than a minute, and was astonished at the swift numbness that smote them. It certainly was cold. He pulled on the mitten hastily, and beat the hand savagely across his chest.

At twelve o'clock the day was at its brightest. Yet the sun was too far south on its winter journey to clear the horizon. The bulge of the earth intervened between it and Henderson Creek, where the man walked under a clear sky at noon and cast no shadow. At half-past twelve, to the minute, he arrived at the forks of the creek. He was pleased at the speed he had made. If he kept it up, he would certainly be with the boys by six. He unbuttoned his jacket and shirt and drew forth his lunch. The action consumed no more than a quarter of a minute, yet in that brief moment the numbness laid hold of the exposed fingers. He did not put the mitten on, but, instead, struck the fingers a dozen sharp smashes against his leg. Then he sat down on a snow-covered log to eat. The sting that followed upon the striking of his fingers against his leg ceased so quickly that he was startled. He had had no chance to take a bite of biscuit. He struck the fingers repeatedly and returned them to the mitten, baring the other hand for the purpose of eating. He tried to take a mouthful, but the ice muzzle prevented. He had forgotten to build a fire and thaw out. He chuckled at his foolishness, and as he chuckled he noted the numbness creeping into the exposed fingers. Also, he noted that the stinging which had first come to his toes when he sat down was already passing away. He wondered whether the toes were warm or numb. He moved them inside the moccasins and decided that they were numb.

He pulled the mitten on hurriedly and stood up. He was a bit frightened. He stamped up and down until the stinging returned into the feet. It certainly was cold, was his thought. That man from Sulphur Creek had spoken the truth when telling how cold it sometimes got in the country. And he had laughed at him at the time! That showed one must not be too sure of things. There was no mistake about it, it *was* cold. He strode up and down, stamping his feet and threshing his arms, until reassured by the returning warmth. Then he got out matches and proceeded to make a fire. From the undergrowth, where high water of the previous spring had lodged a supply of seasoned twigs, he got his firewood. Working carefully from a small beginning, he soon had a roaring fire, over which he thawed the ice from his face and in the protection of which he ate his biscuits. For the moment the cold of space was outwitted. The dog took satisfaction in the fire, stretching out close enough for warmth and far enough away to escape being singed.

When the man had finished, he filled his pipe and took his comfortable time over a smoke. Then he pulled on his mittens, settled the ear-flaps of his cap firmly about his ears, and took the creek trail up the left fork. The dog was disappointed and yearned back towards the fire. This man did not know cold. Possibly all the generations of his ancestry had been ignorant of cold, of real cold, of cold one hundred and seven degrees below freezing point. But the dog knew; all its ancestry knew, and it had inherited the knowledge. And it knew that it was not good to walk abroad in such fearful cold. It was the time to lie snug in a hole in the snow and wait for a curtain of cloud to be drawn across the face of outer space whence this cold came. On the other hand, there was no keen intimacy between the dog and the man. The one was the toil slave of the other, and the only caresses it had ever received were the caresses of the whip lash and of harsh and menacing throat sounds that threatened the whip lash. So the dog made no effort to communicate its apprehension to the man. It was not concerned in the welfare of the man; it was for its own sake that it yearned back towards the fire. But the man whistled, and spoke to it with the sound of whip lashes, and the dog swung in at the man's heels and followed after.

The man took a chew of tobacco and proceeded to start a new amber beard. Also, his moist breath quickly powdered with white his moustache, eyebrows, and lashes. There did not seem to be so many springs on the left fork of the Henderson, and for half an hour the man saw no signs of any. And then it happened. At a place where there were no signs, where the soft, unbroken snow seemed to advertise solidity beneath, the man broke through. It was not deep. He wet himself half-way to the knees before he floundered out to the firm crust.

He was angry, and cursed his luck aloud. He had hoped to get into camp with the boys at six o'clock, and this would delay him an hour, for he would have to build a fire and dry out his footgear. This was imperative at that low temperature—he knew that much; and he turned aside to the bank, which he climbed. On top, tangled in the underbrush about the trunks of several small spruce trees, was a high-water deposit of dry firewood—sticks and twigs, principally, but also larger portions of seasoned branches and fine, dry, last year's grasses. He threw down several large pieces on top of the snow. This served for a foundation and prevented the young flame from drowning itself in the snow it otherwise would melt. The flame he got by touching a match to a small shred of birch bark that he took from his pocket. This burned even more readily than paper. Placing it on the foundation, he fed the young flame with wisps of dry grass and with the tiniest dry twigs.

He worked slowly and carefully, keenly aware of his danger. Gradually, as the flame grew stronger, he increased the size of the twigs with which he fed it. He squatted in the snow pulling the twigs out from their entanglement in the brush and feeding directly to the flame. He knew there must be no failure. When it is seventy-five below zero, a man must not fail in his first attempt to build a fire—that is, if his feet are wet. If his feet are dry, and he fails, he can run along the trail for half a mile and restore his circulation. But the circulation of wet and freezing feet cannot be restored by running when it is seventy-five below. No matter how fast he runs, the wet feet will freeze the harder.

All this the man knew. The old-timer on Sulphur Creek had told him about it the previous fall, and now he was appreciating the advice. Already all sensation had gone out of his feet. To build the fire he had been forced to remove his mittens, and the fingers had quickly gone numb. His pace of four miles an hour had kept his heart pumping blood to the surface of his body and to all the extremities. But the instant he stopped, the action of the pump eased down. The cold of space smote the unprotected tip of the planet, and he, being on that unprotected tip, received the full force of the blow. The blood of his body recoiled before it. The blood was alive, like the dog, and like the dog it wanted to hide away and cover itself up from the fearful cold. So long as he walked four miles an hour, he pumped that blood, willy-nilly, to the surface; but now it ebbed away and sank down into the recesses of his body. The extremities were the first to feel its absence. His wet feet froze the faster, and his exposed fingers numbed the faster, though they had not yet begun to freeze. Nose and cheeks were already freezing, while the skin of all his body chilled as it lost its blood.

But he was safe. Toes and nose and cheeks would be only touched by the frost, for the fire was beginning to burn with strength. He was feeding it with twigs the size of his finger. In another minute he would be able to feed it with branches the size of his wrist, and then he could remove his wet footgear, and, while it dried, he could keep his naked feet warm by the fire, rubbing them at first, of course, with snow. The fire was a success. He was safe. He remembered the advice of the old-timer on Sulphur Creek, and smiled. The old-timer had been very serious in laying down the law that no man must travel alone in the Klondike after fifty below. Well, here he was; he had had the accident;

he was alone; and he had saved himself. Those old-timers were rather womanish, some of them, he thought. All a man had to do was to keep his head, and he was all right. Any man who was a man could travel alone. But it was surprising, the rapidity with which his cheeks and nose were freezing. And he had not thought his fingers could go lifeless in so short a time. Lifeless they were, for he could scarcely make them move together to grip a twig, and they seemed remote from his body and from him. When he touched a twig, he had to look and see whether or not he had hold of it. The wires were pretty well down between him and his finger ends.

All of which counted for little. There was the fire, snapping and crackling and promising life with every dancing flame. He started to untie his moccasins. They were coated with ice; the thick German socks were like sheaths of iron halfway to the knees; and the moccasin strings were like rods of steel all twisted and knotted as by some conflagration. For a moment he tugged with his numb fingers, then, realizing the folly of it, he drew his sheath knife.

But before he could cut the strings, it happened. It was his own fault or, rather, his mistake. He should not have built the fire under the spruce tree. He should have built it in the open. But it had been easier to pull the twigs from the brush and drop them directly on the fire. Now the tree under which he had done this carried a weight of snow on its boughs. No wind had blown for weeks, and each bough was fully freighted. Each time he had pulled a twig he had communicated a slight agitation to the tree—an imperceptible agitation, so far as he was concerned, but an agitation sufficient to bring about the disaster. High up in the tree one bough capsized its load of snow. This fell on the boughs beneath, capsizing them. This process continued, spreading out and involving the whole tree. It grew like an avalanche, and it descended without warning upon the man and the fire, and the fire was blotted out! Where it had burned was a mantle of fresh and disordered snow.

The man was shocked. It was as though he had just heard his own sentence of death. For a moment he sat and stared at the spot where the fire had been. Then he grew very calm. Perhaps the old-timer on Sulphur Creek was right. If he had only had a trail mate he would have been in no danger now. The trail mate could have built the fire. Well, it was up to him to build the fire over again, and this second time there must be no failure. Even if he succeeded, he would most likely lose some toes. His feet must be badly frozen by now, and there would be some time before the second fire was ready.

Such were his thoughts, but he did not sit and think them. He was busy all the time they were passing through his mind. He made a new foundation for a fire, this time in the open, where no treacherous tree could blot it out. Next he gathered dry grasses and tiny twigs from the high-water flotsam. He could not bring his fingers together to pull them out, but he was able to gather them by the handful. In this way he got many rotten twigs and bits of green moss that were undesirable, but it was the best he could do. He worked methodically, even collecting an armful of the larger branches to be used later when the fire gathered strength. And all the while the dog sat and watched him, a certain yearning wistfulness in its eyes, for it looked upon him as the fire provider, and the fire was slow in coming.

When all was ready, the man reached in his pocket for a second piece of birch bark. He knew the bark was there, and, though he could not feel it with his fingers, he could hear its crisp rustling as he fumbled for it. Try as he would, he could not clutch hold of it. And all the time, in his consciousness, was the knowledge that each instant his feet were freezing. This thought tended to put him in a panic, but he fought against it and kept calm. He pulled on his mittens with his teeth, and threshed his arms back and forth, beating his hands with all his might against his sides. He did this sitting down, and he stood up to do it; and all the while the dog sat in the snow, its wolf brush of a tail curled around warmly over its forefront, its sharp wolf ears pricked forward intently as it watched the man. And the man, as he beat and threshed with his arms and hands, felt a great surge of envy as he regarded the creature that was warm and secure in its natural covering.

After a time he was aware of the first faraway signals of sensation in his beaten fingers. The faint tingling grew stronger till it evolved into a stinging ache that was excruciating, but which the man hailed with satisfaction. He stripped the mitten from his right hand and fetched forth the birch bark. The exposed fingers were quickly going numb again. Next he brought out his bunch of sulphur matches. But the tremendous cold had already driven the life out of his fingers. In his effort to separate one match from the others, the whole bunch fell in the snow. He tried to pick it out of the snow, but failed. The dead fingers could neither touch nor clutch. He was very careful. He drove the thought of his freezing feet, and nose, and cheeks, out of his mind, devoting his whole soul to the matches. He watched, using the sense of vision in place of that touch, and when he saw his fingers on each side of the bunch, he closed them—that is, he willed to close them, for the wires were down, and the fingers did not obey. He pulled the mitten on the right hand, and beat it fiercely against his knee. Then with both mittened hands, he scooped the bunch of matches, along with much snow, into his lap. Yet he was no better off.

After some manipulation he managed to get the bunch between the heels of his mittened hands. In this fashion he carried it to his mouth. The ice crackled and snapped when by a violent effort he opened his mouth. He drew the lower jaw in, curled the upper lip out of the way, and scraped the bunch with his upper teeth in order to separate a match. He succeeded in getting one, which he dropped on his lap. He was no better off. He could not pick it up. Then he devised a way. He picked it up in his teeth and scratched it on his leg. Twenty times he scratched before he succeeded in lighting it. As it flamed he held it with his teeth to the birch bark. But the burning brimstone went up his nostrils and into his lungs, causing him to cough spasmodically. The match fell into the snow and went out.

The old-timer on Sulphur Creek was right, he thought in the moment of controlled despair that ensued: after fifty below, a man should travel with a partner. He beat his hands, but failed in exciting any sensation. Suddenly he bared both hands, removing the mittens with his teeth. He caught the whole bunch between the heels of his hands. His arm muscles not being frozen enabled him to press the hand heels tightly against the matches. Then he scratched the bunch along his leg. It flared into flame, seventy sulphur matches at once! There was no wind to blow them out. He kept his head to one side to escape the strangling fumes, and held the blazing bunch to the birch bark. As he so held it, he became aware of sensation in his hand. His flesh was burning. He could smell it. Deep down below the surface he could feel it. The sensation developed into pain that grew acute. And still he endured it, holding the flame of the matches clumsily to the bark that would not light readily because his own burning hands were in the way, absorbing most of the flame.

At last, when he could endure no more, he jerked his hands apart. The blazing matches fell sizzling into the snow, but the birch bark was alight. He began laying dry grasses and the tiniest twigs on the flame. He could not pick and choose, for he had to lift the fuel between the heels of his hands. Small pieces of rotten wood and green moss clung to the twigs, and he bit them off as well as he could with his teeth. He cherished the flame carefully and awkwardly. It meant life, and it must not perish. The withdrawal of blood from the surface of his body now made him begin to shiver, and he grew more awkward. A large piece of green moss fell squarely on the little fire. He tried to poke it out with his fingers, but his shivering frame made him poke too far, and he disrupted the nucleus of the little fire, the burning grasses and tiny twigs separating and scattering. He tried to poke them together again, but in spite of the tenseness of the effort, his shivering got away with him, and the twigs were hopelessly scattered. Each twig gushed a puff of smoke and went out. The fire provider had failed. As he looked apathetically about him, his eyes chanced on the dog, sitting across the ruins of the fire from him, in the snow, making restless, hunching movements, slightly lifting one forefoot and then the other, shifting its weight back and forth on them with wistful eagerness.

The sight of the dog put a wild idea into his head. He remembered the tale of the man, caught in a blizzard, who killed a steer and crawled inside the carcass, and so was saved. He would kill the dog and bury his hands in the warm body until the numbness went out of them. Then he could build another fire. He spoke to the dog, calling it to him; but in his voice was a strange note of fear that frightened the animal, who had never known the man to speak in such a way before. Something was the matter, and its suspicious nature sensed danger—it knew not what danger, but somewhere, somehow, in its brain arose an apprehension of the man. It flattened its ears down at the sound of the man's voice, and its restless, hunching movements and the liftings and shiftings of its forefeet became more pronounced; but it would not come to the man. He got on his hands and knees and crawled towards the dog. This unusual posture again excited suspicion, and the animal sidled mincingly away.

The man sat up in the snow for a moment and struggled for calmness. Then he pulled on his mittens, by means of his teeth, and got upon his feet. He glanced down at first in order to assure himself that he was really standing up, for the absence of sensation in his feet left him unrelated to the earth. His erect position in itself started to drive the webs of suspicion from the dog's mind; and when he spoke peremptorily, with the sound of whip lashes in his voice, the dog rendered its customary allegiance and came to him. As it came within reaching distance, the man lost his control. His arms flashed out to the dog, and he experienced genuine surprise when he discovered that his hands could not clutch, that there was neither bend nor feeling in the fingers. He had forgotten for the moment that they were frozen and that they were freezing more and more. All this happened quickly, and before the animal could get away, he encircled its body with his arms. He sat down in the snow, and in this fashion held the dog, while it snarled and whined and struggled.

But it was all he could do, hold its body encircled in his arms and sit there. He realized he could not kill the dog. There was no way to do it. With his helpless hands he could neither draw nor hold his sheath knife nor throttle the animal. He released it, and it plunged wildly away, with tail between its legs, and still snarling. It halted forty feet away and surveyed him curiously, with ears sharply pricked forward.

The man looked down at his hands in order to locate them, and found them hanging on the ends of his arms. It struck him as curious that one should have to use his eyes in order to find out where his hands were. He began threshing his arms back and forth, beating the mittened hands against his sides. He did this for five minutes, violently, and his heart pumped enough blood up to the surface to put a stop to his shivering. But no sensation was aroused in the hands. He had an impression that they hung like weights on the ends of his arms, but when he tried to run the impression down, he could not find it.

A certain fear of death, dull and oppressive, came to him. This fear quickly became poignant as he realized that it was no longer a mere matter of freezing his fingers and toes, or of losing his hands and feet, but that it was a matter of life and death with the chances against him. This threw him into a panic, and he turned and ran up the creek bed along the old, dim trail. The dog joined in behind him and kept up with him. He ran blindly, without intention, in fear such as he had never known in his life. Slowly, as he ploughed and floundered through the snow, he began to see things again—the banks of the creek, the old timber jams, the leafless aspens, and the sky. The running made him feel better. He did not shiver. Maybe, if he ran on, his feet would thaw out; and, anyway, if he ran far enough, he would reach camp and the boys. Without doubt he would lose some fingers and toes and some of his face; but the boys would take care of him, and save the rest of him when he got there. And at the same time there was another thought in his mind that said he would never get to the camp and the boys; that it was too many miles away, that the freezing had too great a start on him, and that he would soon be stiff and dead. This thought he kept in the background and refused to consider. Sometimes it pushed itself forward and demanded to be heard, but he thrust it back and strove to think of other things.

It struck him as curious that he could run at all on feet so frozen that he could not feel them when they struck the earth and took the weight of his body. He seemed to himself to skim along above the surface, and to have no connection with the earth. Somewhere he had once seen a winged Mercury, and he wondered if Mercury felt as he felt when skimming over the earth.

His theory of running until he reached camp and the boys had one flaw in it: he lacked the endurance. Several times he stumbled, and finally he tottered, crumpled up, and fell. When he tried to rise, he failed. He must sit and rest, he decided, and next time he would merely walk and keep on going. As he sat and regained his breath, he noted that he was feeling quite warm and comfortable. He was not shivering, and it even seemed that a warm glow had come to his chest and trunk. And yet, when he touched his nose or cheeks, there was no sensation. Running would not thaw them out. Nor would it thaw out his hands and feet. Then the thought came to him that the frozen portions of his body must be extending. He tried to keep this thought down, to forget it, to think of something else; he was aware of the panicky feeling that it caused, and he was afraid of the panic. But the thought asserted itself, and persisted, until it produced a vision of his body totally frozen. This was too much, and he made another wild run along the trail. Once he slowed down to a walk, but the thought of the freezing extending itself made him run again.

And all the time the dog ran with him, at his heels. When he fell down a second time, it curled its tail over its forefeet and sat in front of him, facing him, curiously eager and intent. The warmth and security of the animal angered him, and he cursed it till it flattened down its ears appeasingly. This time the shivering came more quickly upon the man. He was losing in his battle with the frost. It was creeping into his body from all sides. The thought of it drove him on, but he ran no more than a hundred feet, when he staggered and pitched headlong. It was his last panic. When he had recovered his breath and control, he sat up and entertained in his mind the conception of meeting death with dignity. However, the conception did not come to him in such terms. His idea of it was that he had been making a fool of himself, running around like a chicken with its head cut off—such was the simile that occurred to him. Well, he was bound to freeze anyway, and he might as well take it decently. With this new-found peace of mind came the first glimmerings of drowsiness. A good idea, he thought, to sleep off to death. It was like taking an anaesthetic. Freezing was not so bad as people thought. There were lots worse ways to die.

He pictured the boys finding his body next day. Suddenly he found himself with them, coming along the trail looking for himself. And, still with them, he came around a turn in the trail and found himself lying in the snow. He did not belong with himself any more, for even then he was out of himself, standing with the boys and looking at himself in the snow. It certainly was cold, was his thought. When he got back to the States he could tell the folks what real cold was. He drifted on from this to a vision of the old-timer on Sulphur Creek. He could see him quite clearly, warm and comfortable, and smoking a pipe.

"You were right, old hoss; you were right," the man mumbled to the old-timer of Sulphur Creek.

Then the man drowsed off into what seemed to him the most comfortable and satisfying sleep he had ever known. The dog sat facing him and waiting. The brief day drew to a close in a long, slow twilight. There were no signs of a fire to be made, and, besides, never in the dog's experience had it known a man to sit like that in the snow and make no fire. As the twilight drew on, its eager yearning for the fire mastered it, and with a great lifting and shifting of forefeet, it whined softly, then flattened its ears down in anticipation of being chidden by the man. But the man remained silent. Later the dog whined loudly. And still later it crept close to the man and caught the scent of death. This made the animal bristle and back away. A little longer it delayed, howling under the stars that leaped and danced and shone brightly in the cold sky. Then it turned and trotted up the trail in the direction of the camp it knew, where were the other food providers and fire providers.

1908

DISCUSSION QUESTIONS

1. Compare the opening three paragraphs of the first version with the first paragraph of the second version. Examine the *tone* and mood of these two introductions by reading them aloud. What makes the first introduction appropriate for a story about a man who ultimately survives his bitter experience, and the second introduction suitable for one who does not?

2. Why, in version 2, does the man need to excuse himself when he pauses for breath at the top of the earth bank? What does this tell us about him? Relate it to his belief that "those old-timers were rather womanish" (page 19) and to Vincent's notion that nose straps are "feminine contraptions" (page 5).

3. Why did London add the dog to his second version? Explain the following statement: "The blood was alive, like the dog, and like the dog it wanted to hide away and cover itself up from the fearful cold" (page 18). What have the man and dog in common? What distinguishes them?

4. Just before Vincent, in version 1, steps unknowingly into the ice-skinned pool, he reflects boastfully: "Strong as were the elements, he was stronger. . . . He was a man, a master of things" (page 5). Find an equally presumptuous boast in the second version, followed by a comparably *ironic* mishap.

5. Compare the attitude of each narrator toward the event he is describing:

But at the moment he was adding the first thick twigs to the fire a grievous thing happened. The pine boughs above his head were burdened with a four months' snowfall, and so finely adjusted were the burdens that his slight movement in collecting the twigs had been sufficient to disturb the balance. (page 6)

But before he could cut the strings, it happened. It was his own fault or, rather, his mistake. He should not have built the fire under the spruce tree. He should have built it in the open. But it had been easier to pull the twigs from the brush and drop them directly on the fire. Now the tree under which he had done this carried a weight of snow on its boughs. No wind had blown for weeks, and each bough was fully freighted. (page 19)

6. Such statements in version 2 as "Each time he had pulled a twig he

had communicated a slight agitation to the tree—an imperceptible agitation, so far as he was concerned" (page 19) and "he sat up and entertained in his mind the conception of meeting death with dignity. However, the conception did not come to him in such terms" (page 24) suggest the presence of a narrator superior to the protagonist in knowledge and intelligence. Find some other passages to confirm this. Is a similar narrator present in the first version, and if so, can you find evidence of his presence?

7. We are told in version 2 that "the absence of sensation in his feet left him unrelated to the earth" (page 22) and that he "seemed to himself to skim along above the surface, and to have no connection with the earth" (page 23). What wider *symbolical* significance does this sense of alienation imply? Relate your answer to the following statement: "He did not belong with himself any more, for even then he was out of himself, standing with the boys and looking at himself in the snow" (page 24).

8. After much panic and fear, the protagonist of version 2 determines to meet death "with dignity." How do you account for such a change? Is it consistent with his personality? Would Tom Vincent have been capable of a similar resolution? Explain.

9. Which of the two endings do you prefer? Why?

10. For his second version, London added about 4,500 words. Identify his principal additions and changes by comparing the *structure* of the two versions.

11. London wrote the original story for *Youth's Companion,* a boy's magazine, and rewrote it for publication in an adult magazine. How is this difference in audience reflected in the *diction* (choice of words), *didacticism, theme,* and choice of ending of each version?

ANALYSIS AND APPLICATION

1. Why is "Fifty degrees below zero" repeated three times in the third paragraph of the second version? Find another example of repetition in this paragraph and explain its purpose. Examine the first sentence of the paragraph in context and explain its purpose. Compare it with the following modified version: But all this—the tremendous cold, the

strangeness and weirdness of it all, the mysterious, far-reaching hairline trail, and the absence of sun from the sky—made no impression on the man. Which version do you prefer? Why?

2. Discuss the appropriateness of the *similes* in the following sentence: "They were coated with ice; the thick German socks were like sheaths of iron halfway to the knees; and the moccasin strings were like rods of steel all twisted and knotted as by some conflagration" (page 19). What qualities are being transferred to the socks and moccasin strings? What makes "as by some conflagration" *ironic?* Rewrite the sentence by substituting your own similes.

AN ACCOUNT OF THE TRAGIC DEATH OF THE WILLEY FAMILY

THE NOTCH of the White Mountains will long be remembered for the tragical fate of a whole family, who were swept away by a *slide,* or avalanche of earth from the side of the mountain, on the night of the 28th of August, 1826. This family by the name of *Willey,* occupied what was called the Notch House, in a very narrow interval between the bases of the two mountains. No knowledge of any accident from the mountain in former times, existed to create any apprehension of danger in their situation. Their dwelling stood alone, many miles from the residence of any human being, and there was an aspect of rural neatness, simplicity and content, in their manners and life, that

Samuel Griswold Goodrich, ed., *A System of Universal Geography* (Boston: Carter Hendee, 1833), p. 27.

strongly interested the traveller whom chance or curiosity led into their neighborhood. For two seasons previous, the mountains had been very dry, and on the 28th of June there was a slide not far from the house, which so far alarmed them, that they erected a temporary encampment a short distance from their dwelling, as a place of refuge.

On the morning of August 28th it began raining very hard with strong and tempestuous wind. The storm continued through that day and night, but it appears the family retired to rest without the least apprehension of any disaster. Among them were five beautiful children, from two to twelve years of age. At midnight, the clouds which had gathered about the mountain, seemed to burst instantaneously, and pour their contents down in one tremendous flood of rain. The soil which had been previously soaked through, was suddenly loosened by the flood, and the trees pushed and wrung by fierce winds, acted as levers in breaking up the earth. The avalanche, began upon the mountain top immediately above the house, and moved down the mountain in a direct line toward it, in a sweeping torrent which seemed like a river pouring from the clouds, full of trees, earth and rocks.

On reaching the house it divided in a singular manner within six feet of it, and passed on either side, sweeping away the stable and horses, and completely surrounding the dwelling. The night was dark and frightfully tempestuous. The family, it appears, sprang from their beds, and fled naked into the open air, where they were instantly carried away by the torrent and over whelmed. The slide took everything with it, forest, earth and stones down to the solid rock of the mountain.

In the morning, a most frightful scene of desolation was exhibited. All the bridges over the streams were gone. The road was torn away to the depth of 15 or 20 feet, or covered with immense heaps of earth, rocks and trees.

In the Notch, and along the deep defile below it for a mile and a half, the steep sides of the mountain had slidden down into this narrow passage, and formed a complete mass of fragments. The barn was crushed, and under its ruins were two dead horses, but the house was uninjured. The beds appeared to have been just quitted; their coverings were turned down, and the clothes of the several members of the family lay upon the chairs and floor. The little green in front of the house was undisturbed, and a flock of sheep remained there in quiet, though the torrent forming a curve on both sides, had swept completely round them, and united below, covering the meadows and orchard with ruins. The bodies of seven of the family were dug out of the drift wood and mountain ruins, on the banks of the Saco.

THE AMBITIOUS GUEST

NATHANIEL HAWTHORNE

ONE SEPTEMBER night a family had gathered round their hearth, and piled it high with the driftwood of mountain streams, the dry cones of the pine, and the splintered ruins of great trees that had come crashing down the precipice. Up the chimney roared the fire, and brightened the room with its broad blaze. The faces of the father and mother had a sober gladness; the children laughed; the eldest daughter was the image of Happiness at seventeen; and the aged grandmother, who sat knitting in the warmest place, was the image of Happiness grown old. They had found the "herb, heart's-ease," in the bleakest spot of all New England. This family were situated in the Notch of the White Hills, where the wind was sharp throughout the year, and pitilessly cold in the winter,—giving their cottage all its fresh inclemency before it descended on the valley of the Saco. They dwelt in a cold spot and a dangerous one; for a mountain towered above their heads, so steep, that the stones would often rumble down its sides and startle them at midnight.

The daughter had just uttered some simple jest that filled them all with mirth, when the wind came through the Notch and seemed to pause before their cottage—rattling the door, with a sound of wailing and lamentation, before it passed into the valley. For a moment it saddened them, though there was nothing unusual in the tones. But the family were glad again when they perceived that the latch was lifted by some traveller, whose footsteps had been unheard amid the dreary blast which heralded his approach, and wailed as he was entering, and went moaning away from the door.

Though they dwelt in such a solitude, these people held daily converse with the world. The romantic pass of the Notch is a great artery, through which the life-blood of internal commerce is continually throbbing between Maine, on one side, and the Green Mountains and the shores of the St. Lawrence, on the other. The stage-coach always drew up before the door of the cottage. The wayfarer, with no companion but his staff, paused here to exchange a word, that the sense of loneliness might not utterly overcome him ere he could pass through the cleft of the mountain, or reach the first house in the valley. And here the teamster, on his way to Portland market, would put up for the night; and, if a bachelor, might sit an hour beyond the usual bedtime, and steal a kiss from the mountain maid at parting. It was one of those primitive taverns where the traveller pays only for food and lodging, but meets with a homely kindness beyond all price. When the footsteps were heard, therefore, between the outer door and the inner one, the whole family rose up, grandmother, children, and all, as if about to welcome some one who belonged to them, and whose fate was linked with theirs.

The door was opened by a young man. His face at first wore the melancholy expression, almost despondency, of one who travels a wild and bleak road, at nightfall and alone, but soon brightened up when he saw the kindly warmth of his reception. He felt his heart spring forward to meet them all, from the old woman, who wiped a chair with her apron, to the little child that held out its arms to him. One glance and smile placed the stranger on a footing of innocent familiarity with the eldest daughter.

"Ah, this fire is the right thing!" cried he; "especially when there is such a pleasant circle round it. I am quite benumbed; for the Notch is just like the pipe of a great pair of bellows; it has blown a terrible blast in my face all the way from Bartlett."

"Then you are going towards Vermont?" said the master of the house, as he helped to take a light knapsack off the young man's shoulders.

"Yes; to Burlington, and far enough beyond," replied he. "I meant to have been at Ethan Crawford's[1] to-night; but a pedestrian lingers along such a road as this. It is no matter; for, when I saw this good fire, and all your cheerful faces, I felt as if you had kindled it on purpose for me, and were waiting my arrival. So I shall sit down among you, and make myself at home."

The frank-hearted stranger had just drawn his chair to the fire when something like a heavy footstep was heard without, rushing down the steep side of the mountain, as with long and rapid strides, and taking such a leap in passing the cottage as to strike the opposite precipice. The family held their breath, because they knew the sound, and their guest held his by instinct.

"The old mountain has thrown a stone at us, for fear we should forget him," said the landlord, recovering himself. "He sometimes nods his head and threatens to come down; but we are old neighbors, and agree together pretty well upon the whole. Besides we have a sure place of refuge hard by if he should be coming in good earnest."

Let us now suppose the stranger to have finished his supper of bear's meat; and, by his natural felicity of manner, to have placed himself on a footing of kindness with the whole family, so that they talked as freely together as if he belonged to their mountain brood. He was of a proud, yet gentle spirit—haughty and reserved among the rich and great; but ever ready to stoop his head to the lowly cottage door, and be like a brother or a son at the poor man's fireside. In the household of the Notch he found warmth and simplicity of feeling, the pervading intelligence of New England, and a poetry of native growth, which they had gathered when they little thought of it from the mountain peaks and chasms, and at the very threshold of their romantic and dangerous abode. He had travelled far and alone; his whole life, indeed, had been a solitary path; for, with the lofty caution of his nature, he had kept himself apart from those who might otherwise have been his com-

[1] Ethan Allen Crawford (1792–1846), at whose popular inn Hawthorne stayed in September 1832.

panions. The family, too, though so kind and hospitable, had that consciousness of unity among themselves, and separation from the world at large, which, in every domestic circle, should still keep a holy place where no stranger may intrude. But this evening a prophetic sympathy impelled the refined and educated youth to pour out his heart before the simple mountaineers, and constrained them to answer him with the same free confidence. And thus it should have been. Is not the kindred of a common fate a closer tie than that of birth?

The secret of the young man's character was a high and abstracted ambition. He could have borne to live an undistinguished life, but not to be forgotten in the grave. Yearning desire had been transformed to hope; and hope, long cherished, had become like certainty, that, obscurely as he journeyed now, a glory was to beam on all his pathway,—though not, perhaps, while he was treading it. But when posterity should gaze back into the gloom of what was now the present, they would trace the brightness of his footsteps, brightening as meaner glories faded, and confess that a gifted one had passed from his cradle to his tomb with none to recognize him.

"As yet," cried the stranger—his cheek glowing and his eye flashing with enthusiasm—"as yet, I have done nothing. Were I to vanish from the earth to-morrow, none would know so much of me as you: that a nameless youth came up at nightfall from the valley of the Saco, and opened his heart to you in the evening, and passed through the Notch by sunrise, and was seen no more. Not a soul would ask, 'Who was he? Whither did the wanderer go?' But I cannot die till I have achieved my destiny. Then, let Death come! I shall have built my monument!"

There was a continual flow of natural emotion, gushing forth amid abstracted reverie, which enabled the family to understand this young man's sentiments, though so foreign from their own. With quick sensibility of the ludicrous, he blushed at the ardor into which he had been betrayed.

"You laugh at me," said he, taking the eldest daughter's hand, and laughing himself. "You think my ambition as nonsensical as if I were to freeze myself to death on the top of Mount Washington, only that people might spy at me from the country round about. And, truly, that would be a noble pedestal for a man's statue!"

"It is better to sit here by this fire," answered the girl, blushing, "and be comfortable and contented, though nobody thinks about us."

"I suppose," said her father, after a fit of musing, "there is something natural in what the young man says; and if my mind had been turned that way, I might have felt just the same. It is strange, wife, how his talk has set my head running on things that are pretty certain never to come to pass."

"Perhaps they may," observed the wife. "Is the man thinking what he will do when he is a widower?"

"No, no!" cried he, repelling the idea with reproachful kindness. "When I think of your death, Esther, I think of mine, too. But I was wishing we had a good farm in Bartlett, or Bethlehem, or Littleton, or some other township round the White Mountains; but not where they could tumble on our heads. I should want to stand well with my neighbors and be called Squire, and sent to General Court for a term or two; for a plain, honest man may do as much good there as a lawyer. And when I should be grown quite an old man, and you an old woman, so as not to be long apart, I might die happy enough in my bed, and leave you all crying around me. A slate gravestone would suit me as well as a marble one—with just my name and age, and a verse of a hymn, and something to let people know that I lived an honest man and died a Christian."

"There now!" exclaimed the stranger; "it is our nature to desire a monument, be it slate or marble, or a pillar of granite, or a glorious memory in the universal heart of man."

"We're in a strange way, to-night," said the wife, with tears in her eyes. "They say it's a sign of something, when folks' minds go a wandering so. Hark to the children!"

They listened accordingly. The younger children had been put to bed in another room, but with an open door between, so that they could be heard talking busily among themselves. One and all seemed to have caught the infection from the fireside circle, and were outvying each other in wild wishes, and childish projects of what they would do when they came to be men and women. At length a little boy, instead of addressing his brothers and sisters, called out to his mother.

"I'll tell you what I wish, mother," cried he. "I want you and father and grandma'm, and all of us, and the stranger too, to start right away, and go and take a drink out of the basin of the Flume!"

Nobody could help laughing at the child's notion of leaving a warm bed, and dragging them from a cheerful fire, to visit the basin of the Flume,—a brook, which tumbles over the precipice, deep within the Notch. The boy had hardly spoken when a wagon rattled along the road, and stopped a moment before the door. It appeared to contain two or three men, who were cheering their hearts with the rough chorus of a song, which resounded, in broken notes, between the cliffs, while the singers hesitated whether to continue their journey or put up here for the night.

"Father," said the girl, "they are calling you by name."

But the good man doubted whether they had really called him, and was unwilling to show himself too solicitous of gain by inviting people to patronize his house. He therefore did not hurry to the door; and the lash being soon applied, the travellers plunged into the Notch, still singing and laughing, though their music and mirth came back drearily from the heart of the mountain.

"There, mother!" cried the boy, again. "They'd have given us a ride to the Flume."

Again they laughed at the child's pertinacious fancy for a night ramble. But it happened that a light cloud passed over the daughter's spirit; she looked gravely into the fire, and drew a breath that was almost a sigh. It forced its way, in spite of a little struggle to repress it. Then starting and blushing, she looked quickly round the circle, as if they had caught a glimpse into her bosom. The stranger asked what she had been thinking of.

"Nothing," answered she, with a downcast smile. "Only I felt lonesome just then."

"Oh, I have always had a gift of feeling what is in other people's hearts," said he, half seriously. "Shall I tell the secrets of yours? For I know what to think when a young girl shivers by a warm hearth, and complains of lonesomeness at her mother's side. Shall I put these feelings into words?"

"They would not be a girl's feelings any longer if they could be put into words," replied the mountain nymph, laughing, but avoiding his eye.

All this was said apart. Perhaps a germ of love was springing in their hearts, so pure that it might blossom in Paradise, since it could not be matured on earth; for women worship such gentle dignity as his; and the proud, contemplative, yet kindly soul is oftenest captivated by simplicity like hers. But while they spoke softly, and he was watching the happy sadness, the lightsome shadows, the shy yearnings of a maiden's nature, the wind through the Notch took a deeper and drearier sound. It seemed, as the fanciful stranger said, like the choral strain of the spirits of the blast, who in old Indian times had their dwelling among these mountains, and made their heights and recesses a sacred region. There was a wail along the road, as if a funeral were passing. To chase away the gloom, the family threw pine branches on their fire, till the dry leaves crackled and the flame arose, discovering once again a scene of peace and humble happiness. The light hovered about them fondly, and caressed them all. There were the little faces of the children, peeping from their bed apart, and here the father's frame of strength, the mother's subdued and careful mien, the high-browed youth, the budding girl, and the good old grandam, still knitting in the warmest place. The aged woman looked up from her task, and, with fingers ever busy, was the next to speak.

"Old folks have their notions," said she, "as well as young ones. You've been wishing and planning; and letting your heads run on one thing and another, till you've set my mind a wandering too. Now what should an old woman wish for, when she can go but a step or two before she comes to her grave? Children, it will haunt me night and day till I tell you."

"What is it, mother?" cried the husband and wife at once.

Then the old woman, with an air of mystery which drew the circle closer round the fire, informed them that she had provided her grave-clothes some years before,—a nice linen shroud, a cap with a muslin ruff, and everything of a finer sort than she had worn since her wedding day. But this evening an old superstition had strangely recurred to her. It used to be said, in her younger days, that if anything were amiss with a corpse, if only the ruff were not smooth, or the cap did not set right, the corpse in the coffin and beneath the clods would strive to put up its cold hands and arrange it. The bare thought made her nervous.

"Don't talk so, grandmother!" said the girl, shuddering.

"Now,"—continued the old woman, with singular earnestness, yet smiling strangely at her own folly,—"I want one of you, my children—when your mother is dressed and in the coffin—I want one of you to hold a looking-glass over my face. Who knows but I may take a glimpse at myself, and see whether all's right?"

"Old and young, we dream of graves and monuments," murmured the stranger youth. "I wonder how mariners feel when the ship is sinking, and they, unknown and undistinguished, are to be buried together in the ocean—that wide and nameless sepulchre?"

For a moment, the old woman's ghastly conception so engrossed the minds of her hearers that a sound abroad in the night, rising like the roar of a blast, had grown broad, deep, and terrible, before the fated group were conscious of it. The house and all within it trembled; the foundations of the earth seemed to be shaken, as if this awful sound were the peal of the last trump. Young and old exchanged one wild glance, and remained an instant, pale, affrighted, without utterance, or power to move. Then the same shriek burst simultaneously from all their lips.

"The Slide! The Slide!"

The simplest words must intimate, but not portray, the unutterable horror of the catastrophe. The victims rushed from their cottage, and sought refuge in what they deemed a safer spot—where, in contemplation of such an emergency, a sort of barrier had been reared. Alas! they had quitted their security, and fled right into the pathway of destruction. Down came the whole side of the mountain, in a cataract of ruin. Just before it reached the house, the stream broke into two branches—shivered not a window there, but overwhelmed the whole vicinity, blocked up the road, and annihilated everything in its dreadful course. Long ere the thunder of the great Slide had ceased to roar among the mountains, the mortal agony had been endured, and the victims were at peace. Their bodies were never found.

The next morning, the light smoke was seen stealing from the cottage chimney up the mountain side. Within, the fire was yet smouldering on the hearth, and the chairs in a circle round it, as if the inhabitants had but gone forth to view the devastation of the Slide, and would shortly return, to thank Heaven for their miraculous escape. All had left separate tokens, by which those who had known the family were made to shed a tear for each. Who has not heard their name? The story has been told far and wide, and will forever be a legend of these mountains. Poets have sung their fate.

There were circumstances which led some to suppose that a stranger had been received into the cottage on this awful night, and had shared the catastrophe of all its inmates. Others denied that there were sufficient grounds for such a conjecture. Woe for the high-souled youth, with his dream of Earthly Immortality! His name and person utterly unknown; his history, his way of life, his plans, a mystery never to be solved, his death and his existence equally a doubt! Whose was the agony of that death moment?

1835

DISCUSSION QUESTIONS

1. Compare the first sentence of the historical account with Hawthorne's first sentence. Why is one specific and the other vague? What function does each sentence serve?

2. Which part of the historical account might possibly have given Hawthorne the inspiration for his story?

3. In the historical account, the victims appear to have been asleep when the avalanche occurred. Why does Hawthorne keep them awake up to the time of the disaster?

4. Though we are never told how the guest plans to achieve immortal fame, he does claim to possess "a gift of feeling what is in other people's hearts" (page 36). How does this admission help to identify his ambition or calling?

5. We are told that the children "caught the infection from the fireside circle" (page 35). Explain the nature of the "infection" and its cause.

6. What significance do you attach to the fact that if the family had complied with the little boy's fanciful wish, instead of laughing at it, they would have saved themselves?

7. Why does a "light cloud [pass] over the daughter's spirit" (page 36) while everyone is laughing at the boy's supposed whim?

8. Although for most of his story Hawthorne keeps his readers in the dark about the ultimate fate of his characters, he does prepare us by permeating his story with a carefully cultivated sense of foreboding. Beginning with the first sentence, identify the specific means used to create this *atmosphere.* Why do we need such *foreshadowing* to prepare us for the catastrophe when in real life disaster often strikes without any warning? What would have been our reaction if Hawthorne had merely described the family's perilous situation at the outset and then dropped the subject entirely until the avalanche begins?

9. Just before the avalanche kills them, the narrator calls its victims "the fated group." Since fate denotes a chain of predetermined circumstances that we are powerless to prevent, why is this particular operation of fate so *ironic?*

10. The foreknowledge that a second reading bestows gives us a new, more detached perspective from which to view "The Ambitious Guest."

We are now in a position to see the discrepancy between the characters' expectations and the actual outcome of events (*dramatic irony*). How does your own emotional reaction to the events change? How do you react, for example, to the following statement: "I felt as if you had kindled it on purpose for me, and were waiting my arrival" (page 33), knowing what will soon occur? Likewise, how do you respond to the little boy who wants everybody "to start right away" for the "basin of the Flume" or the men who "hesitated whether to continue their journey or put up here for the night" (page 36)?

ANALYSIS AND APPLICATION

1. Compare Hawthorne's first sentence with the following modified version: One September night a family had gathered round their hearth, and piled it high with the driftwood of mountain streams, the splintered ruins of great trees that had come crashing down the precipice, and the dry cones of the pine. Which version do you prefer? Why?

2. Analyze the following *extended metaphor:* "The romantic pass of the Notch is a great artery, through which the life-blood of internal commerce is continually throbbing . . ." (page 32). Identify each point of comparison and comment on its appropriateness.

THE CHILD-WHO-WAS-TIRED

KATHERINE MANSFIELD

SHE WAS just beginning to walk along a little white road with tall black trees on either side, a little road that led to nowhere, and where nobody walked at all, when a hand gripped her shoulder, shook her, slapped her ear.

"Oh, oh, don't stop me," cried the Child-Who-Was-Tired. "Let me go."

"Get up, you good-for-nothing brat," said a voice; "get up and light the oven or I'll shake every bone out of your body."

With an immense effort she opened her eyes, and saw the Frau standing by, the baby bundled under one arm. The three other children who shared the same bed with the Child-Who-Was-Tired, accustomed to brawls, slept on peacefully. In a corner of the room the Man was fastening his braces.

"What do you mean by sleeping like this the whole night through—like a sack of potatoes? You've let the baby wet his bed twice."

She did not answer, but tied her petticoat string, and buttoned on her plaid frock with cold, shaking fingers.

"There, that's enough. Take the baby into the kitchen with you, and heat that cold coffee on the spirit lamp for the master, and give him the loaf of black bread out of the table drawer. Don't guzzle it yourself or I'll know."

The Frau staggered across the room, flung herself on to her bed, drawing the pink bolster round her shoulders.

It was almost dark in the kitchen. She laid the baby on the wooden settle, covering him with a shawl, then poured the coffee from the earthenware jug into the saucepan, and set it on the spirit lamp to boil.

"I'm sleepy," nodded the Child-Who-Was-Tired, kneeling on the floor and splitting the damp pine logs into little chips. "That's why I'm not awake."

The oven took a long time to light. Perhaps it was cold, like herself, and sleepy.... Perhaps it had been dreaming of a little white road with black trees on either side, a little road that led to nowhere.

Then the door was pulled violently open and the Man strode in.

"Here, what are you doing, sitting on the floor?" he shouted. "Give me my coffee. I've got to be off. Ugh! You haven't even washed over the table."

She sprang to her feet, poured his coffee into an enamel cup, and gave him bread and a knife, then, taking a wash rag from the sink, smeared over the black linoleumed table.

"Swine of a day—swine's life," mumbled the Man, sitting by the table and staring out of the window at the bruised sky, which seemed to bulge heavily over the dull land. He stuffed his mouth with bread and then swilled it down with the coffee.

The Child drew a pail of water, turned up her sleeves, frowning the while at her arms, as if to scold them for being so thin, so much like little stunted twigs, and began to mop over the floor.

"Stop sousing about the water while I'm here," grumbled the man. "Stop the baby snivelling; it's been going on like that all night."

The Child gathered the baby into her lap and sat rocking him.

"Ts—ts—ts," she said. "He's cutting his eye teeth, that's what makes him cry so. *And* dribble—I never seen a baby dribble like this one."

She wiped his mouth and nose with a corner of her skirt. "Some babies get their teeth without you knowing it," she went on, "and some take on this way all the time. I once heard of a baby that died, and they found all its teeth in its stomach."

The Man got up, unhooked his cloak from the back of the door, and flung it round him.

"There's another coming," said he.

"What—a tooth!" exclaimed the Child, startled for the first time that morning out of her dreadful heaviness, and thrusting her finger into the baby's mouth.

"No," he said grimly, "another baby. Now, get on with your work; it's time the others got up for school." She stood a moment quite silently, hearing his heavy steps on the stone passage, then the gravel walk, and finally the slam of the front gate.

"Another baby! Hasn't she finished having them *yet?*" thought the Child. "Two babies getting eye teeth—two babies to get up for in the night—two babies to carry about and wash their little piggy clothes!" She looked with horror at the one in her arms, who, seeming to understand the contemptuous loathing of her tired glance, doubled his fists, stiffened his body, and began violently screaming.

"Ts—ts—ts." She laid him on the settle and went back to her floor-washing. He never ceased crying for a moment, but she got quite used to it and kept time with her broom. Oh, how tired she was! Oh, the heavy broom handle and the burning spot just at the back of her neck that ached so, and a funny little fluttering feeling just at the back of her waistband, as though something were going to break.

The clock struck six. She set the pan of milk in the oven, and went into the next room to wake and dress the three children. Anton and Hans lay together in attitudes of mutual amity which certainly never existed out of their sleeping hours. Lena was curled up, her knees under her chin, only a straight, standing-up pigtail of hair showing above the bolster.

"Get up," cried the Child, speaking in a voice of immense authority, pulling off the bedclothes and giving the boys sundry pokes and digs. "I've been calling you this last half-hour. It's late, and I'll tell on you if you don't get dressed this minute."

Anton awoke sufficiently to turn over and kick Hans on a tender part, whereupon Hans pulled Lena's pigtail until she shrieked for her mother.

"Oh, do be quiet," whispered the Child. "Oh, do get up and dress. You know what will happen. There—I'll help you."

But the warning came too late. The Frau got out of bed, walked in a determined fashion into the kitchen, returning with a bundle of twigs in her hand fastened together with a strong cord. One by one she laid the children across her knee and severely beat them, expending a final burst of energy on the Child-Who-Was-Tired, then returned to bed, with a comfortable sense of her maternal duties in good working order for the day. Very subdued, the three allowed themselves to be dressed and washed by the Child, who even laced the boys' boots, having found through experience that if left to themselves they hopped about for at least five minutes to find a comfortable ledge for their foot, and then spat on their hands and broke the bootlaces.

While she gave them their breakfast they became uproarious, and the baby would not cease crying. When she filled the tin kettle with milk, tied on the rubber teat, and, first moistening it herself, tried with little coaxing words to make him drink, he threw the bottle on to the floor and trembled all over.

"Eye teeth!" shouted Hans, hitting Anton over the head with his empty cup; "he's getting the evil-eye teeth, I should say."

"Smarty!" retorted Lena, poking out her tongue at him, and then, when he promptly did the same, crying at the top of her voice, "Mother, Hans is making faces at me!"

"That's right," said Hans; "go on howling, and when you're in bed to-night I'll wait till you're asleep, and then I'll creep over and take a little tiny piece of your arm and twist and twist it until—" He leant over the table making the most horrible faces at Lena, not noticing that Anton was standing behind his chair until the little boy bent over and spat on his brother's shaven head.

"Oh, weh! oh! weh!"

The Child-Who-Was-Tired pushed and pulled them apart, muffled them into their coats, and drove them out of the house.

"Hurry, hurry! the second bell's rung," she urged, knowing perfectly well she was telling a story, and rather exulting in the fact. She washed up the breakfast things, then went down to the cellar to look out the potatoes and beetroot.

Such a funny, cold place the coal cellar! With potatoes banked on one corner, beetroot in an old candle box, two tubs of sauerkraut, and a twisted mass of dahlia roots—that looked as real as though they were fighting one another, thought the Child.

She gathered the potatoes into her skirt, choosing big ones with few eyes because they were easier to peel, and bending over the dull heap in the silent cellar, she began to nod.

"Here, you, what are you doing down there?" cried the Frau, from the top of the stairs. "The baby's fallen off the settle, and got a bump as big as an egg over his eye. Come up here, and I'll teach you!"

"It wasn't me—it wasn't me!" screamed the Child, beaten from one side of the hall to the other, so that the potatoes and beetroot rolled out of her skirt.

The Frau seemed to be as big as a giant, and there was a certain heaviness in all her movements that was terrifying to anyone so small.

"Sit in the corner, and peel and wash the vegetables, and keep the baby quiet while I do the washing."

Whimpering she obeyed, but as to keeping the baby quiet, that was impossible. His face was hot, little beads of sweat stood all over his head, and he stiffened his body and cried. She held him on her knees, with a pan of cold water beside her for the cleaned vegetables and the ducks' bucket for the peelings.

"Ts—ts—ts!" she crooned, scraping and boring; "there's going to be another soon, and you can't both keep on crying. Why don't you go to sleep, baby? I would, if I were you. I'll tell you a dream. Once upon a time there was a little white road—"

She shook back her head, a great lump ached in her throat and then the tears ran down her face on to the vegetables.

"That's no good," said the Child, shaking them away. "Just stop crying until I've finished this, baby, and I'll walk you up and down."

But by that time she had to peg out the washing for the Frau. A wind had sprung up. Standing on tiptoe in the yard, she almost felt she would be blown away. There was a bad smell coming from the ducks' coop, which was half full of manure water, but away in the meadow she saw the grass blowing like little green hairs. And she remembered having heard of a child who had once played for a whole day in just such a meadow with real sausages and beer for her dinner—and not a little bit of tiredness. Who had told her that story? She could not remember, and yet it was so plain.

The wet clothes flapped in her face as she pegged them; danced and jigged on the line, bulged out and twisted. She walked back to the house with lagging steps, looking longingly at the grass in the meadow.

"What must I do now, please?" she said.

"Make the beds and hang the baby's mattress out of the window, then get the waggon and take him for a little walk along the road. In front of the house, mind—where I can see you. Don't stand there, gaping! Then come in when I call you and help me cut up the salad."

When she had made the beds the Child stood and looked at them. Gently she stroked the pillow with her hand, and then, just for one moment, let her head rest there. Again the smarting lump in her throat, the stupid tears that fell and kept on falling as she dressed the baby and dragged the little waggon up and down the road.

A man passed, driving a bullock waggon. He wore a long, queer feather in his hat, and whistled as he passed. Two girls with bundles on their shoulders came walking out of the village—one wore a red handkerchief about her head and one a blue. They were laughing and holding each other by the hand. Then the sun pushed by a heavy fold of grey cloud and spread a warm yellow light over everything.

"Perhaps," thought the Child-Who-Was-Tired, "if I walked far enough up this road I might come to a little white one, with tall black trees on either side—a little road—"

"Salad, salad!" cried the Frau's voice from the house.

Soon the children came home from school, dinner was eaten, the Man took the Frau's share of pudding as well as his own, and the three children seemed to smear themselves all over with whatever they ate. Then more dish-washing and more cleaning and baby-minding. So the afternoon dragged coldly through.

Old Frau Gerathwohl came in with a fresh piece of pig's flesh for the Frau, and the Child listened to them gossiping together.

"Frau Manda went on her 'journey to Rome' last night, and brought back a daughter. How are you feeling?"

"I was sick twice this morning," said the Frau. "My insides are all twisted up with having children too quickly."

"I see you've got a new help," commented old Mother Gerathwohl.

"Oh, dear Lord"—the Frau lowered her voice—"don't you know her? She's the free-born one—daughter of the waitress at the railway station. They found her mother trying to squeeze her head in the wash-hand jug, and the child's half silly."

"Ts—ts—ts!" whispered the free-born one to the baby.

As the day drew in the Child-Who-Was-Tired did not know how to fight her sleepiness any longer. She was afraid to sit down or stand still. As she sat at supper the Man and the Frau seemed to swell to an immense size as she watched them, and then become smaller than dolls, with little voices that seemed to come from outside the window. Looking at the baby, it suddenly had two heads, and then no head. Even his crying made her feel worse. When she thought of the nearness of bedtime she shook all over with excited joy. But as eight o'clock approached there was the sound of wheels on the road, and presently in came a party of friends to spend the evening.

Then it was:

"Put on the coffee."

"Bring me the sugar tin."

"Carry the chairs out of the bedroom."

"Set the table."

And, finally, the Frau sent her into the next room to keep the baby quiet.

There was a little piece of candle burning in the enamel bracket. As she walked up and down she saw her great big shadow on the wall like a grown-up person with a grown-up baby. Whatever would it look like when she carried two babies so!

"Ts—ts—ts! Once upon a time she was walking along a little white road, with oh! such great big black trees on either side."

"Here, you!" called the Frau's voice, "bring me my new jacket from behind the door." And as she took it into the warm room one of the women said, "She looks like an owl. Such children are seldom right in their heads."

"Why don't you keep that baby quiet?" said the Man, who had just drunk enough beer to make him feel very brave and master of his house.

"If you don't keep that baby quiet you'll know why later on."

They burst out laughing as she stumbled back into the bedroom.

"I don't believe Holy Mary could keep him quiet," she murmured. "Did Jesus cry like this when He was little? If I was not so tired perhaps I could do it; but the baby just knows that I want to go to sleep. And there is going to be another one."

She flung the baby on the bed, and stood looking at him with terror.

From the next room there came the jingle of glasses and the warm sound of laughter.

And she suddenly had a beautiful marvellous idea.

She laughed for the first time that day, and clapped her hands.

"Ts—ts—ts!" she said, "lie there, silly one; you *will* go to sleep. You'll not cry any more or wake up in the night. Funny, little ugly baby."

He opened his eyes, and shrieked loudly at the sight of the Child-Who-Was-Tired. From the next room she heard the Frau call out to her.

"One moment—he is almost asleep," she cried.

And then gently, smiling, on tiptoe, she brought the pink bolster from the Frau's bed and covered the baby's face with it, pressed with all her might as he struggled, "like a duck with its head off, wriggling," she thought.

She heaved a long sigh, then fell back on to the floor, and was walking along a little white road with tall black trees on either side, a little road that led to nowhere, and where nobody walked at all—nobody at all.

1911

SLEEPY

ANTON CHEKHOV

NIGHT. VARKA, the little nurse, a girl of thirteen, is rocking the cradle in which the baby is lying, and humming hardly audibly:

Hush-a-bye, my baby wee,
While I sing a song for thee.

A little green lamp is burning before the ikon; there is a string stretched from one end of the room to the other, on which baby-clothes and a pair of big black trousers are hanging. There is a big patch of green on the ceiling from the ikon-lamp, and the baby-clothes and the

Reprinted with permission of Macmillan Publishing Co., Inc. from *The Cook's Wedding and Other Stories* by Anton Chekhov. Translated from the Russian by Constance Garnett. Copyright 1922 by Macmillan Publishing Co., Inc., renewed 1950 by David Garnett. Also reprinted with permission of David Garnett and Chatto & Windus from *Select Tales of Tchehov* Volume I, Barnes & Noble, translated by Constance Garnett.

trousers throw long shadows on the stove, on the cradle, and on Varka. . . . When the lamp begins to flicker, the green patch and the shadows come to life, and are set in motion, as though by the wind. It is stuffy. There is a smell of cabbage soup, and of the inside of a boot-shop.

The baby is crying. For a long while he has been hoarse and exhausted with crying; but he still goes on screaming, and there is no knowing when he will stop. And Varka is sleepy. Her eyes are glued together, her head droops, her neck aches. She cannot move her eyelids or her lips, and she feels as though her face is dried and wooden, as though her head has become as small as the head of a pin.

"Hush-a-bye, my baby wee," she hums, "while I cook the groats for thee. . . ."

A cricket is churring in the stove. Through the door in the next room the master and the apprentice Afanasy are snoring. . . . The cradle creaks plaintively, Varka murmurs—and it all blends into that soothing music of the night to which it is so sweet to listen, when one is lying in bed. Now that music is merely irritating and oppressive, because it goads her to sleep, and she must not sleep; if Varka—God forbid!—should fall asleep, her master and mistress would beat her.

The lamp flickers. The patch of green and the shadows are set in motion, forcing themselves on Varka's fixed, half-open eyes, and in her half-slumbering brain are fashioned into misty visions. She sees dark clouds chasing one another over the sky, and screaming like the baby. But then the wind blows, the clouds are gone, and Varka sees a broad high-road covered with liquid mud; along the high-road stretched files of wagons, while people with wallets on their backs are trudging along and shadows flit backwards and forwards; on both sides she can see forests through the cold harsh mist. All at once the people with their wallets and their shadows fall on the ground in the liquid mud. "What is that for?" Varka asks. "To sleep, to sleep!" they answer her. And they fall sound asleep, and sleep sweetly, while crows and magpies sit on the telegraph wires, scream like the baby, and try to wake them.

"Hush-a-bye, my baby wee, and I will sing a song to thee," murmurs Varka, and now she sees herself in a dark stuffy hut.

Her dead father, Yefim Stepanov, is tossing from side to side on the floor. She does not see him, but she hears him moaning and rolling on the floor from pain. "His guts have burst," as he says; the pain is so violent that he cannot utter a single word, and can only draw in his breath and clack his teeth like the rattling of a drum:

"Boo—boo—boo—boo. . . ."

Her mother, Pelageya, has run to the master's house to say that Yefim is dying. She has been gone a long time, and ought to be back. Varka lies awake on the stove, and hears her father's "boo—boo—boo." And then she hears someone has driven up to the hut. It is a young doctor from the town, who has been sent from the big house where he is staying on a visit. The doctor comes into the hut; he cannot be seen in the darkness, but he can be heard coughing and rattling the door.

"Light a candle," he says.

"Boo—boo—boo," answers Yefim.

Pelageya rushes to the stove and begins looking for the broken pot with the matches. A minute passes in silence. The doctor, feeling in his pocket, lights a match.

"In a minute, sir, in a minute," says Pelageya. She rushes out of the hut, and soon afterwards comes back with a bit of candle.

Yefim's cheeks are rosy and his eyes are shining, and there is a peculiar keenness in his glance, as though he were seeing right through the hut and the doctor.

"Come, what is it? What are you thinking about?" says the doctor, bending down to him. "Aha! have you had this long?"

"What? Dying, your honour, my hour has come. . . . I am not to stay among the living. . . ."

"Don't talk nonsense! We will cure you!"

"That's as you please, your honour, we humbly thank you, only we understand. . . . Since death has come, there it is."

The doctor spends a quarter of an hour over Yefim, then he gets up and says:

"I can do nothing. You must go into the hospital, there they will operate on you. Go at once. . . . You must go! It's rather late, they will all be asleep in the hospital, but that doesn't matter, I will give you a note. Do you hear?"

"Kind sir, but what can he go in?" says Pelageya. "We have no horse."

"Never mind. I'll ask your master, he'll let you have a horse."

The doctor goes away, the candle goes out, and again there is the sound of "boo—boo—boo." Half an hour later someone drives up to the hut. A cart has been sent to take Yefim to the hospital. He gets ready and goes. . . .

But now it is a clear bright morning. Pelageya is not at home; she has gone to the hospital to find what is being done to Yefim. Somewhere there is a baby crying, and Varka hears someone singing with her own voice:

"Hush-a-bye, my baby wee, I will sing a song to thee."

Pelageya comes back; she crosses herself and whispers:

"They put him to rights in the night, but towards morning he gave up his soul to God. . . . The Kingdom of Heaven be his and peace everlasting. . . . They say he was taken too late. . . . He ought to have gone sooner. . . ."

Varka goes out into the road and cries there, but all at once someone hits her on the back of her head so hard that her forehead knocks against a birch-tree. She raises her eyes, and sees facing her, her master, the shoemaker.

"What are you about, you scabby slut?" he says. "The child is crying, and you are asleep!"

He gives her a sharp slap behind the ear, and she shakes her head, rocks the cradle, and murmurs her song. The green patch and the shadows from the trousers and the baby-clothes move up and down, nod to her, and soon take possession of her brain again. Again she sees the high-road covered with liquid mud. The people with wallets on their backs and the shadows have lain down and are fast asleep. Looking at them, Varka has a passionate longing for sleep; she would lie down with enjoyment, but her mother Pelageya is walking beside her, hurrying her on. They are hastening together to the town to find situations.

"Give alms, for Christ's sake!" her mother begs of the people they meet. "Show us the Divine Mercy, kind-hearted gentlefolk!"

"Give the baby here!" a familiar voice answers. "Give the baby here!" the same voice repeats, this time harshly and angrily. "Are you asleep, you wretched girl?"

Varka jumps up, and looking round grasps what is the matter: there is no high-road, no Pelageya, no people meeting them, there is only her mistress, who has come to feed the baby, and is standing in the middle of the room. While the stout, broad-shouldered woman nurses the child and soothes it, Varka stands looking at her and waiting till she has done. And outside the windows the air is already turning blue, the shadows and the green patch on the ceiling are visibly growing pale, it will soon be morning.

"Take him," says her mistress, buttoning up her chemise over her bosom; "he is crying. He must be bewitched."

Varka takes the baby, puts him in the cradle, and begins rocking it again. The green patch and the shadows gradually disappear, and now there is nothing to force itself on her eyes and cloud her brain. But she is as sleepy as before, fearfully sleepy! Varka lays her head on the edge of the cradle, and rocks her whole body to overcome her sleepiness, but yet her eyes are glued together, and her head is heavy.

"Varka, heat the stove!" she hears the master's voice through the door.

So it is time to get up and set to work. Varka leaves the cradle, and runs to the shed for firewood. She is glad. When one moves and runs about, one is not so sleepy as when one is sitting down. She brings the wood, heats the stove, and feels that her wooden face is getting supple again, and that her thoughts are growing clearer.

"Varka, set the samovar!" shouts her mistress.

Varka splits a piece of wood, but has scarcely time to light the splinters and put them in the samovar, when she hears a fresh order:

"Varka, clean the master's goloshes!"

She sits down on the floor, cleans the goloshes, and thinks how nice it would be to put her head into a big deep golosh, and have a little nap in it.... And all at once the golosh grows, swells, fills up the whole room. Varka drops the brush, but at once shakes her head, opens her eyes wide, and tries to look at things so that they may not grow big and move before her eyes.

"Varka, wash the steps outside; I am ashamed for the customers to see them!"

Varka washes the steps, sweeps and dusts the rooms, then heats another stove and runs to the shop. There is a great deal of work: she hasn't one minute free.

But nothing is so hard as standing in the same place at the kitchen table peeling potatoes. Her head droops over the table, the potatoes dance before her eyes, the knife tumbles out of her hand while her fat, angry mistress is moving about near her with her sleeves tucked up, talking so loud that it makes a ringing in Varka's ears. It is agonizing, too, to wait at dinner, to wash, to sew, there are minutes when she longs to flop on to the floor regardless of everything, and to sleep.

The day passes. Seeing the windows getting dark, Varka presses her temples that feel as though they were made of wood, and smiles, though she does not know why. The dusk of evening caresses her eyes that will hardly keep open, and promises her sound sleep soon. In the evening visitors come.

"Varka, set the samovar!" shouts her mistress.

The samovar is a little one, and before the visitors have drunk all the tea they want, she has to heat it five times. After tea Varka stands for a whole hour on the same spot, looking at the visitors, and waiting for orders.

"Varka, run and buy three bottles of beer!"

She starts off, and tries to run as quickly as she can, to drive away sleep.

"Varka, fetch some vodka! Varka, where's the corkscrew? Varka, clean a herring!"

But now, at last, the visitors have gone; the lights are put out, the master and mistress go to bed.

"Varka, rock the baby!" she hears the last order.

The cricket churrs in the stove; the green patch on the ceiling and the shadows from the trousers and the baby-clothes force themselves on Varka's half-opened eyes again, wink at her and cloud her mind.

"Hush-a-bye, my baby wee," she murmurs, "and I will sing a song to thee."

And the baby screams, and is worn out with screaming. Again Varka sees the muddy high-road, the people with wallets, her mother Pelageya, her father Yefim. She understands everything, she recognizes everyone, but through her half-sleep she cannot understand the force which binds her, hand and foot, weighs upon her, and prevents her from living. She looks round, searches for that force that she may escape from it, but she cannot find it. At last, tired to death, she does her very utmost, strains her eyes, looks up at the flickering green patch, and, listening to the screaming, finds the foe who will not let her live.

That foe is the baby.

She laughs. It seems strange to her that she has failed to grasp such a simple thing before. The green patch, the shadows, and the cricket seem to laugh and wonder too.

The hallucination takes possession of Varka. She gets up from her stool, and with a broad smile on her face and wide unblinking eyes, she walks up and down the room. She feels pleased and tickled at the thought that she will be rid directly of the baby that binds her hand and foot. . . . Kill the baby and then sleep, sleep, sleep. . . .

Laughing and winking and shaking her fingers at the green patch, Varka steals up to the cradle and bends over the baby. When she has strangled him, she quickly lies down on the floor, laughs with delight that she can sleep, and in a minute is sleeping as sound as the dead.

1888

Translated by Constance Garnett

DISCUSSION QUESTIONS

1. Varka's dream, in which she recalls her father's death, explains the circumstances that have led to her present plight. Without this *flashback,* would we feel differently toward Varka and her act of murder? Explain. Does Mansfield provide any comparable *exposition?*

2. Define the *atmosphere* (prevailing mood) Chekhov creates in his second paragraph through his description of the *setting.* Which of our five senses is stimulated by the *imagery?* A part of it, "the green patch and the shadows," recurs frequently, recalling earlier associations. Explain the function of this *motif* in the story.

3. The Child looks at the baby with "contemptuous loathing." Does Varka feel any comparable animosity toward her charge before the last four paragraphs of the story? If so, how does Chekhov convey it?

4. Such *ironic* statements as those indicating that the Frau "returned to bed, with a comfortable sense of her maternal duties in good working order for the day" (page 44) and that the Man "had just drunk enough beer to make him feel very brave and master of his house (page 47) make Mansfield's contempt explicit. What is Chekhov's attitude toward Varka's employers and how does he convey it?

5. What "force . . . binds [Varka], hand and foot, weighs upon her, and prevents her from living" (page 54)? In what terms does Mansfield's Child picture "living"? What comparable "force" stifles her?

6. Explain the significance of Chekhov's recurring *imagery* of men sleeping in the liquid mud of the highway.

7. Likewise, what is the significance of Mansfield's recurring *imagery* of "a little white road with tall black trees on either side, a little road that led to nowhere, and where nobody walked at all"?

8. What specific factors and chain of circumstances induce each girl to murder her charge? Compare the two endings carefully.

9. How does each writer prepare us for the murder? Of the two protagonists, whose actions seem more plausible? Why? Do Mansfield's broad hints that the Child is mentally retarded improve or weaken the story?

10. Which do you judge to be the better story? Why?

ANALYSIS AND APPLICATION

1. Compare the following modified passage with Mansfield's original on page 45: She stood on tiptoe in the yard and almost felt she would be blown away. There was a bad smell coming from the duck's coop because it was half full of water, and away in the meadow she saw the grass blowing like little green hairs. Explain the effect of each specific change. Which version do you prefer? Why?

2. Compare the last paragraph of "Sleepy" with another translation of the same passage:

And smiling and blinking and threatening the green spot with her fingers, Varka steals to the cradle and bends over the child.... And having smothered the child, she drops to the floor, and, laughing with joy at the thought that she can sleep, in a moment sleeps as soundly as the child.[1]

Identify individual differences and give reasons for your preferences. Which translation do you prefer? Why?

3. Examine the following *implied metaphor:* "the bruised sky, which seemed to bulge heavily over the dull land" (page 42). To what is the sky being compared? How appropriate is the comparison, and what is its purpose within the context of the story?

[1] Anton Chekhov, *Works* (New York: Walter J. Black, 1929), p. 320.

From TRICKS AND DEFEATS OF SPORTING GENIUS

SAMUEL SEABOUGH

JOE B– –, formerly of Calaveras county, was, is, and always will be a "sport." He bets on every game, but has a particular penchant for "dead things," such as thimble-rig and French monte,[1] and from some cause, always a mystery, of course, he was generally "dead broke." Well, one day he was in a neck of woods where poker games were as thick as blackberries in the angles of an Old Virginia fence, and those who played them, as much sharper than himself as a cambric needle is sharper than the Big Tree stump.

Joe borrowed an X, and set his wits to work for a raise. Lounging on an old log that lay over a prospect hole—now eloquent with the

From San Andreas *Independent*, 11 December 1858, p. 2.

[1] A form of the card game known as monte.

croaking of a hundred frogs, he observed a small, trim-built musical little cuss, doing some of the tallest kind of leaping. Joe gave chase—over banks of rubbish, through bogs and down into a deep hole went his frogship, and down went Joe, up to his eyes in mud and water. Joe had an "idee," *he had!* The frog was quickly fished out, and away he went to the landlord, as jolly an old Boniface as ever drew cork from a bottle of ale.

"I'll bet an X," said Joe, "that this 'ere's a blooded race-frog, an' kin jist outjump any other croakin varmint in the nineteen States."

"Take that bet," said Boniface.

"Come *down* with yer spondulicks,[2]" retorted Joe—and the cash was staked.

The champions were soon brought to the scratch, and at the word, away they went—and away went the landlord's X—losing by a foot and a-half.

Boniface was not satisfied. He offered to double the bet and jump in the morning.

"Done," said Joe, and down went two 20's.

That night, tidings of the "new game" spread throughout the neighboring gulches, and down the road as far as "Sucker creek," and "Sardine hill." In they crowded—"Sucker" and "Sardine,"[3] with the "greeneys"[4] from "Tadpole bar," and down went their dust[5] on the new game. Jack H– –, who was an old turfman, and never deceived in the "pints an' muscle uv a hoss," bet *his* money on Joe's nag, and all "Suckerdom" and all the "Tadpole" boys went in on Jack's judgment. Old Boniface had his friends who knew he was "weighty" on a repeat.

So next morning the frogs were brought to the score, surrounded by three hundred interested spectators. The word was given, and away they went—alas for poor Joe, and the "Suckers," and the "Tadpoles," with a most disastrous result to them! The "blooded frog" let down, worse than "Gray Eagle," in his renowned race with "Wagoner."

"Hello," said one, "he's sick, they've dragged 'im."

"Light'nin *hes* struck the critter," dryly remarked Boniface.

"Throw-off," muttered another.

Old Weaseleye, pushed through the crowd and picking up the dis-

[2] Money.
[3] Connotes immaturity or inexperience, as does "Tadpole."
[4] Greenhorns; persons who are inexperienced, naive, and gullible.
[5] Tiny gold particles derived from washing gold deposits; money.

comfited racer, and holding him above his head, squeezed out of his stomach about a pound of bird-shot, which Boniface had fed him in the night, mistaking them for flies.

Forty high-pressure boats, puffing against the current of the Mississippi, or a hundred howling wolves would be a dead silence to the roars and yells that followed Joe as his coat tail disappeared behind the next hill.

THE NOTORIOUS JUMPING FROG OF CALAVERAS[1] COUNTY

MARK TWAIN

IN COMPLIANCE with the request of a friend of mine, who wrote me from the East, I called on good-natured, garrulous old Simon Wheeler, and inquired after my friend's friend, Leonidas W. Smiley, as requested to do, and I hereunto append the result. I have a lurking suspicion that *Leonidas W.* Smiley is a myth; that my friend never knew such a personage; and that he only conjectured that if I asked old Wheeler about him, it would remind him of his infamous *Jim* Smiley, and he would go to work and bore me to death with some exasperating reminiscence of him as long and as tedious as it should be useless to me. If that was the design, it succeeded.

[1] Pronounced Cal-e-*va*-ras.

I found Simon Wheeler dozing comfortably by the barroom stove of the dilapidated tavern in the decayed mining camp of Angel's, and I noticed that he was fat and bald-headed, and had an expression of winning gentleness and simplicity upon his tranquil countenance. He roused up, and gave me good-day. I told him a friend of mine had commissioned me to make some inquiries about a cherished companion of his boyhood named *Leonidas W.* Smiley—*Rev. Leonidas W.* Smiley, a young minister of the Gospel, who he had heard was at one time a resident of Angel's Camp. I added that if Mr. Wheeler could tell me anything about this Rev. Leonidas W. Smiley, I would feel under many obligations to him.

Simon Wheeler backed me into a corner and blockaded me there with his chair, and then sat down and reeled off the monotonous narrative which follows this paragraph. He never smiled, he never frowned, he never changed his voice from the gentle-flowing key to which he tuned his initial sentence, he never betrayed the slightest suspicion of enthusiasm; but all through the interminable narrative there ran a vein of impressive earnestness and sincerity, which showed me plainly that, so far from his imagining that there was anything ridiculous or funny about his story, he regarded it as a really important matter, and admired its two heroes as men of transcendent genius in *finesse.* I let him go on in his own way, and never interrupted him once.

"Rev. Leonidas W. H'm, Reverend Le—well, there was a feller here once by the name of *Jim* Smiley, in the winter of '49—or may be it was the spring of '50—I don't recall exactly, somehow, though what makes me think it was one or the other is because I remember the big flume warn't finished when he first come to the camp; but any way, he was the curiosest man about always betting on anything that turned up you ever see, if he could get anybody to bet on the other side; and if he couldn't he'd change sides. Any way that suited the other man would suit *him*—any way just so's he got a bet, *he* was satisfied. But still he was lucky, uncommon lucky; he most always come out winner. He was always ready and laying for a chance; there couldn't be no solit'ry thing mentioned but that feller'd offer to bet on it, and take ary side you please, as I was just telling you. If there was a horse-race, you'd find him flush or you'd find him busted at the end of it; if there was a dog-fight, he'd bet on it; if there was a cat-fight, he'd bet on it; if there was a chicken-fight, he'd bet on it; why, if there was two birds setting on a fence, he would bet you which one would fly first; or if there was a camp-meeting, he would be there reg'lar to bet on Parson Walker, which he judged to be the best exhorter about here, and so he was too, and a good man. If he even see a straddle-bug start to go anywheres, he would bet you how long it would take him to get to—to wherever he was going to, and if you took him up, he would foller that straddle-bug to Mexico but what he would find out where he was bound for and how long he was on the road. Lots of the boys here has seen that Smiley, and can tell you about him. Why, it never made no difference to *him*—he'd bet on *any* thing—the dangdest feller. Parson Walker's wife laid very sick once, for a good while, and it seemed as if they warn't going to save her; but one morning he come in, and Smiley up and asked him how she was, and he said she was considable better—thank the Lord for his inf'nite mercy—and coming on so smart that with the blessing of Prov'dence she'd get well yet; and Smiley, before he thought, says, 'Well, I'll resk two-and-a-half she don't anyway."

Thish-yer Smiley had a mare—the boys called her the fifteen-minute nag, but that was only in fun, you know, because of course she was faster than that—and he used to win money on that horse, for all she was so slow and always had the asthma, or the distemper, or the consumption, or something of that kind. They used to give her two or three hundred yards start, and then pass her under way; but always at the fag end of the race she'd get excited and desperate like, and come cavorting and straddling up, and scattering her legs around limber, sometimes in the air, and sometimes out to one side among the fences, and kicking up m-o-r-e dust and raising m-o-r-e racket with her coughing and sneezing and blowing her nose—and *always* fetch up at the stand just about a neck ahead, as near as you could cipher it down.

And he had a little small bull-pup, that to look at him you'd think he warn't worth a cent but to set around and look ornery and lay for a chance to steal something. But as soon as money was up on him he was a different dog; his under-jaw'd begin to stick out like the fo'castle of a steamboat, and his teeth would uncover and shine like the furnaces. And a dog might tackle him and bully-rag him, and bite him, and throw him over his shoulder two or three times, and Andrew Jackson—which was the name of the pup—Andrew Jackson would never let on but what *he* was satisfied, and hadn't expected nothing else—and the bets being doubled and doubled on the other side all the time, till the money was all up; and then all of a sudden he would grab that other dog jest by the j'int of his hind leg and freeze to it—not chaw, you understand, but only just grip and hang on till they throwed up the sponge, if it was a year. Smiley always come out winner on that pup, till he harnessed a dog once that didn't have no hind legs, because they'd been sawed off in a circular saw, and when the thing had gone along far enough, and the money was all up, and he come to make a snatch for his pet holt, he see in a minute how he'd been imposed on, and how the other dog had him in the door, so to speak, and he 'peared surprised, and then he looked sorter discouraged-like, and didn't try no more to win the fight, and so he got shucked out bad. He give Smiley a look, as much as to say his heart was broke, and it was *his* fault, for putting up a dog that hadn't no hind legs for him to take holt of, which was his main dependence in a fight, and then he limped off a piece and laid down and died. It was a good pup, was that Andrew Jackson, and would have made a name for hisself if he'd lived, for the stuff was in him and he had genius—I know it, because he hadn't no opportunities to speak of, and it don't stand to reason that a dog could make such a fight as he could under them circumstances if he hadn't no talent. It always makes me feel sorry when I think of that last fight of his'n, and the way it turned out.

Well, thish-yer Smiley had rat-tarriers, and chicken cocks, and tomcats and all them kind of things, till you couldn't rest, and you couldn't fetch nothing for him to bet on but he'd match you. He ketched a frog one day, and took him home, and said he cal'lated to educate him; and so he never done nothing for three months but set in his back yard and learn that frog to jump. And you bet you he *did* learn him, too. He'd give him a little punch behind, and the next minute you'd see that frog whirling in the air like a doughnut—see him turn one summerset, or may be a couple, if he got a good start, and come down flat-footed and all right, like a cat. He got him up so in the matter of ketching flies, and kep' him in practice so constant, that he'd nail a fly every time as fur as he could see him. Smiley said all a frog wanted was education, and he could do 'most anything—and I believe him. Why, I've seen him set Dan'l Webster down here on this floor—Dan'l Webster was the name of the frog—and sing out, "Flies, Dan'l, flies!" and quicker'n you could wink he'd spring straight up and snake a fly off'n the counter there, and flop down on the floor ag'in as solid as a gob of mud, and fall to scratching the side of his head with his hind foot as indifferent as if he hadn't no idea he'd been doin' any more'n any frog might do. You never see a frog so modest and straightfor'ard as he was, for all he was so gifted. And when it come to fair and square jumping on a dead level, he could get over more ground at one straddle than any animal of his breed you ever see. Jumping on a dead level was his strong suit, you understand; and when it come to that, Smiley would ante up money on him as long as he had a red.[2] Smiley was monstrous proud of his frog, and well he might be, for fellers that had traveled and been everywheres all said he laid over any frog that ever *they* see.

Well, Smiley kep' the beast in a little lattice box, and he used to fetch him down town sometimes and lay for a bet. One day a feller—a stranger in the camp, he was—come acrost him with his box, and says:

"What might it be that you've got in the box?"

And Smiley says, sorter indifferent-like, "It might be a parrot, or it might be a canary, maybe, but it ain't—its only just a frog."

And the feller took it, and looked at it careful, and turned it round this way and that, and says, "H'm—so 'tis. Well, what's *he* good for?"

"Well," Smiley says, easy and careless, "he's good enough for *one* thing, I should judge—he can outjump any frog in Calaveras county."

The feller took the box again, and took another long, particular look, and give it back to Smiley, and says, very deliberate, "Well," he says, "I don't see no p'ints about that frog that's any better'n any other frog."

"Maybe you don't," Smiley says. "Maybe you understand frogs and maybe you don't understand 'em; maybe you've had experience, and maybe you ain't only a amature, as it were. Anyways, I've got *my* opinion, and I'll resk forty dollars that he can outjump any frog in Calaveras county."

And the feller studied a minute, and then says, kinder sad like, "Well, I'm only a stranger here, and I ain't got no frog; but if I had a frog, I'd bet you."

And then Smiley says, "That's all right—that's all right—if you'll hold my box a minute, I'll go and get you a frog." And so the feller took the box, and put up his forty dollars along with Smiley's, and set down to wait.

So he set there a good while thinking and thinking to hisself, and then he got the frog out and prized his mouth open and took a teaspoon and filled him full of quail shot—filled him pretty near up to his chin—and set him on the floor. Smiley he went to the swamp and slopped around in the mud for a long time, and finally he ketched a frog, and fetched him in, and give him to this feller, and says:

"Now, if you're ready, set him alongside of Dan'l, with his forepaws just even with Dan'l's, and I'll give the word." Then he says, "One—two—three—*git!*" and him and the feller touched up the frogs from

[2] Cent (formerly made of copper).

behind, and the new frog hopped off lively, but Dan'l give a heave, and hysted up his shoulders—so—like a Frenchman, but it warn't no use—he couldn't budge; he was planted as solid as a church, and he couldn't no more stir than if he was anchored out. Smiley was a good deal surprised, and he was disgusted too, but he didn't have no idea what the matter was, of course.

The feller took the money and started away; and when he was going out at the door, he sorter jerked his thumb over his shoulder—so—at Dan'l, and says again, very deliberate, "Well," he says, "I don't see no p'ints about that frog that's any better'n any other frog."

Smiley he stood scratching his head and looking down at Dan'l a long time, and at last he says, "I do wonder what in the nation that frog throw'd off for—I wonder if there ain't something the matter with him—he 'pears to look mighty baggy, somehow." And he ketched Dan'l by the nap of the neck, and hefted him, and says, "Why blame my cats if he don't weigh five pound!" and turned him upside down and he belched out a double handful of shot. And then he see how it was, and he was the maddest man—he set the frog down and took out after that feller, but he never ketched him. And—"

[Here Simon Wheeler heard his name called from the front yard, and got up to see what was wanted.] And turning to me as he moved away, he said: "Just set where you are, stranger, and rest easy—I ain't going to be gone a second."

But, by your leave, I did not think that a continuation of the history of the enterprising vagabond *Jim* Smiley would be likely to afford me much information concerning the Rev. *Leonidas W.* Smiley, and so I started away.

At the door I met the sociable Wheeler returning, and he buttonholed me and re-commenced:

"Well, thish-yer Smiley had a yaller one-eyed cow that didn't have no tail, only just a short stump like a bannanner, and—"

However, lacking both time and inclination, I did not wait to hear about the afflicted cow, but took my leave.

1865

DISCUSSION QUESTIONS

1. Compare and contrast Joe B-- with Jim Smiley. Why does Joe decide to get a frog to wager on? How does each man obtain a winning frog?

2. Specifically, how and why is each man outsmarted? Whose defeat seems more surprising? Why?

3. Compare and contrast Boniface with Twain's stranger. Does either man have anything in common with Simon Wheeler? Support your answer with specific details.

4. Identify the parts of the story Twain added to the original and explain their purposes. What specific function does the *narrative frame* serve?

5. The narrator claims that Simon Wheeler can see nothing "ridiculous or funny" in his story. Is that true? If not, why does Wheeler tell his tale in such an expressionless manner?

6. What similarities can you find between Smiley's encounter with the stranger and the narrator's meeting with Wheeler? Explain the significance of Wheeler addressing the narrator as "stranger" at the end of the story. The narrator complains that Wheeler's story is useless to him. Is he right? Explain.

7. Contrast the narrator with Simon Wheeler. Support your answer with specific details. What basic difference in values distinguishes them?

8. What do Smiley's pup and mare have in common? How does Daniel Webster differ from them? How does this difference affect the outcome of Smiley's encounter with the stranger?

ANALYSIS AND APPLICATION

1. The first paragraph of Wheeler's tale is made up of eight examples to demonstrate Smiley's penchant for betting "on anything that turned up." Are the illustrations arranged according to any order or are they arbitrarily thrown together? Explain. Are all eight examples introduced in a similar way or does the manner of presentation change as the paragraph progresses? Explain.

2. Analyze the following *similes:* "his under-jaw'd begin to stick out like the fo'castle of a steamboat, and his teeth would uncover and shine like the furnaces" (page 63). Is the obvious incongruity of these comparisons justified within the context of the story? Explain. Find two other similes in Twain's story and determine whether they are equally extravagant.

REPENTANCE

FRANK O'CONNOR

HE KNEW he should have been overjoyed, but he wasn't. Preparation for his first confession and first Holy Communion involved the importation into the school of a horrid old devil of a woman in a big black bonnet and black-beaded cloak who kept them in for an extra half-hour during the whole week. While she talked Micky's attention wandered from her beard, which was large, to her rings, which were many. She was supposed to be enormously rich, and somehow the story had gone the rounds that she would give them sweets. She gave them no sweets at all, and when on her first visit she opened her large handbag it was only to produce a candle and a box of matches. She staggered

Reprinted by permission of Harriet O'Donovan Sheehy. Originally appeared in *Lovat Dickson's Magazine,* January 1935.

from her seat to the mantelpiece, wagging her big rheumaticky buttocks, and lit the candle. Then with fat, yellow, half-dead fingers that shone with rings she opened her purse and took out a crown-piece. A thrill of expectation ran through the roomful of ragged little boys; Micky's heart leaped wildly, and in the silence that followed, the silly song of a blackbird rose and fell from the green boughs that tapped the high square schoolwindow.

"I will give five shillings," she said in a solemn voice, "five shillings in silver I will now give to any little boy who will hold one finger, only one finger, in that candle flame for five minutes."

They looked from her to the crown-piece and from that to the candle, chagrin and disappointment seizing all their hearts.

"One shilling for every minute," she said, head lowered, bonnet wagging. "Oh, my, isn't that high wages? What? No little boy wants to earn five shillings?"

No one answered. Micky thought it was more than his mother earned for a week's work.

"For the last time," she said, her tone growing more solemn.

Still no one replied.

"And yet," she went on, her voice rising shrilly, "by offending against Almighty God you run the risk of burning, not your finger but your whole body and soul, not for five nor ten nor twenty minutes, but for all eternity, for ever and ever. For ever—do you understand the meaning of that?"

"Yes, ma'am," they chorused.

"You don't like school, do you?"

"No, ma'am," replied a few of the bolder spirits.

"And you're all wishing it was half-past three so that you could go home and have your dinners and play?"

"Yes, ma'am," they agreed with a little more unanimity; all but one sponger who chimed in with "No, ma'am, we likes listening to you."

"Hell," she intoned, "is a school from which you will never get out. Never! Three o'clock will come, half-past three, four, but no devil will ever say 'School is over.'" She chuckled grimly, and, leaning with one hand on the back of her chair, she poked her index finger at one after another of them. "And it won't be any use holding up your hands then and saying, 'Please may I go home now?'"

In the gloomy silence that followed while she pulled up her skirts and resumed her seat, nodding her black bonnet menacingly, Micky, listening to the blackbird's silly piping, wished that the good God had permitted him to be born a blackbird, so that he could perch on a bough and look in the school window and whistle derisively at the poor dejected urchins within, trying to cope with the twin horrors of sums and hell.

As if that wasn't enough there was the sight of his grandmother to upset him when he came home to dinner. His grandmother, his father's mother, had come to live with them and he hated her. He hated her wrinkled face and untidy grey hair; he hated her snuff-taking and the bare dirty feet on which she plodded about the kitchen; he hated the great meal of potatoes she cooked for herself morning and evening, the way she spread a potful on the table, peeled them with her fingers, dipped them in a heap of salt and then ate them. He hated her blind fumbling for things, and the way she produced snuff-box and purse and even sweets from her bosom, unpinning her blouse and shivering. He hatred her and everything about her, and was quite irreconcilable. Neither beatings from his father nor coaxings from his mother would induce him to tolerate the old woman. Nora, his elder sister, was on excellent terms with her, did messages for her and got pennies in reward, but even the pennies, even when Nora grigged[1] him with them till she drove him into hysterics, even these did not induce him to speak nicely to his grandmother.

As ill-luck would have it his mother had got a week's work picking fruit in the nurseries, and to spite him, Nora refused to give him his dinner in the front room, as his mother did to take him from under the old woman's eyes.

"I wants me dinner in the room," he said.

"Well, you won't get it," snapped Nora. "As if you hadn't us heart-scalded enough as it is! You'll take it in here or do without it."

"I wants it in the room," he repeated, and began to sob.

"Och, aye," said his grandmother sourly, drawing the old knitted shawl more tightly about her shoulders. "I suppose 'tis all my fault. Give it to him in the room, Nora girl. Give it to him in the room, and he can do without his pinny on Saturday."

"I wo' not," replied Nora. "The dirty spoiled suppurating little caffler![2] . . . Shut up now or I'll scratch your eyes out."

Micky wailed louder than before.

" 'Tis all me ma's fault," continued his sister. "Giving him bad habits."

[1] Tantalized.

[2] One who makes excuses or prevaricates.

His grandmother took another pinch of snuff and smoothed down her dirty grey hair in the middle.

"I won't be a trouble to ye long," she declared, her voice trembling with self-pity. "I know I'm a bother to ye, but 'twill soon be over whin ye carry me to me long home. Soon enough, soon enough ye'll be rid of the poor ould woman. Up in Kilcronin 'tisn't there they'll refuse me or be ashamed to sit with me."

"Eat your dinner, you plague!" shouted Nora, catching him a clout over the ear.

"I will not! I will not!" he screamed, and when she grabbed him he shouted and kicked and tore and bit.

There was a terrible scene that ended by his taking refuge beneath the table in the darkness, sobbing madly. He had a bread knife in one hand and a small heavy pot in the other with which he lashed out at Nora whenever she tried to crawl underneath to dislodge him. His grandmother and Nora knew there would be trouble if his mother came in and found him like that, so their approaches became more and more tender until at last they were offering him sweets and pennies to come out and eat his dinner in the room. But the softer they grew the more savage he became, and at last his mother did come in and find him. They caught it, and Micky was petted and fed back to sanity.

Then they had their innings. Nora, the little spy, told his father all about it; his father tried to beat him, his mother intervened, and there was another scene. It always worked out that way, that his father and Nora were on one side, his mother and he on the other, and between them the intruder, the big, dirty old peasant woman with her rosary beads twined about her wrist.

Next day the black-bonneted instructress was there again with her dolman and her rings. This time it was to tell them what a terrible crime it was to keep a secret from the priest. Oh, a terrible crime that was! No sin, however dreadful in itself, could be as bad as the sin of concealing it and making a bad confession. She had a long rigmarole of a story about a man who once did such a thing and, to all appearances, became very holy afterwards. All the people admired and respected him, and when he died, they were so certain that his soul had gone straight to heaven that they didn't even bother to pray for him. But some time later his ghost appeared and went about telling everyone his secret sin and how he had been damned because of it. And even while it was speaking his ghost had not ceased to burn and writhe, and after it had disappeared the room was full of the smell of roasted flesh.

This story made a great impression on Micky and exasperated his already strained nerves.

At home another scene. This time it was really his fault. Neither Nora nor his grandmother was speaking to him, and Micky sat in a corner reading his book, an adventure story full of pirates and desert islands. The old woman went to brew a cup of tea for herself, and when he heard her bare feet padding across the kitchen, in spite of himself he looked up, all his hatred concentrated on her in an instant. Then as she reached for the cup from the shelf something broke in him and he began to cry. She heard him and looked round and raised her dirty hand to heaven.

"Oh, the malice!" she said in a horrified tone. "The malice!"

And so a terrible week passed, and Saturday came, the day he was to make his first confession. Because of the distance he had to come he was allowed to make it by himself in the parish church. Nora brought him down by the hand, and all the way kept telling him what a doing-over the priest would give him. Outside the church he stuck his two feet in the pathway and refused to enter. She dragged him after her, only turning to address a whoop of glee or a fresh threat to him.

"Ah," she said, "I hope he'll give you the pinitintial psalms. That'll cure you, you caffler!"

"I don't want to go," whined Micky.

"You'll have to go, you'll have to go," she chanted triumphantly. "Or the parish priest will be up to the house with a stick looking for you."

The church was an old one with two iron gates and an old stone front. All about the yard were trees. There was no stained glass in it, and the white light was broken here and there by boughs that lifted themselves against the windowpanes. Once within the door the fear of God came on Micky. He gave himself up for lost and allowed himself to be led noisily through the vaulted silence, the intense and magical silence that seemed to have frozen within the ancient walls, buttressing them and lifting upon its shoulders the high pointed wooden roof. In the street outside, yet seeming a million miles away, in another world, a ballad-singer was drawling a ballad Micky knew well, and over which he had often shed a patriotic tear.

> Adieu, adieu to Dublin town, for I must now away,
> Likewise Cork city where I spent so many a happy day.
> When I am in Bermudas, the view I shall deplore,
> Farewell, farewell, my native land, I mean the shamrock shore.

Nora sat in front of him on the bench beside the confessional box. There were a few old women before her, and afterwards a thin, sad-looking man with long hair came and sat beside Micky. In the intense silence of the church that seemed to grow deeper from the plaintive moaning of the ballad-singer he could hear the buzz-buzz-buzz of a woman's voice in the box; buzz-buzz-buzz and then the ba-ba-ba of the priest's. And then the soft thud of something that signalled the end of the confession, and out came the woman, head lowered, hands joined, looking neither to right nor left and tiptoed up the altar to say her penance. And again the buzz-buzz, a rush of sibilants, and the stern deep note of the priest's voice.

It seemed only a matter of seconds before Nora rose, and with a whispered injunction disappeared from his sight. He was all alone. Alone, and next to be heard, and with the fear of damnation in his soul, knowing as he did that he was about to make a bad confession and that nothing could save him. He looked at the sad-faced man. He was gazing at the roof with hands joined in prayer. A woman in a red blouse and black shawl had taken her place below him. She put a pin in her teeth, fluffed her hair out roughly with her hand, brushed it sharply back, then, with bowed head, caught it in a knot and pinned it on her neck. Micky heard the slide go, and Nora emerged. He rose, and looked at her with a hatred that was quite inappropriate to the occasion and the place. Her hands were joined as far down as she could possibly hold them, her eyes were modestly lowered, and her face had an expression of the most rapt and tender recollection. With death in his heart Micky crept into the box and closed the door behind him.

He was in pitch-darkness. He could see no priest or anything else. And anything he had ever heard of confession simply rose in tumult in his mind. He knelt to the right-hand wall and said, "Bless me, father, for I have sinned. This is my first confession." Nothing happened. The wall made no reply. He repeated it, louder. Still it gave no answer. Then he turned to the opposite wall, genuflected first, then again went on his knees and repeated the charm. This time he was certain he would receive a reply, but none came. He repeated the process with the remaining wall, again without effect. He had the feeling of someone with an unfamiliar machine, of pressing buttons at random. And finally the thought struck him that God knew, God knew all about the bad confession he had intended to make, and had made him deaf and blind so that he could neither hear nor discern the priest.

Then, as his eyes grew accustomed to the blackness, he perceived something he had not noticed up to this; a sort of shelf at about the height of his head. The purpose of this eluded him for a moment but then he understood. It was for kneeling on.

He had always prided himself upon his powers of climbing, but this was a tougher proposition than a gas-lamp or a telegraph pole, and there wasn't as much as a foothold to be discovered. He slipped twice before he even succeeded in getting his knee on it, and the strain of drawing the rest of himself up was almost more than he was capable of. However, he did at last get his two knees on it, there was just room for those, but his legs hung down uncomfortably and the edge of the shelf bruised his shin. He joined his hands and pressed the last remaining button. He uttered his "Open Sesame" to the corner.

At the same moment the slide was pushed back and a dim light streamed into the little box. There was an uncomfortable silence, and then an alarmed voice asked "Who's there? What's wrong?" Micky found it was extremely difficult to speak into the grille, which was on a level with his knees, but he got a firm grip of the moulding above it, bent his head sideways and up and found himself looking almost upside down through the grille. The priest also had his head cocked sideways and up, and Micky, whose knees were being tortured by this new position, felt it was a very queer way to hear confessions.

" 'Tis me," he piped.

"What?" exclaimed a deep, frightened and angry voice, and the sombre figure at the other side of the grille stood bolt upright, disappearing almost entirely from Micky's view. "What's this? What are you doing there? What's the meaning of it, I say?"

And with the shock Micky felt his hands lose their grip and his legs their balance. He discovered himself tumbling into space, and tumbling he knocked his head against the door, the door shot open, and he fell clear into the centre of the aisle. The middle door opened and out came a small, dark-haired priest with the biretta forward on his head. At the same moment Nora came skeltering madly down the aisle.

"Lord God!" she cried. "The sniffling little caffler. I knew he'd do it. I knew he'd disgrace me." He received a clout across the ear which suddenly reminded him that for some strange reason he hadn't yet begun to cry, and that people might possibly think he wasn't hurt at all. He did cry then, with a vengeance. Nora slapped him again.

"What's this? What's this?" cried the priest. "Don't attempt to beat the child, you little vixen!"

"I can't do me pinance with him," cried Nora shrilly, cocking a shocked eye up at the priest as though wondering how he dared to interfere on behalf of disorder. "He have me driven mad. Stop your crying, you ignorant scut![3] Crying in the chapel! Stop it now or I'll make you cry at the other side of your ugly face."

"Run away out of this and let the unfortunate child alone!" growled the priest. He suddenly began to laugh, took out his pocket-handkerchief and wiped Micky's face. "You're not hurt, sure you're not? What's your name?"

Through his sobs, Micky told him.

"Well, Micky, you're a grand young fellow, you are so! Never mind your old sister.... Show us your head.... Ah, 'tis only a tiny bump; 'twill be better before you're twice married.... So you're coming to confession?"

"I am, father," replied Micky, his tears dwindling to sobs.

"Is it your first?"

" 'Tis, father."

"Well now, Micky, wait five minutes till I get rid of these two old ones, and we'll have a great old talk. Will you?"

"I will, father."

With a feeling of great importance that somehow glowed through his tears like a sunrift behind a shower, Micky took his seat opposite the confessional. Nora stuck out her tongue at him, but he did not even bother to reply. A great feeling of relief was welling up within him. The sense of oppression that had been weighing him down for a week, the knowledge that he was about to make a bad confession, disappeared. It was all old women and girls and their talk. He would tell everything, everything, to this priest, and take whatever punishment was coming to him like a man. There was nothing to show he had been weeping but an occasional sniff.

This time the priest kept the slide open for him and showed him what to do and where to kneel. And then they had a great chat, all about where Micky went to school, and who was teaching him, and what his father's job was, and what he wanted to be when he grew up. And when the time came to tell his sins, Micky, not wishing to keep the priest in doubt a moment longer about the type of child he had to deal with, bowed his head, clenched his fists and replied:

"Father, I made it up to kill me grandmother."

"Oh," said the priest with polite interest. "Your grandmother."

So then Micky had to explain what sort of woman his grandmother

[3] A contemptible fellow.

was, that she drank porter, took snuff and went about the house in her bare feet. It was all made infinitely easier because the priest never once took his eyes off Micky's face, and at every few words interrupted with a sympathetic "Tut-tut!" or "Well! well!" As he seemed to be so interested and understanding, Micky thought he might as well tell him the whole thing; how he had planned to come behind her while she was eating a meal of potatoes and hit her over the head with a hatchet. They had a discussion about the hatchet. The priest thought a knife would have been better, as there would be a danger that the old woman would scream. Micky admitted that he hadn't thought of that, but this wasn't quite true, as he had thought of it vaguely, but had rejected it because he couldn't imagine himself running a knife into her. On the other hand, the priest considered his plan for disposing of the body most ingenious. He proposed to make a cart out of an orange box which he could get at the shop for threepence and take her out that way in pieces. The pieces he intended to bury in a deserted field a few hundred yards away from the house. He told how he had rehearsed the burial on two occasions after dark, stealing out with a cardboard box and a trowel, and burying it by starlight.

"Lord!" exclaimed the priest. "You must have been frightened."

"Ah, no, only a bit," said Micky.

"But wouldn't they see the blood on the cart?"

"They would not. I'd wrap up the bits in paper."

"I suppose you could do that," admitted the priest. "But all the same I don't know. I often thought of killing people myself, but I'm not like you. I'd never have the nerve. And hanging is an awful death."

"Is it?" asked Micky, responding to the brightness of a new theme.

"Oh, an awful blooming death!"

"Did you ever see a fellow hanged?"

"Me? Hundreds of them, and they all died roaring. No, Micky, I'm afraid I'd never be brave enough for it. And besides, what would your father do?"

"How, father?"

"Well, what would you do if someone went and bashed your mother's head in with a hatchet . . . and then cut her up in bits and took her away in a cart to bury her?"

"Lord, father," said Micky, catching his lip with horror, "I never thought of that."

"Well, there you are! No, Micky, before you do a thing like that you ought to consider the consequences. Think it over well, and come back and tell me. Only, mind, I'm not going to help you. . . . When I think of the fellows I saw being hanged . . ."

For three years Micky went to confession to him every Saturday. Then one day it all came back to him, he grew hot and cold by turns, and afterwards he went to that priest no more. When he saw him in the street he ran miles to avoid him. As he died some years later they never spoke again. But one night in a Paris hotel Micky remembered it all, and it was as if tears were falling within his mind, and then it seemed as though window or door were suddenly opened and magic caught him by the hair.

1935

FIRST CONFESSION

FRANK O'CONNOR

ALL THE trouble began when my grandfather died and my grandmother—my father's mother—came to live with us. Relations in the one house are a strain at the best of times, but, to make matters worse, my grandmother was a real old countrywoman and quite unsuited to the life in town. She had a fat, wrinkled old face, and, to Mother's great indignation, went round the house in bare feet—the boots had her crippled, she said. For dinner she had a jug of porter and a pot of potatoes with—sometimes—a bit of salt fish, and she poured out the potatoes on the table and ate them slowly, with great relish, using her fingers by way of a fork.

Now, girls are supposed to be fastidious, but I was the one who suffered most from this. Nora, my sister, just sucked up to the old woman for the penny she got every Friday out of the old-age pension, a thing I could not do. I was too honest, that was my trouble; and when I was playing with Bill Connell, the sergeant-major's son, and saw my grandmother steering up the path with the jug of porter sticking out from beneath her shawl I was mortified. I made excuses not to let him come into the house, because I could never be sure what she would be up to when we went in.

When Mother was at work and my grandmother made the dinner I wouldn't touch it. Nora once tried to make me, but I hid under the table from her and took the bread-knife with me for protection. Nora let on to be very indignant (she wasn't, of course, but she knew Mother saw through her, so she sided with Gran) and came after me. I lashed out at her with the bread-knife, and after that she left me alone. I stayed there till Mother came in from work and made my dinner, but when Father came in later Nora said in a shocked voice: "Oh, Dadda, do you know what Jackie did at dinnertime?" Then, of course, it all came out; Father gave me a flaking;[1] Mother interfered, and for days after that he didn't speak to me and Mother barely spoke to Nora. And all because of that old woman! God knows, I was heart-scalded.

Then, to crown my misfortunes, I had to make my first confession and communion. It was an old woman called Ryan who prepared us for these. She was about the one age with Gran; she was well-to-do, lived in a big house on Montenotte, wore a black cloak and bonnet, and came every day to school at three o'clock when we should have been going home, and talked to us of hell. She may have mentioned the other place as well, but that could only have been by accident, for hell had the first place in her heart.

She lit a candle, took out a new half-crown, and offered it to the first boy who would hold one finger—only one finger!—in the flame for five minutes by the school clock. Being always very ambitious I was tempted to volunteer, but I thought it might look greedy. Then she asked were we afraid of holding one finger—only one finger—in a little candle flame for five minutes and not afraid of burning all over in roasting hot furnaces for all eternity. "All eternity! Just think of that! A whole lifetime goes by and it's nothing, not even a drop in the ocean of your

[1] Beating.

sufferings." The woman was really interesting about hell, but my attention was all fixed on the half-crown. At the end of the lesson she put it back in her purse. It was a great disappointment; a religious woman like that, you wouldn't think she'd bother about a thing like a half-crown.

Another day she said she knew a priest who woke up one night to find a fellow he didn't recognize leaning over the end of his bed. The priest was a bit frightened—naturally enough—but he asked the fellow what he wanted, and the fellow said in a deep, husky voice that he wanted to go to confession. The priest said it was an awkward time and wouldn't it do in the morning, but the fellow said that last time he went to confession, there was one sin he kept back, being ashamed to mention it, and now it was always on his mind. Then the priest knew it was a bad case, because the fellow was after making a bad confession and committing a mortal sin. He got up to dress, and just then the cock crew in the yard outside, and—lo and behold!—when the priest looked round there was no sign of the fellow, only a smell of burning timber, and when the priest looked at his bed didn't he see the print of two hands burned in it? That was because the fellow had made a bad confession. This story make a shocking impression on me.

But the worst of all was when she showed us how to examine our conscience. Did we take the name of the Lord, our God, in vain? Did we honour our father and our mother? (I asked her did this include grandmothers and she said it did.) Did we love our neighbors as ourselves? Did we covet our neighbor's goods? (I thought of the way I felt about the penny that Nora got every Friday.) I decided that, between one thing and another, I must have broken the whole ten commandments, all on account of that old woman, and so far as I could see, so long as she remained in the house I had no hope of ever doing anything else.

I was scared to death of confession. The day the whole class went I let on to have a toothache, hoping my absence wouldn't be noticed; but at three o'clock, just as I was feeling safe, along comes a chap with a message from Mrs. Ryan that I was to go to confession myself on Saturday and be at the chapel for communion with the rest. To make it worse, Mother couldn't come with me and sent Nora instead.

Now, that girl had ways of tormenting me that Mother never knew of. She held my hand as we went down the hill, smiling sadly and saying how sorry she was for me, as if she were bringing me to the hospital for an operation.

"Oh, God help us!" she moaned. "Isn't it a terrible pity you weren't a good boy? Oh, Jackie, my heart bleeds for you! How will you ever think of all your sins? Don't forget you have to tell him about the time you kicked Gran on the shin."

"Lemme go!" I said, trying to drag myself free of her. "I don't want to go to confession at all."

"But sure, you'll have to go to confession, Jackie," she replied in the same regretful tone. "Sure, if you didn't, the parish priest would be up to the house, looking for you. 'Tisn't, God knows, that I'm not sorry for you. Do you remember the time you tried to kill me with the bread-knife under the table? And the language you used to me? I don't know what he'll do with you at all, Jackie. He might have to send you up to the bishop."

I remember thinking bitterly that she didn't know the half of what I had to tell—if I told it. I knew I couldn't tell it, and understood perfectly why the fellow in Mrs. Ryan's story made a bad confession; it seemed to me a great shame that people wouldn't stop criticizing him. I remember that steep hill down to the church, and the sunlit hillsides beyond the valley of the river, which I saw in the gaps between the houses like Adam's last glimpse of Paradise.

Then, when she had manœuvred me down the long flight of steps to the chapel yard, Nora suddenly changed her tone. She became the raging malicious devil she really was.

"There you are!" she said with a yelp of triumph, hurling me through the church door. "And I hope he'll give you the penitential psalms, you dirty little caffler.[2]"

I knew then I was lost, given up to eternal justice. The door with the coloured-glass panels swung shut behind me, the sunlight went out and gave place to deep shadow, and the wind whistled outside so that the silence within seemed to crackle like ice under my feet. Nora sat in front of me by the confession box. There were a couple of old women ahead of her, and then a miserable-looking poor devil came and wedged me in at the other side, so that I couldn't escape even if I had the courage. He joined his hands and rolled his eyes in the direction of the roof, muttering aspirations in an anguished tone, and I wondered had he a grandmother too. Only a grandmother could account for a fellow behaving in that heartbroken way, but he was better off than I, for he at least could go and confess his sins; while I would make a bad con-

[2] One who makes excuses or prevaricates.

fession and then die in the night and be continually coming back and burning people's furniture.

Nora's turn came, and I heard the sound of something slamming, and then her voice as if butter wouldn't melt in her mouth, and then another slam, and out she came. God, the hypocrisy of women! Her eyes were lowered, her head was bowed, and her hands were joined very low down on her stomach, and she walked up the aisle to the side altar looking like a saint. You never saw such an exhibition of devotion; and I remembered the devilish malice with which she had tormented me all the way from our door, and wondered were all religious people like that, really. It was my turn now. With the fear of damnation in my soul I went in, and the confessional door closed of itself behind me.

It was pitch-dark and I couldn't see priest or anything else. Then I really began to be frightened. In the darkness it was a matter between God and me, and He had all the odds. He knew what my intentions were before I even started; I had no chance. All I had ever been told about confession got mixed up in my mind, and I knelt to one wall and said: "Bless me, father, for I have sinned; this is my first confession." I waited for a few minutes, but nothing happened, so I tried it on the other wall. Nothing happened there either. He had me spotted all right.

It must have been then that I noticed the shelf at about one height with my head. It was really a place for grown-up people to rest their elbows, but in my distracted state I thought it was probably the place you were supposed to kneel. Of course, it was on the high side and not very deep, but I was always good at climbing and managed to get up all right. Staying up was the trouble. There was room only for my knees, and nothing you could get a grip on but a sort of wooden moulding a bit above it. I held on to the moulding and repeated the words a little louder, and this time something happened all right. A slide was slammed back; a little light entered the box, and a man's voice said: "Who's there?"

" 'Tis me, father," I said for fear he mightn't see me and go away again. I couldn't see him at all. The place the voice came from was under the moulding, about level with my knees, so I took a good grip of the moulding and swung myself down till I saw the astonished face of a young priest looking up at me. He had to put his head on one side to see me, and I had to put mine on one side to see him, so we were more or less talking to one another upside-down. It struck me as a queer way of hearing confessions, but I didn't feel it my place to criticize.

"Bless me, father, for I have sinned; this is my first confession," I rattled off all in one breath, and swung myself down the least shade more to make it easier for him.

"What are you doing up there?" he shouted in an angry voice, and the strain the politeness was putting on my hold of the moulding, and the shock of being addressed in such an uncivil tone, were too much for me. I lost my grip, tumbled, and hit the door an unmerciful wallop before I found myself flat on my back in the middle of the aisle. The people who had been waiting stood up with their mouths open. The priest opened the door of the middle box and came out, pushing his biretta back from his forehead; he looked something terrible. Then Nora came scampering down the aisle.

"Oh, you dirty little caffler!" she said. "I might have known you'd do it. I might have known you'd disgrace me. I can't leave you out of my sight for one minute."

Before I could even get to my feet to defend myself she bent down and gave me a clip across the ear. This reminded me that I was so stunned I had even forgotten to cry, so that people might think I wasn't hurt at all, when in fact I was probably maimed for life. I gave a roar out of me.

"What's all this about?" the priest hissed, getting angrier than ever and pushing Nora off me. "How dare you hit the child like that, you little vixen?"

"But I can't do my penance with him, father," Nora cried, cocking an outraged eye up at him.

"Well, go and do it, or I'll give you some more to do," he said, giving me a hand up. "Was it coming to confession you were, my poor man?" he asked me.

" 'Twas, father," said I with a sob.

"Oh," he said respectfully, "a big hefty fellow like you must have terrible sins. Is this your first?"

" 'Tis, father," said I.

"Worse and worse," he said gloomily. "The crimes of a lifetime. I don't know will I get rid of you at all today. You'd better wait now till I'm finished with these old ones. You can see by the looks of them they haven't much to tell."

"I will, father," I said with something approaching joy.

The relief of it was really enormous. Nora stuck out her tongue at me from behind his back, but I couldn't even be bothered retorting. I knew from the very moment that man opened his mouth that he was intelligent above the ordinary. When I had time to think, I saw how right I was. It only stood to reason that a fellow confessing after seven years would have more to tell than people that went every week. The crimes of a lifetime, exactly as he said. It was only what he expected, and the rest was the cackle of old women and girls with their talk of hell, the bishop, and the penitential psalms. That was all they knew. I started to make my examination of conscience, and barring the one bad business of my grandmother it didn't seem so bad.

The next time, the priest steered me into the confession box himself and left the shutter back the way I could see him get in and sit down at the further side of the grille from me.

"Well, now," he said, "what do they call you?"

"Jackie, father," said I.

"And what's a-trouble to you, Jackie?"

"Father," I said, feeling I might as well get it over while I had him in good humour, "I had it all arranged to kill my grandmother."

He seemed a bit shaken by that, all right, because he said nothing for quite a while.

"My goodness," he said at last, "that'd be a shocking thing to do. What put that into your head?"

"Father," I said, feeling very sorry for myself, "she's an awful woman."

"Is she?" he asked. "What way is she awful?"

"She takes porter, father," I said, knowing well from the way Mother talked of it that this was a mortal sin, and hoping it would make the priest take a more favourable view of my case.

"Oh, my!" he said, and I could see he was impressed.

"And snuff, father," said I.

"That's a bad case, sure enough, Jackie," he said.

"And she goes round in her bare feet, father," I went on in a rush of self-pity, "and she knows I don't like her, and she gives pennies to Nora and none to me, and my da sides with her and flakes me, and one night I was so heart-scalded I made up my mind I'd have to kill her."

"And what would you do with the body?" he asked with great interest.

"I was thinking I could chop that up and carry it away in a barrow I have," I said.

"Begor, Jackie," he said, "do you know you're a terrible child?"

"I know, father," I said, for I was just thinking the same thing myself. "I tried to kill Nora too with a bread-knife under the table, only I missed her."

"Is that the little girl that was beating you just now?" he asked.

" 'Tis, father."

"Someone will go for her with a bread-knife one day, and he won't miss her," he said rather cryptically. "You must have great courage. Between ourselves, there's a lot of people I'd like to do the same to but I'd never have the nerve. Hanging is an awful death."

"Is it, father?" I asked with the deepest interest—I was always very keen on hanging. "Did you ever see a fellow hanged?"

"Dozens of them," he said solemnly. "And they all died roaring."

"Jay!" I said.

"Oh, a horrible death!" he said with great satisfaction. "Lots of the fellows I saw killed their grandmothers too, but they all said 'twas never worth it."

He had me there for a full ten minutes talking, and then walked out the chapel yard with me. I was genuinely sorry to part with him, because he was the most entertaining character I'd ever met in the religious line. Outside, after the shadow of the church, the sunlight was like the roaring of waves on a beach; it dazzled me; and when the frozen silence melted and I heard the screech of trams on the road my heart soared. I knew now I wouldn't die in the night and come back, leaving marks on my mother's furniture. It would be a great worry to her, and the poor soul had enough.

Nora was sitting on the railing, waiting for me, and she put on a very sour puss when she saw the priest with me. She was mad jealous because a priest had never come out of the church with her.

"Well," she asked coldly, after he left me, "what did he give you?"

"Three Hail Marys," I said.

"Three Hail Marys," she repeated incredulously. "You mustn't have told him anything."

"I told him everything," I said confidently.

"About Gran and all?"

"About Gran and all."

(All she wanted was to be able to go home and say I'd made a bad confession.)

"Did you tell him you went for me with the bread-knife?" she asked with a frown.

"I did to be sure."

"And he only gave you three Hail Marys?"

"That's all."

She slowly got down from the railing with a baffled air. Clearly, this was beyond her. As we mounted the steps back to the main road she looked at me suspiciously.

"What are you sucking?" she asked.

"Bullseyes."

"Was it the priest gave them to you?"

" 'Twas."

"Lord God," she wailed bitterly, "some people have all the luck! 'Tis no advantage to anybody trying to be good. I might just as well be a sinner like you."

1951

DISCUSSION QUESTIONS

1. Compare the *scenes* of each version that lead up to going to first confession. Which of these scenes occur in both versions? Which order of these similar scenes is more effective? Why? Identify each scene occurring in only one version and explain its purpose.

2. How is the boy's hostility toward his grandmother explained in each version? What effect has this difference on the way you feel toward Micky and Jackie? Why does each boy refuse to eat his dinner? Why does each wish to kill his grandmother?

3. Why does each boy fear confession? Why does each resolve to make a bad confession though he knows "what a terrible crime it was to keep a secret from the priest"?

4. Why does each boy feel relieved after the priest tells him to wait? Which reaction do you prefer? Why? Why does each boy decide to confess all? Which reaction seems more plausible? Why?

5. In "First Confession," what function is served by the addition of the paragraph that begins: "He had me there for a full ten minutes . . ."? Relate it to the earlier description of Jackie entering the church. Explain the significance of the reappearing "sunlight" and the melting "frozen silence."

6. Compare the priests of the two versions. How do they differ in the ways in which they handle the boy? Which priest seems more adept at it? Why?

7. Which narrator seems to you more effective: the *undramatized narrator* recounting Micky's story and presenting the boy's thoughts (inner view) or Jackie describing his own experience? Give reasons and examples in support of your preference.

8. Choose three comical passages from "First Confession" in which the humor stems from Jackie's natural innocence and naiveté. Try to adapt them to fit "Repentance." Specifically, what changes were necessary? How successful were your adaptations? What specific problems did you encounter?

9. Such a statement as "Relations in the one house are a strain at the best of times" (page 79) obviously implies an intelligence far beyond the grasp of a seven-year-old and suggests that in "First Confession" an older and maturer Jackie is recounting his earlier experience. Find

several other instances in which this older narrator makes use of his superior intelligence and hindsight to obtrude between us and his younger self.

10. Such a sentence as "He rose, and looked at her with a hatred that was quite inappropriate to the occasion and the place" (page 74) obviously stems from the impersonal narrator in "Repentance" offering his own comment rather than Micky's thought. In other instances, the distinction is more blurred: "She staggered from her seat to the mantelpiece, wagging her big rheumaticky buttocks" (pages 69–70); "This time it was really his fault" (page 73); "her voice trembling with self-pity" (page 72). Do these statements reflect Micky's or the narrator's judgment? Why should the *point of view* of "Repentance" produce more such ambiguities than the point of view of "First Confession"?

11. Compare the last paragraph of "Repentance" with the last *scene* (meeting Nora outside the church) of "First Confession." Which seems the more effective resolution of the *action?* Why?

12. Which of the two boys do you admire more? Why? Which version of O'Connor's story did you enjoy more? Why?

ANALYSIS AND APPLICATION

1. Compare corresponding parts of the following passages:

He discovered himself tumbling into space, and tumbling he knocked his head against the door, the door shot open, and he fell clear into the centre of the aisle. The middle door opened and out came a small, dark-haired priest with the biretta forward on his head. (page 75)

I lost my grip, tumbled, and hit the door an unmerciful wallop before I found myself flat on my back in the middle of the aisle. The people who had been waiting stood up with their mouths open. The priest opened the door of the middle box and came out, pushing his biretta back from his forehead; he looked something terrible. (page 84)

Is O'Connor justified in leaving out "the door shot open" in "First Confession"? Explain. Why did O'Connor add the second sentence in the second passage? Specifically, how has the last sentence of the first passage been altered? Is it an improvement? Explain. Which passage do you prefer? Why?

2. Analyze and compare the following parallel passages:

He gave himself up for lost and allowed himself to be led noisily through the vaulted silence, the intense and magical silence that seemed to have frozen within the ancient walls, buttressing them and lifting upon its shoulders the high pointed wooden roof. (page 73)

I knew then I was lost, given up to eternal justice. The door with the coloured-glass panels swung shut behind me, the sunlight went out and gave place to deep shadow, and the wind whistled outside so that the silence within seemed to crackle like ice under my feet. (page 82)

Which of the two descriptions better expresses the boy's feeling of despair? Why?

THE DEATH IN THE FOREST

SHERWOOD ANDERSON

IT WAS December and snowing when Mrs. Ike Marvin—we knew her as Ma Marvin—died in the little hollow in the center of Grimes' woods, about two miles south of our Ohio town. I was a boy then and had a job in Will Hunt's general store. Well, you see, Christmas time was approaching and there was a merry tinkling thing in the air. On Friday the snow that had been falling heavily since Tuesday had let up. Everyone said the sleighing would be good over the holiday time and even though we did not own a horse and sleigh, there was a kind of gladness in the air one felt. For one thing farmers began to drive into town in bobsleds and boys, more fortunate than myself in not being tied up with a job indoors, could catch rides. Crowds of boys ran along in the deep snow in Main Street, flipping on the runners of bobs, being thrown into the deep snow, shouting and laughing.

Even at that time there were two or three young women of our place whose fathers were up far enough in the world to send their daughters away to the city to school and they had now come home. They walked past on the sidewalk outside our general store, young women with a kind of air our own girls hadn't picked up yet. It had a kind of effect I can't explain. One felt one's town putting its nose up in the air like a fine pointer dog or something like that. You know what I mean. "Well we belong to the world. We aren't just a town stuck off here on a branch railroad," one whispered to oneself.

And there was young Ben Lewis home too. He was the son of our principal lawyer and five years ago had gone off to Chicago where he had worked himself up to be reporter on the Chicago Daily News. It was said he got twenty-five dollars a week, but Will Hunt declared he would never believe any such nonsense. Anyway there was the day just as I have described, and the sun breaking through masses of white clouds now and then, and sleighs covered with the dust from haylofts dragged out, boys laughing, girls and young women walking on newly swept sidewalks, Ben Lewis with such a grand overcoat on as I had never seen before (all silk lined and everything) standing in front of Huntley's Jewelry and telling how he discovered a clue to a murder in a hammer found back of an ice chest in a Chicago house and got a scoop for the Daily News, and men and boys listening and admiring and filled with envy and at the same time with gladness that such a fellow as Ben had come from our town.

It was, right enough, a day to remember and feel right about afterward, when, along about three o'clock news came into town of how Ma Marvin had died.

Things went bang then, like putting a light out in a room where a man sits looking at a book and a woman is playing a piano and children are cutting pictures out of newspapers on the floor. There you are and then "bang" there you aren't. What I mean is everyone is fumbling around in a queer sort of way.

I remember that, at the very moment the news came, Will Hunt was counting eggs out of Mrs. John Graham's basket into a bushel basket under the counter. The big iron stove at the back of the store was just booming—there was all the smells a boy loves to smell in the winter time when he is always hungry—cheese and coffee and brown sugar in barrels and dried herring and the smell of bolts of calico over on the other side of the store too.

Mrs. Graham was going to trade the eggs she had brought for goods. Will counted them, three eggs in each hand making a half dozen every time his two hands dropped to the bushel basket. What big fat red hands.

"Five, six, seven dozen and eight Mrs. Graham. Yes mam. Eggs is nineteen cents today. They are holding up pretty well. I guess it's the Christmas coming on. There'll be a lot of cakes and pies baked these next few days. Is John going to haul his corn in or will he hold? Ed Pearson said he was going to hold until March. Sometimes it pays. Sometimes it don't. Yes 'em the sledding is bound to be pretty good. There's a good bottom to the roads. That's the best part."

That's the way it was. That's the feel of how things were when the news of Ma Marvin's death came.

Two young fellows, the Passley boys, who had been out hunting rabbits brought the news into town. They had stumbled upon the poor woman's body, all covered with snow as they tramped through Grimes' woods, or perhaps their dog had found it. Anyway they ran nearly all the way to town and it was amazing how the news spread. Now that I think back on it all—the two young men, with the shot guns over their shoulders, half running, half walking over snow covered fields, climbing fences into the road, hurrying hurrying through the deep white fresh snow, shouting to drivers of passing bobsleds, shouting to farm women who came to front doors, to farm men too, standing in barnyards, getting to the scattered houses at the edge of town, running into Main Street, shouting and telling the news, well now, after all these years their two figures become in my imagination not quite human. They are more like Gods that run pushing before them dark clouds that shut out the sun on the snow and make the light in the houses dim.

Because, with their coming, and right away, everything in town changed. Boys quit laughing and flipping on and off bobs, Mrs. John Graham forgot what she wanted in goods in exchange for the eggs she had brought in, Ben Lewis stopped telling his wonder tale of the Chicago murder, done with the hammer he had found back of an ice box. Even the day changed. White clouds became a smokey grey. The sun went away. And we all closed up the stores and went out to Grimes' woods. Even women who had no babies to look after went. Right away there was the whole town tramping, strange little silent black massed dots moving over the white snow, climbing fences, tearing rail fences down, going across white fields and under black bare trees to the little white open space in Grimes' wood.

It was a simple poor little story after all. Everyone had known for a long time that Ma Marvin, although she couldn't have been more than thirty-five or six, was about worn out. That with cooking and slaving for that big lazy brute of an Ike Marvin and her three equally big lazy brutes of sons, all of them always getting drunk and raising the devil, that with the work and worry poor Ma Marvin had lived through, what was one to expect?

The whole story was just as plain as though there had been an eye witness to her death there to tell the tale.

Ma Marvin had been into town for supplies. That must have been on Tuesday, the day when the snow storm began. It was just like the Marvin men to let her come afoot. There were two or three old bony horses still left about the Marvin place, but no doubt the men had wanted them to drive off to some other nearby town and sell a load of stove wood to get money with which to get drunk and raise the devil.

So Ma Marvin, poor little old thing, had come just as you could see, by the path through the wood to our town, and she had got a sack of flour, potatoes, a chunk of salt pork, coffee, a small sack of sugar and other things. I remember there was a small cloth bag of salt.

And of course a pack of the big ugly dogs one always saw lying in the shadow over about Ike Marvin's ruined saw mill on Sugar Creek had come with her.

She had put all of the supplies into an old grain bag and had tried to carry it over her shoulder. "Lord Amighty," Will Hunt said, "I never sold her them things. Look at that bag of things. It is almost as big as she is, poor little old thing. Tom Friend must have sold her them things. He never ought to have let her set out with no such load."

It is odd what one remembers and doesn't remember. There was the white, half frozen little old figure, pitched a little forward (she had stopped to rest, sitting on the ground by a little pile of stones) and the Marvin dogs had grown bold after she was dead and had torn the grain bag and got at the hunk of salt pork within.

She must have come over to town on Tuesday and when she started home the storm began—the wind howling, the blinding snow, the woman, old before her time, putting down her load to rest a moment.

Then the stillness of death coming softly, night and the cold. My boy's mind couldn't grasp it then. We all stood about for a long time before some men, directed by Ben Lewis, got a barn door from a nearby barn, put the dead woman's body upon it and tramped off to the Marvin place, two more miles away.

It was said later about town that they found but two of the Marvin men at home and they both drunk and quarreling. There was even talk of lynching on our Main Street later but nothing came of it.

What I am myself trying to say is that as we stood about the dead figure in the snow, Ben Lewis seemed suddenly to feel that it was his part, as a city man among us, to do something. I happened to stand near him and he jerked off his overcoat and gave it to me to hold. Then he grew excited and went off with the others to carry the body home and there was I with that precious garment in my charge and night coming on. There was nothing to do of course but to carry it home with me and keep it safe for him until the next morning.

That I did and the charge lay upon me with a delicious weight. Could men, actual flesh and blood men, who had been raised in our town wear such gorgeous garments? Did such unbelievable things happen to young fellows who left our town and become reporters on city newspapers?

The coat was of broad yellow and green plaid and to my fingers the touch of it was delicious. How I wanted to put my hands into the pockets.

And it was lined with silk. How reverently I carried it home to our house and how good and kind I thought my mother when she laughingly permitted me to have the coat hanging in my own room over night.

I slept but little that night and often crept out of bed to touch the coat again. How deliciously soft the fabric. I thought it like touching the soft fur of a cat in the darkness and all night I remembered that in the afternoon in the woods when Ben Lewis had unbuttoned his coat and when it was still light enough to see, the lining was a reddish running color that changed in the light. The death of Ma Marvin in the snow in the wood was forgotten. Ben Lewis had gone from our town to the city and now wore a coat such as a king might wear. Would I, could I, sometime, grow up, go away to a city, get a job on a newspaper and like Ben Lewis wear a coat like a king? The thought thrilled me beyond words and so, as the dead frozen body of Ma Marvin lay in the tumble down house five miles away, I lay awake dreaming of a triumphant life wherein one was on a newspaper and wore plaid overcoats lined with silk such as only nobles and kings might wear.

As to the actual story of Ma Marvin's death—I found all about it in a rather queer way nearly twenty years later. Now I will tell you of that.

DEATH IN THE WOODS

SHERWOOD ANDERSON

SHE WAS an old woman and lived on a farm near the town in which I lived. All country and small-town people have seen such old women, but no one knows much about them. Such an old woman comes into town driving an old worn-out horse or she comes afoot carrying a basket. She may own a few hens and have eggs to sell. She brings them in a basket and takes them to a grocer. There she trades them in. She gets some salt pork and some beans. Then she gets a pound or two of sugar and some flour.

Afterwards she goes to the butcher's and asks for some dog-meat. She may spend ten or fifteen cents, but when she does she asks for something. Formerly the butchers gave liver to any one who wanted to carry it away. In our family we were always having it. Once one of my brothers got a whole cow's liver at the slaughter-house near the fair-grounds in our town. We had it until we were sick of it. It never cost a cent. I have hated the thought of it ever since.

The old farm woman got some liver and a soupbone. She never visited with any one, and as soon as she got what she wanted she lit out for home. It made quite a load for such an old body. No one gave her a lift. People drive right down a road and never notice an old woman like that.

There was such an old woman who used to come into town past our house one Summer and Fall when I was a young boy and was sick with what was called inflammatory rheumatism. She went home later carrying a heavy pack on her back. Two or three large gaunt-looking dogs followed at her heels.

The old woman was nothing special. She was one of the nameless ones that hardly any one knows, but she got into my thoughts. I have just suddenly now, after all these years, remembered her and what happened. It is a story. Her name was Grimes, and she lived with her husband and son in a small unpainted house on the bank of a small creek four miles from town.

The husband and son were a tough lot. Although the son was but twenty-one, he had already served a term in jail. It was whispered about that the woman's husband stole horses and ran them off to some other county. Now and then, when a horse turned up missing, the man had also disappeared. No one ever caught him. Once, when I was loafing at Tom Whitehead's livery-barn, the man came there and sat on the bench in front. Two or three other men were there, but no one spoke to him. He sat for a few minutes and then got up and went away. When he was leaving he turned around and stared at the men. There was a look of defiance in his eyes. "Well, I have tried to be friendly. You don't want to talk to me. It has been so wherever I have gone in this town. If, some day, one of your fine horses turns up missing, well, then what?" He did not say anything actually. "I'd like to bust one of you on the jaw," was about what his eyes said. I remember how the look in his eyes made me shiver.

The old man belonged to a family that had had money once. His name was Jake Grimes. It all comes back clearly now. His father, John Grimes, had owned a sawmill when the country was new, and had made money. Then he got to drinking and running after women. When he died there wasn't much left.

Jake blew in the rest. Pretty soon there wasn't any more lumber to cut and his land was nearly all gone.

He got his wife off a German farmer, for whom he went to work one June day in the wheat harvest. She was a young thing then and scared to death. You see, the farmer was up to something with the girl—she was, I think, a bound girl and his wife had her suspicions. She took it out on the girl when the man wasn't around. Then, when the wife had to go off to town for supplies, the farmer got after her. She told young Jake that nothing really ever happened, but he didn't know whether to believe it or not.

He got her pretty easy himself, the first time he was out with her. He wouldn't have married her if the German farmer hadn't tried to tell him where to get off. He got her to go riding with him in his buggy one night when he was threshing on the place, and then he came for her the next Sunday night.

She managed to get out of the house without her employer's seeing, but when she was getting into the buggy he showed up. It was almost dark, and he just popped up suddenly at the horse's head. He grabbed the horse by the bridle and Jake got out his buggy-whip.

They had it out all right! The German was a tough one. Maybe he didn't care whether his wife knew or not. Jake hit him over the face and shoulders with the buggy-whip, but the horse got to acting up and he had to get out.

Then the two men went for it. The girl didn't see it. The horse started to run away and went nearly a mile down the road before the girl got him stopped. Then she managed to tie him to a tree beside the road. (I wonder how I know all this. It must have stuck in my mind from small-town tales when I was a boy.) Jake found her there after he got through with the German. She was huddled up in the buggy seat, crying, scared to death. She told Jake a lot of stuff, how the German had tried to get her, how he chased her once into the barn, how another time, when they happened to be alone in the house together, he tore her dress open clear down the front. The German, she said, might have got her that time if he hadn't heard his old woman drive in at the gate. She had been off to town for supplies. Well, she would be putting the horse in the barn. The German managed to sneak off to the fields without his wife seeing. He told the girl he would kill her if she told. What could she do? She told a lie about ripping her dress in the barn when she was feeding the stock. I remember now that she was a bound girl and did not know where her father and mother were. Maybe she did not have any father. You know what I mean.

Such bound children were often enough cruelly treated. They were children who had no parents, slaves really. There were very few orphan homes then. They were legally bound into some home. It was a matter of pure luck how it came out.

II

She married Jake and had a son and daughter, but the daughter died. Then she settled down to feed stock. That was her job. At the German's place she had cooked the food for the German and his wife. The wife was a strong woman with big hips and worked most of the time in the fields with her husband. She fed them and fed the cows in the barn, fed the pigs, the horses and the chickens. Every moment of every day, as a young girl, was spent feeding something.

Then she married Jake Grimes and he had to be fed. She was a slight thing, and when she had been married for three or four years, and after the two children were born, her slender shoulders became stooped.

Jake always had a lot of big dogs around the house, that stood near the unused sawmill near the creek. He was always trading horses when he wasn't stealing something and had a lot of poor bony ones about. Also he kept three or four pigs and a cow. They were all pastured in the few acres left of the Grimes place and Jake did little enough work.

He went into debt for a threshing outfit and ran it for several years, but it did not pay. People did not trust him. They were afraid he would steal the grain at night. He had to go a long way off to get work and it cost too much to get there. In the Winter he hunted and cut a little firewood, to be sold in some nearby town. When the son grew up he was just like the father. They got drunk together. If there wasn't anything to eat in the house when they came home the old man gave his old woman a cut over the head. She had a few chickens of her own and had to kill one of them in a hurry. When they were all killed she wouldn't have any eggs to sell when she went to town, and then what would she do?

She had to scheme all her life about getting things fed, getting the pigs fed so they would grow fat and could be butchered in the Fall. When they were butchered her husband took most of the meat off to town and sold it. If he did not do it first the boy did. They fought sometimes and when they fought the old woman stood aside trembling.

She had got the habit of silence anyway—that was fixed. Sometimes, when she began to look old—she wasn't forty yet—and when the husband and son were both off, trading horses or drinking or hunting or stealing, she went around the house and the barnyard muttering to herself.

How was she going to get everything fed?—that was her problem. The dogs had to be fed. There wasn't enough hay in the barn for the horses and the cow. If she didn't feed the chickens how could they lay eggs? Without eggs to sell how could she get things in town, things she had to have to keep the life of the farm going? Thank heaven, she did not have to feed her husband—in a certain way. That hadn't lasted long after their marriage and after the babies came. Where he went on his long trips she did not know. Sometimes he was gone from home for weeks, and after the boy grew up they went off together.

They left everything at home for her to manage and she had no money. She knew no one. No one ever talked to her in town. When it was Winter she had to gather sticks of wood for her fire, had to try to keep the stock fed with very little grain.

The stock in the barn cried to her hungrily, the dogs followed her about. In the Winter the hens laid few enough eggs. They huddled in the corners of the barn and she kept watching them. If a hen lays an egg in the barn in the Winter and you do not find it, it freezes and breaks.

One day in Winter the old woman went off to town with a few eggs and the dogs followed her. She did not get started until nearly three o'clock and the snow was heavy. She hadn't been feeling very well for several days and so she went muttering along, scantily clad, her shoulders stooped. She had an old grain bag in which she carried her eggs, tucked away down in the bottom. There weren't many of them, but in Winter the price of eggs is up. She would get a little meat in exchange for the eggs, some salt pork, a little sugar, and some coffee perhaps. It might be the butcher would give her a piece of liver.

When she had got to town and was trading in her eggs the dogs lay by the door outside. She did pretty well, got the things she needed, more than she had hoped. Then she went to the butcher and he gave her some liver and some dog-meat.

It was the first time any one had spoken to her in a friendly way for a long time. The butcher was alone in his shop when she came in and was annoyed by the thought of such a sick-looking old woman out on such a day. It was bitter cold and the snow, that had let up during the afternoon, was falling again. The butcher said something about her husband and her son, swore at them, and the old woman stared at him, a look of mild surprise in her eyes as he talked. He said that if either the husband or the son were going to get any of the liver or the heavy bones with scraps of meat hanging to them that he had put into the grain bag, he'd see him starve first.

Starve, eh? Well, things had to be fed. Men had to be fed, and the horses that weren't any good but maybe could be traded off, and the poor thin cow that hadn't given any milk for three months.

Horses, cows, pigs, dogs, men.

III

The old woman had to get back before darkness came if she could. The dogs followed at her heels, sniffing at the heavy grain bag she had fastened on her back. When she got to the edge of town she stopped by a fence and tied the bag on her back with a piece of rope she had carried in her dress-pocket for just that purpose. That was an easier way to carry it. Her arms ached. It was hard when she had to crawl over fences and once she fell over and landed in the snow. The dogs went frisking about. She had to struggle to get to her feet again, but she made it. The point of climbing over the fences was that there was a short cut over a hill and through a woods. She might have gone around by the road, but it was a mile farther that way. She was afraid she couldn't make it. And then, besides, the stock had to be fed. There was a little hay left and a little corn. Perhaps her husband and son would bring some home when they came. They had driven off in the only buggy the Grimes family had, a rickety thing, a rickety horse hitched to the buggy, two other rickety horses led by halters. They were going to trade horses, get a little money if they could. They might come home drunk. It would be well to have something in the house when they came back.

The son had an affair on with a woman at the county seat, fifteen miles away. She was a rough enough woman, a tough one. Once, in the Summer, the son had brought her to the house. Both she and the son had been drinking. Jake Grimes was away and the son and his woman ordered the old woman about like a servant. She didn't mind much; she was used to it. Whatever happened she never said anything. That was her way of getting along. She had managed that way when she was a young girl at the German's and ever since she had married Jake. That time her son brought his woman to the house they stayed all night, sleeping together just as though they were married. It hadn't shocked the old woman, not much. She had got past being shocked early in life.

With the pack on her back she went painfully along across an open field, wading in the deep snow, and got into the woods.

There was a path, but it was hard to follow. Just beyond the top of the hill, where the woods was thickest, there was a small clearing. Had some one once thought of building a house there? The clearing was as large as a building lot in town, large enough for a house and a garden. The path ran along the side of the clearing, and when she got there the old woman sat down to rest at the foot of a tree.

It was a foolish thing to do. When she got herself placed, the pack against the tree's trunk, it was nice, but what about getting up again? She worried about that for a moment and then quietly closed her eyes.

She must have slept for a time. When you are about so cold you can't get any colder. The afternoon grew a little warmer and the snow came thicker than ever. Then after a time the weather cleared. The moon even came out.

There were four Grimes dogs that had followed Mrs. Grimes into town, all tall gaunt fellows. Such men as Jake Grimes and his son always keep just such dogs. They kick and abuse them, but they stay. The Grimes dogs, in order to keep from starving, had to do a lot of foraging for themselves, and they had been at it while the old woman slept with her back to the tree at the side of the clearing. They had been chasing rabbits in the woods and in adjoining fields and in their ranging had picked up three other farm dogs.

After a time all the dogs came back to the clearing. They were excited about something. Such nights, cold and clear and with a moon, do things to dogs. It may be that some old instinct, come down from the time when they were wolves and ranged the woods in packs on Winter nights, comes back into them.

The dogs in the clearing, before the old woman, had caught two or three rabbits and their immediate hunger had been satisfied. They began to play, running in circles in the clearing. Round and round they ran, each dog's nose at the tail of the next dog. In the clearing, under the snow-laden trees and under the wintry moon they made a strange picture, running thus silently, in a circle their running had beaten in the soft snow. The dogs made no sound. They ran around and around in the circle.

It may have been that the old woman saw them doing that before she died. She may have awakened once or twice and looked at the strange sight with dim old eyes.

She wouldn't be very cold now, just drowsy. Life hangs on a long time. Perhaps the old woman was out of her head. She may have dreamed of her girlhood, at the German's, and before that, when she was a child and before her mother lit out and left her.

Her dreams couldn't have been very pleasant. Not many pleasant things had happened to her. Now and then one of the Grimes dogs left the running circle and came to stand before her. The dog thrust his face close to her face. His red tongue was hanging out.

The running of the dogs may have been a kind of death ceremony. It may have been that the primitive instinct of the wolf, having been aroused in the dogs by the night and the running, made them somehow afraid.

"Now we are no longer wolves. We are dogs, the servants of men. Keep alive, man! When man dies we become wolves again."

When one of the dogs came to where the old woman sat with her back against the tree and thrust his nose close to her face he seemed satisfied and went back to run with the pack. All the Grimes dogs did it at some time during the evening, before she died. I knew all about it afterward, when I grew to be a man, because once in a woods in Illinois, on another Winter night, I saw a pack of dogs act just like that. The dogs were waiting for me to die as they had waited for the old woman that night when I was a child, but when it happened to me I was a young man and had no intention whatever of dying.

The old woman died softly and quietly. When she was dead and when one of the Grimes dogs had come to her and had found her dead all the dogs stopped running.

They gathered about her.

Well, she was dead now. She had fed the Grimes dogs when she was alive, what about now?

There was the pack on her back, the grain bag containing the piece of salt pork, the liver the butcher had given her, the dog-meat, the soup bones. The butcher in town, having been suddenly overcome with a feeling of pity, had loaded her grain bag heavily. It had been a big haul for the old woman.

It was a big haul for the dogs now.

IV

One of the Grimes dogs sprang suddenly out from among the others and began worrying the pack on the old woman's back. Had the dogs really been wolves that one would have been the leader of the pack. What he did, all the others did.

All of them sank their teeth into the grain bag the old woman had fastened with ropes to her back.

They dragged the old woman's body out into the open clearing. The worn-out dress was quickly torn from her shoulders. When she was found, a day or two later, the dress had been torn from her body clear to the hips, but the dogs had not touched her body. They had got the meat out of the grain bag, that was all. Her body was frozen stiff when it was found, and the shoulders were so narrow and the body so slight that in death it looked like the body of some charming young girl.

Such things happened in towns of the Middle West, on farms near town, when I was a boy. A hunter out after rabbits found the old woman's body and did not touch it. Something, the beaten round path in the little snow-covered clearing, the silence of the place, the place where the dogs had worried the body trying to pull the grain bag away or tear it open—something startled the man and he hurried off to town.

I was in Main street with one of my brothers who was town newsboy and who was taking the afternoon papers to the stores. It was almost night.

The hunter came into a grocery and told his story. Then he went to a hardware-shop and into a drugstore. Men began to gather on the sidewalks. Then they started out along the road to the place in the woods.

My brother should have gone on about his business of distributing papers but he didn't. Every one was going to the woods. The undertaker went and the town marshal. Several men got on a dray and rode out to where the path left the road and went into the woods, but the horses weren't very sharply shod and slid about on the slippery roads. They made no better time than those of us who walked.

The town marshal was a large man whose leg had been injured in the Civil War. He carried a heavy cane and limped rapidly along the road. My brother and I followed at his heels, and as we went other men and boys joined the crowd.

It had grown dark by the time we got to where the old woman had left the road but the moon had come out. The marshal was thinking there might have been a murder. He kept asking the hunter questions. The hunter went along with his gun across his shoulders, a dog following at his heels. It isn't often a rabbit hunter has a chance to be so conspicuous. He was taking full advantage of it, leading the procession with the town marshal. "I didn't see any wounds. She was a beautiful young girl. Her face was buried in the snow. No, I didn't know her." As a matter of fact, the hunter had not looked closely at the body. He had been frightened. She might have been murdered and some one might spring out from behind a tree and murder him. In a woods, in the late afternoon, when the trees are all bare and there is white snow on the ground, when all is silent, something creepy steals over the mind and body. If something strange or uncanny has happened in the neighborhood all you think about is getting away from there as fast as you can.

The crowd of men and boys had got to where the old woman had crossed the field and went, following the marshal and the hunter, up the slight incline and into the woods.

My brother and I were silent. He had his bundle of papers in a bag slung across his shoulder. When he got back to town he would have to go on distributing his papers before he went home to supper. If I went along, as he had no doubt already determined I should, we would both be late. Either mother or our older sister would have to warm our supper.

Well, we would have something to tell. A boy did not get such a chance very often. It was lucky we just happened to go into the grocery when the hunter came in. The hunter was a country fellow. Neither of us had ever seen him before.

Now the crowd of men and boys had got to the clearing. Darkness comes quickly on such Winter nights, but the full moon made everything clear. My brother and I stood near the tree, beneath which the old woman had died.

She did not look old, lying there in that light, frozen and still. One of the men turned her over in the snow and I saw everything. My body trembled with some strange mystical feeling and so did my brother's. It might have been the cold.

Neither of us had ever seen a woman's body before. It may have been the snow, clinging to the frozen flesh, that made it look so white and lovely, so like marble. No woman had come with the party from town; but one of the men, he was the town blacksmith, took off his overcoat and spread it over her. Then he gathered her into his arms and started off to town, all the others following silently. At that time no one knew who she was.

V

I had seen everything, had seen the oval in the snow, like a miniature race-track, where the dogs had run, had seen how the men were mystified, had seen the white bare young-looking shoulders, had heard the whispered comments of the men.

The men were simply mystified. They took the body to the undertaker's, and when the blacksmith, the hunter, the marshal and several others had got inside they closed the door. If father had been there perhaps he could have got in, but we boys couldn't.

I went with my brother to distribute the rest of his papers and when we got home it was my brother who told the story.

I kept silent and went to bed early. It may have been I was not satisfied with the way he told it.

Later, in the town, I must have heard other fragments of the old woman's story. She was recognized the next day and there was an investigation.

The husband and son were found somewhere and brought to town and there was an attempt to connect them with the woman's death, but it did not work. They had perfect enough alibis.

However, the town was against them. They had to get out. Where they went I never heard.

I remember only the picture there in the forest, the men standing about, the naked girlish-looking figure, face down in the snow, the tracks made by the running dogs and the clear cold Winter sky above. White fragments of clouds were drifting across the sky. They went racing across the little open space among the trees.

The scene in the forest had become for me, without my knowing it, the foundation for the real story I am now trying to tell. The fragments, you see, had to be picked up slowly, long afterwards.

Things happened. When I was a young man I worked on the farm of a German. The hired-girl was afraid of her employer. The farmer's wife hated her.

I saw things at that place. Once later, I had a half-uncanny, mystical adventure with dogs in an Illinois forest on a clear, moon-lit Winter night. When I was a schoolboy, and on a Summer day, I went with a boy friend out along a creek some miles from town and came to the house where the old woman had lived. No one had lived in the house since her death. The doors were broken from the hinges; the window lights were all broken. As the boy and I stood in the road outside, two dogs, just roving farm dogs no doubt, came running around the corner of the house. The dogs were tall, gaunt fellows and came down to the fence and glared through at us, standing in the road.

The whole thing, the story of the old woman's death, was to me as I grew older like music heard from far off. The notes had to be picked up slowly one at a time. Something had to be understood.

The woman who died was one destined to feed animal life. Anyway, that is all she ever did. She was feeding animal life before she was born, as a child, as a young woman working on the farm of the German, after she married, when she grew old and when she died. She fed animal life in cows, in chickens, in pigs, in horses, in dogs, in men. Her daughter had died in childhood and with her one son she had no articulate relations. On the night when she died she was hurrying homeward, bearing on her body food for animal life.

She died in the clearing in the woods and even after her death continued feeding animal life.

You see it is likely that, when my brother told the story, that night when we got home and my mother and sister sat listening, I did not think he got the point. He was too young and so was I. A thing so complete has its own beauty.

I shall not try to emphasize the point. I am only explaining why I was dissatisfied then and have been ever since. I speak of that only that you may understand why I have been impelled to try to tell the simple story over again.

1933

DISCUSSION QUESTIONS

1. The first eight paragraphs of "The Death in the Forest" are intended to give "the feel of how things were when the news of Ma Marvin's death came." Why did Anderson delete them from his final version?

2. Is Ma Marvin or the narrator the main character of the first version? What function does Ben Lewis's overcoat serve in the story?

3. The dead Ma Marvin is a "half frozen little old figure," while Mrs. Grimes's corpse "looked like the body of some charming young girl." What was Anderson's purpose in making this change? In what respects do the narrators of the two versions differ? What change of emphasis occurs?

4. Aside from the first sentence, at what point in the story does the narrator begin specifically to talk about Mrs. Grimes? What purpose do the preceding paragraphs serve?

5. At what point in "Death in the Woods" does *summary* end and *scene* (concrete action set in a specific time and place) begin?

6. Explain how Mrs. Grimes had "to feed her husband—in a certain way" (page 101). In what sense did she feed "animal life before she was born" and "even after her death" (page 108)? How does she feed the narrator when he sees her body in the clearing?

7. To get at the grain bag, the dogs tear Mrs. Grimes's dress "from her shoulders." Under what earlier circumstances had her dress also been torn? What is the significance of this parallel?

8. The dogs fear their primitive instincts: "When man dies we become wolves again" (page 104). How has this statement broader application in the story?

9. While recounting Mrs. Grimes's life with a German farmer, the narrator asks himself: "I wonder how I know all this. It must have stuck in my mind from small-town tales when I was a boy" (page 99). Yet near the end of the story, he admits working on a German's farm where the "hired-girl was afraid of her employer" (page 107). How do you account for this apparent inconsistency? Are there any other instances where the narrator admits the use of personal experiences that occurred after Mrs. Grimes's death? Why is there no need for such admissions in "The Death in the Forest"?

10. How do you explain the fact that although the boy's limited *point of view* prevents us from witnessing the scene at the undertaker's, earlier in the story we were given an inner view (thoughts) of Mrs. Grimes?

11. Near the beginning, we are told that what happened to Mrs. Grimes "is a story" (page 98) while near the end, the narrator refers to "the real story" (page 107). Do the two usages of the term suggest any difference in meaning?

12. Compare your feelings toward Ma Marvin and Mrs. Grimes. How do you account for differences in the ways in which you respond to the two versions of the same character? In what way does the fact that you get an inner view only in the case of Mrs. Grimes affect your response?

ANALYSIS AND APPLICATION

1. Contrast the following modified passage with the original version in "Death in the Woods" (page 104), noting and evaluating all changes:

There was the pack on her back, the grain bag containing the piece of salt pork, the soup bones, the dog-meat, the liver the butcher had given her. Because the butcher had been suddenly overcome with a feeling of pity, he had loaded her grain bag heavily so that it had been a big haul for the old woman.

Which version is more effective? Why?

2. Contrast the following passage from "The Death in the Forest": "even though we did not own a horse and sleigh, there was a kind of gladness in the air one felt" (page 91) with a modified version of it: even though we did not own a horse and sleigh, one felt there was a kind of gladness in the air. How does the change in word order alter the meaning? Which version is more effective? Why?

3. Describing the Passley boys spreading the news in "The Death in the Forest," the narrator exclaims: "They are more like Gods that run pushing before them dark clouds that shut out the sun on the snow and make the light in the houses dim" (page 93). How effective is the comparison? Explain. How well does it express the narrator's emotional experience? Is it the kind of *simile* that one expects from this narrator? Explain. Find another simile in "The Death in the Forest." Apply the same questions to it.

THE GERANIUM

FLANNERY O'CONNOR

OLD DUDLEY folded into the chair he was gradually molding to his own shape and looked out the window fifteen feet away into another window framed by blackened red brick. He was waiting for the geranium. They put it out every morning about ten and they took it in at five-thirty. Mrs. Carson back home had a geranium in her window. There were plenty of geraniums at home, better-looking geraniums. Ours are sho nuff geraniums, Old Dudley thought, not any er this pale pink business with green, paper bows. The geranium they would put in the window reminded him of the Grisby boy at home who had polio and had to be wheeled out every morning and left in the sun to blink.

Lutisha could have taken that geranium and stuck it in the ground and had something worth looking at in a few weeks. Those people across the alley had no business with one. They set it out and let the hot sun bake it all day and they put it so near the ledge the wind could almost knock it over. They had no business with it, no business with it. It shouldn't have been there. Old Dudley felt his throat knotting up. Lutish could root anything. Rabie too. His throat was drawn taut. He laid his head back and tried to clear his mind. There wasn't much he could think of to think about that didn't do his throat that way.

His daughter came in. "Don't you want to go for a walk?" she asked. She looked provoked.

He didn't answer her.

"Well?"

"No." He wondered how long she was going to stand there. She made his eyes feel like his throat. They'd get watery and she'd see. She had seen before and had looked sorry for him. She'd looked sorry for herself too; but she could er saved herself, Old Dudley thought, if she'd just have let him alone—let him stay where he was back home and not be so taken up with her damn duty. She moved out of the room, leaving an audible sigh, to crawl over him and remind him again of that one minute—that wasn't her fault at all—when suddenly he had wanted to go to New York to live with her.

He could have got out of going. He could have been stubborn and told her he'd spend his life where he'd always spent it, send him or not send him the money every month, he'd get along with his pension and odd jobs. Keep her damn money—she needed it worse than he did. She would have been glad to have had her duty disposed of like that. Then she could have said if he died without his children near him, it was his own fault; if he got sick and there wasn't anybody to take care of him, well, he'd asked for it, she could have said. But there was that thing inside him that had wanted to see New York. He had been to Atlanta once when he was a boy and he had seen New York in a picture show. *Big Town Rhythm* it was. Big towns were important places. The thing inside him had sneaked up on him for just one instant. The place like he'd seen in the picture show had room for him! It was an important place and it had room for him! He'd said yes, he'd go.

He must have been sick when he said it. He couldn't have been well and said it. He had been sick and she had been so taken up with her damn duty, she had wangled it out of him. Why did she have to come down there in the first place to pester him? He had been doing all right.

There was his pension that could feed him and odd jobs that kept him his room in the boarding house.

The window in that room showed him the river—thick and red as it struggled over rocks and around curves. He tried to think how it was besides red and slow. He added green blotches for trees on either side of it and a brown spot for trash somewhere upstream. He and Rabie had fished it in a flat-bottom boat every Wednesday. Rabie knew the river up and down for twenty miles. There wasn't another nigger in Coa County that knew it like he did. He loved the river, but it hadn't meant anything to Old Dudley. The fish were what he was after. He liked to come in at night with a long string of them and slap them down in the sink. "Few fish I got," he'd say. It took a man to get those fish, the old girls at the boarding house always said. He and Rabie would start out early Wednesday morning and fish all day. Rabie would find the spots and row; Old Dudley always caught them. Rabie didn't care much about catching them—he just loved the river. "Ain't no use settin' yo' line down dere, boss," he'd say. "Ain't no fish dere. Dis ol' riber ain't hidin' none nowhere 'round hyar, nawsuh." And he would giggle and shift the boat downstream. That was Rabie. He could steal cleaner than a weasel but he knew where the fish were. Old Dudley always gave him the little ones.

Old Dudley had lived upstairs in the corner room of the boarding house ever since his wife died in '22. He protected the old ladies. He was the man in the house and he did the things a man in the house was supposed to do. It was a dull occupation at night when the old girls crabbed and crocheted in the parlor and the man in the house had to listen and judge the sparrow-like wars that rasped and twittered intermittently. But in the daytime there was Rabie. Rabie and Lutisha lived down in the basement. Lutish cooked and Rabie took care of the cleaning and the vegetable garden; but he was sharp at sneaking off with half his work done and going to help Old Dudley with some current project—building a hen house or painting a door. He liked to listen, he liked to hear about Atlanta when Old Dudley had been there and about how guns were put together on the inside and all the other things the old man knew.

Sometimes at night they would go 'possum hunting. They never got a 'possum but Old Dudley liked to get away from the ladies once in a while and hunting was a good excuse. Rabie didn't like 'possum hunting. They never got a 'possum; they never even treed one; and besides, he was mostly a water nigger. "We ain't gonna go huntin' no 'possum tonight, is we, boss? I got a lil' business I wants tuh tend tuh," he'd say when Old Dudley would start talking about hounds and guns. "Whose chickens you gonna steal tonight?" Dudley would grin. "I reckon I be huntin' 'possum tonight," Rabie'd sigh.

Old Dudley would get out his gun and take it apart and, as Rabie cleaned the pieces, would explain the mechanism to him. Then he'd put it together again. Rabie always marveled at the way he could put it together again. Old Dudley would have liked to have explained New York to Rabie. If he could have showed it to Rabie, it wouldn't have been so big—he wouldn't have felt pressed down every time he went out in it. "It ain't so big," he would have said. "Don't let it get you down, Rabie. It's just like any other city and cities ain't all that complicated."

But they were. New York was swishing and jamming one minute and dirty and dead the next. His daughter didn't even live in a house. She lived in a building—the middle in a row of buildings all alike, all blackened-red and gray with rasp-mouthed people hanging out their windows looking at other windows and other people just like them looking back. Inside you could go up and you could go down and there were just halls that reminded you of tape measures strung out with a door every inch. He remembered he'd been dazed by the building the first week. He'd wake up expecting the halls to have changed in the night and he'd look out the door and there they stretched like dog runs. The streets were the same way. He wondered where he'd be if he walked to the end of one of them. One night he dreamed he did and ended at the end of the building—nowhere.

The next week he had become more conscious of the daughter and son-in-law and their boy—no place to be out of their way. The son-in-law was a queer one. He drove a truck and came in only on the weekends. He said "nah" for "no" and he'd never heard of a 'possum. Old Dudley slept in the room with the boy, who was sixteen and couldn't be talked to. But sometimes when the daughter and Old Dudley were alone in the apartment, she would sit down and talk to him. First she had to think of something to say. Usually it gave out before what she considered was the proper time to get up and do something else, so he would have to say something. He always tried to think of something he hadn't said before. She never listened the second time. She was seeing that her father spent his last years with his own family and not in a decayed boarding house full of old women whose heads jiggled. She was doing her duty. She had brothers and sisters who were not.

Once she took him shopping with her but he was too slow. They went in a "subway"—a railroad underneath the ground like a big cave.

People boiled out of trains and up steps and over into the streets. They rolled off the street and down steps and into trains—black and white and yellow all mixed up like vegetables in soup. Everything was boiling. The trains swished in from tunnels, up canals, and all of a sudden stopped. The people coming out pushed through the people coming in and a noise rang and the train swooped off again. Old Dudley and the daughter had to go in three different ones before they got where they were going. He wondered why people ever went out of their houses. He felt like his tongue had slipped down in his stomach. She held him by the coat sleeve and pulled him through the people.

They went on an overhead train too. She called it an "El." They had to go up on a high platform to catch it. Old Dudley looked over the rail and could see the people rushing and the automobiles rushing under him. He felt sick. He put one hand on the rail and sank down on the wooden floor of the platform. The daughter screamed and pulled him over from the edge. "Do you want to fall off and kill yourself?" she shouted.

Through a crack in the boards he could see the cars swimming in the street. "I don't care," he murmured, "I don't care if I do or not."

"Come on," she said, "you'll feel better when we get home."

"Home?" he repeated. The cars moved in a rhythm below him.

"Come on," she said, "here it comes; we've just got time to make it." They'd just had time to make all of them.

They made that one. They came back to the building and the apartment. The apartment was too tight. There was no place to be where there wasn't somebody else. The kitchen opened into the bathroom and the bathroom opened into everything else and you were always where you started from. At home there was upstairs and the basement and the river and downtown in front of Fraziers . . . damn his throat.

The geranium was late today. It was ten-thirty. They usually had it out by ten-fifteen.

Somewhere down the hall a woman shrilled something unintelligible out to the street; a radio was bleating the worn music to a soap serial; and a garbage can crashed down a fire escape. The door to the next apartment slammed and a sharp footstep clipped down the hall. "That would be the nigger," Old Dudley muttered. "The nigger with the shiny shoes." He had been there a week when the nigger moved in. That Thursday he was looking out the door at the dog-run halls when this nigger went into the next apartment. He had on a gray, pin-stripe suit and a tan tie. His collar was stiff and white and made a clear-cut line next to his neck. His shoes were shiny tan—they matched his tie and his skin. Old

Dudley scratched his head. He hadn't known the kind of people that would live thick in a building could afford servants. He chuckled. Lot of good a nigger in a Sunday suit would do them. Maybe this nigger would know the country around here—or maybe how to get to it. They might could hunt. They might could find them a stream somewhere. He shut the door and went to the daughter's room. "Hey!" he shouted, "the folks next door got 'em a nigger. Must be gonna clean for them. You reckon they gonna keep him every day?"

She looked up from making the bed. "What are you talking about?"

"I say they got 'em a servant next door—a nigger—all dressed up in a Sunday suit."

She walked to the other side of the bed. "You must be crazy," she said. "The next apartment is vacant and besides, nobody around here can afford any servant."

"I tell you I saw him," Old Dudley snickered. "Going right in there with a tie and a white collar on—and sharp-toed shoes."

"If he went in there, he's looking at it for himself," she muttered. She went to the dresser and started fidgeting with things.

Old Dudley laughed. She could be right funny when she wanted to. "Well," he said, "I think I'll go over and see what day he gets off. Maybe I can convince him he likes to fish," and he'd slapped his pocket to make the two quarters jingle. Before he got out in the hall good, she came tearing behind him and pulled him in. "Can't you hear?" she'd yelled. "I meant what I said. He's renting that himself if he went in there. Don't you go asking him any questions or saying anything to him. I don't want any trouble with niggers."

"You mean," Old Dudley murmured, "he's gonna live next door to you?"

She shrugged. "I suppose he is. And you tend to your own business," she added. "Don't have anything to do with him."

That's just the way she'd said it. Like he didn't have any sense at all. But he'd told her off then. He'd stated his say and she knew what he meant. "You ain't been raised that way!" he'd said thundery-like. "You ain't been raised to live tight with niggers that think they're just as good as you, and you think I'd go messin' around with one er that kind! If you think I want anything to do with them, you're crazy." He had had to slow down then because his throat was tightening. She'd stood stiff up and said they lived where they could afford to live and made the best of it. Preaching to him! Then she'd walked stiff off without a word more. That was her. Trying to be holy with her shoulders curved around and her neck in the air. Like he was a fool. He knew Yankees let niggers in their front doors and let them set on their sofas but he didn't know his own daughter that was raised proper would stay next door to them—and then think he didn't have no more sense than to want to mix with them. Him!

He got up and took a paper off another chair. He might as well appear to be reading when she came through again. No use having her standing up there staring at him, believing she had to think up something for him to do. He looked over the paper at the window across the alley. The geranium wasn't there yet. It had never been this late before. The first day he'd seen it, he had been sitting there looking out the window at the other window and he had looked at his watch to see how long it had been since breakfast. When he looked up, it was there. It startled him. He didn't like flowers, but the geranium didn't look like a flower. It looked like the sick Grisby boy at home and it was the color of the drapes the old ladies had in the parlor and the paper bow on it looked like the one behind Lutish's uniform she wore on Sundays. Lutish had a fondness for sashes. Most niggers did, Old Dudley thought.

The daughter came through again. He had meant to be looking at the paper when she came through. "Do me a favor, will you?" she asked as if she had just thought up a favor he could do.

He hoped she didn't want him to go to the grocery again. He got lost the time before. All the blooming buildings looked alike. He nodded.

"Go down to the third floor and ask Mrs. Schmitt to lend me the shirt pattern she uses for Jake."

Why couldn't she just let him sit? She didn't need the shirt pattern. "All right," he said. "What number is it?"

"Number 10—just like this. Right below us three floors down."

Old Dudley was always afraid that when he went out in the dog runs, a door would suddenly open and one of the snipe-nosed men that hung off the window ledges in his undershirt would growl, "What are you doing here?" The door to the nigger's apartment was open and he could see a woman sitting in a chair by the window. "Yankee niggers," he muttered. She had on rimless glasses and there was a book in her lap. Niggers don't think they're dressed up till they got on glasses, Old Dudley thought. He remembered Lutish's glasses. She had saved up thirteen dollars to buy them. Then she went to the doctor and asked him to look at her eyes and tell her how thick to get the glasses. He made her look at animals' pictures through a mirror and he stuck a light through her eyes and looked in her head. Then he said she didn't need any glasses. She was so mad she burned the corn bread three days in a row, but she bought her some glasses anyway at the ten-cent store. They didn't cost her but $1.98 and she wore them every Saddey. "That was niggers," Old Dudley chuckled. He realized he had made a noise, and covered his mouth with his hand. Somebody might hear him in one of the apartments.

He turned down the first flight of stairs. Down the second he heard footsteps coming up. He looked over the banisters and saw it was a woman—a fat woman with an apron on. From the top, she looked kind er like Mrs. Benson at home. He wondered if she would speak to him. When they were four steps from each other, he darted a glance at her but she wasn't looking at him. When there were no steps between them, his eyes fluttered up for an instant and she was looking at him cold in the face. Then she was past him. She hadn't said a word. He felt heavy in his stomach.

He went down four flights instead of three. Then he went back up one and found number 10. Mrs. Schmitt said O.K., wait a minute and she'd get the pattern. She sent one of the children back to the door with it. The child didn't say anything.

Old Dudley started back up the stairs. He had to take it more slowly. It tired him going up. Everything tired him, looked like. Not like having Rabie to do his running for him. Rabie was a light-footed nigger. He could sneak in a hen house 'thout even the hens knowing it and get him the fattest fryer in there and not a squawk. Fast too. Dudley had always been slow on his feet. It went that way with fat people. He remembered one time him and Rabie was hunting quail over near Molton. They had 'em a hound dog that could find a covey quickern any fancy pointer going. He wasn't no good at bringing them back but he could find them every time and then set like a dead stump while you aimed at the birds. This one time the hound stopped cold-still. "Dat gonna be a big 'un," Rabie whispered, "I feels it." Old Dudley raised the gun slowly as they walked along. He had to be careful of the pine needles. They covered the ground and made it slick. Rabie shifted his weight from side to side, lifting and setting his feet on the waxen needles with unconscious care. He looked straight ahead and moved forward swiftly. Old Dudley kept one eye ahead and one on the ground. It would slope and he would be sliding forward dangerously, or in pulling himself up an incline, he would slide back down.

"Ain't I better get dem birds dis time, boss?" Rabie suggested. "You ain't never easy on yo' feets on Monday. If you falls in one dem slopes, you gonna scatter dem birds fo' you gits dat gun up."

Old Dudley wanted to get the covey. He could er knocked four out of it easy. "I'll get 'em," he muttered. He lifted the gun to his eye and leaned forward. Something slipped beneath him and he slid backward on his heels. The gun went off and the covey sprayed into the air.

"Dem was some mighty fine birds we let get away from us," Rabie sighed.

"We'll find another covey," Old Dudley said. "Now get me out of this damn hole."

He could er got five er those birds if he hadn't fallen. He could er shot 'em off like cans on a fence. He drew one hand back to his ear and extended the other forward. He could er knocked 'em out like clay pigeons. Bang! A squeak on the staircase made him wheel around—his arms still holding the invisible gun. The nigger was clipping up the steps toward him, an amused smile stretching his trimmed mustache. Old Dudley's mouth dropped open. The nigger's lips were pulled down like he was trying to keep from laughing. Old Dudley couldn't move. He stared at the clear-cut line the nigger's collar made against his skin.

"What are you hunting, old-timer?" the Negro asked in a voice that sounded like a nigger's laugh and a white man's sneer.

Old Dudley felt like a child with a pop-pistol. His mouth was open and his tongue was rigid in the middle of it. Right below his knees felt hollow. His feet slipped and he slid three steps and landed sitting down.

"You better be careful," the Negro said. "You could easily hurt yourself on these steps." And he held out his hand for Old Dudley to pull up on. It was a long narrow hand and the tips of the fingernails were clean and cut squarely. They looked like they might have been filed. Old Dudley's hands hung between his knees. The nigger took him by the arm and pulled up. "Whew!" he gasped, "you're heavy. Give a little help here." Old Dudley's knees unbended and he staggered up. The nigger had him by the arm. "I'm going up anyway," he said. "I'll help you." Old Dudley looked frantically around. The steps behind him seemed to close up. He was walking with the nigger up the stairs. The nigger was waiting for him on each step. "So you hunt?" the nigger was saying. "Well, let's see. I went deer hunting once. I believe we used a Dodson .38 to get those deer. What do you use?"

Old Dudley was staring through the shiny tan shoes. "I use a gun," he mumbled.

"I like to fool with guns better than hunting," the nigger was saying. "Never was much at killing anything. Seems kind of a shame to deplete the game reserve. I'd collect guns if I had the time and the money, though." He was waiting on every step till Old Dudley got on it. He was explaining guns and makes. He had on gray socks with a black fleck in them. They finished the stairs. The nigger walked down the hall with him, holding him by the arm. It probably looked like he had his arm locked in the nigger's.

They went right up to Old Dudley's door. Then the nigger asked, "You from around here?"

Old Dudley shook his head, looking at the door. He hadn't looked at the nigger yet. All the way up the stairs, he hadn't looked at the nigger. "Well," the nigger said, "it's a swell place—once you get used to it." He patted Old Dudley on the back and went into his own apartment. Old Dudley went into his. The pain in his throat was all over his face now, leaking out his eyes.

He shuffled to the chair by the window and sank down in it. His throat was going to pop. His throat was going to pop on account of a nigger—a damn nigger that patted him on the back and called him "old-timer." Him that knew such as that couldn't be. Him that had come from a good place. A good place. A place where such as that couldn't be. His eyes felt strange in their sockets. They were swelling in them and in a minute there wouldn't be any room left for them there. He was trapped in this place where niggers could call you "old-timer." He wouldn't be trapped. He wouldn't be. He rolled his head on the back of the chair to stretch his neck that was too full.

A man was looking at him. A man was in the window across the alley looking straight at him. The man was watching him cry. That was where the geranium was supposed to be and it was a man in his undershirt, watching him cry, waiting to watch his throat pop. Old Dudley looked back at the man. It was supposed to be the geranium. The geranium belonged there, not the man. "Where is the geranium?" he called out of his tight throat.

"What you cryin' for?" the man asked. "I ain't never seen a man cry like that."

"Where is the geranium?" Old Dudley quavered. "It ought to be there. Not you."

"This is my window," the man said. "I got a right to set here if I want to."

"Where is it?" Old Dudley shrilled. There was just a little room left in his throat.

"It fell off if it's any of your business," the man said.

Old Dudley got up and peered over the window ledge. Down in the alley, way six floors down, he could see a cracked flower pot scattered over a spray of dirt and something pink sticking out of a green paper bow. It was down six floors. Smashed down six floors.

Old Dudley looked at the man who was chewing gum and waiting to see the throat pop. "You shouldn't have put it so near the ledge," he murmured. "Why don't you pick it up?"

"Why don't you, pop?"

Old Dudley stared at the man who was where the geranium should have been.

He would. He'd go down and pick it up. He'd put it in his own window and look at it all day if he wanted to. He turned from the window and left the room. He walked slowly down the dog run and got to the steps. The steps dropped down like a deep wound in the floor. They opened up through a gap like a cavern and went down and down. And he had gone up them a little behind the nigger. And the nigger had pulled him up on his feet and kept his arm in his and gone up the steps with him and said he hunted deer, "old-timer," and seen him holding a gun that wasn't there and sitting on the steps like a child. He had shiny tan shoes and he was trying not to laugh and the whole business was laughing. There'd probably be niggers with black flecks in their socks on every step, pulling down their mouths so as not to laugh. The steps dropped down and down. He wouldn't go down and have niggers pattin' him on the back. He went back to the room and the window and looked down at the geranium.

The man was sitting over where it should have been. "I ain't seen you pickin' it up," he said.

Old Dudley stared at the man.

"I seen you before," the man said. "I seen you settin' in that old chair every day, starin' out the window, looking in my apartment. What I do in my apartment is my business, see? I don't like people looking at what I do."

It was at the bottom of the alley with its roots in the air.

"I only tell people once," the man said and left the window.

1946

JUDGEMENT DAY

FLANNERY O'CONNOR

TANNER WAS conserving all his strength for the trip home. He meant to walk as far as he could get and trust to the Almighty to get him the rest of the way. That morning and the morning before, he had allowed his daughter to dress him and had conserved that much more energy. Now he sat in the chair by the window—his blue shirt buttoned at the collar, his coat on the back of the chair, and his hat on his head—waiting for her to leave. He couldn't escape until she got out of the way. The window looked out on a brick wall and down into an alley full of New York air, the kind fit for cats and garbage. A few snow flakes drifted past the window but they were too thin and scattered for his failing vision.

The daughter was in the kitchen washing dishes. She dawdled over everything, talking to herself. When he had first come, he had answered her, but that had not been wanted. She glowered at him as if, old fool that he was, he should still have had sense enough not to answer a woman talking to herself. She questioned herself in one voice and answered herself in another. With the energy he had conserved yesterday letting her dress him, he had written a note and pinned it in his pocket. IF FOUND DEAD SHIP EXPRESS COLLECT TO COLEMAN PARRUM, CORINTH, GEORGIA. Under this he had continued: COLEMAN SELL MY BELONGINGS AND PAY THE FREIGHT ON ME & THE UNDERTAKER. ANYTHING LEFT OVER YOU CAN KEEP. YOURS TRULY T. C. TANNER. P.S. STAY WHERE YOU ARE. DON'T LET THEM TALK YOU INTO COMING UP HERE. ITS NO KIND OF PLACE. It had taken him the better part of thirty minutes to write the paper; the script was wavery but decipherable with patience. He controlled one hand by holding the other on top of it. By the time he had got it written, she was back in the apartment from getting her groceries.

Today he was ready. All he had to do was push one foot in front of the other until he got to the door and down the steps. Once down the steps, he would get out of the neighborhood. Once out of it, he would hail a taxi cab and go to the freight yards. Some bum would help him onto a car. Once he got in the freight car, he would lie down and rest. During the night the train would start South, and the next day or the morning after, dead or alive, he would be home. Dead or alive. It was being there that mattered; the dead or alive did not.

If he had had good sense he would have gone the day after he arrived; better sense and he would not have arrived. He had not got desperate until two days ago when he had heard his daughter and son-in-law taking leave of each other after breakfast. They were standing in the front door, she seeing him off for a three-day trip. He drove a long distance moving van. She must have handed him his leather headgear. "You ought to get you a hat," she said, "a real one."

"And sit all day in it," the son-in-law said, "like him in there. Yah! All he does is sit all day with that hat on. Sits all day with that damn black hat on his head. Inside!"

"Well you don't even have you a hat," she said. "Nothing but that leather cap with flaps. People that are somebody wear hats. Other kinds wear those leather caps like you got on."

"People that are somebody!" he cried. "People that are somebody! That kills me! That really kills me!" The son-in-law had a stupid muscular face and a yankee voice to go with it.

"My daddy is here to stay," his daughter said. "He ain't going to last long. He was somebody when he was somebody. He never worked for nobody in his life but himself and had people—other people—working for him."

"Yah? Niggers is what he had working for him," the son-in-law said. "That's all. I've worked a nigger or two myself."

"Those were just nawthun niggers you worked," she said, her voice suddenly going lower so that Tanner had to lean forward to catch the words. "It takes brains to work a real nigger. You got to know how to handle them."

"Yah so I don't have brains," the son-in-law said.

One of the sudden, very occasional, feelings of warmth for the daughter came over Tanner. Every now and then she said something that might make you think she had a little sense stored away somewhere for safe keeping.

"You got them," she said. "You don't always use them."

"He has a stroke when he sees a nigger in the building," the son-in-law said, "and she tells me . . ."

"Shut up talking so loud," she said. "That's not why he had the stroke."

There was a silence. "Where you going to bury him?" the son-in-law asked, taking a different tack.

"Bury who?"

"Him in there."

"Right here in New York," she said. "Where do you think? We got a lot. I'm not taking that trip down there again with nobody."

"Yah. Well I just wanted to make sure," he said.

When she returned to the room, Tanner had both hands gripped on the chair arms. His eyes were trained on her like the eyes of an angry corpse. "You promised you'd bury me there," he said. "Your promise ain't any good. Your promise ain't any good. Your promise ain't any good." His voice was so dry it was barely audible. He began to shake, his hands, his head, his feet. "Bury me here and burn in hell!" he cried and fell back into his chair.

The daughter shuddered to attention. "You ain't dead yet!" She threw out a ponderous sigh. "You got a long time to be worrying about that." She turned and began to pick up parts of the newspaper scattered on the floor. She had gray hair that hung to her shoulders and a round face, beginning to wear. "I do every last living thing for you," she muttered, "and this is the way you carry on." She stuck the papers under her arm and said, "And don't throw hell at me. I don't believe in it.

That's a lot of hardshell Baptist hooey." Then she went into the kitchen.

He kept his mouth stretched taut, his top plate gripped between his tongue and the roof of his mouth. Still the tears flooded down his cheeks; he wiped each one furtively on his shoulder.

Her voice rose from the kitchen. "As bad as having a child. He wanted to come and now he's here, he don't like it."

He had not wanted to come.

"Pretended he didn't but I could tell. I said if you don't want to come I can't make you. If you don't want to live like decent people there's nothing I can do about it."

"As for me," her higher voice said, "when I die that ain't the time I'm going to start getting choosey. They can lay me in the nearest spot. When I pass from this world I'll be considerate of them that stay in it. I won't be thinking of just myself."

"Certainly not," the other voice said, "You never been that selfish. You're the kind that looks out for other people."

"Well I try," she said, "I try."

He laid his head on the back of the chair for a moment and the hat tilted down over his eyes. He had raised three boys and her. The three boys were gone, two in the war and one to the devil and there was nobody left who felt a duty toward him but her, married and childless, in New York City like Mrs. Big and ready when she came back and found him living the way he was to take him back with her. She had put her face in the door of the shack and had stared, expressionless, for a second. Then all at once she had screamed and jumped back.

"What's that on the floor?"

"Coleman," he said.

The old Negro was curled up on a pallet asleep at the foot of Tanner's bed, a stinking skin full of bones, arranged in what seemed vaguely human form. When Coleman was young, he had looked like a bear; now that he was old he looked like a monkey. With Tanner it was the opposite; when he was young he had looked like a monkey but when he got old, he looked like a bear.

The daughter stepped back onto the porch. There were the bottoms of two cane chairs tilted against the clapboard but she declined to take a seat. She stepped out about ten feet from the house as if it took that much space to clear the odor. Then she had spoken her piece.

"If you don't have any pride I have and I know my duty and I was raised to do it. My mother raised me to do it if you didn't. She was from plain people but not the kind that likes to settle in with niggers."

At that point the old Negro roused up and slid out the door, a doubled-up shadow which Tanner just caught sight of gliding away.

She had shamed him. He shouted so they both could hear. "Who you think cooks? Who you think cuts my firewood and empties my slops? He's paroled to me. That no-good scoundrel has been on my hands for thirty years. He ain't a bad nigger."

She was unimpressed. "Whose shack is this anyway?" she had asked. "Yours or his?"

"Him and me built it," he said. "You go on back up there. I wouldn't come with you for no million dollars or no sack of salt."

"It looks like him and you built it. Whose land is it on?"

"Some people that live in Florida," he said evasively. He had known then that it was land up for sale but he thought it was too sorry for anyone to buy. That same afternoon he had found out different. He had found out in time to go back with her. If he had found out a day later, he might still be there, squatting on the doctor's land.

When he saw the brown porpoise-shaped figure striding across the field that afternoon, he had known at once what had happened; no one had to tell him. If that nigger had owned the whole world except for one runty rutted peafield and he acquired it, he would walk across it that way, beating the weeds aside, his thick neck swelled, his stomach a throne for his gold watch and chain. Doctor Foley. He was only part black. The rest was Indian and white.

He was everything to the niggers—druggist and undertaker and general counsel and real estate man and sometimes he got the evil eye off them and sometimes he put it on. Be prepared, he said to himself, watching him approach, to take something off him, nigger though he be. Be prepared, because you ain't got a thing to hold up to him but the skin you come in, and that's no more use to you now than what a snake would shed. You don't have a chance with the government against you.

He was sitting on the porch in the piece of straight chair tilted against the shack. "Good evening, Foley," he said and nodded as the doctor came up and stopped short at the edge of the clearing, as if he had only just that minute seen him though it was plain he had sighted him as he crossed the field.

"I be out here to look at my property," the doctor said. "Good evening." His voice was quick and high.

Ain't been your property long, he said to himself. "I seen you coming," he said.

"I acquired this here recently," the doctor said and proceeded without looking at him again to walk around to one side of the shack. In a moment he came back and stopped in front of him. Then he stepped boldly to the door of the shack and put his head in. Coleman was in there that time too, asleep. He looked for a moment and then turned aside. "I know that nigger," he said. "Coleman Parrum—how long does it take him to sleep off that stump liquor you all make?"

Tanner took hold of the knobs on the chair bottom and held them hard. "This shack ain't in your property. Only on it, by my mistake," he said.

The doctor removed his cigar momentarily from his mouth. "It ain't my mis-take," he said and smiled.

He had only sat there, looking ahead.

"It don't pay to make this kind of mis-take," the doctor said.

"I never found nothing that paid yet," he muttered.

"Everything pays," the Negro said, "if you knows how to make it," and he remained there smiling, looking the squatter up and down. Then he turned and went around the other side of the shack. There was a silence. He was looking for the still.

Then would have been the time to kill him. There was a gun inside the shack and he could have done it as easy as not, but, from childhood, he had been weakened for that kind of violence by the fear of hell. He had never killed one, he had always handled them with his wits and with luck. He was known to have a way with niggers. There was an art to handling them. The secret of handling a nigger was to show him his brains didn't have a chance against yours; then he would jump on your back and know he had a good thing there for life. He had had Coleman on his back for thirty years.

Tanner had first seen Coleman when he was working six of them at a saw mill in the middle of a pine forest fifteen miles from nowhere. They were as sorry a crew as he had worked, the kind that on Monday they didn't show up. What was in the air had reached them. They thought there was a new Lincoln elected who was going to abolish work. He managed them with a very sharp penknife. He had had something wrong with his kidney then that made his hands shake and he had taken to whittling to force that waste motion out of sight. He did not intend them to see that his hands shook of their own accord and he did not intend to see it himself or to countenance it. The knife had moved constantly, violently, in his quaking hands and here and there small crude figures—that he never looked at again and could not have said what they were if he had—dropped to the ground. The Negroes picked them up and took them home; there was not much time between them and darkest Africa. The knife glittered constantly in his hands. More than once he had stopped short and said in an off-hand voice to some half-reclining, head-averted Negro, "Nigger, this knife is in my hand now but if you don't quit wasting my time and money, it'll be in your gut shortly." And the Negro would begin to rise—slowly, but he would be in the act—before the sentence was completed.

A large black loose-jointed Negro, twice his own size, had begun hanging around the edge of the saw mill, watching the others work and when he was not watching, sleeping, in full view of them, sprawled like a gigantic bear on his back. "Who is that?" he had asked. "If he wants to work, tell him to come here. If he don't, tell him to go. No idlers are going to hang around here."

None of them knew who he was. They knew he didn't want to work. They knew nothing else, not where he had come from, nor why, though he was probably brother to one, cousin to all of them. He had ignored him for a day; against the six of them he was one yellow-faced scrawny white man with shaky hands. He was willing to wait for trouble, but not forever. The next day the stranger came again. After the six Tanner worked had seen the idler there for half the morning, they quit and began to eat, a full thirty minutes before noon. He had not risked ordering them up. He had gone to the source of the trouble.

The stranger was leaning against a tree on the edge of the clearing, watching with half-closed eyes. The insolence on his face barely covered the wariness behind it. His look said, this ain't much of a white man so why he come on so big, what he fixing to do?

He had meant to say, "Nigger, this knife is in my hand now but if you ain't out of my sight . . ." but as he drew closer he changed his mind. The Negro's eyes were small and bloodshot. Tanner supposed there was a knife on him somewhere that he would as soon use as not. His own penknife moved, directed solely by some intruding intelligence that worked in his hands. He had no idea what he was carving, but when he reached the Negro, he had already made two holes the size of half dollars in the piece of bark.

The Negro's gaze fell on his hands and was held. His jaw slackened. His eyes did not move from the knife tearing recklessly around the bark. He watched as if he saw an invisible power working on the wood.

He looked himself then and, astonished, saw the connected rims of a pair of spectacles.

He held them away from him and looked through the holes past a pile of shavings and on into the woods to the edge of the pen where they kept their mules.

"You can't see so good, can you, boy?" he said and began scraping the ground with his foot to turn up a piece of wire. He picked up a small piece of haywire; in a minute he found another, shorter piece and picked that up. He began to attach these to the bark. He was in no hurry now that he knew what he was doing. When the spectacles were finished, he handed them to the Negro. "Put these on," he said. "I hate to see anybody can't see good."

There was an instant when the Negro might have done one thing or another, might have taken the glasses and crushed them in his hand or grabbed the knife and turned it on him. He saw the exact instant in the muddy liquor-swollen eyes when the pleasure of having a knife in this white man's gut was balanced against something else, he could not tell what.

The Negro reached for the glasses. He attached the bows carefully behind his ears and looked forth. He peered this way and that with exaggerated solemnity. And then he looked directly at Tanner and grinned, or grimaced, Tanner could not tell which, but he had an instant's sensation of seeing before him a negative image of himself, as if clownishness and captivity had been their common lot. The vision failed him before he could decipher it.

"Preacher," he said, "what you hanging around here for?" He picked up another piece of bark and began, without looking at it, to carve again. "This ain't Sunday."

"This here ain't Sunday?" the Negro said.

"This is Friday," he said. "That's the way it is with you preachers—drunk all week so you don't know when Sunday is. What you see through those glasses?"

"See a man."

"What kind of a man?"

"See the man make theseyer glasses."

"Is he white or black?"

"He white!" the Negro said as if only at that moment was his vision sufficiently improved to detect it. "Yessuh, he white!" he said.

"Well, you treat him like he was white," Tanner said. "What's your name?"

"Name Coleman," the Negro said.

And he had not got rid of Coleman since. You make a monkey out of one of them and he jumps on your back and stays there for life, but let one make a monkey out of you and all you can do is kill him or disappear. And he was not going to hell for killing a nigger. Behind the shack he heard the doctor kick over a bucket. He sat and waited.

In a moment the doctor appeared again, beating his way around the other side of the house, whacking at scattered clumps of Johnson grass with his cane. He stopped in the middle of the yard, about where that morning the daughter had delivered her ultimatum.

"You don't belong here," he began. "I could have you prosecuted."

Tanner remained there, dumb, staring across the field.

"Where's your still?" the doctor asked.

"If it's a still around here, it don't belong to me," he said and shut his mouth tight.

The Negro laughed softly. "Down on your luck, ain't you?" he murmured. "Didn't you used to own a little piece of land over acrost the river and lost it?"

He had continued to study the woods ahead.

"If you want to run the still for me, that's one thing," the doctor said. "If you don't, you might as well had be packing up."

"I don't have to work for you," he said. "The governmint ain't got around yet to forcing the white folks to work for the colored."

The doctor polished the stone in his ring with the ball of his thumb. "I don't like the governmint no bettern you," he said. "Where you going instead? You going to the city and get you a soot of rooms at the Biltmo' Hotel?"

Tanner said nothing.

"The day coming," the doctor said, "when the white folks IS going to be working for the colored and you mights well to git ahead of the crowd."

"That day ain't coming for me," Tanner said shortly.

"Done come for you," the doctor said. "Ain't come for the rest of them."

Tanner's gaze drove on past the farthest blue edge of the tree line into the pale empty afternoon sky. "I got a daughter in the north," he said. "I don't have to work for you."

The doctor took his watch from his watch pocket and looked at it and put it back. He gazed for a moment at the back of his hands. He appeared to have measured and to know secretly the time it would take everything to change finally upside down. "She don't want no old daddy like you," he said. "Maybe she say she do, but that ain't likely. Even if you rich," he said, "they don't want you. They got they own ideas. The black ones they rares and they pitches. I made mine," he said, "and I ain't done none of that." He looked again at Tanner. "I be back here next week," he said, "and if you still here, I know you going to work for me." He remained there a moment, rocking on his heels, waiting for some answer. Finally he turned and started beating his way back through the overgrown path.

Tanner had continued to look across the field as if his spirit had been sucked out of him into the woods and nothing was left on the chair but a shell. If he had known it was a question of this—sitting here looking out of this window all day in this no-place, or just running a still for a nigger, he would have run the still for the nigger. He would have been a nigger's white nigger any day. Behind him he heard the daughter come in from the kitchen. His heart accelerated but after a second he heard her plump herself down on the sofa. She was not yet ready to go. He did not turn and look at her.

She sat there silently a few moments. Then she began. "The trouble with you is," she said, "you sit in front of that window all the time where there's nothing to look out at. You need some inspiration and an out-let. If you would let me pull your chair around to look at the TV, you would quit thinking about morbid stuff, death and hell and judgement. My Lord."

"The Judgement is coming," he muttered. "The sheep'll be separated from the goats. Them that kept their promises from them that didn't. Them that did the best they could with what they had from them that didn't. Them that honored their father and their mother from them that cursed them. Them that . . ."

She heaved a mammoth sigh that all but drowned him out. "What's the use in me wasting my good breath?" she asked. She rose and went back in the kitchen and began knocking things about.

She was so high and mighty! At home he had been living in a shack but there was at least air around it. He could put his feet on the ground. Here she didn't even live in a house. She lived in a pigeon-hutch of a building, with all stripes of foreigner, all of them twisted in the tongue. It was no place for a sane man. The first morning here she had taken him sightseeing and he had seen in fifteen minutes exactly how it was. He had not been out of the apartment since. He never wanted to set foot again on the underground railroad or the steps that moved under you while you stood still or any elevator to the thirty-fourth floor. When he was safely back in the apartment again, he had imagined going over it with Coleman. He had to turn his head every few seconds to make sure Coleman was behind him. Keep to the inside or these people'll knock you down, keep right behind me or you'll get left, keep your hat on, you damn idiot, he had said, and Coleman had come on with his bent running shamble, panting and muttering, What we doing here? Where you get this fool idea coming here?

I come to show you it was no kind of place. Now you know you were well off where you were.

I knowed it before, Coleman said. Was you didn't know it.

When he had been here a week, he had got a postcard from Coleman that had been written for him by Hooten at the railroad station. It was written in green ink and said, "This is Coleman—X—howyou boss." Under it Hooten had written from himself, "Quit frequenting all those nitespots and come on home, you scoundrel, yours truly. W. P. Hooten." He had sent Coleman a card in return, care of Hooten, that said, "This place is alrite if you like it. Yours truly, W. T. Tanner." Since the daughter had to mail the card, he had not put on it that he was returning as soon as his pension check came. He had not intended to tell her but to leave her a note. When the check came, he would hire himself a taxi to the bus station and be on his way. And it would have made her as happy as it made him. She had found his company dour and her duty irksome. If he had sneaked out, she would have had the pleasure of having tried to do it and to top that off, the pleasure of his ingratitude.

As for him, he would have returned to squat on the doctor's land and to take his orders from a nigger who chewed ten-cent cigars. And to think less about it than formerly. Instead he had been done in by a nigger actor, or one who called himself an actor. He didn't believe the nigger was any actor.

There were two apartments on each floor of the building. He had been with the daughter three weeks when the people in the next hutch moved out. He had stood in the hall and watched the moving-out and the next day he had watched a moving-in. The hall was narrow and dark and he stood in the corner out of the way, offering only a suggestion every now and then to the movers that would have made their work easier for them if they had paid any attention. The furniture was new and cheap so he decided the people moving in might be a newly married couple and he would just wait around until they came and wish them well. After a while a large Negro in a light blue suit came lunging up the stairs, carrying two canvas suitcases, his head lowered against the strain. Behind him stepped a young tan-skinned woman with bright copper-colored hair. The Negro dropped the suitcases with a thud in front of the door of the next apartment.

"Be careful, Sweetie," the woman said. "My make-up is in there."

It broke upon him then just what was happening.

The Negro was grinning. He took a swipe at one of her hips.

"Quit it," she said, "there's an old guy watching."

They both turned and looked at him.

"Had-do," he said and nodded. Then he turned quickly into his own door.

His daughter was in the kitchen. "Who you think's rented that apartment over there?" he asked, his face alight.

She looked at him suspiciously. "Who?" she muttered.

"A nigger!" he said in a gleeful voice. "A South Alabama nigger if I ever saw one. And got him this high-yeller, high-stepping woman with red hair and they two are going to live next door to you!" He slapped his knee. "Yes siree!" he said. "Damn if they ain't!" It was the first time since coming up here that he had had occasion to laugh.

Her face squared up instantly. "All right now you listen to me," she said. "You keep away from them. Don't you go over there trying to get friendly with him. They ain't the same around here and I don't want any trouble with niggers, you hear me? If you have to live next to them, just you mind your business and they'll mind theirs. That's the way people were meant to get along in this world. Everybody can get along if they just mind their business. Live and let live." She began to wrinkle her nose like a rabbit, a stupid way she had. "Up here everybody minds their own business and everybody gets along. That's all you have to do."

"I was getting along with niggers before you were born," he said. He went back out into the hall and waited. He was willing to bet the nigger would like to talk to someone who understood him. Twice while he waited, he forgot and in his excitement, spit his tobacco juice against the baseboard. In about twenty minutes, the door of the apartment opened again and the Negro came out. He had put on a tie and a pair of horn-rimmed spectacles and Tanner noticed for the first time that he had a small almost invisible goatee. A real swell. He came on without appearing to see there was anyone else in the hall.

"Haddy, John," Tanner said and nodded, but the Negro brushed past without hearing and went rattling rapidly down the stairs.

Could be deaf and dumb, Tanner thought. He went back into the apartment and sat down but each time he heard a noise in the hall, he got up and went to the door and stuck his head out to see if it might be the Negro. Once in the middle of the afternoon, he caught the Negro's eye just as he was rounding the bend of the stairs again but before he could get out a word, the man was in his own apartment and had slammed the door. He had never known one to move that fast unless the police were after him.

He was standing in the hall early the next morning when the woman came out of her door alone, walking on high gold-painted heels. He wished to bid her good morning or simply to nod but instinct told him to beware. She didn't look like any kind of woman, black or white, he had ever seen before and he remained pressed against the wall, frightened more than anything else, and feigning invisibility.

The woman gave him a flat stare, then turned her head away and stepped wide of him as if she were skirting an open garbage can. He held his breath until she was out of sight. Then he waited patiently for the man.

The Negro came out about eight o'clock.

This time Tanner advanced squarely in his path. "Good morning, Preacher," he said. It had been his experience that if a Negro tended to be sullen, this title usually cleared up his expression.

The Negro stopped abruptly.

"I seen you move in," Tanner said. "I ain't been up here long myself. It ain't much of a place if you ask me. I reckon you wish you were back in South Alabama."

The Negro did not take a step or answer. His eyes began to move. They moved from the top of the black hat, down to the collarless blue shirt, neatly buttoned at the neck, down the faded galluses to the gray trousers and the high-top shoes and up again, very slowly, while some unfathomable dead-cold rage seemed to stiffen and shrink him.

"I thought you might know somewhere around here we could find us a pond, Preacher," Tanner said in a voice growing thinner but still with considerable hope in it.

A seething noise came out of the Negro before he spoke. "I'm not from South Alabama," he said in a breathless wheezing voice. "I'm from New York City. And I'm not no preacher! I'm an actor."

Tanner chortled. "It's a little actor in most preachers, ain't it?" he said and winked. "I reckon you just preach on the side."

"I don't preach!" the Negro cried and rushed past him as if a swarm of bees had suddenly come down on him out of nowhere. He dashed down the stairs and was gone.

Tanner stood here for some time before he went back in the apartment. The rest of the day he sat in his chair and debated whether he would have one more try at making friends with him. Every time he heard a noise on the stairs he went to the door and looked out, but the Negro did not return until late in the afternoon. Tanner was standing in the hall waiting for him when he reached the top of the stairs. "Good evening, Preacher," he said, forgetting that the Negro called himself an actor.

The Negro stopped and gripped the banister rail. A tremor racked him from his head to his crotch. Then he began to come forward slowly. When he was close enough he lunged and grasped Tanner by both shoulders. "I don't take no crap," he whispered, "off no wool-hat[1] red-neck[2] son-of-a-bitch peckerwood[3] old bastard like you." He caught his breath. And then his voice came out in the sound of an exasperation so profound that it rocked on the verge of a laugh. It was high and piercing and weak, "And I'm not no preacher! I'm not even no Christian. I don't believe that crap. There ain't no Jesus and there ain't no God."

The old man felt his heart inside him hard and tough as an oak knot. "And you ain't black," he said. "And I ain't white!"

The Negro slammed him against the wall. He yanked the black hat down over his eyes. Then he grabbed his shirt front and shoved him backwards to his open door and knocked him through it. From the kitchen the daughter saw him blindly hit the edge of the inside hall door and fall reeling into the living room.

For days his tongue appeared to be frozen in his mouth. When it unthawed it was twice its normal size and he could not make her understand him. What he wanted to know was if the government check had come because he meant to buy a bus ticket with it and go home. After a few days, he made her understand. "It came," she said, "and it'll just pay the first two weeks' doctor-bill and please tell me how you're going home when you can't talk or walk or think straight and you got one eye crossed yet? Just please tell me that?"

It had come to him then slowly just what his present situation was. At least he would have to make her understand that he must be sent home to be buried. They could have him shipped back in a refrigerated car so that he would keep for the trip. He didn't want any undertaker up here messing with him. Let them get him off at once and he would come in on the early morning train and they could wire Hooten to get Coleman and Coleman would do the rest; she would not even have to

[1] Yokel.

[2] Refers disparagingly to someone belonging to the rural laboring class of the South.

[3] A poor white.

go herself. After a lot of argument, he wrung the promise from her. She would ship him back.

After that he slept peacefully and improved a little. In his dreams he could feel the cold early morning air of home coming in through the cracks of the pine box. He could see Coleman waiting, red-eyed, on the station platform and Hooten standing there with his green eye-shade and black alpaca sleeves. If the old fool had stayed at home where he belonged, Hooten would be thinking, he wouldn't be arriving on the 6:03 in no box. Coleman had turned the borrowed mule and cart so that they could slide the box off the platform onto the open end of the wagon. Everything was ready and the two of them, shut-mouthed, inched the loaded coffin toward the wagon. From inside he began to scratch on the wood. They let go as if it had caught fire.

They stood looking at each other, then at the box.

"That him," Coleman said. "He in there his self."

"Naw," Hooten said, "must be a rat got in there with him."

"That him. This here one of his tricks."

"If it's a rat he might as well stay."

"That him. Git a crowbar."

Hooten went grumbling off and got the crowbar and came back and began to pry open the lid. Even before he had the upper end pried open, Coleman was jumping up and down, wheezing and panting from excitement. Tanner gave a thrust upward with both hands and sprang up in the box. "Judgement Day! Judgement Day!" he cried. "Don't you two fools know it's Judgement Day?"

Now he knew exactly what her promises were worth. He would do as well to trust to the note pinned in his coat and to any stranger who found him dead in the street or in the boxcar or wherever. There was nothing to be looked for from her except that she would do things her way. She came out of the kitchen again, holding her hat and coat and rubber boots.

"Now listen," she said, "I have to go to the store. Don't you try to get up and walk around while I'm gone. You've been to the bathroom and you shouldn't have to go again. I don't want to find you on the floor when I get back."

You won't find me atall when you get back, he said to himself. This was the last time he would see her flat dumb face. He felt guilty. She had been good to him and he had been nothing but a nuisance to her.

"Do you want you a glass of milk before I go?" she asked.

"No," he said. Then he drew breath and said, "You got a nice place here. It's a nice part of the country. I'm sorry if I've give you a lot of trouble getting sick. It was my fault trying to be friendly with that nigger." And I'm a damned liar besides, he said to himself to kill the outrageous taste such a statement made in his mouth.

For a moment she stared as if he were losing his mind. Then she seemed to think better of it. "Now don't saying something pleasant like that once in a while make you feel better?" she asked and sat down on the sofa.

His knees itched to unbend. Git on, git on, he fumed silently. Make haste and go.

"It's great to have you here," she said. "I wouldn't have you any other place. My own daddy." She gave him a big smile and hoisted her right leg up and began to pull on her boot. "I wouldn't wish a dog out on a day like this," she said, "but I got to go. You can sit here and hope I don't slip and break my neck." She stamped the booted foot on the floor and then began to tackle the other one.

He turned his eyes to the window. The snow was beginning to stick and freeze to the outside pane. When he looked at her again, she was standing there like a big doll stuffed into its hat and coat. She drew on a pair of green knitted gloves. "Okay," she said, "I'm gone. You sure you don't want anything?"

"No," he said, "go ahead on."

"Well so long then," she said.

He raised the hat enough to reveal a bald palely speckled head. The hall door closed behind her. He began to tremble with excitement. He reached behind him and drew the coat into his lap. When he got it on, he waited until he had stopped panting, then he gripped the arms of the chair and pulled himself up. His body felt like a great heavy bell whose clapper swung from side to side but made no noise. Once up, he remained standing a moment, swaying until he got his balance. A sensation of terror and defeat swept over him. He would never make it. He would never get there dead or alive. He pushed one foot forward and did not fall and his confidence returned. "The Lord is my shepherd," he muttered, "I shall not want." He began moving toward the sofa where he would have support. He reached it. He was on his way.

By the time he got to the door, she would be down the four flights of steps and out of the building. He got past the sofa and crept along by the wall, keeping his hand on it for support. Nobody was going to bury him here. He was as confident as if the woods of home lay at the bottom of the stairs. He reached the front door of the apartment and opened it and peered into the hall. This was the first time he had looked into it since the actor had knocked him down. It was dank-smelling and empty. The thin piece of linoleum stretched its moldy length to the door of the other apartment, which was closed. "Nigger actor," he said.

The head of the stairs was ten or twelve feet from where he stood and he bent his attention to getting there without creeping around the long way with a hand on the wall. He held his arms a little way out from his sides and pushed forward directly. He was halfway there when all at once his legs disappeared, or felt as if they had. He looked down, bewildered, for they were still there. He fell forward and grasped the banister post with both hands. Hanging there, he gazed for what seemed the longest time he had ever looked at anything down the steep unlighted steps; then he closed his eyes and pitched forward. He landed upside down in the middle of the flight.

He felt presently the tilt of the box as they took it off the train and got it on the baggage wagon. He made no noise yet. The train jarred and slid away. In a moment the baggage wagon was rumbling under him, carrying him back to the station side. He heard footsteps rattling closer and closer to him and he supposed that a crowd was gathering. Wait until they see this, he thought.

"That him," Coleman said, "one of his tricks."

"It's a damn rat in there," Hooten said.

"It's him. Git the crowbar."

In a moment a shaft of greenish light fell on him. He pushed through it and cried in a weak voice, "Judgement Day! Judgement Day! You idiots didn't know it was Judgement Day, did you?"

"Coleman?" he murmured.

The Negro bending over him had a large surly mouth and sullen eyes.

"Ain't any coal man, either," he said. This must be the wrong station, Tanner thought. Those fools put me off too soon. Who is this nigger? It ain't even daylight here.

At the Negro's side was another face, a woman's—pale, topped with a pile of copper-glinting hair and twisted as if she had just stepped in a pile of dung.

"Oh," Tanner said, "it's you."

The actor leaned closer and grasped him by the front of his shirt. "Judgement day," he said in a mocking voice. "Ain't no judgement day, old man. Cept this. Maybe this here judgement day for you."

Tanner tried to catch hold of a banister-spoke to raise himself but his hand grasped air. The two faces, the black one and the pale one, appeared to be wavering. By an effort of will he kept them focused before him while he lifted his hand, as light as a breath, and said in his jauntiest voice, "Hep me up, Preacher. I'm on my way home!"

His daughter found him when she came in from the grocery store. His hat had been pulled down over his face and his head and arms thrust between the spokes of the banister; his feet dangled over the stairwell like those of a man in the stocks. She tugged at him frantically and then flew for the police. They cut him out with a saw and said he had been dead about an hour.

She buried him in New York City, but after she had done it she could not sleep at night. Night after night she turned and tossed and very definite lines began to appear in her face, so she had him dug up and shipped the body to Corinth. Now she rests well at night and her good looks have mostly returned.

1965

DISCUSSION QUESTIONS

1. Compare Dudley's and Tanner's motives for going to New York. Whose seem more convincing?

2. Why would New York have not seemed so big for Dudley "if he could have showed it to Rabie" (page 114)? Explain and contrast the role Dudley assigns here to Rabie with the role Tanner attributes to Coleman during an imaginary tour of New York.

3. Tanner calls Coleman a "no-good scoundrel" who has been "paroled" to him. In reality, what are Tanner's true feelings toward him? Give supporting evidence. Define their relationship. Explain why, during their first meeting, Tanner saw in Coleman "a negative image of himself" (page 130)? What do they actually have in common?

4. Define the relationship between Dudley and Rabie. Give supporting evidence. Compare it with the relationship Tanner has with Coleman.

5. Dudley's black neighbor calls New York "a swell place—once you get used to it" (page 120). What prevents each of the *protagonists* from adjusting to it?

6. Why does Dudley try to avoid his black neighbor, while Tanner goes persistently out of his way to meet him? Why did O'Connor make this change in her story? Why does Dudley feel "trapped" after his neighbor helps him up the stairs?

7. Compare the black neighbors in the two versions. Do not neglect to note differences in manners and appearance. Why has O'Connor made this change?

8. In contrast to Tanner, both his daughter and the black actor lack religious belief. Do they have anything else in common in their relationship with him? Are there any comparable religious overtones in "The Geranium"?

9. Why is Tanner so eager to get home "dead or alive"? Does the dream of going home in a coffin have any *symbolical* significance? Why doesn't Dudley make any comparable effort to get home?

10. Determine what the geranium *symbolizes* by examining each detail about it.

11. Analyze and compare the time schemes of the two stories. Define each version's present time or frame of reference, the starting point for

scenes reverting to an earlier time sequence, and explain why O'Connor chose to focus on that particular moment. Explain the purpose of each *flashback* and dream. Why is one flashback implanted within another in "Judgement Day"?

12. Since endings are one of the most reliable ways of determining writers' attitudes toward their characters, what insights do you gain from examining and comparing O'Connor's two endings?

13. Which of the two protagonists, Dudley or Tanner, do you feel more sympathy for? Why? Whom do you admire more? Why? Which version of O'Connor's story do you prefer? Why?

ANALYSIS AND APPLICATION

1. Analyze the following passage from "The Geranium":

> People boiled out of trains and up steps and over into the streets. They rolled off the street and down steps and into trains—black and white and yellow all mixed up like vegetables in soup. Everything was boiling. The trains swished in from tunnels, up canals, and all of a sudden stopped. (page 115).

Which verbs in this passage seem incongruous and are used as *implied metaphors?* Identify the comparison implied by each *metaphor.* Do the metaphors, plus the *simile,* fit together to form an *extended metaphor?* If so, explain. Are the metaphors merely decorative or do they define an attitude or feeling? Explain.

2. Examine the *implied metaphor* in the following sentence from "Judgement Day": "Tanner had continued to look across the field as if his spirit had been sucked out of him into the woods and nothing was left on the chair but a shell" (page 132). To what is Tanner implicitly being compared? What qualities are being transferred metaphorically to Tanner? What role does Dr. Foley serve in this comparison?

ODOUR OF CHRYSANTHEMUMS

Version 1

D. H. LAWRENCE

THE SMALL locomotive engine, Number 4, came clanking, stumbling down from Selston with seven full waggons. It appeared round the corner with loud threats of speed, but the colt that it startled from among the gorse, which still flickered indistinctly in the raw afternoon, outdistanced it at a canter. A woman, walking up the railway-line to Underwood, drew back into the hedge, held her basket aside, and watched the footplate of the engine advancing. The trucks thumped heavily past, one by one, with slow inevitable movement, as she stood insignificantly trapped beneath the jolting black waggons and the hedge; then they curved away towards the coppice where the

Reprinted by permission of Laurence Pollinger Ltd. and the Estate of the late Mrs. Frieda Lawrence. Acknowledgement is also made to the University of Nottingham MS LaB 3, and to Professor J. T. Boulton of the University of Birmingham.

ODOUR OF CHRYSANTHEMUMS

Version 3

D. H. LAWRENCE

THE SMALL locomotive engine, Number 4, came clanking, stumbling down from Selston with seven full waggons. It appeared round the corner with loud threats of speed, but the colt that it startled from among the gorse, which still flickered indistinctly in the raw afternoon, outdistanced it at a canter. A woman, walking up the railway line to Underwood, drew back into the hedge, held her basket aside, and watched the footplate of the engine advancing. The trucks thumped heavily past, one by one, with slow inevitable movement, as she stood insignificantly trapped between the jolting black waggons and the hedge; then they curved away towards the coppice where the withered oak withered oak-leaves dropped noiselessly, while the birds, pulling at the scarlet hips beside the track, made off into the dusk that had already crept into the spinney. In the open, the smoke from the engine sank and cleaved to the rough grass. The fields were dreary and forsaken, and in the marshy strip that led to the whimsey, a reedy pit-pond, the fowls had already abandoned their run among the shaggy black alders, to roost in the tarred fowl-house. The pit-bank loomed up beyond the pond, flames like red sores licking its ashy sides, in the afternoon's stagnant light. Just beyond rose the tapering chimneys and the clumsy black headstocks of Brinsley Colliery. The two wheels were spinning fast up against the sky, and the winding-engine rapped out its little spasms. The miners were being turned up.

The engine whistled as it came near the rows of trucks that were standing in the bay of railway-lines by Brinsley pit. Already among the waggons the men were moving: those who were going up to Underwood stood aside to let the train jolt past, lifting their blackened faces to call something to the driver. Then they passed on, loudly talking, their shapeless grey-black figures seeming of a piece with the raw November afternoon, the tea-bottles rolling in their pockets, while the stumbling of their great boots across the sleepers resounded from afar.

The train slowed down as it drew near a small cottage squat beside the great bay of railway-lines. Four black steps, old sleepers, led down from the cinder-track to the threshold of the house, which was small and grimy, a large bony vine scrambling over it, as if trying to claw down the tiled roof. Round the small bricked yard was a rim of sooty garden with a few chill primroses. Beyond, a long garden sloped down to a tree-hidden brook course. There were twiggy apple-trees and winter-crack trees,[1] forlorn and black, and a number of ragged cabbages. Beside the path there hung torn and scattered groups of dishevelled pink chrysanthemums. A woman came bending out of the felt-covered fowl-house half-way down the garden. She closed and padlocked the door, then drew herself erect, having brushed some bits from her white apron.

She was a tall woman of imperious mien, handsome, with definite black eyebrows. Her smooth black hair was parted exactly. For a few moments she stood steadily watching the miners as they passed along the railway: then she turned towards the brook-course. There was no quickness, no lightness, in her movements. Her face was calm and proud with defiance, her mouth was closed with disillusionment. After a moment she called:

[1] Small green plum trees with late-ripening fruit.

leaves dropped noiselessly, while the birds, pulling at the scarlet hips beside the track, made off into the dusk that had already crept into the spinney. In the open, the smoke from the engine sank and cleaved to the rough grass. The fields were dreary and forsaken, and in the marshy strip that led to the whimsey, a reedy pit-pond, the fowls had already abandoned their run among the alders, to roost in the tarred fowl-house. The pit-bank loomed up beyond the pond, flames like red sores licking its ashy sides, in the afternoon's stagnant light. Just beyond rose the tapering chimneys and the clumsy black headstocks of Brinsley Colliery. The two wheels were spinning fast up against the sky, and the winding-engine rapped out its little spasms. The miners were being turned up.

The engine whistled as it came into the wide bay of railway lines beside the colliery, where rows of trucks stood in harbour.

Miners, single, trailing and in groups, passed like shadows diverging home. At the edge of the ribbed level of sidings squat a low cottage, three steps down from the cinder track. A large bony vine clutched at the house, as if to claw down the tiled roof. Round the bricked yard grew a few wintry primroses. Beyond, the long garden sloped down to a bush-covered brook course. There were some twiggy apple trees, winter-crack trees, and ragged cabbages. Beside the path hung dishevelled pink chrysanthemums, like pink cloths hung on bushes. A woman came stooping out of the felt-covered fowl-house, half-way down the garden. She closed and padlocked the door, then drew herself erect, having brushed some bits from her white apron.

She was a tall woman of imperious mien, handsome, with definite black eyebrows. Her smooth black hair was parted exactly. For a few moments she stood steadily watching the miners as they passed along the railway: then she turned towards the brook course. Her face was calm and set, her mouth was closed with disillusionment. After a moment she called:

"John!" There was no answer. She waited, and then said distinctly: "Where are you?"

"Here!" replied a child's sulky voice from among the bushes that crowded darkly on the bank of the brook. The woman looked piercingly through the dusk.

"Are you at that brook?" she asked sternly.

For answer the child showed himself before the raspberry-canes that rose like whips towards alders. He was a small, sturdy boy of five, and he stood quite still, like some "farouche" creature.

"Oh!" said the mother, conciliated. "I thought you were down at that wet brook—and you remember what I told you——"

The boy did not move or answer.

"Come, come on in," she said more gently, "it's getting dark and cold—and listen, there's your grandfather's engine coming down the line!"

The lad came slowly forward, with resentful, taciturn movement. He was dressed in trousers and waistcoat of cloth that was too thick and hard for the size of the garments. They were evidently cut down from a man's clothes. He wore no coat, and his mother looked at his little flannelette shirt-sleeves as she waited for him to precede her up the path.

"You'll be catching cold, out at nightfall without your jacket," she said.

As they went slowly towards the house he tore at the ragged pink locks of the pale chrysanthemums and dropped the petals in handfuls along the path.

"Don't do that—it *does* look nasty," said his mother. He refrained, and she, suddenly pitiful, broke off a twig with three or four small, wan flowers and held them against her face. When they reached the yard her hand hesitated, and instead of throwing the flower away, she pushed it in her apron band. Mother and boy stood at the foot of the wooden steps looking across the bay of lines at the passing home of the miners The trundle of the small train was imminent. Suddenly the engine loomed past the house and came to a stop opposite the gate.

The engine-driver, a short man with round grey beard, leaned out of the cab high above the woman.

"Ive just come right for a cup of tea," he said in a merry little fashion.

"I haven't mashed[2] it yet. If you'll wait just a minute though—the kettle is on the boil," she replied.

[2] Brewed.

"John!" There was no answer. She waited, and then said distinctly: "Where are you?"

"Here!" replied a child's sulky voice from among the bushes. The woman looked piercingly through the dusk.

"Are you at that brook?" she asked sternly.

For answer the child showed himself before the raspberry-canes that rose like whips. He was a small, sturdy boy of five. He stood quite still, defiantly.

"Oh!" said the mother, conciliated. "I thought you were down at that wet brook—and you remember what I told you——"

The boy did not move or answer.

"Come, come on in," she said more gently, "it's getting dark. There's your grandfather's engine coming down the line!"

The lad advanced slowly, with resentful, taciturn movement. He was dressed in trousers and waistcoat of cloth that was too thick and hard for the size of the garments. They were evidently cut down from a man's clothes.

As they went slowly towards the house he tore at the ragged wisps of chrysanthemums and dropped the petals in handfuls along the path.

"Don't do that—it does look nasty," said his mother. He refrained, and she, suddenly pitiful, broke off a twig with three or four wan flowers and held them against her face. When mother and son reached the yard her hand hesitated, and instead of laying the flower aside, she pushed it in her apron-band. The mother and son stood at the foot of the three steps looking across the bay of lines at the passing home of the miners. The trundle of the small train was imminent. Suddenly the engine loomed past the house and came to a stop opposite the gate.

The engine-driver, a short man with round grey beard, leaned out of the cab high above the woman.

"Have you got a cup of tea?" he said in a cheery, hearty fashion.

It was her father. She went in, saying she would mash. Directly, she returned.

"Never mind, never mind—no, don't bother—no——" It was in vain he cried his remonstrances; the woman went indoors. Directly, she returned.

"I didn't come and see you on Sunday," began the little grey-bearded man. "I'd promised——"

"I didn't expect you," said his daughter coldly.

The little engine-driver winced; then, trying to resume his merry, airy manner, he said:

"Oh, have you heard then? I thought they'd be running to tell you! And what do you think——?"

"I think it is soon enough," she replied.

At her brief, cold censure the little man made an impatient gesture, and said coaxingly, excusing himself:

"Well, what's a man to do? It's no sort of life living with strangers, a man of my years. I'm used to sitting on my own hearth with my own woman. And if you're going to marry again it may as well be soon as late—a few months make no difference."

The woman did not reply, but turned and went into the house. The little man in the engine-cab stared about in much discomfort till she returned with a cup of tea and a piece of bread and butter on a plate. She went up the steps and stood near the footplate of the dark, looming engine.

"You needn't 'a brought me bread an' butter as well," said the little man. "But a cup of tea"—he sipped appreciatively—"it's very nice." He sipped a moment or two, then: "I hear as Walter's no better than he was," he said.

"We don't expect him to be any better," said the woman bitterly.

"I heered tell of him in the 'Lord Nelson' braggin' as he was going to spend that b—— afore he went: half a sovereign that was."

"When?" asked the woman, very curtly.

"A' Sat'day night—an' I know it's true."

"Very likely," laughed the woman with great bitterness. "He is doing pretty well—an' gives me twenty-three shillings. I'd rather have bad times than good, he hasn't so much to spend."

"It's a crying shame, he wants horsewhipping!" said the little man. The woman turned her head with weary impatience. Her father swallowed the last of his tea, and handed her the cup.

"Ay," he sighed, wiping his mouth. "I've repented the day I ever let you have him."

He put his hand on the lever. The little engine strained and groaned, and the train rumbled towards the crossing. The woman again looked

"I didn't come to see you on Sunday," began the little grey-bearded man.

"I didn't expect you," said his daughter.

The engine-driver winced; then, reassuming his cheery, airy manner, he said:

"Oh, have you heard then? Well, and what do you think——?"

"I think it is soon enough," she replied.

At her brief censure the little man made an impatient gesture, and said coaxingly, yet with dangerous coldness:

"Well, what's a man to do? It's no sort of life for a man of my years, to sit at my own hearth like a stranger. And if I'm going to marry again it may as well be soon as late—what does it matter to anybody?"

The woman did not reply, but turned and went into the house. The man in the engine-cab stood assertive, till she returned with a cup of tea and a piece of bread and butter on a plate. She went up the steps and stood near the footplate of the hissing engine.

"You needn't 'a' brought me bread an' butter," said her father. "But a cup of tea"—he sipped appreciatively—"it's very nice." He sipped for a moment or two, then: "I hear as Walter's got another bout on," he said.

"When hasn't he?" said the woman bitterly.

"I heered tell of him in the 'Lord Nelson' braggin' as he was going to spend that b—— afore he went: half a sovereign that was."

"When?" asked the woman.

"A' Sat'day night—I know that's true."

"Very likely," she laughed bitterly. "He gives me twenty-three shillings."

"Aye, it's a nice thing, when a man can do nothing with his money but make a beast of himself!" said the grey-whiskered man. The woman turned her head away. Her father swallowed the last of his tea and handed her the cup.

"Aye," he sighed, wiping his mouth. "It's a settler,[1] it is——"

He put his hand on the lever. The little engine strained and groaned, and the train rumbled towards the crossing. The woman again looked

[1] A crushing, or finishing, blow.

across the metals.[3] Darkness was settling over the spaces of the railway and the trucks: the miners, in grey sombre groups were still passing home. The winding-engine was pulsing hurriedly, with brief pauses. The woman looked at the dreary flow of men, then she went indoors.

"Is tea ready?" asked the boy, standing with his arms on the table, which was laid with a cloth and cups and saucers.

"Take your arms off the table! Yes, when your father or Annie comes in. They're turning the soft coal men up——"

"Can I 'ave summat t' eat?"

" 'Summat t' eat'—who says that! You can have 'something to eat' when you have your tea."

The boy dragged his way to the foot of the stairs, two white wooden steps of which intruded into the kitchen.

"Don't drag your feet!" said the mother, watching him, "They want mending often enough."

The kitchen was small and full of ruddy firelight. The fierce coals piled their beautiful, glowing life up to the chimney mouth. The white hearth looked hot, and the redness was on the bright steel fender. The uncovered floor was worn with hollows, but its soft deep red was unsullied. The tea-table shone white and comfortable, and the scarlet chinz on the sofa under the window was warm and full of invitation. The boy sat on the lowest stair, in the far corner, cutting a piece of white wood with a blunt knife. He struggled with determined little fists. His mother moved about the oven, and glanced at the clock. Then she tried the potatoes and pulled the saucepan back on the hob from the fire. She left the oven door slightly ajar, and the room was full of the smell of stewed meat. She glanced at the clock again, and began cutting bread and butter. It was half-past four. When she had cut four or five thick slices, the woman stood, with nothing to do but wait. The boy still bent over his piece of wood.

"What are you doing?" she asked.

He did not answer.

"What are you making?" she repeated.

"A tram," he answered, meaning a little truck such as is used down pit.

"Don't make a litter," she said.

"They on'y go on th' steerfoot mat," he replied.

"Very well," said his mother, repeating his words to correct their

[3] Broken stones used for railroad beds.

across the metals. Darkness was settling over the spaces of the railway and trucks: the miners, in grey sombre groups, were still passing home. The winding-engine pulsed hurriedly, with brief pauses. Elizabeth Bates looked at the dreary flow of men, then she went indoors. Her husband did not come.

The kitchen was small and full of firelight; red coals piled glowing up the chimney mouth. All the life of the room seemed in the white, warm hearth and the steel fender reflecting the red fire. The cloth was laid for tea; cups glinted in the shadows. At the back, where the lowest stairs protruded into the room, the boy sat struggling with a knife and a piece of whitewood. He was almost hidden in the shadow. It was half-past four. They had but to await the father's coming to begin tea.

vulgar pronunciation, "see they do only go on the stairfoot mat, and then shake it when you've done."

She turned away. Her son was very much like herself, yet something in him always pained her, and roused her opposition. He had his father's brutality, without his father's frank boisterousness. She glanced again at the clock, and took the potatoes to strain them in the yard. The garden and the fields beyond the brook were closed in uncertain darkness. When she rose with the saucepan, leaving the grate steaming into the night behind her, she saw the yellow lamps were lit along the highway that went up the hill away beyond the space of the railway-lines and the field. Then again, she watched the men trooping home, fewer now, and fewer.

Indoors the highest flush of the fire had passed and the night pressed round the ruddy glowing room. The woman put her saucepan on the hob, and set a batter pudding[4] near the mouth of the oven. Then she stood unmoving. Irritation and suspense gathered like the thickening darkness: then, gratefully, came quick young steps to the door. A child hung on the latch a moment, and a little girl entered.

"Oh!" she exclaimed, sniffing, "Stew! Can I have some, mother?"

She began pulling off her clothes, dragging a mass of curls just ripening from gold to brown over her eyes with her hat.

"Well," said her mother. "Shut the door! You're late, aren't you?"

"Why, what time is it? We had a lovely game of king o' the mountain down Nethergreen. Oh, mother, is tea ready? I thought of it against the crossing, an' I run, for it did seem beautiful—tea."

She hung her grey scarf and her clothes on the door. Her mother chid her for coming late from school, and said she would have to keep her at home the dark winter days.

"Why, mother, it's hardly a bit dark. The lamp's not lighted, and my father's not home yet."

"No, he isn't. But it's quarter to five! Did you see anything of him?"

The child became serious. She looked at her mother with large, wistful blue eyes.

"No, mother, I've never seen him. Why? Has he come up an' gone down Old Brinsley? He hasn't, mother, 'cos I never saw him."

"He'd watch that," said the mother bitterly, "he'd take care as you didn't see him, child. But you may depend upon it, he's seated in the 'Prince o' Wales.' He wouldn't be this late."

[4] Unsweetened pudding of flour, eggs, and milk or cream that is boiled or baked.

As the mother watched her son's sullen little struggle with the wood, she saw herself in his silence and pertinacity; she saw the father in her child's indifference to all but himself. She seemed to be occupied by her husband. He had probably gone past his home, slunk past his own door, to drink before he came in, while his dinner spoiled and wasted in waiting. She glanced at the clock, then took the potatoes to strain them in the yard. The garden and fields beyond the brook were closed in uncertain darkness. When she rose with the saucepan, leaving the drain steaming into the night behind her, she saw the yellow lamps were lit along the high road that went up the hill away beyond the space of the railway lines and the field.

Then again she watched the men trooping home, fewer now and fewer.

Indoors the fire was sinking and the room was dark red. The woman put her saucepan on the hob, and set a batter pudding near the mouth of the oven. Then she stood unmoving. Directly, gratefully, came quick young steps to the door. Someone hung on the latch a moment, then a little girl entered and began pulling off her outdoor things, dragging a mass of curls, just ripening from gold to brown, over her eyes with her hat.

Her mother chid her for coming late from school, and said she would have to keep her at home the dark winter days.

"Why, mother, it's hardly a bit dark yet. The lamp's not lighted, and my father's not home."

"No, he isn't. But it's a quarter to five! Did you see anything of him?"

The child became serious. She looked at her mother with large, wistful blue eyes.

"No, mother, I've never seen him. Why? Has he come up an' gone past, to Old Brinsley? He hasn't, mother, 'cos I never saw him."

"He'd watch that," said the mother bitterly, "he'd take care as you didn't see him. But you may depend upon it, he's seated in the 'Prince o' Wales.' He wouldn't be this late."

The girl looked at her mother piteously. The boy sat with his head bowed over his bit of wood. The mother let loose, now, the silent anger and bitterness that coiled within her. She said little, but there was the grip of "trouble," like the tentacle of an octopus, round the hearts of the children.

"Let's have our teas, mother, should we?" said the girl plaintively; with woman's instinct for turning aside from the thing she feared. The mother called John to table. He took the mat to shake the bits in the fire first.

"Nay," said his mother, "that's a sloven's trick!" and she put him back with her hand. "Take it outside."

He went very slowly. She opened the door for him and leaned out to look across the darkness of the lines. All was deserted: she could not hear the winding-engines.

"Perhaps," she said to herself, "he's stopped to get some ripping[5] done."

They sat down to tea. John, at the end of the table near the door, was almost lost in the darkness. Their faces were hidden from each other. After the first piece of bread, the girl asked: "Can I have cobbler's toast, mother?"

"Can I?" said John.

The mother hesitated awhile.

"Yes," she said at last, "only it's a waste of butter, and you generally want twice as much if you have toast."

The girl crouched against the fender slowly moving a thick piece of bread before the fire. The lad, his face a dusky mark on the shadow, sat watching her, transfigured as she was in the hot red glow.

"I do think it's beautiful to look in the fire," said she pensively.

"Do you?" said her mother. "Why?"

"It's so red, and full of little hot caves—and it feels nice so, and you can fair smell it."

"It'll want mending directly," replied her mother. "And then if your father comes he'll carry on and say there never is a fire when a man comes home wet from the pit. A public house is always warm enough though."

There was silence till the boy said complainingly: "Make haste, our Annie."

"Well, I am! I can't make the fire do it no faster, can I?"

"She keeps waflin[6] it about so's to make 'er slow," grumbled the boy.

[5] To take down the roof of an underground road in a coal mine in order to increase its height.

[6] Waving.

The girl looked at her mother piteously.

"Let's have our teas, mother, should we?" said she.

The mother called John to table. She opened the door once more and looked out across the darkness of the lines. All was deserted: she could not hear the winding-engines.

"Perhaps," she said to herself, "he's stopped to get some ripping done."

They sat down to tea. John, at the end of the table near the door, was almost lost in the darkness. Their faces were hidden from each other. The girl crouched against the fender slowly moving a thick piece of bread before the fire. The lad, his face a dusky mark on the shadow, sat watching her who was transfigured in the red glow.

"I do think it's beautiful to look in the fire," said the child.

"Do you?" said her mother. "Why?"

"It's so red, and full of little caves—and it feels so nice, and you can fair smell it."

"It'll want mending directly," replied her mother, "and then if your father comes he'll carry on and say there never is a fire when a man comes home sweating from the pit—A public-house is always warm enough."

There was silence till the boy said complainingly: "Make haste, our Annie."

"Well, I am doing! I can't make the fire do it no faster, can I?"

"She keeps wafflin' it about so's to make 'er slow," grumbled the boy.

"Don't have such an evil imagination, child," replied her mother. "I'm sure it's done now, Annie, you're only making all the butter drip out. Look!"

"I don't like it soft on the buttery side," complained the girl quietly, looking at her piece of bread where the butter was bubbling in places, with patches browning elsewhere.

Soon the room was busy in the darkness with the crisp sound of crunching. The mother ate very little. She drank her tea determinedly, and sat thinking, full of anger. When she rose and took the Yorkshire pudding from the oven her accumulated anger was evident in the stern, unbending head. She looked at the pudding in the fender, and broke out:

"It *is* a scandalous thing as a man can't even come in to his dinner. If it's crozzled[7] up to a cinder I don't see why I should care. Past his very door he goes to get to a public house, and here I sit with his dinner waiting for him——"

She went out of the house, returning directly with a dustpan of coal, with which she mended the fire. As she dropped piece after piece of coal on the red fire, the shadows fell on the walls, till the room was almost in total darkness.

"I canna see," grumbled the invisible John. In spite of herself, the mother laughed.

"You know the way to your mouth," she said. She set the dustpan outside the door, and came in, going across to the pantry to wash her hands. When she came again like a tall shadow on to the hearth, the lad repeated, complaining sulkily:

"I canna see."

"Good gracious!" cried the mother irritably, "you're as bad as your father if it's a bit dusk!"

Nevertheless she took a paper spill from a sheaf on the mantelpiece and proceeded to light the lamp that hung from the ceiling in the middle of the room. As she reached up her figure displayed itself just rounding with maternity.

"Oh mother——!" exclaimed the girl.

"What?" said the woman, suspended in the act of putting the lamp-glass over the flame. The copper reflector shone handsomely on her, as she stood with uplifted arm, turning her face to her daughter.

"You've got a flower in your apron!" said the child, in a little rapture at this unusual event.

[7] Burned.

"Don't have such an evil imagination, child," replied the mother.

Soon the room was busy in the darkness with the crisp sound of crunching. The mother ate very little. She drank her tea determinedly, and sat thinking. When she rose her anger was evident in the stern unbending of her head. She looked at the pudding in the fender, and broke out:

"It is a scandalous thing as a man can't even come home to his dinner! If it's crozzled up to a cinder I don't see why I should care. Past his very door he goes to get to a public-house, and here I sit with his dinner waiting for him——"

She went out. As she dropped piece after piece of coal on the red fire, the shadows fell on the walls, till the room was almost in total darkness.

"I canna see," grumbled the invisible John. In spite of herself, the mother laughed.

"You know the way to your mouth," she said. She set the dustpan outside the door. When she came again like a shadow on the hearth, the lad repeated, complaining sulkily:

"I canna see."

"Good gracious!" cried the mother irritably, "you're as bad as your father if it's a bit dusk!"

Nevertheless she took a paper spill from a sheaf on the mantelpiece and proceeded to light the lamp that hung from the ceiling in the middle of the room. As she reached up, her figure displayed itself just rounding with maternity.

"Oh, mother——!" exclaimed the girl.

"What?" said the woman, suspended in the act of putting the lamp-glass over the flame. The copper reflector shone handsomely on her, as she stood with uplifted arm, turning to face her daughter.

"You've got a flower in your apron!" said the child, in a little rapture at this unusual event.

"Goodness me!" exclaimed the woman, relieved, and a little annoyed. "One would think the house was afire." She replaced the glass and waited a moment before turning up the wick. A pale shadow seemed to be floating weirdly on the floor.

"Let me smell!" said the child, still rapturously, coming forward and putting her face to her mother's waist.

"Go along, silly!" said the mother, turning up the lamp. The light seemed to reveal all the suspense and suppressed wrath that held the little room. The woman felt it almost unbearable. Annie was still bending at her waist. Irritably, the mother took the flowers from out of her apron band.

"Oh mother—don't take them out!" cried Annie, catching her hand, and trying to replace the flowers.

"Such nonsense!" said the mother, turning away. The child put the pale chrysanthemums to her lips, with exaggerated tenderness, murmuring:

"Don't they smell beautiful!"

Her mother gave a short laugh.

"Hateful!" she said. "I hate them. It was chrysanthemums when I married him, and chrysanthemums when you were born, and the first time they ever brought him home drunk he'd got brown chrysanthemums in his coat. When I smell them I could always think of that, me dragging at him to get his coat off——"

She looked at the children. Their eyes and their little parted lips were piteous. The mother sat rocking in silence for some time. Then she looked at the clock.

"Twenty minutes to six!" In a tone of fine bitter carelessness she continued: "Eh, he'll not come now till they bring him. There he'll stick! He needn't come rolling in here in his pit-dirt, for *I* won't wash him. He can lie on the floor——Eh, what a fool I've been, what a fool! And this is what I came here for, to this dirty hole, rats and all, for him to slink past his very door. Twice last week—he's begun now——"

She silenced herself, and rose to clear the table. When she was actively engaged she could endure, but as she sat still her fury seemed to sway like fighting imps within her, and to break out of her control.

Annie trotted after her mother with the tea-things, and helped to wipe them, chattering all the time, almost feverishly chattering. Anything was better than the clouds of silence that would settle on them. When there was no more housework to be done Annie stood disconsolate for a moment. She felt almost unequal to the struggle with the

"Goodness me!" exclaimed the woman, relieved. "One would think the house was afire." She replaced the glass and waited a moment before turning up the wick. A pale shadow was seen floating vaguely on the floor.

"Let me smell!" said the child, still rapturously, coming forward and putting her face to her mother's waist.

"Go along, silly!" said the mother, turning up the lamp. The light revealed their suspense so that the woman felt it almost unbearable. Annie was still bending at her waist. Irritably, the mother took the flowers out from her apron-band.

"Oh, mother—don't take them out!" Annie cried, catching her hand and trying to replace the sprig.

"Such nonsense!" said the mother, turning away. The child put the pale chrysanthemums to her lips, murmuring:

"Don't they smell beautiful!"

Her mother gave a short laugh.

"No," she said, "not to me. It was chrysanthemums when I married him, and chrysanthemums when you were born, and the first time they ever brought him home drunk, he'd got brown chrysanthemums in his button-hole."

She looked at the children. Their eyes and their parted lips were wondering. The mother sat rocking in silence for some time. Then she looked at the clock.

"Twenty minutes to six!" In a tone of fine bitter carelessness she continued: "Eh, he'll not come now till they bring him. There he'll stick! But he needn't come rolling in here in his pit-dirt, for *I* won't wash him. He can lie on the floor—— Eh, what a fool I've been, what a fool! And this is what I came here for, to this dirty hole, rats and all, for him to slink past his very door. Twice last week—he's begun now——"

She silenced herself, and rose to clear the table.

pressure of the trouble. Yet, in childish dread of abnormal states, in terror of an approaching climax, she forced herself to play.

"Our John, should we play at gipsies?"

They hung an old red table cloth from the sofa to their father's large arm-chair, and in the corner behind it was their gipsy caravan. They played with peculiar intentness, were brilliantly fertile in inventions, united in terror against the oncoming of they knew not what. John was a tinker and Annie sold clothes-pegs. They knocked at the dresser and interviewed an imaginary housewife; they knocked at the pantry door, and an imaginary dog flew at them, when John had the pleasure of kicking it under the jaw, they knocked at the stairfoot door, and sold two pegs, putting them under the mat, they could make no one hear at the parlour door; then John returned to the pantry and was given a lading can to mend. Whilst he soldered it Annie washed the clothes. When it was finished he took it back: "And did you get tenpence, John? Oh that's very nice! Now what should we have for dinner?"

"A hedgehog," suggested John gruffly.

"Oh, no, not hedgehog!"

But he insisted, and it had to be baked in clay. In a few seconds it was done: a pair of the father's stockings, black specked with red, rolled in a duster for clay. Annie was forced to pretend to eat, though she dithered at the bare idea.

At last they wore the game out, and John demanded "pit." This Annie hated, but she would have played anything to avoid a crisis.

John crept under the sofa, and, lying on his side as his father had taught him, pretended to be hacking a hole in the wall with a little stick—"holing a stint," he said. Meanwhile Annie dragged up a little box on wheels, and put in it all the boots and slippers—"loading a waggon"—and then "taking a carfle to the bottom." John could grunt and sweat in safety under the sofa, but Annie had only her horse to address: "Gee Dobbin! Whoa!" and the game at last grew to be too much of a burden to her. She had no more heart to play.

The mother all this time sat in her rocking-chair making a "singlet" of thick cream-coloured flannel, which gave a dull sound when she tore off the grey strip at the edge. She worked at her sewing with energy, listening to the children, and her anger wearied itself of pacing backwards and forwards like an impotent caged creature, and lay down to rest, its eyes always open and steadily watching, its ears raised to listen. Sometimes, even her anger quailed and shrank, and the mother suspended her sewing, tracing the footsteps that thudded along the sleepers outside; she would lift her head sharply to bid the children "hush," but

While for an hour or more the children played, subduedly intent, fertile of imagination, united in fear of the mother's wrath, and in dread of their father's home-coming, Mrs. Bates sat in her rocking-chair making a "singlet" of thick cream-coloured flannel, which gave a dull wounded sound as she tore off the grey edge. She worked at her sewing with energy, listening to the children, and her anger wearied itself, lay down to rest, opening its eyes from time to time and steadily watching, its ears raised to listen. Sometimes even her anger quailed and shrank, and the mother suspended her sewing, tracing the footsteps that thudded along the sleepers outside; she would lift her head sharply to bid the children "hush," but she recovered herself in time, and the footsteps she recovered herself in time, and the footsteps went past the gate, and the children were not dragged out of their play-world.

But at last Annie sighed, and gave in. She glanced at her waggon of slippers, and loathed it. Hesitating, faltering, she dragged it to a corner and left it, turning plaintively to her mother.

"Read us a tale, mother!" she pleaded.

Her mother had bent her head over her sewing. If there was one thing she shrank from doing, it was from lifting up her voice, which was like a child in rebellion, and would need all her efforts to command; sulky, it was, with shut lips.

"Shall you, mother?" insisted the girl. John, under the sofa, lay still to hear the answer. The mother looked at the clock. It was a quarter to seven, and they were not to be undressed for bed till seven. A quarter of an hour may be an age.

"Which one?" she asked, temporising.

"The Fir Tree!" and gladly the girl turned to the dresser and took from one of the drawers an old volume of Andersen.[8]

"Now look," she said, "let me get it!" and she quickly found the place. The child's demonstration of gaiety loosened the lips of the mother's silence, and she began to read, listening to the sound of her own voice. John crept out like a frog from under the sofa. His mother looked up:

"Yes," she said. "Just look at those shirt-sleeves!"

The boy held them out to look at them, and said nothing. The reproof was a sign that the mother had in some measure recovered her usual equilibrium, and as such was grateful. The tale began well, but somebody called in a hoarse voice down the line, and the old silence woke up and bristled in the room, till two people had gone by outside, talking. Then the mother continued to read, but it was a mere barrenness of words. The same subtle determination that had kept the children playing made the mother read the tale to the end, though it had no meaning for anybody. At last it was finished, and:

"There!" she exclaimed in relief. "You must go to bed now—it's past seven o'clock."

"My father hasn't come," said Annie plaintively, giving way at last. But her mother was primed with courage:

"Never mind. They'll bring him when he does come—like a log." She meant there would be no scene. "And he may sleep on the floor till he wakes himself. I know he'll not go to work to-morrow after this!"

[8] Hans Christian Andersen (1805–1875), Danish writer of fairy tales.

went past the gate, and the children were not flung out of their playworld.

But at last Annie sighed, and gave in. She glanced at her waggon of slippers, and loathed the game. She turned plaintively to her mother.

"Mother!"—but she was inarticulate.

John crept out like a frog from under the sofa. His mother glanced up.

"Yes," she said, "just look at those shirt-sleeves!"

The boy held them out to survey them, saying nothing. Then somebody called in a hoarse voice away down the line, and suspense bristled in the room, till two people had gone by outside, talking.

"It is time for bed," said the mother.

"My father hasn't come," wailed Annie plaintively. But her mother was primed with courage.

"Never mind. They'll bring him when he does come—like a log." She meant there would be no scene. "And he may sleep on the floor till he wakes himself. I know he'll not go to work to-morrow after this!"

The children had their hands and faces wiped with the flannel,[9] and were undressed on the hearthrug. They were very quiet. When they had put on their nightdresses, they kneeled down, and the girl hid her face in her mother's lap, and the boy put his face in his mother's skirt at the side, and they said their prayers, the boy mumbling. She looked down at them, at the brown silken bush of intertwining curls in the nape of the girl's neck, and the little black head of the boy, and in front of her eyes shone love and pity, and close behind pity stood anger, with shadowy hate, like a phantom, and scorn, glittering and dangerous; all these on the darkened stage of the mother's soul, with pity and love in front. The children hid their faces in her skirts, and were full of comfort and safety, and they prayed to her, for she was the God of their prayers. Then she lighted the candle and took them to bed.

When she came down, the room was strangely empty, with a tension of expectancy. The mother took up her sewing and stitched for some time without raising her head. Meantime her anger was accumulating. She broke the spell sharply at last, and looked up. It was ten minutes to eight. She sat staring at the pudding in the fender, and at the saucepan to the inside of which bits of dried potato were sticking. Then, for the first time, fear arrived in the room, and stood foremost. The expression of her face changed, and she sat thinking acutely.

The clock struck eight and she rose suddenly, dropping her sewing on her chair. She went to the stairfoot door, opened it, and stood listening. The children were evidently asleep. Very softly the mother shut the door, and, without hesitating, fetched an iron screen from the pantry, and hung it before the fire, turned back the rug, and put on her hat and a large grey cloth shawl. Then she went out, locking the door behind her.

Something scuffled down the yard as she went out, and she started, though she knew it was only the rats, with which the place was overrun. The night was very dark. In the great bay of railway-lines where the black trucks rose up obscurely there was no trace of light, only away back she could see a few yellow lamps at the pit-top, and the red smear of the burning pit-bank on the night. She could see the street lamps threading down hill beyond the railway and the field, shining large where the road crossed the lines, and tangling like fireflies in a blur of light where she looked straight down into Old Brinsley. She hurried along the edge of the track, stepping carefully over the levers of the points, and, crossing the converging lines, came to the stile by the great

[9] Washcloth.

The children had their hands and faces wiped with a flannel. They were very quiet. When they had put on their nightdresses, they said their prayers, the boy mumbling. The mother looked down at them, at the brown silken bush of intertwining curls in the nape of the girl's neck, at the little black head of the lad, and her heart burst with anger at their father who caused all three such distress. The children hid their faces in her skirts for comfort.

When Mrs. Bates came down, the room was strangely empty, with a tension of expectancy. She took up her sewing and stitched for some time without raising her head. Meantime her anger was tinged with fear.

II

The clock struck eight and she rose suddenly, dropping her sewing on her chair. She went to the stairfoot door, opened it, listening. Then she went out, locking the door behind her.

Something scuffled in the yard, and she started, though she knew it was only the rats with which the place was overrun. The night was very dark. In the great bay of railway lines, bulked with trucks, there was no trace of light, only away back she could see a few yellow lamps at the pit-top, and the red smear of the burning pit-bank on the night. She hurried along the edge of the track, then, crossing the converging lines, came to the stile by the white gates, whence she emerged on the white gates near the weighing machine, whence she emerged on the road. Then the fear which had led her by the hand unhesitating loosed its hold, and shrank back. People were walking up to New Brinsley; she saw the light in the window of his mother's house below the road by the crossing; twenty yards further on were the great windows of the "Prince of Wales," very warm and bright, and the loud voices of men could be heard distinctly. What a fool she had been to imagine that anything had happened to him! Here, in the commonplace movement of the sordid village, her sense of tragedy, with its dignity, vanished. He was merely drinking over there at the "Prince of Wales." She faltered. She had never yet been to fetch him, and she never would. Yet, while she was out, she must get some satisfaction. So she continued her walk, with the black wooden fence and the railway on her right, and, across the road, the long straggling line of houses standing blank on the highway. She went across the road, and entered a passage between the houses.

This entry sloped down sharply, as the houses were built on the drop to the brook, and had downstair kitchens. The houses were in pairs, as is usual, the back doors facing each other, and between them a small breadth of bricked yard. She did not know for certain which was the house of Jack Rigley, one of her husband's fellow butties.[10] She asked at the wrong house.

"No, Rigleys is next door—there look!" And Elizabeth Bates turned round, moved past the big, lighted kitchen windows of the two houses, and knocked at the other door.

"Mr. Rigley?—Yes! Did you want him? No, he's not in at this minute."

The raw-boned woman leaned forward from her dark scullery and peered at the other, upon whom fell a dim light through the blind of the kitchen window.

"Is it Mrs. Bates?" she asked in a tone tinged with respect.

"Yes. I wondered if your Master was at home. Mine hasn't come yet."

" 'Asn't 'e! Oh, Jack's been 'ome an 'ad 'is dinner long since. E's just gone for 'alf an 'our afore bed-time, but 'e won't be long. Did you call at th' 'Prince of Wales'?"

"No——"

"No, you didn't like——! Its not very nice, is it?" the other woman was indulgent and kind. There was an awkward pause. "Jack never said nothink about—about your Mester," she added.

[10] Buddy, mate.

road. Then the fear which had led her shrank. People were walking up to New Brinsley; she saw the lights in the houses; twenty yards further on were the broad windows of the "Prince of Wales," very warm and bright, and the loud voices of men could be heard distinctly. What a fool she had been to imagine that anything had happened to him! He was merely drinking over there at the "Prince of Wales." She faltered. She had never yet been to fetch him, and she never would go. So she continued her walk towards the long straggling line of houses, standing blank on the highway. She entered a passage between the dwellings.

"Mr. Rigley?—Yes! Did you want him? No, he's not in at this minute."

The raw-boned woman leaned forward from her dark scullery and peered at the other, upon whom fell a dim light through the blind of the kitchen window.

"Is it Mrs. Bates?" she asked in a tone tinged with respect.

"Yes. I wondered if your Master was at home. Mine hasn't come yet."

" 'Asn't 'e! Oh, Jack's been 'ome an 'ad 'is dinner an' gone out. E's just gone for 'alf an hour afore bedtime. Did you call at the 'Prince of Wales'?"

"No——"

"No, you didn't like——! It's not very nice." The other woman was indulgent. There was an awkward pause. "Jack never said nothink about—about your Mester," she said.

"No!—I expect he's stuck in there!"

Elizabeth Bates said this bitterly, and with recklessness. She knew that the woman across the yard was standing at her door listening, but she was sick, and did not care. She was turning away.

"Stop a minute! I'll just go an' ask Jack if 'e knows anythink," said Mrs. Rigley.

"Oh, no—I wouldn't like to put——!"

"Yes, I will, if you'll just step inside an' see as th' childer doesn't come downstairs and set theirselves afire."

Elizabeth Bates, murmuring a remonstrance, stepped inside, hesitating at the kitchen door.

"Come in! Sit you down. I shanna be a minute. Dunna look at th' 'ouse, Ah'n on'y just got 'em off to bed."

The kitchen needed apology. There were little frocks and trousers and childish undergarments on the squab[11] and on the floor, and a litter of playthings everywhere. On the black American cloth[12] of the table were pieces of bread and cake, crusts, and a teapot with cold tea.

"Eh, ours is just as bad," said Elizabeth Bates, looking at the woman, not at the house. Mrs. Rigley put a shawl over her head and hurried out, saying:

"I shanna be a minute."

The other sat quite still, waiting, noting with faint disapproval the general untidiness of the room, which was clean, if littered. Then she fell, with womanly curiosity, to counting the shoes of various sizes scattered over the room. There were twelve. She sighed and said to herself, "No wonder!"—glancing again over the litter. Then came the scratching of two pairs of feet across the yard, and the Rigleys entered. Elizabeth Bates rose. Rigley was a big man, with very large bones. His head looked particularly bony. Across his temple was a large blue scar, caused by a wound got in the pit, a wound in which the coal-dust remained blue like tattooing.

" 'Asna 'e come whom yit?" asked the man, without any form of greeting, but with a fine rough sympathy, and some concern: "I dunna think there's owt amiss—'e's non ower theer, though!"—he jerked his head to signify the "Prince of Wales."

"E's 'appen[13] gone up to th' 'Yew,' " said Mrs. Rigley, gently, showing by her tone that she was upset.

[11] Couch.

[12] Sturdy oilcloth.

[13] Perhaps, maybe.

"No!—I expect he's stuck in there!"

Elizabeth Bates said this bitterly, and with recklessness. She knew that the woman across the yard was standing at her door listening, but she did not care. As she turned:

"Stop a minute! I'll just go an' ask Jack if 'e knows anythink," said Mrs. Rigley.

"Oh, no—I wouldn't like to put——!"

"Yes, I will, if you'll just step inside an' see as th' childer doesn't come downstairs and set theirselves afire."

Elizabeth Bates, murmuring a remonstrance, stepped inside. The other woman apologized for the state of the room.

The kitchen needed apology. There were little frocks and trousers and childish undergarments on the squab and on the floor, and a litter of playthings everywhere. On the black American cloth of the table were pieces of bread and cake, crusts, slops, and a teapot with cold tea.

"Eh, ours is just as bad," said Elizabeth Bates, looking at the woman, not at the house. Mrs. Rigley put a shawl over her head and hurried out, saying:

"I shanna be a minute."

The other sat, noting with faint disapproval the general untidiness of the room. Then she fell to counting the shoes of various sizes scattered over the floor. There were twelve. She sighed and said to herself, "No wonder!"—glancing at the litter. There came the scratching of two pairs of feet on the yard, and the Rigleys entered. Elizabeth Bates rose. Rigley was a big man, with very large bones. His head looked particularly bony. Across his temple was a blue scar, caused by a wound got in the pit, a wound in which the coal-dust remained blue like tattooing.

" 'Asna 'e come whoam yit?" asked the man, without any form of greeting, but with deference and sympathy. "I couldna say wheer he is—'e's non ower theer!"—he jerked his head to signify the "Prince of Wales."

" 'E's 'appen gone up to th' 'Yew,' " said Mrs. Rigley.

"I bet that's wheer 'e is!" adjoined the husband. "Else at Jack Salmon's. 'E's very likely at Jack Salmon's, tha' knows 'is daughter wor married yisterday."

There was another pause. Rigley had evidently something to get off his mind:

"Ah left 'im finishin' a stint," he began. "Loose—a'[14] 'ad bin gone about ten minutes when we com'n away, an' I shouted, 'Are ter comin', Walt?' an' 'e said, 'Go on, Ah shanna be but alf minnit,' so we com'n ter th' bottom, me an' Bower, an' I thowt 'e wor just behint us. Ah'd a ta'en a hoath as 'e wor just behint—an' 'ud come up i' th' next bantle——"[15]

He stood perplexed and concerned, as if answering a charge of desertion of his mate. Elizabeth Bates, now again certain of disaster, hastened to reassure him:

"I expect 'e's gone to th' 'Yew Tree,' as you say. It's not the first time. I've fretted myself into a fever before now. He'll come home when they carry him."

"Ay, isn't it a bit too bad of 'em!" deplored the other woman.

"I'll just step up to Salmon's an' see if 'e *is* theer," offered the man, afraid of appearing concerned, and afraid of taking liberties with this woman. The bounds of intimacy are very dangerous to overstep.

"Oh, I wouldn't think of bothering you that far," said Elizabeth Bates, with the decision of a woman who knows her own affairs.

"It wouldna be no bother to *me*," urged the man. Elizabeth Bates hesitated.

"Yes—go on, Jack!" said his wife persuasively. "You can go up th' line an' across th' fields. It's as near as any way, an' then you can go with 'er to th' gate"—she looked at him significantly.

Elizabeth Bates understood quite well that this meant "you can call at the pit top and get them to telephone down to the deputy," but she gave no sign.

"Ah, that's what I can do!" said Rigley with relief. He put on his cap again, and they went out.

"Good night, Mrs. Bates. I'm sure it'll be all right! Don't you bother now!"

As they went up the entry, Elizabeth Bates heard Rigley's wife run across the yard and open her neighbour's door. Then suddenly all the blood in her body seemed to switch away from her heart.

[14] Signal to leave off work and return to the surface.

[15] The car of the elevator that brings coal miners to the surface.

There was another pause. Rigley had evidently something to get off his mind:

"Ah left 'im finishin' a stint," he began. "Loose-all 'ad bin gone about ten minutes when we com'n away, an' I shouted, 'Are ter comin', Walt?' an' 'e said, 'Go on, Ah shanna be but a'ef a minnit,' so we com'n ter th' bottom, me an' Bowers, thinkin' as 'e wor just behint, an' 'ud come up i' th' next bantle——"

He stood perplexed, as if answering a charge of deserting his mate. Elizabeth Bates, now again certain of disaster, hastened to reassure him:

"I expect 'e's gone up to th' 'Yew Tree,' as you say. It's not the first time. I've fretted myself into a fever before now. He'll come home when they carry him."

"Ay, isn't it too bad!" deplored the other woman.

"I'll just step up to Dick's an' see if 'e *is* theer," offered the man, afraid of appearing alarmed, afraid of taking liberties.

"Oh, I wouldn't think of bothering you that far," said Elizabeth Bates, with emphasis, but he knew she was glad of his offer.

As they stumbled up the entry, Elizabeth Bates heard Rigley's wife run across the yard and open her neighbour's door. At this, suddenly all the blood in her body seemed to switch away from her heart.

"Mind!" warned Rigley. "Ah've said many a time as Ah'd fill up them ruts in this entry, sumb'dy 'll be breakin' their legs yit."

She recovered herself and walked quickly along with the miner. She wanted to get home—for fear there should be anything.

"I don't like leaving the children in bed, and nobody in the house," she said.

"No, you dunna!" he replied, with all his courtesy and sympathy in his tones. They were soon at the gate of the cottage. All was still.

"Well, I shanna be many minutes. Dunna thee be frettin' now, 'e'll be a' right," said the butty.

"Thank you very much, Mr. Rigley," she replied, and the pathos and gratitude of her voice upset him.

"It's a' right—dunna mention it—you quite welcome!" he stammered, moving away. "I shanna be many minutes."

The house was quiet. Elizabeth Bates took off her hat and shawl, and rolled back the rug. Then she turned up the lamp and began to straighten the house. She took the pudding and the stew jar into the pantry, emptied the potatoes on a plate, and put these away too. She was in a hurry to straighten the house, even to lay the children's clothes neatly on the sofa arm. Somebody would be coming, she knew. She folded her sewing and put it in the dresser cupboard. She would do no more of it that night; this also she knew. When she had finished all her tasks, she sat down. It was a few minutes past nine. She was startled by the rapid chuff[16] of the winding-engine at the pit, and the sharp whirr of the brakes on the rope as it descended. Again she felt the painful sharp sweep of her blood, and she put her hand to her side, saying aloud, "Good gracious!—it's only the nine o'clock deputy going down," rebuking herself.

She sat still, listening, her whole body gripped in suspense. Half an hour of this, and she was wearied out.

"What am I working myself up like this for?" she said pitiably to herself, "I s'll only be doing myself some damage."

She did not mean herself alone.

What could she do to occupy herself? She took out her sewing again, but it was a pit singlet, and the thought of that took away her energy. She would have liked to begin and make some cake—but she couldn't have those things about when somebody was coming in. So she began to patch the elbow of one of the boy's coat-sleeves.

At a quarter to ten there were footsteps. She sat quite still, listening.

[16] Regularly repeated puffing sounds.

"Mind!" warned Rigley. "Ah've said many a time as Ah'd fill up them ruts in this entry, sumb'dy 'll be breakin' their legs yit."

She recovered herself and walked quickly along with the miner.

"I don't like leaving the children in bed, and nobody in the house," she said.

"No, you dunna!" he replied courteously. They were soon at the gate of the cottage.

"Well, I shanna be many minnits. Dunna you be frettin' now, 'e'll be all right," said the butty.

"Thank you very much, Mr. Rigley," she replied.

"You're welcome!" he stammered, moving away. "I shanna be many minnits."

The house was quiet. Elizabeth Bates took off her hat and shawl, and rolled back the rug. When she had finished, she sat down. It was a few minutes past nine. She was startled by the rapid chuff of the winding-engine at the pit, and the sharp whirr of the brakes on the rope as it descended. Again she felt the painful sweep of her blood, and she put her hand to her side, saying aloud, "Good gracious!—it's only the nine o'clock deputy going down," rebuking herself.

She sat still, listening. Half an hour of this, and she was wearied out.

"What am I working myself up like this for?" she said pitiably to herself, "I s'll only be doing myself some damage."

She took out her sewing again.

At a quarter to ten there were footsteps. One person! She watched

One person! She watched for the door to open. It was an elderly woman, in a black bonnet and a black woollen shawl—his mother. This was a short woman of sixty or thereabouts, pale, with blue eyes, and her face all shapen to lines of old lamentation and self-commiseration. She shut the door and came straight to her daughter, and put her old hand on the other's strong, capable hands.

"Eh, Lizzie, whatever shall we do, whatever shall we do!" she wailed.

Elizabeth drew back a little, sharply.

"What is it, mother?" she said.

The elderly woman went and seated herself on the sofa. The tears were running down the furrows which her old laments had left.

"I don't know, child, I can't tell you!"—she shook her head slowly and with despair. Elizabeth sat watching her, anxious and vexed.

"I don't know," replied the grandmother, sighing very deeply. "Trouble never leaves us, it doesn't. The things I've gone through, and now this——!" She wept without wiping her eyes, the tears running freely. She seemed to be looking back down the long dark avenue of her troubles.

"But mother," interrupted Elizabeth decisively. "What have you got to tell me? Let me know!"

The grandmother slowly wiped her eyes. The loose fountains of her tears were stopped by Elizabeth's sharpness. She wiped her eyes slowly. She knew it was aggravating, but then—her daughter-in-law had nettled her; and she could not rise too abruptly out of the luxurious bed of her grief.

"Poor child! eh, you poor thing!" she wailed. "I don't know what we're going to do, I don't—and you as you are—it's an awful thing, it is indeed, an awful thing!"

Elizabeth sat strangling in the cords of suspense.

"Is he dead?" she asked, and at the words her heart swung violently, though she felt a slight flush of shame at the ultimate extravagance of the idea. The question sufficiently startled the old lady.

"Don't say so, Elizabeth! The Lord won't let it be as bad as that; no, the Lord will spare us that, Elizabeth. Jack Rigley came just as I was sittin' down to a glass afore going to bed, an' 'e said, ' 'Appen you'll go down th' line, Mrs. Bates. Walt's had an accident. 'Appen you'll go an' sit wi' 'er till we can get him home.' I hadn't time to ask him a word, afore he was gone. An' I put my bonnet on an' come straight down to you, Lizzie. I thought to myself, 'Eh, that poor blessed child, if anybody should come an' tell her of a sudden, there's no tellin' what'll 'appen to 'er.' You mustn't let it upset you, Lizzie—you mustn't child. Think for the door to open. It was an elderly woman, in a black bonnet and a black woollen shawl—his mother. She was about sixty years old, pale, with blue eyes, and her face all wrinkled and lamentable. She shut the door and turned to her daughter-in-law peevishly.

"Eh, Lizzie, whatever shall we do, whatever shall we do!" she cried.

Elizabeth drew back a little, sharply.

"What is it, mother?" she said.

The elder woman seated herself on the sofa.

"I don't know, child, I can't tell you!"—she shook her head slowly. Elizabeth sat watching her, anxious and vexed.

"I don't know," replied the grandmother, sighing very deeply. "There's no end to my troubles, there isn't. The things I've gone through, I'm sure it's enough——!" She wept without wiping her eyes, the tears running.

"But, mother," interrupted Elizabeth, "what do you mean? What is it?"

The grandmother slowly wiped her eyes. The fountains of her tears were stopped by Elizabeth's directness. She wiped her eyes slowly.

"Poor child! Eh, you poor thing!" she moaned. "I don't know what we're going to do, I don't—and you as you are—it's a thing, it is indeed!"

Elizabeth waited.

"Is he dead?" she asked, and at the words her heart swung violently, though she felt a slight flush of shame at the ultimate extravagance of the question. Her words sufficiently frightened the old lady, almost brought her to herself.

"Don't say so, Elizabeth! We'll hope it's not as bad as that; no, may the Lord spare us that, Elizabeth. Jack Rigley came just as I was sittin' down to a glass afore going to bed, an' 'e said, ' 'Appen you'll go down th' line, Mrs. Bates. Walt's had an accident. 'Appen you'll go an' sit wi' 'er till we can get him home.' I hadn't time to ask him a word afore he was gone. An' I put my bonnet on an' come straight down, Lizzie. I thought to myself, 'Eh, that poor blessed child, if anybody should come an' tell her of a sudden, there's no knowin' what'll 'appen to 'er.' You mustn't let it upset you, Lizzie—or you know what to expect. How of that poor little thing as isn't here by six months—or is it five, Lizzie? Ay!"—the old woman shook her head—"time slips on, it slips on! Ay! How long is it since you had 'im, Lizzie?"

Elizabeth's thoughts were busy elsewhere. If he was killed—would she be able to manage on the little pension and what she could earn?—she counted up rapidly. If he was hurt—they wouldn't take him to the hospital—how tiresome he would be to nurse!—but perhaps she'd get him away from the drink and his hateful ways. She would—while he was ill. The tears came to her eyes at the picture. Then in thought she arose once more—he had killed her "sentiment"—and began to consider the children. At any rate she was absolutely necessary for them; she must save herself for them. She clung to the thought of the children; and, covering the ugly image of him, rose her pity, a deep womanly pity, which is only akin to love when its object is physically struck down. He would be weak, and she would have him in her hands. Then she was full of tenderness. Her mother startled her. She captured the echo of the question.

"How long? It's eight years come Christmas."

"Eight years!" repeated the old woman, "an' it seems but a week or two since he brought me his first wages. Ay—he was a good lad, Elizabeth, he was a good lad. I don't know—I don't know why he got such a trouble, I don't. He was a good lad at home, a dear lad. But there's no mistake he's been a handful o' trouble, a handful o' trouble, he has! I hope the Lord'll spare him to mend his ways, I hope so, I hope so. You've had a sight o' trouble with him, Elizabeth, you have indeed. But I'm sure he was a good lad wi' me, he was, there's no denying. I don't know how it is... Eh! they don't turn out well, they don't! They run your legs off, an' make you tired out when they're little, an' when they're big, you sit still wi' more trouble than you can well carry because of 'em. It is so——"

The old woman continued to think aloud, a monotonous plaintive sound, while Elizabeth drove her thoughts fiercely here and there, arrested once, when she heard the winding-engine chuff quickly again, and the brakes skirr[17] with a shriek. Then she heard the engine more slowly, and the brakes made no sound. The old woman did not notice. Elizabeth sat in a coil of half-twisted suspense. The old woman talked, with lapses into silence.

"But he wasn't your son, Lizzie—an' it makes a difference. What-

[17] Move rapidly.

long is it, six months—or is it five, Lizzie? Ay!"—the old woman shook her head—"time slips on, it slips on! Ay!"

Elizabeth's thoughts were busy elsewhere. If he was killed—would she be able to manage on the little pension and what she could earn?—she counted up rapidly. If he was hurt—they wouldn't take him to the hospital—how tiresome he would be to nurse!—but perhaps she'd be able to get him away from the drink and his hateful ways. She would—while he was ill. The tears offered to come to her eyes at the picture. But what sentimental luxury was this she was beginning?—She turned to consider the children. At any rate she was absolutely necessary for them. They were her business.

"Ay!" repeated the old woman, "it seems but a week or two since he brought me his first wages. Ay—he was a good lad, Elizabeth, he was, in his way. I don't know why he got to be such a trouble, I don't. He was a happy lad at home, only full of spirits. But there's no mistake he's been a handful of trouble, he has! I hope the Lord'll spare him to mend his ways. I hope so, I hope so. You've had a sight o' trouble with him, Elizabeth, you have indeed. But he was a jolly enough lad wi' me, he was, I can assure you. I don't know how it is. . . ."

The old woman continued to muse aloud, a monotonous irritating sound, while Elizabeth thought concentratedly, startled once, when she heard the winding-engine chuff quickly, and the brakes skirr with a shriek. Then she heard the engine more slowly, and the brakes made no sound. The old woman did not notice. Elizabeth waited in suspense. The mother-in-law talked, with lapses into silence.

"But he wasn't your son, Lizzie, an' it makes a difference. Whatever

ever he was, I remember him when he was little, a beautiful little lad, as ever your eyes could wish."

It was half-past ten, and the old woman was saying: "You've nothing left—but trouble; and you're never too old for trouble, never too old for that——" when the gate banged, and there were heavy feet on the steps.

"I'll go, Lizzie, let me go," cried the old woman, rising. But Elizabeth was at the door. It was a man in pit-clothes.

"They're bringin' 'im, Missis," he said, simply. Elizabeth's life halted a moment within her. Then it switched on again, almost suffocating her.

"Is he—is it bad?" she asked.

The man nodded and turned away, looking at the garden:

"The doctor says 'e'd been dead hours. 'E saw 'im i' th' lamp cabin."

The old woman, who stood just behind Elizabeth, dropped into a chair, and folded her hands, crying: "Oh, my boy, my boy."

"Hush!" said Elizabeth, with a sharp twitch of a frown. "Be still, mother, don't waken th' children: I wouldn't have them down for anything!"

The old woman moaned softly, rocking herself. The man was turning away. Elizabeth took a step forward.

"How was it?" she asked.

"Well, it wor this like," the man replied, very ill at ease. " 'E wor finishin' a stint, an' th' butties 'ad gone, an' a lot o' stuff come down atop 'n 'im."

"And is he much—has it made a mess of him?" asked the widow, with a shudder. She dreaded most of all at this moment that he should look ghastly; she felt she could not stand it.

"No," said the man, "it fell at th' back on 'im. 'E wor under th' face, tha sees, an' it niver touched 'im. It shut 'im in. 'E wor smothered."

Elizabeth shrank back with a low cry. The thought of it was like a weapon against her life. She heard the old woman behind her say:

"What?—did 'e say 'e was suffocated?"

The man replied, more loudly: "Yes—that's 'ow it wor!"

Then the old woman wailed aloud, and this calmed Elizabeth.

"Oh, mother," she said, putting her arms round the old woman, "don't waken th' children, don't waken the children."

She wept a little, while the old woman rocked herself and moaned. Elizabeth did not think of it—she did not think of him. She only thought that they were bringing him home, and she must be ready, and whatever happened, she must not forget the children. "They'll lay him he was, I remember him when he was little, an' I learned to understand him and to make allowances. You've got to make allowances for them—"

It was half-past ten, and the old woman was saying: "But it's trouble from beginning to end; you're never too old for trouble, never too old for that——" when the gate banged back, and there were heavy feet on the steps.

"I'll go, Lizzie, let me go," cried the old woman, rising. But Elizabeth was at the door. It was a man in pit-clothes.

"They're bringin' 'im, Missis," he said. Elizabeth's heart halted a moment. Then it surged on again, almost suffocating her.

"Is he—is it bad?" she asked.

The man turned away, looking at the darkness:

"The doctor says 'e'd been dead hours. 'E saw 'im i' th' lamp-cabin."

The old woman, who stood just behind Elizabeth, dropped into a chair, and folded her hands, crying: "Oh, my boy, my boy!"

"Hush!" said Elizabeth, with a sharp twitch of a frown. "Be still, mother, don't waken th' children: I wouldn't have them down for anything!"

The old woman moaned softly, rocking herself. The man was drawing away. Elizabeth took a step forward.

"How was it?" she asked.

"Well, I couldn't say for sure," the man replied, very ill at ease. " 'E wor finishin' a stint an' th' butties 'ad gone, an' a lot o' stuff come down atop 'n 'im."

"And crushed him?" cried the widow, with a shudder.

"No," said the man, "it fell at th' back of 'im. 'E wor under th' face, an' it niver touched 'im. It shut 'im in. It seems 'e wor smothered."

Elizabeth shrank back. She heard the old woman behind her cry:

"What?—what did 'e say it was?"

The man replied, more loudly: " 'E wor smothered!"

Then the old woman wailed aloud, and this relieved Elizabeth.

"Oh, mother," she said, putting her hand on the old woman, "don't waken th' children, don't waken th' children."

She wept a little, unknowing, while the old mother rocked herself and moaned. Elizabeth remembered that they were bringing him home, and she must be ready. "They'll lay him in the parlour," she said to in the parlour," she said to herself, standing a moment pale and perplexed.

Then she lighted a candle and went into the tiny room. The air was cold and damp, but she could not make a fire, there was no fireplace. She set down the candle and looked round. There was a sofa, and four chairs, and a chiffonier, and the room was crowded. The candle-light glittered on the lustreglasses,[18] and on the two glass vases that held some of the pink chrysanthemums. There was a cold deathly smell of chrysanthemums in the room. Elizabeth stood looking at the flowers. Vaguely, they recalled her wedding. She turned away, and calculated whether they would have room to lay him on the floor, between the couch and the chiffonier. She pushed the couch down against the narrow wall, and put the chairs at that end also. There would be room to lay him down and to step round him. Then she fetched the old red table-cloth, and another old cloth, spreading them down to save her bit of carpet. She shivered on leaving the parlour; so, from the dresser drawer she took a clean shirt and put it at the fire to air. All the time her mother-in-law was rocking herself in the chair and moaning.

"You'll have to move from there, mother," said Elizabeth. "They'll be bringing him in. Come in the rocker."

The old mother rose mechanically, and seated herself by the fire, continuing to "keen." The parlour door was open, and inside it looked very dim and cold, with one yellow candle on the dark red chiffonier. Elizabeth went into the pantry for another candle, and there, in the little place under the naked tiles, she heard them coming. She stood still in the pantry doorway, listening. She heard them pass the end of the house, and come awkwardly down the three steps, a jumble of shuffling footsteps and muttering voices. The old mother rose and stood silent. The men were in the yard.

Then Elizabeth heard Matthews, the manager of the pit, say: "You go in first, Jim. Mind!"

The door came open, and the two women saw a collier backing into the room, holding one end of a stretcher, on which they could see the great pit-boots of the dead man. The two carriers halted, the man at the head stooping to the lintel of the door.

"Wheer will you have him?" asked the old manager, a short, white-bearded man.

Elizabeth roused herself and came away from the pantry, carrying the unlighted candle.

[18] Prismatic glass pendants attached to a decorative object.

herself, standing a moment pale and perplexed.

Then she lighted a candle and went into the tiny room. The air was cold and damp, but she could not make a fire, there was no fireplace. She set down the candle and looked round. The candlelight glittered on the lustre-glasses, on the two vases that held some of the pink chrysanthemums, and on the dark mahogany. There was a cold, deathly smell of chrysanthemums in the room. Elizabeth stood looking at the flowers. She turned away, and calculated whether there would be room to lay him on the floor, between the couch and the chiffonier. She pushed the chairs aside. There would be room to lay him down and to step round him. Then she fetched the old red tablecloth, and another old cloth, spreading them down to save her bit of carpet. She shivered on leaving the parlour; so, from the dresser-drawer she took a clean shirt and put it at the fire to air. All the time her mother-in-law was rocking herself in the chair and moaning.

"You'll have to move from there, mother," said Elizabeth. "They'll be bringing him in. Come in the rocker."

The old mother rose mechanically, and seated herself by the fire, continuing to lament. Elizabeth went into the pantry for another candle, and there, in the little penthouse under the naked tiles, she heard them coming. She stood still in the pantry doorway, listening. She heard them pass the end of the house, and come awkwardly down the three steps, a jumble of shuffling footsteps and muttering voices. The old woman was silent. The men were in the yard.

Then Elizabeth heard Matthews, the manager of the pit, say: "You go in first, Jim. Mind!"

The door came open, and the two women saw a collier backing into the room, holding one end of a stretcher, on which they could see the nailed pit-boots of the dead man. The two carriers halted, the man at the head stooping to the lintel of the door.

"Wheer will you have him?" asked the manager, a short, white-bearded man.

Elizabeth roused herself and came from the pantry carrying the unlighted candle.

"In the parlour," she said.

"In there Jim!" pointed the manager, and the carriers backed round into the tiny room. The coat with which they had covered the body fell off as they awkwardly turned through the two doorways, and the women saw their man, naked to the waist, lying stripped for work. Immediately the old woman began to moan in a low voice, "My boy!" Elizabeth followed to see where they laid him, and she came face to face with the manager, who was on the heels of the second bearer. Neither noticed the other.

"Lay th' stretcher at th' side," snapped the manager, "an' put *'im* on th' cloths. Mind now, mind! Look you now——!"

One of the men had knocked off a vase of chrysanthemums. He stared awkwardly, then they set down the stretcher. Elizabeth did not look at her husband. As soon as she could get in the room, she went and picked up the broken vase, and the flowers.

"Wait a minute!" she said.

The three men waited in silence while she put the bits of glass and the flowers in the ashpan, and mopped up the water with a duster. Then they lifted the body and put it on the cloths, and stood up with a sigh, keeping their eyes on the man.

"Eh, what a job, what a job, to be sure!" the manager was saying, rubbing his brow with trouble and perplexity. "Never knew such a thing in my life, never! They'd no business to ha' left 'im, you know, no business to ha' left him. I never knew such a thing in my life! Fell over him clean as a whistle, an' shut him in. Not ten feet of space, there wasn't—yet it never bruised him."

He looked down at the dead man, lying serene, half naked, all grimed with coal-dust.

"'Sphyxiated,' the doctor said. I never knew anything like it. It seems as if it had to be. Clean over him, an' shut 'im in, like a vault"—he made a sweeping gesture with his hand.

"It *wor* that!" corroborated one of the men.

They forced the horror of the thing upon the woman's imagination, and it gripped her as in some great invisible hand.

"Don't take on!" said the manager, "it's no good now, Missis, it isna. It's a bad job, I know it is, but——"

Then they heard the girl's voice upstairs calling shrilly: "Mother, mother—who is it? Mother!—who is it?"

Elizabeth hurried to the foot of the stairs and opened the door:

"Go to sleep!" she commanded sharply. "What are you shouting about? Go to sleep at once—there's nothing——"

"In the parlour," she said.

"In there, Jim!" pointed the manager, and the carriers backed round into the tiny room. The coat with which they had covered the body fell off as they awkwardly turned through the two doorways, and the women saw their man, naked to the waist, lying stripped for work. The old woman began to moan in a low voice of horror.

"Lay th' stretcher at th' side," snapped the manager, "an' put 'im on th' cloths. Mind now, mind! Look you now——!"

One of the men had knocked off a vase of chrysanthemums. He stared awkwardly, then they set down the stretcher. Elizabeth did not look at her husband. As soon as she could get in the room, she went and picked up the broken vase and the flowers.

"Wait a minute!" she said.

The three men waited in silence while she mopped up the water with a duster.

"Eh, what a job, what a job, to be sure!" the manager was saying, rubbing his brow with trouble and perplexity. "Never knew such a thing in my life, never! He'd no business to ha' been left. I never knew such a thing in my life! Fell over him clean as a whistle, an' shut him in. Not four foot of space, there wasn't—yet it scarce bruised him."

He looked down at the dead man, lying prone, half naked, all grimed with coal-dust.

" 'Sphyxiated,' the doctor said. It *is* the most terrible job I've ever known. Seems as if it was done o' purpose. Clean over him, an' shut 'im in, like a mouse-trap"—he made a sharp, descending gesture with his hand.

The colliers standing by jerked aside their heads in hopeless comment.

The horror of the thing bristled upon them all.

Then they heard the girl's voice upstairs calling shrilly: "Mother, mother—who is it? Mother, who is it?"

Elizabeth hurried to the foot of the stairs and opened the door:

"Go to sleep!" she commanded sharply. "What are you shouting about? Go to sleep at once—there's nothing——"

Then she began to mount the stairs. They could hear her on the boards, and on the plaster floor of the little bedroom. They could hear her distinctly:

"What's the matter now?—what's the matter with you, silly thing?"—her voice was much gentler than when she had called from the foot of the stairs.

"I thought it was some men come," said the plaintive voice of the child.

"They only brought your father home. There's nothing to make a fuss about. Go to sleep now, like a good child."

They could imagine her smoothing the bedclothes over the shoulders of the soothed children.

"Is he drunk?" the girl asked, timidly, faintly.

"No! Don't be a silly. He—he's asleep."

"Is he asleep downstairs?"

"Yes . . . and don't wake him."

There was a silence for a moment, then the men heard the frightened child again:

"What's that noise? Is it him asleep?"

"Yes! He's all right, what are you bothering for?"

The noise was the grandmother moaning. She was quite oblivious of everything, sitting on her chair rocking and moaning. The manager put his hand on her arm and bade her "Sh—sh!!"

The old woman opened her eyes and looked at him. She was stung by this interruption, but she became quiet, very pitiful and forlorn.

"What time is it?"—the plaintive thin voice of the child, reassured, sinking back to sleep, asked this last question.

"Ten o'clock," answered the mother softly. Then she must have bent down and kissed them, and they heard the soft level flight of her voice, but could not tell what she said.

Matthews beckoned the men to come away. They put on their caps and took up the stretcher. Then, stepping over the body, they tiptoed out of the house. None of them spoke till they were far from the wakeful children.

When Elizabeth came down she found her mother alone on the parlour floor, with the face of her son between her hands, the tears dropping on him.

"We must lay him out," she whispered softly. She went and put on the kettle, then returned and kneeling at the feet, began to unfasten the knotted leather laces. The room was very dim with only one candle, and she had to bend her face almost to the floor. At last she got off the

Then she began to mount the stairs. They could hear her on the boards, and on the plaster floor of the little bedroom. They could hear her distinctly:

"What's the matter now?—what's the matter with you, silly thing?"—her voice was much agitated, with an unreal gentleness.

"I thought it was some men come," said the plaintive voice of the child. "Has he come?"

"Yes, they've brought him. There's nothing to make a fuss about. Go to sleep now, like a good child."

They could hear her voice in the bedroom, they waited whilst she covered the children under the bedclothes.

"Is he drunk?" asked the girl, timidly, faintly.

"No! No—he's not! He—he's asleep."

"Is he asleep downstairs?"

"Yes—and don't make a noise."

There was silence for a moment, then the men heard the frightened child again:

"What's that noise?"

"It's nothing, I tell you, what are you bothering for?"

The noise was the grandmother moaning. She was oblivious of everything, sitting on her chair rocking and moaning. The manager put his hand on her arm and bade her "Sh—sh!!"

The old woman opened her eyes and looked at him. She was shocked by this interruption, and seemed to wonder.

"What time is it?"—the plaintive thin voice of the child, sinking back unhappily into sleep, asked this last question.

"Ten o'clock," answered the mother more softly. Then she must have bent down and kissed the children.

Matthews beckoned to the men to come away. They put on their caps and took up the stretcher. Stepping over the body, they tiptoed out of the house. None of them spoke till they were far from the wakeful children.

When Elizabeth came down she found her mother alone on the parlour floor, leaning over the dead man, the tears dropping on him.

"We must lay him out," the wife said. She put on the kettle, then returning knelt at the feet, and began to unfasten the knotted leather laces. The room was clammy and dim with only one candle, so that she had to bend her face almost to the floor. At last she got off the heavy

heavy boots and took them away. Then she pulled off his stockings, with dirty tape garters: black and red "mingled" stockings, like those of the children's hedgehog. She unfastened the thick leather belt from round his waist.

"We must get his trousers off," she whispered to the little old woman, and together, with difficulty, they did so.

When they rose and looked at him lying naked in the beauty of death, the women experienced suddenly the same feeling; that of motherhood, mixed with some primeval awe. But the pitiful mother-feeling prevailed. Elizabeth knelt down and put her arms round him, and laid her cheek on his breast. His mother had his face between her hands again, and was murmuring and sobbing. Elizabeth touched him and kissed him with her cheek and her lips. Then suddenly she felt jealous that the old woman had his face.

She rose, and went into the kitchen, where she poured some warm water into a bowl, and brought soap and flannel and a towel.

"I must wash him," she said decisively. Then the old mother rose stiffly, and watched Elizabeth as she gently washed his face, tenderly, as if he were a child, brushing the big blonde moustache from his mouth with the flannel. Then the old woman, jealous, said:

"Let me wipe him!"—and she kneeled on the other side and slowly dried him as Elizabeth washed, her big black bonnet sometimes brushing the dark head of her daughter. They worked thus in silence for a long time, lovingly, with meticulous care. Sometimes they forgot it was death, and the touch of the man's body gave them strange thrills, different in each of the women; secret thrills that made them turn one from the other, and left them with a keen sadness.

At last it was finished. He was a man of handsome figure and genial face, which showed traces of the disfigurement of drink. He was blonde, full-fleshed, with fine round limbs.

"Bless him," whispered his mother, looking always at his face, "he looks as if he was just waking up. He's smiling a bit, bless him. Look, he's smiling a bit, just in his old way——" She spoke in a faint, sibilant rapture.

Elizabeth sank down again to the floor, and put her face against his neck, and sobbed till she was tired. The old woman wept too, slow noiseless tears, touching him, regarding him with endless fondness and unwearying interest.

"White as milk he is, clear as a twelvemonth baby, bless him, the darling!" she whispered to herself. "Not a mark on him, clear and clean boots and put them away.

"You must help me now," she whispered to the old woman. Together they stripped the man.

When they arose, saw him lying in the naïve dignity of death, the women stood arrested in fear and respect. For a few moments they remained still, looking down, the old mother whimpering. Elizabeth felt countermanded. She saw him, how utterly inviolable he lay in himself. She had nothing to do with him. She could not accept it. Stooping, she laid her hand on him, in claim. He was still warm, for the mine was hot where he had died. His mother had his face between her hands, and was murmuring incoherently. The old tears fell in succession as drops from wet leaves; the mother was not weeping, merely her tears flowed. Elizabeth embraced the body of her husband, with cheek and lips. She seemed to be listening, inquiring, trying to get some connection. But she could not. She was driven away. He was impregnable.

She rose, went into the kitchen, where she poured warm water into a bowl, brought soap and flannel and a soft towel.

"I must wash him," she said.

Then the old mother rose stiffly, and watched Elizabeth as she carefully washed his face, carefully brushing the big blonde moustache from his mouth with the flannel. She was afraid with a bottomless fear, so she ministered to him. The old woman, jealous, said:

"Let me wipe him!"—and she kneeled on the other side drying slowly as Elizabeth washed, her big black bonnet sometimes brushing the dark head of her daughter. They worked thus in silence for a long time. They never forgot it was death, and the touch of the man's dead body gave them strange emotions, different in each of the women; a great dread possessed them both, the mother felt the lie was given to her womb, she was denied; the wife felt the utter isolation of the human soul, the child within her was a weight apart from her.

At last it was finished. He was a man of handsome body, and his face showed no traces of drink. He was blonde, full-fleshed, with fine limbs. But he was dead.

"Bless him," whispered his mother, looking always at his face, and speaking out of sheer terror. "Dear lad—bless him!" She spoke in a faint, sibilant ecstasy of fear and mother love.

Elizabeth sank down again to the floor, and put her face against his neck, and trembled and shuddered. But she had to draw away again. He was dead, and her living flesh had no place against his. A great dread and weariness held her: she was so unavailing. Her life was gone like this.

"White as milk he is, clear as a twelve-month baby, bless him, the darling!" the old mother murmured to herself. "Not a mark on him, and white, as beautiful as ever a child was made," she murmured with pride. Elizabeth kept her face hidden, sobbing.

"He went peaceful, Lizzie—as peaceful as sleep. Look, Lizzie, he's smiling a bit; and he knew how to laugh, he did, when I had him. That hearty! He's my lad again now, Lizzie."

Elizabeth, who had sobbed herself weary, looked up. Then she put her arms round him, and kissed him again on the smooth ripples below the breasts, and held him to her. She loved him very much now—so beautiful, and gentle, and helpless. He must have suffered! What must he have suffered! Her tears started hot again. Ah, she was so sorry, sorrier than she could ever tell. She was sorry for him, that he had suffered so, and got lost in the dark places of death. But the poignancy of her grief was that she loved him again—ah, so much! She did not want him to wake up, she did not want him to speak. She had him again, now, and it was Death which had brought him. She kissed him, so that she might kiss Death which had taken the ugly things from him. Think how he might have come home—not white and beautiful, gently smiling.... Ugly, befouled, with hateful words on an evil breath, reeking with disgust. She loved him so much now; her life was mended again, and her faith looked up with a smile; he had come home to her, beautiful. How she had loathed him! It was strange he could have been such as he had been. How wise of death to be so silent! If he spoke, even now, her anger and her scorn would lift their heads like fire. He would not speak—no, just gently smile, with wide eyes. She was sorry to have to disturb him to put on his shirt—but she must, he could not lie like that. The shirt was aired by now. But it would be cruel hard work to get him into it. He was so heavy, and helpless, more helpless than a baby, poor dear!—and so beautiful.

1910 *Version 1*

Version 2, The Ending

"He went peaceful, Lizzie—peaceful as sleep. Isn't it wonderful? You'd think he was smiling a bit. 'Appen he made it all right, Lizzie, shut in there. He'd have time. He wouldn't look like this if he hadn't made his peace. He's smiling a bit. Eh, but he used to have a hearty clear and clean and white, beautiful as ever a child was made," she murmured with pride. Elizabeth kept her face hidden.

"He went peaceful, Lizzie—peaceful as sleep. Isn't he beautiful, the lamb? Ay—he must ha' made his peace, Lizzie. 'Appen he made it all right, Lizzie, shut in there. He'd have time. He wouldn't look like this if he hadn't made his peace. The lamb, the dear lamb. Eh, but he had a hearty laugh. I loved to hear it. He had the heartiest laugh, Lizzie, as a lad——"

Elizabeth looked up. The man's mouth was fallen back, slightly open under the cover of the moustache. The eyes, half shut, did not show glazed in the obscurity. Life with its smoky burning gone from him, had left him apart and utterly alien to her. And she knew what a stranger he was to her. In her womb was ice of fear, because of this separate stranger with whom she had been living as one flesh. Was this what it all meant—utter, intact separateness, obscured by heat of living? In dread she turned her face away. The fact was too deadly. There had been nothing between them, and yet they had come together, exchanging their nakedness repeatedly. Each time he had taken her, they had been two isolated beings, far apart as now. He was no more responsible than she. The child was like ice in her womb. For as she looked at the dead man, her mind, cold and detached, said clearly: "Who am I? What have I been doing? I have been fighting a husband who did not exist. *He* existed all the time. What wrong have I done? What was that I have been living with? There lies the reality, this man."—And her soul died in her for fear: she knew she had never seen him, he had never seen her, they had met in the dark and had fought in the dark, not knowing whom they met nor whom they fought. And now she saw, and turned silent in seeing. For she had been wrong. She had said he was something he was not; she had felt familiar with him. Whereas he was apart all the while, living as she never lived, feeling as she never felt.

In fear and shame she looked at his naked body, that she had known falsely. And he was the father of her children. Her soul was torn from her body and stood apart. She looked at his naked body and was ashamed, as if she had denied it. After all, it was itself. It seemed awful to her. She looked at his face, and she turned her own face to the wall. For his look was other than hers, his way was not her way. She had denied him what he was—she saw it now. She had refused him as himself.—And this had been her life, and his life.—She was grateful to death, which restored the truth. And she knew she was not dead.

And all the while her heart was bursting with grief and pity for him. What had he suffered? What stretch of horror for this helpless man!

laugh. I loved to hear it. He's like he was when *I* had him, Lizzie. The heartiest laugh he had——"

Elizabeth looked up. The man's mouth was fallen back, slightly open under the cover of the moustache. The eyes, half shut, did not show glazed by the small candlelight. His wife looked at him. He seemed to be dreaming back, half awake. Life with its smoky burning gone from him, had left a purity and a candour like an adolescent's moulded upon his reverie. His intrinsic beauty was evident now. She had not been mistaken in him, as often she had bitterly confessed to herself she was. The beauty of his youth, of his eighteen years, of the time when life had settled on him, as in adolescence it settles on youth, bringing a mission to fulfil and equipment therefor, this beauty shone almost unstained again. It was this adolescent "he," the young man looking round to see which way, that Elizabeth had loved. He had come from the discipleship of youth, through the Pentecost of adolescence, pledged to keep with honour his own individuality, to be steadily and unquenchably himself, electing his own masters and serving them till the wages were won. He betrayed himself in his search for amusement. Let Education teach us to amuse ourselves, necessity will train us to work. Once out of the pit, there was nothing to interest this man. He sought the public-house, where, by paying the price of his own integrity, he found amusement; destroying the clamours for activity, because he knew not what form the activities might take. The miner turned miscreant to himself, easing the ache of dissatisfaction by destroying the part of him which ached. Little by little the recreant maimed and destroyed himself.

It was this recreant his wife had hated so bitterly, had fought against so strenuously. She had strove, all the years of his falling off, had strove with all her force to save the man she had known new-bucklered with beauty and strength. In a wild and bloody passion she fought the recreant. Now this lay killed, the clean young knight was brought home to her. Elizabeth bowed her head upon the body and wept.

She put her arms round him, kissed the smooth ripples below his breasts, bowed her forehead on him in submission. Faithful to her deeper sense of honour, she uttered no word of sorrow in her heart. Upright in soul are women, however they bow the swerving body. She owned the beauty of the blow.

And all the while her heart was bursting with grief and pity for him. What had he suffered? What stretch of horror for this helpless man! She wept herself almost in agony. She had not been able to help him. Never again would she be able to help him. It was grief unutterable to think that now all was over between them. Even if it were a case of

She was rigid with agony. She had not been able to help him. He had been cruelly injured, this naked man, this other being, and she could make no reparation. There were the children—but the children belonged to life. This dead man had nothing to do with them. He and she were only channels through which life had flowed to issue in the children. She was a mother—but how awful she knew it now to have been a wife. And he, dead now, how awful he must have felt it to be a husband. She felt that in the next world he would be a stranger to her. If they met there, in the beyond, they would only be ashamed of what had been before. The children had come, for some mysterious reason, out of both of them. But the children did not unite them. Now he was dead, she knew how eternally he was apart from her, how eternally he had nothing more to do with her. She saw this episode of her life closed. They had denied each other in life. Now he had withdrawn. An anguish came over her. It was finished then: it had become hopeless between them long before he died. Yet he had been her husband. But how little!

"Have you got his shirt, 'Lizabeth?"

Elizabeth turned without answering, though she strove to weep and behave as her mother-in-law expected. But she could not, she was silenced. She went into the kitchen and returned with the garment.

"It is aired," she said, grasping the cotton shirt here and there to try. She was almost ashamed to handle him; what right had she or anyone to lay hands on him; but her touch was humble on his body. It was hard work to clothe him. He was so heavy and inert. A terrible dread gripped her all the while: that he could be so heavy and utterly inert, unresponsive, apart. The horror of the distance between them was almost too much for her—it was so infinite a gap she must look across.

At last it was finished. They covered him with a sheet and left him lying, with his face bound. And she fastened the door of the little parlour, lest the children should see what was lying there. Then, with peace sunk heavy on her heart, she went about making tidy the kitchen. She knew she submitted to life, which was her immediate master. But from death, her ultimate master, she winced with fear and shame.

1914 *Version 3*

meeting in the next world, he would not need her there; it would be different. She saw the great episode of her life closed with him, and grief was a passion. The old mother was hushed in awe. She, the elder, less honourable woman, had said: "She drives him to it, she makes him ten thousand times worse." But now the old mother bowed down in respect for the wife. As the passion of Elizabeth's grief grew more, the old woman shrank and tried to avoid it.

"Have you got his shirt, 'Lizabeth?"

Elizabeth wept without answering, though she strove to lull and recover. At last she rose and went into the kitchen. Returning:

"It is aired," she said, grasping the cotton shirt here and there to try. She was sorry to disturb him, but he could not lie naked. It was hard work to clothe him. He was so heavy and helpless, more helpless than a baby fallen heavily asleep. They had to struggle with him as if he were a rebellious child. This made Elizabeth's heart weep again.

Yet more joy was mixed in her emotion than she knew. He might have come home ugly, befouled, so that she would have had a loathly, strange creature to combat. Ah! how she had fought that him, the disfigured coward, which gradually replaced her man! How wise of death to be so silent! Even now her fear could not trust him to speak. Yet he was restored to her fair, unblemished, fresh as for the splendour of a fight.

1911 *Version 2*

DISCUSSION QUESTIONS

1. Which parts and aspects of the story underwent the most drastic reductions? What does the story gain or lose through these cuts? What change of emphasis do they produce?

2. Compare and contrast the first and third versions of the paragraph beginning with "When they rose" (page 188) and "When they arose" (page 189), respectively. What basic change has occurred? In both instances, Elizabeth embraces her husband, but for different reasons. Distinguish between the two motives. What insight does Elizabeth attain in the third version? In a similar way, compare and explain changes made in the first and third versions of the paragraph beginning with "Let me wipe him!" (pages 188–189). Do the same for the one beginning with "Elizabeth sank down again" (pages 188–189).

3. In the first two versions of the ending, Walter seems transfigured by death. Describe the qualities of her husband that Elizabeth discovers in each of these versions. Explain the differences of emphasis and *tone* in these two endings.

4. In the third version of the ending, Elizabeth is also "grateful to death," but now because death has "restored the truth." In your own words, explain the "truth" she has discovered. Lawrence had earlier prepared the reader for her insight through specific changes in her mother-in-law's comments. Find these revised passages. Contrast Elizabeth's present attitude toward Walter with the ones expressed in the first two versions.

5. In the third version, explain the following statement: "I have been fighting a husband who did not exist. *He* existed all the time" (page 191). Who is *he?*

6. In each of the three endings, Elizabeth realizes how her husband "must have suffered." While the first two versions refer to the agony of Walter's death, what meaning does his suffering take on in the third version through the addition of "He had been cruelly injured, this naked man, this other being, and she could make no reparation" (page 193). In line with this change, explain Lawrence's reason for altering "shut 'im in, like a vault" to "shut 'im in, like a mouse-trap (pages 184 and 185).

7. Determine the *symbolical* meaning of the chrysanthemums by examining each reference to the flowers in either complete version. How do you explain the fact that Elizabeth scolds the boy for destroying them, and carries them around in her apron, yet later voices her distaste for them (in fact, hates them in the first version)?

8. A second reading of a story often gives us an *ironic* perspective because knowing the outcome enables us to see implications in a character's words and actions very different from those intended. Find several instances of such incongruity (called *dramatic irony*) in either complete version of the story.

9. Analyze the descriptive passage that opens the third version of the story, up to the fourth sentence of the third paragraph. What mood does it evoke? How appropriate is it to the story? Explain. How does the description, particularly of the woman, relate to and *foreshadow* Lawrence's story?

ANALYSIS AND APPLICATION

1. In each of the following pairs, the second passage represents a shortened version of the first. Study each of Lawrence's alterations; consider what meaning, if any, has been lost or changed; and explain why you consider Lawrence's changes justified or unjustified.

a. "The kitchen was small and full of ruddy firelight. The fierce coals piled their beautiful, glowing life up to the chimney mouth." (page 152)

"The kitchen was small and full of firelight; red coals piled glowing up the chimney mouth. (page 153)

b. "In the great bay of railway-lines where the black trucks rose up obscurely" (page 166)

"In the great bay of railway lines bulked with trucks" (page 167)

2. In each of the following pairs, changes stem largely from alterations in *diction* (choice of words). Discuss the effect of each change within the context of the story, paying close attention to both the *denotative* and *connotative* meanings of individual words. Explain why you consider each change justified or unjustified.

a. "and the children were not dragged out of their play-world" (page 164)

"and the children were not flung out of their play-world" (page 165)

b. "but with a fine rough sympathy, and some concern" (page 170)

"but with deference and sympathy" (page 171)

3. For each of the following pairs, explain why Lawrence made the change and why you consider it justified or unjustified within the context of the story:

a. "—her voice was much gentler than when she had called from the foot of the stairs." (page 186)

"—her voice was much agitated, with an unreal gentleness." (page 187)

b. "The room was very dim with only one candle, and she had to bend her face almost to the floor." (page 186)

"The room was clammy and dim with only one candle, so that she had to bend her face almost to the floor." (page 187)

THE JEWELRY

GUY DE MAUPASSANT

HAVING MET the girl one evening, at the house of the office-superintendent, M. Lantin became enveloped in love as in a net.

She was the daughter of a country-tutor, who had been dead for several years. Afterward she had come to Paris with her mother, who made regular visits to several *bourgeois* families of the neighbourhood, in hopes of being able to get her daughter married. They were poor and respectable, quiet and gentle. The young girl seemed to be the very ideal of that pure good woman to whom every young man dreams of entrusting his future. Her modest beauty had a charm of angelic shyness; and the slight smile that always dwelt about her lips seemed a reflection of her heart.

Everybody sang her praises; all who knew her kept saying: "The man who gets her will be lucky. No one could find a nicer girl than that."

M. Lantin, who was then chief clerk in the office of the Minister of the Interior, with a salary of 3,500 francs a year, demanded her hand, and married her.

He was unutterably happy with her. She ruled his home with an economy so adroit that they really seemed to live in luxury. It would be impossible to conceive of any attentions, tendernesses, playful caresses which she did not lavish upon her husband; and such was the charm of her person that, six years after he married her, he loved her even more than he did the first day.

There were only two points upon which he ever found fault with her,—her love of the theatre, and her passion for false jewelry.

Her lady-friends (she was acquainted with the wives of several small office holders) were always bringing her tickets for the theatres; whenever there was a performance that made a sensation, she always had her *loge* secured, even for first performances; and she would drag her husband with her to all these entertainments, which used to tire him horribly after his day's work. So at last he begged her to go to the theatre with some lady-acquaintances who would consent to see her home afterward. She refused for quite a while;—thinking it would not look very well to go out thus unaccompanied by her husband. But finally she yielded, just to please him; and he felt infinitely grateful to her therefor.

Now this passion for the theatre at last evoked in her the desire of dress. It was true that her toilette remained simple, always in good taste, but modest; and her sweet grace, her irresistible grace, ever smiling and shy, seemed to take fresh charm from the simplicity of her robes. But she got into the habit of suspending in her pretty ears two big cut pebbles, fashioned in imitation of diamonds; and she wore necklaces of false pearls, bracelets of false gold, and haircombs studded with paste-imitations of precious stones.

Her husband, who felt shocked by this love of tinsel and show, would often say:—"My dear, when one has not the means to afford real jewelry, one should appear adorned with one's natural beauty and grace only,—and these gifts are the rarest of jewels."

But she would smile sweetly and answer: "What does it matter? I like those things—that is my little whim. I know you are right; but one can't make oneself over again. I've always loved jewelry so much!"

And then she would roll the pearls of the necklaces between her fingers, and make the facets of the cut crystals flash in the light, repeating: "Now look at them—see how well the work is done. You would swear it was real jewelry."

He would then smile in his turn, and declare to her: "You have the tastes of a regular Gipsy."

Sometimes, in the evening, when they were having a chat by the fire, she would rise and fetch the morocco box in which she kept her "stock" (as M. Lantin called it),—would put it on the tea-table, and begin to examine the false jewelry with passionate delight, as if she experienced some secret and mysterious sensations of pleasure in their contemplation; and she would insist on putting one of the necklaces round her husband's neck, and laugh till she couldn't laugh any more, crying out: "Oh! how funny you look!" Then she would rush into his arms, and kiss him furiously.

One winter's night, after she had been to the Opera, she came home chilled through, and trembling. Next day she had a bad cough. Eight days after that, she died of pneumonia.

Lantin was very nearly following her into the tomb. His despair was so frightful that in one single month his hair turned white. He wept from morning till night, feeling his heart torn by inexpressible suffering,—ever haunted by the memory of her, by the smile, by the voice, by all the charm of the dead woman.

Time did not assuage his grief. Often during office hours his fellow-clerks went off to a corner to chat about this or that topic of the day,—his cheeks might have been seen to swell up all of a sudden, his nose wrinkle, his eyes fill with water;—he would pull a frightful face, and begin to sob.

He had kept his dead companion's room just in the order she had left it, and he used to lock himself up in it every evening to think about her;—all the furniture, and even all her dresses, remained in the same place they had been on the last day of her life.

But life became hard for him. His salary, which, in his wife's hands, had amply sufficed for all household needs, now proved scarcely sufficient to supply his own few wants. And he asked himself in astonishment how she had managed always to furnish him with excellent wines and with delicate eating which he could not now afford at all with his scanty means.

He got a little into debt, like men obliged to live by their wits. At last one morning that he happened to find himself without a cent in his pocket, and a whole week to wait before he could draw his monthly salary, he thought of selling something; and almost immediately it occurred to him to sell his wife's "stock,"—for he had always borne a secret grudge against the flash-jewelry that used to annoy him so much in former days. The mere sight of it, day after day, somewhat spoiled the sad pleasure of thinking of his darling.

He tried a long time to make a choice among the heap of trinkets she had left behind her;—for up to the very last day of her life she had kept obstinately buying them, bringing home some new thing almost every night;—and finally he resolved to take the big pearl necklace which she used to like the best of all, and which he thought ought certainly to be worth six or eight francs, as it was really very nicely mounted for an imitation necklace.

He put it in his pocket, and walked toward the office, following the boulevards, and looking for some jewelry-store on the way, where he could enter with confidence.

Finally he saw a place and went in; feeling a little ashamed of thus exposing his misery, and of trying to sell such a trifling object.

"Sir," he said to the jeweler, "please tell me what this is worth."

The jeweler took the necklace, examined it, weighed it, took up a magnifying glass, called his clerk, talked to him in whispers, put down the necklace on the counter, and drew back a little bit to judge of its effect at a distance.

M. Lantin, feeling very much embarrassed by all these ceremonies, opened his mouth and began to declare:—"Oh! I know it can't be worth much" . . . when the jeweler interrupted him by saying:

"Well, sir, that is worth between twelve and fifteen thousand francs; but I cannot buy it unless you can let me know exactly how you came by it."

The widower's eyes opened enormously, and he stood gaping,—unable to understand. Then after a while he stammered out: "You said? . . . Are you sure?" The jeweler, misconstruing the cause of this astonishment, replied in a dry tone:—"Go elsewhere if you like, and see if you can get any more for it. The very most I would give for it is fifteen thousand. Come back and see me again, if you can't do better."

M. Lantin, feeling perfectly idiotic, took his necklace and departed; obeying a confused desire to find himself alone and to get a chance to think.

But the moment he found himself in the street again, he began to laugh, and he muttered to himself: "The fool!—oh! what a fool! If I had only taken him at his word. Well, well!—a jeweler who can't tell paste from real jewelry!"

And he entered another jewelry-store, at the corner of the Rue de la

Paix. The moment the jeweler set eyes on the necklace, he exclaimed:— "Hello! I know that necklace well.—it was sold here!"

M. Lantin, very nervous, asked:

"What's it worth?"

"Sir, I sold it for twenty-five thousand francs. I am willing to buy it back again for eighteen thousand,—if you can prove to me satisfactorily, according to legal prescriptions, how you came into possession of it."— This time, M. Lantin was simply paralyzed with astonishment. He said: "Well . . . but please look at it again, sir. I always thought until now that it was . . . was false."

The jeweler said:

"Will you give me your name, sir?"

"Certainly. My name is Lantin; I am employed at the office of the Minister of the Interior. I live at No. 16, Rue des Martyrs."

The merchant opened the register, looked, and said: "Yes; this necklace was sent to the address of Madame Lantin, 16 Rue des Martyrs, on July 20th, 1876."

And the two men looked into each other's eyes;—the clerk wild with surprise; the jeweler suspecting he had a thief before him.

The jeweler resumed:

"Will you be kind enough to leave this article here for twenty-four hours only—I'll give you a receipt."

M. Lantin stuttered: "Yes—ah! certainly." And he went out, folding up the receipt, which he put in his pocket.

Then he crossed the street, went the wrong way, found out his mistake, returned by way of the Tuileries, crossed the Seine, found out he had taken the wrong road again, and went back to the Champs-Elysées without being able to get one clear idea into his head. He tried to reason, to understand. His wife could never have bought so valuable an object as that. Certainly not. But then, it must have been a present! . . . A present from whom? What for?

He stopped and stood stock-still in the middle of the avenue.

A horrible suspicion swept across his mind. . . . She? . . . But then all those other pieces of jewelry must have been presents also! . . . Then it seemed to him that the ground was heaving under his feet; that a tree, right in front of him, was falling toward him; he thrust out his arms instinctively, and fell senseless.

He recovered his consciousness again in a drug-store to which some bystanders had carried him. He had them lead him home, and he locked himself into his room.

Until nightfall he cried without stopping, biting his handkerchief to keep himself from screaming out. Then, completely worn out with grief and fatigue, he went to bed, and slept a leaden sleep.

A ray of sunshine awakened him, and he rose and dressed himself slowly to go to the office. It was hard to have to work after such a shock. Then he reflected that he might be able to excuse himself to the superintendent, and he wrote to him. Then he remembered he would have to go back to the jeweler's; and shame made his face purple. He remained thinking a long time. Still he could not leave the necklace there; he put on his coat and went out.

It was a fine day; the sky extended all blue over the city, and seemed to make it smile. Strollers were walking aimlessly about, with their hands in their pockets.

Lantin thought as he watched them passing: "How lucky the men are who have fortunes! With money a man can even shake off grief:—you can go where you please—travel,—amuse yourself! Oh! if I were only rich!"

He suddenly discovered he was hungry,—not having eaten anything since the evening before. But his pockets were empty; and he remembered the necklace. Eighteen thousand francs! Eighteen thousand francs!—that was a sum—that was!

He made his way to the Rue de la Paix and began to walk backward and forward on the sidewalk in front of the store. Eighteen thousand francs! Twenty times he started to go in; but shame always kept him back.

Still he was hungry—very hungry,—and had not a cent. He made one brusque resolve, and crossed the street almost at a run, so as not to let himself have time to think over the matter; and he rushed into the jeweler's.

As soon as he saw him, the merchant hurried forward, and offered him a chair with smiling politeness. Even the clerks came forward to stare at Lantin, with gayety in their eyes and smiles about their lips.

The jeweler said: "Sir, I made inquiries; and if you are still so disposed, I am ready to pay you down the price I offered you."

The clerk stammered: "Why, yes—sir, certainly."

The jeweler took from a drawer eighteen big bills, counted them, and held them out to Lantin, who signed a little receipt, and thrust the money feverishly into his pocket.

Then, as he was on the point of leaving, he turned to the ever-smiling merchant, and said, lowering his eyes: "I have some—I have some other jewelry, which came to me in the same—from the same inheritance. Would you purchase them also from me?"

The merchant bowed, and answered: "Why, certainly, sir—certainly. . . ." One of the clerks rushed out to laugh at his ease; another kept blowing his nose as hard as he could.

Lantin, impassive, flushed and serious, said: "I will bring them to you."

And he hired a cab to get the jewelry.

When he returned to the store, an hour later, he had not yet breakfasted. They examined the jewelry,—piece by piece,—putting a value on each. Nearly all had been purchased from that very house.

Lantin, now, disputed estimates made, got angry, insisted on seeing the books, and talked louder and louder the higher the estimates grew.

The big diamond earrings were worth 20,000 francs; the bracelets, 35,000; the brooches, rings, and medallions, 16,000; a set of emeralds and sapphires, 14,000; solitaire, suspended to a gold neckchain, 40,000; the total value being estimated at 196,000 francs.

The merchant observed with mischievous good nature: "The person who owned these must have put all her savings into jewelry."

Lantin answered with gravity: "Perhaps that is as good a way of saving money as any other." And he went off, after having agreed with the merchant that an expert should make a counter-estimate for him the next day.

When he found himself in the street again, he looked at the Column Vendôme[1] with the desire to climb it, as if it were a May pole. He felt jolly enough to play leapfrog over the Emperor's head,—up there in the blue sky.

He breakfasted at Voisin's restaurant, and ordered wine at 20 francs a bottle.

Then he hired a cab and drove out to the Bois.[2] He looked at the carriages passing with a sort of contempt, and a wild desire to yell out to the passers-by: "I am rich, too—I am! I have 200,000 francs!"

The recollection of the office suddenly came back to him. He drove there, walked right into the superintendent's private room, and said: "Sir, I come to give you my resignation. I have just come into a fortune of *three* hundred thousand francs." Then he shook hands all round with his fellow-clerks; and told them all about his plans for a new career. Then he went to dinner at the Café Anglais.[3]

[1] Famous Parisian column at Place Vendôme, surmounted by statue of Napoleon I.

[2] Bois de Boulogne: a large park on the western fringe of Paris.

[3] One of the most famous and expensive Parisian restaurants during the reign of Napoleon III.

Finding himself seated at the same table with a man who seemed to him quite genteel, he could not resist the itching desire to tell him, with a certain air of coquetry, that he had just inherited a fortune of *four* hundred thousand francs.

For the first time in his life he went to the theatre without feeling bored by the performance; and he passed the night in revelry and debauch.

Six months after he married again. His second wife was the most upright of spouses, but had a terrible temper. She made his life very miserable.

1883

Translated by Lafcadio Hearn

PASTE

HENRY JAMES

'I'VE FOUND a lot more things,' her cousin said to her the day after the second funeral; 'they're up in her room—but they're things I wish *you'd* look at.'

The pair of mourners, sufficiently stricken, were in the garden of the vicarage together, before luncheon, waiting to be summoned to that meal, and Arthur Prime had still in his face the intention, she was moved to call it rather than the expression, of feeling something or other. Some such appearance was in itself of course natural within a week of his stepmother's death, within three of his father's; but what was most present to the girl, herself sensitive and shrewd, was that he seemed

From *The Soft Side* by Henry James. Reprinted by permission of Alexander R. James, Literary Executor.

somehow to brood without sorrow, to suffer without what she in her own case would have called pain. He turned away from her after this last speech—it was a good deal his habit to drop an observation and leave her to pick it up without assistance. If the vicar's widow, now in her turn finally translated, had not really belonged to him it was not for want of her giving herself, so far as he ever would take her; and she had lain for three days all alone at the end of the passage, in the great cold chamber of hospitality, the dampish, greenish room where visitors slept and where several of the ladies of the parish had, without effect, offered, in pairs and successions, piously to watch with her. His personal connection with the parish was now slighter than ever, and he had really not waited for this opportunity to show the ladies what he thought of them. She felt that she herself had, during her doleful month's leave from Bleet, where she was governess, rather taken her place in the same snubbed order; but it was presently, none the less, with a better little hope of coming in for some remembrance, some relic, that she went up to look at the things he had spoken of, the identity of which, as a confused cluster of bright objects on a table in the darkened room, shimmered at her as soon as she had opened the door.

They met her eyes for the first time, but in a moment, before touching them, she knew them as things of the theatre, as very much too fine to have been, with any verisimilitude, things of the vicarage. They were too dreadfully good to be true, for her aunt had had no jewels to speak of, and these were coronets and girdles, diamonds, rubies, and sapphires. Flagrant tinsel and glass, they looked strangely vulgar, but if, after the first queer shock of them, she found herself taking them up, it was for the very proof, never yet so distinct to her, of a far-off faded story. An honest widowed cleric with a small son and a large sense of Shakespeare had, on a brave latitude of habit as well as of taste—since it implied his having in very fact dropped deep into the 'pit'—conceived for an obscure actress, several years older than himself, an admiration of which the prompt offer of his reverend name and hortatory hand was the sufficiently candid sign. The response had perhaps, in those dim years, in the way of eccentricity, even bettered the proposal, and Charlotte, turning the tale over, had long since drawn from it a measure of the career renounced by the undistinguished *comédienne*—doubtless also tragic, or perhaps pantomimic, at a pinch—of her late uncle's dreams. This career could not have been eminent and must much more probably have been comfortless.

'You see what it is—old stuff of the time she never liked to mention.'

Our young woman gave a start; her companion had, after all, rejoined her and had apparently watched a moment her slightly scared recognition. 'So I said to myself,' she replied. Then, to show intelligence, yet keep clear of twaddle: 'How peculiar they look!'

'They look awful,' said Arthur Prime. 'Cheap gilt, diamonds as big as potatoes. These are trappings of a ruder age than ours. Actors do themselves better now.'

'Oh, now,' said Charlotte, not to be less knowing, 'actresses have real diamonds.'

'Some of them.' Arthur spoke drily.

'I mean the bad ones—the nobodies too.'

'Oh, some of the nobodies have the biggest. But mamma wasn't of that sort.'

'A nobody?' Charlotte risked.

'Not a nobody to whom somebody—well, not a nobody with diamonds. It isn't all worth, this trash, five pounds.'

There was something in the old gewgaws that spoke to her, and she continued to turn them over. 'They're relics. I think they have their melancholy and even their dignity.'

Arthur observed another pause. 'Do you care for them?' he then asked. 'I mean,' he promptly added, 'as a souvenir.'

'Of you?' Charlotte threw off.

'Of me? What have I to do with it? Of your poor dead aunt who was so kind to you,' he said with virtuous sternness.

'Well, I would rather have them than nothing.'

'Then please take them,' he returned in a tone of relief which expressed somehow more of the eager than of the gracious.

'Thank you.' Charlotte lifted two or three objects up and set them down again. Though they were lighter than the materials they imitated they were so much more extravagant that they struck her in truth as rather an awkward heritage, to which she might have preferred even a matchbox or a penwiper. They were indeed shameless pinchbeck. 'Had you any idea she had kept them?'

'I don't at all believe she *had* kept them or knew they were there, and I'm very sure my father didn't. They had quite equally worked off any tenderness for the connection. These odds and ends, which she thought had been given away or destroyed, had simply got thrust into a dark corner and been forgotten.'

Charlotte wondered. 'Where then did you find them?'

'In that old tin box'—and the young man pointed to the receptacle from which he had dislodged them and which stood on a neighbouring chair. 'It's rather a good box still, but I'm afraid I can't give you *that*.'

The girl gave the box no look; she continued only to look at the trinkets. 'What corner had she found?'

'She hadn't "found" it,' her companion sharply insisted; 'she had simply lost it. The whole thing had passed from her mind. The box was on the top shelf of the old schoolroom closet, which, until one put one's head into it from a step-ladder, looked, from below, quite cleared out. The door is narrow and the part of the closet to the left goes well into the wall. The box had stuck there for years.'

Charlotte was conscious of a mind divided and a vision vaguely troubled, and once more she took up two or three of the subjects of this revelation; a big bracelet in the form of a gilt serpent with many twists and beady eyes, a brazen belt studded with emeralds and rubies, a chain, of flamboyant architecture, to which, at the Theatre Royal, Little Peddlington, Hamlet's mother had probably been careful to attach the portrait of the successor to Hamlet's father.[1] 'Are you very sure they're not really worth something? Their mere weight alone—!' she vaguely observed, balancing a moment a royal diadem that might have crowned one of the creations of the famous Mrs. Jarley.[2]

But Arthur Prime, it was clear, had already thought the question over and found the answer easy. 'If they had been worth anything to speak of she would long ago have sold them. My father and she had unfortunately never been in a position to keep any considerable value locked up.' And while his companion took in the obvious force of this he went on with a flourish just marked enough not to escape her: 'If they're worth anything at all—why, you're only the more welcome to them.'

Charlotte had now in her hand a small bag of faded, figured silk—one of those antique conveniences that speak to us, in the terms of evaporated camphor and lavender, of the part they have played in some personal history; but, though she had for the first time drawn the string, she looked much more at the young man than at the questionable treasure it appeared to contain. 'I shall like them. They're all I have.'

'All you have—?'

'That belonged to her.'

He swelled a little, then looked about him as if to appeal—as against her avidity—to the whole poor place. 'Well, what else do you want?'

'Nothing. Thank you very much.' With which she bent her eyes

[1] After the death of her husband, Gertrude marries his brother Claudius in Shakespeare's *Hamlet* (1603).

[2] The owner and exhibitor of Jarley's Wax-Works in Charles Dickens's novel *The Old Curiosity Shop* (1841).

on the article wrapped, and now only exposed, in her superannuated satchel—a necklace of large pearls, such as might once have graced the neck of a provincial Ophelia[3] and borne company to a flaxen wig. 'This perhaps *is* worth something. Feel it.' And she passed him the necklace, the weight of which she had gathered for a moment into her hand.

He measured it in the same way with his own, but remained quite detached. 'Worth at most thirty shillings.'

'Not more?'

'Surely not if it's paste?'

'But *is* it paste?'

He gave a small sniff of impatience. 'Pearls nearly as big as filberts?'

'But they're heavy,' Charlotte declared.

'No heavier than anything else.' And he gave them back with an allowance for her simplicity. 'Do you imagine for a moment they're real?'

She studied them a little, feeling them, turning them round. 'Mightn't they possibly be?'

'Of that size—stuck away with that trash?'

'I admit it isn't likely,' Charlotte presently said. 'And pearls are so easily imitated.'

'That's just what—to a person who knows—they're not. These have no lustre, no play.'

'No—they *are* dull. They're opaque.'

'Besides,' he lucidly inquired, 'how could she ever have come by them?'

'Mightn't they have been a present?'

Arthur stared at the question as if it were almost improper. 'Because actresses are exposed—?' He pulled up, however, not saying to what, and before she could supply the deficiency had, with the sharp ejaculation of 'No, they mightn't!' turned his back on her and walked away. His manner made her feel that she had probably been wanting in tact, and before he returned to the subject, the last thing that evening, she had satisfied herself of the ground of his resentment. They had been talking of her departure the next morning, the hour of her train and the fly that would come for her, and it was precisely these things that gave him his effective chance. 'I really can't allow you to leave the house under the impression that my stepmother was at *any* time of her life the sort of person to allow herself to be approached—'

'With pearl necklaces and that sort of thing?' Arthur had made for

[3] A principal character in Shakespeare's *Hamlet.*

her somehow the difficulty that she couldn't show him she understood him without seeming pert.

It at any rate only added to his own gravity. 'That sort of thing, exactly.'

'I didn't think when I spoke this morning—but I see what you mean.'

'I mean that she was beyond reproach,' said Arthur Prime.

'A hundred times yes.'

'Therefore if she couldn't, out of her slender gains, ever have paid for a row of pearls—'

'She couldn't, in that atmosphere, ever properly have had one? Of course she couldn't. I've seen perfectly since our talk,' Charlotte went on, 'that that string of beads isn't even, as an imitation, very good. The little clasp itself doesn't seem even gold. With false pearls, I suppose,' the girl mused, 'it naturally wouldn't be.'

'The whole thing's rotten paste,' her companion returned as if to have done with it. 'If it were *not,* and she had kept it all these years hidden—'

'Yes?' Charlotte sounded as he paused.

'Why, I shouldn't know what to think!'

'Oh, I see.' She had met him with a certain blankness, but adequately enough, it seemed, for him to regard the subject as dismissed; and there was no reversion to it between them before, on the morrow, when she had with difficulty made a place for them in her trunk, she carried off these florid survivals.

At Bleet she found small occasion to revert to them and, in an air charged with such quite other references, even felt, after she had laid them away, much enshrouded, beneath various piles of clothing, as if they formed a collection not wholly without its note of the ridiculous. Yet she was never, for the joke, tempted to show them to her pupils, though Gwendolen and Blanche, in particular, always wanted, on her return, to know what she had brought back; so that without an accident by which the case was quite changed they might have appeared to enter on a new phase of interment. The essence of the accident was the sudden illness, at the last moment, of Lady Bobby, whose advent had been so much counted on to spice the five days' feast laid out for the coming of age of the eldest son of the house; and its equally marked effect was the despatch of a pressing message, in quite another direction, to Mrs. Guy, who, could she by a miracle be secured—she was always engaged ten parties deep—might be trusted to supply, it was believed, an element of exuberance scarcely less active. Mrs. Guy was already known to several of the visitors already on the scene, but she was not yet known to our young lady, who found her, after many wires and counterwires had at last determined the triumph of her arrival, a strange, charming little red-haired, black-dressed woman, with the face of a baby and the authority of a commodore. She took on the spot the discreet, the exceptional young governess into the confidence of her designs and, still more, of her doubts; intimating that it was a policy she almost always promptly pursued.

'To-morrow and Thursday are all right,' she said frankly to Charlotte on the second day, 'but I'm not half satisfied with Friday.'

'What improvement then do you suggest?'

'Well, my strong point, you know, is *tableaux vivants*.'

'Charming. And what is your favourite character?'

'Boss!' said Mrs. Guy with decision; and it was very markedly under that ensign that she had, within a few hours, completely planned her campaign and recruited her troop. Every word she uttered was to the point, but none more so than, after a general survey of their equipment, her final inquiry of Charlotte. She had been looking about, but half appeased, at the muster of decoration and drapery. 'We shall be dull. We shall want more colour. You've nothing else?'

Charlotte had a thought. 'No—I've *some* things.'

'Then why don't you bring them?'

The girl hesitated. 'Would you come to my room?'

'No,' said Mrs. Guy—'bring them to-night to mine.'

So Charlotte, at the evening's end, after candlesticks had flickered through brown old passages bedward, arrived at her friend's door with the burden of her aunt's relics. But she promptly expressed a fear. 'Are they too garish?'

When she had poured them out on the sofa Mrs. Guy was but a minute, before the glass, in clapping on the diadem. 'Awfully jolly—we can do Ivanhoe![4]'

'But they're only glass and tin.'

'Larger than life they are, *rather!*—which is exactly what, for tableaux, is wanted. *Our* jewels, for historic scenes, don't tell—the real thing falls short. Rowena must have rubies as big as eggs. Leave them with me,' Mrs. Guy continued—'they'll inspire me. Good-night.'

The next morning she was in fact—yet very strangely—inspired. 'Yes, *I'll* do Rowena. But I don't, my dear, understand.'

'Understand what?'

Mrs. Guy gave a very lighted stare. 'How you come to have such things.'

[4] Novel (1819) by Sir Walter Scott, of which Rowena is the heroine.

Poor Charlotte smiled. 'By inheritance.'

'Family jewels?'

'They belonged to my aunt, who died some months ago. She was on the stage a few years in early life, and these are a part of her trappings.'

'She left them to you?'

'No; my cousin, her stepson, who naturally has no use for them, gave them to me for remembrance of her. She was a dear kind thing, always so nice to me, and I was fond of her.'

Mrs. Guy had listened with visible interest. 'But it's *he* who must be a dear kind thing!'

Charlotte wondered. 'You think so?'

'Is *he,*' her friend went on, 'also "always so nice" to you?'

The girl, at this, face to face there with the brilliant visitor in the deserted breakfast-room, took a deeper sounding. 'What is it?'

'Don't you know?'

Something came over her. 'The pearls——?' But the question fainted on her lips.

'Doesn't *he* know?'

Charlotte found herself flushing. 'They're *not* paste?'

'Haven't you looked at them?'

She was conscious of two kinds of embarrassment. '*You* have?'

'Very carefully.'

'And they're real?'

Mrs. Guy became slightly mystifying and returned for all answer: 'Come again, when you've done with the children, to my room.'

Our young woman found she had done with the children, that morning, with a promptitude that was a new joy to them, and when she reappeared before Mrs. Guy this lady had already encircled a plump white throat with the only ornament, surely, in all the late Mrs. Prime's—the effaced Miss Bradshaw's—collection, in the least qualified to raise a question. If Charlotte had never yet once, before the glass, tied the string of pearls about her own neck, this was because she had been capable of no such condescension to approved 'imitation'; but she had now only to look at Mrs. Guy to see that, so disposed, the ambiguous objects might have passed for frank originals. 'What in the world have you done to them?'

'Only handled them, understood them, admired them, and put them on. That's what pearls want; they want to be worn—it wakes them up. They're alive, don't you see? How *have* these been treated? They must have been buried, ignored, despised. They were half dead. Don't you *know* about pearls?' Mrs. Guy threw off as she fondly fingered the necklace.

'How *should* I? Do *you?*'

'Everything. These were simply asleep, and from the moment I really touched them—well,' said their wearer lovingly, 'it only took one's eye!'

'It took more than mine—though I did just wonder; and than Arthur's,' Charlotte brooded. She found herself almost panting. 'Then their value——?'

'Oh, their value's excellent.'

The girl, for a deep moment, took another plunge into the wonder, the beauty and mystery, of them. 'Are you *sure?*'

Her companion wheeled round for impatience. 'Sure? For what kind of an idiot, my dear, do you take me?'

It was beyond Charlotte Prime to say. 'For the same kind as Arthur—and as myself,' she could only suggest. 'But my cousin didn't know. He thinks they're worthless.'

'Because of the rest of the lot? Then your cousin's an ass. But what—if, as I understood you, he gave them to you—has he to do with it?'

'Why, if he gave them to me as worthless and they turn out precious—'

'You must give them back? I don't see that—if he was such a fool. He took the risk.'

Charlotte fed, in fancy, on the pearls, which, decidedly, were exquisite, but which at the present moment somehow presented themselves much more as Mrs. Guy's than either as Arthur's or as her own. 'Yes—he did take it; even after I had distinctly hinted to him that they looked to me different from the other pieces.'

'Well, then!' said Mrs. Guy with something more than triumph—with a positive odd relief.

But it had the effect of making our young woman think with more intensity. 'Ah, you see he thought they couldn't be different, because—so peculiarly—they shouldn't be.'

'Shouldn't? I don't understand.'

'Why, how would she have got them?'—so Charlotte candidly put it.

'She? Who?' There was a capacity in Mrs. Guy's tone for a sinking of persons—!

'Why, the person I told you of: his stepmother, my uncle's wife—among whose poor old things, extraordinarily thrust away and out of sight, he happened to find them.'

Mrs. Guy came a step nearer to the effaced Miss Bradshaw. 'Do you mean she may have stolen them?'

'No. But she had been an actress.'

'Oh, well then,' cried Mrs. Guy, 'wouldn't that be just how?'

'Yes, except that she wasn't at all a brilliant one, nor in receipt of large pay.' The girl even threw off a nervous joke. 'I'm afraid she couldn't have been our Rowena.'

Mrs. Guy took it up. 'Was she very ugly?'

'No. She may very well, when young, have looked rather nice.'

'Well, then!' was Mrs. Guy's sharp comment and fresh triumph.

'You mean it was a present? That's just what he so dislikes the idea of her having received—a present from an admirer capable of going such lengths.'

'Because she wouldn't have taken it for nothing? *Speriamo*[5]—that she wasn't a brute. The "length" her admirer went was the length of a whole row. Let us hope she was just a little kind!'

'Well,' Charlotte went on, 'that she was "kind" might seem to be shown by the fact that neither her husband, nor his son, nor I, his niece, knew or dreamed of her possessing anything so precious; by her having kept the gift all the rest of her life beyond discovery—out of sight and protected from suspicion.'

'As if, you mean'—Mrs. Guy was quick—'she had been wedded to it and yet was ashamed of it? Fancy,' she laughed while she manipulated the rare beads, 'being ashamed of *these!*'

'But you see she had married a clergyman.'

'Yes, she must have been "rum." But at any rate he had married *her*. What did he suppose?'

'Why, that she had never been of the sort by whom such offerings are encouraged.'

'Ah, my dear, the sort by whom they are *not*——!' But Mrs. Guy caught herself up. 'And her stepson thought the same?'

'Overwhelmingly.'

'Was he, then, if only her stepson——'

'So fond of her as that comes to? Yes; he had never known, consciously, his real mother, and, without children of her own, she was very patient and nice with him. And *I* liked her so,' the girl pursued, 'that at the end of ten years, in so strange a manner, to "give her away"——'

'Is impossible to you? Then don't!' said Mrs. Guy with decision.

[5] Let us hope.

'Ah, but if they're real I can't keep them!' Charlotte, with her eyes on them, moaned in her impatience. 'It's too difficult.'

'Where's the difficulty, if he has such sentiments that he would rather sacrifice the necklace than admit it, with the presumption it carries with it, to be genuine? You've only to be silent.'

'And keep it? How can *I* ever wear it?'

'You'd have to hide it, like your aunt?' Mrs. Guy was amused. 'You can easily sell it.'

Her companion walked round her for a look at the affair from behind. The clasp was certainly, doubtless intentionally, misleading, but everything else was indeed lovely. 'Well, I must think. Why didn't *she* sell them?' Charlotte broke out in her trouble.

Mrs. Guy had an instant answer. 'Doesn't that prove what they secretly recalled to her? You've only to be silent!' she ardently repeated.

'I must think—I must think!'

Mrs. Guy stood with her hands attached but motionless.

'Then you want them back?'

As if with the dread of touching them Charlotte retreated to the door. 'I'll tell you to-night.'

'But may I wear them?'

'Meanwhile?'

'This evening—at dinner.'

It was the sharp, selfish pressure of this that really, on the spot, determined the girl; but for the moment, before closing the door on the question, she only said: 'As you like!'

They were busy much of the day with preparation and rehearsal, and at dinner, that evening, the concourse of guests was such that a place among them for Miss Prime failed to find itself marked. At the time the company rose she was therefore alone in the schoolroom, where, towards eleven o'clock, she received a visit from Mrs. Guy. This lady's white shoulders heaved, under the pearls, with an emotion that the very red lips which formed, as if for the full effect, the happiest opposition of colour, were not slow to translate. 'My dear, you should have seen the sensation—they've had a success!'

Charlotte, dumb a moment, took it all in. 'It *is* as if they knew it—they're more and more alive. But so much the worse for both of us! I can't,' she brought out with an effort, 'be silent.'

'You mean to return them?'

'If I don't I'm a thief.'

Mrs. Guy gave her a long, hard look: what was decidedly not of the baby in Mrs. Guy's face was a certain air of established habit in the eyes. Then, with a sharp little jerk of her head and a backward reach of her bare beautiful arms, she undid the clasp and, taking off the necklace, laid it on the table. 'If you do, you're a goose.'

'Well, of the two—!' said our young lady, gathering it up with a sigh. And as if to get it, for the pang it gave, out of sight as soon as possible, she shut it up, clicking the lock, in the drawer of her own little table; after which, when she turned again, her companion, without it, looked naked and plain. 'But what will you say?' it then occurred to her to demand.

'Downstairs—to explain?' Mrs. Guy was, after all, trying at least to keep her temper. 'Oh, I'll put on something else and say that clasp is broken. And you won't of course name *me* to him,' she added.

'As having undeceived me? No—I'll say that, looking at the thing more carefully, it's my own private idea.'

'And does he know how little you really know?'

'As an expert—surely. And he has much, always, the conceit of his own opinion.'

'Then he won't believe you—as he so hates to. He'll stick to his judgment and maintain his gift, and we shall have the darlings back!' With which reviving assurance Mrs. Guy kissed her good-night.

She was not, however, to be gratified or justified by any prompt event, for, whether or no paste entered into the composition of the ornament in question, Charlotte shrank from the temerity of despatching it to town[6] by post. Mrs. Guy was thus disappointed of the hope of seeing the business settled—'by return,' she had seemed to expect—before the end of the revels. The revels, moreover, rising to a frantic pitch, pressed for all her attention, and it was at last only in the general confusion of leave-taking that she made, parenthetically, a dash at her young friend.

'Come, what will you take for them?'

'The pearls? Ah, you'll have to treat with my cousin.'

Mrs. Guy, with quick intensity, lent herself. 'Where then does he live?'

'In chambers in the Temple.[7] You can find him.'

'But what's the use, if *you* do neither one thing nor the other?'

'Oh, I *shall* do the "other," ' Charlotte said; 'I'm only waiting till I

[6] London.

[7] Inns of Court, centers of the legal profession.

go up. You want them so awfully?' She curiously, solemnly again, sounded her.

'I'm dying for them. There's a special charm in them— I don't know what it is: they tell so their history.'

'But what do you know of that?'

'Just what they themselves say. It's all *in* them—and it comes out. They breathe a tenderness—they have the white glow of it. My dear,' hissed Mrs. Guy in supreme confidence and as she buttoned her glove—'they're things of love!'

'Oh!' our young woman vaguely exclaimed.

'They're things of passion!'

'Mercy!' she gasped, turning short off. But these words remained, though indeed their help was scarce needed, Charlotte being in private face to face with a new light, as she by this time felt she must call it, on the dear dead, kind, colourless lady whose career had turned so sharp a corner in the middle. The pearls had quite taken their place as a revelation. She might have received them for nothing—admit that; but she couldn't have kept them so long and so unprofitably hidden, couldn't have enjoyed them only in secret, for nothing; and she had mixed them, in her reliquary, with false things, in order to put curiosity and detection off the scent. Over this strange fact poor Charlotte interminably mused: it became more touching, more attaching for her than she could now confide to any ear. How bad, or how happy—in the sophisticated sense of Mrs. Guy and the young man at the Temple—the effaced Miss Bradshaw must have been to have had to be so mute! The little governess at Bleet put on the necklace now in secret sessions; she wore it sometimes under her dress; she came to feel, verily, a haunting passion for it. Yet in her penniless state she would have parted with it for money; she gave herself also to dreams of what in this direction it would do for her. The sophistry of her so often saying to herself that Arthur had after all definitely pronounced her welcome to any gain from his gift that might accrue—this trick remained innocent, as she perfectly knew it for what it was. Then there was always the possibility of his—as she could only picture it—rising to the occasion. Mightn't he have a grand magnanimous moment?—mightn't he just say: 'Oh, of course I couldn't have afforded to let you have it if I had known; but since you *have* got it, and have made out the truth by your own wit, I really can't screw myself down to the shabbiness of taking it back'?

She had, as it proved, to wait a long time—to wait till, at the end of several months, the great house of Bleet had, with due deliberation, for the season, transferred itself to town; after which, however, she fairly snatched at her first freedom to knock, dressed in her best and armed with her disclosure, at the door of her doubting kinsman. It was still with doubt and not quite with the face she had hoped that he listened to her story. He had turned pale, she thought, as she produced the necklace, and he appeared, above all, disagreeably affected. Well, perhaps there was reason, she more than ever remembered; but what on earth was one, in close touch with the fact, to do? She had laid the pearls on his table, where, without his having at first put so much as a finger to them, they met his hard, cold stare.

'I don't believe in them,' he simply said at last.

'That's exactly, then,' she returned with some spirit, 'what I wanted to hear!'

She fancied that at this his colour changed; it was indeed vivid to her afterwards—for she was to have a long recall of the scene—that she had made him quite angrily flush. 'It's a beastly unpleasant imputation, you know!'—and he walked away from her as he had always walked at the vicarage.

'It's none of *my* making, I'm sure,' said Charlotte Prime. 'If you're afraid to believe they're real——'

'Well?'—and he turned, across the room, sharp round at her.

'Why, it's not my fault.'

He said nothing more, for a moment, on this; he only came back to the table. 'They're what I originally said they were. They're rotten paste.'

'Then I may keep them?'

'No. I want a better opinion.'

'Than your own?'

'Than *your* own.' He dropped on the pearls another queer stare, then, after a moment, bringing himself to touch them, did exactly what she had herself done in the presence of Mrs. Guy at Bleet—gathered them together, marched off with them to a drawer, put them in and clicked the key. 'You say I'm afraid,' he went on as he again met her; 'but I shan't be afraid to take them to Bond Street.[8]'

'And if the people say they're real——?'

He hesitated—then had his strangest manner. 'They won't say it! They shan't!'

There was something in the way he brought it out that deprived poor Charlotte, as she was perfectly aware, of any manner at all. 'Oh!'

[8] Fashionable London shopping street.

she simply sounded, as she had sounded for her last word to Mrs. Guy; and, within a minute, without more conversation, she had taken her departure.

A fortnight later she received a communication from him, and towards the end of the season one of the entertainments in Eaton Square was graced by the presence of Mrs. Guy. Charlotte was not at dinner, but she came down afterwards, and this guest, on seeing her, abandoned a very beautiful young man on purpose to cross and speak to her. The guest had on a lovely necklace and had apparently not lost her habit of overflowing with the pride of such ornaments.

'Do you see?' She was in high joy.

They were indeed splendid pearls—so far as poor Charlotte could feel that she knew, after what had come and gone, about such mysteries. Charlotte had a sickly smile. 'They're almost as fine as Arthur's.'

'Almost? Where, my dear, are your eyes? They *are* "Arthur's!" ' After which, to meet the flood of crimson that accompanied her young friend's start: 'I tracked them—after your folly, and, by miraculous luck, recognised them in the Bond Street window to which he had disposed of them.'

'*Disposed* of them?' the girl gasped. 'He wrote me that I had insulted his mother and that the people had shown him he was right—had pronounced them utter paste.'

Mrs. Guy gave a stare. 'Ah, I told you he wouldn't bear it! No. But I had, I assure you,' she wound up, 'to drive my bargain!'

Charlotte scarce heard or saw; she was full of her private wrong. 'He wrote me,' she panted, 'that he had smashed them.'

Mrs. Guy could only wonder and pity. 'He's really morbid!' But it was not quite clear which of the pair she pitied; though Charlotte felt really morbid too after they had separated and she found herself full of thought. She even went the length of asking herself what sort of a bargain Mrs. Guy had driven and whether the marvel of the recognition in Bond Street had been a veracious account of the matter. Hadn't she perhaps in truth dealt with Arthur directly? It came back to Charlotte almost luridly that she had had his address.

1899

DISCUSSION QUESTIONS

1. In each story, seemingly false jewelry turns out to be genuine. In which work is the event handled more plausibly? Why?

2. Compare and contrast Arthur's and Lantin's situations and characters. How does each respond to the revelation that the jewelry is genuine? In what ways, if any, are we prepared for their reactions?

3. Although Arthur is very eager to believe his stepmother to have been "beyond reproach," at the outset of the story we see him, through Charlotte's *point of view,* as an insensitive, even callous mourner of his stepmother. Reconcile these two sides of Arthur's personality.

4. What specifically makes Arthur decide to have the pearls appraised when all along he has called them "rotten paste"?

5. Why does Charlotte seem to "dread . . . touching" (page 215) the pearls after Mrs. Guy has convinced her of their genuineness? Why does she later "put on the necklace" secretly and develop "a haunting passion for it" (page 217)? Explain Charlotte's "new light" (page 217) and the change she undergoes. Does Lantin also undergo a change in his attitude toward his dead wife? Explain.

6. Since "in her penniless state she would have parted with it for money" (page 217), why does Charlotte, nevertheless, return the necklace to Arthur? What specifically brings about her decision? Do you agree with it? Does James agree with her decision? Support your answer with evidence.

7. What is Charlotte's social position and how does it affect her relationship with Arthur and Mrs. Guy? Give examples.

8. Explain the "two kinds of embarrassment" of which Charlotte becomes "conscious" (page 212).

9. On page 214, how could Mrs. Prime have been *kind* to her admirer in Mrs. Guy's sense of the word? How would she have been *kind* to her family? How might the second form of kindness prove the first?

10. By what means does each author keep the reader as much in the dark about the genuineness of the jewelry as is each *protagonist?* Cite examples. Which author uses the more effective technique? Explain.

11. In what way is our inner view of Lantin more limited than our inner view of Charlotte? Cite examples. What effect has this difference

on our conception of the two characters? By what means could Maupassant have achieved as extensive an inner view as James? What effect would this change have had on his story?

12. Which author's ending do you prefer? Why? Which story do you prefer? Why?

ANALYSIS AND APPLICATION

1. Try to rearrange the series of verbs in each of the following sentences from "Paste" without perverting their meaning. Be prepared to justify your new order.

a. "Only handled them, understood them, admired them, and put them on." (page 212)

b. "They must have been buried, ignored, despised." (page 212)

2. Identify all transitions in paragraph 8 on page 216 of "Paste." Try to replace each transition with an equally effective substitute.

3. Compare each of the following modified versions with its original in "The Jewelry." Which version is more effective? Why?

a. Having afterward come to Paris with her mother, she made regular visits to several *bourgeois* families of the neighborhood, in hopes of being able to get her daughter married.

"Afterward she had come to Paris with her mother, who made regular visits to several *bourgeois* families of the neighborhood, in hopes of being able to get her daughter married." (page 197)

b. Having been carried to a drug-store by some bystanders, he recovered his consciousness again.

"He recovered his consciousness again in a drug-store to which some bystanders had carried him." (page 201)

BOULE DE SUIF

GUY DE MAUPASSANT

For several consecutive days, the remnants of a shattered army had been passing through the town. They were no longer a disciplined body, but a disorganized rabble. Their beards were unkempt and neglected, their uniforms ragged, and the men, separated from their colours and their regiments, marched listlessly. All of them seemed crushed and worn out, incapable of thought or initiative. They marched on from mere force of habit and, as soon as a man stopped moving, he collapsed. The bulk of them were civilians who had been called to the colours, easy-going citizens, who seemed bent down by the weight of their rifles, or undersized conscripts of the last line, quick of apprehension,

From *Short Stories* by Guy de Maupassant, translated by Marjorie Laurie, published by T. Werner Laurie. Reprinted with the permission of The Bodley Head.

as prone to panic as to enthusiasm, as ready for attack as for flight. Some regular soldiers in red breeches, sole survivors of a division ground to powder in a great battle, and some sombre gunners, mingled with these nondescript infantry men, and here and there appeared the flashing helmet of a booted dragoon, with difficulty keeping pace with the more lightly shod foot-soldier.

Detachments of *francs-tireurs,*[1] who looked like bandits but bore grandiloquent names, such as 'Avengers of Defeat,' 'Citizens of the Grave,' 'The Brotherhood of Death,' passed through in their turn. Their leaders, all flannel and gold lace and armed to the teeth, were retired drapers, corn chandlers, dealers in soap and tallow, who had turned soldier by force of circumstance, and had been elected officers by virtue of their money or their moustaches. In loud, braggart tones, they discussed plans of campaign, as though they alone were sustaining France in her death agony upon their vainglorious shoulders. But they went in fear of their own men, who were a ruffianly gang and, though often desperately brave, could not be withheld from looting and debauchery.

There was a rumour that the Prussians were about to enter Rouen. The National Guard, who, for the last two months, had been engaged in reconnoitring cautiously the neighbouring woods, sometimes shooting their own sentries, and preparing for action every time a rabbit stirred in a bush, had returned to their firesides. Their arms, their uniforms, all the apparatus of slaughter, with which they had formerly terrorized every milestone within a radius of three leagues, had suddenly vanished.

The last of the French army had just crossed the Seine, making for Pont-Audemer by way of Saint-Sever and Bourg-Achard. The rear was brought up by the general marching on foot between two aides-de-camp. In despair, unable to attempt anything with this medley of broken units, he felt overwhelmed in the utter ruin of a people, hitherto accustomed to victory, but now, despite its heroic prestige, disastrously defeated.

And now, a deep calm, an atmosphere of shuddering, silent apprehension brooded over the city. Many a plump citizen, whose manhood had been sapped by commerce, anxiously awaited the conquerors, in dread lest his spits and his big kitchen knives should be regarded as weapons. Life seemed at a standstill. The shops were closed; the streets silent. Here and there a stray citizen, awed by the stillness, hurried along, keeping close to the wall. Such was the agony of suspense that the arrival of the enemy was looked forward to as a relief.

[1] Rifle clubs and unofficial military societies that were organized into small guerrilla units during the Franco-Prussian War (1870–1871).

On the afternoon of the day following the departure of the French troops, some Uhlans, sprung no one knew whence, galloped through the town. A little later, dark masses of troops came pouring down the hill of St. Catherine, while two further torrents of invaders streamed along the roads from Darnetal and Boisguillaume. The advance guards of the three corps effected a well-timed junction in the square before the town hall, and down every street leading to the square the German army poured in, battalion after battalion, while the paved streets rang under their hard, measured tread.

Orders, shouted in strange guttural voices, resounded along the walls of houses, which seemed dead and deserted, though behind the closed shutters eyes were spying upon the victors, who by the rules of war were masters of the city, masters of the property and lives of all. In their darkened rooms, the inhabitants had succumbed to that dazed condition produced by natural cataclysms, devastating convulsions of the earth, against which neither strength nor wisdom avails. This sensation is experienced whenever the established order of things is overturned, when no feeling of security remains, and all that is usually protected by the laws of men or nature is at the mercy of blind and brutal force. The earthquake burying a whole nation beneath the ruins of their houses; the river bursting its banks, drowning peasants and their cattle, tearing rafters from roofs and sweeping all away; the triumphant army slaughtering all who resist, making prisoners of the rest, pillaging in the name of the sword and giving thanks to God amid the roar of cannon: all alike are terrifying visitations which shatter our belief in eternal justice and the confidence we have been taught to place in divine protection and human reason.

Small squads of men knocked at the door of every house and disappeared inside. This was the occupation, the sequel of the invasion. It was now the duty of the vanquished to show themselves courteous to the conquerors.

When the first panic had subsided, a new sort of calm succeeded. In many families, the Prussian officer sat at table with his hosts. If he happened to be a well-bred man, he politely deplored the woes of France and expressed his personal repugnance to the war. His hosts were grateful for these generous sentiments, and, besides, any day they might need his protection. If they humoured him, they might perhaps have fewer men billeted on them. Why should they hurt the man's feelings when they were entirely in his power? To do so would be an act of foolhardiness rather than courage, and foolhardiness is no longer a defect in the character of the burgesses of Rouen, however it might have been in the days of the heroic defences which made their city illustrious. Eventually, appealing to the traditions of French urbanity, they reasoned that it was quite permissible to treat the alien soldier with courtesy within doors, provided that there was no fraternization in public. Though they did not recognize him in the street, at home they were ready to talk to him, and the German soldier sat longer and longer every evening, warming himself at the domestic hearth.

Little by little, the town itself began to resume its normal appearance. For the present, the French population remained indoors, but the streets were swarming with Prussian soldiers. After all, the officers of the Blue Hussars, arrogantly trailing their great sabres along the pavement, did not treat the plain townsmen so very much more contemptuously than did their own light cavalry officers, who had sat drinking in the same cafés the year before.

Yet for all that there was something in the air, some indefinable and subtle quality, a strange and intolerable atmosphere, a diffused exhalation—the effluvium of invasion. It penetrated into private houses and public places, tainting the food, producing an unhomelike feeling, as of exile in distant lands among tribes of hostile savages.

The victorious army demanded money, vast sums of money. The inhabitants went on paying up, and indeed they could afford to do so. But the wealthier he is, the more keenly the Norman trader feels the smallest sacrifice, the transfer of the least fraction of his property into the hands of another.

It was true that a few miles down the Seine, in the vicinity of Croisset, Dieppedalle or Biessart, bargemen and fishermen often brought up from the bottom the bloated corpse of a German soldier in uniform, who had been stabbed or kicked to death, or pushed into the water off a bridge, or had had his head battered in by a stone. The mud of the river engulfed the victims of these surreptitious acts of vengeance, savage yet justifiable, these deeds of obscure heroism, these secret assaults, more perilous than open battle and without the meed of fame. Hatred of the foreigner will always nerve some valiant soul to die for an idea.

At length, finding that the invaders, although subjecting the town to rigorous discipline, had not perpetrated any of the atrocities with which rumour had credited them throughout the whole course of their triumphant march, the population plucked up courage and the tradesmen's business instincts began to revive. Some of them had weighty interests at Havre, which was still held by the French, and were anxious to make an attempt to reach that port, travelling overland to Dieppe and embarking there. Through the influence of German officers, whose acquaintance they had made, a permit for leaving Rouen could be obtained from the general in command.

A large four-horse coach was accordingly engaged for the journey; ten persons had reserved seats in it, and it was agreed to set out one Tuesday morning, before daybreak, so as to avoid exciting attention. For some time there had been a hard frost; on the Monday afternoon great black clouds gathered from the north, and snow fell incessantly all that evening and the following night.

At half-past four in the morning, the travellers met in the yard of the Hôtel de Normandie, where they were to take the coach. They were still half asleep and shivered with cold under their wraps. It was too dark for them to see one another clearly. Under their accumulations of heavy winter clothes, they all resembled corpulent priests in long cassocks. Two men, however, recognized each other; a third joined them, and they entered into conversation.

'I have brought my wife,' said one.

'So have I.'

'And I, too.'

The first speaker added: 'We don't intend returning to Rouen. If the Prussians advance on Havre we shall make our way to England.'

All three were of the same pattern and had the same plans.

Meanwhile, there was no sign of the horses. An ostler carrying a little lantern emerged from time to time from one mysterious door only to disappear through another. Horses' hoofs could be heard stamping on the ground, the noise muffled by stable litter, and from the far end of the building came the voice of a man talking to the animals and swearing. The tinkling of little bells proclaimed that the harness was being got ready, and this sound soon developed into a clear, continuous jingling, in rhythm with the horses' movements, now and then ceasing, only to begin again with a sudden jerk, to the accompaniment of the dull clang of an iron-shod hoof on the stable floor. The door suddenly closed and everything was still. The half-frozen travellers stopped talking and stood there stiff and motionless. A curtain of glistening snowflakes descended towards the earth, veiling every human form and covering inanimate objects with an icy fleece. In the intense stillness of the town, plunged in the deep repose of winter, no sound was audible save that vague, indefinable, fluttering whisper of the falling snow, felt rather than heard, the mingling of airy atoms, which seemed to fill all space and envelop the whole world.

The man with the lantern reappeared, dragging along by a rope a dejected and reluctant horse. He put the horse alongside the carriage-pole and spent a long time adjusting the harness, for he could only use one hand, as the other held the light. As he was going off to fetch the second horse, he noticed the travellers all standing there motionless and already white with snow.

'Why don't you get inside the coach?' he said. 'You would at least be under cover.'

Apparently this had not occurred to them, and they made a rush for the coach. The three husbands installed their wives at the far end and seated themselves beside them. The other veiled and vague forms took the remaining places without uttering a word.

Their feet sank into the straw which covered the floor. The ladies at the far end had brought little copper foot-warmers with a chemical preparation of charcoal which they lighted, and for some time, in subdued voices, they dwelt upon the advantages of these apparatuses, assuring one another of facts of which they had all long been aware.

At last the coach was ready. It had a team of six horses instead of four in consideration of the bad state of the roads. A voice from without asked: 'Is every one in?' A voice from within replied: 'Yes,' and they set off.

The progress of the coach was laborious and very slow. The wheels sank into the snow. Every joint in the whole structure creaked and moaned. The smoking horses slipped and panted, the driver's immense whip cracked incessantly, flickering in all directions, now tying itself into knots and uncoiling itself again like a slender snake, now stinging a bulging hind quarter and inciting its owner to more strenuous efforts. Imperceptibly, day began to dawn. The fall of ethereal snowflakes, which one of the travellers, a true-born native of Rouen, had compared to a shower of cotton, had ceased. A livid light filtered through the dense and lowering clouds, whose blackness set off the dazzling whiteness of the landscape. Here and there stood out a row of tall, frosted trees, or a cottage under a hood of snow.

Inside the carriage, the passengers scrutinized one another inquisitively by the melancholy light of dawn.

Dozing opposite each other in the best places at the end sat Monsieur and Madame Loiseau, wholesale wine merchants of the Rue Grand-pont. Originally a clerk in an office, after his employer's bankruptcy, Loiseau had bought the business and made a fortune. He sold very bad wine at very low prices to small retailers in country places. He was regarded by his friends and acquaintances as a knowing rascal and a true Norman, a jovial fellow, up to every dodge. His reputation for sharp practice was so notorious that one evening at a party at the Prefecture, Monsieur Tournel, a local celebrity, author of some songs and stories and a man of shrewd and caustic wit, proposed to the ladies, who seemed to him somewhat drowsy, a game of *Loiseau vole,* 'The bird steals away.' The jest flew through the Prefect's drawing-rooms and thence to all the other drawing-rooms in the town, and for a month it set the whole province laughing. Loiseau himself was famous for practical jokes of all kinds, good-natured and otherwise, so that no one mentioned his name without adding: 'That fellow Loiseau is really priceless.' He was short, his stomach bulged like a balloon and was surmounted by a red face fringed with grizzled whiskers. His wife, a tall, stout, determined woman, loud-voiced and positive, was the methodical and financial factor in the business, while he brought to it his own exuberant vitality.

Next to them, with the dignity of a higher class, sat Monsieur Carré-Lamadon, a man of good standing in the cotton business, owner of three spinning-mills, officer of the Legion of Honour and member of the Conseil Général.[2] Under the Empire,[3] he posed as leader of a benevolent opposition, solely in order to sell at a higher price his desertion to the side against which he had fought, though always, as he said, with weapons of courtesy. Madame Carré-Lamadon was much younger than her husband. She had been a great comfort to officers of good family, garrisoned at Rouen. A slight, dainty figure, muffled in furs, she sat opposite her husband, staring disconsolately at the deplorable interior of the coach.

Their neighbours were the Count and Countess Hubert de Bréville, who bore one of the oldest and most aristocratic names in Normandy. The count, an old nobleman of dignified demeanour, took pains to accentuate by tricks of the toilet his natural likeness to King Henry IV.[4] According to a legend of which the family were very proud, that monarch had seduced a Madame de Bréville, and in return, had made her husband a count and governor of a province. He was associated with Monsieur Carré-Lamadon on the Conseil Général, and was the local representative of the Orléanist party.[5] The story of his marriage with the daughter of a petty shipowner of Nantes had always been a mystery. But thanks to her stately air, her genius for entertaining, and the rumour that one of the sons of Louis Philippe[6] had been her lover, all

[2] General Council, the principal governing body of the *département* (French administrative district).

[3] Reign of Napoleon III (1852–1870).

[4] Known as Henry of Navarre, King of France (1589–1610).

[5] Supporters of the Count of Paris, a descendant of the Duke of Orleans (younger brother of Louis XIV), as constitutional monarch.

[6] King of France (1830–1848), called the Citizen King.

the local *noblesse* paid court to her. Her *salon* held its own as the first in the neighbourhood. Access to it was not easy, and it was the only drawing-room where old-world courtesy survived. The fortune of the Brévilles, all in landed estate, was said to yield an income of half a million francs.

These six were the backbone of the party. They represented the wealthy, placid, solid element of society, respectable, influential persons of religion and principle.

It so happened that all the women were seated on the same side. Next to the countess sat two nuns telling their long rosaries and muttering paternosters and aves. One of them was old; her skin was deeply pitted with smallpox as if she had received a charge of shot full in the face. Her companion was a puny creature with a pretty but sickly face and the narrow chest of a consumptive, a prey to that burning faith which creates visionaries and martyrs.

Opposite the two nuns sat a man and a woman who excited every one's interest. The man was Cornudet, a notorious democrat, the terror of all respectable people. For the last twenty years he had been dipping his long red beard in mugs of beer at every democratic pothouse. With the help of his boon companions, he had frittered away a respectable fortune which he had inherited from his father, a retired confectioner; and he looked forward eagerly to the coming of the Republic, when he would enter upon the office he had earned by all his libations to the Revolution. On the fourth of September,[7] probably in consequence of a practical joke, he got the idea into his head that he had been elected prefect; but when he essayed to take up his duties, the clerks at the prefecture, who remained in sole possession, refused to recognize him and he was forced to beat a retreat. For all that, he was a very good fellow, harmless and obliging, and he had thrown himself heart and soul into organizing the defence of the town. He had had pits dug in the open country, had had all the young trees in the neighbouring forests cut down and traps set on all the roads, and, satisfied with his preparations, he had, at the approach of the enemy, scuttled back to the city. He felt now that he would be more useful at Havre, where fresh entrenchments would be needed.

The woman beside him was one of those who are technically called gay. She was famous for her premature portliness, which had earned

[7] Date in 1870 on which the Third French Republic was proclaimed, ending the reign of Napoleon III.

for her the nickname of Boule de Suif, ball of lard, 'tallow-keech.'[8] Short, perfectly spherical, fat as dripping, with puffy fingers, dented at the joints like strings of sausages, her skin shining and smooth, her enormous breasts swelling beneath her bodice, she had nevertheless remained so fresh and blooming that she continued to fascinate and allure. Her face was like a ruddy apple or a peony bud ready to burst into flower. Her magnificent black eyes were shaded and deepened by long, thick lashes. Her charming, pouting mouth, ripe for kisses, revealed two rows of tiny dazzling teeth. It was whispered that she had many other priceless qualities.

As soon as they recognized her, the respectable women began to murmur among themselves, and the words 'prostitute,' 'open shame' were whispered so audibly that she looked up. She bestowed upon her companions a glance so bold and challenging that a deep silence ensued and every one sat with downcast eyes, except Loiseau, who stole arch glances at her.

But very soon, the three ladies, united in a sudden friendship verging on intimacy by the intrusion of that brazen hussy, resumed their conversation. They felt that they must ensconce themselves behind the dignity of their wedded estate in face of this shameless hireling. For legalized love always assumes airs of superiority over its random brother.

The three husbands, on the other hand, were drawn together by a common defensive instinct at the sight of Cornudet. They discussed money matters in tones that implied their scorn of poorer folk. Count Hubert alluded to the losses in stolen cattle and ruined crops he had sustained at the hands of the Prussians in the negligent manner of a magnate worth ten millions, who is fully aware that the inconvenience will hardly be felt in a year's time.

Monsieur Carré-Lamadon, a cotton merchant of wide experience, had taken the precaution to send to England six hundred thousand francs as a provision for a rainy day. As for Loiseau, he had arranged to sell to the French Commissariat all the common wines still in his cellars, so that the State owed him a handsome sum which he counted on receiving at Havre.

The three men exchanged quick, friendly glances. Though of different standing, they were linked together by the common tie of money, members of that wide freemasonry of the well-to-do who can thrust their hands into their trouser pockets and jingle the gold there.

[8] Tallow-lump.

The coach moved so slowly that by ten o'clock they had not accomplished more than ten miles. On three occasions, the men got out and walked up the hills. They all began to feel uneasy. They had intended to lunch at Tôtes[9], but they had small hopes now of arriving there before nightfall. Every one was on the look out for a wayside inn, when the diligence plunged into a snowdrift from which they were not extricated for two hours. Their increasing hunger began to depress their spirits. There was no sign of the meanest tavern or wine shop; all the tradespeople had fled in terror before the advance of the Prussians and the retreat of the starving French troops. The men tried to get food from the farm-houses by the roadside, but could not obtain even plain bread, for the cautious peasants had hidden away their stores for fear of being plundered by the soldiers, desperate with hunger, who seized by force anything they could lay their hands on. Towards one o'clock, Loiseau announced that he was distinctly conscious of a painful vacuum in his interior. For some time every one had been suffering from the same complaint, and the steadily increasing pangs of hunger had put a stop to conversation. From time to time, one of the travellers yawned; and another would follow suit. One after the other, in accord with individual character, manners, and social position, they opened their mouths, some noisily, others quietly, hastily putting their hands up to hide the gaping chasm from which the breath issued in a cloud of steam.

Boule de Suif stooped down now and then as if looking for something under her petticoats. She would hesitate for a moment, glance at her neighbours, then quietly sit up again. The faces of all the travellers were pale and drawn. Loiseau vowed that he would give a thousand francs for a knuckle of ham. His wife made as if to protest but restrained herself. It was always painful to her to hear of money being squandered and she could not bear even a joke on that subject.

'I don't feel at all well,' said the count. 'Why didn't I think of bringing some provisions?'

Every one blamed himself for the same omission. Cornudet, however, had a flask of rum; he offered it to his companions, but they coldly declined. Loiseau alone took a couple of sips and thanked him as he returned the flask:

'That's some good, anyhow; it warms one up and cheats one's hunger.'

The spirits put him in a good humour, and he suggested that they should do as they did in the song about the little boat, eat the fattest of the company. This sly allusion to Boule de Suif shocked his more

[9] Town about midway between Rouen and Dieppe.

refined companions. They made no reply; only Cornudet smiled. The two nuns had left off telling their beads; they sat motionless, their hands thrust into their long sleeves; their eyes steadfastly downcast, doubtless offering as a sacrifice to Heaven the sufferings which it had imposed upon them.

At last, at three o'clock, when the coach was making its way across an interminable plain without a village in sight, Boule de Suif briskly bent down and drew from under the seat a large basket covered with a white napkin. First she took from it a little earthenware plate, next a dainty silver cup, and then a large dish containing two carved fowls embedded in their jelly. The basket revealed glimpses of other good things carefully packed—pies, fruit, dainties, sufficient provisions for a three days' journey without having to fall back on the cookery of the inns.

The necks of four bottles protruded from among the parcels of food. Taking the wing of a chicken, she began daintily to eat it, with one of those rolls of bread called *régence* in Normandy.

All eyes were fixed on her. The pleasant aroma of food was wafted abroad, and the result was seen in distended nostrils, watering mouths, and spasmodic contractions of the muscles of the jaw.

The ladies' contempt for the hussy rose to a fury; they were yearning to kill her or throw her out of the carriage into the snow, her, and her cup and her basket and her provisions.

Loiseau's eyes devoured the dish of fowls.

'Congratulations!' he said. 'Madame has been more foreseeing than the rest of us. Some people always think of everything.'

She turned towards him.

'Will you have some, sir?' she asked. 'It is hard to go fasting all day.'

He bowed.

'Frankly,' he replied, 'I cannot refuse; I am at my last gasp. Any port in a storm, as they say.' And casting a glance around him, he added: 'One is lucky to find a friend in need on an occasion like this.'

He spread a newspaper over his knees to save his trousers, and, with the point of a knife which he always carried in his pocket, he transfixed a leg of chicken thickly coated with jelly, tore at it with his teeth, and chewed it with such obvious enjoyment that his companions could not restrain a deep sigh of anguish.

In a low, gentle voice, Boule de Suif invited the two nuns to share her meal. They accepted with alacrity and, without raising their eyes, murmured their thanks and quickly set to work. Nor did Cornudet decline his neighbour's invitation, and between them they made a sort of table by spreading newspapers on their knees. Their jaws worked feverishly; they chewed and swallowed the food with ravenous haste.

Loiseau, busy in his corner, quietly pressed his wife to follow his example. She held out for a long time, but at last a piercing pang of hunger induced her to give way. Her husband with a well-turned phrase asked his 'charming companion' if he might offer Madame Loiseau a small portion.

'Why, certainly, sir,' she replied, with a pleasant smile, and handed him the dish.

A difficulty arose when the first bottle of Bordeaux was opened; there was only one cup. But they passed it round, each wiping it in turn. Cornudet alone, in a spirit of gallantry, set his lips to the rim still moist from the lips of his fair neighbour.

With people eating and drinking all around them, the Count and Countess de Bréville and Monsieur and Madame Carré-Lamadon, enveloped in the odour of food, endured the torments of Tantalus. Suddenly the manufacturer's wife gave a sigh which drew every one's attention. She was as white as the snow outside; her eyes closed, her head drooped, she had fainted. Her distracted husband uttered a general appeal for help. The other passengers were utterly at a loss, but the elder nun raised the patient's head, held Boule de Suif's cup to her lips, and induced her to swallow a few drops of wine. The pretty creature moved, opened her eyes, smiled, and in a faint voice declared that she felt perfectly well again. But, as a precaution, the nun made her drink a whole glass of Bordeaux, saying:

'It is nothing but sheer hunger.'

Blushing in confusion, Boule de Suif looked at the four travellers who were still fasting, and stammered out:

'Oh, dear, if only I might venture to offer these ladies and gentlemen . . .' She broke off, in dread of a snub.

Loiseau took the floor:

'Upon my soul, in cases like this, we are all brothers and should help one another. Come, ladies, the devil take ceremony; accept her offer. Why, we don't know whether we shall even find a night's lodging. At this rate, we shan't be at Tôtes before midday to-morrow.'

They all hesitated, no one caring to take the responsibility of saying 'Yes.'

It was the count who cut the knot. Turning to the embarrassed young women, and assuming his grandest air, he said:

'Madame, we gratefully accept your offer.'

The first step was the only difficulty. The Rubicon once crossed, they fell to with a will. The basket was emptied. It still contained a *pâté de foie gras,* a *pâté* of larks, smoked tongue, some Crassane pears, a Pont l'Évêque cheese, some little cakes, and a jar of pickled gherkins and onions. For, like all women, Boule de Suif had a taste for crude flavours.

It was impossible to eat the woman's food and not talk to her. They entered into conversation, at first with some reserve, but presently, in view of her admirable behaviour, with increasing freedom. Madame de Bréville and Madame Carré-Lamadon, who were women of the world, were tactful and courteous. The countess, in particular, treated Boule de Suif with the gracious condescension of very great ladies, whom no touch can soil, and was charming to her. Only stout Madame Loiseau, who had the soul of a gendarme, remained obdurate, saying little but eating all the more.

The conversation turned naturally upon the war, the horrors perpetrated by the Prussians, and the gallant deeds of the French. All these people, who were running away, paid tribute to the courage of those who remained behind. Presently they came to personal experiences, and Boule de Suif, with real feeling and that fervent eloquence that sometimes characterizes her class when carried away by emotion, gave her reasons for leaving Rouen:

'At first, I thought I could stay. My house was well stocked with food and I preferred to feed a few soldiers rather than go into exile, God knows where. But when I saw those Prussians, it was too much for me. They made my blood boil, and I cried with shame all day long. Oh, if only I were a man! I watched them out of my window, those fat swine with their spiked helmets, and my maid had to hold my hands to stop me from hurling chairs and tables on their heads. Then some of them were billeted on me. I sprang at the throat of the first one; they are no more difficult to strangle than any one else. I should have done for him too if they had not dragged me off by my hair. After that I had to hide. So when I saw a chance, I came away, and here I am.'

They congratulated her warmly. She rose in the estimation of her companions, who had not shown such pluck. Cornudet listened to her with a benevolent and apostolic smile, like a priest who hears one of his flock praising God, for these long-bearded democrats think they have the monopoly of patriotism just as the men in cassocks are monopolists in religion. Speaking in his turn, he laid down the law with a pomposity borrowed from the proclamations posted up on the walls day after day; and he wound up with a burst of eloquence, in which he inveighed magisterially against that blackguard Badinguet, as he designated Napoleon III.

But Boule de Suif at once fired up, for she was a Bonapartist. She flushed as red as a cherry and stammered with rage: 'I should just like to see fellows like you in his position. A nice mess you would have made of it. It's your sort who betrayed the man. There would be nothing for it but to leave France if it were governed by scoundrels like you.'

Cornudet was unmoved and continued to smile his disdainful superior smile. But a violent outburst of abuse was only averted by the count, who, not without difficulty, contrived to pacify the angry young woman, authoritatively declaring that all sincere opinions were entitled to respect. But the countess and Madame Carré-Lamadon, who cherished the unreasonable hatred felt by all respectable people for the Republic, and the instinctive devotion with which every woman regards despotic governments with their pomps and ceremonies, felt themselves involuntarily drawn towards this prostitute of unbending convictions and sentiments so closely allied to their own.

The basket was empty. Ten hungry people had made short work of its contents. Their only regret was that it had not been larger. Conversation continued for a while, but it grew more constrained when the repast was over.

Night fell; the darkness gradually deepened, and the cold, always more keenly felt after a meal, made Boule de Suif shiver, well-covered though she was. At this, Madame de Bréville offered her her foot-warmer, in which the charcoal had been renewed several times since the morning. Boule de Suif accepted it with alacrity as her feet were like ice. Madame Carrê-Lamadon and Madame Loiseau gave their foot-warmers to the two nuns.

The driver had lighted the lamps, which cast a vivid glare upon the cloud of steam rising from the reeking quarters of the wheelers, and upon the roadside snow which seemed to be unrolling itself under the shifting radiance. Within the carriage all was dark, but suddenly there was some by-play between Boule de Suif and Cornudet. Loiseau, straining his eyes through the gloom, thought he saw the man with the long beard start violently away, as if he had received a forcible but noiseless cuff.

On the road ahead, little points of light began to twinkle. It was Tôtes. They had been thirteen hours on the way, including four halts of half an hour each to rest and feed the horses. They entered the town and drew up at the Hôtel du Commerce.

The door of the carriage was flung open. A familiar sound made all the travellers shudder. It was the jingling of a scabbard on the ground. At the same time they heard an exclamation in a German voice.

Though the coach had stopped, no one got out. It was as if the travellers expected to be massacred as soon as they emerged. Then the driver came to the door, flashing his lamps into the farthest recesses of the coach and lighting up two rows of frightened faces with open mouths and eyes bulging with surprise and terror. Beside the driver, in the full glare of the lamp, stood a German officer, a tall, fair young man, extremely slender, squeezed into his uniform like a girl into her corset, wearing on one side his polished flat cap which gave him the appearance of a porter at an English hotel. His huge, long, straight moustache tapered on either side to a point consisting of a single yellow hair, so fine that the extremity was invisible. Its weight seemed to depress the corners of his mouth and by dragging down his cheeks to give to his lips the appearance of drooping. In the French of Alsace, he invited the travellers to alight, saying in a severe voice:

'Will you get out, ladies and gentlemen?'

The two nuns were the first to obey, with the docility of women habituated by their vows to implicit obedience. Next came the count and countess, followed by the manufacturer and his wife; then Loiseau, pushing his better half before him. When he set foot on the ground, Loiseau, from prudence rather than politeness, said to the officer: 'Good evening, sir.' The latter, with the insolence of authority, stared at him without reply. Boule de Suif and Cornudet, though nearest to the door, were the last to emerge, confronting the enemy with a grave and lofty air. The stout young woman endeavoured to control herself and to remain calm. The democrat twisted his long red beard with a histrionic gesture, defiant, yet timid. Conscious that in an encounter such as this, each individual is in some measure the representative of his country, they were anxious to preserve their dignity. Both alike were disgusted at their companions' servility. Boule de Suif desired to prove herself of loftier spirit than those honest women, her fellow-travellers, while Cornudet, realizing that it behoved him to set an example, continued by his attitude the task of resistance which he had begun when he dug up the roads. They went into the great kitchen of the inn, where the German officer, having demanded their permit for departure, signed by the general in command, in which were set forth the names, description, and profession of each of the travellers, minutely examined them all, comparing their appearance with the written record. Then he said abruptly: 'All right!' and disappeared.

They breathed once more. Being still hungry, they ordered supper.

It was promised in half an hour; and while two maids were busy preparing it, they went to look at the bedrooms, all of which opened into a long passage, with a glazed door at the end.

Just as they were sitting down to supper, the host appeared. He was a retired horse-dealer, a stout man troubled with asthma, constantly wheezing, coughing and clearing his throat. His father had bequeathed to him the name of Follenvie.

'Mademoiselle Élisabeth Rousset?' he asked.

Boule de Suif turned to him in alarm.

'Yes?'

'Mademoiselle, the Prussian officer wishes to speak to you at once.'

'To me?'

'Yes, if you are really Mademoiselle Élisabeth Rousset?'

She hesitated for a moment in dismay, then she said roundly: 'He may want me, but I shan't go.'

This caused a sensation among the company. Every one gave his opinion, discussing the reason for the summons. The count went up to Boule de Suif:

'You are wrong, madam; for your refusal may have serious consequences, not only for yourself but all your companions. One should never resist those who have the upper hand. Compliance surely cannot involve you in any danger; no doubt it is on account of some formality which has been omitted.'

The others seconded him; they begged, urged, and lectured Boule de Suif till finally they persuaded her. For they dreaded the complications which might result from her rashness. At last she said:

'Well, remember it's for your sakes I do it.'

The countess clasped her hand.

'You have our grateful thanks,' she said.

Boule de Suif left the room. The others awaited her return before sitting down to supper. Every one regretted not having been sent for instead of that headstrong, passionate girl, and each rehearsed in his mind suitable platitudes in case he should be summoned in his turn. In ten minutes' time, she returned, breathless, scarlet in the face, choking with rage and gasping out: 'The cad! The cad!'

They were eager to hear what had happened, but she would not say a word. And when the count insisted, she replied with much dignity:

'No, it doesn't concern you; I can't tell you.'

They gathered round a large soup-tureen which emitted a smell of cabbage. In spite of the disturbing incident, it was a merry supper. The cider was good. Monsieur and Madame Loiseau and the nuns drank it from motives of economy. All the others sent for wine, except Cornudet, who demanded beer. He had his own way of opening the bottle, frothing up the liquor and contemplating it, first tilting his glass, then holding it up to the light to admire the colour. When he drank, his long beard, which was tinged with the colour of his favourite beverage, seemed to quiver with emotion; he squinted in his anxiety not to lose sight of his mug, and it seemed as if he were discharging the one function for which he had been created. One felt that he was effecting in his mind a junction; establishing an affinity between the two ruling passions of his life: Pale Ale and the Revolution. Clearly he could not taste the one without thinking of the other.

Monsieur and Madame Follenvie supped at the other end of the table. The innkeeper, wheezing like a broken-winded engine, suffered from a constriction of the chest, which prevented him from talking while he ate; but his wife's tongue clacked without ceasing. She gave a detailed account of all her feelings on the arrival of the Prussians, of everything they had done and said, abusing them first because they cost her money, next because she had two sons in the army. She addressed most of her remarks to the countess, flattered by the thought that she was speaking to a lady of quality. Presently she lowered her voice and entered upon such delicate topics, that her husband, every now and then, interrupted her with: 'You had much better keep quiet, Madame Follenvie!' But she paid no attention to him, and went on:

'Yes, madam, those fellows do nothing but eat potatoes and pork, and then more pork and potatoes. And they have filthy habits, and if you could only see them drilling in a field, hour after hour, day after day, marching and wheeling and turning in all directions. It isn't as if they worked on the land or mended the roads in their own country. No, madam, these soldiers are of no use to any one. And yet the poor have to support them, simply for them to learn how to slaughter people. It's true I'm only an ignorant old woman; but when I see these men wearing themselves out, tramping about from morning till night, I say to myself: "When there are people finding out so many useful things, why should others take all that trouble to destroy? Isn't it really abominable to kill people, whether they are Prussians or English or Poles or French? If you take revenge on someone who has wronged you, it's a crime, or you wouldn't be punished; but if you shoot down our lads like game, I suppose it's all right, as those who kill most are given decorations." I tell you, it's a thing I shall never understand.'

Cornudet raised his voice:

'War is barbarous when it's an attack on a peaceful neighbour. It is a sacred duty in the defence of one's country.'

The old woman nodded:

'Oh, yes, self-defence is quite another thing. But wouldn't it be better to kill all the kings, who make war for their own pleasure?'

Cornudet's eyes flashed.

'Bravo, citizeness,' he cried.

Monsieur Carré-Lamadon was plunged in deep thought. Though he had a passionate admiration for great soldiers, this peasant woman's common sense made him think of all the wealth that would accrue to a country, if all these idle hands, now a drain on its finances, all the sterile power it had to maintain, were employed on vast industrial enterprises, which in the present circumstances it would take centuries to achieve.

Loiseau, however, left his chair for a quiet talk with the fat innkeeper, who laughed and coughed and spat; his enormous paunch quivered with joy at his neighbour's jests, and he gave him an order for six half-hogsheads of Bordeaux to be delivered in the spring after the Prussians had gone.

Supper was hardly finished when the travellers, tired to death, went off to bed.

But Loiseau had been taking everything in. He sent his wife to bed and then applied ear and eye by turns to the keyhole with a view to discovering what he called 'the mysteries of the corridor.'

After about an hour, he heard a rustling sound, and hastily peeping out he saw Boule de Suif, looking fatter than ever in a blue cashmere dressing-gown, trimmed with white lace. She carried a candle and was making for the glazed door at the end of the corridor. Another door was cautiously opened, and when she presently returned, Cornudet came out in his shirtsleeves and followed her. There was a whispered conversation; then they came to a standstill. Boule de Suif seemed to be protesting energetically against Cornudet's entry into her bedroom. Loiseau was unfortunately unable to hear all that was said, but as they raised their voices, he at last caught a word here and there. Cornudet was insisting eagerly.

'Come now, don't be silly,' he said. 'What can it matter to you?'

She answered indignantly:

'No, my dear, there are times when these things are not done. Just now, it would be scandalous!'

Evidently he did not see her point, and pressed her for a reason. Roused to wrath, she exclaimed in still louder tones:

'You ask why? Don't you see why? When there are Prussians in the house, perhaps even in the next room!'

He was silenced. The patriotic delicacy of this poor outcast, who would not submit to an embrace while the enemy was within the gates, must have revived his waning sense of decency; for, after one kiss, he tiptoed back to his own room.

His senses stirred, Loiseau left the key-hole, cut a caper about the room, put on his night-cap, and turning back the sheet which covered the gaunt form of his spouse, woke her with a kiss, murmuring:

'Do you love me, darling?'

Silence then fell on the house. But soon there arose from some quarter difficult to define, which might have been the cellar or the garret, a powerful, monotonous, rhythmic snore, long drawn out, and vibrant as an engine boiler under pressure. Monsieur Follenvie slept.

As it had been arranged to start at eight o'clock the next morning, the party assembled in the kitchen at an early hour. But the coach, its top covered with snow, stood forlornly in the middle of the courtyard without horses or driver. They hunted vainly for the latter in stables, granary, and coach-house. The men then decided to go out and scour the country for him. They reached the market-place with the church at its far end, and on either side a row of low-roofed houses, where they caught sight of Prussian soldiers. The first one they saw was peeling potatoes. The next, a little farther on, was washing down the barber's shop. Another bearded warrior was petting a tiny child and endeavouring to check its tears by rocking it on his knees. The buxom peasant women, whose men had gone to the war, indicated by means of signs what tasks they desired their docile conquerors to undertake: wood to be split, or the coffee to be ground, or the soup to be poured on the bread. One soldier was actually doing the washing for his hostess, a helpless old grandam.

In surprise, the count questioned the beadle as he came out of the presbytery. The old church rat replied:

'Oh, this lot are not at all bad; they are not Prussians, I'm told, but come from farther off, I don't exactly know where. And every man of them has left a wife and children in his own country. The war is no joke to them, I'll be bound. Their women, too, are crying for their men-folk and are every bit as miserable as our own women here. However, just now we are not so badly off; the soldiers do no harm and are ready for any odd job just as if they were at home. You see, sir, poor folk must help one another. It is the great ones who make the wars.'

Cornudet felt indignant at the friendly feeling that united conquerors and conquered, and went off, preferring to shut himself up in the inn. Loiseau had his little joke:

'They are restocking the country.'

But Monsieur Carré-Lamadon solemnly said:

'They are making reparation.'

The driver was nowhere to be seen. At last they ran him to earth in the village café, fraternizing with the officer's orderly. The count addressed him:

'Weren't you ordered to have the carriage ready by eight o'clock?'

'Yes, to be sure, but I had another order afterwards.'

'What order?'

'Not to get ready at all.'

'Who gave you that order?'

'Why, the Prussian commandant.'

'For what reason?'

'I don't know. Go and ask him. I was told not to get it ready. So I didn't, and there you are.'

'Did he give you the order in person?'

'No, sir, it was through the innkeeper.'

'When was that?'

'Yesterday evening, as I was going to bed.'

The three men returned to the inn, feeling very uneasy. They asked for Monsieur Follenvie, but the maid answered that her master, on account of his asthma, never got up before ten o'clock. He had given strict orders that he was never to be called at an earlier hour, except in case of fire. They then desired to see the officer, but that was absolutely out of the question, although he was staying in the hotel. Monsieur Follenvie alone was authorized to speak to him on civil business. So they had to wait. The ladies went back to their rooms and passed the time in trifling occupations.

Cornudet installed himself in the kitchen chimney corner, where a mighty fire was blazing. A pot of beer stood on a table in front of him; and he took out his pipe which, in democratic circles, was regarded with almost as much respect as its owner, as if in serving Cornudet it served the State. It was a fine meerschaum with a curved stem, beautifully coloured, as black as its master's teeth, redolent and shining, an old friend and a characteristic adjunct to his physiognomy. He sat perfectly still, his eyes now on the blazing hearth, now on the froth of his mug of beer, and whenever he had taken a pull he would pass his long, lean fingers through his greasy locks, while he sucked the froth from his moustache with an air of content.

Under pretext of stretching his legs, Loiseau went out to sell his wine to the local retailers. The count and the manufacturer talked politics and speculated as to the future of France. The one believed in the house of Orleans, the other looked for an unknown saviour, a hero who would come to the rescue when all seemed lost; a du Guesclin,[10] perhaps, or a Joan of Arc, or a second Napoleon. Ah, if only the Prince Imperial[11] were not so young! Cornudet listened with the smile of one who knows the secrets of destiny. The aroma of his pipe filled the kitchen.

On the stroke of ten, Monsieur Follenvie appeared. To their eager questions, he had only one reply, which he repeated two or three times.

'The officer said to me just like this: "Monsieur Follenvie, you will give orders not to have the carriage ready to-morrow for those travellers. I do not wish them to proceed without my consent. You understand? . . . Very good!" '

They then asked to see the officer. The count sent in his card, on which Monsieur Carré-Lamadon had written his name and all his distinctions. The Prussian sent word that he would receive them after luncheon, about one o'clock.

The ladies came down and, in spite of their uneasiness, they partook of a light meal. Boule de Suif seemed out of sorts and terribly worried. As they were finishing their coffee, the orderly came for the two gentlemen, and Loiseau joined the count and Monsieur Carré-Lamadon. They tried to enlist Cornudet to add weight to the deputation, but he declared haughtily that he was resolved never to hold any communication with Germans; and he sat down again in his chimney corner, and called for another pot of beer.

The three men went upstairs and were ushered into the best room of the inn, where the officer received them. Lolling in an arm-chair, with both feet on the mantelpiece, he was smoking a long porcelain pipe and was wrapped in a gaudy dressing-gown, doubtless looted from the deserted house of some middle-class person of execrable taste. He neither rose nor saluted, nor even looked at them. He was a perfect specimen of the insolence which is natural to a victorious soldiery.

At last, after some moments had elapsed, he said:

'What do you want?'

The count was the spokesman:

'Sir, we wish to continue our journey.'

'You can't.'

'Might I venture to ask the reason of your refusal?'

'I don't wish you to go.'

[10] Bertrand du Guesclin (1320?–1380), Constable of France, drove the English out of most of their French possessions.

[11] Napoleon Eugène Louis (1856–1879), only son of Napoleon III.

'I would respectfully bring to your notice, sir, that the general in command has given us a permit to go to Dieppe; I am not aware that we have done anything to deserve this harsh treatment.'

'I don't wish it. That's all. You may go.'

The three delegates bowed and withdrew.

They spent a melancholy afternoon. Unable to interpret the capricious behaviour of the German officer, they were tormented by the most fantastic ideas. Gathered in the kitchen, they engaged in endless discussions and hazarded the wildest conjectures. Perhaps it was intended to keep them as hostages—but for what purpose?—or to take them away as prisoners, or, more likely still, to exact a substantial ransom? . . . At this suggestion they were panic-stricken. The wealthier they were the more they were horrified. They saw themselves forced to purchase their lives with bags of gold poured into the lap of that insolent soldier. They racked their brains to devise plausible falsehoods for disguising their wealth, and for passing themselves off for very poor people indeed. Loiseau took off his watch chain and hid it in his pocket. With nightfall, their fears increased. The lamp was lit, and as there were still two hours till dinner, Madame Loiseau proposed a game of *trente-et-un*[12] to pass the time. Every one welcomed this suggestion, including Cornudet, who, out of politeness, extinguished his pipe.

The count shuffled the cards and dealt. Boule de Suif in the very first round held thirty-one. Very soon, in the excitement of the game, their haunting fears subsided. Cornudet, however, noticed that the two Loiseaus were helping each other to cheat.

Just as they were sitting down to dinner, Monsieur Follenvie came in. In his husky voice, he said:

'The Prussian officer wishes to know if Mademoiselle Élisabeth Rousset has changed her mind yet.'

Boule de Suif turned pale. She remained standing. But suddenly she flushed crimson, choking with rage, unable to utter a word. At last she broke out:

'You may tell that blackguard, that dirty scoundrel, that filthy Prussian, that I never will. Have you got it? Never, never, never.'

The fat innkeeper went off. The others gathered round Boule de Suif, teasing her with questions, imploring her to reveal the mystery of her interview with the Prussian. At first she stood out, but finally, carried away by her resentment, she cried:

12 Thirty-one.

'What does he want? ... What does he want? ... He wants to sleep with me!'

So keen was their indignation that no one was shocked at the phrase. Cornudet brought his mug so violently down on the table that he broke it. There was a general outcry against this ruffianly soldier. Swept by a common gust of anger, they resolved unanimously upon resistance, as if each of them had been called upon to contribute to the sacrifice.

With an air of disgust, the count declared that these fellows were behaving like the barbarians of old. The ladies, in particular, lavished upon Boule de Suif vehement demonstrations of sympathy. The nuns, who appeared only at meal times, bowed their heads and held their peace.

After the first burst of anger had subsided, they dined, but conversation languished; every one was pensive.

The ladies retired early; the men smoked and got up a game of écarté in which they invited Monsieur Follenvie to join, with the object of skilfully eliciting from him the best means of overcoming the officer's opposition. But he devoted his whole attention to the cards, listened to no questions, and made no reply; calling out continually: 'Play, gentlemen, play!' His attention was so closely fixed that he even forgot to spit, an omission which was liable to produce organ effects in his chest. His wheezing lungs ran through the whole asthmatical gamut, from deep bass notes to the shrill squawk of a cockerel trying to crow. He declined to go to bed when his wife, dropping with fatigue, came to look for him. So she went off alone, for she was an early bird, always up with the sun; while her husband preferred late hours and was always ready to make a night of it with his friends. He called out to her: 'Put my egg-flip[13] before the fire,' and went on with the game.

When they saw that they could get nothing out of him, they declared that it was time for them to stop, and they all went off to bed.

They were up early again next morning, filled with a vague hope, an increasing desire to be gone, and a dread of another day in that horrible little inn.

Alas! the horses remained in the stable, and the driver was still invisible. For want of anything better to do, they hung about the coach.

Luncheon was a gloomy meal. A certain coldness began to manifest itself towards Boule de Suif. Taking counsel of their pillows had somewhat modified her companions' view of the case. By this time, they

[13] Hot drink made of beer or ale, eggs, sugar, and nutmeg.

were almost ready to blame the girl for not having secretly sought out the Prussian officer, with a view to providing a pleasant surprise for her fellow-travellers the next morning. Could anything have been simpler? After all, who would have been the wiser? She could have saved her face by letting the officer know that she had taken pity on her fellow-travellers' distress. It would have been such a small matter for her. But as yet no one uttered these thoughts aloud.

In the afternoon, to relieve their devastating boredom, the count suggested a walk on the outskirts of the village. Carefully wrapped up, the little party set out, with the exception of Cornudet, who preferred to stay by the fire, and the nuns who were spending their days in church or at the parsonage. The cold, which was daily increasing in intensity, sharply nipped their ears and noses; their feet ached so painfully that each step was torture. And the open country, under its pall of snow, stretching away beyond range of sight, produced upon them such a terrible impression of dreariness that they turned home, chilled and oppressed in heart and soul. The four women walked on ahead, while the three men followed at a little distance.

Loiseau, who had grasped the situation, suddenly asked if the 'wench' meant to keep them hanging on much longer like this. Chivalrous as ever, the count declared that they could not ask a woman to make so painful a sacrifice; it must be voluntary. Monsieur Carré-Lamadon observed that if the French, as was thought likely, turned and took the offensive by way of Dieppe, the engagement could only take place at Tôtes, a reflection which made the others uneasy.

'Suppose we escape on foot?' said Loiseau.

'Out of the question in all this snow, and with our wives too,' said the count shrugging his shoulders. 'Besides, they would be after us in no time; we should be caught within ten minutes and brought back as prisoners at the mercy of the soldiers.'

There was no answer to this, and they relapsed into silence.

The ladies discussed fashions, but a feeling of constraint seemed to disturb the harmony.

Suddenly, the Prussian officer appeared at the end of the street. His tall, wasp-waisted, uniformed figure stood out sharply against the snowy background. He walked with his knees well apart, with the gait characteristic of military men who are anxious not to splash their beautifully polished boots. He bowed as he passed the ladies, but glanced contemptuously at the men, who, for their part, did not lower themselves so far as to take off their hats, though Loiseau made as if to do so.

Boule de Suif blushed up to the eyes, and the three married women felt deeply mortified at having been seen by the officer in the company of the young woman whom he had treated so cavalierly.

Then they discussed him, criticizing his face and figure. Madame Carré-Lamadon, who had known a great many officers and spoke with the authority of an expert, declared that he was not at all unprepossessing. It was a pity, she actually said, that he was not a Frenchman; he would have made a very smart hussar, and all the women would have been crazy about him.

When they returned to the inn, they were at their wits' end for something to do. Sharp words were exchanged on the slightest provocation. Dinner was a short and silent meal, and every one went to bed, hoping to kill time by going to sleep. The next morning they came downstairs with jaded looks and nerves on edge. The women would hardly speak to Boule de Suif.

The church bell rang for a christening. Boule de Suif had a child of her own, who was being brought up in a peasant family at Yvetot. She saw it scarcely once a year and never troubled her head about it. But now the thought of the infant about to be christened awoke in her a sudden burst of tender feeling towards her own baby, and nothing would do but she must be present at the ceremony.

As soon as she had left the inn, the others exchanged glances and drew their chairs close together, for they felt that it was really time they came to some decision. Loiseau had an inspiration. His suggestion was to invite the officer to keep back Boule de Suif by herself and to let the others go. Monsieur Follenvie undertook to convey this message, but he came back almost at once. The German, who knew what men were, had turned him out of the room. He intended to keep the whole party till he had attained his desire.

At this, the innate vulgarity of Madame Loiseau broke out:

'Anyhow, we are not going to stay here till we die of old age. It's the wretched creature's trade. One man is as good as another from her point of view. What right has she to pick and choose? I ask you. She never refused any one who came along at Rouen, not even coachmen. Yes, indeed, madam, she carried on with the mayor's coachman. I know all about it because he buys his wine from us. And now, when it's a question of getting us out of a mess, she put on airs, the slut. Really, I think the officer is behaving very well. He has probably had no opportunities for a long time; and here are we three whom he would no doubt have preferred. But no, he is ready to content himself with a common woman. He has a proper respect for married women. Remember, he is master here. He has only to raise a finger, and his soldiers would seize us for him by force.'

The other women gave a little shudder. Pretty Madame Carré-Lamadon's eyes sparkled and she turned a little pale, as if she already felt herself forcibly seized by the officer.

The men, who had been privately conferring, now joined the ladies. Loiseau, in a fury, was for delivering the wretch, bound hand and foot, to the enemy. But the count, who was sprung from three generations of ambassadors and was himself a diplomat by instinct, counselled strategy.

'We must persuade her,' he said.

So they proceeded to concoct a plan.

The women put their heads together. Voices were lowered and the discussion became general, every one giving an opinion. It was all conducted with the utmost propriety. The ladies displayed a special aptitude for expressing the most outrageous ideas by polite euphemisms and refined phrases. They were so careful of the conventions of speech that a stranger would have understood nothing. But since the veneer of modesty with which every woman is provided is purely superficial, they threw themselves heart and soul into this unsavoury affair, secretly revelling in it, perfectly in their element and dallying with the idea of the liaison with all the sensual emotion of a cook, himself a gourmand, preparing another person's supper.

Their spirits rose again at the humorous aspect of the adventure. The count ventured upon some rather risky jokes which were so neatly turned that no one could help smiling. Loiseau indulged in broader pleasantries, and even these were not resented. Every one was thinking of Madame Loiseau's brutally frank remark: 'It's her trade, so why should she pick and choose?' Indeed, charming Madame Carré-Lamadon seemed to think that if she were in her place she would rather have him than another.

A plan of blockade was carefully considered, as if for the investment of a fortress. To each conspirator a separate role was assigned, including appropriate arguments and manœuvres. A plan of attack, with strategic openings and surprise methods of assault, was agreed upon with a view to forcing this citadel of flesh and blood to admit the enemy.

Cornudet alone remained aloof, unwilling to have anything to do with the affair.

They were so deeply engrossed that they did not hear Boule de Suif come in, till, at the count's whispered 'Hush!' every one looked up and saw her.

Conversation ceased abruptly and at first a feeling of embarrassment deterred them from addressing her. The countess, however, was more of an adept than her companions in social insincerity.

'Was it a pretty christening?' she asked.

Not without emotion, Boule de Suif described the whole proceedings, the congregation, the ceremony, and the church itself. She added:

'It does one good to say one's prayers now and then.'

Up to luncheon-time the ladies contented themselves with being pleasant to her, with the object of gaining her confidence and making her amenable to their advice. But as soon as they sat down to table the siege was opened. They began with a vague discussion of the virtue of self-sacrifice. Instances from antiquity were quoted: Judith and Holofernes,[14] then, with utter inconsequence, Lucretia and Sextus, [15] and Cleopatra, admitting to her bed all the enemy generals and making them her obedient slaves. Next was unfolded a fantastic story, hatched in the imagination of these ignorant plutocrats, of how the Roman women betook themselves to Capua and lulled to sleep in their arms Hannibal, his officers, and his phalanxes of mercenaries.[16] They told of women who had stayed the tide of conquest, offering their persons as a battle-field and making of their own beauty an effective weapon; heroines whose caresses had compassed the overthrow of the vilest and most hateful of mankind, and who had sacrificed their chastity in a fervour of vengeance and self-immolation.

All these stories were told with due regard to propriety and good taste, with frequent outbursts of studied enthusiasm calculated to excite to emulation.

By the time they had finished, one would have supposed that the whole duty of woman here below was the repeated sacrifice of her person, a continual surrender of herself to a licentious soldiery.

Deep in their meditations, the two nuns did not seem to be listening, and Boule de Suif said not a word.

All that afternoon they left her to her own reflections. Only, instead of addressing her as 'Madame,' as they had hitherto done, they now

[14] Hebrew heroine of a book of the Apocrypha who delivered her people by slaying the Assyrian general Holofernes.

[15] According to Roman legend, Lucretia, the virtuous wife of Collatinus, stabbed herself to death after being raped by Sextus Tarquinius, son of King Tarquin. Her suicide led to a revolt and the establishment of the Roman Republic.

[16] In 216 B.C., Hannibal, the great Carthaginian general, made Capua, a city celebrated for its wealth and luxury, the winter quarters of his army in his war against Rome. That his soldiers were supposed to have been enervated and demoralized by Capua became a popular legend in later ages.

said simply 'Mademoiselle,' no one quite knew why, unless it was to detract from the position of respect to which she had attained, and to bring home to her the shame of her calling.

While the soup was being served, Monsieur Follenvie appeared again, and repeated the question of the previous evening:

'The Prussian officer wishes to know if Mademoiselle Élisabeth Rousset has changed her mind yet.'

'No,' said Boule de Suif, curtly.

During dinner, the coalition showed signs of weakening. Loiseau made two or three unfortunate remarks. All the conspirators vainly racked their brains in search of fresh examples, when the countess, probably without design, and simply with a vague idea of showing respect to religion, questioned the elder nun about the main incidents in the lives of the saints. It appeared that many of the saints had been guilty of deeds which would be considered crimes in our eyes. But the Church makes no difficulty about granting absolution for heinous offences, provided that they are committed for the glory of God or the good of one's neighbour. Here was a powerful argument, and the countess jumped at it. It was either a case of that tacit understanding, that veiled connivance, for which all who wear the garb of the Church develop a special faculty, or simply the result of a fortunate lack of intelligence, an opportune stupidity. Whatever the cause, the old nun rendered yeoman's service to the intriguers. In spite of her apparent timidity, she showed herself bold, eloquent, forcible. She, for one, did not trouble to grope among the mazes of casuistry; her doctrine was as rigid as an iron bar; her faith was unswerving; her conscience knew no scruple. She regarded Abraham's sacrifice[17] as perfectly natural, for she herself would have had no hesitation in slaying both father and mother at a command from on high. No act, she believed, could be displeasing to the Lord if the intention was praiseworthy. Taking advantage of the pious authority of this unexpected ally, the countess induced her to deliver an edifying exposition of the moral axiom: 'The end justifies the means.'

'Then, sister,' she said, 'you believe that all means are acceptable to God and that He will pardon any act if only the motive be pure?'

'Who can doubt it, madam? An act culpable in itself often becomes meritorious because of the idea which inspires it.'

And they continued in this strain, interpreting the will of God, anticipating His judgments, and involving Him in matters which were really no concern of His. And the whole drift of their discussion was

[17] God tests Abraham by enjoining him to sacrifice his son Isaac, but restrains him as he is about to obey (Gen. 22:1–18).

veiled, insidious, discreet. Every word uttered by the holy woman in the nun's coif made a breach in the courtesan's fierce resistance. Presently the conversation took a somewhat different turn. She of the rosary spoke of the houses of her order, her superior, herself, her charming companion, dear Sister Saint-Nicéphore. They had been summoned to Havre to nurse in the hospitals hundreds of soldiers suffering from smallpox. She depicted these poor fellows, giving a detailed description of their disease. And while they were held up on their journey for a whim of this Prussian, scores of Frenchmen were perhaps dying, whom their ministrations might have saved. Nursing soldiers was her specialty. She had been in the Crimea, in Italy, in Austria. In relating her campaigns, she suddenly revealed herself as one of those nuns of fife and drum, whose destiny is to follow the armies and bring in the wounded, cast up by the back-wash of battles, and whose word is more effective than a general's in subduing undisciplined soldiers. She was a real Sister Rub-a-dub,[18] and her worn face, seamed with countless wrinkles, was like a symbol of the havoc of war.

The effect of her speech seemed so admirable that when she ceased no one said another word. As soon as dinner was over, the whole party retired at once to their rooms and did not come down till rather late the next morning. Luncheon passed quietly. The seed, which had been sown on the previous evening, was given time to germinate and bear fruit.

In the afternoon, the countess suggested a walk. The count, as had been arranged, gave his arm to Boule de Suif and lingered with her behind the others. He adopted towards her that familiar, paternal, somewhat supercilious manner, with which men of a certain position treat young women of her class, calling her 'my dear child' with the condescension arising from his social rank and his unquestioned respectability.

He went straight to the root of the matter:

'Then, you prefer to keep us here, exposed like yourself to all the outrages which would ensue if the Prussian troops suffered a reverse, rather than grant a favour which you have conceded so often as a matter of course?'

Boule de Suif made no reply.

He tried her with kindness, argument, appeals to sentiment, yet he never forgot his rank, even though obliged to pay court, to lavish compliments—in short, to make himself agreeable. He magnified the service

[18] Sister of the drum.

she would render her companions and spoke of their gratitude; finally, with gay familiarity, he exclaimed:

'And you know, my dear, he will be able to boast of having enjoyed a prettier girl than he could often find in his own country.'

Boule de Suif still made no reply and caught up the others. As soon as she returned home she withdrew to her room and did not come down again. The rest of the party were greatly perturbed. What did she mean to do? If she still held out, it would be very awkward.

The dinner hour came, but they waited for her in vain. Then Monsieur Follenvie appeared and said that Mademoiselle Rousset was indisposed and that they might begin. They all pricked up their ears. The count went up to the innkeeper and asked in a whisper; 'Is it all right?' 'Yes,' he was told. From a sense of propriety, he said nothing to his companions, but he slightly nodded his head. Every one uttered a sigh of relief and every face lighted up. Loiseau exclaimed: 'Glory be! I'll stand champagne, if there is any in the house!' and Madame Loiseau writhed in agony when the host came back with four bottles. Every one at once became voluble and noisy. They were bubbling over with joy. The count appeared to awake to Madame Carré-Lamadon's charms; the manufacturer addressed compliments to the countess. The tone of the conversation grew lively, merry, and racy.

Suddenly, Loiseau raised his hands with an air of anxiety, and shouted: 'Silence!' Surprised, almost frightened, the whole party sat mute. He made a sign to them to keep still; stood in an attitude of attention, his eyes raised to the ceiling, and listened again. Then in his ordinary voice, he said: 'Be easy; all is well.' Slowly his meaning dawned upon them and they exchanged smiles.

A quarter of an hour later he went through the same performance, which he repeated at intervals throughout the evening. He pretended to be addressing questions to someone on the floor above, and proffering advice, which had a double meaning characteristic of his bagman's[19] wit. With a sorrowful expression, he would sigh: 'Poor girl,' or he would murmur between his teeth as in a fury: 'Get out, you Prussian brute.' Sometimes, when the others were off their guard, he would cry repeatedly in a thrilling voice: 'Have done! Have done!' adding, as if to himself: 'I only hope we may see her again and that that scoundrel won't be the death of her.'

Though these jests were in deplorable taste, every one enjoyed them and no one was shocked. Like any other sentiment, virtuous indignation

[19] Traveling salesman's.

is the result of environment, and gradually an atmosphere had been created which was laden with obscene suggestion. At dessert, even the women, who had drunk a good deal and whose eyes were sparkling, made discreet but waggish allusions.

The count, who preserved, even when he fell from grace, his grave and lofty bearing, drew a comparison, which was much relished, between their condition and that of ice-bound mariners at the Pole, rejoicing because winter is over and the way to the south open once more.

Loiseau jumped up, a glass of champagne in his hand: 'I drink to our deliverance!' Every one rose and drank the toast with acclamation. Even the two nuns yielded to the importunity of the other ladies and took a sip of the bubbling wine, which they had never tasted before. They said it was like effervescent lemonade, but admitted that it had a finer flavour.

Loiseau summed up the situation:

'What a pity we haven't a piano; we might have managed a quadrille.'

Cornudet had not uttered a word or made a sign. He seemed, indeed, as if plunged in serious thought, and now and then with a furious gesture he tugged at his great beard, as if he wished to make it longer still. At last, towards midnight, as the party was about to break up, Loiseau reeled up to him and poked him in the ribs.

'You're not in good form this evening, old chap. Have you lost your tongue?'

Cornudet raised his head sharply and, glaring ferociously at the company, said:

'I tell you all that you have done an infamous thing.' He rose and made his way to the door.

'Infamous!' he repeated and disappeared.

The immediate effect of his words was to cast a blight on every one. Loiseau was utterly taken aback and stood there like a fool. But he quickly recovered himself. Convulsed with laughter, he exclaimed:

'The grapes are sour, old boy; the grapes are sour.'

As no one understood, he told his story of the mysteries of the corridor. There was a fresh outburst of gaiety. The ladies nearly died of laughing. The count and Monsieur Carré-Lamadon laughed till they cried. They could not believe their ears.

'What! are you sure? He really wanted to——?'

'I tell you I saw it!'

'And she refused?'

'Yes, because the Prussian was in the next room.'

'Is it possible?'

'I'll take my oath.'

The count suffocated with laughter and the manufacturer held his sides. Loiseau resumed:

'And now you know why he didn't think it at all funny this evening!'

The three men exploded again, until they were out of breath and weak with laughing. Then they all went upstairs and the party dispersed.

Madame Loiseau, who was as spiteful as a stinging nettle, said to her husband as soon as they were in bed:

'That affected little minx, Madame Carré-Lamadon, was laughing on the wrong side of her mouth all the evening. When it comes to a uniform, you know, some women don't care whether it is French or Prussian; it's all one to them. Good Lord, isn't it revolting?'

All that night the darkened corridor was alive with rustling sounds, so light as to be almost inaudible, the pattering of bare feet, the faint creaking of boards. From the gleams of light that showed beneath the doors for a long time, it was obvious that no one went to sleep till a late hour. Champagne is said to make one restless.

Next morning, the snow glittered dazzlingly in the bright winter sun. The coach, ready at last, was standing at the door, while a flock of white pigeons, pink-eyed with black pupils, were preening their luxuriant plumage and stalking solemnly in and out between the legs of the six horses, picking up their sustenance.

Wrapped in his sheepskin, the driver was seated on the box, pulling at his pipe, and the delighted travellers were all of them busy packing up provisions for the rest of the journey. All they were now waiting for was Boule de Suif.

Presently she appeared. She seemed somewhat ill at ease and ashamed, and as she moved timidly towards her fellow-travellers, they all unanimously turned away as if they had not seen her. The count, with a dignified air, took his wife's arm and drew her away from that contaminating contact.

Boule de Suif stood for a moment in amazement, then plucking up courage, she greeted the manufacturer's wife with a humble 'Good morning, madam.' The latter, however, merely returned an insolent little nod and a glance of virtuous indignation. Every one seemed to have a great deal to do and held aloof from her, as if she carried some infection in her petticoats. Then they made a rush for the coach. Boule de Suif was the last to reach it, and quietly slipped into the seat she had occupied during the first stage of her journey.

They pretended not to see or recognize her, but Madame Loiseau shot an indignant glance at her from a distance, and whispered audibly to her husband: 'I'm glad I'm not sitting next to her.'

The heavy coach lurched off and the journey was resumed. At first every one was silent. Boule de Suif did not venture to look up. She was disgusted with her companions and at the same time ashamed of having submitted to the defiling embraces of the Prussian officer, into whose arms she had been flung by these hypocrites.

Presently, turning to Madame Carré-Lamadon, the countess broke the painful silence:

'I think you know Madame d'Étrelles?'

'Yes, she is a friend of mine.'

'What a charming woman!'

'Perfectly delightful! Really distinguished, well-educated, and artistic to the finger-tips. She sings divinely and draws exquisitely.'

The manufacturer talked to the count; above the rattling of the windows, a word was now and then audible: 'dividend warrant—fall due—premium—mature.'

Loiseau, who had annexed from the inn its pack of old cards, greasy with five years' contact with dirty tables, played bezique with his wife.

The nuns, taking the long rosaries hanging at their waists, crossed themselves, and their lips began to move with ever-increasing speed, as though their muttered prayers were running a race. Every now and then they kissed a medallion, crossed themselves again, and resumed their rapid, continuous babbling.

Cornudet sat motionless, plunged in thought.

After they had been three hours or so on the way, Loiseau gathered up the cards, saying:

'I feel hungry!'

His wife produced a packet tied with string from which she took a piece of cold veal. She cut it into neat, thin slices and they both began to eat.

'Suppose we do the same,' said the countess. Her husband agreed and she unpacked the provisions brought for themselves and the Carré-Lamadons. They consisted of an oblong dish with a hare in earthenware on the lid, which was an indication of the contents, a savoury hare-pie, in which the dark flesh, mixed with other finely chopped meat, was set off by streaks of white fat. There was also a fine piece of Gruyère, wrapped in a newspaper, with *Faits divers*[20] impressed on its unctuous surface.

The two nuns took out a piece of sausage smelling of garlic; while

[20] News in brief.

Cornudet, thrusting both hands at once into the wide pockets of his loose greatcoat, extracted from one four hard-boiled eggs, from the other a crust of bread. Throwing the shells into the straw at his feet, he set to work on the eggs, scattering on his spreading beard yellow specks of yolk, which shone there like stars.

When she got up that morning Boule de Suif had been too much flustered and agitated to think of anything. Choking with rage and indignation, she watched all these people calmly eating away. Seething with fury, she opened her mouth to tell them what she thought of them, and a torrent of abuse rose to her lips; but her exasperation strangled her utterance. No one gave her a look or a thought. She felt overwhelmed by the contempt of these miserable churls, these respectable people, who had first sacrificed her and then flung her away like a thing useless and unclean. And then she remembered her big basket full of good things which they had greedily devoured, her two fowls in shining jelly, her *pâtés,* her pears, her four bottles of Bordeaux. Her rage suddenly gave way like a snapping cord and she felt on the verge of tears. She made a violent effort to brace herself and swallowed down her sobs as a child does; but tears rose to her eyes, glistened on her eyelashes, and soon two great drops rolled slowly down her cheeks. Then the tears came faster and faster, like drops of water trickling from a rock, and falling in regular succession on to her swelling bosom. She sat erect and looked straight before her, her face pale and set, in the hope that her distress would pass unnoticed. But the countess remarked it and with a gesture drew her husband's attention to it. He shrugged his shoulders as if to say: 'Well, what of it? It's not my fault.'

Madame Loiseau, with a silent laugh of mockery, murmured:

'She is crying for shame.'

After wrapping up the remainder of their sausage, the two nuns returned to their prayers.

Cornudet, who was digesting his eggs, put up his long legs on the opposite seat, leant back with folded arms, and smiled like a man who has thought of a good joke. He began to whistle the *Marseillaise.*[21]

Every face grew overcast. The song of the people certainly did not appeal to his companions in the least. They fidgeted nervously, and each looked ready to howl, like a dog at the sound of a barrel-organ. He realized this, and went on for all that. He even hummed a verse:

[21] French Republican national anthem, written in 1792.

Amour sacré de la patrie,
Conduis, soutiens nos bras vengeurs,
Liberté, liberté, chérie,
Combats avec tes défenseurs![22]

As the snow hardened, their progress became more rapid. All the way to Dieppe, throughout the long weary hours of the journey; above the jolting of the coach, in the gathering gloom, in the subsequent deep darkness which filled the carriage, with savage resolution he kept up his monotonous, vindictive whistling. He forced their jaded, exasperated brains to follow the song from end to end, word by word, and note by note. All the time Boule de Suif never ceased to weep, and now and then, at a pause in the song, a sob that she could not repress was heard in the darkness.

1880

Translated by Marjorie Laurie

[22] Sacred love of the fatherland, / Direct, support our avenging arms, / Liberty, beloved liberty, / Fight along with your defenders!

THE HEROINE

ISAK DINESEN

THERE WAS a young Englishman, named Frederick Lamond, who was the descendant of a long line of clergymen and scholars, and himself a student of religious philosophy, and who when he was twenty years old attracted his teacher's attention by his talent and tenacity. In the year of 1870 he got a travelling legacy, and went away to Germany. He meant to write a book upon the doctrine of atonement, and had his mind all filled with his subject.

Frederick had lived a seclusive life amongst books; now every day brought him new impressions. The world itself, like a big old book, fell open, and slowly, on its own, turned one leaf after another. The first great phenomenon that met him within it was the art of painting. One day he went up into the gallery of Das Altes Museum to look at Venusti's picture of Christ on the Mount of Olives,[1] of which a friend had told him. He was amazed to find himself surrounded by paintings connected with his study. He had not known that there were so many pictures in the world. He returned to see them again, and from the sacred paintings he turned to the profane work of the great masters. He was a simple young man. He had nobody to guide him, and no illusions as to his own knowledge of art; he came back to the pictures because he was happy amongst them. In the end he felt at home in the galleries. He recognized most Biblical characters by sight, and stood in a friendly relation to the mythological and allegorical figures as well. These indeed were the people of Berlin whom he knew best, for outside the galleries he was slow in making acquaintances.

While he was thus wandering in his own thoughts, the world of hard facts round him was not standing still, but was, on the contrary, moving with feverish haste. A great war was about to break out.

The situation was first made clear to him on a hot day in July, when he met a young man from the manor by his father's rectory, who greeted him proudly with a quotation from *Hamlet:* "Upon my life, Lamond!"[2] and went on to unburden to him his wild young mind, all seething with rumours of the coming Franco-Prussian war. The young man had a brother at the Embassy in Paris, and he explained to Frederick that there was not a button lacking in a gaiter in the French army, and that in Paris the crowds were crying: *"À Berlin!"*[3] Frederick now realized that he had already for some time known of all this, from talk in the cafés where he dined, but only, as it were, with the surface of his mind. He also found that his sympathies were with France. "I had better get out of Berlin," he thought.

He collected his manuscripts and packed his clothes. Then he went to say good-bye to the pictures, and prayed that the coming siege and storm of Berlin might not affect them. And so he made for the frontier.

[1] Marcello Venusti (1515–1579), minor Venetian painter, was a close follower of Michelangelo; the picture is probably Venusti's *Prayers on the Mount of Olives,* which hangs in Sant' Ignazio at Viterbo, Italy. It is on the Mount of Olives that Jesus tells Peter that he will thrice deny Him before the cock crows (Matt. 26:30–35).

[2] Laertes's response to Claudius's reference to "a gentleman of Normandy" who praised Laertes's skill as a swordsman (*Hamlet,* act 4, sc. 7, line 93).

[3] "On to Berlin!" Ironically, it was not the French who reached their enemies' capital during the Franco-Prussian War (1870–71), but the Prussians.

But he had not gone far before he found that he had been too slow. By this time travelling was difficult; he could get neither forward nor back. He changed his plans and decided to go to Metz, where he knew people, but he could not get to Metz either. In the end he had to content himself on being allowed to stay in a small town, named Saarburg, near the border.

In the modest hotel of Saarburg there were many stranded French travellers. Amongst them was an old priest, who came from a college in Bavaria, and two old nuns from a convent school, a widow who kept a hotel in a provincial town, a rich wine-grower, and a commercial traveller. All these people were in the greatest agitation of mind. The optimists amongst them hoped to get permission to pass the frontier of the Duchy of Luxembourg and to get to France that way; the pessimists repeated alarming tales of how Frenchmen were accused of espionage, and shot. The landlord of the hotel was unkindly disposed towards his guests, for some of them had hurried from their homes without luggage or money, and besides he was an atheist, and disliked the Church.

The refugees now found a kind of sedative in the unconcernedness of the young English scholar; they came and talked to him of their troubles. He and the old priest, to pass the time, carried on long theological discussions. The old man confided to him that he had, in his young days, composed a treatise upon the denial of Peter.[4] At that, Frederick translated bits of his manuscript to him.

Within the last days of July the air and ground of Saarburg began to boil and smoke with coming events. It was rumoured that German troops would arrive here on their way to France. In the foreshadow of their mightiness the landlord hardened in his manner to the Frenchmen; he made the two old nuns weep, and the widow, after a great scene with him, fainted, and went to bed. The rest of the party lay as low as they could.

In the midst of these trials a French lady, with her maid, arrived at the hotel from Wiesbaden, and immediately became the central figure of its small world.

She bore a name which to Frederick had all the sound of heroic French history. He first read it on a number of boxes and trunks in the hall of the hotel, and expected to see an old majestic lady, like a spectre out of the grand past. But when she appeared she was as young as himself, flourishing like a rose, a great beauty. He thought: "It is

[4] Matt. 26:69–75.

as if a lioness had calmly walked among a flock of sheep." She had been, he reflected, so slow to leave Wiesbaden because she had it not in her to believe that any inconvenience could ever hit her personally; she refused to believe so now. She was not in the least afraid. She met the anxiety of the pale assembly of the hotel with undaunted forbearance, as if she realized that they must needs have been looking forward in suspense to her arrival. Confronted with the danger of the moment, the timidity of the little group and the hostility of its surroundings, she became still more heraldic, like a lioness in a coat of arms. In spite of her youthfulness and fragility, to Frederick she seemed, from hour to hour, and even as to her carriage, mien and speech, to grow into the orthodox and ideal figure of a "*dame haute et puissante,*"[5] and an embodiment of ancient France.

The refugees took shelter behind her. She wafted the landlord out of existence, changed the servants' manners, and improved the table. She had the bills paid, and sent for a doctor for Madame Bellot. In these matters she had need of a courier, and thus she and Frederick became acquainted.

If Frederick had met this lady six months earlier, before he left England, he would have felt shy and embarrassed in her society. Now he was familiar, if not with herself, at least with sisters and kinswomen of hers. For although she was so elegantly modern, she had all the looks of the goddesses of Titian[6] and Veronese.[7] Her long silky curls shone with the same pale golden tint as their tresses; her carriage had that female majesty with which they sit enthroned or dance, and her flesh had the mysterious freshness and lustre of their flesh.

She had on a small chasseur hat with a pink ostrich feather, a dove-grey silk dress of unbelievable voluminousness, long suede gloves, and round her white throat a narrow black velvet ribbon. She had pearls in her ears and on her neck, and diamond rings on her fingers. He had never seen anything the least like her in real life, but she might well have sat within a gold frame in the gallery of Das Altes Museum. He learned that she was a widow, having been married very young, but not much more about her. But he knew, without being told, where she had spent the years till they now met: amongst the luminous marble columns, in the sweet verdure, in front of the burning blue sea and the

[5] Grand and mighty lady.

[6] Tiziano Vecelli (Titian), 1477–1576, leader of the Venetian school of painters.

[7] Paolo Caliari (Veronese), 1528–1588, last of the great Venetian painters.

silvery and coralline clouds, which he had seen in the paintings. Perhaps she had had a small Negro servant to wait on her. At times his thoughts would wander, and he would see her in divinely negligent attitudes—yes, in the attire of Venus herself.[8] But these fancies of his were candid and impersonal; he would not offend her for the world.

She was kind to him in an elder-sisterly way, but was at times a little curt, as if impatient with a world so much less perfect than herself. Frederick reflected that he and she had got something in common. They agreed in overlooking many facts of existence, which to other people were of the greatest importance. Only in his case this disregard arose from a sense of remoteness from, or estrangement to, the world in general. "While with her," he thought, "it springs from the circumstance that she masters the world, and will stand no nonsense from it. She is the descendant, and the rightful heiress, of conquerors and commanders, even of tyrants, of this world." Her Christian name, he learned from the trunks, was Heloïse.

In the consciousness of Madame Heloïse's power the refugees of the hotel lived through one or two happy days. In the end they all somewhat overdid their gallant assurance. At supper, over a roast chicken and some excellent wine, they talked freely and hopefully, and the commercial traveller, who was a small, timid man, but had a sweet voice, gave them a number of songs. There was a piano in the dining room, and the old priest accompanied him on it. At last the whole party joined in the hymn of: *"Partant pour la Syrie."*[9] In the midst of a verse there was a knocking, like thunder, on the door. They did not mind, they sang on, and parted for the night confidently. The next day the German troops made their entry into Saarburg, in a storm of excitement and triumph, and in the afternoon the refugees of the hotel, with the exception of Madame Bellot, who was still in bed, were arrested, and brought before the magistrate.

To his surprise Frederick learned that he was, together with the old priest, accused of espionage, and that their long talks, and his manuscript and notes, formed the material for the accusation. The magistrate would have it that his quotations from Isaiah, 53.8: "For the transgression of my people" had reference to the hour, date and month of the German advance. Frederick reflected that he had, before now, heard Isaiah interpreted to strange purposes, and patiently tried to

[8] Naked.

[9] "Leaving for Syria."

reason with the magistrate. But he found this gentleman obsessed by the great emotions of the hour, and inaccessible to arguments. The old priest would not, or could not, speak.

Slowly, in the course of the day, it became clear to Frederick that he might in very earnest be shot before night. The certitude gave him a strange, deep tremor. "I shall know now," he thought, "if there is a life after death." He realized that the priest would know it as soon as he. The idea was difficult to conceive; the old man had been such a doctrinairian. But by sunset the magistrate himself grew tired of the case, and had both the accused brought before a party of officers, who were in residence in a big villa outside the town, from which the owners had fled in fear of a French invasion. They found the rest of the group from the hotel here.

The atmosphere of the villa was very different from that of the municipality office. The three German officers had found it convenient to dine in the ease of the salon, which was richly done up in crimson brocade, with heavy curtains and large paintings on the walls. Their dessert and wine were still on the table before them. They were flushed with wine, but even more with triumph, for they had, an hour ago, had news of the action of Wissenburg,[10] and the telegram lay by their glasses.

One of the three was an erect, grey-haired man with a lean face, another seemed to be the leading spirit, or the spoiled child, amongst them. He was left a free hand in the cross-examination of the prisoners, for he spoke French better than the others, and amused them by his exuberant vitality. He was quite young, a giant in stature, and strikingly fair, with a fullness, or heaviness, that gave him the appearance of a young god. He met the people from the hotel with laughing surprise and disdain, and seemed to fear neither God nor the Devil—and still less any Frenchman—until he caught sight of Madame Heloïse. From then the case became a matter between him and her.

Frederick could see that much. But he was no judge of this kind of warfare; and, although after the first glance she did not once look at the man, while his light, protruding eyes did not for a moment leave her face or figure, he could not have decided whether, in very truth, the offensive lay with him or with her.

The two were alike, and might have been brother and sister. They were obviously afraid of one another. As the interview proceeded the

[10] Small border town where on 4 August 1870, the French met their first defeat, having been overwhelmed by a superior German force.

German sweated with dread, and she grew pale, still nothing could have held them apart. Frederick was certain that they met here for the first time; all the same it was an old feud which was about to be settled in the salon of the villa. Was it, he wondered, a hereditary national combat, or would he have to go further back, and deeper down, to discover the root of it?

The young German began by stating that he now hardly found it worth his while to proceed to Paris. He asked her how she had got into her present company, and whether she considered her compeers to be more dangerous than herself? She replied curtly, her chin lifted. Frederick was aware that his own fate, with that of his fellows, now rested with her. He reflected that no human being, and least of all this young soldier, would for long put up with her look and manner, and still in his heart he applauded the fine display of insolence that she gave them. It was inevitable that in the end the German should come up close to her; as he held a paper up for her inspection he spoke straight into her face. At that, in a gentle movement, she swept back the ample skirt of her dress, so that it should get in no contact with him.

He stopped short in the midst of his speech, and gasped for breath. "I am not, Madame," he said very slowly, "going to touch your dress. I am going to make you a proposal. I shall write out the passport for you and your friends to get into Luxembourg, which you want from me. You may come and fetch it in half an hour. But you will have to come without that skirt, which you do, rightly, take such trouble to keep away from me. You will, in fact, have to come for your passports dressed like the goddess Venus. That is," he added after a moment's breathless silence, "at any rate, a handsome proposition, Madame." At his own words he suddenly blushed dark crimson.

Frederick's heart ceased to beat for a moment, with disgust or horror, and with sadness. The sentence was a distortion of his own beautiful fancies about Heloïse. The blasphemy made of the world a place of nauseating baseness, and of him an accomplice.

As to Heloïse herself, the insult changed her as if it had set fire to her. She turned straight upon the insulter, and Frederick had never seen her so abundant in vitality or arrogance; she seemed about to laugh in her adversary's face. The sordidness of the world, he thought with deep ecstatic gratitude, did not touch her; she was above it all. Only for a moment her hand went up to the collar of her mantilla, as if, choking under the wave of her disdain, she must free herself of it. But again the next moment she stood still; her hand sank down, and with it the blood from her cheeks; she became very pale. She turned to her fellow-prisoners, and slowly let her gaze run over their white, horrified faces.

The two older officers stirred in their chairs. The young man wafted his paper at them. "Why!" he cried. "He was wounded for our transgressions! For the transgressions of my people we are stricken! With chapter and verse to it! We have a whole gang of spies before us, Sirs, with her—" he pointed a shaking finger at Heloïse, "at the head of them. Why must she come here of all places? Could she not have left us, at any rate, alone?"

He spoke to her again; he could not let go his hold of her. "Are you sure you have understood me?" he screamed. "No, I am not sure," said she. "The French language will lend itself badly to your proposition. Will you please repeat it in German?" This was difficult for him to do; still he did it. Heloïse took off her hat, so that her golden hair shone in the lamplight. During the rest of the interview she kept it in her hands behind her slim waist, and it gave her a look of having her hands tied upon her back.

"Why do you ask me?" she said. "Ask those who are with me. These are poor people, hard-working, and used to hardships. Here is a French priest," she went on very slowly, "the consoler of many poor souls; here are two French sisters, who have nursed the sick and dying. The two others have children in France, who will fare ill without them. Their salvation is, to each one of them, more important than mine. Let them decide for themselves if they will buy it at your price. You will be answered, by them, in French."

The old priest took a step forward. He had been given to long speeches, in the hotel, but here he did not say a word. He only stretched his right arm upwards, and waved it to and fro. The one old nun threw herself back towards the wall, as if already facing the fusillading squad. She lifted both arms and cried: "No!" The other nun burst into terrible sobs, her legs gave way under her, she fell down upon her knees and repeated: "No. No. No."

It was the commercial traveller who made a speech. He took a long step towards the young officer, looked up to his great height and said: "You believe that we are afraid of you? Yes, so we are. We are afraid ever to come to look as you do." Frederick did not speak; he looked the officer in the face, and could not help smiling a little.

The German stared down at the commercial traveller, and then over his head at Heloïse. He cried out: "Then away with you. Let it have an end. Away with you all!" He called on two soldiers from the adjoining room. "Take these people down," he commanded, "into the courtyard. For further orders." And once more he cried to the prisoners: "You will have it your own way now. Let me have peace. Let me have peace only." The last thing that Frederick saw in the room was his face, as Heloïse passed him and looked at him. The whole party was rushed down the stairs, and out of the house.

As they came down in the courtyard the night was clear and the stars began to show in the sky. There was a low wall running along the one side of the court, fencing the garden of the villa; from the other side of it came the smell of stock. One by one the tired refugees, ignorant of their fate, went and took their place by this wall. Heloïse, who stood bareheaded in the court, looked up to the sky, then after a while said to Frederick: "There was a falling star. You might have wished."

When they had stood in the courtyard for half an hour three soldiers came out of the house; one of them carried a lamp. One of the others, who seemed to be a superintendent, looked round at the prisoners, went up to the old priest and handed him a paper. "This is your permission to go to Luxembourg," he said. "It is for all of you. The trains are filled up; you will have to get a carriage in town. You had better leave at once."

As soon as he had finished, another of the soldiers stepped forward and addressed himself to Heloïse, and they were surprised to see that he was holding a big bouquet of roses, which had been upon the table of the salon. He made a military salute. "The Colonel," he said, "asks Madame to accept these. With his compliments. To a heroine." Heloïse took the bouquet from him as if she did not see either him or it.

They managed to get carriages at the hotel. While they were kept waiting for them they had a hurried, spare meal of bread and wine, for none of them had eaten anything since morning. It was no renewal of their gallant supper of last night; it seemed to have no connection with it. Their existence, since then, had been set on another plane. They held one another's hands, each of them owed his life to each of the others.

Heloïse was still the central figure of their communion, but in a new way, as an object infinitely precious to them all. Her pride, her glory was theirs, since they had been ready to die for it. She was still very pale; she looked like a child amongst the old people, and laughed at what they said to her. As she insisted on taking all her trunks and boxes with her, evidently regarding them as part of herself and not to be left in the hands of the enemy, and as Frederick had to load them up, he and she came to drive together, behind the others, and in a small fiacre, to the frontier.

Frederick all his life remembered this drive, even to the curves of the road. The moon was up, and the stretch of sky between her and the low horizon was as if powdered with gold-dust. When the dew fell, Heloïse drew her shawl over her head; within its dark folds she looked like a village girl, and still she sat enthroned, like a muse, by his side. He had read in books, before now, of heroics and heroines; the episode he had lived through and the young woman beside him were like the books, and all the same she was so gently and simply vivid, like no book in the world. Her silent, triumphant happiness was as sweet to him as the smell of the ripe cornfield through which they drove. All of a sudden she took his hand.

It was early when they passed the frontier and came to the small station of Wasserbillig, where they found the rest of their party. While they waited for the train, which was to take them into France, and once more turned their faces to Paris, his French friends, Frederick felt, became like one family, to which he no longer belonged. When the train at last came in, they seemed almost ignorant of his existence.

But at the last moment Heloïse gave him a long, deep, tender glance. It followed him from behind the window of her compartment. Then suddenly she was gone.

Frederick stood on the platform and watched the train disappear in a dim morning landscape. He felt that the curtain had gone down upon a great event in his life. His heart was aching both with happiness and with woe. The lately born artist within him, Venusti's friend, received the adventure in a humble, ecstatic spirit, and *"Domine, non sum dignus"*[11] was his response to it. But when he was once more alone, the searcher and inquirer, his old self of the universities of England took hold, craved for more than that, and demanded to be enlightened, to know and understand. There was, within the phenomena of the heroic mind, still something left uncomprehended, an unexplored, a mysterious area.

It would be, he reflected, this moment of incompleted investigation and unobtained insight, which now caused him to stand at the station of Wasserbillig with an almost choking feeling of loss or privation, as if a cup had been withdrawn from his lips before his thirst was quenched.

The true seeker is sometimes helped to his end by the hand of fate. So was Frederick in his research on the heroic mind. He only had to wait for a while.

In England he went back to his books. He finished his treatise on the doctrine of atonement, and later on wrote another book. With time

[11] "Lord, I am not worthy": the centurion's answer to Jesus (Matt. 8:8 and Luke 7:6).

he strolled from the area of religious philosophy to that of history of religion in general. He was holding a good position amongst the young men of letters of his generation, and was engaged to a girl, whom he had known from the time when they were both children, when, five or six years after his adventure at Saarburg, he had to go to Paris to attend a course of lectures by a great French historian.

He looked up an old friend there, a brother of the boy who, in Berlin, had first given him news of the war. This young man's name was Arthur, and he was still, as then, in the same office at the Embassy. Arthur was at a loss to know how to entertain a student of theology in Paris. He invited Frederick out to dine at a select restaurant, and, while they were dining, asked him how he liked Paris, and what he had been seeing there. Frederick answered that he had seen a multitude of beautiful things, and had been to the museums of the Louvre and Luxembourg. They talked for some time of classic and modern art. Then suddenly Arthur exclaimed: "If you like to look at beautiful things I know what we will do. We will go and see Heloïse." "Heloïse?" said Frederick. "Not a word more," said Arthur. "It cannot be described; it shall be seen."

He took Frederick to a small, select and exquisite music hall. "We are just in time," he said. Then he laughed and added: "Although you really ought to have seen her at the time of the Empire.[12] Some people have it that she is as stupid as a goose, but you cannot believe it when you look at her legs. *La jambe c'est la femme!*[13] They also tell me that her private life is quite respectable. I do not know."

The show which they were to see was called *Diana's Revenge* and affected the classic style, but was elegantly modern in its details. A great number of lovely young dancers danced and posed, as nymphs in a forest, and were all very scantily dressed. But the climax of the whole performance was the appearance of the goddess Diana herself, with nothing on at all.

As she stepped forward bending her golden bow, a noise like a long sigh went through the house. The beauty of her body came as a surprise and an ecstasy even to those who had seen her before; they hardly believed their eyes.

Arthur regarded her in his opera-glasses, then generously handed them on to Frederick. But he noticed that Frederick did not make use of

[12] Reign of Napoleon III, Second Empire of France (1852–1870), which ended with Napoleon's defeat and capture at Sedan.

[13] The leg is the woman.

them, and, after a moment, that he had become very still. He wondered if he was shocked. *"C'est une chose incroyable,"* he said, *"que la beauté de cette femme.*[14] What do you say?"

"Yes," said Frederick. "But I know her. I have seen her before now." "But not in this thing?" said Arthur. "No. Not in that," said Frederick. After a little while he added: "Perhaps she will remember me. I shall send up my card." Arthur smiled. The page who had taken up Frederick's card came back with a small letter for him. "Is that from her?" Arthur asked. "Yes," said Frederick. "She remembers me. She will come and see us when the performance is over." "Heloïse?" exclaimed Arthur. "Well, you English professors of religious philosophy! When did you meet her? Was it when you were writing upon the mysteries of the Egyptian Adonis?[15]" "No, I was writing on another theme then," said Frederick. Arthur ordered a table and wine and a big bouquet of roses.

Heloïse came into the theatre, and made all heads turn towards her, like a bed of sunflowers towards the sun. She was in black, with a long train and long gloves, ostrich feathers and pearls. "All that black," sighed the house in its heart, "to cover up all that white!"

She was perhaps a little fuller of bosom, and thinner in the face, than she had been six years ago, but she still moved in the same way, like one of the great Felidae,[16] and had, in her countenance and mien, that brevity or impatience which had then charmed Frederick. Frederick rose to greet her, and Arthur, who had thought him sadly awkward amongst the elegant public of the theatre, was struck by his friend's dignity, and, as he and Heloïse looked at each other, by the completely identical expression of deep happy earnestness in their two faces. They gave him the impression that they would have liked to kiss as they met, but were held back by something other than the presence of people round them. They kept standing up, as if they had forgotten the human faculty of sitting down.

Heloïse beamed on Frederick. "I am so happy that you have come to see me," she said, with his hand in hers. Frederick at first could not find a word to say; in the end he asked a stupid question. "Have any of the others," he asked, "been here to see you?" "No," said Heloïse.

[14] The beauty of that woman is unbelievable.

[15] Just as Adonis, in Greek legend, is reborn after his death to live half of each year with Aphrodite, so is his Egyptian counterpart, Osiris, resurrected after his death by Isis, his sister-wife. Both legends are associated with agriculture and primitive fertility rituals.

[16] Feline (cat family).

"No, none of them." Here Arthur succeeded in making them sit down, opposite each other, by his table. "You know," said Heloïse, "that poor old Father Lamarque has died?" "No!" said Frederick. "I have not been in touch with any of them." "Yes, he died," said Heloïse. "When he came to Paris, then, he asked to be sent to the army. He did wonders there; he was a hero! But he got wounded, later, here in Paris, by the soldiers of Versailles. When I heard of it I ran to the hospital, but alas, it was too late."

To make up for his countryman's silence Arthur poured out the champagne to her with a compliment.

"Oh, they were good people," she cried, taking her glass. "What a fine time it was! The two old sisters, too, how good they were! And so were all of them.

"But they were not exactly very brave," she added, setting down the glass again. "They were all in a deadly funk that night at the villa. They were already seeing the muzzles of the German rifles, pointing at them. And, good God, they were running a risk then, too, and a worse one than they ever knew themselves."

"How do you mean?" Frederick asked.

"Yes, a worse risk to them," said Heloïse. "For they would have made me do as the German demanded. They would have made me do it, to save their lives, if he had put it straight to them at first, or if they had been left to themselves. And then they would never have got over it. They would have repented it all their lives, and have held themselves to be great sinners. They were not the people for that kind of business, they, who had never before done a mean thing in their life. That is why it was a sad thing that they should have been so badly frightened. I tell you, my friend, for those people it would have been better to be shot than to live on with a bad conscience. They were not used to that, you see; they would not have known how to live with it."

"How do you know all that?" asked Frederick.

"Oh, I know that kind of people well," said Heloïse. "I was brought up amongst poor, honest people myself. My grandmother had a sister who was a nun, and it was an old poor priest, like Father Lamarque, who taught me to read."

Frederick put his elbow on the table, and his chin in his hand, and sat and looked at her. "Then your triumph afterwards," he said very slowly, "was really all on our behalf? Because we had behaved so well?" "You did behave well, did you not?" said she smiling at him. "So you were a greater heroine, even," said Frederick in the same way, "than I knew at the time." "My dear friend!" said she.

He asked her, "Did you believe, at the moment, that you might really be shot?" "Yes," said she. "He might very well have had me shot, and all of you with me. That might well have been his fashion of making love. And all the same," she added thoughtfully, "he was honest, an honest young man. He could really want a thing. Many men have not got that in them."

She drank, had her glass refilled, and looked at Frederick. "You," she said, "you were not like the others. If you and I had been alone there, everything would have been different. You might have made me save my life, in the way he told me, quite simply, and have thought nothing of it afterwards. I saw it, at the time. And when we drove together to the frontier, and you did not say a word, I knew it, in that fiacre. I liked it in you, and I do not know where you have learned it, seeing that after all you are an Englishman." Frederick thought her words over. "Yes," he said slowly, "if you had proposed it yourself, of your own free will." Heloïse laughed at that.

"But do you know," she suddenly cried, "what was good luck both for you and me, and for all of us? That there were no women with us at the time! A woman would have made me do it, quick, had I been ever so distressed. And where, in that case, would all our greatness have been?" "But there were women with us," said Frederick. "There were the nuns." "Nay, they do not count," said Heloïse. "A nun is not a woman in that sense. No, I mean a married woman, or an old maid, an honest woman. If Madame Bellot had not had stomach-ache with fear, she would have had everything off me in no time, I can promise you. Her I could never have talked round."

Heloïse fell into thought, with her eyes on Frederick's face, and after a minute or two said: "What a man you have become! I believe that you have grown. You were only a boy then. We were both so much younger," "Tonight," said he, "it does not seem to me a long time ago." "But it is a long time, all the same," said she, "only to you it does not matter. You are a man, a writer, are you not? You are on the upward path. You will be writing many more books, I feel that. Do you remember, now, how when we went out for a walk, in Saarburg, you told me about the books of a Jew in Amsterdam? He had a pretty name, like a woman's. I might have chosen it for myself, instead of the one I have got, which also a learned man selected for me.[17] I suppose

[17] Heloïse (1101?–1164) became the mistress and eventually the wife of her teacher, the French theologian and philosopher Pierre Abélard (1079–1142). After her uncle had Abélard castrated, she retired to the convent of Argenteuil.

that only very learned people would know it at all. What was it, now?" "Spinoza," said Frederick. "Yes," said Heloïse, "Spinoza.[18] He cut diamonds. It was very interesting. No, to you time does not matter. One is happy to meet one's friends again," she said, "and yet it is then that one realizes how time flies. It is we who feel it, the women. From us time takes away so much. And in the end: everything." She looked up at Frederick, and none of the faces which the great masters paint had ever given him such a vision of life, and of the world. "How I wish, my dear friend," she said, "that you had seen me then."

1942

[18] Baruch or Benedict de Spinoza (1632–1677), Dutch-Jewish philosopher, who earned his living as a lens grinder.

DISCUSSION QUESTIONS

1. After describing the three married couples accompanying Élisabeth Rousset (Boule de Suif), the narrator calls them "respectable, influential persons of religion and principle" (page 230). Judging from their subsequent behavior, the statement is obviously meant to be *ironic.* Find three other examples in which the narrator, through a feigned matter-of-fact *tone,* pretends to accept a character's viewpoint only in order to mock it. Find several examples in which the narrator is openly critical of a character. Compare this narrator with the one Maupassant used in "The Jewelry." Specifically, how do they differ? Why?

2. By what means does Maupassant arouse our sympathy for Élisabeth early in the story? Why does she wait until 3 P.M. to eat her lunch?

3. The saying "the end justifies the means" is in "Boule de Suif" assumed to be a "moral axiom" (page 250). Do you agree? Explain. Describe the narrator's attitude toward this dictum. Give supporting evidence.

4. The ten travelers form a social hierarchy from lowly harlot to count. Through three or four examples, show how Maupassant exploits this class distinction psychologically as well as comically.

5. Besides the obvious satisfaction of escaping the Prussians, what other pleasure do the travelers derive from Élisabeth's yielding to the officer? Cite examples.

6. Why do we get an extended inner view of Élisabeth only near the end of the story? In what way, if any, would the story and our attitude toward her have been different if we had been exposed to Élisabeth's thoughts and feelings from the beginning?

7. Through whose *point of view* is "The Heroine" narrated? When does Dinesen switch temporarily to another point of view? At what point does the narrator momentarily comment on the action?

8. Contrast Élisabeth's attitude toward the officer with Heloïse's. Why is the latter's response more complex, even ambivalent? Explain the nature of her "warfare" with the German. Why is Frederick "no judge" of it?

9. How is the officer's demand a "distortion of his [Frederick's] own beautiful fancies about Heloïse" (page 265)? Explain how each man sees Heloïse. What do her final words to Frederick mean? Why does

she call the officer "an honest young man"? Could Frederick "really want a thing" (page 272)? Explain.

10. Compare Élisabeth's and Heloïse's personalities and actions. Do the same for the two officers. Which officer seems more believable? Why?

11. While Élisabeth's reward for saving her fellow refugees is their contempt, Heloïse gains their veneration by persuading them to risk their lives for her. What specific conditions bring about this difference?

12. Heloïse claims that her companions would have accepted the German's proposal if "he had put it straight to them at first, or if they had been left to themselves" (page 271). In contrast, how does she manage to make them reject the proposal? How is her use of *salvation* an ironic *pun* (a play on two meanings of a word)? What results stem from Élisabeth's fellow travelers being "left to themselves"? What difference in situation originates from Élisabeth's profession being known and Heloïse's unknown?

13. Why is Heloïse willing to risk her life and that of her companions in order to avoid appearing naked before the officer, even though nudity in public is for her an everyday occurrence?

ANALYSIS AND APPLICATION

1. Compare each of the following modified versions with its original in "Boule de Suif." Which is more effective within the context of the story? Why?

a. Only the first step was difficult. They fell to with a will once the Rubicon was crossed and emptied the basket.

"The first step was the only difficulty. The Rubicon once crossed, they fell to with a will. The basket was emptied." (page 235)

b. Being still hungry, supper was ordered.

"Being still hungry, they ordered supper." (page 237)

c. The others seconded him and lectured, begged, and urged Boule de Suif till finally they persuaded her, dreading the complications which might result from her rashness.

"The others seconded him; they begged, urged, and lectured Boule de

Suif till finally they persuaded her. For they dreaded the complications which might result from her rashness." (page 238)

d. After the coach had stopped, no one got out due to the fact that the travellers expected to be massacred as soon as they emerged.

"Though the coach had stopped, no one got out. It was as if the travellers expected to be massacred as soon as they emerged." (page 237)

e. Stout Madame Loiseau, however, who had the soul of a gendarme, saying little but eating all the more, remained obdurate.

"Only stout Madame Loiseau, who had the soul of a gendarme, remained obdurate, saying little but eating all the more." (page 235)

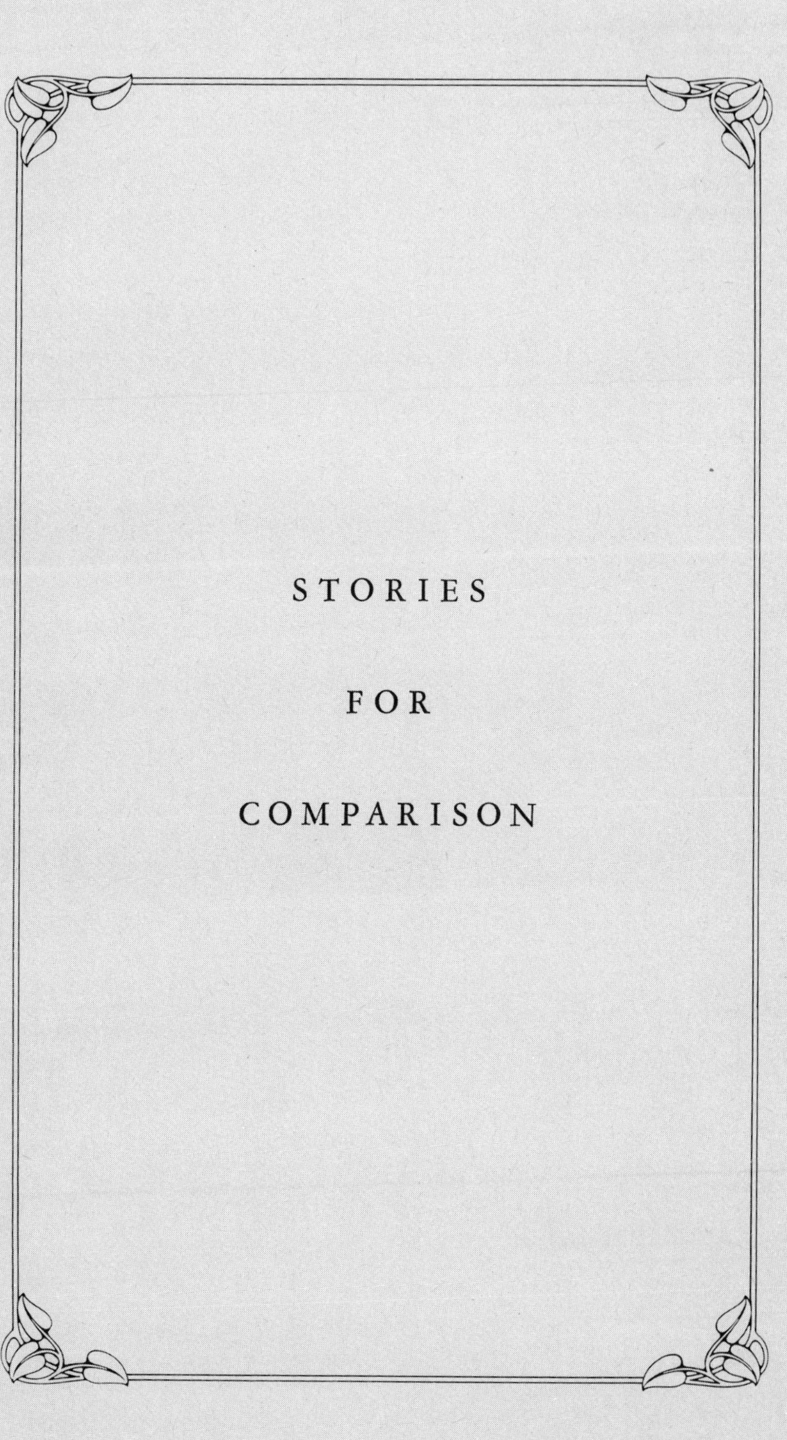

STORIES

FOR

COMPARISON

THAT EVENING SUN

WILLIAM FAULKNER

MONDAY IS no different from any other weekday in Jefferson now. The streets are paved now, and the telephone and electric companies are cutting down more and more of the shade trees—the water oaks, the maples and locusts and elms—to make room for iron poles bearing clusters of bloated and ghostly and bloodless grapes, and we have a city laundry which makes the rounds on Monday morning, gathering the bundles of clothes into bright-colored, specially-made motor cars: the soiled wearing of a whole week now flees apparitionlike behind alert and irritable electric horns, with a long diminishing noise of rubber and asphalt like tearing silk, and even the Negro women who still take in white people's washing after the old custom, fetch and deliver it in automobiles.

But fifteen years ago, on Monday morning the quiet, dusty, shady streets would be full of Negro women with, balanced on their steady, turbaned heads, bundles of clothes tied up in sheets, almost as large as cotton bales, carried so without touch of hand between the kitchen door of the white house and the blackened washpot beside a cabin door in Negro Hollow.

Nancy would set her bundle on the top of her head, then upon the bundle in turn she would set the black straw sailor hat which she wore winter and summer. She was tall, with a high, sad face sunken a little where her teeth were missing. Sometimes we would go a part of the way down the lane and across the pasture with her, to watch the balanced bundle and the hat that never bobbed nor wavered, even when she walked down into the ditch and up the other side and stooped through the fence. She would go down on her hands and knees and crawl through the gap, her head rigid, uptilted, the bundle steady as a rock or a balloon, and rise to her feet again and go on.

Sometimes the husbands of the washing women would fetch and deliver the clothes, but Jesus never did that for Nancy, even before father told him to stay away from our house, even when Dilsey was sick and Nancy would come to cook for us.

And then about half the time we'd have to go down the lane to Nancy's cabin and tell her to come on and cook breakfast. We would stop at the ditch, because father told us to not have anything to do with Jesus—he was a short black man, with a razor scar down his face—and we would throw rocks at Nancy's house until she came to the door, leaning her head around it without any clothes on.

"What yawl mean, chunking my house?" Nancy said. "What you little devils mean?"

"Father says for you to come on and get breakfast," Caddy said. "Father says it's over a half an hour now, and you've got to come this minute."

"I aint studying[1] no breakfast," Nancy said. "I going to get my sleep out."

"I bet you're drunk," Jason said. "Father says you're drunk. Are you drunk, Nancy?"

[1] Considering.

"Who says I is?" Nancy said. "I got to get my sleep out. I aint studying no breakfast."

So after a while we quit chunking the cabin and went back home. When she finally came, it was too late for me to go to school. So we thought it was whisky until that day they arrested her again and they were taking her to jail and they passed Mr. Stovall. He was the cashier in the bank and a deacon in the Baptist church, and Nancy began to say:

"When you going to pay me, white man? When you going to pay me, white man? It's been three times now since you paid me a cent—" Mr Stovall knocked her down, but she kept on saying, "When you going to pay me, white man? It's been three times now since—" until Mr Stovall kicked her in the mouth with his heel and the marshal caught Mr Stovall back, and Nancy lying in the street, laughing. She turned her head and spat out some blood and teeth and said, "It's been three times now since he paid me a cent."

That was how she lost her teeth, and all that day they told about Nancy and Mr Stovall, and all that night the ones that passed the jail could hear Nancy singing and yelling. They could see her hands holding to the window bars, and a lot of them stopped along the fence, listening to her and to the jailer trying to make her stop. She didn't shut up until almost daylight, when the jailer began to hear a bumping and scraping upstairs and he went up there and found Nancy hanging from the window bar. He said that it was cocaine and not whisky, because no nigger would try to commit suicide unless he was full of cocaine, because a nigger full of cocaine wasn't a nigger any longer.

The jailer cut her down and revived her; then he beat her, whipped her. She had hung herself with her dress. She had fixed it all right, but when they arrested her she didn't have on anything except a dress and so she didn't have anything to tie her hands with and she couldn't make her hands let go of the window ledge. So the jailer heard the noise and ran up there and found Nancy hanging from the window, stark naked, her belly already swelling out a little, like a little balloon.

When Dilsey was sick in her cabin and Nancy was cooking for us, we could see her apron swelling out; that was before father told Jesus to stay away from the house. Jesus was in the kitchen, sitting behind the stove, with his razor scar on his black face like a piece of dirty string. He said it was a watermelon that Nancy had under her dress.

"It never come off of your vine, though," Nancy said.

"Off of what vine?" Caddy said.

"I can cut down the vine it did come off of," Jesus said.

"What makes you want to talk like that before these children?" Nancy said. "Whyn't you go on to work? You done et. You want Mr Jason to catch you hanging around his kitchen, talking that way before these chillen?"

"Talking what way?" Caddy said. "What vine?"

"I cant hang around white man's kitchen," Jesus said. "But white man can hang around mine. White man can come in my house, but I cant stop him. When white man want to come in my house, I aint got no house. I cant stop him, but he cant kick me outen it. He cant do that."

Dilsey was still sick in her cabin. Father told Jesus to stay off our place. Dilsey was still sick. It was a long time. We were in the library after supper.

"Isn't Nancy through in the kitchen yet?" mother said. "It seems to me that she has had plenty of time to have finished the dishes."

"Let Quentin go and see," father said. "Go and see if Nancy is through, Quentin. Tell her she can go on home."

I went to the kitchen. Nancy was through. The dishes were put away and the fire was out. Nancy was sitting in a chair, close to the cold stove. She looked at me.

"Mother wants to know if you are through," I said.

"Yes," Nancy said. She looked at me. "I done finished." She looked at me.

"What is it?" I said. "What is it?"

"I aint nothing but a nigger," Nancy said. "It aint none of my fault."

She looked at me, sitting in the chair before the cold stove, the sailor hat on her head. I went back to the library. It was the cold stove and all, when you think of a kitchen being warm and busy and cheerful. And with a cold stove and the dishes all put away, and nobody wanting to eat at that hour.

"Is she through?" mother said.

"Yessum," I said.

"What is she doing?" mother said.

"She's not doing anything. She's through."

"I'll go and see," father said.

"Maybe she's waiting for Jesus to come and take her home," Caddy said.

"Jesus is gone," I said. Nancy told us how one morning she woke up and Jesus was gone.

"He quit me," Nancy said. "Done gone to Memphis, I reckon. Dodging them city *po*-lice for a while, I reckon."

"And a good riddance," father said. "I hope he stays there."

"Nancy's scaired of the dark," Jason said.

"So are you," Caddy said.

"I'm not," Jason said.

"Scairy cat," Caddy said.

"I'm not," Jason said.

"You, Candace!" mother said. Father came back.

"I am going to walk down the lane with Nancy," he said. "She says that Jesus is back."

"Has she seen him?" mother said.

"No. Some Negro sent her word that he was back in town. I won't be long."

"You'll leave me alone, to take Nancy home?" mother said. "Is her safety more precious to you than mine?"

"I wont be long," father said.

"You'll leave these children unprotected, with that Negro about?"

"I'm going too," Caddy said. "Let me go, Father."

"What would he do with them, if he were unfortunate enough to have them?" father said.

"I want to go, too," Jason said.

"Jason!" mother said. She was speaking to father. You could tell that by the way she said the name. Like she believed that all day father had been trying to think of doing the thing she wouldn't like the most, and that she knew all the time that after a while he would think of it. I stayed quiet, because father and I both knew that mother would want him to make me stay with her if she just thought of it in time. So father didn't look at me. I was the oldest. I was nine and Caddy was seven and Jason was five.

"Nonsense," father said. "We wont be long."

Nancy had her hat on. We came to the lane. "Jesus always been good to me," Nancy said. "Whenever he had two dollars, one of them was mine." We walked in the lane. "If I can just get through the lane," Nancy said, "I be all right then."

The lane was always dark. "This is where Jason got scared on Hallowe'en," Caddy said.

"I didn't," Jason said.

"Cant Aunt Rachel do anything with him?" father said. Aunt Rachel was old. She lived in a cabin beyond Nancy's, by herself. She had white hair and she smoked a pipe in the door, all day long; she didn't work any more. They said she was Jesus' mother. Sometimes she said she was and sometimes she said she wasn't any kin to Jesus.

"Yes, you did," Caddy said. "You were scairder than Frony. You were scairder than T.P. even. Scairder than niggers."

"Cant nobody do nothing with him," Nancy said. "He say I done woke up the devil in him and aint but one thing going to lay it down again."

"Well, he's gone now," father said. "There's nothing for you to be afraid of now. And if you'd just let white men alone."

"Let what white men alone?" Caddy said. "How let them alone?"

"He aint gone nowhere," Nancy said. "I can feel him. I can feel him now, in this lane. He hearing us talk, every word, hid somewhere, waiting. I aint seen him, and I aint going to see him again but once more, with that razor in his mouth. That razor on that string down his back, inside his shirt. And then I aint going to be even surprised."

"I wasn't scaired," Jason said.

"If you'd behave yourself, you'd have kept out of this," father said. "But it's all right now. He's probably in St. Louis now. Probably got another wife by now and forgot all about you."

"If he has, I better not find out about it," Nancy said. "I'd stand there right over them, and every time he wropped[2] her, I'd cut that arm off. I'd cut his head off and I'd slit her belly and I'd shove—"

"Hush," father said.

"Slit whose belly, Nancy?" Caddy said.

"I wasn't scaired," Jason said. "I'd walk right down this lane by myself."

"Yah," Caddy said. "You wouldn't dare to put your foot down in it if we were not here too."

II

Dilsey was still sick, so we took Nancy home every night until mother said, "How much longer is this going on? I to be left alone in this big house while you take home a frightened Negro?"

We fixed a pallet in the kitchen for Nancy. One night we waked up, hearing the sound. It was not singing and it was not crying, coming up the dark stairs. There was a light in mother's room and we heard father going down the hall, down the back stairs, and Caddy and I went into the hall. The floor was cold. Our toes curled away from it while we listened to the sound. It was like singing and it wasn't like singing, like the sounds that Negroes make.

[2] Embraced.

Then it stopped and we heard father going down the back stairs, and we went to the head of the stairs. Then the sound began again, in the stairway, not loud, and we could see Nancy's eyes halfway up the stairs, against the wall. They looked like cat's eyes do, like a big cat against the wall, watching us. When we came down the steps to where she was, she quit making the sound again, and we stood there until father came back up from the kitchen, with his pistol in his hand. He went back down with Nancy and they came back with Nancy's pallet.

We spread the pallet in our room. After the light in mother's room went off, we could see Nancy's eyes again. "Nancy," Caddy whispered, "are you asleep, Nancy?"

Nancy whispered something. It was oh or no, I dont know which. Like nobody had made it, like it came from nowhere and went nowhere, until it was like Nancy was not there at all; that I had looked so hard at her eyes on the stairs that they had got printed on my eyeballs, like the sun does when you have closed your eyes and there is no sun. "Jesus," Nancy whispered. "Jesus."

"Was it Jesus?" Caddy said. "Did he try to come into the kitchen?"

"Jesus," Nancy said. Like this: Jeeeeeeeeeeeeeeeesus, until the sound went out, like a match or a candle does.

"It's the other Jesus she means," I said.

"Can you see us, Nancy?" Caddy whispered. "Can you see our eyes too?"

"I aint nothing but a nigger," Nancy said. "God knows. God knows."

"What did you see down there in the kitchen?" Caddy whispered. "What tried to get in?"

"God knows," Nancy said. We could see her eyes. "God knows."

Dilsey got well. She cooked dinner. "You'd better stay in bed a day or two longer," father said.

"What for?" Dilsey said. "If I had been a day later, this place would be to rack and ruin. Get on out of here now, and let me get my kitchen straight again."

Dilsey cooked supper too. And that night, just before dark, Nancy came into the kitchen.

"How do you know he's back?" Dilsey said. "You aint seen him."

"Jesus is a nigger," Jason said.

"I can feel him," Nancy said. "I can feel him laying yonder in the ditch."

"Tonight?" Dilsey said. "Is he there tonight?"

"Dilsey's a nigger too," Jason said.

"You try to eat something," Dilsey said.

"I dont want nothing," Nancy said.

"I aint a nigger," Jason said.

"Drink some coffee," Dilsey said. She poured a cup of coffee for Nancy. "Do you know he's out there tonight? How come you know it's tonight?"

"I know," Nancy said. "He's there, waiting. I know. I done lived with him too long. I know what he is fixing to do fore he know it himself."

"Drink some coffee," Dilsey said. Nancy held the cup to her mouth and blew into the cup. Her mouth pursed out like a spreading adder's, like a rubber mouth, like she had blown all the color out of her lips with blowing the coffee.

"I aint a nigger," Jason said. "Are you a nigger, Nancy?"

"I hellborn, child," Nancy said. "I wont be nothing soon. I going back where I come from soon."

III

She began to drink the coffee. While she was drinking, holding the cup in both hands, she began to make the sound again. She made the sound into the cup and the coffee sploshed out onto her hands and her dress. Her eyes looked at us and she sat there, her elbows on her knees, holding the cup in both hands, looking at us across the wet cup, making the sound. "Look at Nancy," Jason said. "Nancy cant cook for us now. Dilsey's got well now."

"You hush up," Dilsey said. Nancy held the cup in both hands, looking at us, making the sound, like there were two of them: one looking at us and the other making the sound. "Whyn't you let Mr. Jason telefoam the marshal?" Dilsey said. Nancy stopped then, holding the cup in her long brown hands. She tried to drink some coffee again, but it sploshed out of the cup, onto her hands and her dress, and she put the cup down. Jason watched her.

"I cant swallow it," Nancy said. "I swallows but it wont go down me."

"You go down to the cabin," Dilsey said. "Frony will fix you a pallet and I'll be there soon."

"Wont no nigger stop him," Nancy said.

"I aint a nigger," Jason said. "Am I, Dilsey?"

"I reckon not," Dilsey said. She looked at Nancy. "I dont reckon so. What you going to do, then?"

Nancy looked at us. Her eyes went fast, like she was afraid there wasn't time to look, without hardly moving at all. She looked at us, at all three of us at one time. "You member that night I stayed in yawls' room?" she said. She told about how we waked up early the next morning, and played. We had to play quiet, on her pallet, until father woke up and it was time to get breakfast. "Go and ask your maw to let me stay here tonight," Nancy said. "I wont need no pallet. We can play some more."

Caddy asked mother. Jason went too. "I cant have Negroes sleeping in the bedrooms," mother said. Jason cried. He cried until mother said he couldn't have any dessert for three days if he didn't stop. Then Jason said he would stop if Dilsey would make a chocolate cake. Father was there.

"Why dont you do something about it?" mother said. "What do we have officers for?"

"Why is Nancy afraid of Jesus?" Caddy said. "Are you afraid of father, mother?"

"What could the officers do?" father said. "If Nancy hasn't seen him, how could the officers find him?"

"Then why is she afraid?" mother said.

"She says he is there. She says she knows he is there tonight."

"Yet we pay taxes," mother said. "I must wait here alone in this big house while you take a Negro woman home."

"You know that I am not lying outside with a razor," father said.

"I'll stop if Dilsey will make a chocolate cake," Jason said. Mother told us to go out and father said he didn't know if Jason would get a chocolate cake or not, but he knew what Jason was going to get in about a minute. We went back to the kitchen and told Nancy.

"Father said for you to go home and lock the door, and you'll be all right," Caddy said. "All right from what, Nancy? Is Jesus mad at you?" Nancy was holding the coffee cup in her hands again, her elbows on her knees and her hands holding the cup between her knees. She was looking into the cup. "What have you done that made Jesus mad?" Caddy said. Nancy let the cup go. It didn't break on the floor, but the coffee spilled out, and Nancy sat there with her hands still making the shape of the cup. She began to make the sound again, not loud. Not singing and not unsinging. We watched her.

"Here," Dilsey said. "You quit that, now. You get aholt of yourself. You wait here. I going to get Versh to walk home with you." Dilsey went out.

We looked at Nancy. Her shoulders kept shaking, but she quit making the sound. We watched her. "What's Jesus going to do to you?" Caddy said. "He went away."

Nancy looked at us. "We had fun that night I stayed in yawls' room, didn't we?"

"I didn't," Jason said. "I didn't have any fun."

"You were asleep in mother's room," Caddy said. "You were not there."

"Let's go down to my house and have some more fun," Nancy said.

"Mother wont let us," I said. "It's too late now."

"Dont bother her," Nancy said. "We can tell her in the morning. She wont mind."

"She wouldn't let us," I said.

"Dont ask her now," Nancy said. "Dont bother her now."

"She didn't say we couldn't go," Caddy said.

"We didn't ask," I said.

"If you go, I'll tell," Jason said.

"We'll have fun," Nancy said. "They won't mind, just to my house. I been working for yawl a long time. They won't mind."

"I'm not afraid to go," Caddy said. "Jason is the one that's afraid. He'll tell."

"I'm not," Jason said.

"Yes, you are," Caddy said. "You'll tell."

"I won't tell," Jason said. "I'm not afraid."

"Jason ain't afraid to go with me," Nancy said. "Is you, Jason?"

"Jason is going to tell," Caddy said. The lane was dark. We passed the pasture gate. "I bet if something was to jump out from behind that gate, Jason would holler."

"I wouldn't," Jason said. We walked down the lane. Nancy was talking loud.

"What are you talking so loud for, Nancy?" Caddy said.

"Who; me?" Nancy said. "Listen at Quentin and Caddy and Jason saying I'm talking loud."

"You talk like there was five of us here," Caddy said. "You talk like father was here too."

"Who; me talking loud, Mr Jason?" Nancy said.

"Nancy called Jason 'Mister,' " Caddy said.

"Listen how Caddy and Quentin and Jason talk," Nancy said.

"We're not talking loud," Caddy said. "You're the one that's talking like father—"

"Hush," Nancy said; "hush, Mr Jason."

"Nancy called Jason 'Mister' aguh—"

"Hush," Nancy said. She was talking loud when we crossed the ditch and stooped through the fence where she used to stoop through with the clothes on her head. Then we came to her house. We were going fast then. She opened the door. The smell of the house was like the lamp and the smell of Nancy was like the wick, like they were waiting for one another to begin to smell. She lit the lamp and closed the door and put the bar up. Then she quit talking loud, looking at us.

"What're we going to do?" Caddy said.

"What do yawl want to do?" Nancy said.

"You said we would have some fun," Caddy said.

There was something about Nancy's house; something you could smell besides Nancy and the house. Jason smelled it, even. "I don't want to stay here," he said. "I want to go home."

"Go home, then," Caddy said.

"I don't want to go by myself," Jason said.

"We're going to have some fun," Nancy said.

"How?" Caddy said.

Nancy stood by the door. She was looking at us, only it was like she had emptied her eyes, like she had quit using them. "What do you want to do?" she said.

"Tell us a story," Caddy said. "Can you tell a story?"

"Yes," Nancy said.

"Tell it," Caddy said. We looked at Nancy. "You don't know any stories."

"Yes," Nancy said. "Yes, I do."

She came and sat in a chair before the hearth. There was a little fire there. Nancy built it up, when it was already hot inside. She built a good blaze. She told a story. She talked like her eyes looked, like her eyes watching us and her voice talking to us did not belong to her. Like she was living somewhere else, waiting somewhere else. She was outside the cabin. Her voice was inside and the shape of her, the Nancy that could stoop under a barbed wire fence with a bundle of clothes balanced on her head as though without weight, like a balloon, was there. But that was all. "And so this here queen come walking up to the ditch, where that bad man was hiding. She was walking up to the ditch, and she say, 'If I can just get past this here ditch,' was what she say . . ."

"What ditch?" Caddy said. "A ditch like that one out there? Why did a queen want to go into a ditch?"

"To get to her house," Nancy said. She looked at us. "She had to cross the ditch to get into her house quick and bar the door."

"Why did she want to go home and bar the door?" Caddy said.

IV

Nancy looked at us. She quit talking. She looked at us. Jason's legs stuck straight out of his pants where he sat on Nancy's lap. "I don't think that's a good story," he said. "I want to go home."

"Maybe we had better," Caddy said. She got up from the floor. "I bet they are looking for us right now." She went toward the door.

"No," Nancy said. "Don't open it." She got up quick and passed Caddy. She didn't touch the door, the wooden bar.

"Why not?" Caddy said.

"Come back to the lamp," Nancy said. "We'll have fun. You don't have to go."

"We ought to go," Caddy said. "Unless we have a lot of fun." She and Nancy came back to the fire, the lamp.

"I want to go home," Jason said. "I'm going to tell."

"I know another story," Nancy said. She stood close to the lamp. She looked at Caddy, like when your eyes look up at a stick balanced on your nose. She had to look down to see Caddy, but her eyes looked like that, like when you are balancing a stick.

"I won't listen to it," Jason said. "I'll bang on the floor."

"It's a good one," Nancy said. "It's better than the other one."

"What's it about?" Caddy said. Nancy was standing by the lamp. Her hand was on the lamp, against the light, long and brown.

"Your hand is on that hot globe," Caddy said. "Don't it feel hot to your hand?"

Nancy looked at her hand on the lamp chimney. She took her hand away, slow. She stood there, looking at Caddy, wringing her long hand as though it were tied to her wrist with a string.

"Let's do something else," Caddy said.

"I want to go home," Jason said.

"I got some popcorn," Nancy said. She looked at Caddy and then at Jason and then at me and then at Caddy again. "I got some popcorn."

"I don't like popcorn," Jason said. "I'd rather have candy."

Nancy looked at Jason. "You can hold the popper." She was still wringing her hand; it was long and limp and brown.

"All right," Jason said. "I'll stay a while if I can do that. Caddy can't hold it. I'll want to go home again if Caddy holds the popper."

Nancy built up the fire. "Look at Nancy putting her hands in the fire," Caddy said. "What's the matter with you, Nancy?"

"I got popcorn," Nancy said. "I got some." She took the popper from under the bed. It was broken. Jason began to cry.

"Now we can't have any popcorn," he said.

"We ought to go home, anyway," Caddy said. "Come on, Quentin."

"Wait," Nancy said; "wait. I can fix it. Don't you want to help me fix it?"

"I don't think I want any," Caddy said. "It's too late now."

"You help me, Jason," Nancy said. "Don't you want to help me?"

"No," Jason said. "I want to go home."

"Hush," Nancy said; "hush. Watch. Watch me. I can fix it so Jason can hold it and pop the corn." She got a piece of wire and fixed the popper.

"It won't hold good," Caddy said.

"Yes, it will," Nancy said. "Yawl watch. Yawl help me shell some corn."

The popcorn was under the bed too. We shelled it into the popper and Nancy helped Jason hold the popper over the fire.

"It's not popping," Jason said. "I want to go home."

"You wait," Nancy said. "It'll begin to pop. We'll have fun then." She was sitting close to the fire. The lamp was turned up so high it was beginning to smoke.

"Why don't you turn it down some?" I said.

"It's all right," Nancy said. "I'll clean it. Yawl wait. The popcorn will start in a minute."

"I don't believe it's going to start," Caddy said. "We ought to start home, anyway. They'll be worried."

"No," Nancy said. "It's going to pop. Dilsey will tell um yawl with me. I been working for yawl long time. They won't mind if yawl at my house. You wait, now. It'll start popping any minute now."

Then Jason got some smoke in his eyes and he began to cry. He dropped the popper into the fire. Nancy got a wet rag and wiped Jason's face, but he didn't stop crying.

"Hush," she said. "Hush." But he didn't hush. Caddy took the popper out of the fire.

"It's burned up," she said. "You'll have to get some more popcorn, Nancy."

"Did you put all of it in?" Nancy said.

"Yes," Caddy said. Nancy looked at Caddy. Then she took the popper and opened it and poured the cinders into her apron and began to sort the grains, her hands long and brown, and we watching her.

"Haven't you got any more?" Caddy said.

"Yes," Nancy said; "yes. Look. This here ain't burnt. All we need to do is—"

"I want to go home," Jason said. "I'm going to tell."

"Hush," Caddy said. We all listened. Nancy's head was already turned toward the barred door, her eyes filled with red lamplight. "Somebody is coming," Caddy said.

Then Nancy began to make that sound again, not loud, sitting there above the fire, her long hands dangling between her knees; all of a sudden water began to come out on her face in big drops, running down her face, carrying in each one a little turning ball of firelight like a spark until it dropped off her chin. "She's not crying," I said.

"I ain't crying," Nancy said. Her eyes were closed. "I ain't crying. Who is it?"

"I don't know," Caddy said. She went to the door and looked out. "We've got to go now," she said. "Here comes father."

"I'm going to tell," Jason said. "Yawl made me come."

The water still ran down Nancy's face. She turned in her chair. "Listen. Tell him. Tell him we going to have fun. Tell him I take good care of yawl until in the morning. Tell him to let me come home with yawl and sleep on the floor. Tell him I won't need no pallet. We'll have fun. You member last time how we had so much fun?"

"I didn't have fun," Jason said. "You hurt me. You put smoke in my eyes. I'm going to tell."

V

Father came in. He looked at us. Nancy did not get up.

"Tell him," she said.

"Caddy made us come down here," Jason said. "I didn't want to."

Father came to the fire. Nancy looked up at him. "Can't you go to Aunt Rachel's and stay?" he said. Nancy looked up at father, her hands between her knees. "He's not here," father said. "I would have seen him. There's not a soul in sight."

"He in the ditch," Nancy said. "He waiting in the ditch yonder."

"Nonsense," father said. He looked at Nancy. "Do you know he's there?"

"I got the sign," Nancy said.

"What sign?"

"I got it. It was on the table when I come in. It was a hogbone, with blood meat still on it, laying by the lamp. He's out there. When yawl walk out that door, I gone."

"Gone where, Nancy?" Caddy said.

"I'm not a tattletale," Jason said.

"Nonsense," father said.

"He out there," Nancy said. "He looking through that window this minute, waiting for yawl to go. Then I gone."

"Nonsense," father said. "Lock up your house and we'll take you on to Aunt Rachel's."

" 'Twont do no good," Nancy said. She didn't look at father now, but he looked down at her, at her long, limp, moving hands. "Putting it off wont do no good."

"Then what do you want to do?" father said.

"I don't know," Nancy said. "I can't do nothing. Just put it off. And that don't do no good. I reckon it belong to me. I reckon what I going to get ain't no more than mine."

"Get what?" Caddy said. "What's yours?"

"Nothing," father said. "You all must get to bed."

"Caddy made me come," Jason said.

"Go on to Aunt Rachel's," father said.

"It won't do no good," Nancy said. She sat before the fire, her elbows on her knees, her long hands between her knees. "When even your own kitchen wouldn't do no good. When even if I was sleeping on the floor in the room with your chillen, and the next morning there I am, and blood—"

"Hush," father said. "Lock the door and put out the lamp and go to bed."

"I scared of the dark," Nancy said. "I scared for it to happen in the dark."

"You mean you're going to sit right here with the lamp lighted?" father said. Then Nancy began to make the sound again, sitting before the fire, her long hands between her knees. "Ah, damnation," father said. "Come along, chillen. It's past bedtime."

"When yawl go home, I gone," Nancy said. She talked quieter now, and her face looked quiet, like her hands. "Anyway, I got my coffin money saved up with Mr. Lovelady." Mr. Lovelady was a short, dirty man who collected the Negro insurance, coming around to the cabins or the kitchens every Saturday morning, to collect fifteen cents. He and his wife lived at the hotel. One morning his wife committed suicide. They had a child, a little girl. He and the child went away. After a week or two he came back alone. We would see him going along the lanes and the back streets on Saturday mornings.

"Nonsense," father said. "You'll be the first thing I'll see in the kitchen tomorrow morning."

"You'll see what you'll see, I reckon," Nancy said. "But it will take the Lord to say what that will be."

VI

We left her sitting before the fire.

"Come and put the bar up," father said. But she didn't move. She didn't look at us again, sitting quietly there between the lamp and the fire. From some distance down the lane we could look back and see her through the open door.

"What, Father?" Caddy said. "What's going to happen?"

"Nothing," father said. Jason was on father's back, so Jason was the tallest of all of us. We went down into the ditch. I looked at it, quiet. I couldn't see much where the moonlight and the shadows tangled.

"If Jesus is hid here, he can see us, cant he?" Caddy said.

"He's not there," father said. "He went away a long time ago."

"You made me come," Jason said, high; against the sky it looked like father had two heads, a little one and a big one. "I didn't want to."

We went up out of the ditch. We could still see Nancy's house and the open door, but we couldn't see Nancy now, sitting before the fire with the door open, because she was tired. "I just done got tired," she said. "I just a nigger. It ain't no fault of mine."

But we could hear her, because she began just after we came up out of the ditch, the sound that was not singing and not unsinging. "Who will do our washing now, Father?" I said.

"I'm not a nigger," Jason said, high and close above father's head.

"You're worse," Caddy said, "you are a tattletale. If something was to jump out, you'd be scairder than a nigger."

"I wouldn't," Jason said.

"You'd cry," Caddy said.

"Caddy," father said.

"I wouldn't!" Jason said.

"Scairy cat," Caddy said.

"Candace!" father said.

1931

DISCUSSION QUESTIONS

1. Who is the main character of the story? Why has Faulkner made a nine-year-old boy the narrator? What changes would the story have undergone if Caddy or Jason had been the narrator? What if an *undramatized narrator* had told the story?

2. Since much of what the adults say is incomprehensible to the children, whose responses often seem irrelevant, why do the children play such a prominent role in the dialogue? What effect would the elimination of their questions and squabbles have on the story?

3. How sympathetic is each child to Nancy's plight? How, specifically, do Caddy and Jason take advantage of Nancy's fears? Who, under earlier circumstances, also exploited Nancy?

4. Do you agree or disagree with Nancy's claim that "It aint none of my fault" (page 282)? Why? Is the father right when he tells Nancy, "If you'd behave yourself, you'd have kept out of this" (page 284)? Give reasons for your answer. How well has the father treated Nancy?

5. Why does Nancy's threat to kill Jesus if she finds him with another woman seem *ironic?* What changes does Nancy undergo during the story? How does Faulkner convey them? By what means does he convey her terror?

6. Examine and compare how each of the following characters responds to darkness: Jason, Caddy, the mother, and Nancy. Explain the significance of the story title, which was "That Evening Sun Go Down" in an earlier version.

THE KILLERS

ERNEST HEMINGWAY

THE DOOR of Henry's lunch-room opened and two men came in. They sat down at the counter.

"What's yours?" George asked them.

"I don't know," one of the men said. "What do you want to eat, Al?"

"I don't know," said Al. "I don't know what I want to eat."

Outside it was getting dark. The street-light came on outside the window. The two men at the counter read the menu. From the other end of the counter Nick Adams watched them. He had been talking to George when they came in.

"I'll have a roast pork tenderloin with apple sauce and mashed potatoes," the first man said.

"It isn't ready yet."

"What the hell do you put it on the card for?"

"That's the dinner," George explained. "You can get that at six o'clock."

George looked at the clock on the wall behind the counter.

"It's five o'clock."

"The clock says twenty minutes past five," the second man said.

"It's twenty minutes fast."

"Oh, to hell with the clock," the first man said. "What have you got to eat?"

"I can give you any kind of sandwiches," George said. "You can have ham and eggs, bacon and eggs, liver and bacon, or a steak."

"Give me chicken croquettes with green peas and cream sauce and mashed potatoes."

"That's the dinner."

"Everything we want's the dinner, eh? That's the way you work it."

"I can give you ham and eggs, bacon and eggs, liver——"

"I'll take ham and eggs," the man called Al said. He wore a derby hat and a black overcoat buttoned across the chest. His face was small and white and he had tight lips. He wore a silk muffler and gloves.

"Give me bacon and eggs," said the other man. He was about the same size as Al. Their faces were different, but they were dressed like twins. Both wore overcoats too tight for them. They sat leaning forward, their elbows on the counter.

"Got anything to drink?" Al asked.

"Silver beer, bevo, ginger-ale," George said.

"I mean you got anything to *drink?*"

"Just those I said."

"This is a hot town," said the other. "What do they call it?"

"Summit."

"Ever hear of it?" Al asked his friend.

"No," said the friend.

"What do you do here nights?" Al asked.

"They eat the dinner," his friend said. "They all come here and eat the big dinner."

"That's right," George said.

"So you think that's right?" Al asked George.

"Sure."

"You're a pretty bright boy, aren't you?"

"Sure," said George.

"Well, you're not," said the other little man. "Is he, Al?"

"He's dumb," said Al. He turned to Nick. "What's your name?"

"Adams."

"Another bright boy," Al said. "Ain't he a bright boy, Max?"

"The town's full of bright boys," Max said.

George put the two platters, one of ham and eggs, the other of bacon and eggs, on the counter. He set down two side-dishes of fried potatoes and closed the wicket into the kitchen.

"Which is yours?" he asked Al.

"Don't you remember?"

"Ham and eggs."

"Just a bright boy," Max said. He leaned forward and took the ham and eggs. Both men ate with their gloves on. George watched them eat.

"What are *you* looking at?" Max looked at George.

"Nothing."

"The hell you were. You were looking at me."

"Maybe the boy meant it for a joke, Max," Al said.

George laughed.

"*You* don't have to laugh," Max said to him. "*You* don't have to laugh at all, see?"

"All right," said George.

"So he thinks it's all right." Max turned to Al. "He thinks it's all right. That's a good one."

"Oh, he's a thinker," Al said. They went on eating.

"What's the bright boy's name down the counter?" Al asked Max.

"Hey, bright boy," Max said to Nick. "You go around on the other side of the counter with your boy friend."

"What's the idea?" Nick asked.

"There isn't any idea."

"You better go around, bright boy," Al said. Nick went around behind the counter.

"What's the idea?" George asked.

"None of your damn business," Al said. "Who's out in the kitchen?"

"The nigger."

"What do you mean the nigger?"

"The nigger that cooks."

"Tell him to come in."

"What's the idea?"

"Tell him to come in."

"Where do you think you are?"

"We know damn well where we are," the man called Max said. "Do we look silly?"

"You talk silly," Al said to him. "What the hell do you argue with this kid for? Listen," he said to George, "tell the nigger to come out here."

"What are you going to do to him?"

"Nothing. Use your head, bright boy. What would we do to a nigger?"

George opened the slit that opened back into the kitchen. "Sam," he called. "Come in here a minute."

The door to the kitchen opened and the nigger came in. "What was it?" he asked. The two men at the counter took a look at him.

"All right, nigger. You stand right there," Al said.

Sam, the nigger, standing in his apron, looked at the two men sitting at the counter. "Yes, sir," he said. Al got down from his stool.

"I'm going back to the kitchen with the nigger and bright boy," he said. "Go on back to the kitchen, nigger. You go with him, bright boy." The little man walked after Nick and Sam, the cook, back into the kitchen. The door shut after them. The man called Max sat at the counter opposite George. He didn't look at George but looked in the mirror that ran along back of the counter. Henry's had been made over from a saloon into a lunch-counter.

"Well, bright boy," Max said, looking into the mirror, "why don't you say something?"

"What's it all about?"

"Hey, Al," Max called, "bright boy wants to know what it's all about."

"Why don't you tell him?" Al's voice came from the kitchen.

"What do you think it's all about?"

"I don't know."

"What do you think?"

Max looked into the mirror all the time he was talking.

"I wouldn't say."

"Hey, Al, bright boy says he wouldn't say what he thinks it's all about."

"I can hear you, all right," Al said from the kitchen. He had propped open the slit that dishes passed through into the kitchen with a catsup bottle. "Listen, bright boy," he said from the kitchen to George. "Stand a little further along the bar. You move a little to the left, Max." He was like a photographer arranging for a group picture.

"Talk to me, bright boy," Max said. "What do you think's going to happen?"

George did not say anything.

"I'll tell you," Max said. "We're going to kill a Swede. Do you know a big Swede named Ole Andreson?"

"Yes."

"He comes here to eat every night, don't he?"

"Sometimes he comes here."

"He comes here at six o'clock, don't he?"

"If he comes."

"We know all that, bright boy," Max said. "Talk about something else. Ever go to the movies?"

"Once in a while."

"You ought to go to the movies more. The movies are fine for a bright boy like you."

"What are you going to kill Ole Andreson for? What did he ever do to you?"

"He never had a chance to do anything to us. He never even seen us."

"And he's only going to see us once," Al said from the kitchen.

"What are you going to kill him for, then?" George asked.

"We're killing him for a friend. Just to oblige a friend, bright boy."

"Shut up," said Al from the kitchen. "You talk too goddam much."

"Well, I got to keep bright boy amused. Don't I, bright boy?"

"You talk too damn much," Al said. "The nigger and my bright boy are amused by themselves. I got them tied up like a couple of girl friends in the convent."

"I suppose you were in a convent."

"You never know."

"You were in a kosher convent. That's where you were."

George looked up at the clock.

"If anybody comes in you tell them the cook is off, and if they keep after it, you tell them you'll go back and cook yourself. Do you get that, bright boy?"

"All right," George said. "What you going to do with us afterward?"

"That'll depend," Max said. "That's one of those things you never know at the time."

George looked up at the clock. It was a quarter past six. The door from the street opened. A street-car motorman came in.

"Hello, George," he said. "Can I get supper?"

"Sam's gone out," George said. "He'll be back in about half an hour."

"I'd better go up the street," the motorman said. George looked at the clock. It was twenty minutes past six.

"That was nice, bright boy," Max said. "You're a regular little gentleman."

"He knew I'd blow his head off," Al said from the kitchen.

"No," said Max. "It ain't that. Bright boy is nice. He's a nice boy. I like him."

At six-fifty-five George said: "He's not coming."

Two other people had been in the lunch-room. Once George had gone out to the kitchen and made a ham-and-egg sandwich "to go" that a man wanted to take with him. Inside the kitchen he saw Al, his derby hat tipped back, sitting on a stool beside the wicket with the muzzle of a sawed-off shotgun resting on the ledge. Nick and the cook were back to back in the corner, a towel tied in each of their mouths. George had cooked the sandwich, wrapped it up in oiled paper, put it in a bag, brought it in, and the man had paid for it and gone out.

"Bright boy can do everything," Max said. "He can cook and everything. You'd make some girl a nice wife, bright boy."

"Yes?" George said. "Your friend, Ole Andreson, isn't going to come."

"We'll give him ten minutes," Max said.

Max watched the mirror and the clock. The hands of the clock marked seven o'clock, and then five minutes past seven.

"Come on, Al," said Max. "We better go. He's not coming."

"Better give him five minutes," Al said from the kitchen.

In the five minutes a man came in, and George explained that the cook was sick.

"Why the hell don't you get another cook?" the man asked. "Aren't you running a lunch-counter?" He went out.

"Come on, Al," Max said.

"What about the two bright boys and the nigger?"

"They're all right."

"You think so?"

"Sure. We're through with it."

"I don't like it," said Al. "It's sloppy. You talk too much."

"Oh, what the hell," said Max. "We got to keep amused, haven't we?"

"You talk too much, all the same," Al said. He came out from the kitchen. The cut-off barrels of the shotgun made a slight bulge under the waist of his too tight-fitting overcoat. He straightened his coat with his gloved hands.

"So long, bright boy," he said to George. "You got a lot of luck."

"That's the truth," Max said. "You ought to play the races, bright boy."

The two of them went out the door. George watched them, through the window, pass under the arc-light and cross the street. In their tight overcoats and derby hats they looked like a vaudeville team. George went back through the swinging-door into the kitchen and untied Nick and the cook.

"I don't want any more of that," said Sam, the cook. "I don't want any more of that."

Nick stood up. He had never had a towel in his mouth before.

"Say," he said. "What the hell?" He was trying to swagger it off.

"They were going to kill Ole Andreson," George said. "They were going to shoot him when he came in to eat."

"Ole Andreson?"

"Sure."

The cook felt the corners of his mouth with his thumbs.

"They all gone?" he asked.

"Yeah," said George. "They're gone now."

"I don't like it," said the cook. "I don't like any of it at all."

"Listen," George said to Nick. "You better go see Ole Andreson."

"All right."

"You better not have anything to do with it at all," Sam, the cook, said. "You better stay way out of it."

"Don't go if you don't want to," George said.

"Mixing up in this ain't going to get you anywhere," the cook said. "You stay out of it."

"I'll go see him," Nick said to George. "Where does he live?"

The cook turned away.

"Little boys always know what they want to do," he said.

"He lives up at Hirsch's rooming-house," George said to Nick.

"I'll go up there."

Outside the arc-light shone through the bare branches of a tree. Nick walked up the street beside the car-tracks and turned at the next arc-light down a side-street. Three houses up the street was Hirsch's rooming-house. Nick walked up the two steps and pushed the bell. A woman came to the door.

"Is Ole Andreson here?"

"Do you want to see him?"

"Yes, if he's in."

Nick followed the woman up a flight of stairs and back to the end of a corridor. She knocked on the door.

"Who is it?"

"It's somebody to see you, Mr. Andreson," the woman said.

"It's Nick Adams."

"Come in."

Nick opened the door and went into the room. Ole Andreson was lying on the bed with all his clothes on. He had been a heavyweight prizefighter and he was too long for the bed. He lay with his head on two pillows. He did not look at Nick.

"What was it?" he asked.

"I was up at Henry's," Nick said, "and two fellows came in and tied up me and the cook, and they said they were going to kill you."

It sounded silly when he said it. Ole Andreson said nothing.

"They put us out in the kitchen," Nick went on. "They were going to shoot you when you came in to supper."

Ole Andreson looked at the wall and did not say anything.

"George thought I better come and tell you about it."

"There isn't anything I can do about it," Ole Andreson said.

"I'll tell you what they were like."

"I don't want to know what they were like," Ole Andreson said. He looked at the wall. "Thanks for coming to tell me about it."

"That's all right."

Nick looked at the big man lying on the bed.

"Don't you want me to go and see the police?"

"No," Ole Andreson said. "That wouldn't do any good."

"Isn't there something I could do?"

"No. There ain't anything to do."

"Maybe it was just a bluff."

"No. It ain't just a bluff."

Ole Andreson rolled over toward the wall.

"The only thing is," he said, talking toward the wall, "I just can't make up my mind to go out. I been in here all day."

"Couldn't you get out of town?"

"No," Ole Andreson said. "I'm through with all that running around."

He looked at the wall.

"There ain't anything to do now."

"Couldn't you fix it up some way?"

"No. I got in wrong." He talked in the same flat voice. "There ain't anything to do. After a while I'll make up my mind to go out."

"I better go back and see George," Nick said.

"So long," said Ole Andreson. He did not look toward Nick. "Thanks for coming around."

Nick went out. As he shut the door he saw Ole Andreson with all his clothes on, lying on the bed looking at the wall.

"He's been in his room all day," the landlady said down-stairs. "I guess he don't feel well. I said to him: 'Mr. Andreson, you ought to go out and take a walk on a nice fall day like this,' but he didn't feel like it."

"He doesn't want to go out."

"I'm sorry he don't feel well," the woman said. "He's an awfully nice man. He was in the ring, you know."

"I know it."

"You'd never know it except from the way his face is," the woman said. They stood talking just inside the street door. "He's just as gentle."

"Well, good-night, Mrs. Hirsch," Nick said.

"I'm not Mrs. Hirsch," the woman said. "She owns the place. I just look after it for her. I'm Mrs. Bell."

"Well, good-night, Mrs. Bell," Nick said.

"Good-night," the woman said.

Nick walked up the dark street to the corner under the arc-light, and then along the car-tracks to Henry's eating-house. George was inside, back of the counter.

"Did you see Ole?"

"Yes," said Nick. "He's in his room and he won't go out."

The cook opened the door from the kitchen when he heard Nick's voice.

"I don't even listen to it," he said and shut the door.

"Did you tell him about it?" George asked.

"Sure. I told him but he knows what it's all about."

"What's he going to do?"

"Nothing."

"They'll kill him."

"I guess they will."

"He must have got mixed up in something in Chicago."

"I guess so," said Nick.

"It's a hell of a thing."

"It's an awful thing," Nick said.

They did not say anything. George reached down for a towel and wiped the counter.

"I wonder what he did?" Nick said.

"Double-crossed somebody. That's what they kill them for."

"I'm going to get out of this town," Nick said.

"Yes," said George. "That's a good thing to do."

"I can't stand to think about him waiting in the room and knowing he's going to get it. It's too damned awful."

"Well," said George, "you better not think about it."

1927

DISCUSSION QUESTIONS

1. Although Al and Max are "dressed like twins," their personalities show marked differences. Describe these differences. Which one seems more ruthless? Why does Max advise George "to go to the movies more" (page 301)? Why do the two killers wear derby hats, tight overcoats, silk mufflers, and gloves?

2. The narrator compares Al and Max to a "vaudeville team." In what ways are they deliberately funny? How do they seem unwittingly funny? Analyze the source of the humor in each case. Does this comical element make them appear more or less frightening? Why?

3. What kind of narrator does Hemingway use? How, if at all, does the narrator influence your attitude toward the story? What changes to the story would have occurred if Nick had been the narrator? What if George had been the narrator?

4. Does Andreson's attitude toward death seem heroic or cowardly? Explain. Is the main character Andreson or Nick? Why? Give evidence to support your answer.

5. Why does telling Andreson about being tied up by two gangsters who plan to kill the Swede sound "silly" to Nick?

6. Compare the attitudes of Nick, George, and Sam toward the two gangsters and their plan to kill Andreson. How does each of them behave when Nick returns from seeing Andreson? Whose response do you admire most? Why?

1. Compare Nancy with Ole Andreson. What do the two victims have in common? In what, if any, significant ways do they differ? While Nancy dominates Faulkner's story, Andreson makes only a brief appearance in "The Killers." How do these varying degrees of participation result in differences between the two stories?

2. Compare Jesus with Al and Max. Contrast their motives for contemplating murder. Whose motives seem more reprehensible? Why? While Al and Max play dominant roles in Hemingway's main scene, Jesus appears only briefly in Faulkner's story. How do these varying degrees of participation result in differences between the two stories?

3. Compare Quentin with Nick. In what ways are their situations similar? How do they differ? What differences result from the fact that Nick is much older than Quentin? What does each boy learn from his experience?

4. Has each author chosen the best *point of view* from which to tell his particular story, or is one author's narrative angle more effective than the other's? Explain and give reasons for your answer. Which do you think is the better story? Why?

ANALYSIS AND APPLICATION

1. Since "That Evening Sun" is told from a child's *point of view,* most of it is narrated through short simple or compound sentences. Make one complex sentence out of each of the following sequences of sentences by subordinating lesser ideas to the main idea and clarifying their relationship to it. Which version seems to you more effective? Why?

a. "I went to the kitchen. Nancy was through. The dishes were put away and the fire was out." (page 282)

b. "Aunt Rachel was old. She lived in a cabin beyond Nancy's, by herself. She had white hair and she smoked a pipe in the door, all day long; she didn't work anymore." (page 283)

c. "There was a little fire there. Nancy built it up, when it was already hot inside. She built a good blaze." (page 289)

2. Do the same for each of the following sequences of sentences from "The Killers," which also has a deliberately simple *style.* Which version do you prefer? Why?

a. "The door shut after them. The man called Max sat at the counter opposite George. He didn't look at George but looked in the mirror that ran along back of the counter." (page 300)

b. "George looked up at the clock. It was a quarter past six. The door from the street opened. A street-car motorman came in." (page 301)

AN OCCURRENCE AT OWL CREEK BRIDGE

AMBROSE BIERCE

A MAN stood upon a railroad bridge in northern Alabama, looking down into the swift water twenty feet below. The man's hands were behind his back, the wrists bound with a cord. A rope closely encircled his neck. It was attached to a stout cross-timber above his head and the slack fell to the level of his knees. Some loose boards laid upon the sleepers supporting the metals of the railway supplied a footing for him and his executioners—two private soldiers of the Federal army, directed by a sergeant who in civil life may have been a deputy sheriff. At a short remove upon the same temporary platform was an officer in the uniform of his rank, armed. He was a captain. A sentinel at each end

From *In the Midst of Life* by Ambrose Bierce.

of the bridge stood with his rifle in the position known as "support," that is to say, vertical in front of the left shoulder, the hammer resting on the forearm thrown straight across the chest—a formal and unnatural position, enforcing an erect carriage of the body. It did not appear to be the duty of these two men to know what was occurring at the centre of the bridge; they merely blockaded the two ends of the foot planking that traversed it.

Beyond one of the sentinels nobody was in sight; the railroad ran straight away into a forest for a hundred yards, then, curving, was lost to view. Doubtless there was an outpost farther along. The other bank of the stream was open ground—a gentle acclivity topped with a stockade of vertical tree trunks, loopholed for rifles, with a single embrasure through which protruded the muzzle of a brass cannon commanding the bridge. Midway of the slope between bridge and fort were the spectators—a single company of infantry in line, at "parade rest," the butts of the rifles on the ground, the barrels inclining slightly backward against the right shoulder, the hands crossed upon the stock. A lieutenant stood at the right of the line, the point of his sword upon the ground, his left hand resting upon his right. Excepting the group of four at the centre of the bridge, not a man moved. The company faced the bridge, staring stonily, motionless. The sentinels, facing the banks of the stream, might have been statues to adorn the bridge. The captain stood with folded arms, silent, observing the work of his subordinates, but making no sign. Death is a dignitary who when he comes announced is to be received with formal manifestations of respect, even by those most familiar with him. In the code of military etiquette silence and fixity are forms of deference.

The man who was engaged in being hanged was apparently about thirty-five years of age. He was a civilian, if one might judge from his habit, which was that of a planter. His features were good—a straight nose, firm mouth, broad forehead, from which his long, dark hair was combed straight back, falling behind his ears to the collar of his well-fitting frock-coat. He wore a mustache and pointed beard, but no whiskers; his eyes were large and dark gray, and had a kindly expression which one would hardly have expected in one whose neck was in the hemp. Evidently this was no vulgar assassin. The liberal military code makes provision for hanging many kinds of persons, and gentlemen are not excluded.

The preparations being complete, the two private soldiers stepped aside and each drew away the plank upon which he had been standing.

The sergeant turned to the captain, saluted and placed himself immediately behind that officer, who in turn moved apart one pace. These movements left the condemned man and the sergeant standing on the two ends of the same plank, which spanned three of the cross-ties of the bridge. The end upon which the civilian stood almost, but not quite, reached a fourth. This plank had been held in place by the weight of the captain; it was now held by that of the sergeant. At a signal from the former the latter would step aside, the plank would tilt and the condemned man go down between two ties. The arrangement commended itself to his judgment as simple and effective. His face had not been covered nor his eyes bandaged. He looked a moment at his "unsteadfast footing," then let his gaze wander to the swirling water of the stream racing madly beneath his feet. A piece of dancing driftwood caught his attention and his eyes followed it down the current. How slowly it appeared to move! What a sluggish stream!

He closed his eyes in order to fix his last thoughts upon his wife and children. The water, touched to gold by the early sun, the brooding mists under the banks at some distance down the stream, the fort, the soldiers, the piece of drift—all had distracted him. And now he became conscious of a new disturbance. Striking through the thought of his dear ones was a sound which he could neither ignore nor understand, a sharp, distinct, metallic percussion like the stroke of a blacksmith's hammer upon the anvil; it had the same ringing quality. He wondered what it was, and whether immeasurably distant or near by—it seemed both. Its recurrence was regular, but as slow as the tolling of a death knell. He awaited each stroke with impatience and—he knew not why—apprehension. The intervals of silence grew progressively longer; the delays became maddening. With their greater infrequency the sounds increased in strength and sharpness. They hurt his ear like the thrust of a knife; he feared he would shriek. What he heard was the ticking of his watch.

He unclosed his eyes and saw again the water below him. "If I could free my hands," he thought, "I might throw off the noose and spring into the stream. By diving I could evade the bullets and, swimming vigorously, reach the bank, take to the woods and get away home. My home, thank God, is as yet outside their lines; my wife and little ones are still beyond the invader's farthest advance."

As these thoughts, which have here to be set down in words, were flashed into the doomed man's brain rather than evolved from it the captain nodded to the sergeant. The sergeant stepped aside.

II

Peyton Farquhar was a well-to-do planter, of an old and highly respected Alabama family. Being a slave owner and like other slave owners a politician he was naturally an original secessionist and ardently devoted to the Southern cause. Circumstances of an imperious nature, which it is unnecessary to relate here, had prevented him from taking service with the gallant army that had fought the disastrous campaigns ending with the fall of Corinth,[1] and he chafed under the inglorious restraint, longing for the release of his energies, the larger life of the soldier, the opportunity for distinction. That opportunity, he felt, would come, as it comes to all in war time. Meanwhile he did what he could. No service was too humble for him to perform in aid of the South, no adventure too perilous for him to undertake if consistent with the character of a civilian who was at heart a soldier, and who in good faith and without too much qualification assented to at least a part of the frankly villainous dictum that all is fair in love and war.

One evening while Farquhar and his wife were sitting on a rustic bench near the entrance to his grounds, a gray-clad soldier rode up to the gate and asked for a drink of water. Mrs. Farquhar was only too happy to serve him with her own white hands. While she was fetching the water her husband approached the dusty horseman and inquired eagerly for news from the front.

"The Yanks are repairing the railroads," said the man, "and are getting ready for another advance. They have reached the Owl Creek bridge, put it in order and built a stockade on the north bank. The commandant has issued an order, which is posted everywhere, declaring that any civilian caught interfering with the railroad, its bridges, tunnels or trains will be summarily hanged. I saw the order."

"How far is it to the Owl Creek bridge?" Farquhar asked.

"About thirty miles."

"Is there no force on this side the creek?"

"Only a picket post half a mile out, on the railroad, and a single sentinel at this end of the bridge."

"Suppose a man—a civilian and student of hanging—should elude the picket post and perhaps get the better of the sentinel," said Farquhar, smiling, "what could he accomplish?"

The soldier reflected. "I was there a month ago," he replied. "I ob-

[1] Northern victory at the Battle of Shiloh, Tennessee, 6–7 April 1862, led Confederate troops to retreat to Corinth, Mississippi, which they were forced to abandon a month later.

served that the flood of last winter had lodged a great quantity of driftwood against the wooden pier at this end of the bridge. It is now dry and would burn like tow."

The lady had now brought the water, which the soldier drank. He thanked her ceremoniously, bowed to her husband and rode away. An hour later, after nightfall, he repassed the plantation, going northward in the direction from which he had come. He was a Federal scout.

III

As Peyton Farquhar fell straight downward through the bridge he lost consciousness and was as one already dead. From this state he was awakened—ages later, it seemed to him—by the pain of a sharp pressure upon his throat, followed by a sense of suffocation. Keen, poignant agonies seemed to shoot from his neck downward through every fibre of his body and limbs. These pains appeared to flash along well-defined lines of ramification and to beat with an inconceivably rapid periodicity. They seemed like streams of pulsating fire heating him to an intolerable temperature. As to his head, he was conscious of nothing but a feeling of fulness—of congestion. These sensations were unaccompanied by thought. The intellectual part of his nature was already effaced; he had power only to feel, and feeling was torment. He was conscious of motion. Encompassed in a luminous cloud, of which he was now merely the fiery heart, without material substance, he swung through unthinkable arcs of oscillation, like a vast pendulum. Then all at once, with terrible suddenness, the light about him shot upward with the noise of a loud plash; a frightful roaring was in his ears, and all was cold and dark. The power of thought was restored; he knew that the rope had broken and he had fallen into the stream. There was no additional strangulation; the noose about his neck was already suffocating him and kept the water from his lungs. To die of hanging at the bottom of a river!—the idea seemed to him ludicrous. He opened his eyes in the darkness and saw above him a gleam of light, but how distant, how inaccessible! He was still sinking, for the light became fainter and fainter until it was a mere glimmer. Then it began to grow and brighten, and he knew that he was rising toward the surface—knew it with reluctance, for he was now very comfortable. "To be hanged and drowned," he thought, "that is not so bad; but I do not wish to be shot. No; I will not be shot; that is not fair."

He was not conscious of an effort, but a sharp pain in his wrist apprised him that he was trying to free his hands. He gave the struggle his attention, as an idler might observe the feat of a juggler, without interest in the outcome. What splendid effort!—what magnificent, what superhuman strength! Ah, that was a fine endeavor! Bravo! The cord fell away; his arms parted and floated upward, the hands dimly seen on each side in the growing light. He watched them with a new interest as first one and then the other pounced upon the noose at his neck. They tore it away and thrust it fiercely aside, its undulations resembling those of a water-snake. "Put it back, put it back!" He thought he shouted these words to his hands, for the undoing of the noose had been succeeded by the direst pang that he had yet experienced. His neck ached horribly; his brain was on fire; his heart, which had been fluttering faintly, gave a great leap, trying to force itself out at his mouth. His whole body was racked and wrenched with an insupportable anguish! But his disobedient hands gave no heed to the command. They beat the water vigorously with quick, downward strokes, forcing him to the surface. He felt his head emerge; his eyes were blinded by the sunlight; his chest expanded convulsively, and with a supreme and crowning agony his lungs engulfed a great draught of air, which instantly he expelled in a shriek!

He was now in full possession of his physical senses. They were, indeed, preternaturally keen and alert. Something in the awful disturbance of his organic system had so exalted and refined them that they made record of things never before perceived. He felt the ripples upon his face and heard their separate sounds as they struck. He looked at the forest on the bank of the stream, saw the individual trees, the leaves and the veining of each leaf—saw the very insects upon them: the locusts, the brilliant-bodied flies, the gray spiders stretching their webs from twig to twig. He noted the prismatic colors in all the dewdrops upon a million blades of grass. The humming of the gnats that danced above the eddies of the stream, the beating of the dragon-flies' wings, the strokes of the water-spiders' legs, like oars which had lifted their boat—all these made audible music. A fish slid along beneath his eyes and he heard the rush of its body parting the water.

He had come to the surface facing down the stream; in a moment the visible world seemed to wheel slowly round, himself the pivotal point, and he saw the bridge, the fort, the soldiers upon the bridge, the captain, the sergeant, the two privates, his executioners. They were in silhouette against the blue sky. They shouted and gesticulated, pointing at him. The captain had drawn his pistol, but did not fire; the others were unarmed. Their movements were grotesque and horrible, their forms gigantic.

Suddenly he heard a sharp report and something struck the water smartly within a few inches of his head, spattering his face with spray. He heard a second report, and saw one of the sentinels with his rifle at his shoulder, a light cloud of blue smoke rising from the muzzle. The man in the water saw the eye of the man on the bridge gazing into his own through the sights of the rifle. He observed that it was a gray eye and remembered having read that gray eyes were keenest, and that all famous marksmen had them. Nevertheless, this one had missed.

A counter-swirl had caught Farquhar and turned him half round; he was again looking into the forest on the bank opposite the fort. The sound of a clear, high voice in a monotonous singsong now rang out behind him and came across the water with a distinctness that pierced and subdued all other sounds, even the beating of the ripples in his ears. Although no soldier, he had frequented camps enough to know the dread significance of that deliberate, drawling, aspirated chant; the lieutenant on shore was taking a part in the morning's work. How coldly and pitilessly—with what an even, calm intonation, presaging, and enforcing tranquillity in the men—with what accurately measured intervals fell those cruel words:

"Attention, company! . . . Shoulder arms! . . . Ready! . . . Aim! . . . Fire!"

Farquhar dived—dived as deeply as he could. The water roared in his ears like the voice of Niagara, yet he heard the dulled thunder of the volley and, rising again toward the surface, met shining bits of metal, singularly flattened, oscillating slowly downward. Some of them touched him on the face and hands, then fell away, continuing their descent. One lodged between his collar and neck; it was uncomfortably warm and he snatched it out.

As he rose to the surface, gasping for breath, he saw that he had been a long time under water; he was perceptibly farther down stream—nearer to safety. The soldiers had almost finished reloading; the metal ramrods flashed all at once in the sunshine as they were drawn from the barrels, turned in the air, and thrust into their sockets. The two sentinels fired again, independently and ineffectually.

The hunted man saw all this over his shoulder; he was now swimming vigorously with the current. His brain was as energetic as his arms and legs; he thought with the rapidity of lightning.

"The officer," he reasoned, "will not make that martinet's error a second time. It is as easy to dodge a volley as a single shot. He has probably already given the command to fire at will. God help me, I cannot dodge them all!"

An appalling plash within two yards of him was followed by a loud, rushing sound, *diminuendo*, which seemed to travel back through the air to the fort and died in an explosion which stirred the very river to its deeps! A rising sheet of water curved over him, fell down upon him, blinded him, strangled him! The cannon had taken a hand in the game. As he shook his head free from the commotion of the smitten water he heard the deflected shot humming through the air ahead, and in an instant it was cracking and smashing the branches in the forest beyond.

"They will not do that again," he thought; "the next time they will use a charge of grape. I must keep my eye upon the gun; the smoke will apprise me—the report arrives too late; it lags behind the missile. That is a good gun."

Suddenly he felt himself whirled round and round—spinning like a top. The water, the banks, the forests, the now distant bridge, fort and men—all were commingled and blurred. Objects were represented by their colors only; circular horizontal streaks of color—that was all he saw. He had been caught in a vortex and was being whirled on with a velocity of advance and gyration that made him giddy and sick. In a few moments he was flung upon the gravel at the foot of the left bank of the stream—the southern bank—and behind a projecting point which concealed him from his enemies. The sudden arrest of his motion, the abrasion of one of his hands on the gravel, restored him, and he wept with delight. He dug his fingers into the sand, threw it over himself in handfuls and audibly blessed it. It looked like diamonds, rubies, emeralds; he could think of nothing beautiful which it did not resemble. The trees upon the bank were giant garden plants; he noted a definite order in their arrangement, inhaled the fragrance of their blooms. A strange, roseate light shone through the spaces among their trunks and the wind made in their branches the music of æolian harps. He had no wish to perfect his escape—was content to remain in that enchanting spot until retaken.

A whiz and rattle of grapeshot among the branches high above his head roused him from his dream. The baffled cannoneer had fired him a random farewell. He sprang to his feet, rushed up the sloping bank, and plunged into the forest.

All that day he traveled, laying his course by the rounding sun. The forest seemed interminable; nowhere did he discover a break in it, not even a woodman's road. He had not known that he lived in so wild a region. There was something uncanny in the revelation.

By nightfall he was fatigued, footsore, famishing. The thought of his wife and children urged him on. At last he found a road which led him in what he knew to be the right direction. It was as wide and straight as a city street, yet it seemed untraveled. No fields bordered it, no dwelling anywhere. Not so much as the barking of a dog suggested human habitation. The black bodies of the trees formed a straight wall on both sides, terminating on the horizon in a point, like a diagram in a lesson in perspective. Overhead, as he looked up through this rift in the wood, shone great golden stars looking unfamiliar and grouped in strange constellations. He was sure they were arranged in some order which had a secret and malign significance. The wood on either side was full of singular noises, among which—once, twice, and again—he distinctly heard whispers in an unknown tongue.

His neck was in pain and lifting his hand to it he found it horribly swollen. He knew that it had a circle of black where the rope had bruised it. His eyes felt congested; he could no longer close them. His tongue was swollen with thirst; he relieved its fever by thrusting it forward from between his teeth into the cold air. How softly the turf had carpeted the untraveled avenue—he could no longer feel the roadway beneath his feet!

Doubtless, despite his suffering, he had fallen asleep while walking, for now he sees another scene—perhaps he has merely recovered from a delirium. He stands at the gate of his own home. All is as he left it, and all bright and beautiful in the morning sunshine. He must have traveled the entire night. As he pushes open the gate and passes up the wide white walk, he sees a flutter of female garments; his wife, looking fresh and cool and sweet, steps down from the veranda to meet him. At the bottom of the steps she stands waiting, with a smile of ineffable joy, an attitude of matchless grace and dignity. Ah, how beautiful she is! He springs forward with extended arms. As he is about to clasp her he feels a stunning blow upon the back of the neck; a blinding white light blazes all about him with a sound like the shock of a cannon—then all is darkness and silence!

Peyton Farquhar was dead; his body, with a broken neck, swung gently from side to side beneath the timbers of the Owl Creek bridge.

1891

DISCUSSION QUESTIONS

1. What function does each part of the story serve? Why did Bierce place part I before part II? What would happen if the order of the first two parts were reversed?

2. The story is told by three different narrators. Identify the characteristics of each, give supporting evidence, and show what portions of the story each narrates. Note that some parts of the story involve more than one narrator.

3. How can the stream be "racing madly beneath his feet" and immediately after appear slow and "sluggish" (page 311)? Explain why the intervals of silence between "the ticking of his watch" grow "progressively longer" while the "sounds increased in strength and sharpness (page 311). What purpose do these impressions serve in Bierce's story?

4. We are told that Farquhar's senses have become "preternaturally keen and alert" (page 314). Name some other preternatural aspects of Farquhar's experience. Do such subjective phenomena seem believable before you come to the surprise ending or only afterward?

5. Farquhar's thoughts, at the end of part I, "were flashed into the doomed man's brain rather than evolved from it." If they do not stem from the brain, from what human faculty do they evolve?

6. What elements of the story make Farquhar's escape seem real? What specific aspects make it seem unreal? When a "sheet of water" falls down on him, Farquhar feels "strangled" (page 316). What other instances can you find in which the actual sensations of strangulation reinforce the imagined impressions of escaping?

THE SECRET MIRACLE

JORGE LUIS BORGES

> And God made him die during the course of a hundred years and then He revived him and said:
> "How long have you been here?"
> "A day, or part of a day," he replied.
>
> *The Koran,* II 261

ON THE night of March 14, 1939, in an apartment on the Zelternergasse in Prague, Jaromir Hladík, author of the unfinished tragedy *The Enemies,* of a *Vindication of Eternity,* and of an inquiry into the indirect Jewish sources of Jakob Boehme,[1] dreamt a long-drawn-

[1] Influential German theosophist and mystic (1575–1624).

out chess game. The antagonists were not two individuals, but two illustrious families. The contest had begun many centuries before. No one could any longer describe the forgotten prize, but it was rumored that it was enormous and perhaps infinite. The pieces and the chessboard were set up in a secret tower. Jaromir (in his dream) was the first-born of one of the contending families. The hour for the next move, which could not be postponed, struck on all the clocks. The dreamer ran across the sands of a rainy desert—and he could not remember the chessmen or the rules of chess. At this point he awoke. The din of the rain and the clangor of the terrible clocks ceased. A measured unison, sundered by voices of command, arose from the Zelternergasse. Day had dawned, and the armored vanguards of the Third Reich were entering Prague.

On the nineteenth, the authorities received an accusation against Jaromir Hladík; on the same day, at dusk, he was arrested. He was taken to a barracks, aseptic and white, on the opposite bank of the Moldau. He was unable to refute a single one of the charges made by the Gestapo: his maternal surname was Jaroslavski, his blood was Jewish, his study of Boehme was Judaizing, his signature had helped to swell the final census of those protesting the *Anschluss*. In 1928, he had translated the *Sepher Yezirah*[2] for the publishing house of Hermann Barsdorf; the effusive catalogue issued by this firm had exaggerated, for commercial reasons, the translator's renown; this catalogue was leafed through by Julius Rothe, one of the officials in whose hands lay Hladík's fate. The man does not exist who, outside his own specialty, is not credulous: two or three adjectives in Gothic script sufficed to convince Julius Rothe of Hladík's preeminence, and of the need for the death penalty, *pour encourager les autres*.[3] The execution was set for the twenty-ninth of March, at nine in the morning. This delay (whose importance the reader will appreciate later) was due to a desire on the part of the authorities to act slowly and impersonally, in the manner of planets or vegetables.

Hladík's first reaction was simply one of horror. He was sure he would not have been terrified by the gallows, the block, or the knife; but to die before a firing squad was unbearable. In vain he repeated to himself that the pure and general act of dying, not the concrete circumstances, was the dreadful fact. He did not grow weary of imagining

[2] Book of Creation: mystical work of cosmology, written between the third and sixth centuries A.D. in Babylonia or Palestine.

[3] In order to encourage others [to obey].

these circumstances: he absurdly tried to exhaust all the variations. He infinitely anticipated the process, from the sleepless dawn to the mysterious discharge of the rifles. Before the day set by Julius Rothe, he died hundreds of deaths, in courtyards whose shapes and angles defied geometry, shot down by changeable soldiers whose number varied and who sometimes put an end to him from close up and sometimes from far away. He faced these imaginary executions with true terror (perhaps with true courage). Each simulacrum lasted a few seconds. Once the circle was closed, Jaromir returned interminably to the tremulous eve of his death. Then he would reflect that reality does not tend to coincide with forecasts about it. With perverse logic he inferred that to foresee a circumstantial detail is to prevent its happening. Faithful to this feeble magic, he would invent, *so that they might not happen,* the most atrocious particulars. Naturally, he finished by fearing that these particulars were prophetic. During his wretched nights he strove to hold fast somehow to the fugitive substance of time. He knew that time was precipitating itself toward the dawn of the twenty-ninth. He reasoned aloud: *I am now in the night of the twenty-second. While this night lasts (and for six more nights to come) I am invulnerable, immortal.* His nights of sleep seemed to him deep, dark pools into which he might submerge. Sometimes he yearned impatiently for the firing squad's definitive volley, which would redeem him, for better or for worse, from the vain compulsion of his imagination. On the twenty-eighth, as the final sunset reverberated across the high barred windows, he was distracted from all these abject considerations by thought of his drama, *The Enemies.*

Hladík was past forty. Apart from a few friendships and many habits, the problematic practice of literature constituted his life. Like every writer, he measured the virtues of other writers by their performance, and asked that they measure him by what he conjectured or planned. All of the books he had published merely moved him to a complex repentance. His investigation of the work of Boehme, of Ibn Ezra,[4] and of Fludd[5] was essentially a product of mere application; his translation of the *Sepher Yezirah* was characterized by negligence, fatigue, and conjecture. He judged his *Vindication of Eternity* to be perhaps less deficient: the first volume is a history of the diverse eternities de-

[4] Ibn Ezra, Abraham Ben Meir (1090?–1167?), Spanish Jew, poet, grammarian, who disseminated Arabic learning in Western Europe.

[5] Robert Fludd (1574–1637), British physician and mystic, developed his own pantheistic theosophy.

vised by man, from the immutable Being of Parmenides[6] to the alterable past of Hinton;[7] the second volume denies (with Francis Bradley)[8] that all the events in the universe make up a temporal series. He argues that the number of experiences possible to man is not infinite, and that a single "repetition" suffices to demonstrate that time is a fallacy.... Unfortunately, the arguments that demonstrate this fallacy are not any less fallacious. Hladík was in the habit of running through these arguments with a certain disdainful perplexity. He had also written a series of expressionist poems; these, to the discomfiture of the author, were included in an anthology in 1924, and there was no anthology of later date which did not inherit them. Hladík was anxious to redeem himself from his equivocal and languid past with his verse drama, *The Enemies.* (He favored the verse form in the theater because it prevents the spectators from forgetting unreality, which is the necessary condition of art.)

This opus preserved the dramatic unities (time, place, and action). It transpires in Hradcany, in the library of the Baron Roemerstadt, on one of the last evenings of the nineteenth century. In the first scene of the first act, a stranger pays a visit to Roemerstadt. (A clock strikes seven, the vehemence of a setting sun glorifies the window panes, the air transmits familiar and impassioned Hungarian music.) This visit is followed by others; Roemerstadt does not know the people who come to importune him, but he has the uncomfortable impression that he has seen them before: perhaps in a dream. All the visitors fawn upon him, but it is obvious—first to the spectators of the drama, and then to the Baron himself—that they are secret enemies, sworn to ruin him. Roemerstadt manages to outwit, or evade, their complex intrigues. In the course of the dialogue, mention is made of his betrothed, Julia de Weidenau, and of a certain Jaroslav Kubin, who at one time had been her suitor. Kubin has now lost his mind and thinks he is Roemerstadt. ... The dangers multiply. Roemerstadt, at the end of the second act, is forced to kill one of the conspirators. The third and final act begins. The incongruities gradually mount up: actors who seemed to have been discarded from the play reappear; the man who had been killed by Roemerstadt returns, for an instant. Someone notes that the time of day has not advanced: the clock strikes seven, the western sun reverberates

[6] Greek philosopher of the fifth century B.C., leader of the Eleatic school of philosophy.

[7] James Hinton (1822–1875), British mystic and ear specialist.

[8] British Idealist philosopher (1864–1924).

in the high windowpanes, impassioned Hungarian music is carried on the air. The first speaker in the play reappears and repeats the words he had spoken in the first scene of the first act. Roemerstadt addresses him without the least surprise. The spectator understands that Roemerstadt is the wretched Jaroslav Kubin. The drama has never taken place: it is the circular delirium which Kubin unendingly lives and relives.

Hladík had never asked himself whether this tragicomedy of errors was preposterous or admirable, deliberate or casual. Such a plot, he intuited, was the most appropriate invention to conceal his defects and to manifest his strong points, and it embodied the possibility of redeeming (symbolically) the fundamental meaning of his life. He had already completed the first act and a scene or two of the third. The metrical nature of the work allowed him to go over it continually, rectifying the hexameters, without recourse to the manuscript. He thought of the two acts still to do, and of his coming death. In the darkness, he addressed himself to God. *If I exist at all, if I am not one of Your repetitions and errata, I exist as the author of* The Enemies. *In order to bring this drama, which may serve to justify me, to justify You, I need one more year. Grant me that year, You to whom belong the centuries and all time.* It was the last, the most atrocious night, but ten minutes later sleep swept over him like a dark ocean and drowned him.

Toward dawn, he dreamt he had hidden himself in one of the naves of the Clementine Library. A librarian wearing dark glasses asked him: *What are you looking for?* Hladík answered: *God.* The Librarian told him: *God is in one of the letters on one of the pages of one of the 400,000 volumes of the Clementine. My fathers and the fathers of my fathers have sought after that letter. I've gone blind looking for it.* He removed his glasses, and Hladík saw that his eyes were dead. A reader came in to return an atlas. *This atlas is useless,* he said, and handed it to Hladík, who opened it at random. As if through a haze, he saw a map of India. With a sudden rush of assurance, he touched one of the tiniest letters. An ubiquitous voice said: *The time for your work has been granted.* Hladík awoke.

He remembered that the dreams of men belong to God, and that Maimonides[9] wrote that the words of a dream are divine, when they are all separate and clear and are spoken by someone invisible. He dressed. Two soldiers entered his cell and ordered him to follow them.

From behind the door, Hladík had visualized a labyrinth of passage-

[9] Rabbi Moses ben Maimon (1135–1204), Spanish-born Jewish philosopher and physician.

ways, stairs, and connecting blocks. Reality was less rewarding: the party descended to an inner courtyard by a single iron stairway. Some soldiers —uniforms unbuttoned—were testing a motorcycle and disputing their conclusions. The sergeant looked at his watch: it was 8:44. They must wait until nine. Hladík, more insignificant than pitiful, sat down on a pile of firewood. He noticed that the soldiers' eyes avoided his. To make his wait easier, the sergeant offered him a cigarette. Hladík did not smoke. He accepted the cigarette out of politeness or humility. As he lit it, he saw that his hands shook. The day was clouding over. The soldiers spoke in low tones, as though he were already dead. Vainly, he strove to recall the woman of whom Julia de Weidenau was the symbol. . . .

The firing squad fell in and was brought to attention. Hladík, standing against the barracks wall, waited for the volley. Someone expressed fear the wall would be splashed with blood. The condemned man was ordered to step forward a few paces. Hladík recalled, absurdly, the preliminary maneuvers of a photographer. A heavy drop of rain grazed one of Hladík's temples and slowly rolled down his cheek. The sergeant barked the final command.

The physical universe stood still.

The rifles converged upon Hladík, but the men assigned to pull the triggers were immobile. The sergeant's arm eternalized an inconclusive gesture. Upon a courtyard flagstone a bee cast a stationary shadow. The wind had halted, as in a painted picture. Hladík began a shriek, a syllable, a twist of the hand. He realized he was paralyzed. Not a sound reached him from the stricken world.

He thought: *I'm in hell, I'm dead.*

He thought: *I've gone mad.*

He thought: *Time has come to a halt.*

Then he reflected that in that case, his thought, too, would have come to a halt. He was anxious to test this possibility: he repeated (without moving his lips) the mysterious Fourth Eclogue of Virgil. He imagined that the already remote soldiers shared his anxiety; he longed to communicate with them. He was astonished that he felt no fatigue, no vertigo from his protracted immobility. After an indeterminate length of time he fell asleep. On awakening he found the world still motionless and numb. The drop of water still clung to his cheek; the shadow of the bee still did not shift in the courtyard; the smoke from the cigarette he had thrown down did not blow away. Another "day" passed before Hladík understood.

He had asked God for an entire year in which to finish his work: His omnipotence had granted him the time. For his sake, God projected a secret miracle: German lead would kill him, at the determined hour, but in his mind a year would elapse between the command to fire and its execution. From perplexity he passed to stupor, from stupor to resignation, from resignation to sudden gratitude.

He disposed of no document but his own memory; the mastering of each hexameter as he added it, had imposed upon him a kind of fortunate discipline not imagined by those amateurs who forget their vague, ephemeral, paragraphs. He did not work for posterity, nor even for God, of whose literary preferences he possessed scant knowledge. Meticulous, unmoving, secretive, he wove his lofty invisible labyrinth in time. He worked the third act over twice. He eliminated some rather too-obvious symbols: the repeated striking of the hour, the music. There were no circumstances to constrain him. He omitted, condensed, amplified; occasionally, he chose the primitive version. He grew to love the courtyard, the barracks; one of the faces endlessly confronting him made him modify his conception of Roemerstadt's character. He discovered that the hard cacophonies which so distressed Flaubert[10] are mere visual superstitions: debilities and annoyances of the written word, not of the sonorous, the sounding one.... He brought his drama to a conclusion: he lacked only a single epithet. He found it: the drop of water slid down his cheek. He began a wild cry, moved his face aside. A quadruple blast brought him down.

Jaromir Hladík died on March 29, at 9:02 in the morning.

1944

Translated by Anthony Kerrigan

DISCUSSION QUESTIONS

1. By what means does Borges prepare us for the secret miracle?

2. Compare Hladík's two dreams. What do they have in common? What makes Hladík successful in finding God when the librarian and his ancestors have all failed? What kind of progression is noticeable between the first and second dream? What kind of change does this fact reveal in Hladík?

3. While Hladík's maternal surname is Jaroslavski, Kubin's forename is

[10] Gustave Flaubert (1821–1880), French novelist.

Jaroslav. What other resemblances are there between the playwright and his protagonist? What effect have these affinities on the way in which we interpret Borges's story?

4. Is there any reliable way to ascertain whether the miracle emanates from God or from the "vain compulsion of his [Hladík's] imagination" (page 321)? What evidence exists for each interpretation? Which one makes for a better story? Why?

5. Identify several circumstances that make Hladík feel "more insignificant than pitiful" (page 324). What makes his death sentence seem *ironic?*

6. Why does Hladík place so much importance on his play? If "He did not work for posterity, nor even for God" (page 325), for whom is he completing *The Enemies?* Why?

1. By what rearrangement of the normal relationship between external clock time and inner psychological time is the death of each *protagonist* held in abeyance? Which man's experience seems more believable? Why?

2. Which of the two stories loses more of your interest on a second reading? Why? What precisely prevents such a loss of interest when rereading the other story?

3. For which of the two *protagonists* do you feel more sympathy? Why? Which author seems more sympathetic toward his character, which more detached? Support your answer with specific evidence.

4. Which do you judge to be the better story? Why?

ANALYSIS AND APPLICATION

1. Few things improve one's *style* more readily than variety in one's sentences: varying their lengths, departing from the normal subject-verb-object pattern, or even developing one of these elements. In the following sentence, which element (subject, verb, or object) is amplified in order to depict fully the nature of Farquhar's distraction? "The water, touched to gold by the early sun, the brooding mists under the banks at some

distance down the stream, the fort, the soldiers, the piece of drift—all had distracted him" (page 311). What function does "—all" serve? What would happen to the sentence without it? How does Bierce achieve variety within his series? Find at least two more similarly constructed sentences in the story. Construct several sentences of your own that duplicate Bierce's structure. What change of emphasis would occur if this sentence were put in the passive voice (He had been distracted by . . .)? How well would such a sentence fit into the context of the paragraph?

2. "His nights of sleep seemed to him deep, dark pools into which he might submerge" (page 321). Find another comparison involving sleep in Borges's story and relate it to this *metaphor.* Construct two *similes* or metaphors of your own that define sleep and are related to each other.

MIRIAM

TRUMAN CAPOTE

FOR SEVERAL years, Mrs. H. T. Miller had lived alone in a pleasant apartment (two rooms with kitchenette) in a remodeled brownstone near the East River. She was a widow: Mr. H. T. Miller had left a reasonable amount of insurance. Her interests were narrow, she had no friends to speak of, and she rarely journeyed farther than the corner grocery. The other people in the house never seemed to notice her: her clothes were matter-of-fact, her hair iron-gray, clipped and casually waved; she did not use cosmetics, her features were plain and inconspicuous, and on her last birthday she was sixty-one. Her activities were seldom spontaneous: she kept the two rooms immaculate, smoked an occasional cigarette, prepared her own meals and tended a canary.

Then she met Miriam. It was snowing that night. Mrs. Miller had finished drying the supper dishes and was thumbing through an afternoon paper when she saw an advertisement of a picture playing at a neighborhood theater. The title sounded good, so she struggled into her beaver coat, laced her galoshes and left the apartment, leaving one light burning in the foyer: she found nothing more disturbing than a sensation of darkness.

The snow was fine, falling gently, not yet making an impression on the pavement. The wind from the river cut only at street crossings. Mrs. Miller hurried, her head bowed, oblivious as a mole burrowing a blind path. She stopped at a drugstore and bought a package of peppermints.

A long line stretched in front of the box office; she took her place at the end. There would be (a tired voice groaned) a short wait for all seats. Mrs. Miller rummaged in her leather handbag till she collected exactly the correct change for admission. The line seemed to be taking its own time and, looking around for some distraction, she suddenly became conscious of a little girl standing under the edge of the marquee.

Her hair was the longest and strangest Mrs. Miller had ever seen: absolutely silver-white, like an albino's. It flowed waist-length in smooth, loose lines. She was thin and fragilely constructed. There was a simple, special elegance in the way she stood with her thumbs in the pockets of a tailored plum-velvet coat.

Mrs. Miller felt oddly excited, and when the little girl glanced toward her, she smiled warmly. The little girl walked over and said, "Would you care to do me a favor?"

"I'd be glad to, if I can," said Mrs. Miller.

"Oh, it's quite easy. I merely want you to buy a ticket for me; they won't let me in otherwise. Here, I have the money." And gracefully she handed Mrs. Miller two dimes and a nickel.

They went into the theater together. An usherette directed them to a lounge; in twenty minutes the picture would be over.

"I feel just like a genuine criminal," said Mrs. Miller gaily, as she sat down. "I mean that sort of thing's against the law, isn't it? I do hope I haven't done the wrong thing. Your mother knows where you are, dear? I mean she does, doesn't she?"

The little girl said nothing. She unbuttoned her coat and folded it across her lap. Her dress underneath was prim and dark blue. A gold chain dangled about her neck, and her fingers, sensitive and musical-looking, toyed with it. Examining her more attentively, Mrs. Miller decided the truly distinctive feature was not her hair, but her eyes; they were hazel, steady, lacking any childlike quality whatsoever and, because of their size, seemed to consume her small face.

Mrs. Miller offered a peppermint. "What's your name, dear?"

"Miriam," she said, as though, in some curious way, it were information already familiar.

"Why, isn't that funny—my name's Miriam, too. And it's not a terribly common name either. Now, don't tell me your last name's Miller!"

"Just Miriam."

"But isn't that funny?"

"Moderately," said Miriam, and rolled the peppermint on her tongue.

Mrs. Miller flushed and shifted uncomfortably. "You have such a large vocabulary for such a little girl."

"Do I?"

"Well, yes," said Mrs. Miller, hastily changing the topic to: "Do you like the movies?"

"I really wouldn't know," said Miriam. "I've never been before."

Women began filling the lounge; the rumble of the newsreel bombs exploded in the distance. Mrs. Miller rose, tucking her purse under her arm. "I guess I'd better be running now if I want to get a seat," she said. "It was nice to have met you."

Miriam nodded ever so slightly.

It snowed all week. Wheels and footsteps moved soundlessly on the street, as if the business of living continued secretly behind a pale but impenetrable curtain. In the falling quiet there was no sky or earth, only snow lifting in the wind, frosting the window glass, chilling the rooms, deadening and hushing the city. At all hours it was necessary to keep a lamp lighted, and Mrs. Miller lost track of the days: Friday was no different from Saturday and on Sunday she went to the grocery: closed, of course.

That evening she scrambled eggs and fixed a bowl of tomato soup. Then, after putting on a flannel robe and cold-creaming her face, she propped herself up in bed with a hot-water bottle under her feet. She was reading the *Times* when the doorbell rang. At first she thought it must be a mistake and whoever it was would go away. But it rang and rang and settled to a persistent buzz. She looked at the clock: a little after eleven; it did not seem possible, she was always asleep by ten.

Climbing out of bed, she trotted barefoot across the living room. "I'm coming, please be patient." The latch was caught; she turned it this way and that way and the bell never paused an instant. "Stop it," she cried. The bolt gave way and she opened the door an inch. "What in heaven's name?"

"Hello," said Miriam.

"Oh . . . why, hello," said Mrs. Miller, stepping hesitantly into the hall. "You're that little girl."

"I thought you'd never answer, but I kept my finger on the button; I knew you were home. Aren't you glad to see me?"

Mrs. Miller did not know what to say. Miriam, she saw, wore the same plum-velvet coat and now she had also a beret to match; her white hair was braided in two shining plaits and looped at the ends with enormous white ribbons.

"Since I've waited so long, you could at least let me in," she said.

"It's awfully late. . . ."

Miriam regarded her blankly. "What difference does that make? Let me in. It's cold out here and I have on a silk dress." Then, with a gentle gesture, she urged Mrs. Miller aside and passed into the apartment.

She dropped her coat and beret on a chair. She was indeed wearing a silk dress. White silk. White silk in February. The skirt was beautifully pleated and the sleeves long; it made a faint rustle as she strolled about the room. "I like your place," she said. "I like the rug, blue's my favorite color." She touched a paper rose in a vase on the coffee table. "Imitation," she commented wanly. "How sad. Aren't imitations sad?" She seated herself on the sofa, daintily spreading her skirt.

"What do you want?" asked Mrs. Miller.

"Sit down," said Miriam. "It makes me nervous to see people stand."

Mrs. Miller sank to a hassock. "What do you want?" she repeated.

"You know, I don't think you're glad I came."

For a second time Mrs. Miller was without an answer; her hand motioned vaguely. Miriam giggled and pressed back on a mound of chintz pillows. Mrs. Miller observed that the girl was less pale than she remembered; her cheeks were flushed.

"How did you know where I lived?"

Miriam frowned. "That's no question at all. What's your name? What's mine?"

"But I'm not listed in the phone book."

"Oh, let's talk about something else."

Mrs. Miller said, "Your mother must be insane to let a child like you wander around at all hours of the night—and in such ridiculous clothes. She must be out of her mind."

Miriam got up and moved to a corner where a covered bird cage hung from a ceiling. She peeked beneath the cover. "It's a canary," she said. "Would you mind if I woke him? I'd like to hear him sing."

"Leave Tommy alone," said Mrs. Miller, anxiously. "Don't you dare wake him."

"Certainly," said Miriam. "But I don't see why I can't hear him sing." And then, "Have you anything to eat? I'm starving! Even milk and a jam sandwich would be fine."

"Look," said Mrs. Miller, arising from the hassock, "look—if I make some nice sandwiches will you be a good child and run along home? It's past midnight, I'm sure."

"It's snowing," reproached Miriam. "And cold and dark."

"Well, you shouldn't have come here to begin with," said Mrs. Miller, struggling to control her voice. "I can't help the weather. If you want anything to eat you'll have to promise to leave."

Miriam brushed a braid against her cheek. Her eyes were thoughtful, as if weighing the proposition. She turned toward the bird cage. "Very well," she said, "I promise."

How old is she? Ten? Eleven? Mrs. Miller, in the kitchen, unsealed a jar of strawberry preserves and cut four slices of bread. She poured a glass of milk and paused to light a cigarette. *And why has she come?* Her hand shook as she held the match, fascinated, till it burned her finger. The canary was singing; singing as he did in the morning and at no other time. "Miriam," she called, "Miriam, I told you not to disturb Tommy." There was no answer. She called again; all she heard was the canary. She inhaled the cigarette and discovered she had lighted the cork-tip end and—oh, really, she mustn't lose her temper.

She carried the food in on a tray and set it on the coffee table. She saw first that the bird cage still wore its night cover. And Tommy was singing. It gave her a queer sensation. And no one was in the room. Mrs. Miller went through an alcove leading to her bedroom; at the door she caught her breath.

"What are you doing?" she asked.

Miriam glanced up and in her eyes there was a look that was not ordinary. She was standing by the bureau, a jewel case opened before her. For a minute she studied Mrs. Miller, forcing their eyes to meet, and she smiled. "There's nothing good here," she said. "But I like this." Her hand held a cameo brooch. "It's charming."

"Suppose—perhaps you'd better put it back," said Mrs. Miller, feeling suddenly the need of some support. She leaned against the door frame; her head was unbearably heavy; a pressure weighted the rhythm of her heartbeat. The light seemed to flutter defectively. "Please, child—a gift from my husband . . ."

"But it's beautiful and I want it," said Miriam. *"Give it to me."*

As she stood, striving to shape a sentence which would somehow save the brooch, it came to Mrs. Miller there was no one to whom she might turn; she was alone; a fact that had not been among her thoughts for a long time. Its sheer emphasis was stunning. But here in her own room in the hushed snow-city were evidences she could not ignore or, she knew with startling clarity, resist.

Miriam ate ravenously, and when the sandwiches and milk were gone, her fingers made cobweb movements over the plate, gathering crumbs. The cameo gleamed on her blouse, the blonde profile like a trick reflection of its wearer. "That was very nice," she sighed, "though now an almond cake or a cherry would be ideal. Sweets are lovely, don't you think?"

Mrs. Miller was perched precariously on the hassock, smoking a cigarette. Her hair net had slipped lopsided and loose strands straggled down her face. Her eyes were stupidly concentrated on nothing and her cheeks were mottled in red patches, as though a fierce slap had left permanent marks.

"Is there a candy—a cake?"

Mrs. Miller tapped ash on the rug. Her head swayed slightly as she tried to focus her eyes. "You promised to leave if I made the sandwiches," she said.

"Dear me, did I?"

"It was a promise and I'm tired and I don't feel well at all."

"Mustn't fret," said Miriam. "I'm only teasing."

She picked up her coat, slung it over her arm, and arranged her beret in front of a mirror. Presently she bent close to Mrs. Miller and whispered, "Kiss me good night."

"Please—I'd rather not," said Mrs. Miller.

Miriam lifted a shoulder, arched an eyebrow. "As you like," she said, and went directly to the coffee table, seized the vase containing the paper roses, carried it to where the hard surface of the floor lay bare, and hurled it downward. Glass sprayed in all directions and she stamped her foot on the bouquet.

Then slowly she walked to the door, but before closing it she looked back at Mrs. Miller with a slyly innocent curiosity.

Mrs. Miller spent the next day in bed, rising once to feed the canary and drink a cup of tea; she took her temperature and had none, yet her dreams were feverishly agitated; their unbalanced mood lingered even as she lay staring wide-eyed at the ceiling. One dream threaded through the others like an elusively mysterious theme in a complicated symphony, and the scenes it depicted were sharply outlined, as though sketched by a hand of gifted intensity: a small girl, wearing a bridal gown and a wreath of leaves, led a gray procession down a mountain path, and among them there was unusual silence till a woman at the rear asked, "Where is she taking us?" "No one knows," said an old man marching in front. "But isn't she pretty?" volunteered a third voice. "Isn't she like a frost flower . . . so shining and white?"

Tuesday morning she woke up feeling better; harsh slats of sunlight, slanting through Venetian blinds, shed a disrupting light on her unwholesome fancies. She opened the window to discover a thawed, mild-as-spring day; a sweep of clean new clouds crumpled against a vastly blue, out-of-season sky; and across the low line of rooftops she could see the river and smoke curving from tugboat stacks in a warm wind. A great silver truck plowed the snow-banked street, its machine sound humming on the air.

After straightening the apartment, she went to the grocer's, cashed a check and continued to Schrafft's where she ate breakfast and chatted happily with the waitress. Oh, it was a wonderful day—more like a holiday—and it would be so foolish to go home.

She boarded a Lexington Avenue bus and rode up to Eighty-sixth Street; it was here that she had decided to do a little shopping.

She had no idea what she wanted or needed, but she idled along, intent only upon the passers-by, brisk and preoccupied, who gave her a disturbing sense of separateness.

It was while waiting at the corner of Third Avenue that she saw the man: an old man, bowlegged and stooped under an armload of bulging packages; he wore a shabby brown coat and a checkered cap. Suddenly she realized they were exchanging a smile: there was nothing friendly about this smile, it was merely two cold flickers of recognition. But she was certain she had never seen him before.

He was standing next to an El pillar, and as she crossed the street he turned and followed. He kept quite close; from the corner of her eye she watched his reflection wavering on the shopwindows.

Then in the middle of the block she stopped and faced him. He stopped also and cocked his head, grinning. But what could she say? Do? Here, in broad daylight, on Eighty-sixth Street? It was useless and, despising her own helplessness, she quickened her steps.

Now Second Avenue is a dismal street, made from scraps and ends; part cobblestone, part asphalt, part cement; and its atmosphere of desertion is permanent. Mrs. Miller walked five blocks without meeting anyone, and all the while the steady crunch of his footfalls in the snow stayed near. And when she came to a florist's shop, the sound was still with her. She hurried inside and watched through the glass door as the old man passed; he kept his eyes straight ahead and didn't slow his pace, but he did one strange, telling thing: he tipped his cap.

"Six white ones, did you say?" asked the florist. "Yes," she told him, "white roses." From there she went to a glassware store and selected a vase, presumably a replacement for the one Miriam had broken, though the price was intolerable and the vase itself (she thought) grotesquely vulgar. But a series of unaccountable purchases had begun, as if by prearranged plan: a plan of which she had not the least knowledge or control.

She bought a bag of glazed cherries, and at a place called the Knickerbocker Bakery she paid forty cents for six almond cakes.

Within the last hour the weather had turned cold again; like blurred lenses, winter clouds cast a shade over the sun, and the skeleton of an early dusk colored the sky; a damp mist mixed with the wind and the voices of a few children who romped high on mountains of gutter snow seemed lonely and cheerless. Soon the first flake fell, and when Mrs. Miller reached the brownstone house, snow was falling in a swift screen and foot tracks vanished as they were printed.

The white roses were arranged decoratively in the vase. The glazed cherries shone on a ceramic plate. The almond cakes, dusted with sugar, awaited a hand. The canary fluttered on its swing and picked at a bar of seed.

At precisely five the doorbell rang. Mrs. Miller *knew* who it was. The hem of her housecoat trailed as she crossed the floor. "Is that you?" she called.

"Naturally," said Miriam, the word resounding shrilly from the hall. "Open this door."

"Go away," said Mrs. Miller.

"Please hurry . . . I have a heavy package."

"Go away," said Mrs. Miller. She returned to the living room, lighted a cigarette, sat down and calmly listened to the buzzer; on and on and on. "You might as well leave. I have no intention of letting you in."

Shortly the bell stopped. For possibly ten minutes Mrs. Miller did not move. Then, hearing no sound, she concluded Miriam had gone. She tiptoed to the door and opened it a sliver; Miriam was half-reclining atop a cardboard box with a beautiful French doll cradled in her arms.

"Really, I thought you were never coming," she said peevishly. "Here help me get this in, it's awfully heavy."

It was not spell-like compulsion that Mrs. Miller felt, but rather a curious passivity; she brought in the box, Miriam the doll. Miriam curled up on the sofa, not troubling to remove her coat or beret, and watched disinterestedly as Mrs. Miller dropped the box and stood trembling, trying to catch her breath.

"Thank you," she said. In the daylight she looked pinched and drawn, her hair less luminous. The French doll she was loving wore an exquisite powdered wig and its idiot glass eyes sought solace in Miriam's. "I have a surprise," she continued. "Look into my box."

Kneeling, Mrs. Miller parted the flaps and lifted out another doll; then a blue dress which she recalled as the one Miriam had worn that first night at the theater; and of the remainder she said, "It's all clothes. Why?"

"Because I've come to live with you," said Miriam, twisting a cherry stem. "Wasn't it nice of you to buy me the cherries . . . ?"

"But you can't! For God's sake go away—go away and leave me alone!"

". . . and the roses and the almond cakes? How really wonderfully generous. You know, these cherries are delicious. The last place I lived was with an old man; he was terribly poor and we never had good things to eat. But I think I'll be happy here." She paused to snuggle her doll closer. "Now, if you'll just show me where to put my things . . ."

Mrs. Miller's face dissolved into a mask of ugly red lines; she began to cry, and it was an unnatural, tearless sort of weeping, as though, not having wept for a long time, she had forgotten how. Carefully she edged backward till she touched the door.

She fumbled through the hall and down the stairs to a landing below. She pounded frantically on the door of the first apartment she came to; a short, red-headed man answered and she pushed past him. "Say, what the hell is this?" he said. "Anything wrong, lover?" asked a young woman who appeared from the kitchen, drying her hands. And it was to her that Mrs. Miller turned.

"Listen," she cried, "I'm ashamed behaving this way but—well, I'm Mrs. H. T. Miller and I live upstairs and . . ." She pressed her hands over her face. "It sounds so absurd. . . ."

The woman guided her to a chair, while the man excitedly rattled pocket change. "Yeah?"

"I live upstairs and there's a little girl visiting me, and I suppose that I'm afraid of her. She won't leave and I can't make her and—she's going to do something terrible. She's already stolen my cameo, but she's about to do something worse—something terrible!"

The man asked, "Is she a relative, huh?"

Mrs. Miller shook her head. "I don't know who she is. Her name's Miriam, but I don't know for certain who she is."

"You gotta calm down, honey," said the woman, stroking Mrs. Miller's arm. "Harry here'll tend to this kid. Go on, lover." And Mrs. Miller said, "The door's open—5A."

After the man left, the woman brought a towel and bathed Mrs. Miller's face. "You're very kind," Mrs. Miller said. "I'm sorry to act like such a fool, only this wicked child. . . ."

"Sure, honey," consoled the woman. "Now, you better take it easy."

Mrs. Miller rested her head in the crook of her arm; she was quiet enough to be asleep. The woman turned a radio dial; a piano and a husky voice filled the silence and the woman, tapping her foot, kept excellent time. "Maybe we oughta go up too," she said.

"I don't want to see her again. I don't want to be anywhere near her."

"Uh huh, but what you shoulda done, you shoulda called a cop."

Presently they heard the man on the stairs. He strode into the room frowning and scratching the back of his neck. "Nobody there," he said, honestly embarrassed. "She musta beat it."

"Harry, you're a jerk," announced the woman. "We been sitting here the whole time and we woulda seen . . ." she stopped abruptly, for the man's glance was sharp.

"I looked all over," he said, "and there just ain't nobody there. Nobody, understand?"

"Tell me," said Mrs. Miller, rising, "tell me, did you see a large box? Or a doll?"

"No, ma'am, I didn't."

And the woman, as if delivering a verdict, said, "Well, for cryinoutloud. . . ."

Mrs. Miller entered her apartment softly; she walked to the center of the room and stood quite still. No, in a sense it had not changed: the roses, the cakes, and the cherries were in place. But this was an empty room, emptier than if the furnishings and familiars were not present, lifeless and petrified as a funeral parlor. The sofa loomed before her with a new strangeness: its vacancy had a meaning that would have been less penetrating and terrible had Miriam been curled on it. She gazed fixedly at the space where she remembered setting the box and, for a moment, the hassock spun desperately. And she looked through the window; surely the river was real, surely snow was falling—but then, one could not be certain witness to anything: Miriam, so vividly *there* —and yet, where was she? Where, where?

As though moving in a dream, she sank to a chair. The room was losing shape; it was dark and getting darker and there was nothing to be done about it; she could not lift her hand to light a lamp.

Suddenly, closing her eyes, she felt an upward surge, like a diver emerging from some deeper, greener depth. In times of terror or immense distress, there are moments when the mind waits, as though for a revelation, while a skein of calm is woven over thought; it is like a sleep, or a supernatural trance; and during this lull one is aware of a force of quiet reasoning: well, what if she had never really known a girl named Miriam? that she had been foolishly frightened on the street? In the end, like everything else, it was of no importance. For the only thing she had lost to Miriam was her identity, but now she knew she had found again the person who lived in this room, who cooked her own meals, who owned a canary, who was someone she could trust and believe in: Mrs. H. T. Miller.

Listening in contentment, she became aware of a double sound: a bureau drawer opening and closing; she seemed to hear it long after completion—opening and closing. Then gradually, the harshness of it was replaced by the murmur of a silk dress and this, delicately faint, was moving nearer and swelling in intensity till the walls trembled with the vibration and the room was caving under a wave of whispers. Mrs. Miller stiffened and opened her eyes to a dull, direct stare.

"Hello," said Miriam.

1945

DISCUSSION QUESTIONS

1. What significance can you attach to the fact that Miriam and Mrs. Miller share the same forename? Look up the etymology of *Miriam.* What similar circumstances are present each of the first two times that Miriam appears?

2. What does the bouquet of paper roses tell us about its owner? What does Miriam's reaction to it reveal about her? Why does Mrs. Miller

forbid Miriam to awaken the canary? Why does the singing bird give Mrs. Miller "a queer sensation" (page 333)? What makes Tommy sing?

3. Why has the realization of being alone "not been among her thoughts for a long time" (page 334)? Relate your answers to the fact that "Her activities were seldom spontaneous" (page 329). Cite other examples to support this statement.

4. When Mrs. Miller walks to the theater, "her head [is] bowed, oblivious as a mole burrowing a blind path" (page 330). How does this *simile* help us to understand her life? Compare this description with her walk on Eighty-sixth Street. What change has occurred? Why? Cite other examples of this change.

5. Why does Mrs. Miller make "a series of unaccountable purchases"? Why would she prepare for Miriam's return with arrangements to please the child and then resolutely try to keep her out? Are there other examples of such *ambivalent* behavior? If so, cite them.

6. Why does Miriam's decision to live with her create fear in Mrs. Miller? Why has she not "wept for a long time," even "forgotten how"? Why does she refer to herself as Mrs. H. T. Miller, rather than as Mrs. Miriam Miller? Explain the statement that "the only thing she had lost to Miriam was her identity" (page 339).

A LITTLE COMPANION

ANGUS WILSON

THEY SAY in the village that Miss Arkwright has never been the same since the war[1] broke out, but she knows that it all began a long time before that—on 24th July, 1936, to be exact, the day of her forty-seventh birthday.

She was in no way a remarkable person. Her appearance was not particularly distinguished and yet she was without any feature that could actively displease. She had enough personal eccentricities to fit into the pattern of English village life, but none so absurd or anti-social that they could embarrass or even arouse gossip beyond what was pleasant to her neighbours. She accepted her position as an old maid with that

[1] The Second World War.

cheerful good humour and occasional irony which are essential to English spinsters since the deification of Jane Austen,[2] or more sacredly Miss Austen, by the upper middle classes, and she attempted to counteract the inadequacy of the unmarried state by quiet, sensible and tolerant social work in the local community. She was liked by nearly everyone, though she was not afraid of making enemies where she knew that her broad but deeply felt religious principles were being opposed. Any socially pretentious or undesirably extravagant conduct, too, was liable to call forth from her an unexpectedly caustic and well-aimed snub. She was invited everywhere and always accepted the invitations. You could see her at every tea or cocktail party, occasionally drinking a third gin, but never more. Quietly but well dressed, with one or two very fine old pieces of jewellery that had come down to her from her grandmother, she would pass from one group to another, laughing or serious as the occasion demanded. She smoked continuously her own, rather expensive, brand of cigarettes—"My one vice," she used to say, "the only thing that stands between me and secret drinking." She listened with patience, but with a slight twinkle in the eye, to Mr. Hodgson's endless stories of life in Dar-es-Salaam or Myra Hope's breathless accounts of her latest system of diet. John Hobday in his somewhat ostentatiously gentleman-farmer attire would describe his next novel about East Anglian life to her before even his beloved daughter had heard of it. Richard Trelawney, just down from Oxford, found that she had read and really knew Donne's[3] sermons, yet she could swop detective stories with Colonel Wright by the hour, and was his main source for quotations when *The Times* crossword was in question. She it was who incorporated little Mrs. Grantham into village life, when that rather underbred, suburban woman came there as Colonel Grantham's second wife, checking her vulgar remarks about "the lower classes" with kindly humour, but defending her against the formidable battery of Lady Vernon's antagonism. Yet she it was also who was first at Lady Vernon's when Sir Robert had his stroke and her unobtrusive kindliness and real services gained her a singular position behind the grim reserve of the Vernon family. She could always banter the vicar away from his hobby horse of the Greek rite when at parish meetings the agenda seemed to have been buried for ever beneath a welter of Euchologia[4] and Menaia.[5] She checked Sir Robert's anti-bolshevik phobia from

[2] Major English novelist (1775–1817).

[3] John Donne (1573–1631), major English poet and cleric.

[4] Books of prayers, liturgies, and rites of the Eastern Orthodox church.

[5] Collections of hymns of the Eastern Orthodox church.

victimizing the County Librarian for her Fabianism, but was fierce in her attack on the local council when she thought that class prejudice had prevented Commander Osborne's widow from getting a council house.[6] She led in fact an active and useful existence, yet when anyone praised her she would only laugh—"My dear," she would say, "hard work's the only excuse old maids like me have got for existing at all, and even then I don't know that they oughtn't to lethalize the lot of us." As the danger of war grew nearer in the 'thirties her favourite remark was, "Well, if they've got any sense this time they'll keep the young fellows at home and put us useless old maids in the trenches," and she said it with real conviction.

With her good carriage, ample figure and large, deep blue eyes, she even began to acquire a certain beauty as middle age approached. People speculated as to why she had never married. She had in fact refused a number of quite personable suitors. The truth was that from girlhood she had always felt a certain repulsion from physical contact. Not that she was in any way prudish; she was remarkable for a rather eighteenth-century turn of coarse phrase. Indeed, verbal freedom was the easier for her in that sexual activity was the more remote. Nor would psychoanalysts have found anything of particular interest in her; she had no abnormal desires. As a child she had never felt any wish to change her sex or observed any peculiarly violent or crude incident that could have resulted in what is called a psychic trauma. She just wasn't interested, and was perhaps as a result a little over-given to talking of "all this fuss and nonsense that's made over sex." She would however have liked to have had a child. She recognized this as a common phenomenon among childless women and accepted it, though she could never bring herself to admit it openly or laugh about it in the commonsensical way in which she treated her position as an old maid. As the middle years approached she found a sudden interest and even sometimes a sudden jealousy over other people's babies and children growing upon her, attacking her unexpectedly and with apparent irrelevancy to time or place. She was equally wide-awake to the dangers of the late forties and resolutely resisted such foolish fancies, though she became as a result a little snappish and over-gruff with the very young. "Now, my dear," she told herself, "you *must* deal with this nonsense or you'll start getting odd." How very odd she could not guess.

The Granthams always gave a little party for her on her birthdays.

[6] Dwelling place owned and rented by the local council (administrative body of the parish, district, or town).

"Awful nonsense at my age," she had been saying now for many years, "but I never say no to a drink." Her forty-seventh birthday party was a particular success. Mary Hatton was staying with the Granthams and like Miss Arkwright she was an ardent Janeite[7] so they'd been able to talk Mr. Collins and Mrs. Elton and the Elliots to their hearts' content, then Colonel Grantham had given her some tips about growing meconopsis[8] and finally Mrs. Osborne had been over to see the new rector at Longhurst, so they had a good-natured but thoroughly enjoyable "cat" about the state of the rectory there. She was just paying dutiful attention to her hostess' long complaint about the grocery deliveries, preparatory to saying good-bye, when suddenly a thin, whining, but remarkably clear, child's voice said loudly in her ear, "Race you home, Mummy." She looked around her in surprise, then decided that her mind must have wandered from the boring details of Mrs. Grantham's saga, but almost immediately the voice sounded again, "Come on, Mummy, you are a slowcoach. I said, 'race you home.'" This time Miss Arkwright was seriously disturbed. She wondered if Colonel Grantham's famous high spirits had got the better of him, but it could hardly have been so, she thought, as she saw his face earnest in conversation—"The point is, Vicar, not so much whether we want to intervene as whether we've got to." She began to feel most uncomfortable and as soon as politeness allowed she made her way home.

The village street seemed particularly hot and dusty, the sunlight on the whitewashed cottages peculiarly glaring as she walked along. "One too many on a hot day, that's your trouble, my dear," she said to herself and felt comforted by so material an explanation. The familiar trimness of her own little house and the cool shade of the walnut tree on the front lawn further calmed her nerves. She stopped for a moment to pick up a basket of lettuce that old Pyecroft had left at the door and then walked in. After the sunlight outside, the hall seemed so dark that she could hardly discern even the shape of the grandfather clock. Out of this shadowy blackness came the child's voice loudly and clearly but if anything more nasal than before. "Beat you to it this time," it said. Miss Arkwright's heart stopped for a moment and her lungs seemed to contract and then almost instantaneously she had seen it—a little white-faced boy, thin, with matchstick arms and legs growing out of shrunken

[7] An enthusiastic admirer of Jane Austen's novels. References to characters in three of her novels follow: Mr. Collins: *Pride and Prejudice* (1813); Mrs. Elton: *Emma* (1816); and the Elliots: *Persuasion* (1818).

[8] Welsh poppy genus.

clothes, with red-rimmed eyes and an adenoidal open-mouthed expression. Instantaneously, because the next moment he was not there, almost like a flickering image against the eye's retina. Miss Arkwright straightened her back, took a deep breath, then she went upstairs, took off her shoes and lay down on her bed.

It was many weeks before anything fresh occurred and she felt happily able to put the whole incident down to cocktails and the heat; indeed she began to remember that she had woken next morning with a severe headache—"You're much too old to start suffering from hangovers," she told herself. But the next experience was really more alarming. She had been up to London to buy a wedding present at Harrods[9] and, arriving somewhat late for the returning train, found herself sitting in a stuffy and overpacked carriage. She felt therefore particularly pleased to see the familiar slate quarries that heralded the approach of Brankston Station, when suddenly a sharp dig drove the bones of her stays into her ribs. She looked with annoyance at the woman next to her—a blowsy creature with feathers in her hat—when she saw to her surprise that the woman was quietly asleep, her arms folded in front of her. Then in her ears there sounded "Chuff, Chuff, Chuff, Chuff," followed by a little snort and a giggle, and then quite unmistakably the whining voice saying, "Rotten old train." After that it seemed to her as though for a few moments pandemonium had broken loose in the carriage—shouts and cries and a monotonous thumping against the woodwork as though someone were beating an impatient rhythm with their foot—yet no other occupant seemed in the slightest degree disturbed. They were for Miss Arkwright moments of choking and agonizing fear. She dreaded that at any minute the noise would grow so loud that the others would notice, for she felt an inescapable responsibility for the incident. Yet had the whole carriage risen and flung her from the window as a witch it would in some degree have been a release from the terrible sense of personal obsession; it would have given objective reality to what now seemed an uncontrollable expansion of her own consciousness into space; it would at the least have shown that others were mad beside herself. But no slightest ripple broke the drowsy torpor of the hot carriage in the August sun. She was deeply relieved when the train at last drew into Brankston and the impatience of her invisible attendant was assuaged, but no sooner had she set foot on the platform than she heard once more the almost puling whine, the too familiar, "Race you home, Mummy." She knew then that whatever it was,

[9] Fashionable London department store.

it had come to stay, that her homecomings would no longer be to the familiar comfort of her house and servants, but that there would always be a childish voice, a childish face to greet her for one moment as she crossed the threshold.

And so it proved. Gradually at first, at more than weekly intervals, and then increasingly, so that even a short spell in the vegetable garden or with the rock plants would mean impatient whining, wanton scattering of precious flowers, overturning of baskets—and then that momentary vision, lengthened now sometimes to five minutes' duration, that sickly, cretinous face. The very squalor of the child's appearance was revolting to Miss Arkwright, for whom cheerful, good health was the first of human qualities. Sometimes the sickliness of the features would be of the thick, flaccid, pasty appearance that suggested rich feeding and late hours, and then the creature would be dressed in a velvet suit and Fauntleroy collar[10] that might have clothed an over-indulged French *bourgeois* child; at other times the appearance was more cretinous, adenoidal and emaciated, and then it would wear the shrunken uniform and thick black boots of an institution idiot. In either case it was a child quite out of keeping with the home it sought to possess—a home of quiet beauty, unostentatious comfort and restrained good taste. Of course, Miss Arkwright argued, it was an emanation from the sick side of herself so that it was bound to be diseased, but this realization did not compensate for dribble marks on her best dresses or for sticky finger marks on her tweed skirts.

At first she tried to ignore the obsession with her deep reserve of stoic patience, but as it continued, she felt the need of the Church. She became a daily communicant and delighted the more "spikey"[11] of her neighbours. She prayed ceaselessly for release or resignation. A lurking sense of sin was roused in her and she wondered if small frivolities and pleasures were the cause of her visitation; she remembered that after all it had first begun when she was drinking gin. Her religion had always been of the "brisk" and "sensible" variety, but now she began to fear that she had been oversuspicious of "enthusiasm" or "pietism." She gave up all but the most frugal meals, distributed a lot of her clothes to the poor, slept on a board and rose at one in the morning to say a special Anglican office from a little book she had once been given by a rather

[10] Wide collar with round corners, after Lord Fauntleroy, protagonist of Frances Hodgson Burnett's novel *Little Lord Fauntleroy* (1886).

[11] Holding rigid High Church views.

despised High Church cousin. The only result seemed to be to cause scandal to her comfortable, old-fashioned parlourmaid and cook. She mentioned her state of sin in general terms to the vicar and he lent her Neale's[12] translations of the Coptic[13] and Nestorian[14] rites, but they proved of little comfort. At Christmas she rather shamefacedly and secretively placed a little bed with a richly filled stocking in the corner of her bedroom, but the child was not to be blackmailed. Throughout the day she could hear faint but unsavory sounds of uncontrolled and slovenly guzzling, like the distant sound of pigs feeding, and when evening came she was pursued by ever louder retching and the disturbing smell of vomit.

On Boxing Day she visited her old and sensible friend the bishop and told him the whole story. He looked at her very steadily with the large, dramatic brown eyes that were so telling in the pulpit, and for a long time he remained silent. Miss Arkwright hoped that he would advise her quickly, for she could feel a growing tugging at her skirt. It was obvious that this quiet, spacious library was no place for a child, and she could not have borne to see these wonderful, old books disturbed even if she was the sole observer of the sacrilege. At last the bishop spoke. "You say that the child appears ill and depraved. Has this evil appearance been more marked in the last weeks?" Miss Arkwright was forced to admit that it had. "My dear old friend," said the bishop and he put his hand on hers. "It is your sick self that you are seeing, and all this foolish abstinence, this extravagant martyrdom are making you more sick." The bishop was a great Broad Churchman of the old school. "Go out into the world and take in its beauty and its colour. Enjoy what is yours and thank God for it." And without more ado, he persuaded Miss Arkwright to go to London for a few weeks.

Established at Berners', she set out to have a good time. She was always fond of expensive meals, but her first attempt to indulge at Claridge's[15] proved an appalling failure, for with every course the voice grew louder and louder in her ears. "Coo! what rotten stuff," it kept on repeating, "I want an ice." Henceforth her meals were taken almost exclusively on Selfridge's[16] roof or in ice-cream parlours, an unsatisfying

[12] John Mason Neale (1818–1866), hymnologist and theologian.

[13] Belonging to the Christian church of Egypt.

[14] Eastern church adhering to the doctrines of Nestorius.

[15] Fashionable London hotel.

[16] Large London department store.

and indigestible diet. Visits to the theatre were at first a greater success. She saw the new adaptation of *The Mill on the Floss,*[17] and a version of *Lear* modelled on the original Kean[18] production. The child had clearly never seen a play before and was held entranced by the mere spectacle. But soon it began to grow restless. A performance of *Hedda Gabbler*[19] was entirely ruined by rustlings, kicks, whispers, giggles and a severe bout of hiccoughs. For a time it was kept quiet by musical comedies and farces, but in the end Miss Arkwright found herself attending only *Where the Rainbow Ends,*[20] *Mother Goose,* and *Buckie's Bears*[21]—it was not a sophisticated child. As the run of Christmas plays drew near their end she became desperate, and one afternoon she left a particularly dusty performance at the Circus and visited her old friend Madge Cleaver—once again to tell all. "Poor Bessie," said Madge Cleaver and she smiled so spiritually, "how real Error can seem," for Madge was a Christian Scientist. "But it's so *un*real, dear, if we can only have the courage to see the Truth. Truth denies Animal Magnetism, Spiritualism and all other false manifestations." She lent Miss Arkwright *Science and Health*[22] and promised that she would give her "absent treatment."

At first Miss Arkwright felt most comforted. Mrs. Eddy's denial of the reality of most common phenomena and in particular of those that are evil seemed to offer a way out. Unfortunately, the child seemed quite unconvinced of its own non-existence. One afternoon Miss Arkwright thought with horror that by adopting a theology that denied the existence of Matter and gave reality only to Spirit she might well be gradually removing herself from the scene, whilst leaving the child in possession. After all her own considerable bulk was testimony enough to her material nature, whilst the child might well in some repulsive way be accounted spirit. Terrified by the prospect before her, she speedily renounced Christian Science.

She returned to her home and by reaction decided to treat the whole phenomenon on the most material basis possible. She submitted her body to every old-fashioned purgative, she even indulged in a little

[17] Based on George Eliot's novel of 1860.

[18] Edmund Kean (1787–1833), British Shakespearean actor.

[19] Drama by Henrik Ibsen, first performed in 1890.

[20] Musical fairy tale by Mrs. Clifford Mills and John Ramsay.

[21] Musical play by Erica Fay and Henry Buffkins.

[22] Written by Mary Baker Eddy (1821–1910), founder of Christian Science, who taught that disease was illusory in nature and caused by mental error.

amateur blood-letting, for might not the creature be some ill humour or sickly emanation of the body itself? But this antiquarian leechcraft only produced serious physical weakness and collapse. She was forced to call in Dr. Kent who at once terminated the purgatives and put her on to port wine and beefsteak.

Failure of material remedies forced Miss Arkwright at last to a conviction which she had feared from the start. The thing, she decided, must be a genuine psychic phenomenon. It cost her much to admit this for she had always been very contemptuous of spiritualism, and regarded it as socially undesirable where it was not consciously fraudulent. But she was by now very desperate and willing to waive the deepest prejudices to free herself from the vulgar and querulous apparition. For a month or more she attended seances in London, but though she received "happy" communications from enough small Indian or Red Indian children to have started a nursery school, no medium or clairvoyant could tell her anything that threw light on her little companion. At one of the seances, however, she met a thin, red-haired, pre-Raphaelite sort of lady in a long grey garment and sandals, who asked her to attend the Circle of the Seventh Pentacle in the Earllands Road. The people she found there did not attract Miss Arkwright; she decided that the servants of the Devil were either common frauds or of exceedingly doubtful morals, but the little group was enthusiastic when she told her story. How could she hope to fight such Black Powers, they asked, unless she was prepared to invoke the White Art? Although she resisted their arguments at first, she finally found herself agreeing to a celebration of the Satanic Mass in her own home. She sent cook and Annie away for a week and prepared to receive the Circle. Their arrival in the village caused a great stir, partly because of their retinue of goats and rabbits. It had been decided that Miss Arkwright should celebrate the Mass herself, an altar had been set up in the drawing room, she had bought an immense white maternity gown from Debenham's and had been busy all the week learning her words, but at the last minute something within her rebelled, she could not bring herself to say the Lord's Prayer backwards and the Mass had to be called off. In the morning the devotees of the Pentacle left with many recriminations. The only result seemed to be that valuable ornaments were missing from the bedrooms occupied by the less reputable, whilst about those rooms in which the Devil's true servants had slept there hung an odour of goat that no fumigation could remove.

Miss Arkwright had long since given up visiting her neighbours, though they had not ceased to speculate about her. A chance remark that she had "two now to provide for," had led them to think that she believed herself pregnant. After this last visitation Lady Vernon decided that the time had come to act. She visited Miss Arkwright early one morning, and seeing the maternity gown which was still lying in the sitting room, she was confirmed in her suspicions. "Bessie dear," she said, "you've got to realize that you're seriously ill, mentally ill," and she packed Miss Arkwright off to a brain specialist in Welbeck Street. This doctor, finding nothing physically wrong, sent her to a psychoanalyst. Poor Miss Arkwright! She was so convinced of her own insanity, that she could think of no argument if they should wish to shut her up. But the analyst, a smart, grey-haired Jew, laughed when she murmured "madness." "We don't talk in those terms any more, Miss Arkwright. You're a century out of date. It's true there are certain disturbingly psychotic features in what you tell me, but nothing, I think, that won't yield to deep analysis," and deep analysis she underwent for eight months or more, busily writing down dreams at night and lying on a couch "freely associating" by day. At the end of that time the analyst began to form a few conclusions. "The child itself," he said, "is unimportant; the fact that you still see it even less so. What is important is that you now surround yourself with vulgarity and whining. You have clearly a need for these things which you have inhibited too long in an atmosphere of refinement." It was decided that Miss Arkwright should sublimate this need by learning the saxophone. Solemnly each day the poor lady sat in the drawing room—that room which had resounded with Bach and Mozart—and practised the alto sax. At last one day when she had got so far as to be able to play the opening bars of "Alligator Stomp," her sense of the ridiculous rebelled and she would play no more, though her little companion showed great restlessness at the disappearance of noises which accorded all too closely with its vulgar taste.

I shall treat myself, she decided, and after long thought she came to the conclusion that the most salient feature of the business lay in the child's constant reiteration of the challenge, "Race you home, Mummy"; with this it had started and with this it had continued. If, thought Miss Arkwright, I were to leave home completely, not only this house, but also England, then perhaps it would withdraw its challenge and depart.

In January, 1938, then, she set out on her travels. All across Europe, in museums and cafés and opera houses, it continued to throw down the gauntlet—"Race you home, Mummy," and there it would be in her hotel bedroom. It seemed, however, anxious to take on local colour and would appear in a diversity of national costumes, often reviving for the purpose peasant dresses seen only at folk-dance festivals or when worn by beggars in order to attract tourists. For Miss Arkwright this rather vulgar and commercial World's Fair aspect of her life was particularly distressing. The child also attempted to alter its own colour, pale brown it achieved in India, in China a faint tinge of lemon, and in America by some misunderstanding of the term Red Indian it emerged bright scarlet. She was especially horrified by the purple swelling with which it attempted to emulate the black of the African natives. But whatever its colour, it was always there.

At last the menace of war in September found Miss Arkwright in Morocco and along with thousands of other British travellers she hurried home, carrying, she felt, her greatest menace with her. It was only really after Munich[23] that she became reconciled to its continued presence, learning gradually to incorporate its noises, its appearance, its whole personality into her daily life. She went out again among her neighbours and soon everyone had forgotten that she had ever been ill. It was true that she was forced to address her companion occasionally with a word of conciliation, or to administer a slap in its direction when it was particularly provoking, but she managed to disguise these peculiarities beneath her normal gestures.

One Saturday evening in September, 1939, she was returning home from the rectory, worried by the threat of approaching war and wondering how she could best use her dual personality to serve her country, when she was suddenly disturbed to hear a clattering of hoofs and a thunderous bellow behind her. She turned to see at some yards distance a furious bull, charging down the village street. She began immediately to run for her home, the little voice whining in her ear, "Race you home, Mummy." But the bull seemed to gain upon her, and in her terror she redoubled her speed, running as she had not run since she was a girl. She heard, it is true, a faint sighing in her ears as of dying breath, but she was too frightened to stop until she was safe at her own door. In she walked and, to her amazement, indeed, to her horror, look where she would, the little child was *not* there. She had taken up his challenge to a race and she had won.

She lay in bed that night depressed and lonely. She realized only too clearly that difficult as it was to get rid of him—now that the child was gone she found herself thinking of "him" rather than "it"—it would

[23] Munich Pact of 29 September 1938, between Great Britain, France, Italy, and Germany, which gave the Sudetenland to Germany.

be well-nigh impossible to get him back. The sirens that declared war next morning seemed only a confirmation of her personal loss. She went into mourning and rarely emerged from the house. For a short while it is true, her spirits were revived when the evacuee children came from the East End; some of the more cretinous and adenoidal seemed curiously like her lost one. But country air and food soon gave them rosy cheeks and sturdy legs and she rapidly lost her interest. Before the year was out she was almost entirely dissociated from the external world, and those few friends, who found time amid the cares of war to visit her in her bedroom, decided that there was little that could be done for one who showed so little response. The vicar, who was busy translating St. Gregory Nazianzen's[24] prayers for victory, spoke what was felt to be the easiest and kindest verdict when he described her as "just another war casualty."

1950

DISCUSSION QUESTIONS

1. How does Wilson prepare the reader for the appearance of the "little white-faced boy"? What is the most natural explanation for Miss Arkwright's hallucination?

2. Miss Arkwright stops playing the saxophone because "her sense of the ridiculous rebelled" (page 350). In what ways does Wilson share his protagonist's sense of the ridiculous? Cite examples. What purpose does he achieve through his use of the ridiculous or the absurd?

3. Each of Miss Arkwright's efforts to get rid of her "little companion" ends not only in failure but usually in her discomfort. Do these *scenes* appeal more to our humor or to our sympathy? Why? Cite examples.

4. Why does the narrator tell us that psychoanalysts would not "have found anything of particular interest in her; she had no abnormal desires" (page 343), when Miss Arkwright later undergoes eight months of "deep analysis"?

5. When all efforts to get rid of the child have failed, why would Miss Arkwright's spontaneous act of "running as she had not run since she was a girl" (page 351) inadvertently bring success?

[24] Theologian and bishop (328?–390).

6. How do you explain Miss Arkwright's reaction to the loss of the child? Were you prepared for it? Does her response seem probable or absurd? How does it influence your interpretation of the story?

1. Compare Mrs. Miller with Miss Arkwright. What are their basic differences? What do they have in common?

2. Examine your feelings toward the two women and their dilemmas. Are you equally sympathetic toward them? If not, what aspects of the two stories (including the narrator's *tone*) create differences in your response? Cite examples.

3. Compare the impact that the two children have on the two women. In what way is each affected and changed by the experience?

4. Which of the two stories seems to you the better one? Why?

ANALYSIS AND APPLICATION

1. In the following descriptive passages, what organizing principle determines the position of each element in the series? Construct a similarly organized series for each passage.

a. "only snow lifting in the wind, frosting the window glass, chilling the rooms, deadening and hushing the city." (page 331)

b. "a sweep of clean new clouds crumpled against a vastly blue, out-of-season sky; and across the low line of rooftops she could see the river and smoke curving from tugboat stacks in a warm wind. A great silver truck plowed the snow-banked street, its machine sound humming on the air." (page 335)

2. In the sentence below, Wilson has used parallel grammatical elements to emphasize the parallel meaning of his three independent clauses. Identify these parallel elements. Construct a sentence of your own that closely imitates Wilson's structure.

> Yet had the whole carriage risen and flung her from the window as a witch it would in some degree have been a release from the terrible sense of personal obsession; it would have given objective reality to what now seemed an uncontrollable expansion of her own consciousness into space; it would at the least have shown that others were mad beside herself. (page 345)

3. In the following sentence, parallelism has been carried much further: Not only are the two clauses nearly perfectly balanced, but they are almost of equal length. List the parallel elements in two facing columns. Why is "for her" implied rather than repeated? Construct two similarly balanced sentences modeled on Wilson's.

"Indeed, verbal freedom was the easier for her in that sexual activity was the more remote." (page 343)

THE DEMON LOVER

ELIZABETH BOWEN

TOWARDS THE end of her day in London Mrs. Drover went round to her shut-up house to look for several things she wanted to take away. Some belonged to herself, some to her family, who were by now used to their country life. It was late August; it had been a steamy, showery day: at the moment the trees down the pavement glittered in an escape of humid yellow afternoon sun. Against the next batch of clouds, already piling up ink-dark, broken chimneys and parapets stood out. In her once familiar street, as in any unused channel, an unfamiliar queerness had silted up; a cat wove itself in and out of railings, but no human eye watched Mrs. Drover's return. Shifting some parcels under her arm, she slowly forced round her latchkey in an unwilling lock, then gave the door, which had warped, a push with her knee. Dead air came out to meet her as she went in.

The staircase window having been boarded up, no light came down into the hall. But one door, she could just see, stood ajar, so she went quickly through into the room and unshuttered the big window in there. Now the prosaic woman, looking about her, was more perplexed than she knew by everything that she saw, by traces of her long former habit of life—the yellow smoke-stain up the white marble mantelpiece, the ring left by a vase on the top of the escritoire; the bruise in the wallpaper where, on the door being thrown open widely, the china handle had always hit the wall. The piano, having gone away to be stored, had left what looked like claw-marks on its part of the parquet. Though not much dust had seeped in, each object wore a film of another kind; and, the only ventilation being the chimney, the whole drawing-room smelled of the cold hearth. Mrs. Drover put down her parcels on the escritoire and left the room to proceed upstairs; the things she wanted were in a bedroom chest.

She had been anxious to see how the house was—the part-time caretaker she shared with some neighbours was away this week on his holiday, known to be not yet back. At the best of times he did not look in often, and she was never sure that she trusted him. There were some cracks in the structure, left by the last bombing, on which she was anxious to keep an eye. Not that one could do anything—

A shaft of refracted daylight now lay across the hall. She stopped dead and stared at the hall table—on this lay a letter addressed to her.

She thought first—then the caretaker *must* be back. All the same, who, seeing the house shuttered, would have dropped a letter in at the box? It was not a circular, it was not a bill. And the post office redirected, to the address in the country, everything for her that came through the post. The caretaker (even if he *were* back) did not know she was due in London to-day—her call here had been planned to be a surprise—so his negligence in the manner of this letter, leaving it to wait in the dusk and the dust, annoyed her. Annoyed, she picked up the letter, which bore no stamp. But it cannot be important, or they would know . . . She took the letter rapidly upstairs with her, without a stop to look at the writing till she reached what had been her bedroom, where she let in light. The room looked over the garden and other gardens: the sun had gone in; as the clouds sharpened and lowered, the trees and rank lawns seemed already to smoke with dark. Her reluctance to look again at the letter came from the fact that she felt intruded upon—and by someone contemptuous of her ways. However, in the tenseness preceding the fall of rain she read it: it was a few lines.

DEAR KATHLEEN,

You will not have forgotten that to-day is our anniversary, and the day we said. The years have gone by at once slowly and fast. In view of the fact that nothing has changed, I shall rely upon you to keep your promise. I was sorry to see you leave London, but was satisfied that you would be back in time. You may expect me, therefore, at the hour arranged.

Until then . . .

K.

Mrs. Drover looked for the date: it was to-day's. She dropped the letter on to the bed-springs, then picked it up to see the writing again—her lips, beneath the remains of lipstick, beginning to go white. She felt so much the change in her own face that she went to the mirror, polished a clear patch in it and looked at once urgently and stealthily in. She was confronted by a woman of forty-four, with eyes starting out under a hat-brim that had been rather carelessly pulled down. She had not put on any more powder since she left the shop where she ate her solitary tea. The pearls her husband had given her on their marriage hung loose round her now rather thinner throat, slipping into the V of the pink wool jumper her sister knitted last autumn as they sat round the fire. Mrs. Drover's most normal expression was one of controlled worry, but of assent. Since the birth of the third of her little boys, attended by a quite serious illness, she had had an intermittent muscular flicker to the left of her mouth, but in spite of this she could always sustain a manner that was at once energetic and calm.

Turning from her own face as precipitately as she had gone to meet it, she went to the chest where the things were, unlocked it, threw up the lid and knelt to search. But as rain began to come crashing down she could not keep from looking over her shoulder at the stripped bed on which the letter lay. Behind the blanket of rain the clock of the church that still stood struck six—with rapidly heightening apprehension she counted each of the slow strokes. "The hour arranged . . . My God," she said, "*what* hour? How should I . . . ? After twenty-five years. . . ."

The young girl talking to the soldier in the garden had not ever completely seen his face. It was dark; they were saying good-bye under a tree. Now and then—for it felt, from not seeing him at this intense moment, as though she had never seen him at all—she verified his presence for these few moments longer by putting out a hand, which he each time pressed, without very much kindness, and painfully, on to one of the breast buttons of his uniform. That cut of the button on the palm of her hand was, principally, what she was to carry away. This was so near the end of a leave from France that she could only wish him already gone. It was August 1916. Being not kissed, being drawn away from and looked at intimidated Kathleen till she imagined spectral glitters in the place of his eyes. Turning away and looking back up the lawn she saw, through branches of trees, the drawing-room window alight: she caught a breath for the moment when she could go running back there into the safe arms of her mother and sister, and cry: "What shall I do, what shall I do? He has gone."

Hearing her catch her breath, her fiancé said, without feeling: "Cold?"

"You're going away such a long way."

"Not so far as you think."

"I don't understand?"

"You don't have to," he said. "You will. You know what we said."

"But that was—suppose you—I mean, suppose."

"I shall be with you," he said, "sooner or later. You won't forget that. You need do nothing but wait."

Only a little more than a minute later she was free to run up the silent lawn. Looking in through the window at her mother and sister, who did not for the moment perceive her, she already felt that unnatural promise drive down between her and the rest of all human kind. No other way of having given herself could have made her feel so apart, lost and foresworn. She could not have plighted a more sinister troth.

Kathleen behaved well when, some months later, her fiancé was reported missing, presumed killed. Her family not only supported her but were able to praise her courage without stint because they could not regret, as a husband for her, the man they knew almost nothing about. They hoped she would, in a year or two, console herself—and had it been only a question of consolation things might have gone much straighter ahead. But her trouble, behind just a little grief, was a complete dislocation from everything. She did not reject other lovers, for these failed to appear: for years she failed to attract men—and with the approach of her 'thirties she became natural enough to share her family's anxiousness on this score. She began to put herself out, to wonder; and at thirty-two she was very greatly relieved to find herself being courted by William Drover. She married him, and the two of them settled down in this quiet, arboreal part of Kensington: in this house the years piled up, her children were born and they all lived till they were driven out by the bombs of the next war. Her movements as Mrs. Drover were circumscribed, and she dismissed any idea that they were still watched.

As things were—dead or living the letter-writer sent her only a threat. Unable, for some minutes, to go on kneeling with her back exposed to the empty room, Mrs. Drover rose from the chest to sit on an upright chair whose back was firmly against the wall. The desuetude of her former bedroom, her married London home's whole air of being a cracked cup from which memory, with its reassuring power, had either evaporated or leaked away, made a crisis—and at just this crisis the letter-writer had, knowledgeably, struck. The hollowness of the house this evening cancelled years on years of voices, habits and steps. Through the shut windows she only heard rain fall on the roofs around. To rally herself, she said she was in a mood—and, for two or three seconds shutting her eyes, told herself that she had imagined the letter. But she opened them—there it lay on the bed.

On the supernatural side of the letter's entrance she was not permitting her mind to dwell. Who, in London, knew she meant to call at the house to-day? Evidently, however, this had been known. The caretaker, *had* he come back, had had no cause to expect her: he would have taken the letter in his pocket, to forward it, at his own time, through the post. There was no other sign that the caretaker had been in—but, if not? Letters dropped in at doors of deserted houses do not fly or walk to tables in halls. They do not sit on the dust of empty tables with the air of certainty that they will be found. There is needed some human hand—but nobody but the caretaker had a key. Under circumstances she did not care to consider, a house can be entered without a key. It was possible that she was not alone now. She might be being waited for, downstairs. Waited for—until when? Until "the hour arranged." At least that was not six o'clock: six has struck.

She rose from the chair and went over and locked the door.

The thing was, to get out. To fly? No, not that: she had to catch her train. As a woman whose utter dependability was the keystone of her family life she was not willing to return to the country, to her husband, her little boys and her sister, without the objects she had come up to fetch. Resuming work at the chest she set about making up a number of parcels in a rapid, fumbling-decisive way. These, with her shopping parcels, would be too much to carry; these meant a taxi—at the thought of the taxi her heart went up and her normal breathing resumed. I will ring up the taxi now; the taxi cannot come too soon: I shall hear the taxi out there running its engine, till I walk calmly down to it through the hall. I'll ring up—But no: the telephone is cut off... She tugged at a knot she had tied wrong.

The idea of flight... He was never kind to me, not really. I don't remember him kind at all. Mother said he never considered me. He was set on me, that was what it was—not love. Not love, not meaning a person well. What did he do, to make me promise like that? I can't remember—But she found that she could.

She remembered with such dreadful acuteness that the twenty-five years since then dissolved like smoke and she instinctively looked for the weal left by the button on the palm of her hand. She remembered not only all that he said and did but the complete suspension of *her* existence during that August week. I was not myself—they all told me so at the time. She remembered—but with one white burning blank as where acid has dropped on a photograph: *under no conditions* could she remember his face.

So, wherever he may be waiting, I shall not know him. You have no time to run from a face you do not expect.

The thing was to get to the taxi before any clock struck what could be the hour. She would slip down the street and round the side of the square to where the square gave on the main road. She would return in the taxi, safe, to her own door, and bring the solid driver into the house with her to pick up the parcels from room to room. The idea of the taxi driver made her decisive, bold: she unlocked her door, went to the top of the staircase and listened down.

She heard nothing—but while she was hearing nothing the *passé* air of the staircase was disturbed by a draught that travelled up to her face. It emanated from the basement: down there a door or window was being opened by someone who chose this moment to leave the house.

The rain had stopped; the pavements steamily shone as Mrs. Drover let herself out by inches from her own front door into the empty street. The unoccupied houses opposite continued to meet her look with their damaged stare. Making towards the thoroughfare and the taxi, she tried not to keep looking behind. Indeed, the silence was so intense—one of those creeks of London silence exaggerated this summer by the damage of war—that no tread could have gained on hers unheard. Where her street debouched on the square where people went on living she grew conscious of and checked her unnatural pace. Across the open end of the square two buses impassively passed each other; women, a perambulator, cyclists, a man wheeling a barrow signalized, once again, the ordinary flow of life. At the square's most populous corner should be—and was—the short taxi rank. This evening, only one taxi—but this, although it presented its blank rump, appeared already to be alertly waiting for her. Indeed, without looking round the driver started his engine as she panted up from behind and put her hand on the door. As she did so, the clock struck seven. The taxi faced the main road: to make the trip back to her house it would have to turn—she had settled back on the seat and the taxi *had* turned before she, surprised by its knowing movement, recollected that she had not "said where." She leaned forward to scratch at the glass panel that divided the driver's head from her own.

The driver braked to what was almost a stop, turned round and slid the glass panel back: the jolt of this flung Mrs. Drover forward till her face was almost into the glass. Through the aperture driver and passenger, not six inches between them, remained for an eternity eye to eye. Mrs. Drover's mouth hung open for some seconds before she could issue her first scream. After that she continued to scream freely and to beat with her gloved hands on the glass all round as the taxi, accelerating without mercy, made off with her into the hinterland of deserted streets.

1945

A WARNING FOR MARRIED WOMEN

[THE DAEMON LOVER][1]

THERE DWELT a fair maid in the West,
  Of worthy birth and fame,
Neer unto Plimouth, stately town,
  Jane Reynolds was her name.

This damsel dearly was belovd
  By many a proper youth,
And what of her is to be said
  Is known for very truth.

[1] Child, no. 243A, Restoration Broadside: "A Warning for Married Women, being an example of Mrs Jane Reynolds (a West-country woman), born near Plymouth, who, having plighted her troth to a Seaman, was afterwards married to a Carpenter, and at last carried away by a Spirit, the manner how shall presently be recited. To a West-country tune called 'The Fair Maid of Bristol,' 'Bateman,' or 'John True.' " *Pepys Ballads* IV, 101.

Among the rest a seaman brave
Unto her a wooing came;
A comely proper youth he was,
James Harris called by name.

The maid and young man was agreed,
As time did them allow,
And to each other secretly
They made a solemn vow,

That they would ever faithfull be
Whilst Heaven afforded life;
He was to be her husband kind,
And she his faithfull wife.

A day appointed was also
When they was to be married;
But before these things were brought to pass
Matters were strangely carried.

All you that faithfull lovers be
Give ear and hearken well,
And what of them became at last
I will directly tell.

The young man he was prest to sea,
And forcëd was to go;
His sweet-heart she must stay behind,
Whether she would or no.

And after he was from her gone
She three years for him staid,
Expecting of his comeing home,
And kept herself a maid.

At last news came that he was dead
Within a forraign land,
And how that he was buried
She well did understand,

For whose sweet sake the maiden she
  Lamented many a day,
And never was she known at all
  The wanton for to play.

A carpenter that livd hard by,
  When he heard of the same,
Like as the other had done before,
  To her a wooing came.

But when that he had gained her love
  They married were with speed,
And four years space, being man and wife,
  They loveingly agreed.

Three pritty children in this time
  This loving couple had,
Which made their father's heart rejoyce,
  And mother wondrous glad.

But as occasion servd, one time
  The good man took his way
Some three days journey from his home,
  Intending not to stay.

But, whilst that he was gone away,
  A spirit in the night
Came to the window of his wife,
  And did her sorely fright.

Which spirit spake like to a man,
  And unto her did say,
'My dear and onely love,' quoth he,
  'Prepare and come away.

'James Harris is my name,' quoth he,
  'Whom thou didst love so dear,
And I have traveld for thy sake
  At least this seven year.

'And now I am returnd again,
To take thee to my wife,
And thou with me shalt go to sea,
To end all further strife.'

'O tempt me not, sweet James,' quoth she,
'With thee away to go;
If I should leave my children small,
Alas! what would they do?

'My husband is a carpenter,
A carpenter of great fame;
I would not for five hundred pounds
That he should know the same.'

'I might have had a king's daughter,
And she would have married me;
But I forsook her golden crown,
And for the love of thee.

'Therefore, if thou 'lt thy husband forsake,
And thy children three also,
I will forgive the[e] what is past,
If thou wilt with me go.'

'If I forsake my husband and
My little children three,
What means hast thou to bring me to,
If I should go with thee?'

'I have seven ships upon the sea;
When they are come to land,
Both marriners and marchandize
Shall be at thy command.

'The ship wherein my love shall sail
Is glorious to behold;
The sails shall be of finest silk,
And the mast of shining gold.'

When he had told her these fair tales,
  To love him she began,
Because he was in human shape,
  Much like unto a man.

And so together away they went
  From off the English shore,
And since that time the woman-kind
  Was never seen no more.

But when her husband he come home
  And found his wife was gone,
And left her three sweet pretty babes
  Within the house alone,

He beat his breast, he tore his hair,
  The tears fell from his eyes,
And in the open streets he run
  With heavy doleful cries.

And in this sad distracted case
  He hangd himself for woe
Upon a tree near to the place;
  The truth of all is so.

The children now are fatherless,
  And left without a guide,
But yet no doubt the heavenly powers
  Will for them well provide.

DISCUSSION QUESTIONS

1. When Mrs. Drover spies the letter on the hall table, she feels annoyed and "intruded upon . . . by someone contemptuous of her ways" (pages 356–357). Why? What does her over-reaction tell us about her mental stability? What other aspects of her behavior help to confirm your theory?

2. Explain the following sentence: "Her movements as Mrs. Drover

were circumscribed, and she dismissed any idea that they were still watched" (page 359). Watched by whom?

3. Explain why the sight of her home makes Mrs. Drover "more perplexed than she knew" (page 356). Analyze the sentence on page 359 beginning with "The desuetude of her former bedroom. . . ." What "memory" has "evaporated or leaked away"? Why? Why had it possessed "reassuring power"? Why has its disappearance "made a crisis"?

4. Since in her *flashback* Kathleen feels intimidated by her lover and wishes "him already gone" (page 358), why does she suffer "a complete dislocation from everything" (page 358) after the news of his death and wait thirteen years before getting married?

5. How *reliable* is Mrs. Drover's assumption that someone is in her basement? How does she know that the taxi driver is her dead lover when she couldn't "remember his face"?

6. Compare "The Demon Lover" with the folk ballad of the same name. What elements do they have in common? In what important ways do they differ?

THE DAEMON LOVER

SHIRLEY JACKSON

SHE HAD not slept well; from one-thirty, when Jamie left and she went lingeringly to bed, until seven, when she at last allowed herself to get up and make coffee, she had slept fitfully, stirring awake to open her eyes and look into the half-darkness, remembering over and over, slipping again into a feverish dream. She spent almost an hour over her coffee—they were to have a real breakfast on the way—and then, unless she wanted to dress early, had nothing to do. She washed her coffee cup and made the bed, looking carefully over the clothes she planned to wear, worried unnecessarily, at the window, over whether it would be a fine day. She sat down to read, thought that she might write a letter to her sister instead, and began, in her finest handwriting, "Dearest Anne, by the time you get this I will be married. Doesn't it sound funny? I can hardly believe it myself, but when I tell you how it happened, you'll see it's even stranger than that. . . ."

Sitting, pen in hand, she hesitated over what to say next, read the lines already written, and tore up the letter. She went to the window and saw that it was undeniably a fine day. It occurred to her that perhaps she ought not to wear the blue silk dress; it was too plain, almost severe, and she wanted to be soft, feminine. Anxiously she pulled through the dresses in the closet, and hesitated over a print she had worn the summer before; it was too young for her, and it had a ruffled neck, and it was very early in the year for a print dress, but still. . . .

She hung the two dresses side by side on the outside of the closet door and opened the glass doors carefully closed upon the small closet that was her kitchenette. She turned on the burner under the coffeepot, and went to the window; it was sunny. When the coffeepot began to crackle she came back and poured herself coffee, into a clean cup. I'll have a headache if I don't get some solid food soon, she thought, all this coffee, smoking too much, no real breakfast. A headache on her wedding day; she went and got the tin box of aspirin from the bathroom closet and slipped it into her blue pocketbook. She'd have to change to a brown pocketbook if she wore the print dress, and the only brown pocketbook she had was shabby. Helplessly, she stood looking from the blue pocketbook to the print dress, and then put the pocketbook down and went and got her coffee and sat down near the window, drinking her coffee, and looking carefully around the one-room apartment. They planned to come back here tonight and everything must be correct. With sudden horror she realized that she had forgotten to put clean sheets on the bed; the laundry was freshly back and she took clean sheets and pillow cases from the top shelf of the closet and stripped the bed, working quickly to avoid thinking consciously of why she was changing the sheets. The bed was a studio bed, with a cover to make it look like a couch, and when it was finished no one would have known she had just put clean sheets on it. She took the old sheets and pillow cases into the bathroom and stuffed them down into the hamper, and put the bathroom towels in the hamper too, and clean towels on the bathroom racks. Her coffee was cold when she came back to it, but she drank it anyway.

When she looked at the clock, finally, and saw that it was after nine, she began at last to hurry. She took a bath, and used one of the clean towels, which she put into the hamper and replaced with a clean one. She dressed carefully, all her underwear fresh and most of it new; she put everything she had worn the day before, including her nightgown, into the hamper. When she was ready for her dress, she hesitated before the closet door. The blue dress was certainly decent, and clean, and fairly becoming, but she had worn it several times with Jamie, and there was nothing about it which made it special for a wedding day. The print dress was overly pretty, and new to Jamie, and yet wearing such a print this early in the year was certainly rushing the season. Finally she thought, This is my wedding day, I can dress as I please, and she took the print dress down from the hanger. When she slipped it on over her head it felt fresh and light, but when she looked at herself in the mirror she remembered that the ruffles around the neck did not show her throat to any great advantage, and the wide swinging skirt looked irresistibly made for a girl, for someone who would run freely, dance, swing it with her hips when she walked. Looking at herself in the mirror she thought with revulsion, It's as though I was trying to make myself look prettier than I am, just for him; he'll think I want to look younger because he's marrying me; and she tore the print dress off so quickly that a seam under the arm ripped. In the old blue dress she felt comfortable and familiar, but unexciting. It isn't what you're wearing that matters, she told herself firmly, and turned in dismay to the closet to see if there might be anything else. There was nothing even remotely suitable for her marrying Jamie, and for a minute she thought of going out quickly to some little shop nearby, to get a dress. Then she saw that it was close on ten, and she had no time for more than her hair and her make-up. Her hair was easy, pulled back into a knot at the nape of her neck, but her make-up was another delicate balance between looking as well as possible, and deceiving as little. She could not try to disguise the sallowness of her skin, or the lines around her eyes, today, when it might look as though she were only doing it for her wedding, and yet she could not bear the thought of Jamie's bringing to marriage anyone who looked haggard and lined. You're thirty-four years old after *all,* she told herself cruelly in the bathroom mirror. Thirty, it said on the license.

It was two minutes after ten; she was not satisfied with her clothes, her face, her apartment. She heated the coffee again and sat down in the chair by the window. Can't do anything more now, she thought, no sense trying to improve anything the last minute.

Reconciled, settled, she tried to think of Jamie and could not see his face clearly, or hear his voice. It's always that way with someone you love, she thought, and let her mind slip past today and tomorrow, into the farther future, when Jamie was established with his writing and she had given up her job, the golden house-in-the-country future they had been preparing for the last week. "I used to be a wonderful cook," she had promised Jamie, "with a little time and practice I could remember how to make angel-food cake. And fried chicken," she said, knowing how the words would stay in Jamie's mind, half-tenderly. "And Hollandaise sauce."

Ten-thirty. She stood up and went purposefully to the phone. She dialed, and waited, and the girl's metallic voice said, ". . . the time will be exactly ten-twenty-nine." Half-consciously she set her clock back a minute; she was remembering her own voice saying last night, in the doorway: "Ten o'clock then. I'll be ready. Is it really *true?*"

And Jamie laughing down the hallway.

By eleven o'clock she had sewed up the ripped seam in the print dress and put her sewing-box away carefully in the closet. With the print dress on, she was sitting by the window drinking another cup of coffee. I could have taken more time over my dressing after all, she thought; but by now it was so late he might come any minute, and she did not dare try to repair anything without starting all over. There was nothing to eat in the apartment except the food she had carefully stocked up for their life beginning together: the unopened package of bacon, the dozen eggs in their box, the unopened bread and the unopened butter; they were for breakfast tomorrow. She thought of running downstairs to the drugstore for something to eat, leaving a note on the door. Then she decided to wait a little longer.

By eleven-thirty she was so dizzy and weak that she had to go downstairs. If Jamie had had a phone she would have called him then. Instead, she opened her desk and wrote a note: "Jamie, have gone downstairs to the drugstore. Back in five minutes." Her pen leaked onto her fingers and she went into the bathroom and washed, using a clean towel which she replaced. She tacked the note on the door, surveyed the apartment once more to make sure that everything was perfect, and closed the door without locking it, in case he should come.

In the drugstore she found that there was nothing she wanted to eat except more coffee, and she left it half-finished because she suddenly realized that Jamie was probably upstairs waiting and impatient, anxious to get started.

But upstairs everything was prepared and quiet, as she had left it, her note unread on the door, the air in the apartment a little stale from too many cigarettes. She opened the window and sat down next to it until she realized that she had been asleep and it was twenty minutes to one.

Now, suddenly, she was frightened. Waking without preparation into the room of waiting and readiness, everything clean and untouched since ten o'clock, she was frightened, and felt an urgent need to hurry. She got up from the chair and almost ran across the room to the bathroom, dashed cold water on her face, and used a clean towel; this time she put the towel carelessly back on the rack without changing it; time enough for that later. Hatless, still in the print dress with a coat thrown on over it, the wrong blue pocketbook with the aspirin inside in her hand, she locked the apartment door behind her, no note this time, and ran down the stairs. She caught a taxi on the corner and gave the driver Jamie's address.

It was no distance at all; she could have walked it if she had not been so weak, but in the taxi she suddenly realized how imprudent it would be to drive brazenly up to Jamie's door, demanding him. She asked the driver, therefore, to let her off at a corner near Jamie's address and, after paying him, waited till he drove away before she started to walk down the block. She had never been here before; the building was pleasant and old, and Jamie's name was not on any of the mailboxes in the vestibule, nor on the doorbells. She checked the address; it was right, and finally she rang the bell marked "Superintendent." After a minute or two the door buzzer rang and she opened the door and went into the dark hall where she hesitated until a door at the end opened and someone said, "Yes?"

She knew at the same moment that she had no idea what to ask, so she moved forward toward the figure waiting against the light of the open doorway. When she was very near, the figure said, "Yes?" again and she saw that it was a man in his shirtsleeves, unable to see her any more clearly than she could see him.

With sudden courage she said, "I'm trying to get in touch with someone who lives in this building and I can't find the name outside."

"What's the name you wanted?" the man asked, and she realized that she would have to answer.

"James Harris," she said. "Harris."

The man was silent for a minute and then he said, "Harris." He turned around to the room inside the lighted doorway and said, "Margie, come here a minute."

"What now?" a voice said from inside, and after a wait long enough for someone to get out of a comfortable chair a woman joined him in the doorway, regarding the dark hall. "Lady here," the man said. "Lady looking for a guy name of Harris, lives here. Anyone in the building?"

"No," the woman said. Her voice sounded amused. "No men named Harris here."

"Sorry," the man said. He started to close the door. "You got the wrong house, lady," he said, and added in a lower voice, "or the wrong guy," and he and the woman laughed.

When the door was almost shut and she was alone in the dark hall she said to the thin lighted crack still showing, "But he *does* live here; I know it."

"Look," the woman said, opening the door again a little, "it happens all the time."

"Please don't make any mistake," she said, and her voice was very dignified, with thirty-four years of accumulated pride. "I'm afraid you don't understand."

"What did he look like?" the woman said wearily, the door still only part open.

"He's rather tall, and fair. He wears a blue suit very often. He's a writer."

"No," the woman said, and then, "Could he have lived on the third floor?"

"I'm not sure."

"There was a fellow," the woman said reflectively. "He wore a blue suit a lot, lived on the third floor for a while. The Roysters lent him their apartment while they were visiting her folks upstate."

"That might be it; I thought, though. . . ."

"This one wore a blue suit mostly, but I don't know how tall he was," the woman said. "He stayed there about a month."

"A month ago is when—"

"You ask the Roysters," the woman said. "They come back this morning. Apartment 3B."

The door closed, definitely. The hall was very dark and the stairs looked darker.

On the second floor there was a little light from a skylight far above. The apartment doors lined up, four on the floor, uncommunicative and silent. There was a bottle of milk outside 2C.

On the third floor, she waited for a minute. There was the sound of music beyond the door of 3B, and she could hear voices. Finally she knocked, and knocked again. The door was opened and the music swept out at her, an early afternoon symphony broadcast. "How do you do," she said politely to this woman in the doorway. "Mrs. Royster?"

"That's right." The woman was wearing a housecoat and last night's make-up.

"I wonder if I might talk to you for a minute?"

"Sure," Mrs. Royster said, not moving.

"About Mr. Harris."

"*What* Mr. Harris?" Mrs. Royster said flatly.

"Mr. James Harris. The gentleman who borrowed your apartment."

"O Lord," Mrs. Royster said. She seemed to open her eyes for the first time. "What'd he do?"

"Nothing. I'm just trying to get in touch with him."

"O Lord," Mrs. Royster said again. Then she opened the door wider and said, "Come in," and then, "Ralph!"

Inside, the apartment was still full of music, and there were suitcases half-unpacked on the couch, on the chairs, on the floor. A table in the corner was spread with the remains of a meal, and the young man sitting there, for a minute resembling Jamie, got up and came across the room.

"What about it?" he said.

"Mr. Royster," she said. It was difficult to talk against the music. "The superintendent downstairs told me that this was where Mr. James Harris has been living."

"Sure," he said. "If that was his name."

"I thought you lent him the apartment," she said, surprised.

"*I* don't know anything about him," Mr. Royster said. "He's one of Dottie's friends."

"Not *my* friends," Mrs. Royster said. "No friend of mine." She had gone over to the table and was spreading peanut butter on a piece of bread. She took a bite and said thickly, waving the bread and peanut butter at her husband. "Not *my* friend."

"You picked him up at one of those damn meetings," Mr. Royster said. He shoved a suitcase off the chair next to the radio and sat down, picking up a magazine from the floor next to him. "I never said more'n ten words to him."

"You said it was okay to lend him the place," Mrs. Royster said before she took another bite. "You never said a word against him, after *all*."

"*I* don't say anything about *your* friends," Mr. Royster said.

"If he'd of been a friend of mine you would have said *plenty,* believe me," Mrs. Royster said darkly. She took another bite and said, "Believe me, he would have said *plenty*."

"That's all I want to hear," Mr. Royster said, over the top of the magazine. "No more, now."

"You see." Mrs. Royster pointed the bread and peanut butter at her husband. "That's the way it is, day and night."

There was silence except for the music bellowing out of the radio next to Mr. Royster, and then she said, in a voice she hardly trusted to be heard over the radio noise, "Has he gone, then?"

"Who?" Mrs. Royster demanded, looking up from the peanut butter jar.

"Mr. James Harris."

"Him? He must've left this morning, before we got back. No sign of him anywhere."

"Gone?"

"Everything was fine, though, perfectly fine. I told you," she said to Mr. Royster, "I told you he'd take care of everything fine. I can always tell."

"You were lucky," Mr. Royster said.

"Not a thing out of place," Mrs. Royster said. She waved her bread and peanut butter inclusively. "Everything just the way we left it," she said.

"Do you know where he is now?"

"Not the slightest idea," Mrs. Royster said cheerfully. "But, like I said, he left everything fine. Why?" she asked suddenly. "You looking for *him?*"

"It's very important."

"I'm sorry he's not here," Mrs. Royster said. She stepped forward politely when she saw her visitor turn toward the door.

"Maybe the super saw him," Mr. Royster said into the magazine.

When the door was closed behind her the hall was dark again, but the sound of the radio was deadened. She was halfway down the first flight of stairs when the door was opened and Mrs. Royster shouted down the stairwell, "If I see him I'll tell him you were looking for him."

What can I do? she thought, out on the street again. It was impossible to go home, not with Jamie somewhere between here and there. She stood on the sidewalk so long that a woman, leaning out of a window across the way, turned and called to someone inside to come and see. Finally, on an impulse, she went into the small delicatessen next door to the apartment house, on the side that led to her own apartment. There was a small man reading a newspaper, leaning against the counter; when she came in he looked up and came down inside the counter to meet her.

Over the glass case of cold meats and cheese she said, timidly, "I'm trying to get in touch with a man who lived in the apartment house next door, and I just wondered if you know him."

"Whyn't you ask the people there?" the man said, his eyes narrow, inspecting her.

It's because I'm not buying anything, she thought, and she said, "I'm sorry. I asked them, but they don't know anything about him. They think he left this morning."

"I don't know what you want *me* to do," he said, moving a little back toward his newspaper. "I'm not here to keep track of guys going in and out next door."

She said quickly, "I thought you might have noticed, that's all. He would have been coming past here, a little before ten o'clock. He was rather tall, and he usually wore a blue suit."

"Now how many men in blue suits go past here every day, lady?" the man demanded. "You think I got nothing to do but—"

"I'm sorry," she said. She heard him say, "For God's sake," as she went out the door.

As she walked toward the corner, she thought, he must have come this way, it's the way he'd go to get to my house, it's the only way for him to walk. She tried to think of Jamie: where would he have crossed the street? What sort of person was he actually—would he cross in front of his own apartment house, at random in the middle of the block, at the corner?

On the corner was a newsstand; they might have seen him there. She hurried on and waited while a man bought a paper and a woman asked directions. When the newsstand man looked at her she said, "Can you possibly tell me if a rather tall young man in a blue suit went past here this morning around ten o'clock?" When the man only looked at her, his eyes wide and his mouth a little open, she thought, he thinks it's a joke, or a trick, and she said urgently, "It's very important, please believe me. I'm not teasing you."

"*Look,* lady," the man began, and she said eagerly, "He's a writer. He might have bought magazines here."

"What do you want him for?" the man asked. He looked at her, smiling, and she realized that there was another man waiting in back of her and the newsdealer's smile included him. "Never mind," she said, but the newsdealer said, "Listen, maybe he did come by here." His smile was knowing and his eyes shifted over her shoulder to the man in back of her. She was suddenly horribly aware of her over-young print dress, and pulled her coat around her quickly. The newsdealer said, with vast thoughtfulness, "Now I don't know for sure, mind you, but there might have been someone like your gentleman friend coming by this morning."

"About ten?"

"About ten," the newsdealer agreed. "Tall fellow, blue suit. I wouldn't be at all surprised."

"Which way did he go?" she said eagerly. "Uptown?"

"Uptown," the newsdealer said, nodding. "He went uptown. That's just exactly it. What can I do for you, sir?"

She stepped back, holding her coat around her. The man who had been standing behind her looked at her over his shoulder and then he and the newsdealer looked at one another. She wondered for a minute whether or not to tip the newsdealer but when both men began to laugh she moved hurriedly on across the street.

Uptown, she thought, that's right, and she started up the avenue, thinking: He wouldn't have to cross the avenue, just go up six blocks and turn down my street, so long as he started uptown. About a block farther on she passed a florist's shop; there was a wedding display in the window and she thought, This is my wedding day after all, he might have gotten flowers to bring me, and she went inside. The florist came out of the back of the shop, smiling and sleek, and she said, before he could speak, so that he wouldn't have a chance to think she was buying anything: "It's *terribly* important that I get in touch with a gentleman who may have stopped in here to buy flowers this morning. *Terribly* important."

She stopped for breath, and the florist said, "Yes, what sort of flowers were they?"

"I don't know," she said, surprised. "He never—" She stopped and said, "He was a rather tall young man, in a blue suit. It was about ten o'clock."

"I see," the florist said. "Well, *really,* I'm afraid. . . ."

"But it's *so* important," she said. "He may have been in a hurry," she added helpfully.

"Well," the florist said. He smiled genially, showing all his small teeth. "For a *lady,*" he said. He went to a stand and opened a large book. "Where were they to be sent?" he asked.

"Why," she said, "I don't think he'd have sent them. You see, he was coming—that is, he'd *bring* them."

"Madam," the florist said; he was offended. His smile became deprecatory, and he went on, "Really, you must realize that unless I have *something* to go on. . . ."

"*Please* try to remember," she begged. "He was tall, and had a blue suit, and it was about ten this morning."

The florist closed his eyes, one finger to his mouth, and thought deeply. Then he shook his head. "I simply *can't,*" he said.

"Thank you," she said despondently, and started for the door, when the florist said, in a shrill, excited voice, "Wait! Wait just a moment, madam." She turned and the florist, thinking again, said finally, "Chrysanthemums?" He looked at her inquiringly.

"Oh, *no,*" she said; her voice shook a little and she waited for a minute before she went on. "Not for an occasion like this, I'm sure."

The florist tightened his lips and looked away coldly. "Well, of *course* I don't know the *occasion,*" he said, "but I'm almost certain that the gentleman you were inquiring for came in this morning and purchased one dozen chrysanthemums. No delivery."

"You're *sure?*" she asked.

"Positive," the florist said emphatically. "That was absolutely the man." He smiled brilliantly, and she smiled back and said, "Well, thank you very much."

He escorted her to the door. "Nice corsage?" he said, as they went through the shop. "Red roses? Gardenias?"

"It was very kind of you to help me," she said at the door.

"Ladies always look their best in flowers," he said, bending his head toward her. "Orchids, perhaps?"

"No, thank you," she said, and he said, "I hope you find your young man," and gave it a nasty sound.

Going on up the street she thought, Everyone thinks it's so *funny:* and she pulled her coat tighter around her, so that only the ruffle around the bottom of the print dress was showing.

There was a policeman on the corner, and she thought, Why don't I go to the police—you go to the police for a missing person. And then thought, What a fool I'd look like. She had a quick picture of herself standing in a police station, saying, "Yes, we were going to be married today, but he didn't come," and the policemen, three or four of them standing around listening, looking at her, at the print dress, at her too-bright make-up, smiling at one another. She couldn't tell them any more than that, could not say, "Yes, it looks silly, doesn't it, me all dressed up and trying to find the young man who promised to marry me, but what about all of it you don't know? I have more than this, more than you can see: talent, perhaps, and humor of a sort, and I'm a lady and I have pride and affection and delicacy and a certain clear view of life that might make a man satisfied and productive and happy; there's more than you think when you look at me."

The police were obviously impossible, leaving out Jamie and what he might think when he heard she'd set the police after him. "No, no," she said aloud, hurrying her steps, and someone passing stopped and looked after her.

On the coming corner—she was three blocks from her own street—was a shoeshine stand, an old man sitting almost asleep in one of the chairs. She stopped in front of him and waited, and after a minute he opened his eyes and smiled at her.

"Look," she said, the words coming before she thought of them, "I'm sorry to bother you, but I'm looking for a young man who came up this way about ten this morning, did you see him?" And she began her description, "Tall, blue suit, carrying a bunch of flowers?"

The old man began to nod before she was finished. "I saw him," he said. "Friend of yours?"

"Yes," she said, and smiled back involuntarily.

The old man blinked his eyes and said, "I remember I thought, You're going to see your girl, young fellow. They all go to see their girls," he said, and shook his head tolerantly.

"Which way did he go? Straight on up the avenue?"

"That's right," the old man said. "Got a shine, had his flowers, all dressed up, in an awful hurry. You got a girl, I thought."

"Thank you," she said, fumbling in her pocket for her loose change.

"She sure must of been glad to see him, the way he looked," the old man said.

"Thank you," she said again, and brought her hand empty from her pocket.

For the first time she was really sure he would be waiting for her, and she hurried up the three blocks, the skirt of the print dress swinging under her coat, and turned into her own block. From the corner she could not see her own windows, could not see Jamie looking out, waiting for her, and going down the block she was almost running to get to him. Her key trembled in her fingers at the downstairs door, and as she glanced into the drugstore she thought of her panic, drinking coffee there this morning, and almost laughed. At her own door she could wait no longer, but began to say, "Jamie, I'm here, I was so worried," even before the door was open.

Her own apartment was waiting for her, silent, barren, afternoon shadows lengthening from the window. For a minute she saw only the empty coffee cup, thought, He has been here waiting, before she recognized it as her own, left from the morning. She looked all over the room, into the closet, into the bathroom.

"I never saw him," the clerk in the drugstore said. "I know because I would of noticed the flowers. No one like that's been in."

The old man at the shoeshine stand woke up again to see her standing in front of him. "Hello again," he said, and smiled.

"Are you *sure?*" she demanded. "Did he go on up the avenue?"

"I watched him," the old man said, dignified against her tone. "I thought, There's a young man's got a girl, and I watched him right into the house."

"What house?" she said remotely.

"Right there," the old man said. He leaned forward to point. "The next block. With his flowers and his shine and going to see his girl. Right into her house."

"Which one?" she said.

"About the middle of the block," the old man said. He looked at her with suspicion, and said, "What you trying to do, anyway?"

She almost ran, without stopping to say "Thank you." Up on the next block she walked quickly, searching the houses from the outside to see if Jamie looked from a window, listening to hear his laughter somewhere inside.

A woman was sitting in front of one of the houses, pushing a baby carriage monotonously back and forth the length of her arm. The baby inside slept, moving back and forth.

The question was fluent, by now. "I'm sorry, but did you see a young man go into one of these houses about ten this morning? He was tall, wearing a blue suit, carrying a bunch of flowers."

A boy about twelve stopped to listen, turning intently from one to the other, occasionally glancing at the baby.

"Listen," the woman said tiredly, "the kid has his bath at ten. Would I see strange men walking around? I ask you."

"Big bunch of flowers?" the boy asked, pulling at her coat. "Big bunch of flowers? I seen him, missus."

She looked down and the boy grinned insolently at her. "Which house did he go in?" she asked wearily.

"You gonna divorce him?" the boy asked insistently.

"That's not nice to ask the lady," the woman rocking the carriage said.

"Listen," the boy said, "I seen him. He went in there." He pointed to the house next door. "I followed him," the boy said. "He give me a quarter." The boy dropped his voice to a growl, and said, " 'This is a big day for me, kid,' he says. Give me a quarter."

She gave him a dollar bill. "Where?" she said.

"Top floor," the boy said. "I followed him till he give me the quarter.

Way to the top." He backed up the sidewalk, out of reach, with the dollar bill. "You gonna divorce him?" he asked again.

"Was he carrying flowers?"

"Yeah," the boy said. He began to screech. "You gonna divorce him, missus? You got something on him?" He went careening down the street, howling, "She's got something on the poor guy," and the woman rocking the baby laughed.

The street door of the apartment house was unlocked; there were no bells in the outer vestibule, and no lists of names. The stairs were narrow and dirty; there were two doors on the top floor. The front one was the right one; there was a crumpled florist's paper on the floor outside the door, and a knotted paper ribbon, like a clue, like the final clue in the paper-chase.

She knocked, and thought she heard voices inside, and she thought, suddenly, with terror, What shall I say if Jamie is there, if he comes to the door? The voices seemed suddenly still. She knocked again and there was silence, except for something that might have been laughter far away. He could have seen me from the window, she thought, it's the front apartment and that little boy made a dreadful noise. She waited, and knocked again, but there was silence.

Finally she went to the other door on the floor, and knocked. The door swung open beneath her hand and she saw the empty attic room, bare lath on the walls, floorboards unpainted. She stepped just inside, looking around; the room was filled with bags of plaster, piles of old newspapers, a broken trunk. There was a noise which she suddenly realized as a rat, and then she saw it, sitting very close to her, near the wall, its evil face alert, bright eyes watching her. She stumbled in her haste to be out with the door closed, and the skirt of the print dress caught and tore.

She knew there was someone inside the other apartment, because she was sure she could hear low voices and sometimes laughter. She came back many times, every day for the first week. She came on her way to work, in the mornings; in the evenings, on her way to dinner alone, but no matter how often or how firmly she knocked, no one ever came to the door.

1949

THE PHANTOM LOVER[1]

Two Excerpts

SHIRLEY JACKSON

EXCERPT I[2]

STRANGE ISN'T really the word, she thought suddenly, remembering their decision the night before. There was a small secret smile on her face and she thought, it's exciting and wonderful but now that it's happened at last it doesn't seem at all strange. "Jamie," she had said—and she could almost hear her own voice still, echoing in the room—"I don't want to go on like this any longer."

"What's the matter?" he had said.

She had intended to force him out of his assumed indifference. He

[1] An earlier version of "The Daemon Lover."

[2] This excerpt is preceded by two paragraphs that are almost identical to the opening paragraph of "The Daemon Lover."

hated sentiment and like a shy boy put on a deliberately brutal manner to cover emotion. So she had said comically, "I don't even know if your intentions are honorable or not."

"They're not," he had said and she laughed again, remembering.

"Anyway—" Her voice had been faint and clear in the silence of the room. "All joking aside, I think we ought to plan on getting married."

There had been a pause and then: "We've got plenty of time to think about *that,*" Jamie had said.

Evasiveness, unkindness—his defenses against being hurt. He should know by now that I wouldn't hurt him, she had thought and made her voice gentler. "Seriously, you need someone to take care of you."

"That's quite a job for one girl," Jamie had said.

Poor proud Jamie. She had gone over and sat down on the arm of his chair and put her head down on top of his. "We could get a house in the country and you could write and we could be together all the time and, really, I'd take good care of you."

"Look," he had said and moved away from her and turned to watch her in the dim light, "I don't want to think about marriage. Yet."

"Please don't." She had reached out to put her hand over his mouth. "Please don't get to feeling mean just because I'm not afraid to sound sentimental. I don't care what you say, because I know how you really feel and I know how much you need me. And nothing is ever going to stop me," she had said with a great show of affectionate defiance, getting up from the arm of the chair to walk around and face him. "I fully intend to marry you, young man, so you might as well give in."

"Ye gods," he had said, "I never—" Then he had stared at her for a minute and finally dropped his hands helplessly. "Okay," he had said. "Anything you say."

"Then you'll marry me?"

"Sure."

"When?" She was insistent then, because the subject must be settled at once since she would never be equal to another such effort.

"What?" he had said. Then, "Oh—tomorrow."

"Jamie," she had said and, remembering, she said it again, "Oh, Jamie." Then she had begun to laugh and she had put her hand under his chin and turned his face up to look at her. "Poor cowardly Jamie. So I finally had to ask him!"

EXCERPT 2, THE ENDING[3]

She stood in front of the door and lifted her hand to knock, and while she stood there with her hand raised, she heard voices inside. Then with terror she thought, what shall I say if Jamie is there, if he comes to the door? Jamie, who should be laughing with her by the fireside. To be accosted here in this strange doorway, with strange people peering at her over his shoulder, all waiting while she said, "Jamie, I came to be married."

The voices were still. There was silence on the top floor of the apartment building except for something that might have been laughter far away. Could he have seen me from the window, she wondered. It's the front apartment and that little boy made a dreadful noise. She backed away from the door, her knees suddenly weak.

Her step backward carried her against the other door on the floor and she felt it swing open behind her. She turned quickly and saw a closet, with mops standing in the corner and piles of old newspapers. I can always hide in here if someone opens the other door, she told herself and the idea puzzled her—hiding from Jamie after seeking him so long.

She gathered her courage together and approached the apartment door again. Was it laughter she heard, faint and remote? Or did she imagine it?

As she stood wondering, she was suddenly assailed by new laughter from inside the apartment, unmistakable this time, Jamie's laughter, hilarious and deep, alongside the shrill giggle of a girl.

But at the instant she recognized that it *was* Jamie, her mind rebelled. It *couldn't* be, she thought. She pushed back violently the doubts that had been slipping into her mind all morning—the gnawing question that she herself might have created a relationship between them that Jamie had never really shared.

The girl's voice said clearly, "Now I *know* you've been seeing another girl." The laughter rose and echoed into the hall and she backed hastily away from the door. No, no, she thought, and almost said it aloud, *that's* not Jamie. I was wrong to come. Jamie and I, she thought, we're people of taste and understanding; we have low well-bred voices and we don't shout. No rough laughter, no insinuating remarks: that charming young Mr. and Mrs. Harris.

[3] The paragraph that precedes this excerpt closely resembles the fourth-from-last paragraph of "The Daemon Lover."

The voices were softer now, the laughter subdued. Jamie is *another* sort of person, she thought and put both hands over her eyes.

Quietly, without having knocked, she turned away. It was important now to leave without disturbing the people inside the apartment, important that they should never know she had been there. He wouldn't be in a horrible place like this, he's off somewhere else—the ideas came through her mind quickly, not distinctly but following one another as her feet went down the stairs—there must be some good reason why he didn't come; after all, he loves me. He *did* love me. Even if I never find Jamie, he's shy and gentle and modest and we could have lived in the country. I was so wrong to come.

Poor proud Jamie, she was thinking as she went home through the dusk, dear silly frightened Jamie.

1949

DISCUSSION QUESTIONS

1. Why does the protagonist tear off the print dress as soon as she has put it on? Why does she put the dress back on an hour later? Why does she try to hide it under her coat?

2. When the protagonist goes to the drugstore she leaves the door unlocked and a note for Jamie. Why does she fail to do either of these things when she again leaves her apartment? What change of mood does it suggest? Why doesn't she replace the used towel as she had done earlier?

3. "Everyone thinks it's so *funny*" (page 379), she says bitterly to herself after leaving the florist. Whom does "everyone" actually include? What specifically do they find "funny"? Why?

4. In "The Phantom Lover," why doesn't Jamie show up for his wedding? What gave his fiancée the false impression that he would? In the revised version, with the *flashback* to "the night before" removed, what clues, if any, remain to explain Jamie's behavior and his fiancée's false expectations?

5. Compare the two versions of the ending in detail. What effect results from making Jamie's presence in the apartment uncertain in "The Daemon Lover"? How does Jamie's near obliteration shift the emphasis in Jackson's second version?

6. Why does the mop closet become an "empty attic room" in "The Daemon Lover"? Explain the significance of the rat and the fact that the protagonist tears her print dress in trying to escape from it.

1. Why have Bowen's and Jackson's stories almost identical titles? What specifically creates the supernatural atmosphere in each work?

2. Explain and compare the effect that time has on each protagonist. Give specific examples.

3. Why can neither protagonist clearly remember her lover's face?

4. Which do you think is the better story? Why?

ANALYSIS AND APPLICATION

1. "In her once *familiar* street, as in any unused *channel*, an *unfamiliar* queerness had *silted* up; a cat wove itself in and out of railings, but no human eye watched Mrs. Drover's return" (page 355). How do the italicized words help to make the first part of the sentence coherent? Specifically, how is the second part of the sentence related to the first? Why are the two parts separated by a semicolon? Could any other punctuation mark be substituted?

2. "Waking without preparation into the room of waiting and readiness, everything clean and untouched since ten o'clock, she was frightened, and felt an urgent need to hurry" (pages 372–373). Construct a sentence of your own that closely duplicates Jackson's structure.

3. Which of these versions seems to you more effective? Why?

They would probably come back here tonight, so everything must be correct. ("The Phantom Lover")

They planned to come back here tonight and everything must be correct. ("The Daemon Lover")

DRY SEPTEMBER

WILLIAM FAULKNER

THROUGH THE bloody September twilight, aftermath of sixty-two rainless days, it had gone like a fire in dry grass—the rumor, the story, whatever it was. Something about Miss Minnie Cooper and a Negro. Attacked, insulted, frightened: none of them, gathered in the barber shop on that Saturday evening where the ceiling fan stirred, without freshening it, the vitiated air, sending back upon them, in recurrent surges of stale pomade and lotion, their own stale breath and odors, knew exactly what had happened.

"Except it wasn't Will Mayes," a barber said. He was a man of middle age; a thin, sand-colored man with a mild face, who was shaving a client. "I know Will Mayes. He's a good nigger. And I know Miss Minnie Cooper, too."

"What do you know about her?" a second barber said.

"Who is she?" the client said. "A young girl?"

"No," the barber said. "She's about forty, I reckon. She ain't married. That's why I dont believe—"

"Believe, hell!" a hulking youth in a sweat-stained silk shirt said. "Wont you take a white woman's word before a nigger's?"

"I dont believe Will Mayes did it," the barber said. "I know Will Mayes."

"Maybe you know who did it, then. Maybe you already got him out of town, you damn niggerlover."

"I dont believe anybody did anything. I dont believe anything happened. I leave it to you fellows if them ladies that get old without getting married dont have notions that a man cant—"

"Then you are a hell of a white man," the client said. He moved under the cloth. The youth had sprung to his feet.

"You dont?" he said. "Do you accuse a white woman of lying?"

The barber held the razor poised above the half-risen client. He did not look around.

"It's this durn weather," another said. "It's enough to make a man do anything. Even to her."

Nobody laughed. The barber said in his mild, stubborn tone: "I aint accusing nobody of nothing. I just know and you fellows know how a woman that never—"

"You damn niggerlover!" the youth said.

"Shut up, Butch," another said. "We'll get the facts in plenty of time to act."

"Who is? Who's getting them?" the youth said. "Facts, hell! I—"

"You're a fine white man," the client said. "Aint you?" In his frothy beard he looked like a desert rat in the moving pictures. "You tell them, Jack," he said to the youth. "If there aint any white men in this town, you can count on me, even if I aint only a drummer and a stranger."

"That's right, boys," the barber said. "Find out the truth first. I know Will Mayes."

"Well, by God!" the youth shouted. "To think that a white man in this town—"

"Shut up, Butch," the second speaker said. "We got plenty of time."

The client sat up. He looked at the speaker. "Do you claim that anything excuses a nigger attacking a white woman? Do you mean to tell me you are a white man and you'll stand for it? You better go back North where you came from. The South dont want your kind here."

"North what?" the second said. "I was born and raised in this town."

"Well, by God!" the youth said. He looked about with a strained, baffled gaze, as if he was trying to remember what it was he wanted to say or to do. He drew his sleeve across his sweating face. "Damn if I'm going to let a white woman—"

"You tell them, Jack," the drummer said. "By God, if they—"

The screen door crashed open. A man stood in the floor, his feet apart and his heavy-set body poised easily. His white shirt was open at the throat; he wore a felt hat. His hot, bold glance swept the group. His name was McLendon. He had commanded troops at the front in France and had been decorated for valor.

"Well," he said, "are you going to sit there and let a black son rape a white woman on the streets of Jefferson?"

Butch sprang up again. The silk of his shirt clung flat to his heavy shoulders. At each armpit was a dark halfmoon. "That's what I been telling them! That's what I—"

"Did it really happen?" a third said. "This aint the first man scare she ever had, like Hawkshaw says. Wasn't there something about a man on the kitchen roof, watching her undress, about a year ago?"

"What?" the client said. "What's that?" The barber had been slowly forcing him back into the chair; he arrested himself reclining, his head lifted, the barber still pressing him down.

McLendon whirled on the third speaker. "Happen? What the hell difference does it make? Are you going to let the black sons get away with it until one really does it?"

"That's what I'm telling them!" Butch shouted. He cursed, long and steady, pointless.

"Here, here," a fourth said. "Not so loud. Dont talk so loud."

"Sure," McLendon said; "no talking necessary at all. I've done my talking. Who's with me?" He poised on the balls of his feet, roving his gaze.

The barber held the drummer's face down, the razor poised. "Find out the facts first, boys. I know Willy Mayes. It wasn't him. Let's get the sheriff and do this thing right."

McLendon whirled upon him his furious, rigid face. The barber did not look away. They looked like men of different races. The other barbers had ceased also above their prone clients. "You mean to tell me," McLendon said, "that you'd take a nigger's word before a white woman's? Why, you damn niggerloving—"

The third speaker rose and grasped McLendon's arm; he too had been a soldier. "Now, now. Let's figure this thing out. Who knows anything about what really happened?"

"Figure out hell!" McLendon jerked his arm free. "All that're with me get up from there. The ones that aint—" He roved his gaze, dragging his sleeve across his face.

Three men rose. The drummer in the chair sat up. "Here," he said, jerking at the cloth about his neck; "get this rag off me. I'm with him. I don't live here, but by God, if our mothers and wives and sisters—" He smeared the cloth over his face and flung it to the floor. McLendon stood in the floor and cursed the others. Another rose and moved toward him. The remainder sat uncomfortable, not looking at one another, then one by one they rose and joined him.

The barber picked the cloth from the floor. He began to fold it neatly. "Boys, dont do that. Will Mayes never done it. I know."

"Come on," McLendon said. He whirled. From his hip pocket protruded the butt of a heavy automatic pistol. They went out. The screen door crashed behind them reverberant in the dead air.

The barber wiped the razor carefully and swiftly, and put it away, and ran to the rear, and took his hat from the wall. "I'll be back as soon as I can," he said to the other barbers. "I cant let—" He went out, running. The two other barbers followed him to the door and caught it on the rebound, leaning out and looking up the street after him. The air was flat and dead. It had a metallic taste at the base of the tongue.

"What can he do?" the first said. The second one was saying "Jees Christ, Jees Christ" under his breath. "I'd just as lief be Will Mayes as Hawk, if he gets McLendon riled."

"Jees Christ, Jees Christ," the second whispered.

"You reckon he really done it to her?" the first said.

II

She was thirty-eight or thirty-nine. She lived in a small frame house with her invalid mother and a thin, sallow, unflagging aunt, where each morning between ten and eleven she would appear on the porch in a lace-trimmed boudoir cap, to sit swinging in the porch swing until noon. After dinner she lay down for a while, until the afternoon began to cool. Then, in one of the three or four new voile dresses which she had each summer, she would go downtown to spend the afternoon in the stores with the other ladies, where they would handle the goods and haggle over the prices in cold, immediate voices, without any intention of buying.

She was of comfortable people—not the best in Jefferson, but good people enough—and she was still on the slender side of ordinary looking, with a bright, faintly haggard manner and dress. When she was young she had had a slender, nervous body and a sort of hard vivacity which had enabled her for a time to ride upon the crest of the town's social life as exemplified by the high school party and church social period of her contemporaries while still children enough to be unclassconscious.

She was the last to realize that she was losing ground; that those among whom she had been a little brighter and louder flame than any other were beginning to learn the pleasure of snobbery—male—and retaliation—female. That was when her face began to wear that bright, haggard look. She still carried it to parties on shadowy porticoes and summer lawns, like a mask or a flag, with that bafflement of furious repudiation of truth in her eyes. One evening at a party she heard a boy and two girls, all schoolmates, talking. She never accepted another invitation.

She watched the girls with whom she had grown up as they married and got homes and children, but no man ever called on her steadily until the children of the other girls had been calling her "aunty" for several years, the while their mothers told them in bright voices about how popular Aunt Minnie had been as a girl. Then the town began to see her driving on Sunday afternoons with the cashier in the bank. He was a widower of about forty—a high-colored man, smelling always faintly of the barber shop or of whisky. He owned the first automobile in town, a red runabout; Minnie had the first motoring bonnet and veil the town ever saw. Then the town began to say: "Poor Minnie." "But she is old enough to take care of herself," others said. That was when she began to ask her old schoolmates that their children call her "cousin" instead of "aunty."

It was twelve years now since she had been relegated into adultery by public opinion, and eight years since the cashier had gone to a Memphis bank, returning for one day each Christmas, which he spent at an annual bachelors' party at a hunting club on the river. From behind their curtains the neighbors would see the party pass, and during the over-the-way Christmas day visiting they would tell her about him, about how well he looked, and how they heard that he was prospering in the city, watching with bright, secret eyes her haggard, bright face. Usually by that hour there would be the scent of whisky on her breath. It was supplied her by a youth, a clerk at the soda fountain: "Sure; I buy it for the old gal. I reckon she's entitled to a little fun."

Her mother kept to her room altogether now; the gaunt aunt ran the house. Against that background Minnie's bright dresses, her idle and empty days, had a quality of furious unreality. She went out in the evenings only with women now, neighbors, to the moving pictures. Each afternoon she dressed in one of the new dresses and went downtown alone, where her young "cousins" were already strolling in the late afternoons with their delicate, silken heads and thin, awkward arms and conscious hips, clinging to one another or shrieking and giggling with paired boys in the soda fountain when she passed and went on along the serried store fronts, in the doors of which the sitting and lounging men did not even follow her with their eyes any more.

III

The barber went swiftly up the street where the sparse lights, insect-swirled, glared in rigid and violent suspension in the lifeless air. The day had died in a pall of dust; above the darkened square, shrouded by the spent dust, the sky was as clear as the inside of a brass bell. Below the east was a rumor of the twice-waxed moon.

When he overtook them McLendon and three others were getting into a car parked in an alley. McLendon stooped his thick head, peering out beneath the top. "Changed your mind, did you?" he said. "Damn good thing; by God, tomorrow when this town hears about how you talked tonight—"

"Now, now," the other ex-soldier said. "Hawkshaw's all right. Come on, Hawk; jump in."

"Will Mayes never done it, boys," the barber said. "If anybody done it. Why, you all know well as I do there aint any town where they got better niggers than us. And you know how a lady will kind of think things about men when there aint any reason to, and Miss Minnie anyway—"

"Sure, sure," the soldier said. "We're just going to talk to him a little; that's all."

"Talk hell!" Butch said. "When we're through with the—"

"Shut up, for God's sake!" the soldier said. "Do you want everybody in town—"

"Tell them, by God!" McLendon said. "Tell every one of the sons that'll let a white woman—"

"Let's go; let's go: here's the other car." The second car slid squealing out of a cloud of dust at the alley mouth. McLendon started his car and took the lead. Dust lay like fog in the street. The street lights hung nimbused as in water. They drove on out of town.

A rutted lane turned at right angles. Dust hung above it too, and above all the land. The dark bulk of the ice plant, where the Negro Mayes was night watchman, rose against the sky. "Better stop here, hadn't we?" the soldier said. McLendon did not reply. He hurled the car up and slammed to a stop, the headlights glaring on the blank wall.

"Listen here, boys," the barber said; "if he's here, dont that prove he never done it? Dont it? If it was him, he would run. Dont you see he would?" The second car came up and stopped. McLendon got down; Butch sprang down beside him. "Listen, boys," the barber said.

"Cut the lights off!" McLendon said. The breathless dark rushed down. There was no sound in it save their lungs as they sought air in the parched dust in which for two months they had lived; then the diminishing crunch of McLendon's and Butch's feet, and a moment later McLendon's voice:

"Will! . . . Will!"

Below the east the wan hemorrhage of the moon increased. It heaved above the ridge, silvering the air, the dust, so that they seemed to breathe, live, in a bowl of molten lead. There was no sound of nightbird nor insect, no sound save their breathing and a faint ticking of contracting metal about the cars. Where their bodies touched one another they seemed to sweat dryly, for no more moisture came. "Christ!" a voice said; "let's get out of here."

But they didn't move until vague noises began to grow out of the darkness ahead; then they got out and waited tensely in the breathless dark. There was another sound: a blow, a hissing expulsion of breath and McLendon cursing in undertone. They stood a moment longer, then they ran forward. They ran in a stumbling clump, as though they were fleeing something. "Kill him, kill the son," a voice whispered. McLendon flung them back.

"Not here," he said. "Get him into the car." "Kill him, kill the black son!" the voice murmured. They dragged the Negro to the car. The barber had waited beside the car. He could feel himself sweating and he knew he was going to be sick at the stomach.

"What is it, captains?" the Negro said. "I aint done nothing. 'Fore God, Mr John." Someone produced handcuffs. They worked busily about the Negro as though he were a post, quiet, intent, getting in one another's way. He submitted to the handcuffs, looking swiftly and constantly from dim face to dim face. "Who's here, captains?" he said, leaning to peer into the faces until they could feel his breath and smell his sweaty reek. He spoke a name or two. "What you all say I done, Mr John?"

McLendon jerked the car door open. "Get in!" he said.

The Negro did not move. "What you all going to do with me, Mr John? I aint done nothing. White folks, captains, I aint done nothing: I swear 'fore God." He called another name.

"Get in!" McLendon said. He struck the Negro. The others expelled their breath in a dry hissing and struck him with random blows and he whirled and cursed them, and swept his manacled hands across their faces and slashed the barber upon the mouth, and the barber struck him also. "Get him in there," McLendon said. They pushed at him. He ceased struggling and got in and sat quietly as the others took their places. He sat between the barber and the soldier, drawing his limbs in so as not to touch them, his eyes going swiftly and constantly from face to face. Butch clung to the running board. The car moved on. The barber nursed his mouth with his handkerchief.

"What's the matter, Hawk?" the soldier said.

"Nothing," the barber said. They regained the highroad and turned away from town. The second car dropped back out of the dust. They went on, gaining speed; the final fringe of houses dropped behind.

"Goddamn, he stinks!" the soldier said.

"We'll fix that," the drummer in front beside McLendon said. On the running board Butch cursed into the hot rush of air. The barber leaned suddenly forward and touched McLendon's arm.

"Let me out, John," he said.

"Jump out, niggerlover," McLendon said without turning his head. He drove swiftly. Behind them the sourceless lights of the second car glared in the dust. Presently McLendon turned into a narrow road. It was rutted with disuse. It led back to an abandoned brick kiln—a series of reddish mounds and weed- and vine-choked vats without bottom. It had been used for pasture once, until one day the owner missed one of his mules. Although he prodded carefully in the vats with a long pole, he could not even find the bottom of them.

"John," the barber said.

"Jump out, then," McLendon said, hurling the car along the ruts. Beside the barber the Negro spoke:

"Mr Henry."

The barber sat forward. The narrow tunnel of the road rushed up and past. Their motion was like an extinct furnace blast: cooler, but utterly dead. The car bounded from rut to rut.

"Mr Henry," the Negro said.

The barber began to tug furiously at the door. "Look out, there!" the soldier said, but the barber had already kicked the door open and swung onto the running board. The soldier leaned across the Negro and grasped at him, but he had already jumped. The car went on without checking speed.

The impetus hurled him crashing through dust-sheathed weeds, into the ditch. Dust puffed about him, and in a thin, vicious crackling of sapless stems he lay choking and retching until the second car passed and died away. Then he rose and limped on until he reached the highroad and turned toward town, brushing at his clothes with his hands. The moon was higher, riding high and clear of the dust at last, and after a while the town began to glare beneath the dust. He went on, limping. Presently he heard cars and the glow of them grew in the dust behind him and he left the road and crouched again in the weeds until they passed. McLendon's car came last now. There were four people in it and Butch was not on the running board.

They went on; the dust swallowed them; the glare and the sound died away. The dust of them hung for a while, but soon the eternal dust absorbed it again. The barber climbed back onto the road and limped on toward town.

IV

As she dressed for supper on that Saturday evening, her own flesh felt like fever. Her hands trembled among the hooks and eyes, and her eyes had a feverish look, and her hair swirled crisp and crackling under the comb. While she was still dressing the friends called for her and sat while she donned her sheerest underthings and stockings and a new voile dress. "Do you feel strong enough to go out?" they said, their eyes bright too, with a dark glitter. "When you have had time to get over the shock, you must tell us what happened. What he said and did; everything."

In the leafed darkness, as they walked toward the square, she began to breathe deeply, something like a swimmer preparing to dive, until she ceased trembling, the four of them walking slowly because of the terrible heat and out of solicitude for her. But as they neared the square she began to tremble again, walking with her head up, her hands clenched at her sides, their voices about her murmurous, also with that feverish, glittering quality of their eyes.

They entered the square, she in the center of the group, fragile in her fresh dress. She was trembling worse. She walked slower and slower, as children eat ice cream, her head up and her eyes bright in the haggard banner of her face, passing the hotel and the coatless drummers in chairs along the curb looking around at her: "That's the one: see? The one in pink in the middle." "Is that her? What did they do with the nigger? Did they—?" "Sure. He's all right." "All right, is he?" "Sure. He went on a little trip." Then the drug store, where even the young men lounging in the doorway tipped their hats and followed with their eyes the motion of her hips and legs when she passed.

They went on, passing the lifted hats of the gentlemen, the suddenly ceased voices, deferent, protective. "Do you see?" the friends said. Their voices sounded like long, hovering sighs of hissing exultation. "There's not a Negro on the square. Not one."

They reached the picture show. It was like a miniature fairyland with its lighted lobby and colored lithographs of life caught in its terrible and beautiful mutations. Her lips began to tingle. In the dark, when the picture began, it would be all right; she could hold back the laughing so it would not waste away so fast and so soon. So she hurried on before the turning faces, the undertones of low astonishment, and they took their accustomed places where she could see the aisle against the silver glare and the young men and girls coming in two and two against it.

The lights flicked away; the screen glowed silver, and soon life began to unfold, beautiful and passionate and sad, while still the young men and girls entered, scented and sibilant in the half dark, their paired backs in silhouette delicate and sleek, their slim, quick bodies awkward, divinely young, while beyond them the silver dream accumulated, inevitably on and on. She began to laugh. In trying to suppress it, it made more noise than ever; heads began to turn. Still laughing, her friends raised her and led her out, and she stood at the curb, laughing on a high, sustained note, until the taxi came up and they helped her in.

They removed the pink voile and the sheer underthings and the stockings, and put her to bed, and cracked ice for her temples, and sent for the doctor. He was hard to locate, so they ministered to her with hushed ejaculations, renewing the ice and fanning her. While the ice was fresh and cold she stopped laughing and lay still for a time, moaning only a little. But soon the laughing welled again and her voice rose screaming.

"Shhhhhhhhhhh! Shhhhhhhhhhhhhh!" they said, freshening the ice-pack, smoothing her hair, examining it for gray; "poor girl!" Then to one another: "Do you suppose anything really happened?" their eyes darkly aglitter, secret and passionate. "Shhhhhhhhhh! Poor girl! Poor Minnie!"

V

It was midnight when McLendon drove up to his neat new house. It was trim and fresh as a birdcage and almost as small, with its clean, green-and-white paint. He locked the car and mounted the porch and entered. His wife rose from a chair beside the reading lamp. McLendon stopped in the floor and stared at her until she looked down.

"Look at that clock," he said, lifting his arm, pointing. She stood before him, her face lowered, a magazine in her hands. Her face was pale, strained, and weary-looking. "Haven't I told you about sitting up like this, waiting to see when I come in?"

"John," she said. She laid the magazine down. Poised on the balls of his feet, he glared at her with his hot eyes, his sweating face.

"Didn't I tell you?" He went toward her. She looked up then. He caught her shoulder. She stood passive, looking at him.

"Don't, John. I couldn't sleep . . . The heat; something. Please, John. You're hurting me."

"Didn't I tell you?" He released her and half struck, half flung her across the chair, and she lay there and watched him quietly as he left the room.

He went on through the house, ripping off his shirt, and on the dark, screened porch at the rear he stood and mopped his head and shoulders with the shirt and flung it away. He took the pistol from his hip and laid it on the table beside the bed, and sat on the bed and removed his shoes, and rose and slipped his trousers off. He was sweating again already, and he stooped and hunted furiously for the shirt. At last he found it and wiped his body again, and, with his body pressed against the dusty screen, he stood panting. There was no movement, no sound, not even an insect. The dark world seemed to lie stricken beneath the cold moon and the lidless stars.

1931

DISCUSSION QUESTIONS

1. Explain the purpose of each of the five parts of the story. Are the parts arranged in the best order? Why or why not? Originally, the order of the first two parts was reversed. Did Faulkner's change improve or weaken his *structure?* Explain. What aspects of the lynching does Faulkner focus attention on and which does he deliberately ignore? Why?

2. What distinguishes Hawkshaw from both McLendon and Butch as if they were "men of different races" (page 391)? Base your answer not only on what they say and do, but also on their facial features and expressions.

3. Since Hawkshaw wants to save Mayes, why does he hit him? Why does he later jump from the car?

4. What makes McLendon's treatment of his wife *ironic?* What is his real motive for wanting to lynch Mayes?

5. What do Mayes and Minnie Cooper have in common? What do McLendon and Minnie have in common? Why does she fabricate a story about Mayes? Why does she become hysterical at the movies? What immediate circumstances trigger her hysteria?

6. What direct effect has the sixty-two-day drought on the *action* of the story? What do the town's drought and the resulting *atmosphere symbolize?* How many times is the word *dust* used in part III? Why does the moon ride "high and clear of the dust at last" when Hawkshaw is "brushing at his clothes" (page 397)? Why has Faulkner made Mayes a night watchman at an ice plant, while the lynchers seem to live "in a bowl of molten lead"?

GOING TO MEET THE MAN

JAMES BALDWIN

"WHAT'S THE matter?" she asked.

"I don't know," he said, trying to laugh, "I guess I'm tired."

"You've been working too hard," she said. "I keep telling you."

"Well, goddammit, woman," he said, "it's not my fault!" He tried again; he wretchedly failed again. Then he just lay there, silent, angry, and helpless. Excitement filled him like a toothache, but it refused to enter his flesh. He stroked her breast. This was his wife. He could not ask her to do just a little thing for him, just to help him out, just for a little while, the way he could ask a nigger girl to do it. He lay there, and he sighed. The image of a black girl caused a distant excitement in him, like a far-away light; but, again, the excitement was more like pain; instead of forcing him to act, it made action impossible.

"Go to sleep," she said, gently, "you got a hard day tomorrow."

"Yeah," he said, and rolled over on his side, facing her, one hand still on one breast. "Goddamn the niggers. The black stinking coons. You'd think they'd learn. Wouldn't you think they'd learn? I mean, *wouldn't* you?"

"They going to be out there tomorrow," she said, and took his hand away, "get some sleep."

He lay there, one hand between his legs, staring at the frail sanctuary of his wife. A faint light came from the shutters; the moon was full. Two dogs, far away, were barking at each other, back and forth, insistently, as though they were agreeing to make an appointment. He heard a car coming north on the road and he half sat up, his hand reaching for his holster, which was on a chair near the bed, on top of his pants. The lights hit the shutters and seemed to travel across the room and then went out. The sound of the car slipped away, he heard it hit gravel, then heard it no more. Some liver-lipped students, probably, heading back to that college—but coming from where? His watch said it was two in the morning. They could be coming from anywhere, from out of state most likely, and they would be at the court-house tomorrow. The niggers were getting ready. Well, they would be ready, too.

He moaned. He wanted to let whatever was in him out; but it wouldn't come out. Goddamn! he said aloud, and turned again, on his side, away from Grace, staring at the shutters. He was a big, healthy man and he had never had any trouble sleeping. And he wasn't old enough yet to have any trouble getting it up—he was only forty-two. And he was a good man, a God-fearing man, he had tried to do his duty all his life, and he had been a deputy sheriff for several years. Nothing had ever bothered him before, certainly not getting it up. Sometimes, sure, like any other man, he knew that he wanted a little more spice than Grace could give him and he would drive over yonder and pick up a black piece or arrest her, it came to the same thing, but he couldn't do that now, no more. There was no telling what might happen once your ass was in the air. And they were low enough to kill a man then, too, everyone of them, or the girl herself might do it, right while she was making believe you made her feel so good. The niggers. What had the good Lord Almighty had in mind when he made the niggers? Well. They were pretty good at that, all right. Damn. Damn. Goddamn.

This wasn't helping him to sleep. He turned again, toward Grace again, and moved close to her warm body. He felt something he had never felt before. He felt that he would like to hold her, hold her, hold her, and be buried in her like a child and never have to get up in the morning again and go downtown to face those faces, good Christ, they were ugly! and never have to enter that jail house again and smell that smell and hear that singing; never again feel that filthy, kinky, greasy hair under his hand, never again watch those black breasts leap against the leaping cattle prod, never hear those moans again or watch that blood run down or the fat lips split or the sealed eyes struggle open. They were animals, they were no better than animals, what could be done with people like that? Here they had been in a civilized country for years and they still lived like animals. Their houses were dark, with oil cloth or cardboard in the windows, the smell was enough to make you puke your guts out, and there they sat, a whole tribe, pumping out kids, it looked like, every damn five minutes, and laughing and talking and playing music like they didn't have a care in the world, and he reckoned they didn't, neither, and coming to the door, into the sunlight, just standing there, just looking foolish, not thinking of anything but just getting back to what they were doing, saying, Yes suh, Mr. Jesse. I surely will, Mr. Jesse. Fine weather, Mr. Jesse. Why, I thank you, Mr. Jesse. He had worked for a mail-order house for a while and it had been his job to collect the payments for the stuff they bought. They were too dumb to know that they were being cheated blind, but that was no skin off his ass—he was just supposed to do his job. They would be late—they didn't have the sense to put money aside; but it was easy to scare them, and he never really had any trouble. Hell, they all liked him, the kids used to smile when he came to the door. He gave them candy, sometimes, or chewing gum, and rubbed their rough bullet heads—maybe the candy should have been poisoned. Those kids were grown now. He had had trouble with one of them today.

"There was this nigger today," he said; and stopped; his voice sounded peculiar. He touched Grace. "You awake?" he asked. She mumbled something, impatiently, she was probably telling him to go to sleep. It was all right. He knew that he was not alone.

"What a funny time," he said, "to be thinking about a thing like that—you listening?" She mumbled something again. He rolled over on his back. "This nigger's one of the ringleaders. We had trouble with him before. We must have had him out there at the work farm three or four times. Well, Big Jim C. and some of the boys really had to whip that nigger's ass today." He looked over at Grace; he could not tell whether she was listening or not; and he was afraid to ask again.

"They had this line you know, to register"—he laughed, but she did not—"and they wouldn't stay where Big Jim C. wanted them, no, they had to start blocking traffic all around the court house so couldn't nothing or nobody get through, and Big Jim C. told them to disperse and they wouldn't move, they just kept up that singing, and Big Jim C. figured that the others would move if this nigger would move, him being the ringleader, but he wouldn't move and he wouldn't let the others move, so they had to beat him and a couple of the others and they threw them in the wagon—but *I* didn't see this nigger till I got to the jail. They were still singing and I was supposed to make them stop. Well, I couldn't make them stop for me but I knew he could make them stop. He was lying on the ground jerking and moaning, they had threw him in a cell by himself, and blood was coming out his ears from where Big Jim C. and his boys had whipped him. Wouldn't you think they'd learn? I put the prod to him and he jerked some more and he kind of screamed—but he didn't have much voice left. "You make them stop that singing," I said to him, "you hear me? You make them stop that singing." He acted like he didn't hear me and I put it to him again, under his arms, and he just rolled around on the floor and blood started coming from his mouth. He'd pissed his pants already." He paused. His mouth felt dry and his throat was as rough as sandpaper; as he talked, he began to hurt all over with that peculiar excitement which refused to be released. "You all are going to stop your singing, I said to him, and you are going to stop coming down to the court house and disrupting traffic and molesting the people and keeping us from our duties and keeping doctors from getting to sick white women and getting all them Northerners in this town to give our town a bad name—!" As he said this, he kept prodding the boy, sweat pouring from beneath the helmet he had not yet taken off. The boy rolled around in his own dirt and water and blood and tried to scream again as the prod hit his testicles, but the scream did not come out, only a kind of rattle and a moan. He stopped. He was not supposed to kill the nigger. The cell was filled with a terrible odor. The boy was still. "You hear me?" he called. "You had enough?" The singing went on. "You had enough?" His foot leapt out, he had not known it was going to, and caught the boy flush on the jaw. *Jesus,* he thought, *this ain't no nigger, this is a goddamn bull,* and he screamed again, "You had enough? You going to make them stop that singing now?"

But the boy was out. And now he was shaking worse than the boy had been shaking. He was glad no one could see him. At the same time, he felt very close to a very peculiar, particular joy; something deep in him and deep in his memory was stirred, but whatever was in his memory eluded him. He took off his helmet. He walked to the cell door.

"White man," said the boy, from the floor, behind him.

He stopped. For some reason, he grabbed his privates.

"You remember Old Julia?"

The boy said, from the floor, with his mouth full of blood, and one eye, barely open, glaring like the eye of a cat in the dark, "My grandmother's name was Mrs. Julia Blossom. *Mrs.* Julia Blossom. You going to call our women by their right names yet.—And those kids ain't going to stop singing. We going to keep on singing until every one of you miserable white mothers go stark raving out of your minds." Then he closed the one eye; he spat blood; his head fell back against the floor.

He looked down at the boy, whom he had been seeing, off and on, for more than a year, and suddenly remembered him: Old Julia had been one of his mail-order customers, a nice old woman. He had not seen her for years, he supposed that she must be dead.

He had walked into the yard, the boy had been sitting in a swing. He had smiled at the boy, and asked, "Old Julia home?"

The boy looked at him for a long time before he answered. "Don't no Old Julia live here."

"This is her house. I know her. She's lived here for years."

The boy shook his head. "You might know a Old Julia someplace else, white man. But don't nobody by that name live here."

He watched the boy; the boy watched him. The boy certainly wasn't more than ten. *White man.* He didn't have time to be fooling around with some crazy kid. He yelled, "Hey! Old Julia!"

But only silence answered him. The expression on the boy's face did not change. The sun beat down on them both, still and silent; he had the feeling that he had been caught up in a nightmare, a nightmare dreamed by a child; perhaps one of the nightmares he himself had dreamed as a child. It had that feeling—everything familiar, without undergoing any other change, had been subtly and hideously displaced: the trees, the sun, the patches of grass in the yard, the leaning porch and the weary porch steps and the cardboard in the windows and the black hole of the door which looked like the entrance to a cave, and the eyes of the pickaninny, all, all, were charged with malevolence. *White man.* He looked at the boy. "She's gone out?"

The boy said nothing.

"Well," he said, "tell her I passed by and I'll pass by next week." He started to go; he stopped. "You want some chewing gum?"

The boy got down from the swing and started for the house. He said, "I don't want nothing you got, white man." He walked into the house and closed the door behind him.

Now the boy looked as though he were dead. Jesse wanted to go over to him and pick him up and pistol whip him until the boy's head burst open like a melon. He began to tremble with what he believed was rage, sweat, both cold and hot, raced down his body, the singing filled him as though it were a weird, uncontrollable, monstrous howling rumbling up from the depths of his own belly, he felt an icy fear rise in him and raise him up, and he shouted, he howled, "You lucky we *pump* some white blood into you every once in a while—your women! Here's what I got for all the black bitches in the world—!" Then he was, abruptly, almost too weak to stand; to his bewilderment, his horror, beneath his own fingers, he felt himself violently stiffen—with no warning at all; he dropped his hands and he stared at the boy and he left the cell.

"All that singing they do," he said. "All that singing." He could not remember the first time he had heard it; he had been hearing it all his life. It was the sound with which he was most familiar—though it was also the sound of which he had been least conscious—and it had always contained an obscure comfort. They were singing to God. They were singing for mercy and they hoped to go to heaven, and he had even sometimes felt, when looking into the eyes of some of the old women, a few of the very old men, that they were singing for mercy for his soul, too. Of course he had never thought of their heaven or of what God was, or could be, for them; God was the same for everyone, he supposed, and heaven was where good people went—he supposed. He had never thought much about what it meant to be a good person. He tried to be a good person and treat everybody right: it wasn't his fault if the niggers had taken it into their heads to fight against God and go against the rules laid down in the Bible for everyone to read! Any preacher would tell you that. He was only doing his duty: protecting white people from the niggers and the niggers from themselves. And there were still lots of good niggers around—he had to remember that; they weren't all like that boy this afternoon; and the good niggers must be mighty sad to see what was happening to their people. They would thank him when this was over. In that way they had, the best of them, not quite looking him in the eye, in a low voice, with a little smile: We surely thanks you, Mr. Jesse. From the bottom of our hearts, we thanks you. He smiled. They hadn't all gone crazy. This trouble would pass.—He knew that the young people had changed some of the words to the songs. He had scarcely listened to the words before and he did not listen to them now; but he knew that the words were different; he could hear that much. He did not know if the faces were different, he had never, before this trouble began, watched them as they sang, but he certainly did not like what he saw now. They hated him, and this hatred was blacker than their hearts, blacker than their skins, redder than their blood, and harder, by far, than his club. Each day, each night, he felt worn out, aching, with their smell in his nostrils and filling his lungs, as though he were drowning—drowning in niggers; and it was all to be done again when he awoke. It would never end. It would never end. Perhaps this was what the singing had meant all along. They had not been singing black folks into heaven, they had been singing white folks into hell.

Everyone felt this black suspicion in many ways, but no one knew how to express it. Men much older than he, who had been responsible for law and order much longer than he, were now much quieter than they had been, and the tone of their jokes, in a way that he could not quite put his finger on, had changed. These men were his models, they had been friends to his father, and they had taught him what it meant to be a man. He looked to them for courage now. It wasn't that he didn't know that what he was doing was right—he knew that, nobody had to tell him that; it was only that he missed the ease of former years. But they didn't have much time to hang out with each other these days. They tended to stay close to their families every free minute because nobody knew what might happen next. Explosions rocked the night of their tranquil town. Each time each man wondered silently if perhaps this time the dynamite had not fallen into the wrong hands. They thought that they knew where all the guns were; but they could not possibly know every move that was made in that secret place where the darkies lived. From time to time it was suggested that they form a posse and search the home of every nigger, but they hadn't done it yet. For one thing, this might have brought the bastards from the North down on their backs; for another, although the niggers were scattered throughout the town—down in the hollow near the railroad tracks, way west near the mills, up on the hill, the well-off ones, and some out near the college—nothing seemed to happen in one part of town without the niggers immediately knowing it in the other. This meant that they could not take them by surprise. They rarely mentioned it but they *knew* that some of the niggers had guns. It stood to reason, as they said, since, after all, some of them had been in the Army. There were niggers in the Army right now and God knows they wouldn't have had any trouble stealing this half-assed government blind—the whole world was doing it, look at the European countries and all those countries in Africa. They made jokes about it—bitter jokes; and they cursed the government in Washington, which had betrayed them; but they had not yet formed a posse. Now, if their town had been laid out like some towns in the North, where all the niggers lived together in one locality, they could have gone down and set fire to the houses and brought about peace that way. If the niggers had all lived in one place, they could have kept the fire in one place. But the way this town was laid out, the fire could hardly be controlled. It would spread all over town—and the niggers would probably be helping it to spread. Still, from time to time, they spoke of doing it, anyway; so that now there was a real fear among them that somebody might go crazy and light the match.

They rarely mentioned anything not directly related to the war that they were fighting, but this had failed to establish between them the unspoken communication of soldiers during a war. Each man, in the thrilling silence which sped outward from their exchanges, their laughter, and their anecdotes, seemed wrestling, in various degrees of darkness, with a secret which he could not articulate to himself, and which, however directly it related to the war, related yet more surely to his privacy and his past. They could no longer be sure, after all, that they had all done the same things. They had never dreamed that their privacy could contain any element of terror, could threaten, that is, to reveal itself, to the scrutiny of a judgment day, while remaining unreadable and inaccessible to themselves; nor had they dreamed that the past, while certainly refusing to be forgotten, could yet so stubbornly refuse to be remembered. They felt themselves mysteriously set at naught, as no longer entering into the real concerns of other people—while here they were, out-numbered, fighting to save the civilized world. They had thought that people would care—people didn't care; not enough, anyway, to help them. It would have been a help, really, or at least a relief, even to have been forced to surrender. Thus they had lost, probably forever, their old and easy connection with each other. They were forced to depend on each other more and, at the same time, to trust each other less. Who could tell when one of them might not betray them all, for money, or for the ease of confession? But no one dared imagine what there might be to confess. They were soldiers fighting a war, but their relationship to each other was that of accomplices in a crime. They all had to keep their mouths shut.

I stepped in the river at Jordan.

Out of the darkness of the room, out of nowhere, the line came flying up at him, with the melody and the beat. He turned wordlessly toward his sleeping wife. *I stepped in the river at Jordan.* Where had he heard that song?

"Grace," he whispered. "You awake?"

She did not answer. If she was awake, she wanted him to sleep. Her breathing was slow and easy, her body slowly rose and fell.

I stepped in the river at Jordan.
The water came to my knees.

He began to sweat. He felt an overwhelming fear, which yet contained a curious and dreadful pleasure.

I stepped in the river at Jordan.
The water came to my waist.

It had been night, as it was now, he was in the car between his mother and his father, sleepy, his head in his mother's lap, sleepy, and yet full of excitement. The singing came from far away, across the dark fields. There were no lights anywhere. They had said good-bye to all the others and turned off on this dark dirt road. They were almost home.

I stepped in the river at Jordan,
The water came over my head,
I looked way over to the other side,
He was making up my dying bed!

"I guess they singing for him," his father said, seeming very weary and subdued now. "Even when they're sad, they sound like they just about to go and tear off a piece." He yawned and leaned across the boy and slapped his wife lightly on the shoulder, allowing his hand to rest there for a moment. "Don't they?"

"Don't talk that way," she said.

"Well, that's what we going to do," he said, "you can make up your mind to that." He started whistling. "You see? When I begin to feel it, I gets kind of musical, too."

Oh, Lord! Come on and ease my troubling mind!

He had a black friend, his age, eight, who lived nearby. His name was Otis. They wrestled together in the dirt. Now the thought of Otis made him sick. He began to shiver. His mother put her arm around him.

"He's tired," she said.

"We'll be home soon," said his father. He began to whistle again.

"We didn't see Otis this morning," Jesse said. He did not know why he said this. His voice, in the darkness of the car, sounded small and accusing.

"You haven't seen Otis for a couple of mornings," his mother said.

That was true. But he was only concerned about *this* morning.

"No," said his father, "I reckon Otis's folks was afraid to let him show himself this morning."

"But Otis didn't do nothing!" Now his voice sounded questioning.

"Otis *can't* do nothing," said his father, "he's too little." The car lights picked up their wooden house, which now solemnly approached them, the lights falling around it like yellow dust. Their dog, chained to a tree, began to bark.

"We just want to make sure Otis *don't* do nothing," said his father, and stopped the car. He looked down at Jesse. "And you tell him what your Daddy said, you hear?"

"Yes sir," he said.

His father switched off the lights. The dog moaned and pranced, but they ignored him and went inside. He could not sleep. He lay awake, hearing the night sounds, the dog yawning and moaning outside, the sawing of the crickets, the cry of the owl, dogs barking far away, then no sounds at all, just the heavy, endless buzzing of the night. The darkness pressed on his eyelids like a scratchy blanket. He turned, he turned again. He wanted to call his mother, but he knew his father would not like this. He was terribly afraid. Then he heard his father's voice in the other room, low, with a joke in it; but this did not help him, it frightened him more, he knew what was going to happen. He put his head under the blanket, then pushed his head out again, for fear, staring at the dark window. He heard his mother's moan, his father's sigh; he gritted his teeth. Then their bed began to rock. His father's breathing seemed to fill the world.

That morning, before the sun had gathered all its strength, men and women, some flushed and some pale with excitement, came with news. Jesse's father seemed to know what the news was before the first jalopy stopped in the yard, and he ran out, crying, "They got him, then? They got him?"

The first jalopy held eight people, three men and two women and three children. The children were sitting on the laps of the grown-ups. Jesse knew two of them, the two boys; they shyly and uncomfortably greeted each other. He did not know the girl.

"Yes, they got him," said one of the women, the older one, who wore a wide hat and a fancy, faded blue dress. "They found him early this morning."

"How far had he got?" Jesse's father asked.

"He hadn't got no further than Harkness," one of the men said. "Look like he got lost up there in all them trees—or maybe he just got so scared he couldn't move." They all laughed.

"Yes, and you know it's near a graveyard, too," said the younger woman, and they laughed again.

"Is that where they got him now?" asked Jesse's father.

By this time there were three cars piled behind the first one, with everyone looking excited and shining, and Jesse noticed that they were carrying food. It was like a Fourth of July picnic.

"Yeah, that's where he is," said one of the men, "declare, Jesse, you going to keep us here all day long, answering your damn fool questions. Come on, we ain't got no time to waste."

"Don't bother putting up no food," cried a woman from one of the other cars, "we got enough. Just come on."

"Why, thank you," said Jesse's father, "we be right along, then."

"I better get a sweater for the boy," said his mother, "in case it turns cold."

Jesse watched his mother's thin legs cross the yard. He knew that she also wanted to comb her hair a little and maybe put on a better dress, the dress she wore to church. His father guessed this, too, for he yelled behind her, "Now don't you go trying to turn yourself into no movie star. You just come on." But he laughed as he said this, and winked at the men; his wife was younger and prettier than most of the other women. He clapped Jesse on the head and started pulling him toward the car. "You all go on," he said, "I'll be right behind you. Jesse, you go tie up that there dog while I get this car started."

The cars sputtered and coughed and shook; the caravan began to move; bright dust filled the air. As soon as he was tied up, the dog began to bark. Jesse's mother came out of the house, carrying a jacket for his father and a sweater for Jesse. She had put a ribbon in her hair and had an old shawl around her shoulders.

"Put these in the car, son," she said, and handed everything to him. She bent down and stroked the dog, looked to see if there was water in his bowl, then went back up the three porch steps and closed the door.

"Come on," said his father, "ain't nothing in there for nobody to steal." He was sitting in the car, which trembled and belched. The last car of the caravan had disappeared but the sound of singing floated behind them.

Jesse got into the car, sitting close to his father, loving the smell of the car, and the trembling, and the bright day, and the sense of going on a great and unexpected journey. His mother got in and closed the door and the car began to move. Not until then did he ask, "Where are we going? Are we going on a picnic?"

He had a feeling that he knew where they were going, but he was not sure.

"That's right," his father said, "we're going on a picnic. You won't ever forget *this* picnic—!"

"Are we," he asked, after a moment, "going to see the bad nigger—the one that knocked down old Miss Standish?"

"Well, I reckon," said his mother, "that we *might* see him."

He started to ask, *Will a lot of niggers be there? Will Otis be there?* —but he did not ask his question, to which, in a strange and uncomfortable way, he already knew the answer. Their friends, in the other cars, stretched up the road as far as he could see; other cars had joined them; there were cars behind them. They were singing. The sun seemed, suddenly very hot, and he was, at once very happy and a little afraid. He did not quite understand what was happening, and he did not know what to ask—he had no one to ask. He had grown accustomed, for the solution of such mysteries, to go to Otis. He felt that Otis knew everything. But he could not ask Otis about this. Anyway, he had not seen Otis for two days; he had not seen a black face anywhere for more than two days; and he now realized, as they began chugging up the long hill which eventually led to Harkness, that there were no black faces on the road this morning, no black people anywhere. From the houses in which they lived, all along the road, no smoke curled, no life stirred—maybe one or two chickens were to be seen, that was all. There was no one at the windows, no one in the yard, no one sitting on the porches, and the doors were closed. He had come this road many a time and seen women washing in the yard (there were no clothes on the clotheslines) men working in the fields, children playing in the dust; black men passed them on the road other mornings, other days, on foot, or in wagons, sometimes in cars, tipping their hats, smiling, joking, their teeth a solid white against their skin, their eyes as warm as the sun, the blackness of their skin like dull fire against the white of the blue or the grey of their torn clothes. They passed the nigger church—dead-white, desolate, locked up; and the graveyard, where no one knelt or walked, and he saw no flowers. He wanted to ask, *Where are they? Where are they all?* But he did not dare. As the hill grew steeper, the sun grew colder. He looked at his mother and his father. They looked straight ahead, seeming to be listening to the singing which echoed and echoed in this graveyard silence. They were strangers to him now. They were looking at something he could not see. His father's lips had a strange, cruel curve, he wet his lips from time to time, and swallowed. He was terribly aware of his father's tongue, it was as though he had never seen it before. And his father's body suddenly seemed immense, bigger than a mountain. His eyes, which were grey-green, looked yellow in the sunlight; or at least there was a light in them which he had never seen before. His mother patted her hair and adjusted the ribbon, leaning forward to look into the car mirror. "You look all right," said his father, and laughed. "When that nigger looks at you, he's going to swear he throwed his life away for nothing. Wouldn't be surprised if he don't come back to haunt you." And he laughed again.

The singing now slowly began to cease; and he realized that they were nearing their destination. They had reached a straight, narrow, pebbly road, with trees on either side. The sunlight filtered down on them from a great height, as though they were under-water; and the branches of the trees scraped against the cars with a tearing sound. To the right of them, and beneath them, invisible now, lay the town; and to the left, miles of trees which led to the high mountain range which his ancestors had crossed in order to settle in this valley. Now, all was silent, except for the bumping of the tires against the rocky road, the sputtering of motors, and the sound of a crying child. And they seemed to move more slowly. They were beginning to climb again. He watched the cars ahead as they toiled patiently upward, disappearing into the sunlight of the clearing. Presently, he felt their vehicle also rise, heard his father's changed breathing, the sunlight hit his face, the trees moved away from them, and they were there. As their car crossed the clearing, he looked around. There seemed to be millions, there were certainly hundreds of people in the clearing, staring toward something he could not see. There was a fire. He could not see the flames, but he smelled the smoke. Then they were on the other side of the clearing, among the trees again. His father drove off the road and parked the car behind a great many other cars. He looked down at Jesse.

"You all right?" he asked.

"Yes sir," he said.

"Well, come on, then," his father said. He reached over and opened the door on his mother's side. His mother stepped out first. They followed her into the clearing. At first he was aware only of confusion, of his mother and father greeting and being greeted, himself being handled, hugged, and patted, and told how much he had grown. The wind blew the smoke from the fire across the clearing into his eyes and nose. He could not see over the backs of the people in front of him. The sounds of laughing and cursing and wrath—and something else—rolled in waves from the front of the mob to the back. Those in front expressed their delight at what they saw, and this delight rolled backward, wave upon wave, across the clearing, more acrid than the smoke. His father reached down suddenly and sat Jesse on his shoulders.

Now he saw the fire—of twigs and boxes, piled high; flames made pale orange and yellow and thin as a veil under the steadier light of the sun; grey-blue smoke rolled upward and poured over their heads. Beyond the shifting curtain of fire and smoke, he made out first only a length of gleaming chain, attached to a great limb of the tree; then he saw that this chain bound two black hands together at the wrist, dirty yellow palm facing dirty yellow palm. The smoke poured up; the hands dropped out of sight; a cry went up from the crowd. Then the hands slowly came into view again, pulled upward by the chain. This time he saw the kinky, sweating, bloody head—he had never before seen a head with so much hair on it, hair so black and so tangled that it seemed like another jungle. The head was hanging. He saw the forehead, flat and high, with a kind of arrow of hair in the center, like he had, like his father had; they called it a widow's peak; and the mangled eye brows, the wide nose, the closed eyes, and the glinting eye lashes and the hanging lips, all streaming with blood and sweat. His hands were straight above his head. All his weight pulled downward from his hands; and he was a big man, a bigger man than his father, and black as an African jungle Cat, and naked. Jesse pulled upward; his father's hands held him firmly by the ankles. He wanted to say something, he did not know what, but nothing he said could have been heard, for now the crowd roared again as a man stepped forward and put more wood on the fire. The flames leapt up. He thought he heard the hanging man scream, but he was not sure. Sweat was pouring from the hair in his armpits, poured down his sides, over his chest, into his navel and his groin. He was lowered again; he was raised again. Now Jesse knew that he heard him scream. The head went back, the mouth wide open, blood bubbling from the mouth; the veins of the neck jumped out; Jesse clung to his father's neck in terror as the cry rolled over the crowd. The cry of all the people rose to answer the dying man's cry. He wanted death to come quickly. They wanted to make death wait: and it was they who held death, now, on a leash which they lengthened little by little. *What did he do?* Jesse wondered. *What did the man do? What did he do?*—but he could not ask his father. He was seated on his father's shoulders, but his father was far away. There were two older men, friends of his father's, raising and lowering the chain; everyone, indiscriminately, seemed to be responsible for the fire. There was no hair left on the nigger's privates, and the eyes, now, were wide open, as white as the eyes of a clown or a doll. The smoke now carried a terrible odor across the clearing, the odor of something burning which was both sweet and rotten.

He turned his head a little and saw the field of faces. He watched his mother's face. Her eyes were very bright, her mouth was open: she was more beautiful than he had ever seen her, and more strange. He began to feel a joy he had never felt before. He watched the hanging, gleaming body, the most beautiful and terrible object he had ever seen till then. One of his father's friends reached up and in his hands he held a knife: and Jesse wished that he had been that man. It was a long, bright knife and the sun seemed to catch it, to play with it, to caress it—it was brighter than the fire. And a wave of laughter swept the crowd. Jesse felt his father's hands on his ankles slip and tighten. The man with the knife walked toward the crowd, smiling slightly; as though this were a signal, silence fell; he heard his mother cough. Then the man with the knife walked up to the hanging body. He turned and smiled again. Now there was a silence all over the field. The hanging head looked up. It seemed fully conscious now, as though the fire had burned out terror and pain. The man with the knife took the nigger's privates in his hand, one hand, still smiling, as though he were weighing them. In the cradle of the one white hand, the nigger's privates seemed as remote as meat being weighed in the scales; but seemed heavier, too, much heavier, and Jesse felt his scrotum tighten; and huge, huge, much bigger than his father's, flaccid, hairless, the largest thing he had ever seen till then, and the blackest. The white hand stretched them, cradled them, caressed them. Then the dying man's eyes looked straight into Jesse's eyes—it could not have been as long as a second, but it seemed longer than a year. Then Jesse screamed, and the crowd screamed as the knife flashed, first up, then down, cutting the dreadful thing away, and the blood came roaring down. Then the crowd rushed forward, tearing at the body with their hands, with knives, with rocks, with stones, howling and cursing. Jesse's head, of its own weight, fell downward toward his father's head. Someone stepped forward and drenched the body with kerosene. Where the man had been, a great sheet of flame appeared. Jesse's father lowered him to the ground.

"Well, I told you," said his father, "you wasn't never going to forget *this* picnic." His father's face was full of sweat, his eyes were very peaceful. At that moment Jesse loved his father more than he had ever loved him. He felt that his father had carried him through a mighty test, had revealed to him a great secret which would be the key to his life forever.

"I reckon," he said. "I reckon."

Jesse's father took him by the hand and, with his mother a little behind them, talking and laughing with the other women, they walked through the crowd, across the clearing. The black body was on the ground, the chain which had held it was being rolled up by one of his father's friends. Whatever the fire had left undone, the hands and the knives and the stones of the people had accomplished. The head was caved in, one eye was torn out, one ear was hanging. But one had to look carefully to realize this, for it was, now, merely, a black charred object on the black, charred ground. He lay spread-eagled with what had been a wound between what had been his legs.

"They going to leave him here, then?" Jesse whispered.

"Yeah," said his father, "they'll come and get him by and by. I reckon we better get over there and get some of that food before it's all gone."

"I reckon," he muttered now to himself, "I reckon." Grace stirred and touched him on the thigh: the moonlight covered her like glory. Something bubbled up in him, his nature again returned to him. He thought of the boy in the cell; he thought of the man in the fire; he thought of the knife and grabbed himself and stroked himself and a terrible sound, something between a high laugh and a howl, came out of him and dragged his sleeping wife up on one elbow. She stared at him in a moonlight which had now grown cold as ice. He thought of the morning and grabbed her, laughing and crying, crying and laughing, and he whispered, as he stroked her, as he took her, "Come on, sugar, I'm going to do you like a nigger, just like a nigger, come on, sugar, and love me just like you'd love a nigger." He thought of the morning as he labored and she moaned, thought of morning as he labored harder than he ever had before, and before his labors had ended, he heard the first cock crow and the dogs begin to bark, and the sound of tires on the gravel road.

1965

DISCUSSION QUESTIONS

1. Why does Jesse feel "caught up in a nightmare" the first time he meets Julia's grandson?

2. How had his father's friends "taught him what it meant to be a man" (page 407)? What roles do they play at the lynching? What is Jesse's concept of manhood?

3. What advantage does Baldwin derive from having the jailed civil-rights leader turn out to be Julia's grandson? Why does Jesse feel "very close to a very peculiar, particular joy" (page 404) after kicking him?

4. On the way to the lynching, Jesse's father seems a stranger whose "lips had a strange, cruel curve" (pages 412–413). After the lynching, Jesse "loved his father more than he had ever loved him" (page 415). How do you account for this change of attitude? What does it signify? When precisely does it occur?

5. Explain the fact that Jesse wishes to be the man with the knife and simultaneously feels "his scrotum tighten" (page 415). Are there other examples of such *ambivalence* at the lynching?

6. Jesse's father tells him he is going on a picnic. How do his parents' behavior and that of the other people remind one of a picnic? Give specific examples. What makes such behavior *ironic?* How does it affect the story's *atmosphere?*

7. Why specifically does Jesse feel impotent at the beginning of the story and virile at its end? Name some other stories, television plays, or films in which the hero is healed through the recollection of a particular childhood experience. How does Baldwin's *plot* differ from these in a highly *ironic* way?

1. Which character, McLendon or Jesse, do you dislike more? Why? What specific aspects of the stories affect your attitude?

2. Since both Faulkner and Baldwin deal with the lynching of a black, what conditions create such different stories? What specific function does the lynching serve in each story? How could Baldwin, through a shift of emphasis and *point of view,* have made his work resemble Faulkner's? Conversely, how could Faulkner have shaped his story to resemble Baldwin's?

3. What function does Minnie serve in "Dry September"? What effect results from Miss Standish remaining a mere empty name in "Going to Meet the Man"? What function does Hawkshaw serve in "Dry September"? How is his function fulfilled in Baldwin's story?

4. Which of these two stories seems to contain the more complex and realistic characters? What conditions create such a difference in characterization? Does this difference necessarily determine which is the better story? Support your answer with specific reasons.

ANALYSIS AND APPLICATION

1. In one brief paragraph (part II, paragraph 3), Faulkner describes Minnie Cooper's moment of realization that life has passed her by. "Losing ground" relates to what *implied metaphor* in the previous paragraph? In what way is her "bright, haggard look" like a "mask," but also like a "flag"? Relate these two *similes* to "furious repudiation of truth." Note the extreme brevity of the climactic last sentence of the paragraph: half the length of the next shortest sentence. Although the last two sentences of the paragraph have a cause-and-effect relationship, Faulkner avoids combining them through subordination. To determine whether he made the right choice, experiment with a few changes that combine the sentences. Try, for example, to begin the fourth sentence with *when* or *because*. Which form is more effective: one or two sentences? Why?

2. Compare Faulkner's second sentence in part III with the following modified version: The day had passed obscured by dust; above the darkened square, enveloped by the spent dust, the sky was perfectly clear. Although both versions give the same factual information, why is Faulkner's so much richer? What underlying mood, related to his theme, does Faulkner's sentence convey that is missing from the other version? Specifically, how is this mood suggested?

THE BASEMENT ROOM

GRAHAM GREENE

WHEN THE front door had shut the two of them out and the butler Baines had turned back into the dark and heavy hall, Philip began to live. He stood in front of the nursery door, listening until he heard the engine of the taxi die out along the street. His parents were safely gone for a fortnight's holiday; he was 'between nurses', one dismissed and the other not arrived; he was alone in the great Belgravia house with Baines and Mrs Baines.

He could go anywhere, even through the green baize door to the pantry or down the stairs to the basement living-room. He felt a happy stranger in his home because he could go into any room and all the rooms were empty.

You could only guess who had once occupied them: the rack of pipes in the smoking-room beside the elephant tusks, the carved wood tobacco jar; in the bedroom the pink hangings and the pale perfumes and three-quarter finished jars of cream which Mrs Baines had not yet cleared away for her own use; the high glaze on the never-opened piano in the drawing-room, the china clock, the silly little tables and the silver. But here Mrs Baines was already busy, pulling down the curtains, covering the chairs in dust-sheets.

'Be off out of here, Master Philip,' and she looked at him with her peevish eyes, while she moved round, getting everything in order, meticulous and loveless and doing her duty.

Philip Lane went downstairs and pushed at the baize door; he looked into the pantry, but Baines was not there, then he set foot for the first time on the stairs to the basement. Again he had the sense: this is life. All his seven nursery years vibrated with the strange, the new experience. His crowded brain was like a city which feels the earth tremble at a distant earthquake shock. He was apprehensive, but he was happier than he had ever been. Everything was more important than before.

Baines was reading a newspaper in his shirt-sleeves. He said, 'Come in, Phil, and make yourself at home. Wait a moment and I'll do the honours,' and going to a white cleaned cupboard he brought out a bottle of ginger-beer and half a Dundee cake.[1] 'Half past eleven in the morning,' Baines said. 'It's opening time,[2] my boy,' and he cut the cake and poured out the ginger-beer. He was more genial than Philip had ever known him, more at his ease, a man in his own home.

'Shall I call Mrs Baines?' Philip asked, and he was glad when Baines said no. She was busy. She liked to be busy, so why interfere with her pleasure?

'A spot of drink at half-past eleven,' Baines said, pouring himself out a glass of ginger-beer, 'gives an appetite for chop and does no man any harm.'

'A chop?' Philip asked.

'Old Coasters,'[3] Baines said, 'they call all food chop.'

'But it's not a chop?'

'Well, it might be, you know, if cooked with palm oil. And then some paw-paw to follow.'

[1] Rich fruitcake, usually decorated with almonds.

[2] Hour at which pubs are allowed to open to serve alcohol.

[3] White men living on the Gold Coast in West Africa in the late nineteenth and early twentieth centuries.

Philip looked out of the basement window at the dry stone yard, the ash-can and the legs going up and down beyond the railings.

'Was it hot there?'

'Ah, you never felt such heat. Not a nice heat, mind, like you get in the park on a day like this. Wet,' Baines said, 'corruption.' He cut himself a slice of cake. 'Smelling of rot,' Baines said, rolling his eyes round the small basement room, from clean cupboard to clean cupboard, the sense of bareness, of nowhere to hide a man's secrets. With an air of regret for something lost he took a long draught of ginger-beer.

'Why did father live out there?'

'It was his job,' Baines said, 'same as this is mine now. And it was mine then too. It was a man's job. You wouldn't believe it now, but I've had forty niggers under me, doing what I told them to.'

'Why did you leave?'

'I married Mrs Baines.'

Philip took the slice of Dundee cake in his hand and munched it round the room. He felt very old, independent and judicial; he was aware that Baines was talking to him as man to man. He never called him Master Philip as Mrs Baines did, who was servile when she was not authoritative.

Baines had seen the world; he had seen beyond the railings. He sat there over his ginger pop with the resigned dignity of an exile; Baines didn't complain; he had chosen his fate, and if his fate was Mrs Baines he had only himself to blame.

But today—the house was almost empty and Mrs Baines was upstairs and there was nothing to do—he allowed himself a little acidity.

'I'd go back tomorrow if I had the chance.'

'Did you ever shoot a nigger?'

'I never had any call to shoot,' Baines said. 'Of course I carried a gun. But you didn't need to treat them bad. That just made them stupid. Why,' Baines said, bowing his thin grey hair with embarrassment over the ginger pop, 'I loved some of those damned niggers. I couldn't help loving them. There they'd be laughing, holding hands; they liked to touch each other; it made them feel fine to know the other fellow was around. It didn't mean anything we could understand; two of them would go about all day without loosing hold, grown men; but it wasn't love; it didn't mean anything we could understand.'

'Eating between meals,' Mrs Baines said. 'What would your mother say, Master Philip?'

She came down the steep stairs to the basement, her hands full of pots of cream and salve, tubes of grease and paste. 'You oughtn't to encourage him, Baines,' she said, sitting down in a wicker armchair and screwing up her small ill-humoured eyes at the Coty lipstick, Pond's cream, the Leichner rouge and Cyclax powder and Elizabeth Arden astringent.

She threw them one by one into the wastepaper basket. She saved only the cold cream. 'Telling the boy stories,' she said. 'Go along to the nursery, Master Philip, while I get lunch.'

Philip climbed the stairs to the baize door. He heard Mrs Baines's voice like the voice in a nightmare when the small Price light has guttered in the saucer and the curtains move; it was sharp and shrill and full of malice, louder than people ought to speak, exposed.

'Sick to death of your ways, Baines, spoiling the boy. Time you did some work about the house,' but he couldn't hear what Baines said in reply. He pushed open the baize door, came up like a small earth animal in his grey flannel shorts into a wash of sunlight on a parquet floor, the gleam of mirrors dusted and polished and beautified by Mrs Baines.

Something broke downstairs, and Philip sadly mounted the stairs to the nursery. He pitied Baines; it occurred to him how happily they could live together in the empty house if Mrs Baines were called away. He didn't want to play with his Meccano sets;[4] he wouldn't take out his train or his soldiers; he sat at the table with his chin on his hands: this is life; and suddenly he felt responsible for Baines, as if he were the master of the house and Baines an ageing servant who deserved to be cared for. There was not much one could do; he decided at least to be good.

He was not surprised when Mrs Baines was agreeable at lunch; he was used to her changes. Now it was 'another helping of meat, Master Philip', or 'Master Philip, a little more of this nice pudding'. It was a pudding he liked, Queen's pudding[5] with a perfect meringue, but he wouldn't eat a second helping lest she might count that a victory. She was the kind of woman who thought that any injustice could be counterbalanced by something good to eat.

She was sour, but she liked making sweet things; one never had to complain of a lack of jam or plums; she ate well herself and added soft sugar to the meringue and the strawberry jam. The half-light through the basement window set the motes moving above her pale hair like

[4] Steel construction set for children, similar to an erector set.

[5] Dessert made with bread crumbs, eggs, milk, and meringue.

dust as she sifted the sugar, and Baines crouched over his plate saying nothing.

Again Philip felt responsibility. Baines had looked forward to this, and Baines was disappointed: everything was being spoilt. The sensation of disappointment was one which Philip could share; he could understand better than anyone this grief, something hoped for not happening, something promised not fulfilled, something exciting which turned dull. 'Baines,' he said, 'will you take me for a walk this afternoon?'

'No,' Mrs Baines said, 'no. That he won't. Not with all the silver to clean.'

'There's a fortnight to do it in,' Baines said.

'Work first, pleasure afterwards.'

Mrs Baines helped herself to some more meringue.

Baines put down his spoon and fork and pushed his plate away. 'Blast,' he said.

'Temper,' Mrs Baines said, 'temper. Don't you go breaking any more things, Baines, and I won't have you swearing in front of the boy. Master Philip, if you've finished you can get down.'

She skinned the rest of the meringue off the pudding.

'I want to go for a walk,' Philip said.

'You'll go and have a rest.'

'I want to go for a walk.'

'Master Philip,' Mrs Baines said. She got up from the table, leaving her meringue unfinished, and came towards him, thin, menacing, dusty in the basement room. 'Master Philip, you just do as you're told.' She took him by the arm and squeezed it; she watched him with a joyless passionate glitter and above her head the feet of typists trudged back to the Victoria offices after the lunch interval.

'Why shouldn't I go for a walk?'

But he weakened; he was scared and ashamed of being scared. This was life; a strange passion he couldn't understand moving in the basement room. He saw a small pile of broken glass swept into a corner by the wastepaper basket. He looked at Baines for help and only intercepted hate; the sad hopeless hate of something behind bars.

'Why shouldn't I?' he repeated.

'Master Philip,' Mrs Baines said, 'you've got to do as you're told. You mustn't think just because your father's away there's nobody here to—'

'You wouldn't dare,' Philip cried, and was startled by Baines's low interjection:

'There's nothing she wouldn't dare.'

'I hate you,' Philip said to Mrs Baines. He pulled away from her and ran to the door, but she was there before him; she was old, but she was quick.

'Master Philip,' she said, 'you'll say you're sorry.' She stood in front of the door quivering with excitement. 'What would your father do if he heard you say that?'

She put a hand out to seize him, dry and white with constant soda, the nails cut to the quick, but he backed away and put the table between them, and suddenly to his surprise she smiled; she became again as servile as she had been arrogant. 'Get along with you, Master Philip,' she said with glee, 'I see I'm going to have my hands full till your father and mother come back.'

She left the door unguarded and when he passed her she slapped him playfully. 'I've got too much to do today to trouble about you. I haven't covered half the chairs,' and suddenly even the upper part of the house became unbearable to him as he thought of Mrs Baines moving around shrouding the sofas, laying out the dust-sheets.

So he wouldn't go upstairs to get his cap but walked straight out across the shining hall into the street, and again, as he looked this way and looked that way, it was life he was in the middle of.

II

The pink sugar cakes in the window on a paper doily, the ham, the slab of mauve sausage, the wasps driving like small torpedoes across the pane caught Philip's attention. His feet were tired by pavements; he had been afraid to cross the road, had simply walked first in one direction, then in the other. He was nearly home now; the square was at the end of the street; this was a shabby outpost of Pimlico, and he smudged the pane with his nose looking for sweets, and saw between the cakes and ham a different Baines. He hardly recognized the bulbous eyes, the bald forehead. This was a happy, bold and buccaneering Baines, even though it was, when you looked closer, a desperate Baines.

Philip had never seen the girl, but he remembered Baines had a niece. She was thin and drawn, and she wore a white mackintosh; she meant nothing to Philip; she belonged to a world about which he knew nothing at all. He couldn't make up stories about her, as he could make them up about withered Sir Hubert Reed, the Permanent Secretary, about Mrs Wince-Dudley who came up once a year from Penstanley in Suffolk with a green umbrella and an enormous black handbag, as he could make them up about the upper servants in all the houses where he went to tea and games. She just didn't belong. He thought of mermaids and Undine, but she didn't belong there either, nor to the adventures of Emil,[6] nor to the Bastables.[7] She sat there looking at an iced pink cake in the detachment and mystery of the completely disinherited, looking at the half-used pots of powder which Baines had set out on the marble-topped table between them.

Baines was urging, hoping, entreating, commanding, and the girl looked at the tea and the china pots and cried. Baines passed his handkerchief across the table, but she wouldn't wipe her eyes; she screwed it in her palm and let the tears run down, wouldn't do anything, wouldn't speak, would only put up a silent resistance to what she dreaded and wanted and refused to listen to at any price. The two brains battled over the tea-cups loving each other, and there came to Philip outside, beyond the ham and wasps and dusty Pimlico pane, a confused indication of the struggle.

He was inquisitive and he didn't understand and he wanted to know. He went and stood in the doorway to see better, he was less sheltered than he had ever been; other people's lives for the first time touched and pressed and moulded. He would never escape that scene. In a week he had forgotten it, but it conditioned his career, the long austerity of his life; when he was dying, rich and alone, it was said that he asked: 'Who is she?'

Baines had won; he was cocky and the girl was happy. She wiped her face, she opened a pot of powder, and their fingers touched across the table. It occurred to Philip that it might be amusing to imitate Mrs Baines's voice and to call 'Baines' to him from the door.

His voice shrivelled them; you couldn't describe it in any other way, it made them smaller, they weren't together any more. Baines was the first to recover and trace the voice, but that didn't make things as they were. The sawdust was spilled out of the afternoon; nothing you did could mend it, and Philip was scared. 'I didn't mean . . .' He wanted to say that he loved Baines, that he had only wanted to laugh at Mrs Baines. But he had discovered you couldn't laugh at Mrs Baines. She wasn't Sir Hubert Reed, who used steel nibs and carried a pen-wiper in his pocket; she wasn't Mrs Wince-Dudley; she was darkness when the night-light went out in a draught; she was the frozen blocks of

[6] *Emil and the Detectives* (1928), a famous German children's story by Erich Kästner.

[7] The children in a group of juvenile stories by Edith Nesbit.

earth he had seen one winter in a graveyard when someone said, 'They need an electric drill'; she was the flowers gone bad and smelling in the little closet room at Penstanley. There was nothing to laugh about. You had to endure her when she was there and forget about her quickly when she was away, suppress the thought of her, ram it down deep.

Baines said, 'It's only Phil,' beckoned him in and gave him the pink iced cake the girl hadn't eaten, but the afternoon was broken, the cake was like dry bread in the throat. The girl left them at once: she even forgot to take the powder. Like a blunt icicle in her white mackintosh she stood in the doorway with her back to them, then melted into the afternoon.

'Who is she?' Philip asked. 'Is she your niece?'

'Oh, yes,' Baines said, 'that's who she is; she's my niece,' and poured the last drops of water on to the coarse black leaves in the teapot.

'May as well have another cup,' Baines said.

'The cup that cheers,' he said hopelessly, watching the bitter black fluid drain out of the spout.

'Have a glass of ginger pop, Phil?'

'I'm sorry. I'm sorry, Baines.'

'It's not your fault, Phil. Why, I could really believe it wasn't you at all, but her. She creeps in everywhere.' He fished two leaves out of his cup and laid them on the back of his hand, a thin soft flake and a hard stalk. He beat them with his hand: 'Today,' and the stalk detached itself, 'tomorrow, Wednesday, Thursday, Friday, Saturday, Sunday,' but the flake wouldn't come, stayed where it was, drying under his blows, with a resistance you wouldn't believe it to possess. 'The tough one wins,' Baines said.

He got up and paid the bill and out they went into the street. Baines said, 'I don't ask you to say what isn't true. But you needn't actually *tell* Mrs Baines you met us here.'

'Of course not,' Philip said, and catching something of Sir Hubert Reed's manner, 'I understand, Baines.' But he didn't understand a thing; he was caught up in other people's darkness.

'It was stupid,' Baines said. 'So near home, but I hadn't time to think, you see. I'd got to see her.'

'Of course, Baines.'

'I haven't time to spare,' Baines said. 'I'm not young. I've got to see that she's all right.'

'Of course you have, Baines.'

'Mrs Baines will get it out of you if she can.'

'You can trust me, Baines,' Philip said in a dry important Reed voice;

and then, 'Look out. She's at the window watching.' And there indeed she was, looking up at them, between the lace curtains, from the basement room, speculating. 'Need we go in, Baines?' Philip asked, cold lying heavy on his stomach like too much pudding; he clutched Baines's arm.

'Careful,' Baines said softly, 'careful.'

'But need we go in, Baines? It's early. Take me for a walk in the park.'

'Better not.'

'But I'm frightened, Baines.'

'You haven't any cause,' Baines said. 'Nothing's going to hurt you. You just run along upstairs to the nursery. I'll go down by the area[8] and talk to Mrs Baines.' But he stood hesitating at the top of the stone steps pretending not to see her, where she watched between the curtains. 'In at the front door, Phil, and up the stairs.'

Philip didn't linger in the hall; he ran, slithering on the parquet Mrs Baines had polished, to the stairs. Through the drawing-room doorway on the first floor he saw the draped chairs; even the china clock on the mantel was covered like a canary's cage. As he passed, it chimed the hour, muffled and secret under the duster. On the nursery table he found his supper laid out: a glass of milk and a piece of bread and butter, a sweet biscuit, and a little cold Queen's pudding without the meringue. He had no appetite; he strained his ears for Mrs Baines's coming, for the sound of voices, but the basement held its secrets; the green baize door shut off that world. He drank the milk and ate the biscuit, but he didn't touch the rest, and presently he could hear the soft precise footfalls of Mrs Baines on the stairs: she was a good servant, she walked softly; she was a determined woman, she walked precisely.

But she wasn't angry when she came in; she was ingratiating as she opened the night nursery door—'Did you have a good walk, Master Philip?'—pulled down the blinds, laid out his pyjamas, came back to clear his supper. 'I'm glad Baines found you. Your mother wouldn't have liked your being out alone.' She examined the tray. 'Not much appetite, have you, Master Philip? Why don't you try a little of this nice pudding? I'll bring you up some more jam for it.'

'No, no, thank you, Mrs Baines,' Philip said.

'You ought to eat more,' Mrs Baines said. She sniffed round the room like a dog. 'You didn't take any pots out of the wastepaper basket in the kitchen, did you, Master Philip?'

[8] Sunken space or court adjoining basement entrance to building.

'No,' Philip said.

'Of course you wouldn't. I just wanted to make sure.' She patted his shoulder and her fingers flashed to his lapel; she picked off a tiny crumb of pink sugar. 'Oh, Master Philip,' she said, 'that's why you haven't any appetite. You've been buying sweet cakes. That's not what your pocket money's for.'

'But I didn't,' Philip said, 'I didn't.'

She tasted the sugar with the tip of her tongue.

'Don't tell lies to me, Master Philip. I won't stand for it any more than your father would.'

'I didn't, I didn't,' Philip said. 'They gave it me. I mean Baines,' but she had pounced on the word 'they'. She had got what she wanted; there was no doubt about that, even when you didn't know what it was she wanted. Philip was angry and miserable and disappointed because he hadn't kept Baines's secret. Baines oughtn't to have trusted him; grown-up people should keep their own secrets, and yet here was Mrs Baines immediately entrusting him with another.

'Let me tickle your palm and see if you can keep a secret.' But he put his hand behind him; he wouldn't be touched. 'It's a secret between us, Master Philip, that I know all about them. I suppose she was having tea with him,' she speculated.

'Why shouldn't she?' he asked, the responsibility for Baines weighing on his spirit, the idea that he had got to keep her secret when he hadn't kept Baines's making him miserable with the unfairness of life. 'She was nice.'

'She was nice, was she?' Mrs Baines said in a bitter voice he wasn't used to.

'And she's his niece.'

'So that's what he said,' Mrs Baines struck softly back at him like the clock under the duster. She tried to be jocular. 'The old scoundrel. Don't you tell him I know, Master Philip.' She stood very still between the table and the door, thinking very hard, planning something. 'Promise you won't tell. I'll give you that Meccano set, Master Philip . . .'

He turned his back on her; he wouldn't promise, but he wouldn't tell. He would have nothing to do with their secrets, the responsibilities they were determined to lay on him. He was only anxious to forget. He had received already a larger dose of life than he had bargained for, and he was scared. 'A 2A Meccano set, Master Philip.' He never opened his Meccano set again, never built anything, never created anything, died the old dilettante, sixty years later with nothing to show rather than preserve the memory of Mrs Baines's malicious voice saying good night, her soft determined footfalls on the stairs to the basement, going down, going down.

III

The sun poured in between the curtains and Baines was beating a tattoo on the water-can. 'Glory, glory,' Baines said. He sat down on the end of the bed and said, 'I beg to announce that Mrs Baines has been called away. Her mother's dying. She won't be back till tomorrow.'

'Why did you wake me up so early?' Philip complained. He watched Baines with uneasiness; he wasn't going to be drawn in; he'd learnt his lesson. It wasn't right for a man of Baines's age to be so merry. It made a grown person human in the same way that you were human. For if a grown-up could behave so childishly, you were liable to find yourself in their world. It was enough that it came at you in dreams: the witch at the corner, the man with a knife. So 'It's very early,' he whined, even though he loved Baines, even though he couldn't help being glad that Baines was happy. He was divided by the fear and the attraction of life.

'I want to make this a long day,' Baines said. 'This is the best time.' He pulled the curtains back. 'It's a bit misty. The cat's been out all night. There she is, sniffing round the area. They haven't taken in any milk at 59. Emma's shaking out the mats at 63.' He said, 'This was what I used to think about on the Coast: somebody shaking mats and the cat coming home. I can see it today,' Baines said, 'just as if I was still in Africa. Most days you don't notice what you've got. It's a good life if you don't weaken.' He put a penny on the washstand. 'When you've dressed, Phil, run and get a *Mail* from the barrow[9] at the corner. I'll be cooking the sausages.'

'Sausages?'

'Sausages,' Baines said. 'We're going to celebrate today.' He celebrated at breakfast, restless, cracking jokes, unaccountably merry and nervous. It was going to be a long, long day, he kept on coming back to that: for years he had waited for a long day, he had sweated in the damp Coast heat, changed shirts, gone down with fever, lain between the blankets and sweated, all in the hope of this long day, that cat sniffing round the area, a bit of mist, the mats beaten at 63. He propped the *Mail* in front of the coffee-pot and read pieces aloud.

[9] Cart from which newspapers and other items are sold.

He said, 'Cora Down's been married for the fourth time.' He was amused, but it wasn't his idea of a long day. His long day was the Park, watching the riders in the Row,[10] seeing Sir Arthur Stillwater pass beyond the rails ('He dined with us once in Bo;[11] up from Freetown;[12] he was governor there'), lunch at the Corner House for Philip's sake (he'd have preferred himself a glass of stout and some oysters at the York bar), the Zoo,[13] the long bus ride home in the last summer light: the leaves in the Green Park were beginning to turn and the motors nuzzled out of Berkeley Street with the low sun gently glowing on their windscreens. Baines envied no one, not Cora Down, or Sir Arthur Stillwater, or Lord Sandale, who came out on to the steps of the Army and Navy[14] and then went back again—he hadn't anything to do and might as well look at another paper. 'I said don't let me see you touch that black again.' Baines had led a man's life; everyone on top of the bus pricked his ears when he told Philip all about it.

'Would you have shot him?' Philip asked, and Baines put his head back and tilted his dark respectable manservant's hat to a better angle as the bus swerved round the Artillery Memorial.

'I wouldn't have thought twice about it. I'd have shot to kill,' he boasted, and the bowed figure went by, the steel helmet, the heavy cloak, the down-turned rifle and the folded hands.

'Have you got the revolver?'

'Of course I've got it,' Baines said. 'Don't I need it with all the burglaries there've been?' This was the Baines whom Philip loved: not Baines singing and carefree, but Baines responsible, Baines behind barriers, living his man's life.

All the buses streamed out from Victoria like a convoy of aeroplanes to bring Baines home with honour. 'Forty blacks under me,' and there waiting near the area steps was the proper reward, love at lighting-up time.

'It's your niece,' Philip said, recognizing the white mackintosh, but not the happy sleepy face. She frightened him like an unlucky number; he nearly told Baines what Mrs Baines had said; but he didn't want to bother, he wanted to leave things alone.

'Why, so it is,' Baines said. 'I shouldn't wonder if she was going to

10 Rotten Row: area in Hyde Park set aside for horseback riding.

11 Second largest city in Sierra Leone.

12 Capital of Sierra Leone.

13 Zoological garden in Regent's Park.

14 London department store.

have a bit of supper with us.' But, he said, they'd play a game, pretend they didn't know her, slip down the area steps, 'and here,' Baines said, 'we are,' lay the table, put out the cold sausages, a bottle of beer, a bottle of ginger pop, a flagon of harvest burgundy. 'Everyone his own drink,' Baines said. 'Run upstairs, Phil, and see if there's been a post.'

Philip didn't like the empty house at dusk before the lights went on. He hurried. He wanted to be back with Baines. The hall lay there in quiet and shadow prepared to show him something he didn't want to see. Some letters rustled down and someone knocked. 'Open in the name of the Republic.' The tumbrils rolled, the head bobbed in the bloody basket.[15] Knock, knock, and the postman's footsteps going away. Philip gathered the letters. The slit in the door was like the grating in a jeweller's window. He remembered the policeman he had seen peer through. He had said to his nurse, 'What's he doing?' and when she said, 'He's seeing if everything's all right,' his brain immediately filled with images of all that might be wrong. He ran to the baize door and the stairs. The girl was already there and Baines was kissing her. She leant breathless against the dresser.

'Here's Emmy, Phil.'

'There's a letter for you, Baines.'

'Emmy,' Baines said, 'it's from her.' But he wouldn't open it. 'You bet she's coming back.'

'We'll have supper, anyway,' Emmy said. 'She can't harm that.'

'You don't know her,' Baines said. 'Nothing's safe. Damn it,' he said, 'I was a man once,' and he opened the letter.

'Can I start?' Philip asked, but Baines didn't hear; he presented in his stillness an example of the importance grown-up people attached to the written word: you had to write your thanks, not wait and speak them, as if letters couldn't lie. But Philip knew better than that, sprawling his thanks across a page to Aunt Alice who had given him a teddy bear he was too old for. Letters could lie all right, but they made the lie permanent. They lay as evidence against you: they made you meaner than the spoken word.

'She's not coming back till tomorrow night,' Baines said. He opened the bottles, he pulled up the chairs, he kissed Emmy again against the dresser.

'You oughtn't to,' Emmy said, 'with the boy here.'

'He's got to learn,' Baines said, 'like the rest of us,' and he helped

[15] Allusion to the Reign of Terror (1793–1794) during the French Revolution, as is the "tricolour hat" on page 433.

Philip to three sausages. He only took one himself; he said he wasn't hungry, but when Emmy said she wasn't hungry either he stood over her and made her eat. He was timid and rough with her and made her drink the harvest burgundy because he said she needed building up; he wouldn't take no for an answer, but when he touched her his hands were light and clumsy too, as if he was afraid to damage something delicate and didn't know how to handle anything so light.

'This is better than milk and biscuits, eh?'

'Yes,' Philip said, but he was scared, scared for Baines as much as for himself. He couldn't help wondering at every bite, at every draught of the ginger pop, what Mrs Baines would say if she ever learnt of this meal; he couldn't imagine it, there was a depth of bitterness and rage in Mrs Baines you couldn't sound. He said, 'She won't be coming back tonight?' but you could tell by the way they immediately understood him that she wasn't really away at all; she was there in the basement with them, driving them to longer drinks and louder talk, biding her time for the right cutting word. Baines wasn't really happy; he was only watching happiness from close to instead of from far away.

'No,' he said, 'she'll not be back till late tomorrow.' He couldn't keep his eyes off happiness. He'd not played around as much as other men; he kept on reverting to the Coast as if to excuse himself for his innocence. He wouldn't have been so innocent if he'd lived his life in London, so innocent when it came to tenderness. 'If it was you, Emmy,' he said, looking at the white dresser, the scrubbed chairs, 'this'd be like a home.' Already the room was not quite so harsh; there was a little dust in corners, the silver needed a final polish, the morning's paper lay untidily on a chair. 'You'd better go to bed, Phil; it's been a long day.'

They didn't leave him to find his own way up through the dark shrouded house; they went with him, turning on lights, touching each other's fingers on the switches. Floor after floor they drove the night back. They spoke softly among the covered chairs. They watched him undress, they didn't make him wash or clean his teeth, they saw him into bed and lit his night-light and left his door ajar. He could hear their voices on the stairs, friendly like the guests he heard at dinner-parties when they moved down the hall, saying good night. They belonged; wherever they were they made a home. He heard a door open and a clock strike, he heard their voices for a long while, so that he felt they were not far away and he was safe. The voices didn't dwindle, they simply went out, and he could be sure that they were still somewhere not far from him, silent together in one of the many empty rooms, growing sleepy together as he grew sleepy after the long day.

He just had time to sigh faintly with satisfaction, because this too perhaps had been life, before he slept and the inevitable terrors of sleep came round him: a man with a tricolour hat beat at the door on His Majesty's service, a bleeding head lay on the kitchen table in a basket, and the Siberian wolves crept closer. He was bound hand and foot and couldn't move; they leapt round him breathing heavily; he opened his eyes and Mrs Baines was there, her grey untidy hair in threads over his face, her black hat askew. A loose hairpin fell on the pillow and one musty thread brushed his mouth. 'Where are they?' she whispered. 'Where are they?'

IV

Philip watched her in terror. Mrs Baines was out of breath as if she had been searching all the empty rooms, looking under loose covers.

With her untidy grey hair and her black dress buttoned to her throat, her gloves of black cotton, she was so like the witches of his dreams that he didn't dare to speak. There was a stale smell in her breath.

'She's here,' Mrs Baines said, 'you can't deny she's here.' Her face was simultaneously marked with cruelty and misery; she wanted to 'do things' to people, but she suffered all the time. It would have done her good to scream, but she daren't do that: it would warn them. She came ingratiatingly back to the bed where Philip lay rigid on his back and whispered, 'I haven't forgotten the Meccano set. You shall have it to-morrow, Master Philip. We've got secrets together, haven't we? Just tell me where they are.'

He couldn't speak. Fear held him as firmly as any nightmare. She said, 'Tell Mrs Baines, Master Philip. You love your Mrs Baines, don't you?' That was too much; he couldn't speak, but he could move his mouth in terrified denial, wince away from her dusty image.

She whispered, coming closer to him, 'Such deceit. I'll tell your father. I'll settle with you myself when I've found them. You'll smart; I'll see you smart.' Then immediately she was still, listening. A board had creaked on the floor below, and a moment later, while she stooped listening above his bed, there came the whispers of two people who were happy and sleepy together after a long day. The night-light stood beside the mirror and Mrs Baines could see there her own reflection, misery and cruelty wavering in the glass, age and dust and nothing to hope for. She sobbed without tears, a dry, breathless sound, but her cruelty was a kind of pride which kept her going; it was her best quality, she would have been merely pitiable without it. She went out of the door on tiptoe, feeling her way across the landing, going so softly down the stairs that no one behind a shut door could hear her. Then there was complete silence again; Philip could move; he raised his knees; he sat up in bed; he wanted to die. It wasn't fair, the walls were down again between his world and theirs, but this time it was something worse than merriment that the grown people made him share; a passion moved in the house he recognized but could not understand.

It wasn't fair, but he owed Baines everything: the Zoo, the ginger pop, the bus ride home. Even the supper called to his loyalty. But he was frightened; he was touching something he touched in dreams; the bleeding head, the wolves, the knock, knock, knock. Life fell on him with savagery, and you couldn't blame him if he never faced it again in sixty years. He got out of bed. Carefully from habit he put on his bedroom slippers and tiptoed to the door: it wasn't quite dark on the landing below because the curtains had been taken down for the cleaners and the light from the street washed in through the tall windows. Mrs Baines had her hand on the glass door-knob; she was very carefully turning it; he screamed: 'Baines, Baines.'

Mrs Baines turned and saw him cowering in his pyjamas by the banisters; he was helpless, more helpless even than Baines, and cruelty grew at the sight of him and drove her up the stairs. The nightmare was on him again and he couldn't move; he hadn't any more courage left, he couldn't even scream.

But the first cry brought Baines out of the best spare bedroom and he moved quicker than Mrs Baines. She hadn't reached the top of the stairs before he'd caught her round the waist. She drove her black cotton gloves at his face and he bit her hand. He hadn't time to think, he fought her like a stranger, but she fought back with knowledgeable hate. She was going to teach them all and it didn't really matter whom she began with; they had all deceived her; but the old image in the glass was by her side, telling her she must be dignified, she wasn't young enough to yield her dignity; she could beat his face, but she mustn't bite; she could push, but she mustn't kick.

Age and dust and nothing to hope for were her handicaps. She went over the banisters in a flurry of black clothes and fell into the hall; she lay before the front door like a sack of coals which should have gone down the area into the basement. Philip saw; Emmy saw; she sat down suddenly in the doorway of the best spare bedroom with her eyes open as if she were too tired to stand any longer. Baines went slowly down into the hall.

It wasn't hard for Philip to escape; they'd forgotten him completely. He went down the back, the servants' stairs, because Mrs Baines was in the hall. He didn't understand what she was doing lying there; like the pictures in a book no one had read to him, the things he didn't understand terrified him. The whole house had been turned over to the grown-up world; he wasn't safe in the night nursery; their passions had flooded in. The only thing he could do was to get away, by the back stairs, and up through the area, and never come back. He didn't think of the cold, of the need for food and sleep; for an hour it would seem quite possible to escape from people for ever.

He was wearing pyjamas and bedroom slippers when he came up into the square, but there was no one to see him. It was that hour of the evening in a residential district when everyone is at the theatre or at home. He climbed over the iron railings into the little garden: the plane-trees spread their large pale palms between him and the sky. It might have been an illimitable forest into which he had escaped. He crouched behind a trunk and the wolves retreated; it seemed to him between the little iron seat and the tree-trunk that no one would ever find him again. A kind of embittered happiness and self-pity made him cry; he was lost; there wouldn't be any more secrets to keep; he surrendered responsibility once and for all. Let grown-up people keep to their world and he would keep to his, safe in the small garden between the plane-trees.

Presently the door of 48 opened and Baines looked this way and that; then he signalled with his hand and Emmy came; it was as if they were only just in time for a train, they hadn't a chance of saying good-bye. She went quickly by like a face at a window swept past the platform, pale and unhappy and not wanting to go. Baines went in again and shut the door; the light was lit in the basement, and a policeman walked round the square, looking into the areas. You could tell how many families were at home by the lights behind the first-floor[16] curtains.

Philip explored the garden: it didn't take long: a twenty-yard square of bushes and plane-trees, two iron seats and a gravel path, a padlocked gate at either end, a scuffle of old leaves. But he couldn't stay: something stirred in the bushes and two illuminated eyes peered out at him like a Siberian wolf, and he thought how terrible it would be if Mrs Baines found him there. He'd have no time to climb the railings; she'd seize him from behind.

He left the square at the unfashionable end and was immediately

[16] Floor immediately above the ground floor (second floor).

among the fish-and-chip shops, the little stationers selling *Bagatelle*,[17] among the accommodation addresses[18] and the dingy hotels with open doors. There were few people about because the pubs were open, but a blowsy woman carrying a parcel called out to him across the street and the commissionaire[19] outside a cinema would have stopped him if he hadn't crossed the road. He went deeper: you could go farther and lose yourself more completely here than among the plane-trees. On the fringe of the square he was in danger of being stopped and taken back: it was obvious where he belonged; but as he went deeper he lost the marks of his origin. It was a warm night: any child in those free-living parts might be expected to play truant from bed. He found a kind of camaraderie even among grown-up people; he might have been a neighbour's child as he went quickly by, but they weren't going to tell on him, they'd been young once themselves. He picked up a protective coating of dust from the pavements, of smuts from the trains which passed along the backs in a spray of fire. Once he was caught in a knot of children running away from something or somebody, laughing as they ran; he was whirled with them round a turning and abandoned, with a sticky fruit-drop in his hand.

He couldn't have been more lost, but he hadn't the stamina to keep on. At first he feared that someone would stop him; after an hour he hoped that someone would. He couldn't find his way back, and in any case he was afraid of arriving home alone; he was afraid of Mrs Baines, more afraid than he had ever been. Baines was his friend, but something had happened which gave Mrs Baines all the power. He began to loiter on purpose to be noticed, but no one noticed him. Families were having a last breather on the doorsteps, the refuse bins had been put out and bits of cabbage stalks soiled his slippers. The air was full of voices, but he was cut off; these people were strangers and would always now be strangers; they were marked by Mrs Baines and he shied away from them into a deep class-consciousness. He had been afraid of policemen, but now he wanted one to take him home; even Mrs Baines could do nothing against a policeman. He sidled past a constable who was directing traffic, but he was too busy to pay him any attention. Philip sat down against a wall and cried.

[17] Game in which small balls are struck into numbered holes on a board having a semicircular end.

[18] Location to which letters are sent for a person either having no permanent address or wishing to conceal it.

[19] Doorman.

It hadn't occurred to him that that was the easiest way, that all you had to do was to surrender, to show you were beaten and accept kindness.... It was lavished on him at once by two women and a pawnbroker. Another policeman appeared, a young man with a sharp incredulous face. He looked as if he noted everything he saw in pocketbooks and drew conclusions. A woman offered to see Philip home, but he didn't trust her: she wasn't a match for Mrs Baines immobile in the hall. He wouldn't give his address; he said he was afraid to go home. He had his way; he got his protection. 'I'll take him to the station,' the policeman said, and holding him awkwardly by the hand (he wasn't married; he had his career to make) he led him round the corner, up the stone stairs into the little bare over-heated room where Justice lived.

V

Justice waited behind a wooden counter on a high stool; it wore a heavy moustache; it was kindly and had six children ('three of them nippers like yourself'); it wasn't really interested in Philip, but it pretended to be, it wrote the address down and sent a constable to fetch a glass of milk. But the young constable was interested; he had a nose for things.

'Your home's on the telephone, I suppose,' Justice said. 'We'll ring them up and say you are safe. They'll fetch you very soon. What's your name, sonny?'

'Philip.'

'Your other name?'

'I haven't got another name.' He didn't want to be fetched; he wanted to be taken home by someone who would impress even Mrs Baines. The constable watched him, watched the way he drank the milk, watched him when he winced away from questions.

'What made you run away? Playing truant, eh?'

'I don't know.'

'You oughtn't to do it, young fellow. Think how anxious your father and mother will be.'

'They are away.'

'Well, your nurse.'

'I haven't got one.'

'Who looks after you, then?' The question went home. Philip saw Mrs Baines coming up the stairs at him, the heap of black cotton in the hall. He began to cry.

'Now, now, now,' the sergeant said. He didn't know what to do; he wished his wife were with him; even a policewoman might have been useful.

'Don't you think it's funny,' the constable said, 'that there hasn't been an inquiry?'

'They think he's tucked up in bed.'

'You are scared, aren't you?' the constable said. 'What scared you?'

'I don't know.'

'Somebody hurt you?'

'No.'

'He's had bad dreams,' the sergeant said. 'Thought the house was on fire, I expect. I've brought up six of them. Rose is due back. She'll take him home.'

'I want to go home with you,' Philip said; he tried to smile at the constable, but the deceit was immature and unsuccessful.

'I'd better go,' the constable said. 'There may be something wrong.'

'Nonsense,' the sergeant said. 'It's a woman's job. Tact is what you need. Here's Rose. Pull up your stockings, Rose. You're a disgrace to the Force. I've got a job of work for you.' Rose shambled in: black cotton stockings drooping over her boots, a gawky Girl Guide manner, a hoarse hostile voice. 'More tarts, I suppose.'

'No, you've got to see this young man home.' She looked at him owlishly.

'I won't go with her,' Philip said. He began to cry again. 'I don't like her.'

'More of that womanly charm, Rose,' the sergeant said. The telephone rang on his desk. He lifted the receiver. 'What? What's that?' he said. 'Number 48? You've got a doctor?' He put his hand over the telephone mouth. 'No wonder this nipper wasn't reported,' he said. 'They've been too busy. An accident. Woman slipped on the stairs.'

'Serious?' the constable asked. The sergeant mouthed at him; you didn't mention the word death before a child (didn't he know? he had six of them), you made noises in the throat, you grimaced, a complicated shorthand for a word of only five letters anyway.

'You'd better go, after all,' he said, 'and make a report. The doctor's there.'

Rose shambled from the stove; pink apply-dapply cheeks, loose stockings. She stuck her hands behind her. Her large morgue-like mouth was full of blackened teeth. 'You told me to take him and now just because something interesting . . . I don't expect justice from a man . . .'

'Who's at the house?' the constable asked.

'The butler.'

'You don't think,' the constable said, 'he saw . . .'

'Trust me,' the sergeant said. 'I've brought up six. I know 'em through and through. You can't teach me anything about children.'

'He seemed scared about something.'

'Dreams,' the sergeant said.

'What name?'

'Baines.'

'This Mr Baines,' the constable said to Philip, 'you like him, eh? He's good to you?' They were trying to get something out of him; he was suspicious of the whole roomful of them; he said 'yes' without conviction because he was afraid at any moment of more responsibilities, more secrets.

'And Mrs Baines?'

'Yes.'

They consulted together by the desk. Rose was hoarsely aggrieved; she was like a female impersonator, she bore her womanhood with an unnatural emphasis even while she scorned it in her creased stockings and her weather-exposed face. The charcoal shifted in the stove; the room was over-heated in the mild late summer evening. A notice on the wall described a body found in the Thames, or rather the body's clothes: wool vest,[20] wool pants, wool shirt with blue stripes, size ten boots, blue serge suit worn at the elbows, fifteen and a half celluloid collar. They couldn't find anything to say about the body, except its measurements, it was just an ordinary body.

'Come along,' the constable said. He was interested, he was glad to be going, but he couldn't help being embarrassed by his company, a small boy in pyjamas. His nose smelt something, he didn't know what, but he smarted at the sight of the amusement they caused: the pubs had closed and the streets were full again of men making as long a day of it as they could. He hurried through the less frequented streets, chose the darker pavements, wouldn't loiter, and Philip wanted more and more to loiter, pulling at his hand, dragging with his feet. He dreaded the sight of Mrs Baines waiting in the hall: he knew now that she was dead. The sergeant's mouthing had conveyed that; but she wasn't buried, she wasn't out of sight; he was going to see a dead person in the hall when the door opened.

The light was on in the basement, and to his relief the constable made

[20] Undershirt.

for the area steps. Perhaps he wouldn't have to see Mrs Baines at all. The constable knocked on the door because it was too dark to see the bell, and Baines answered. He stood there in the doorway of the neat bright basement room and you could see the sad complacent plausible sentence he had prepared wither at the sight of Philip; he hadn't expected Philip to return like that in the policeman's company. He had to begin thinking all over again; he wasn't a deceptive man. If it hadn't been for Emmy he would have been quite ready to let the truth lead him where it would.

'Mr Baines?' the constable asked.

He nodded; he hadn't found the right words; he was daunted by the shrewd knowing face, the sudden appearance of Philip there.

'This little boy from here?'

'Yes,' Baines said. Philip could tell that there was a message he was trying to convey, but he shut his mind to it. He loved Baines, but Baines had involved him in secrets, in fears he didn't understand. That was what happened when you loved—you got involved; and Philip extricated himself from life, from love, from Baines.

'The doctor's here,' Baines said. He nodded at the door, moistened his mouth, kept his eyes on Philip, begging for something like a dog you can't understand, 'There's nothing to be done. She slipped on these stone basement stairs. I was in here. I heard her fall.' He wouldn't look at the notebook, at the constable's spidery writing which got a terrible lot on one page.

'Did the boy see anything?'

'He can't have done. I thought he was in bed. Hadn't he better go up? It's a shocking thing. O,' Baines said, losing control, 'it's a shocking thing for a child.'

'She's through there?' the constable asked.

'I haven't moved her an inch,' Baines said.

'He'd better then—'

'Go up the area and through the hall,' Baines said, and again he begged dumbly like a dog: one more secret, keep this secret, do this for old Baines, he won't ask another.

'Come along,' the constable said. 'I'll see you up to bed. You're a gentleman. You must come in the proper way through the front door like the master should. Or will you go along with him, Mr. Baines, while I see the doctor?'

'Yes,' Baines said, 'I'll go.' He came across the room to Philip, begging, begging, all the way with his old soft stupid expression: this is Baines, the old Coaster; what about a palm-oil chop, eh?; a man's life;

forty niggers; never used a gun; I tell you I couldn't help loving them; it wasn't what we call love, nothing we could understand. The messages flickered out from the last posts at the border, imploring, beseeching, reminding: this is your old friend Baines; what about an elevenses;[21] a glass of ginger pop won't do you any harm; sausages; a long day. But the wires were cut, the messages just faded out into the vacancy of the scrubbed room in which there had never been a place where a man could hide his secrets.

'Come along, Phil, it's bedtime. We'll just go up the steps . . .' Tap, tap, tap, at the telegraph; you may get through, you can't tell, somebody may mend the right wire. 'And in at the front door.'

'No,' Philip said, 'no. I won't go. You can't make me go. I'll fight. I won't see her.'

The constable turned on them quickly. 'What's that? Why won't you go?'

'She's in the hall,' Philip said. 'I know she's in the hall. And she's dead. I won't see her.'

'You moved her then?' the constable said to Baines. 'All the way down here? You've been lying, eh? That means you had to tidy up. . . . Were you alone?'

'Emmy,' Philip said, 'Emmy.' He wasn't going to keep any more secrets: he was going to finish once and for all with everything, with Baines and Mrs Baines and the grown-up life beyond him. 'It was all Emmy's fault,' he protested with a quaver which reminded Baines that after all he was only a child; it had been hopeless to expect help there; he was a child; he didn't understand what it all meant; he couldn't read this shorthand of terror; he'd had a long day and he was tired out. You could see him dropping asleep where he stood against the dresser, dropping back into the comfortable nursery peace. You couldn't blame him. When he woke in the morning, he'd hardly remember a thing.

'Out with it,' the constable said, addressing Baines with professional ferocity, 'who is she?' just as the old man sixty years later startled his secretary, his only watcher, asking, 'Who is she? Who is she?' dropping lower and lower into death, passing on the way perhaps the image of Baines: Baines hopeless, Baines letting his head drop, Baines 'coming clean'.

1936

[21] Snack with beverage, usually taken around 11 A.M.

DISCUSSION QUESTIONS

1. In what ways would Greene's story be different without Philip's presence? Would it hold your interest? Explain. Specifically, how is Philip entangled in the story's love triangle? How is Mrs. Baines's suspicion about her husband first aroused?

2. Which characters do we see internally? Define the narrator's attitude toward Baines, Mrs. Baines, and Philip. Cite specific examples and show by what means the narrator conveys his attitude toward these characters.

3. What changes would have occurred to the story if it had been narrated exclusively through Philip's or Baines's *point of view?* How does the narrator's foreknowledge help or hinder the story?

4. Why does Philip love "not Baines singing and carefree, but Baines responsible, Baines behind barriers, living his man's life" (page 430)?

5. Describe Philip's two worlds separated by the "green baize door." Explain the following statement: "he wasn't safe in the night nursery; their passions had flooded in" (page 435).

6. What does Philip discover about Mrs. Baines when he stands in the doorway of the tearoom? Explain each of the three *metaphors* by which he describes her. What brings about his insight at this point in the story?

7. What causal relationship is implied in the following quotation, used by Greene in an earlier version of his story: "In the lost childhood of Judas Christ was betrayed"? How is it applicable to "The Basement Room"?

NEXT DOOR

KURT VONNEGUT

THE OLD house was divided into two dwellings by a thin wall that passed on, with high fidelity, sounds on either side. On the north side were the Leonards. On the south side were the Hargers.

The Leonards—husband, wife, and eight-year-old son—had just moved in. And, aware of the wall, they kept their voices down as they argued in a friendly way as to whether or not the boy, Paul, was old enough to be left alone for the evening.

"Shhhhh!" said Paul's father.

"Was I shouting?" said his mother. "I was talking in a perfectly normal tone."

"If I could hear Harger pulling a cork, he can certainly hear you," said his father.

"I didn't say anything I'd be ashamed to have anybody hear," said Mrs. Leonard.

"You called Paul a baby," said Mr. Leonard. "That certainly embarrasses Paul—and it embarrasses me."

"It's just a way of talking," she said.

"It's a way we've got to stop," he said. "And we can stop treating him like a baby, too—*tonight.* We simply shake his hand, walk out, and go to the movie." He turned to Paul. "You're not afraid—are you boy?"

"I'll be all right," said Paul. He was very tall for his age, and thin, and had a soft, sleepy, radiant sweetness engendered by his mother. "I'm fine."

"Damn right!" said his father, clouting him on the back. "It'll be an adventure."

"I'd feel better about this adventure, if we could get a sitter," said his mother.

"If it's going to spoil the picture for you," said his father, "let's take him with us."

Mrs. Leonard was shocked. "Oh—it isn't for children."

"I don't care," said Paul amiably. The why of their not wanting him to see certain movies, certain magazines, certain books, certain television shows was a mystery he respected—even relished a little.

"It wouldn't kill him to see it," said his father.

"You *know* what it's about," she said.

"What *is* it about?" said Paul innocently.

Mrs. Leonard looked to her husband for help, and got none. "It's about a girl who chooses her friends unwisely," she said.

"Oh," said Paul. "That doesn't sound very interesting."

"Are we going, or aren't we?" said Mr. Leonard impatiently. "The show starts in ten minutes."

Mrs. Leonard bit her lip. "All right!" she said bravely. "You lock the windows and the back door, and I'll write down the telephone numbers for the police and the fire department and the theater and Dr. Failey." She turned to Paul. "You *can* dial, can't you, dear?"

"He's been dialing for years!" cried Mr. Leonard.

"Ssssssh!" said Mrs. Leonard.

"Sorry," Mr. Leonard bowed to the wall. "My apologies."

"Paul, dear," said Mrs. Leonard, "what are you going to do while we're gone?"

"Oh—look through my microscope, I guess," said Paul.

"You're not going to be looking at germs, are you?" she said.

"Nope—just hair, sugar, pepper, stuff like that," said Paul.

His mother frowned judiciously. "I think that would be all right, don't you?" she said to Mr. Leonard.

"Fine!" said Mr. Leonard. "Just as long as the pepper doesn't make him sneeze!"

"I'll be careful," said Paul.

Mr. Leonard winced. "Shhhhh!" he said.

Soon after Paul's parents left, the radio in the Harger apartment went on. It was on softly at first—so softly that Paul, looking through his microscope on the living room coffee table, couldn't make out the announcer's words. The music was frail and dissonant—unidentifiable.

Gamely, Paul tried to listen to the music rather than to the man and woman who were fighting.

Paul squinted through the eyepiece of his microscope at a bit of his hair far below, and he turned a knob to bring the hair into focus. It looked like a glistening brown eel, flecked here and there with tiny spectra where the light struck the hair just so.

There—the voices of the man and woman were getting louder again, drowning out the radio. Paul twisted the microscope knob nervously, and the objective lens ground into the glass slide on which the hair rested.

The woman was shouting now.

Paul unscrewed the lens, and examined it for damage.

Now the man shouted back—shouted something awful, unbelievable.

Paul got a sheet of lens tissue from his bedroom, and dusted at the frosted dot on the lens, where the lens had bitten into the slide. He screwed the lens back in place.

All was quiet again next door—except for the radio.

Paul looked down into the microscope, down into the milky mist of the damaged lens.

Now the fight was beginning again—louder and louder, cruel and crazy.

Trembling, Paul sprinkled grains of salt on a fresh slide, and put it under the microscope.

The woman shouted again, a high, ragged, poisonous shout.

Paul turned the knob too hard, and the fresh slide cracked and fell in triangles to the floor. Paul stood, shaking, wanting to shout, too—to shout in terror and bewilderment. It had to stop. Whatever it was, it *had* to stop!

"If you're going to yell, turn up the radio!" the man cried.

Paul heard the clicking of the woman's heels across the floor. The radio volume swelled until the boom of the bass made Paul feel like he was trapped in a drum.

"And now!" bellowed the radio, "for Katy from Fred! For Nancy from Bob, who thinks she's swell! For Arthur, from one who's worshipped him from afar for six weeks! Here's the old Glenn Miller Band and that all-time favorite, *Stardust!* Remember! If you have a dedication, call Milton nine-three-thousand! Ask for All-Night Sam, the record man!"

The music picked up the house and shook it.

A door slammed next door. Now someone hammered on a door.

Paul looked down into his microscope once more, looked at nothing—while a prickling sensation spread over his skin. He faced the truth: The man and woman would kill each other, if he didn't stop them.

He beat on the wall with his fist. "Mr. Harger! Stop it!" he cried. "Mrs. Harger! Stop it!"

"For Ollie from Lavina!" All-Night Sam cried back at him. "For Ruth from Carl, who'll never forget last Tuesday! For Wilbur from Mary, who's lonesome tonight! Here's the Sauter-Finnegan Band asking, *Love, What Are You Doing to My Heart?*"

Next door, crockery smashed, filling a split second of radio silence. And then the tidal wave of music drowned everything again.

Paul stood by the wall, trembling in his helplessness. "Mr. Harger! Mrs. Harger! Please!"

"Remember the number!" said All-Night Sam. "Milton nine-three-thousand!"

Dazed, Paul went to the phone and dialed the number.

"WJCD," said the switchboard operator.

"Would you kindly connect me with All-Night Sam?" said Paul.

"Hello!" said All-Night Sam. He was eating, talking with a full mouth. In the background, Paul could hear sweet, bleating music, the original of what was rending the radio next door.

"I wonder if I might make a dedication," said Paul.

"Dunno why not," said Sam. "Ever belong to any organization listed as subversive by the Attorney General's office?"

Paul thought a moment. "Nossir—I don't think so, sir," he said.

"Shoot," said Sam.

"From Mr. Lemuel K. Harger to Mrs. Harger," said Paul.

"What's the message?" said Sam.

"I love you," said Paul. "Let's make up and start all over again." The woman's voice was so shrill with passion that it cut through the din of the radio, and even Sam heard it.

"Kid—are you in trouble?" said Sam. "Your folks fighting?"

Paul was afraid that Sam would hang up on him if he found out that Paul wasn't a blood relative of the Hargers. "Yessir," he said.

"And you're trying to pull 'em back together again with this dedication?" said Sam.

"Yessir," said Paul.

Sam became very emotional. "O.K., kid," he said hoarsely, "I'll give it everything I've got. Maybe it'll work. I once saved a guy from shooting himself the same way."

"How did you do that?" said Paul, fascinated.

"He called up and said he was gonna blow his brains out," said Sam, "and I played *The Bluebird of Happiness*." He hung up.

Paul dropped the telephone into its cradle. The music stopped, and Paul's hair stood on end. For the first time, the fantastic speed of modern communications was real to him, and he was appalled.

"Folks!" said Sam, "I guess everybody stops and wonders sometimes what the heck he thinks he's doin' with the life the good Lord gave him! It may seem funny to you folks, because I always keep up a cheerful front, no matter how I feel inside, that I wonder sometimes, too! And then, just like some angel was trying to tell me, 'Keep going, Sam, keep going,' something like this comes along."

"Folks!" said Sam, "I've been asked to bring a man and his wife back together again through the miracle of radio! I guess there's no sense in kidding ourselves about marriage! It isn't any bowl of cherries! There's ups and downs, and sometimes folks don't see how they can go on!"

Paul was impressed with the wisdom and authority of Sam. Having the radio turned up high made sense now, for Sam was speaking like the right-hand man of God.

When Sam paused for effect, all was still next door. Already the miracle was working.

"Now," said Sam, "a guy in my business has to be half musician, half philosopher, half psychiatrist, and half electrical engineer! And! If I've learned one thing from working with all you wonderful people out there, it's this: if folks would swallow their self-respect and pride, there wouldn't be any more divorces!"

There were affectionate cooings from next door. A lump grew in

Paul's throat as he thought about the beautiful thing he and Sam were bringing to pass.

"Folks!" said Sam, "that's all I'm gonna say about love and marriage! That's all anybody needs to know! And now, for Mrs. Lemuel K. Harger, from Mr. Harger—I love you! Let's make up and start all over again!" Sam choked up. "Here's Eartha Kitt, and *Somebody Bad Stole De Wedding Bell!*"

The radio next door went off.

The world lay still.

A purple emotion flooded Paul's being. Childhood dropped away, and he hung, dizzy, on the brink of life, rich, violent, rewarding.

There was movement next door—slow, foot-dragging movement.

"So," said the woman.

"Charlotte—" said the man uneasily. "Honey—I swear."

" 'I love you,' " she said bitterly, " 'let's make up and start all over again.' "

"Baby," said the man desperately, "it's another Lemuel K. Harger. It's got to be!"

"You want your wife back?" she said. "All right—I won't get in her way. She can have you, Lemuel—you jewel beyond price, you."

"*She* must have called the station," said the man.

"She can have you, you philandering, two-timing, two-bit Lochinvar,[1]" she said. "But you won't be in very good condition."

"Charlotte—put down that gun," said the man. "Don't do anything you'll be sorry for."

"That's all behind me, you worm," she said.

There were three shots.

Paul ran out into the hall, and bumped into the woman as she burst from the Harger apartment. She was a big, blonde woman, all soft and awry, like an unmade bed.

She and Paul screamed at the same time, and then she grabbed him as he started to run.

"You want candy?" she said wildly. "Bicycle?"

"No, thank you," said Paul shrilly. "Not at this time."

"You haven't seen or heard a thing!" she said. "You know what happens to squealers?"

"Yes!" cried Paul.

She dug into her purse, and brought out a perfumed mulch of face

[1] Hero of a ballad in Sir Walter Scott's poem *Marmion* (1808), who rides off with his sweetheart just as she is about to be married to another.

tissues, bobbypins and cash. "Here!" she panted. "It's yours! And there's more where that came from, if you keep your mouth shut." She stuffed it into his trousers pocket.

She looked at him fiercely, then fled into the street.

Paul ran back into his apartment, jumped into bed, and pulled the covers up over his head. In the hot, dark cave of the bed, he cried because he and All-Night Sam had helped to kill a man.

A policeman came clumping into the house very soon, and he knocked on both apartment doors with his billyclub.

Numb, Paul crept out of the hot, dark cave, and answered the door. Just as he did, the door across the hall opened, and there stood Mr. Harger, haggard but whole.

"Yes, sir?" said Harger. He was a small, balding man, with a hairline mustache. "Can I help you?"

"The neighbors heard some shots," said the policeman.

"Really?" said Harger urbanely. He dampened his mustache with the tip of his little finger. "How bizarre. I heard nothing." He looked at Paul sharply. "Have you been playing with your father's guns again, young man?"

"Oh, nossir!" said Paul, horrified.

"Where are your folks?" said the policeman to Paul.

"At the movies," said Paul.

"You're all alone?" said the policeman.

"Yessir," said Paul. "It's an adventure."

"I'm sorry I said that about the guns," said Harger. "I certainly would have heard any shots in this house. The walls are thin as paper, and I heard nothing."

Paul looked at him gratefully.

"And you didn't hear any shots, either, kid?" said the policeman.

Before Paul could find an answer, there was a disturbance out on the street. A big, motherly woman was getting out of a taxicab and wailing at the top of her lungs. "Lem! Lem, baby."

She barged into the foyer, a suitcase bumping against her leg and tearing her stocking to shreds. She dropped the suitcase, and ran to Harger, throwing her arms around him.

"I got your message, darling," she said, "and I did just what All-Night Sam told me to do. I swallowed my self-respect, and here I am!"

"Rose, Rose, Rose—my little Rose," said Harger. "Don't ever leave me again." They grappled with each other affectionately, and staggered into their apartment.

"Just look at this apartment!" said Mrs. Harger. "Men are just lost without women!" As she closed the door, Paul could see that she was awfully pleased with the mess.

"You *sure* you didn't hear any shots?" said the policeman to Paul.

The ball of money in Paul's pocket seemed to swell to the size of a watermelon. "Yessir," he croaked.

The policeman left.

Paul shut his apartment door, shuffled into his bedroom, and collapsed on the bed.

The next voices Paul heard came from his own side of the wall. The voices were sunny—the voices of his mother and father. His mother was singing a nursery rhyme and his father was undressing him.

"Diddle-diddle-dumpling, my son John," piped his mother, "Went to bed with his stockings on. One shoe off, and one shoe on—diddle-diddle-dumpling, my son John."

Paul opened his eyes.

"Hi, big boy," said his father, "you went to sleep with all your clothes on."

"How's my little adventurer?" said his mother.

"O.K.," said Paul sleepily. "How was the show?"

"It wasn't for children, honey," said his mother. "You would have liked the short subject, though. It was all about bears—cunning little cubs."

Paul's father handed her Paul's trousers, and she shook them out, and hung them neatly on the back of a chair by the bed. She patted them smooth, and felt the ball of money in the pocket. "Little boys' pockets!" she said, delighted. "Full of childhood's mysteries. An enchanted frog? A magic pocketknife from a fairy princess?" She caressed the lump.

"He's not a little boy—he's a big boy," said Paul's father. "And he's too old to be thinking about fairy princesses."

Paul's mother held up her hands. "Don't rush it, don't rush it. When I saw him asleep there, I realized all over again how dreadfully short childhood is." She reached into the pocket and sighed wistfully. "Little boys are so hard on clothes—especially pockets."

She brought out the ball and held it under Paul's nose. "Now, would you mind telling Mommy what we have here?" she said gaily.

The ball bloomed like a frowzy chrysanthemum, with ones, fives, tens, twenties, and lipstick-stained Kleenex for petals. And rising from it, befuddling Paul's young mind, was the pungent musk of perfume.

Paul's father sniffed the air. "What's that smell?" he said.
Paul's mother rolled her eyes. "*Tabu,*" she said.

1955

DISCUSSION QUESTIONS

1. Why does Mrs. Leonard's desire to protect Paul from a movie "about a girl who chooses her friends unwisely" (page 444) become *ironic?* What other aspects of the story become *ironic* on a second reading? Why?

2. Why does Paul damage the lens of his microscope and break a slide? Are we prepared for such a reaction? If so, how? What does the "milky mist of the damaged lens" (page 445) *symbolize?*

3. Why does Paul's plan to end the quarrel next door seem to backfire? Is he to blame for bringing about this reversal in the story? Justify your answer.

4. Paul is "impressed with the wisdom and authority of Sam" (page 447). Are you? Explain. Is Sam's advice about marriage "all anybody needs to know"? Explain. What does the fact that such advice brings Mrs. Harger back to her husband and that Sam's playing of "The Bluebird of Happiness" prevents a suicide tell us about Vonnegut's view of our society?

5. Examine the following two sentences in their context: "'All right!' she said *bravely*" (page 444). "His mother frowned *judiciously*" (page 445). Do the two italicized adverbs accurately characterize Mrs. Leonard's response? If not, why has Vonnegut chosen them?

6. Although Mrs. Leonard's surmise about the contents of Paul's pockets *ironically* misses the mark, how appropriate, nevertheless, is the fairy tale element that she introduces at the end of the story?

1. In what ways do the two stories resemble each other? Characterize each story's dominant mood. How do you account for differences in mood between the two works?

2. Which writer's characters seem to have been more realistically drawn? Give examples. What conditions determine this greater realism? For which characters do you feel more sympathy: Mr. Baines or Mr. Harger, Mrs. Baines or Mrs. Harger, Charlotte or Emmy? Why?

3. Philip's experience is horrifying and traumatic: "Life fell on him with savagery." What prevents us from seeing a similar kind of savagery in Paul's experience? What prevents it from becoming equally traumatic?

4. Does Harger's surprise appearance seem acceptable? Is it consistent with the *tone* of Vonnegut's story? Would such a comic reversal (the reappearance of Mrs. Baines, for example) work in Greene's story? Justify your answer.

ANALYSIS AND APPLICATION

1. Analyze the following passage: "presently he could hear the soft precise footfalls of Mrs. Baines on the stairs: she was a good servant, she walked softly; she was a determined woman, she walked precisely" (page 427). How are the two parts divided by the colon related? How are the parts divided by each of the two commas related? By what means has Greene balanced the four clauses that follow the colon? For what purpose? List the parallel elements in two facing columns. Define the *tone* of these clauses. What effect would the following change have on that tone: since she was a good servant, she walked softly; likewise, because she was a determined woman, she walked precisely. Why would the tone be affected?

2. Explain Greene's statement, "The sawdust was spilled out of the afternoon; nothing you did could mend it" (page 425). To what is *afternoon* implicitly being compared and how appropriate is this *implied metaphor* within the context of the story? Try to restate the two clauses in nonmetaphorical language.

3. What can we deduce about Sam's listeners from the following dedications: "For Nancy from Bob, who thinks she's swell! For Arthur, from one who's worshipped him from afar for six weeks" (page 446)? With how much precision do the listeners communicate their feelings? How original are their means of expression? How much sincerity do they convey? Find five similarly expressed statements in "Next Door."

WILLIAM WILSON

EDGAR ALLAN POE

What say of it? what say [of] CONSCIENCE grim,
That spectre in my path?

Chamberlayne's Pharronida.[1]

LET ME call myself, for the present, William Wilson. The fair page now lying before me need not be sullied with my real appellation. This has been already too much an object for the scorn—for the horror—for the detestation of my race. To the uttermost regions of the globe have not the indignant winds bruited its unparalleled infamy? Oh, outcast of all outcasts most abandoned!—to the earth art thou not forever dead? to its honors, to its flowers, to its golden aspirations?—and a cloud, dense, dismal, and limitless, does it not hang eternally between thy hopes and heaven?

[1] *Pharonnida, an Heroick Poem* (1659) by William Chamberlayne (1619–1689); Poe's epigraph does not appear in *Pharonnida.*

I would not, if I could, here or to-day, embody a record of my later years of unspeakable misery, and unpardonable crime. This epoch—these later years—took unto themselves a sudden elevation in turpitude, whose origin alone it is my present purpose to assign. Men usually grow base by degrees. From me, in an instant, all virtue dropped bodily as a mantle. From comparatively trivial wickedness I passed, with the stride of a giant, into more than the enormities of an Elah-Gabalus.[2] What chance—what one event brought this evil thing to pass, bear with me while I relate. Death approaches; and the shadow which foreruns him has thrown a softening influence over my spirit. I long, in passing through the dim valley, for the sympathy—I had nearly said for the pity—of my fellow men. I would fain have them believe that I have been, in some measure, the slave of circumstances beyond human control. I would wish them to seek out for me, in the details I am about to give, some little oasis of *fatality* amid a wilderness of error. I would have them allow—what they cannot refrain from allowing—that, although temptation may have erewhile existed as great, man was never *thus,* at least, tempted before—certainly, never *thus* fell. And is it therefore that he has never thus suffered? Have I not indeed been living in a dream? And am I not now dying a victim to the horror and the mystery of the wildest of all sublunary visions?

I am the descendant of a race whose imaginative and easily excitable temperament has at all times rendered them remarkable; and, in my earliest infancy, I gave evidence of having fully inherited the family character. As I advanced in years it was more strongly developed; becoming, for many reasons, a cause of serious disquietude to my friends, and of positive injury to myself. I grew self-willed, addicted to the wildest caprices, and a prey to the most ungovernable passions. Weak-minded, and beset with constitutional infirmities akin to my own, my parents could do but little to check the evil propensities which distinguished me. Some feeble and ill-directed efforts resulted in complete failure on their part, and, of course, in total triumph on mine. Thenceforward my voice was a household law; and at an age when few children have abandoned their leading-strings, I was left to the guidance of my own will, and became, in all but name, the master of my own actions.

My earliest recollections of a school-life, are connected with a large, rambling, Elizabethan house, in a misty-looking village of England, where were a vast number of gigantic and gnarled trees, and where all

[2] Heliogabalus, adopted name of the Roman emperor Varius Avitus Bassianus (A.D. 204–222), infamous for his unparalleled profligacy.

the houses were excessively ancient. In truth, it was a dream-like and spirit-soothing place, that venerable old town. At this moment, in fancy, I feel the refreshing chilliness of its deeply-shadowed avenues, inhale the fragrance of its thousand shrubberies, and thrill anew with undefinable delight, at the deep hollow note of the church-bell, breaking, each hour, with sullen and sudden roar, upon the stillness of the dusky atmosphere in which the fretted Gothic steeple lay imbedded and asleep.

It gives me, perhaps, as much of pleasure as I can now in any manner experience, to dwell upon minute recollections of the school and its concerns. Steeped in misery as I am—misery, alas! only too real—I shall be pardoned for seeking relief, however slight and temporary, in the weakness of a few rambling details. These, moreover, utterly trivial, and even ridiculous in themselves, assume, to my fancy, adventitious importance, as connected with a period and a locality when and where I recognize the first ambiguous monitions of the destiny which afterwards so fully overshadowed me. Let me then remember.

The house, I have said, was old and irregular. The grounds were extensive, and a high and solid brick wall, topped with a bed of mortar and broken glass, encompassed the whole. This prison-like rampart formed the limit of our domain; beyond it we saw but thrice a week—once every Saturday afternoon, when, attended by two ushers, we were permitted to take brief walks in a body through some of the neighbouring fields—and twice during Sunday, when we were paraded in the same formal manner to the morning and evening service in the one church of the village. Of this church the principal of our school was pastor. With how deep a spirit of wonder and perplexity was I wont to regard him from our remote pew in the gallery, as, with step solemn and slow, he ascended the pulpit! This reverend man, with countenance so demurely benign, with robes so glossy and so clerically flowing, with wig so minutely powdered, so rigid and so vast,—could this be he who, of late, with sour visage, and in snuffy habiliments, administered, ferule in hand, the Draconian laws of the academy? Oh, gigantic paradox, too utterly monstrous for solution!

At an angle of the ponderous wall frowned a more ponderous gate. It was riveted and studded with iron bolts, and surmounted with jagged iron spikes. What impressions of deep awe did it inspire! It was never opened save for the three periodical egressions and ingressions already mentioned; then, in every creak of its mighty hinges, we found a plenitude of mystery—a world of matter for solemn remark, or for more solemn meditation.

The extensive enclosure was irregular in form, having many capacious recesses. Of these, three or four of the largest constituted the play-ground. It was level, and covered with fine hard gravel. I well remember it had no trees, nor benches, nor anything similar within it. Of course it was in the rear of the house. In front lay a small parterre, planted with box and other shrubs; but through this sacred division we passed only upon rare occasions indeed—such as a first advent to school or final departure thence, or perhaps, when a parent or friend having called for us, we joyfully took our way home for the Christmas or Midsummer holydays.

But the house!—how quaint an old building was this!—to me how veritably a palace of enchantment! There was really no end to its windings—to its incomprehensible subdivisions. It was difficult, at any given time, to say with certainty upon which of its two stories one happened to be. From each room to every other there were sure to be found three or four steps either in ascent or descent. Then the lateral branches were innumerable—inconceivable—and so returning in upon themselves, that our most exact ideas in regard to the whole mansion were not very far different from those with which we pondered upon infinity. During the five years of my residence here, I was never able to ascertain with precision, in what remote locality lay the little sleeping apartment assigned to myself and some eighteen or twenty other scholars.

The school-room was the largest in the house—I could not help thinking, in the world. It was very long, narrow, and dismally low, with pointed Gothic windows and a ceiling of oak. In a remote and terror-inspiring angle was a square enclosure of eight or ten feet, comprising the *sanctum,* "during hours," of our principal, the Reverend Dr. Bransby.[3] It was a solid structure, with massy door, sooner than open which in the absence of the "Dominie," we would all have willingly perished by the *peine forte et dure.*[4] In other angles were two other similar boxes, far less reverenced, indeed, but still greatly matters of awe. One of these was the pulpit of the "classical" usher, one of the "English and mathematical." Interspersed about the room, crossing and recrossing in endless irregularity, were innumerable benches and desks, black, ancient, and time-worn, piled desperately with much-bethumbed books, and so beseamed with initial letters, names at full length, grotesque figures, and other multiplied efforts of the knife, as to have entirely lost what little of original form might have been their portion in days long

[3] The Reverend John Bransby, an actual person, whose school at Stoke Newington, England, Poe attended from 1817 to 1820.

[4] Long and severe pain (torture).

departed. A huge bucket with water stood at one extremity of the room, and a clock of stupendous dimensions at the other.

Encompassed by the massy walls of this venerable academy, I passed, yet not in tedium or disgust, the years of the third lustrum of my life. The teeming brain of childhood requires no external world of incident to occupy or amuse it; and the apparently dismal monotony of a school was replete with more intense excitement than my riper youth has derived from luxury, or my full manhood from crime. Yet I must believe that my first mental development had in it much of the uncommon—even much of the *outré*. Upon mankind at large the events of very early existence rarely leave in mature age any definite impression. All is gray shadow—a weak and irregular remembrance—an indistinct regathering of feeble pleasures and phantasmagoric pains. With me this is not so. In childhood I must have felt with the energy of a man what I now find stamped upon memory in lines as vivid, as deep, and as durable as the *exergues* of the Carthaginian medals.

Yet in fact—in the fact of the world's view—how little was there to remember! The morning's awakening, the nightly summons to bed; the connings, the recitations; the periodical half-holidays, and perambulations; the play-ground, with its broils, its pastimes, its intrigues;—these, by a mental sorcery long forgotten, were made to involve a wilderness of sensation, a world of rich incident, an universe of varied emotion, of excitement the most passionate and spirit-stirring. *"Oh, le bon temps, que ce siècle de fer!"*[5]

In truth, the ardor, the enthusiasm, and the imperiousness of my disposition, soon rendered me a marked character among my schoolmates, and by slow, but natural gradations, gave me an ascendancy over all not greatly older than myself;—over all with a single exception. This exception was found in the person of a scholar, who, although no relation, bore the same Christian and surname as myself;—a circumstance, in fact, little remarkable; for, notwithstanding a noble descent, mine was one of those everyday appellations which seem, by prescriptive right, to have been, time out of mind, the common property of the mob. In this narrative I have therefore designated myself as William Wilson,—a fictitious title not very dissimilar to the real. My namesake alone, of

[5] Oh, what a good time is this Age of Iron! (based on the Greek notion of regression from the ages of Gold and Silver). According to Stuart and Susan Levine, this quotation is from Voltaire's "Le Mondain" (1736), l. 21: "the poet speaks sarcastically about those who refer to the good old times or the golden age." (Stuart Levine and Susan Levine, eds., *The Short Fiction of Edgar Allan Poe: An Annotated Edition* (Indianapolis: Bobbs-Merrill 1975), p. 291.)

those who in school phraseology constituted "our set," presumed to compete with me in the studies of the class—in the sports and broils of the play-ground—to refuse implicit belief in my assertions, and submission to my will—indeed, to interfere with my arbitrary dictation in any respect whatsoever. If there is on earth a supreme and unqualified despotism, it is the despotism of a master mind in boyhood over the less energetic spirits of its companions.

Wilson's rebellion was to me a source of the greatest embarrassment; —the more so as, in spite of the bravado with which in public I made a point of treating him and his pretensions, I secretly felt that I feared him, and could not help thinking the equality which he maintained so easily with myself, a proof of his true superiority; since not to be overcome cost me a perpetual struggle. Yet this superiority—even this equality—was in truth acknowledged by no one but myself; our associates, by some unaccountable blindness, seemed not even to suspect it. Indeed, his competition, his resistance, and especially his impertinent and dogged interference with my purposes, were not more pointed than private. He appeared to be destitute alike of the ambition which urged, and of the passionate energy of mind which enabled me to excel. In his rivalry he might have been supposed actuated solely by a whimsical desire to thwart, astonish, or mortify myself; although there were times when I could not help observing, with a feeling made up of wonder, abasement, and pique, that he mingled with his injuries, his insults, or his contradictions, a certain most inappropriate, and assuredly most unwelcome *affectionateness* of manner. I could only conceive this singular behavior to arise from a consummate self-conceit assuming the vulgar airs of patronage and protection.

Perhaps it was this latter trait in Wilson's conduct, conjoined with our identity of name, and the mere accident of our having entered the school upon the same day, which set afloat the notion that we were brothers, among the senior classes in the academy. These do not usually inquire with much strictness into the affairs of their juniors. I have before said, or should have said, that Wilson was not, in the most remote degree, connected with my family. But assuredly if we *had* been brothers we must have been twins; for, after leaving Dr. Bransby's, I casually learned that my namesake was born on the nineteenth of January, 1813 —and this is a somewhat remarkable coincidence; for the day is precisely that of my own nativity.

It may seem strange that in spite of the continual anxiety occasioned me by the rivalry of Wilson, and his intolerable spirit of contradiction, I could not bring myself to hate him altogether. We had, to be sure, nearly every day a quarrel in which, yielding me publicly the palm of victory, he, in some manner, contrived to make me feel that it was he who had deserved it; yet a sense of pride on my part, and a veritable dignity on his own, kept us always upon what are called "speaking terms," while there were many points of strong congeniality in our tempers, operating to awake in me a sentiment which our position alone, perhaps, prevented from ripening into friendship. It is difficult, indeed, to define, or even to describe, my real feelings towards him. They formed a motley and heterogeneous admixture;—some petulant animosity, which was not yet hatred, some esteem, more respect, much fear, with a world of uneasy curiosity. To the moralist it will be unnecessary to say, in addition, that Wilson and myself were the most inseparable of companions.

It was no doubt the anomalous state of affairs existing between us, which turned all my attacks upon him, (and they were many, either open or covert) into the channel of banter or practical joke (giving pain while assuming the aspect of mere fun) rather than into a more serious and determined hostility. But my endeavours on this head were by no means uniformly successful, even when my plans were the most wittily concocted; for my namesake had much about him, in character, of that unassuming and quiet austerity which, while enjoying the poignancy of its own jokes, has no heel of Achilles in itself, and absolutely refuses to be laughed at. I could find, indeed, but one vulnerable point, and that, lying in a personal peculiarity, arising, perhaps, from constitutional disease, would have been spared by any antagonist less at his wit's end than myself;—my rival had a weakness in the faucial or guttural organs, which precluded him from raising his voice at any time *above a very low whisper*. Of this defect I did not fail to take what poor advantage lay in my power.

Wilson's retaliations in kind were many; and there was one form of his practical wit that disturbed me beyond measure. How his sagacity first discovered at all that so petty a thing would vex me, is a question I never could solve; but, having discovered, he habitually practised the annoyance. I had always felt aversion to my uncourtly patronymic, and its very common, if not plebeian prænomen. The words were venom in my ears; and when, upon the day of my arrival, a second William Wilson came also to the academy, I felt angry with him for bearing the name, and doubly disgusted with the name because a stranger bore it, who would be the cause of its twofold repetition, who would be constantly in my presence, and whose concerns, in the ordinary routine of the school business, must inevitably, on account of the detestable coincidence, be often confounded with my own.

The feeling of vexation thus engendered grew stronger with every circumstance tending to show resemblance, moral or physical, between my rival and myself. I had not then discovered the remarkable fact that we were of the same age; but I saw that we were of the same height, and I perceived that we were even singularly alike in general contour of person and outline of feature. I was galled, too, by the rumor touching a relationship, which had grown current in the upper forms. In a word, nothing could more seriously disturb me, (although I scrupulously concealed such disturbance,) than any illusion to a similarity of mind, person, or condition existing between us. But, in truth, I had no reason to believe that (with the exception of the matter of relationship, and in the case of Wilson himself,) this similarity had ever been made a subject of comment, or even observed at all by our schoolfellows. That *he* observed it in all its bearings, and as fixedly as I, was apparent; but that he could discover in such circumstances so fruitful a field of annoyance, can only be attributed, as I said before, to his more than ordinary penetration.

His cue, which was to perfect an imitation of myself, lay both in words and in actions; and most admirably did he play his part. My dress it was an easy matter to copy; my gait and general manner were, without difficulty, appropriated; in spite of his constitutional defect, even my voice did not escape him. My louder tones were, of course, unattempted, but then the key, it was identical; *and his singular whisper, it grew the very echo of my own.*

How greatly this most exquisite portraiture harassed me, (for it could not justly be termed a caricature,) I will not now venture to describe. I had but one consolation—in the fact that the imitation, apparently, was noticed by myself alone, and that I had to endure only the knowing and strangely sarcastic smiles of my namesake himself. Satisfied with having produced in my bosom the intended effect, he seemed to chuckle in secret over the sting he had inflicted, and was characteristically disregardful of the public applause which the success of his witty endeavours might have so easily elicited. That the school, indeed, did not feel his design, perceive its accomplishment, and participate in his sneer, was, for many anxious months, a riddle I could not resolve. Perhaps the *gradation* of his copy rendered it not so readily perceptible; or, more possibly, I owed my security to the masterly air of the copyist, who, disdaining the letter, (which in a painting is all the obtuse can see,) gave but the full spirit of his original for my individual contemplation and chagrin.

I have already more than once spoken of the disgusting air of patronage which he assumed toward me, and of his frequent officious interference with my will. This interference often took the ungracious character of advice; advice not openly given, but hinted or insinuated. I received it with a repugnance which gained strength as I grew in years. Yet, at this distant day, let me do him the simple justice to acknowledge that I can recall no occasion when the suggestions of my rival were on the side of those errors or follies so usual to his immature age and seeming inexperience; that his moral sense, at least, if not his general talents and worldly wisdom, was far keener than my own; and that I might, to-day, have been a better, and thus a happier man, had I less frequently rejected the counsels embodied in those meaning whispers which I then but too cordially hated and too bitterly despised.

As it was, I at length grew restive in the extreme under his distasteful supervision, and daily resented more and more openly what I considered his intolerable arrogance. I have said that, in the first years of our connexion as schoolmates, my feelings in regard to him might have been easily ripened into friendship: but, in the latter months of my residence at the academy, although the intrusion of his ordinary manner had, beyond doubt, in some measure, abated, my sentiments, in nearly similar proportion, partook very much of positive hatred. Upon one occasion he saw this, I think, and afterwards avoided, or made a show of avoiding me.

It was about the same period, if I remember aright, that, in an altercation of violence with him, in which he was more than usually thrown off his guard, and spoke and acted with an openness of demeanor rather foreign to his nature, I discovered, or fancied I discovered, in his accent, his air, and general appearance, a something which first startled, and then deeply interested me, by bringing to mind dim visions of my earliest infancy—wild, confused and thronging memories of a time when memory herself was yet unborn. I cannot better describe the sensation which oppressed me than by saying that I could with difficulty shake off the belief of my having been acquainted with the being who stood before me, at some epoch very long ago—some point of the past even infinitely remote. The delusion, however, faded rapidly as it came; and I mention it at all but to define the day of the last conversation I there held with my singular namesake.

The huge old house, with its countless subdivisions, had several large chambers communicating with each other, where slept the greater number of the students. There were, however, (as must necessarily happen in a building so awkwardly planned,) many little nooks or recesses, the odds and ends of the structure; and these the economic ingenuity of Dr. Bransby had also fitted up as dormitories; although, being the merest closets, they were capable of accommodating but a single individual. One of these small apartments was occupied by Wilson.

One night, about the close of my fifth year at the school, and immediately after the altercation just mentioned, finding every one wrapped in sleep, I arose from bed, and, lamp in hand, stole through a wilderness of narrow passages from my own bedroom to that of my rival. I had long been plotting one of those ill-natured pieces of practical wit at his expense in which I had hitherto been so uniformly unsuccessful. It was my intention, now, to put my scheme in operation, and I resolved to make him feel the whole extent of the malice with which I was imbued. Having reached his closet, I noiselessly entered, leaving the lamp, with a shade over it, on the outside. I advanced a step, and listened to the sound of his tranquil breathing. Assured of his being asleep, I returned, took the light, and with it again approached the bed. Close curtains were around it, which, in the prosecution of my plan, I slowly and quietly withdrew, when the bright rays fell vividly upon the sleeper, and my eyes, at the same moment, upon his countenance. I looked;—and a numbness, an iciness of feeling instantly pervaded my frame. My breast heaved, my knees tottered, my whole spirit became possessed with an objectless yet intolerable horror. Gasping for breath, I lowered the lamp in still nearer proximity to the face. Were these—*these* the lineaments of William Wilson? I saw, indeed, that they were his, but I shook as if with a fit of the ague in fancying they were not. What *was* there about them to confound me in this manner? I gazed;—while my brain reeled with a multitude of incoherent thoughts. Not thus he appeared—assuredly not *thus*—in the vivacity of his waking hours. The same name! the same contour of person! the same day of arrival at the academy! And then his dogged and meaningless imitation of my gait, my voice, my habits, and my manner! Was it, in truth, within the bounds of human possibility, that *what I now saw* was the result, merely, of the habitual practice of this sarcastic imitation? Awe-stricken, and with a creeping shudder, I extinguished the lamp, passed silently from the chamber, and left, at once, the halls of that old academy, never to enter them again.

After a lapse of some months, spent at home in mere idleness, I found myself a student at Eton. The brief interval had been sufficient to enfeeble my remembrance of the events at Dr. Bransby's, or at least to effect a material change in the nature of the feelings with which I remembered them. The truth—the tragedy—of the drama was no more. I could now find room to doubt the evidence of my senses; and seldom called up the subject at all but with wonder at the extent of human credulity, and a smile at the vivid force of the imagination which I hereditarily possessed. Neither was this species of scepticism likely to be diminished by the character of the life I led at Eton. The vortex of thoughtless folly into which I there so immediately and so recklessly plunged, washed away all but the froth of my past hours, engulfed at once every solid or serious impression, and left to memory only the veriest levities of a former existence.

I do not wish, however, to trace the course of my miserable profligacy here—a profligacy which set at defiance the laws, while it eluded the vigilance of the institution. Three years of folly, passed without profit, had but given me rooted habits of vice, and added, in a somewhat unusual degree, to my bodily stature, when, after a week of soulless dissipation, I invited a small party of the most dissolute students to a secret carousal in my chambers. We met at a late hour of the night; for our debaucheries were to be faithfully protracted until morning. The wine flowed freely, and there were not wanting other and perhaps more dangerous seductions; so that the grey dawn had already faintly appeared in the east, while our delirious extravagance was at its height. Madly flushed with cards and intoxication, I was in the act of insisting upon a toast of more than wonted profanity, when my attention was suddenly diverted by the violent, although partial unclosing of the door of the apartment, and by the eager voice of a servant from without. He said that some person, apparently in great haste, demanded to speak with me in the hall.

Wildly excited with wine, the unexpected interruption rather delighted than surprised me. I staggered forward at once, and a few steps brought me to the vestibule of the building. In this low and small room there hung no lamp; and now no light at all was admitted, save that of the exceedingly feeble dawn which made its way through the semicircular window. As I put my foot over the threshold, I became aware of the figure of a youth about my own height, and habited in a white kerseymere morning frock, cut in the novel fashion of the one I myself wore at the moment. This the faint light enabled me to perceive; but the features of his face I could not distinguish. Upon my entering he strode hurriedly up to me, and, seizing me by the arm with a gesture of petulant impatience, whispered the words "William Wilson!" in my ear.

I grew perfectly sober in an instant.

There was that in the manner of the stranger, and in the tremulous shake of his uplifted finger, as he held it between my eyes and the light, which filled me with unqualified amazement; but it was not this which had so violently moved me. It was the pregnancy of solemn admonition in the singular, low, hissing utterance; and, above all, it was the character, the tone, *the key,* of those few, simple, and familiar, yet *whispered* syllables, which came with a thousand thronging memories of by-gone days, and struck upon my soul with the shock of a galvanic battery. Ere I could recover the use of my senses he was gone.

Although this event failed not of a vivid effect upon my disordered imagination, yet was it evanescent as vivid. For some weeks, indeed, I busied myself in earnest inquiry, or was wrapped in a cloud of morbid speculation. I did not pretend to disguise from my perception the identity of the singular individual who thus perseveringly interfered with my affairs, and harassed me with his insinuated counsel. But who and what was this Wilson?—and whence came he?—and what were his purposes? Upon neither of these points could I be satisfied; merely ascertaining, in regard to him, that a sudden accident in his family had caused his removal from Dr. Bransby's academy on the afternoon of the day in which I myself had eloped. But in a brief period I ceased to think upon the subject; my attention being all absorbed in a contemplated departure for Oxford. Thither I soon went; the uncalculating vanity of my parents furnishing me with an outfit and annual establishment, which would enable me to indulge at will in the luxury already so dear to my heart—to vie in profuseness of expenditure with the haughtiest heirs of the wealthiest earldoms in Great Britain.

Excited by such appliances to vice, my constitutional temperament broke forth with redoubled ardor, and I spurned even the common restraints of decency in the mad infatuation of my revels. But it were absurd to pause in the detail of my extravagance. Let it suffice, that among spendthrifts I out-Heroded[6] Herod, and that, giving name to a multitude of novel follies, I added no brief appendix to the long catalogue of vices then usual in the most dissolute university of Europe.

It could hardly be credited, however, that I had, even here, so utterly fallen from the gentlemanly estate, as to seek acquaintance with the vilest arts of the gambler by profession, and, having become an adept in his despicable science, to practise it habitually as a means of increasing my already enormous income at the expense of the weak-minded among

[6] To outdo in excess; see *Hamlet,* act 3, sc. 2, line 16.

my fellow-collegians. Such, nevertheless, was the fact. And the very enormity of this offence against all manly and honourable sentiment proved, beyond doubt, the main if not the sole reason of the impunity with which it was committed. Who, indeed, among my most abandoned associates, would not rather have disputed the clearest evidence of his senses, than have suspected of such courses, the gay, the frank, the generous William Wilson—the noblest and most liberal commoner at Oxford—him whose follies (said his parasites) were but the follies of youth and unbridled fancy—whose errors but inimitable whim—whose darkest vice but a careless and dashing extravagance?

I had been now two years successfully busied in this way, when there came to the university a young *parvenu* nobleman, Glendinning—rich, said report, as Herodes Atticus[7]—his riches, too, as easily acquired. I soon found him of weak intellect, and, of course, marked him as a fitting subject for my skill. I frequently engaged him in play, and contrived, with the gambler's usual art, to let him win considerable sums, the more effectually to entangle him in my snares. At length, my schemes being ripe, I met him (with the full intention that this meeting should be final and decisive) at the chambers of a fellow-commoner, (Mr. Preston,) equally intimate with both, but who, to do him justice, entertained not even a remote suspicion of my design. To give to this a better colouring, I had contrived to have assembled a party of some eight or ten, and was solicitously careful that the introduction of cards should appear accidental, and originate in the proposal of my contemplated dupe himself. To be brief upon a vile topic, none of the low finesse was omitted, so customary upon similar occasions that it is a just matter for wonder how any are still found so besotted as to fall its victim.

We had protracted our sitting far into the night, and I had at length effected the manœuvre of getting Glendinning as my sole antagonist. The game, too, was my favorite *écarté*.[8] The rest of the company, interested in the extent of our play, had abandoned their own cards, and were standing around us as spectators. The *parvenu,* who had been induced by my artifices in the early part of the evening, to drink deeply, now shuffled, dealt, or played, with a wild nervousness of manner for which his intoxication, I thought, might partially, but could not altogether account. In a very short period he had become my debtor to a large amount, when, having taken a long draught of port, he did precisely what I had been coolly anticipating—he proposed to double our

[7] Greek rhetorician and public benefactor (A.D. 104?–180?).

[8] Card game for two, played with thirty-two cards.

already extravagant stakes. With a well-feigned show of reluctance, and not until after my repeated refusal had seduced him into some angry words which gave a color of *pique* to my compliance, did I finally comply. The result, of course, did but prove how entirely the prey was in my toils; in less than an hour he had quadrupled his debt. For some time his countenance had been losing the florid tinge lent it by the wine; but now, to my astonishment, I perceived that it had grown to a pallor truly fearful. I say to my astonishment. Glendinning had been represented to my eager inquiries as immeasurably wealthy; and the sums which he had as yet lost, although in themselves vast, could not, I supposed, very seriously annoy, much less so violently affect him. That he was overcome by the wine just swallowed, was the idea which most readily presented itself; and, rather with a view to the preservation of my own character in the eyes of my associates, than from any less interested motive, I was about to insist, peremptorily, upon a discontinuance of the play, when some expressions at my elbow from among the company, and an ejaculation evincing utter despair on the part of Glendinning, gave me to understand that I had effected his total ruin under circumstances which, rendering him an object for the pity of all, should have protected him from the ill offices even of a fiend.

What now might have been my conduct it is difficult to say. The pitiable condition of my dupe had thrown an air of embarrassed gloom over all; and, for some moments, a profound silence was maintained, during which I could not help feeling my cheeks tingle with the many burning glances of scorn or reproach cast upon me by the less abandoned of the party. I will even own that an intolerable weight of anxiety was for a brief instant lifted from my bosom by the sudden and extraordinary interruption which ensued. The wide, heavy folding doors of the apartment were all at once thrown open, to their full extent, with a vigorous and rushing impetuosity that extinguished, as if by magic, every candle in the room. Their light, in dying, enabled us just to perceive that a stranger had entered, about my own height, and closely muffled in a cloak. The darkness, however, was now total; and we could only *feel* that he was standing in our midst. Before any one of us could recover from the extreme astonishment into which this rudeness had thrown all, we heard the voice of the intruder.

"Gentlemen," he said, in a low, distinct, and never-to-be-forgotten *whisper* which thrilled to the very marrow of my bones, "Gentlemen, I make no apology for this behaviour, because in thus behaving, I am but fulfilling a duty. You are, beyond doubt, uninformed of the true character of the person who has to-night won at *écarté* a large sum of money from Lord Glendinning. I will therefore put you upon an expeditious and decisive plan of obtaining this very necessary information. Please to examine, at your leisure, the inner linings of the cuff of his left sleeve, and the several little packages which may be found in the somewhat capacious pockets of his embroidered morning wrapper."

While he spoke, so profound was the stillness that one might have heard a pin drop upon the floor. In ceasing, he departed at once, and as abruptly as he had entered. Can I—shall I describe my sensations?—must I say that I felt all the horrors of the damned? Most assuredly I had little time given for reflection. Many hands roughly seized me upon the spot, and lights were immediately reprocured. A search ensued. In the lining of my sleeve were found all the court cards[9] essential in *écarté,* and, in the pockets of my wrapper, a number of packs, facsimiles of those used at our sittings, with the single exception that mine were of the species called, technically, *arrondées;*[10] the honours[11] being slightly convex at the ends, the lower cards slightly convex at the sides. In this disposition, the dupe who cuts, as customary, at the length of the pack, will invariably find that he cuts his antagonist an honor; while the gambler, cutting at the breadth, will, as certainly, cut nothing for his victim which may count in the records of the game.

Any burst of indignation upon this discovery would have affected me less than the silent contempt, or the sarcastic composure, with which it was received.

"Mr. Wilson," said our host, stooping to remove from beneath his feet an exceedingly luxurious cloak of rare furs, "Mr. Wilson, this is your property." (The weather was cold; and, upon quitting my own room, I had thrown a cloak over my dressing wrapper, putting it off upon reaching the scene of play.) "I presume it is supererogatory to seek here (eyeing the folds of the garment with a bitter smile) for any farther evidence of your skill. Indeed, we have had enough. You will see the necessity, I hope, of quitting Oxford—at all events, of quitting instantly my chambers."

Abased, humbled to the dust as I then was, it is probable that I should have resented this galling language by immediate personal violence, had not my whole attention been at the moment arrested by a fact of the most startling character. The cloak which I had worn was of a rare description of fur; how rare, how extravagantly costly, I shall not ven-

[9] Face cards, playing cards bearing pictures of king, queen, or knave.

[10] Rounded off.

[11] Honor cards, the four or five highest cards in trump or in all suits.

ture to say. Its fashion, too, was of my own fantastic invention; for I was fastidious to an absurd degree of coxcombry, in matters of this frivolous nature. When, therefore, Mr. Preston reached me that which he had picked up upon the floor, and near the folding doors of the apartment, it was with an astonishment nearly bordering upon terror, that I perceived my own already hanging on my arm, (where I had no doubt unwittingly placed it,) and that the one presented me was but its exact counterpart in every, in even the minutest possible particular. The singular being who had so disastrously exposed me, had been muffled, I remembered, in a cloak; and none had been worn at all by any of the members of our party with the exception of myself. Retaining some presence of mind, I took the one offered me by Preston; placed it, unnoticed, over my own; left the apartment with a resolute scowl of defiance; and, next morning ere dawn of day, commenced a hurried journey from Oxford to the continent, in a perfect agony of horror and of shame.

I fled in vain. My evil destiny pursued me as if in exultation, and proved, indeed, that the exercise of its mysterious dominion had as yet only begun. Scarcely had I set foot in Paris ere I had fresh evidence of the detestable interest taken by this Wilson in my concerns. Years flew, while I experienced no relief. Villain!—at Rome, with how untimely, yet with how spectral an officiousness, stepped he in between me and my ambition! At Vienna, too—at Berlin—and at Moscow! Where, in truth, had I *not* bitter cause to curse him within my heart? From his inscrutable tyranny did I at length flee, panic-stricken, as from a pestilence; and to the very ends of the earth *I fled in vain.*

And again, and again, in secret communion with my own spirit, would I demand the questions "Who is he?—whence came he?—and what are his objects?" But no answer was there found. And then I scrutinized, with a minute scrutiny, the forms, and the methods, and the leading traits of his impertinent supervision. But even here there was very little upon which to base a conjecture. It was noticeable, indeed, that, in no one of the multiplied instances in which he had of late crossed my path, had he so crossed it except to frustrate those schemes, or to disturb those actions, which, if fully carried out, might have resulted in bitter mischief. Poor justification this, in truth, for an authority so imperiously assumed! Poor indemnity for natural rights of self-agency so pertinaciously, so insultingly denied!

I had also been forced to notice that my tormentor, for a very long period of time, (while scrupulously and with miraculous dexterity maintaining his whim of an identity of apparel with myself,) had so contrived it, in the execution of his varied interference with my will, that I saw not, at any moment, the features of his face. Be Wilson what he might, *this,* at least, was but the veriest of affectation, or of folly. Could he, for an instant, have supposed that, in my admonisher at Eton—in the destroyer of my honor at Oxford,—in him who thwarted my ambition at Rome, my revenge at Paris, my passionate love at Naples, or what he falsely termed my avarice in Egypt,—that in this, my arch-enemy and evil genius, I could fail to recognize the William Wilson of my school boy days,—the namesake, the companion, the rival,—the hated and dreaded rival at Dr. Bransby's? Impossible!—But let me hasten to the last eventful scene of the drama.

Thus far I had succumbed supinely to this imperious domination. The sentiment of deep awe with which I habitually regarded the elevated character, the majestic wisdom, the apparent omnipresence and omnipotence of Wilson, added to a feeling of even terror, with which certain other traits in his nature and assumptions inspired me, had operated, hitherto, to impress me with an idea of my own utter weakness and helplessness, and to suggest an implicit, although bitterly reluctant submission to his arbitrary will. But, of late days, I had given myself up entirely to wine; and its maddening influence upon my hereditary temper rendered me more and more impatient of control. I began to murmur,—to hesitate,—to resist. And was it only fancy which induced me to believe that, with the increase of my own firmness, that of my tormentor underwent a proportional diminution? Be this as it may, I now began to feel the inspiration of a burning hope, and at length nurtured in my secret thoughts a stern and desperate resolution that I would submit no longer to be enslaved.

It was at Rome, during the Carnival of 18—, that I attended a masquerade in the palazzo of the Neapolitan Duke Di Broglio. I had indulged more freely than usual in the excesses of the wine-table; and now the suffocating atmosphere of the crowded rooms irritated me beyond endurance. The difficulty, too, of forcing my way through the mazes of the company contributed not a little to the ruffling of my temper; for I was anxiously seeking, (let me not say with what unworthy motive) the young, the gay, the beautiful wife of the aged and doting Di Broglio. With a too unscrupulous confidence she had previously communicated to me the secret of the costume in which she would be habited, and now, having caught a glimpse of her person, I was hurrying to make my way into her presence.—At this moment I felt a light hand placed upon my shoulder, and that ever-remembered, low, damnable *whisper* within my ear.

In an absolute phrenzy of wrath, I turned at once upon him who had thus interrupted me, and seized him violently by the collar. He was attired, as I had expected, in a costume altogether similar to my own; wearing a Spanish cloak of blue velvet, begirt about the waist with a crimson belt sustaining a rapier. A mask of black silk entirely covered his face.

"Scoundrel!" I said, in a voice husky with rage, while every syllable I uttered seemed as new fuel to my fury, "scoundrel! impostor! accursed villain! you shall not—you *shall not* dog me unto death! Follow me, or I stab you where you stand!"—and I broke my way from the ball-room into a small ante-chamber adjoining—dragging him unresistingly with me as I went.

Upon entering, I thrust him furiously from me. He staggered against the wall, while I closed the door with an oath, and commanded him to draw. He hesitated but for an instant; then, with a slight sigh, drew in silence, and put himself upon his defence.

The contest was brief indeed. I was frantic with every species of wild excitement, and felt within my single arm the energy and power of a multitude. In a few seconds I forced him by sheer strength against the wainscoting, and thus, getting him at mercy, plunged my sword, with brute ferocity, repeatedly through and through his bosom.

At that instant some person tried the latch of the door. I hastened to prevent an intrusion, and then immediately returned to my dying antagonist. But what human language can adequately portray *that* astonishment, *that* horror which possessed me at the spectacle then presented to view? The brief moment in which I averted my eyes had been sufficient to produce, apparently, a material change in the arrangements at the upper or farther end of the room. A large mirror,—so at first it seemed to me in my confusion—now stood where none had been perceptible before; and, as I stepped up to it in extremity of terror, mine own image, but with features all pale and dabbled in blood, advanced to meet me with a feeble and tottering gait.

Thus it appeared, I say, but was not. It was my antagonist—it was Wilson, who then stood before me in the agonies of his dissolution. His mask and cloak lay, where he had thrown them, upon the floor. Not a thread in all his raiment—not a line in all the marked and singular lineaments of his face which was not, even in the most absolute identity, *mine own!*

It was Wilson; but he spoke no longer in a whisper, and I could have fancied that I myself was speaking while he said:

"You have conquered, and I yield. Yet, henceforward art thou also

dead—dead to the World, to Heaven and to Hope! In me didst thou exist—and, in my death, see by this image, which is thine own, how utterly thou hast murdered thyself."

1839

DISCUSSION QUESTIONS

1. Distinguish Wilson's temperament from that of his namesake when the two boys are at school together. Why are they "the most inseparable of companions" (page 459) despite Wilson's hostility?

2. Wilson claims that his namesake deliberately copies his behavior and dress. If so, why? If you disagree, explain why Wilson would make such a claim. Why is Wilson disturbed by any suggestion of resemblance between himself and his namesake? Why does Wilson flee the "old academy"?

3. Characterize Wilson's feelings toward his rival. Why does Wilson find it so difficult to describe these feelings? Why are they so *ambivalent?* In what manner do they gradually change?

4. Why do "three years of folly" increase Wilson's "bodily stature" (page 463)? Explain the following observation: "with the increase of my own firmness, that of my tormentor underwent a proportional diminution" (page 469). Why, during the duel, is Wilson able to defeat his namesake so quickly?

5. Why does Wilson kill his namesake? Explain the statement, "In me didst thou exist" (page 471). What effect, if any, has his namesake's death on Wilson?

6. What is the narrator's purpose in telling his story? What is his attitude toward his younger self? Distinguish the elder narrator from his youthful counterpart. Support your answer with specific examples. How do you account for his change?

THE SECRET SHARER

JOSEPH CONRAD

On my right hand there were lines of fishing-stakes resembling a mysterious system of half-submerged bamboo fences, incomprehensible in its division of the domain of tropical fishes, and crazy of aspect as if abandoned for ever by some nomad tribe of fishermen now gone to the other end of the ocean; for there was no sign of human habitation as far as the eye could reach. To the left a group of barren islets, suggesting ruins of stone walls, towers, and blockhouses, had its foundations set in a blue sea that itself looked solid, so still and stable did it lie below my feet; even the track of light from the westering sun shone smoothly, without that animated glitter which tells of an imperceptible ripple. And when I turned my head to take a parting glance at the tug which had just left us anchored outside the bar, I saw the straight line of the flat shore joined to the stable sea, edge to edge, with a perfect and unmarked closeness, in one levelled floor half brown, half blue under the enormous dome of the sky. Corresponding in their insignificance to the islets of the sea, two small clumps of trees, one on each side of the only fault in the impeccable joint, marked the mouth of the river Meinam we had just left on the first preparatory stage of our homeward journey; and, far back on the inland level, a larger and loftier mass, the grove surrounding the great Paknam[1] pagoda, was the only thing on which the eye could rest from the vain task of exploring the monotonous sweep of the horizon. Here and there gleams as of a few scattered pieces of silver marked the windings of the great river; and on the nearest of them, just within the bar, the tug steaming right into the land became lost to my sight, hull and funnel and masts, as though the impassive earth had swallowed her up without an effort, without a tremor. My eye followed the light cloud of her smoke, now here, now there, above the plain, according to the devious curves of the stream, but always fainter and farther away, till I lost it at last behind the mitre-shaped hill of the great pagoda. And then I was left alone with my ship, anchored at the head of the Gulf of Siam.

She floated at the starting-point of a long journey, very still in an immense stillness, the shadows of her spars flung far to the eastward by the setting sun. At that moment I was alone on her decks. There was not a sound in her—and around us nothing moved, nothing lived, not a canoe on the water, not a bird in the air, not a cloud in the sky. In this breathless pause at the threshold of a long passage we seemed to be measuring our fitness for a long and arduous enterprise, the appointed task of both our existences to be carried out, far from all human eyes, with only sky and sea for spectators and for judges.

There must have been some glare in the air to interfere with one's sight, because it was only just before the sun left us that my roaming eyes made out beyond the highest ridge of the principal islet of the group something which did away with the solemnity of perfect solitude. The tide of darkness flowed on swiftly; and with tropical suddenness a swarm of stars came out above the shadowy earth, while I lingered yet, my hand resting lightly on my ship's rail as if on the shoulder of a

[1] Local name for Samutprakan, a port on the Gulf of Siam at the mouth of the Chao Phraya or Meinam River in South Thailand.

trusted friend. But, with all that multitude of celestial bodies staring down at one, the comfort of quiet communion with her was gone for good. And there were also disturbing sounds by this time—voices, footsteps forward; the steward flitted along the main-deck, a busily ministering spirit; a hand-bell tinkled urgently under the poop-deck. . . .

I found my two officers waiting for me near the supper-table, in the lighted cuddy. We sat down at once, and as I helped the chief mate, I said:

"Are you aware that there is a ship anchored inside the islands? I saw her mastheads above the ridge as the sun went down."

He raised sharply his simple face, overcharged by a terrible growth of whisker, and emitted his usual ejaculations, "Bless my soul, sir! You don't say so!"

My second mate was a round-cheeked, silent young man, grave beyond his years, I thought; but as our eyes happened to meet I detected a slight quiver on his lips. I looked down at once. It was not my part to encourage sneering on board my ship. It must be said, too, that I knew very little of my officers. In consequence of certain events of no particular significance, except to myself, I had been appointed to the command only a fortnight before. Neither did I know much of the hands forward. All these people had been together for eighteen months or so, and my position was that of the only stranger on board. I mention this because it has some bearing on what is to follow. But what I felt most was my being a stranger to the ship; and if all the truth must be told, I was somewhat of a stranger to myself. The youngest man on board (barring the second mate), and untried as yet by a position of the fullest responsibility, I was willing to take the adequacy of the others for granted. They had simply to be equal to their tasks; but I wondered how far I should turn out faithful to that ideal conception of one's own personality every man sets up for himself secretly.

Meantime the chief mate, with an almost visible effect of collaboration on the part of his round eyes and frightful whiskers, was trying to evolve a theory of the anchored ship. His dominant trait was to take all things into earnest consideration. He was of a painstaking turn of mind. As he used to say, he "liked to account to himself" for practically everything that came in his way, down to a miserable scorpion he had found in his cabin a week before. The why and the wherefore of that scorpion—how it got on board and came to select his room rather than the pantry (which was a dark place and more what a scorpion would be partial to), and how on earth it managed to drown itself in the inkwell of his writing-desk—had exercised him infinitely. The ship within the islands was much more easily accounted for; and just as we were about to rise from table he made his pronouncement. She was, he doubted not, a ship from home lately arrived. Probably she drew too much water to cross the bar except at the top of spring tides. Therefore she went into that natural harbour to wait for a few days in preference to remaining in an open roadstead.

"That's so," confirmed the second mate suddenly, in his slightly hoarse voice. "She draws over twenty feet. She's the Liverpool ship *Sephora* with a cargo of coal. Hundred and twenty-three days from Cardiff."

We looked at him in surprise.

"The tugboat skipper told me when he came on board for your letters, sir," explained the young man. "He expects to take her up the river the day after to-morrow."

After thus overwhelming us with the extent of his information he slipped out of the cabin. The mate observed regretfully that he "could not account for that young fellow's whims." What prevented him telling us all about it at once, he wanted to know.

I detained him as he was making a move. For the last two days the crew had had plenty of hard work, and the night before they had very little sleep. I felt painfully that I—a stranger—was doing something unusual when I directed him to let all hands turn in without setting an anchor-watch. I proposed to keep on deck myself till one o'clock or thereabouts. I would get the second mate to relieve me at that hour.

"He will turn out the cook and the steward at four," I concluded, "and then give you a call. Of course at the slightest sign of any sort of wind we'll have the hands up and make a start at once."

He concealed his astonishment. "Very well, sir." Outside the cuddy he put his head in the second mate's door to inform him of my unheard-of caprice to take a five hours' anchor-watch on myself. I heard the other raise his voice incredulously—"What? The captain himself?" Then a few more murmurs, a door closed, then another. A few moments later I went on deck.

My strangeness, which had made me sleepless, had prompted that unconventional arrangement, as if I had expected in those solitary hours of the night to get on terms with the ship of which I knew nothing, manned by men of whom I knew very little more. Fast alongside a wharf, littered like any ship in port with a tangle of unrelated things, invaded by unrelated shore people, I had hardly seen her yet properly. Now, as she lay cleared for sea, the stretch of her main-deck seemed to me very fine under the stars. Very fine, very roomy for her size, and very inviting. I descended the poop and paced the waist, my mind picturing to myself the coming passage through the Malay Archipelago, down the Indian Ocean, and up the Atlantic. All its phases were familiar enough to me, every characteristic, all the alternatives which were likely to face me on the high seas—everything! . . . except the novel responsibility of command. But I took heart from the reasonable thought that the ship was like other ships, the men like other men, and that the sea was not likely to keep any special surprises expressly for my discomfiture.

Arrived at that comforting conclusion, I bethought myself of a cigar and went below to get it. All was still down there. Everybody at the after end of the ship was sleeping profoundly. I came out again on the quarter-deck, agreeably at ease in my sleeping-suit on that warm, breathless night, barefooted, a glowing cigar in my teeth, and, going forward, I was met by the profound silence of the fore end of the ship. Only as I passed the door of the forecastle I heard a deep, quiet, trustful sigh of some sleeper inside. And suddenly I rejoiced in the great security of the sea as compared with the unrest of the land, in my choice of that untempted life presenting no disquieting problems, invested with an elementary moral beauty by the absolute straightforwardness of its appeal and by the singleness of its purpose.

The riding-light in the fore-rigging burned with a clear, untroubled, as if symbolic, flame, confident and bright in the mysterious shades of the night. Passing on my way aft along the other side of the ship, I observed that the rope side-ladder, put over, no doubt, for the master of the tug when he came to fetch away our letters, had not been hauled in as it should have been. I became annoyed at this, for exactitude in small matters is the very soul of discipline. Then I reflected that I had myself peremptorily dismissed my officers from duty, and by my own act had prevented the anchor-watch being formally set and things properly attended to. I asked myself whether it was wise ever to interfere with the established routine of duties even from the kindest of motives. My action might have made me appear eccentric. Goodness only knew how that absurdly whiskered mate would "account" for my conduct, and what the whole ship thought of that informality of their new captain. I was vexed with myself.

Not from compunction certainly, but, as it were mechanically, I proceeded to get the ladder in myself. Now a side-ladder of that sort is a light affair and comes in easily, yet my vigorous tug, which should have brought it flying on board, merely recoiled upon my body in a totally unexpected jerk. What the devil! . . . I was so astounded by the immovableness of that ladder that I remained stockstill, trying to account for it to myself like that imbecile mate of mine. In the end, of course, I put my head over the rail.

The side of the ship made an opaque belt of shadow on the darkling glassy shimmer of the sea. But I saw at once something elongated and pale floating very close to the ladder. Before I could form a guess, a faint flash of phosphorescent light, which seemed to issue suddenly from the naked body of a man, flickered in the sleeping water with the elusive, silent play of summer lightning in a night sky. With a gasp I saw revealed to my stare a pair of feet, the long legs, a broad livid back immersed right up to the neck in a greenish cadaverous glow. One hand, awash, clutched the bottom rung of the ladder. He was complete but for the head. A headless corpse! The cigar dropped out of my gaping mouth with a tiny plop and a short hiss quite audible in the absolute stillness of all things under heaven. At that I suppose he raised up his face, a dimly pale oval in the shadow of the ship's side. But even then I could only barely make out down there the shape of his black-haired head. However, it was enough for the horrid, frost-bound sensation which had gripped me about the chest to pass off. The moment of vain exclamations was past too. I only climbed on the spare spar and leaned over the rail as far as I could, to bring my eyes nearer to that mystery floating alongside.

As he hung by the ladder, like a resting swimmer, the sea-lightning played about his limbs at every stir; and he appeared in it ghastly, silvery, fish-like. He remained as mute as a fish, too. He made no motion to get out of the water, either. It was inconceivable that he should not attempt to come on board, and strangely troubling to suspect that perhaps he did not want to. And my first words were prompted by just that troubled incertitude.

"What's the matter?" I asked in my ordinary tone, speaking down to the face upturned exactly under mine.

"Cramp," it answered, no louder. Then slightly anxious, "I say, no need to call any one."

"I was not going to," I said.

"Are you alone on deck?"

"Yes."

I had somehow the impression that he was on the point of letting go the ladder to swim away beyond my ken—mysterious as he came. But, for the moment, this being appearing as if he had risen from the bottom of the sea (it was certainly the nearest land to the ship) wanted only to know the time. I told him. And he, down there, tentatively:

"I suppose your captain's turned in?"

"I am sure he isn't," I said.

He seemed to struggle with himself, for I heard something like the low, bitter murmur of doubt. "What's the good?" His next words came out with a hesitating effort.

"Look here, my man. Could you call him out quietly?"

I thought the time had come to declare myself.

"*I* am the captain."

I heard a "By Jove!" whispered at the level of the water. The phosphorescence flashed in the swirl of the water all about his limbs, his other hand seized the ladder.

"My name's Leggatt."

The voice was calm and resolute—a good voice. The self-possession of that man had somehow induced a corresponding state in myself. It was very quietly that I remarked:

"You must be a good swimmer."

"Yes. I've been in the water practically since nine o'clock. The question for me now is whether I am to let go this ladder and go on swimming till I sink from exhaustion, or—to come on board here."

I felt this was no mere formula of desperate speech, but a real alternative in the view of a strong soul. I should have gathered from this that he was young; indeed, it is only the young who are ever confronted by such clear issues. But at the time it was pure intuition on my part. A mysterious communication was established already between us two—in the face of that silent, darkened tropical sea. I was young, too; young enough to make no comment. The man in the water began suddenly to climb up the ladder, and I hastened away from the rail to fetch some clothes.

Before entering the cabin I stood still, listening in the lobby at the foot of the stairs. A faint snore came through the closed door of the chief mate's room. The second mate's door was on the hook, but the darkness in there was absolutely soundless. He, too, was young and could sleep like a stone. Remained the steward, but he was not likely to wake up before he was called. I got a sleeping-suit out of my room, and, coming back on deck, saw the naked man from the sea sitting on the main-hatch, glimmering white in the darkness, his elbows on his knees and his head in his hands. In a moment he had concealed his damp body in a sleeping-suit of the same grey-stripe pattern as the one I was wearing, and followed me like my double on the poop. Together we moved right aft, barefooted, silent.

"What is it?" I asked in a deadened voice, taking the lighted lamp out of the binnacle, and raising it to his face.

"An ugly business."

He had rather regular features; a good mouth; light eyes under somewhat heavy, dark eyebrows; a smooth, square forehead; no growth on his cheeks; a small, brown moustache, and a well-shaped, round chin. His expression was concentrated, meditative, under the inspecting light of the lamp I held up to his face; such as a man thinking hard in solitude might wear. My sleeping-suit was just right for his size. A well-knit young fellow of twenty-five at most. He caught his lower lip with the edge of white, even teeth.

"Yes," I said, replacing the lamp in the binnacle. The warm, heavy tropical night closed upon his head again.

"There's a ship over there," he murmured.

"Yes, I know. The *Sephora.* Did you know of us?"

"Hadn't the slightest idea. I am the mate of her——" He paused and corrected himself. "I should say I *was.*"

"Aha! Something wrong?"

"Yes. Very wrong indeed. I've killed a man."

"What do you mean? Just now?"

"No, on the passage. Weeks ago. Thirty-nine south. When I say a man——"

"Fit of temper," I suggested confidently.

The shadowy, dark head, like mine, seemed to nod imperceptibly above the ghostly grey of my sleeping-suit. It was, in the night, as though I had been faced by my own reflection in the depths of a sombre and immense mirror.

"A pretty thing to have to own up to for a Conway boy," murmured my double distinctly.

"You're a Conway boy?"

"I am," he said, as if startled. Then, slowly . . . "Perhaps you too——"

It was so; but being a couple of years older I had left before he joined. After a quick interchange of dates a silence fell; and I thought suddenly of my absurd mate with his terrific whiskers and the "Bless my soul—you don't say so" type of intellect. My double gave me an inkling of his thoughts by saying:

"My father's a parson in Norfolk. Do you see me before a judge and jury on that charge? For myself I can't see the necessity. There are fellows that an angel from heaven—and I am not that. He was one of those creatures that are just simmering all the time with a silly sort of wickedness. Miserable devils that have no business to live at all. He wouldn't do his duty and wouldn't let anybody else do theirs. But what's the good of talking! You know well enough the sort of ill-conditioned snarling cur——"

He appealed to me as if our experiences had been as identical as our clothes. And I knew well enough the pestiferous danger of such a character where there are no means of legal repression. And I knew well enough also that my double there was no homicidal ruffian. I did not think of asking him for details, and he told me the story roughly in brusque, disconnected sentences. I needed no more. I saw it all going on as though I were myself inside that other sleeping-suit.

"It happened while we were setting a reefed foresail, at dusk. Reefed foresail! You understand the sort of weather. The only sail we had left to keep the ship running; so you may guess what it had been like for days. Anxious sort of job, that. He gave me some of his cursed insolence at the sheet. I tell you I was overdone with this terrific weather that seemed to have no end to it. Terrific, I tell you—and a deep ship. I believe the fellow himself was half crazed with funk. It was no time for gentlemanly reproof, so I turned round and felled him like an ox. He up and at me. We closed just as an awful sea made for the ship. All hands saw it coming and took to the rigging, but I had him by the throat, and went on shaking him like a rat, the men above us yelling, 'Look out! Look out!' Then a crash as if the sky had fallen on my head. They say that for over ten minutes hardly anything was to be seen of the ship—just the three masts and a bit of the forecastle head and of the poop all awash driving along in a smother of foam. It was a miracle that they found us, jammed together behind the forebits. It's clear that I meant business, because I was holding him by the throat still when they picked us up. He was black in the face. It was too much for them. It seems they rushed us aft together, gripped as we were, screaming 'Murder!' like a lot of lunatics, and broke into the cuddy. And the ship running for her life, touch and go all the time, any minute her last in a sea fit to turn your hair grey only a-looking at it. I understand that the skipper, too, started raving like the rest of them. The man had been deprived of sleep for more than a week, and to have this sprung on him at the height of a furious gale nearly drove him out of his mind. I wonder they didn't fling me overboard after getting the carcass of their precious shipmate out of my fingers. They had rather a job to separate us, I've been told. A sufficiently fierce story to make an old judge and a respectable jury sit up a bit. The first thing I heard when I came to myself was the maddening howling of that endless gale, and on that the voice of the old man. He was hanging on to my bunk, staring into my face out of his sou'wester.

" 'Mr. Leggatt, you have killed a man. You can act no longer as chief mate of this ship.' "

His care to subdue his voice made it sound monotonous. He rested a hand on the end of the skylight to steady himself with, and all that time did not stir a limb, so far as I could see. "Nice little tale for a quiet tea-party," he concluded in the same tone.

One of my hands, too, rested on the end of the skylight; neither did I stir a limb, so far as I knew. We stood less than a foot from each other. It occurred to me that if old "Bless my soul—you don't say so" were to put his head up the companion and catch sight of us, he would think he was seeing double, or imagine himself come upon a scene of weird witchcraft; the strange captain having a quiet confabulation by the wheel with his own grey ghost. I became very much concerned to prevent anything of the sort. I heard the other's soothing undertone:

"My father's a parson in Norfolk," it said. Evidently he had forgotten he had told me this important fact before. Truly a nice little tale.

"You had better slip down into my state-room now," I said, moving off stealthily. My double followed my movements; our bare feet made no sound; I let him in, closed the door with care, and, after giving a call to the second mate, returned on deck for my relief.

"Not much sign of any wind yet," I remarked when he approached.

"No, sir. Not much," he assented sleepily in his hoarse voice, with just enough deference, no more, and barely suppressing a yawn.

"Well, that's all you have to look out for. You have got your orders."

"Yes, sir."

I paced a turn or two on the poop and saw him take up his position face forward with his elbow in the ratlines of the mizzen-rigging before I went below. The mate's faint snoring was still going on peacefully. The cuddy lamp was burning over the table on which stood a vase with flowers, a polite attention from the ship's provision merchant—the last flowers we should see for the next three months at the very least. Two bunches of bananas hung from the beam symmetrically, one on each side of the rudder-casing. Everything was as before in the ship—except that two of her captain's sleeping-suits were simultaneously in use, one motionless in the cuddy, the other keeping very still in the captain's state-room.

It must be explained here that my cabin had the form of the capital letter L, the door being within the angle and opening into the short part of the letter. A couch was to the left, the bedplace to the right; my writing-desk and the chronometers' table faced the door. But any one opening it, unless he stepped right inside, had no view of what I call the long (or vertical) part of the letter. It contained some lockers surmounted by a bookcase; and a few clothes, a thick jacket or two, caps, oilskin coat, and such-like, hung on hooks. There was at the bottom of that part a door opening into my bathroom, which could be entered also directly from the saloon. But that way was never used.

The mysterious arrival had discovered the advantage of this particular shape. Entering my room, lighted strongly by a big bulkhead lamp swung on gimbals above my writing-desk, I did not see him anywhere till he stepped out quietly from behind the coats hung in the recessed part.

"I heard somebody moving about, and went in there at once," he whispered.

I, too, spoke under my breath.

"Nobody is likely to come in here without knocking and getting permission."

He nodded. His face was thin and the sunburn faded, as though he had been ill. And no wonder. He had been, I heard presently, kept under arrest in his cabin for nearly seven weeks. But there was nothing sickly in his eyes or in his expression. He was not a bit like me, really; yet, as we stood leaning over my bed-place, whispering side by side, with our dark heads together and our backs to the door, anybody bold enough to open it stealthily would have been treated to the uncanny sight of a double captain busy talking in whispers with his other self.

"But all this doesn't tell me how you came to hang on to our side-ladder," I inquired, in the hardly audible murmurs we used, after he had told me something more of the proceedings on board the *Sephora* once the bad weather was over.

"When we sighted Java Head I had had time to think all those matters out several times over. I had six weeks of doing nothing else, and with only an hour or so every evening for a tramp on the quarter-deck."

He whispered, his arms folded on the side of my bed-place, staring through the open port. And I could imagine perfectly the manner of this thinking out—a stubborn if not a steadfast operation; something of which I should have been perfectly incapable.

"I reckoned it would be dark before we closed with the land," he continued, so low that I had to strain my hearing, near as we were to each other, shoulder touching shoulder almost. "So I asked to speak to the old man. He always seemed very sick when he came to see me—as if he could not look me in the face. You know, that foresail saved the ship. She was too deep to have run long under bare poles. And it was I that managed to set it for him. Anyway, he came. When I had him in my cabin—he stood by the door looking at me as if I had the halter round my neck already—I asked him right away to leave my cabin door unlocked at night while the ship was going through Sunda Straits. There would be the Java coast within two or three miles, off Angier Point. I wanted nothing more. I've had a prize for swimming my second year in the Conway."

"I can believe it," I breathed out.

"God only knows why they locked me in every night. To see some of their faces you'd have thought they were afraid I'd go about at night strangling people. Am I a murdering brute? Do I look it? By Jove! if I had been he wouldn't have trusted himself like that into my room. You'll say I might have chucked him aside and bolted out, there and then—it was dark already. Well, no. And for the same reason I wouldn't think of trying to smash the door. There would have been a rush to stop me at the noise, and I did not mean to get into a confounded scrimmage. Somebody else might have got killed—for I would not have broken out only to get chucked back, and I did not want any more of that work. He refused, looking more sick than ever. He was afraid of the men, and also of that old second mate of his who had been sailing with him for years—a grey-headed old humbug; and his steward, too, had been with him devil knows how long—seventeen years or more—a dogmatic sort of loafer who hated me like poison, just because I was the chief mate. No chief mate ever made more than one voyage in the *Sephora,* you know. Those two old chaps ran the ship. Devil only knows what the skipper wasn't afraid of (all his nerve went to pieces altogether in that hellish spell of bad weather we had)—of what the law would do to him—of his wife, perhaps. Oh yes! she's on board. Though I don't think she would have meddled. She would have been only too glad to have me out of the ship in any way. The 'brand of Cain' business, don't you see? That's all right. I was ready enough to go off wandering on the face of the earth—and that was price enough to pay for an Abel of that sort. Anyhow, he wouldn't listen to me. 'This thing must take its course. I represent the law here.' He was shaking like a leaf. 'So you won't?' 'No!' 'Then I hope you will be able to sleep on that,' I said, and turned my back on him. 'I wonder that *you* can,' cries he, and locks the door.

"Well, after that, I couldn't. Not very well. That was three weeks ago. We have had a slow passage through the Java Sea; drifted about Carimata[2] for ten days. When we anchored here they thought, I suppose, it was all right. The nearest land (and that's five miles) is the ship's destination; the consul would soon set about catching me; and there would have been no object in bolting to these islets there. I don't suppose there's a drop of water on them. I don't know how it was, but to-night that steward, after bringing me my supper went out to let me eat it, and left the door unlocked. And I ate it—all there was, too. After I had finished I strolled out on the quarter-deck. I don't know that I meant to do anything. A breath of fresh air was all I wanted, I believe. Then a sudden temptation came over me. I kicked off my slippers and was in the water before I had made up my mind fairly. Somebody heard the splash and they raised an awful hullabaloo. 'He's gone! Lower the boats! He's committed suicide! No, he's swimming.' Certainly I was swimming. It's not so easy for a swimmer like me to commit suicide by drowning. I landed on the nearest islet before the boat left the ship's side. I heard them pulling about in the dark, hailing, and so on, but after a bit they gave up. Everything quieted down and the anchorage became as still as death. I sat down on a stone and began to think. I felt certain they would start searching for me at daylight. There was no place to hide on those stony things—and if there had been, what would have been the good? But now I was clear of that ship, I was not going back. So after a while I took off all my clothes, tied them up in a bundle with a stone inside, and dropped them in the deep water on the outer side of that islet. That was suicide enough for me. Let them think what they liked, but I didn't mean to drown myself. I meant to swim till I sank—but that's not the same thing. I struck out for another of these little islands, and it was from that one that I first saw your riding-light. Something to swim for. I went on easily, and on the way I came upon a flat rock a foot or two above water. In the daytime, I dare say, you might make it out with a glass from your poop. I scrambled up on it and rested myself for a bit. Then I made another start. That last spell must have been over a mile."

His whisper was getting fainter and fainter, and all the time he stared straight out through the porthole, in which there was not even a star to be seen. I had not interrupted him. There was something that made comment impossible in his narrative, or perhaps in himself; a sort of feeling, a quality, which I can't find a name for. And when he ceased, all I found was a futile whisper, "So you swam for our light?"

[2] Karimata Strait, channel connecting the Java Sea with the South China Sea.

"Yes—straight for it. It was something to swim for. I couldn't see any stars low down because the coast was in the way, and I couldn't see the land, either. The water was like glass. One might have been swimming in a confounded thousand feet deep cistern with no place for scrambling out anywhere; but what I didn't like was the notion of swimming round and round like a crazed bullock before I gave out; and as I didn't mean to go back . . . No. Do you see me being hauled back, stark naked, off one of these little islands by the scruff of the neck and fighting like a wild beast? Somebody would have got killed for certain, and I did not want any of that. So I went on. Then your ladder——"

"Why didn't you hail the ship?" I asked, a little louder.

He touched my shoulder lightly. Lazy footsteps came right over our heads and stopped. The second mate had crossed from the other side of the poop and might have been hanging over the rail, for all we knew.

"He couldn't hear us talking—could he?" My double breathed into my very ear anxiously.

His anxiety was an answer, a sufficient answer, to the question I had put to him. An answer containing all the difficulty of that situation. I closed the porthole quietly, to make sure. A louder word might have been overheard.

"Who's that?" he whispered then.

"My second mate. But I don't know much more of the fellow than you do."

And I told him a little about myself. I had been appointed to take charge while I least expected anything of the sort, not quite a fortnight ago. I didn't know either the ship or the people. Hadn't had the time in port to look about me or size anybody up. And as to the crew, all they knew was that I was appointed to take the ship home. For the rest, I was almost as much of a stranger on board as himself, I said. And at the moment I felt it most acutely. I felt that it would take very little to make me a suspect person in the eyes of the ship's company.

He had turned about meantime; and we, the two strangers in the ship, faced each other in identical attitudes.

"Your ladder——" he murmured, after a silence. "Who'd have thought of finding a ladder hanging over at night in a ship anchored out here! I felt just then a very unpleasant faintness. After the life I've been leading for nine weeks, anybody would have got out of condition. I wasn't capable of swimming round as far as your rudder-chains. And, lo and behold! there was a ladder to get hold of. After I gripped it I said to myself, 'What's the good?' When I saw a man's head looking over I thought I would swim away presently and leave him shouting—in whatever language it was. I didn't mind being looked at. I—I liked it. And then you speaking to me so quietly—as if you had expected me—made me hold on a little longer. It had been a confounded lonely time—I don't mean while swimming. I was glad to talk a little to somebody that didn't belong to the *Sephora.* As to asking for the captain, that was a mere impulse. It could have been no use, with all the ship knowing about me and the other people pretty certain to be round here in the morning. I don't know—I wanted to be seen, to talk with somebody, before I went on. I don't know what I would have said.... 'Fine night, isn't it?' or something of the sort."

"Do you think they will be round here presently?" I asked, with some incredulity.

"Quite likely," he said faintly.

He looked extremely haggard all of a sudden. His head rolled on his shoulders.

"H'm. We shall see then. Meantime get into that bed," I whispered. "Want help? There."

It was a rather high bed-place with a set of drawers underneath. This amazing swimmer really needed the lift I gave him by seizing his leg. He tumbled in, rolled over on his back, and flung one arm across his eyes. And then, with his face nearly hidden, he must have looked exactly as I used to look in that bed. I gazed upon my other self for a while before drawing across carefully the two green serge curtains which ran on a brass rod. I thought for a moment of pinning them together for greater safety, but I sat down on the couch, and once there I felt unwilling to rise and hunt for a pin. I would do it in a moment. I was extremely tired, in a peculiarly intimate way, by the strain of stealthiness, by the effort of whispering, and the general secrecy of this excitement. It was three o'clock by now, and I had been on my feet since nine, but I was not sleepy; I could not have gone to sleep. I sat there, fagged out, looking at the curtains, trying to clear my mind of the confused sensation of being in two places at once, and greatly bothered by an exasperating knocking in my head. It was a relief to discover suddenly that it was not in my head at all, but on the outside of the door. Before I could collect myself, the words "Come in" were out of my mouth, and the steward entered with a tray, bringing in my morning coffee. I had slept, after all, and I was so frightened that I shouted, "This way! I am here, steward," as though he had been miles away. He put down the tray on the table next the couch and only then said, very quietly, "I can see you are here, sir." I felt him give me a keen look, but I dared not meet his eyes just then. He must have wondered why I had drawn the curtains of my bed before going to sleep on the couch. He went out, hooking the door open as usual.

I heard the crew washing decks above me. I knew I would have been told at once if there had been any wind. Calm, I thought, and I was doubly vexed. Indeed, I felt dual more than ever. The steward reappeared suddenly in the doorway. I jumped up from the couch so quickly that he gave a start.

"What do you want here?"

"Close your port, sir—they are washing decks."

"It is closed," I said, reddening.

"Very well, sir." But he did not move from the doorway, and returned my stare in an extraordinary, equivocal manner for a time. Then his eyes wavered, all his expression changed, and in a voice unusually gentle, almost coaxingly:

"May I come in to take the empty cup away, sir?"

"Of course!" I turned my back on him while he popped in and out. Then I unhooked and closed the door and even pushed the bolt. This sort of thing could not go on very long. The cabin was as hot as an oven, too. I took a peep at my double, and discovered that he had not moved, his arm was still over his eyes; but his chest heaved; his hair was wet; his chin glistened with perspiration. I reached over him and opened the port.

"I must show myself on deck," I reflected.

Of course, theoretically, I could do what I liked, with no one to say nay to me within the whole circle of the horizon; but to lock my cabin door and take the key away I did not dare. Directly I put my head out of the companion I saw the group of my two officers, the second mate barefooted, the chief mate in long indiarubber boots, near the break of the poop, and the steward half-way down the poop-ladder talking to them eagerly. He happened to catch sight of me and dived, the second ran down on the main-deck shouting some order or other, and the chief mate came to meet me, touching his cap.

There was a sort of curiosity in his eye that I did not like. I don't know whether the steward had told them that I was "queer" only, or down-right drunk, but I know the man meant to have a good look at me. I watched him coming with a smile which, as he got into point-blank range, took effect and froze his very whiskers. I did not give him time to open his lips.

"Square the yards by lifts and braces before the hands go to breakfast."

It was the first particular order I had given on board that ship; and I stayed on deck to see it executed too. I had felt the need of asserting myself without loss of time. That sneering young cub got taken down a peg or two on that occasion, and I also seized the opportunity of having a good look at the face of every foremast man as they filed past me to go to the after-braces. At breakfast-time, eating nothing myself, I presided with such frigid dignity that the two mates were only too glad to escape from the cabin as soon as decency permitted; and all the time the dual working of my mind distracted me almost to the point of insanity. I was constantly watching myself, my secret self, as dependent on my actions as my own personality, sleeping in that bed, behind that door which faced me as I sat at the head of the table. It was very much like being mad, only it was worse, because one was aware of it.

I had to shake him for a solid minute, but when at last he opened his eyes it was in the full possession of his senses, with an inquiring look.

"All's well so far," I whispered. "Now you must vanish into the bathroom."

He did so, as noiseless as a ghost, and I then rang for the steward, and facing him boldly, directed him to tidy up my state-room while I was having my bath—"and be quick about it." As my tone admitted of no excuses, he said, "Yes, sir," and ran off to fetch his dust-pan and brushes. I took a bath and did most of my dressing, splashing, and whistling softly for the steward's edification, while the secret sharer of my life stood drawn bolt upright in that little space, his face looking very sunken in daylight, his eyelids lowered under the stern, dark line of his eyebrows drawn together by a slight frown.

When I left him there to go back to my room the steward was finishing dusting. I sent for the mate and engaged him in some insignificant conversation. It was, as it were, trifling with the terrific character of his whiskers; but my object was to give him an opportunity for a good look at my cabin. And then I could at last shut, with a clear conscience, the door of my state-room and get my double back into the recessed part. There was nothing else for it. He had to sit still on a small folding stool, half smothered by the heavy coats hanging there. We listened to the steward going into the bathroom out of the saloon, filling the water-bottles there, scrubbing the bath, setting things to rights, whisk, bang, clatter—out again into the saloon—turn the key—click. Such was my scheme for keeping my second self invisible. Nothing better could be contrived under the circumstances. And there we sat: I at my writing-desk ready to appear busy with some papers, he behind me, out of sight of the door. It would not have been prudent to talk in daytime; and I could not have stood the excitement of that queer sense of whispering to myself. Now and then, glancing over my shoulder, I saw him far back there, sitting rigidly on the low stool, his bare feet close together, his arms folded, his head hanging on his breast—and perfectly still. Anybody would have taken him for me.

I was fascinated by it myself. Every moment I had to glance over my shoulder. I was looking at him when a voice outside the door said:

"Beg pardon, sir."

"Well!" . . . I kept my eyes on him, and so, when the voice outside the door announced, "There's a ship's boat coming our way, sir," I saw him give a start—the first movement he had made for hours. But he did not raise his bowed head.

"All right. Get the ladder over."

I hesitated. Should I whisper something to him? But what? His immobility seemed to have been never disturbed. What could I tell him he did not know already? . . . Finally I went on deck.

II

The skipper of the *Sephora* had a thin, red whisker all round his face, and the sort of complexion that goes with hair of that colour; also the particular, rather smeary shade of blue in the eyes. He was not exactly a showy figure; his shoulders were high, his stature but middling —one leg slightly more bandy than the other. He shook hands, looking vaguely around. A spiritless tenacity was his main characteristic, I judged. I behaved with a politeness which seemed to disconcert him. Perhaps he was shy. He mumbled to me as if he were ashamed of what he was saying; gave his name (it was something like Archbold—but at this distance of years I hardly am sure), his ship's name, and a few other particulars of that sort, in the manner of a criminal making a reluctant and doleful confession. He had had terrible weather on the passage out—terrible—terrible—wife aboard, too.

By this time we were seated in the cabin and the steward brought in a tray with a bottle and glasses. "Thanks! No." Never took liquor. Would have some water, though. He drank two tumblerfuls. Terrible thirsty work. Ever since daylight had been exploring the islands round his ship.

"What was that for—fun?" I asked, with an appearance of polite interest.

"No!" He sighed. "Painful duty."

As he persisted in his mumbling, and I wanted my double to hear every word, I hit upon the notion of informing him that I regretted to say I was hard of hearing.

"Such a young man, too!" he nodded, keeping his smeary blue, unintelligent eyes fastened upon me. What was the cause of it—some disease? he inquired, without the least sympathy and as if he thought that, if so, I'd got no more than I deserved.

"Yes; disease," I admitted in a cheerful tone which seemed to shock him. But my point was gained, because he had to raise his voice to give me his tale. It is not worth while to record that version. It was just over two months since all this had happened, and he had thought so much about it that he seemed completely muddled as to its bearings, but still immensely impressed.

"What would you think of such a thing happening on board your own ship? I've had the *Sephora* for these fifteen years. I am a well-known shipmaster."

He was densely distressed—and perhaps I should have sympathised with him if I had been able to detach my mental vision from the unsuspected sharer of my cabin as though he were my second self. There he was on the other side of the bulkhead, four or five feet from us, no more, as we sat in the saloon. I looked politely at Captain Archbold (if that was his name), but it was the other I saw, in a grey sleeping-suit, seated on a low stool, his bare feet close together, his arms folded, and every word said between us falling into the ears of his dark head bowed on his chest.

"I have been at sea now, man and boy, for seven-and-thirty years, and I've never heard of such a thing happening in an English ship. And that it should be my ship. Wife on board, too."

I was hardly listening to him.

"Don't you think," I said, "that the heavy sea which, you told me, came aboard just then might have killed the man? I have seen the sheer weight of a sea kill a man very neatly, by simply breaking his neck."

"Good God!" he uttered impressively, fixing his smeary blue eyes on me. "The sea! No man killed by the sea ever looked like that." He seemed positively scandalised at my suggestion. And as I gazed at him, certainly not prepared for anything original on his part, he advanced his head close to mine and thrust his tongue out at me so suddenly that I couldn't help starting back.

After scoring over my calmness in this graphic way he nodded wisely. If I had seen the sight, he assured me, I would never forget it as long as I lived. The weather was too bad to give the corpse a proper sea burial. So next day at dawn they took it up on the poop, covering its face with a bit of bunting; he read a short prayer, and then, just as it was, in its oilskins and long boots, they launched it amongst those mountainous seas that seemed ready every moment to swallow up the ship herself and the terrified lives on board of her.

"That reefed foresail saved you," I threw in.

"Under God—it did," he exclaimed fervently. "It was by a special mercy, I firmly believe, that it stood some of those hurricane squalls."

"It was the setting of that sail which——" I began.

"God's own hand in it," he interrupted me. "Nothing less could have done it. I don't mind telling you that I hardly dared give the order. It seemed impossible that we could touch anything without losing it, and then our last hope would have been gone."

The terror of that gale was on him yet. I let him go on for a bit, then said casually—as if returning to a minor subject:

"You were very anxious to give up your mate to the shore people, I believe?"

He was. To the law. His obscure tenacity on that point had in it something incomprehensible and a little awful; something, as it were, mystical, quite apart from his anxiety that he should not be suspected of "countenancing any doings of that sort." Seven-and-thirty virtuous years at sea, of which over twenty of immaculate command, and the last fifteen in the *Sephora,* seemed to have laid him under some pitiless obligation.

"And you know," he went on, groping shamefacedly amongst his feelings, "I did not engage that young fellow. His people had some interest with my owners. I was in a way forced to take him on. He looked very smart, very gentlemanly, and all that. But do you know—I never liked him, somehow. I am a plain man. You see, he wasn't exactly the sort for the chief mate of a ship like the *Sephora.*"

I had become so connected in thoughts and impressions with the secret sharer of my cabin that I felt as if I, personally, were being given to understand that I, too, was not the sort that would have done for the chief mate of a ship like the *Sephora.* I had no doubt of it in my mind.

"Not at all the style of man. You understand," he insisted superfluously, looking hard at me.

I smiled urbanely. He seemed at a loss for a while.

"I suppose I must report a suicide."

"Beg pardon?"

"Sui—cide! That's what I'll have to write to my owners directly I get in."

"Unless you manage to recover him before to-morrow," I assented dispassionately.... "I mean, alive."

He mumbled something which I really did not catch, and I turned my ear to him in a puzzled manner. He fairly bawled:

"The land—I say, the mainland is at least seven miles off my anchorage."

"About that."

My lack of excitement, of curiosity, of surprise, of any sort of pronounced interest, began to arouse his distrust. But except for the felicitous pretense of deafness I had not tried to pretend anything. I had felt utterly incapable of playing the part of ignorance properly, and therefore was afraid to try. It is also certain that he had brought some ready-made suspicions with him, and that he viewed my politeness as a strange and unnatural phenomenon. And yet how else could I have received him? Not heartily! That was impossible for psychological reasons, which I need not state here. My only object was to keep off his inquiries. Surlily? Yes, but surliness might have provoked a point-blank question. From its novelty to him and from its nature, punctilious courtesy was the manner best calculated to restrain the man. But there was the danger of his breaking through my defence bluntly. I could not, I think, have met him by a direct lie, also for psychological (not moral) reasons. If he had only known how afraid I was of his putting my feeling of identity with the other to the test! But, strangely enough (I thought of it only afterward), I believe that he was not a little disconcerted by the reverse side of that weird situation, by something in me that reminded him of the man he was seeking—suggested a mysterious similitude to the young fellow he had distrusted and disliked from the first.

However that might have been, the silence was not very prolonged. He took another oblique step.

"I reckon I had no more than a two-mile pull to your ship. Not a bit more."

"And quite enough, too, in this awful heat," I said.

Another pause full of mistrust followed. Necessity, they say, is mother of invention, but fear, too, is not barren of ingenious suggestions. And I was afraid he would ask me point-blank for news of my other self.

"Nice little saloon, isn't it?" I remarked, as if noticing for the first time the way his eyes roamed from one closed door to the other. "And very well fitted out, too. Here, for instance," I continued, reaching over the back of my seat negligently and flinging the door open, "is my bathroom."

He made an eager movement, but hardly gave it a glance. I got up, shut the door of the bathroom, and invited him to have a look round, as if I were very proud of my accommodation. He had to rise and be shown round, but he went through the business without any raptures whatever.

"And now we'll have a look at my state-room," I declared, in a voice as loud as I dared to make it, crossing the cabin to the starboard side with purposely heavy steps.

He followed me in and gazed around. My intelligent double had vanished. I played my part.

"Very convenient—isn't it?"

"Very nice. Very comf . . ." He didn't finish, and went out brusquely as if to escape from some unrighteous wiles of mine. But it was not to be. I had been too frightened not to feel vengeful; I felt I had him on the run, and I meant to keep him on the run. My polite insistence must have had something menacing in it, because he gave in suddenly. And I did not let him off a single item: mate's room, pantry, store-rooms, the very sail-locker, which was also under the poop—he had to look into them all. When at last I showed him out on the quarter-deck he drew a long, spiritless sigh, and mumbled dismally that he must really be going back to his ship now. I desired my mate, who had joined us, to see to the captain's boat.

The man of whiskers gave a blast on the whistle which he used to wear hanging round his neck, and yelled, "*Sephora's* away!" My double down there in my cabin must have heard, and certainly could not feel more relieved than I. Four fellows came running out from somewhere forward and went over the side, while my own men, appearing on deck too, lined the rail. I escorted my visitor to the gangway ceremoniously, and nearly overdid it. He was a tenacious beast. On the very ladder he lingered, and in that unique, guiltily conscientious manner of sticking to the point:

"I say . . . you . . . you don't think that——"

I covered his voice loudly:

"Certainly not. . . . I am delighted. Goodbye."

I had an idea of what he meant to say, and just saved myself by the privilege of defective hearing. He was too shaken generally to insist, but my mate, close witness of that parting, looked mystified, and his face took on a thoughtful cast. As I did not want to appear as if I wished to avoid all communication with my officers, he had the opportunity to address me.

"Seems a very nice man. His boat's crew told our chaps a very extraordinary story, if what I am told by the steward is true. I suppose you had it from the captain, sir?"

"Yes. I had a story from the captain."

"A very horrible affair—isn't it, sir?"

"It is."

"Beats all these tales we hear about murders in Yankee ships."

"I don't think it beats them. I don't think it resembles them in the least."

"Bless my soul—you don't say so! But of course I've no acquaintance whatever with American ships, not I, so I couldn't go against your knowledge. It's horrible enough for me.... But the queerest part is that those fellows seemed to have some idea the man was hidden aboard here. They had really. Did you ever hear of such a thing?"

"Preposterous—isn't it?"

We were walking to and fro athwart the quarter-deck. No one of the crew forward could be seen (the day was Sunday), and the mate pursued:

"There was some little dispute about it. Our chaps took offence. 'As if we would harbour a thing like that,' they said. 'Wouldn't you like to look for him in our coal-hole?' Quite a tiff. But they made it up in the end. I suppose he did drown himself. Don't you, sir?"

"I don't suppose anything."

"You have no doubt in the matter, sir?"

"None whatever."

I left him suddenly. I felt I was producing a bad impression, but with my double down there it was most trying to be on deck. And it was almost as trying to be below. Altogether a nerve-trying situation. But on the whole I felt less torn in two when I was with him. There was no one in the whole ship whom I dared take into my confidence. Since the hands had got to know his story, it would have been impossible to pass him off for any one else, and an accidental discovery was to be dreaded now more than ever....

The steward being engaged in laying the table for dinner, we could talk only with our eyes when I first went down. Later in the afternoon we had a cautious try at whispering. The Sunday quietness of the ship was against us; the stillness of air and water around her was against us; the elements, the men were against us—everything was against us in our secret partnership; time itself—for this could not go on for ever. The very trust in Providence was, I suppose, denied to his guilt. Shall I confess that this thought cast me down very much? And as to the chapter of accidents which counts for so much in the book of success, I could only hope that it was closed. For what favourable accident could be expected?

"Did you hear everything?" were my first words as soon as we took up our position side by side, leaning over my bed-place.

He had. And the proof of it was his earnest whisper, "The man told you he hardly dared to give the order."

I understood the reference to be to that saving foresail.

"Yes. He was afraid of it being lost in the setting."

"I assure you he never gave the order. He may think he did, but he never gave it. He stood there with me on the break of the poop after the maintopsail blew away, and whimpered about our last hope—positively whimpered about it and nothing else—and the night coming on! To hear one's skipper go on like that in such weather was enough to drive any fellow out of his mind. It worked me up into a sort of desperation. I just took it into my own hands and went away from him, boiling, and——But what's the use telling you? *You* know! . . . Do you think that if I had not been pretty fierce with them I should have got the men to do anything? Not it! The bo's'n[3] perhaps? Perhaps! It wasn't a heavy sea—it was a sea gone mad! I suppose the end of the world will be something like that; and a man may have the heart to see it coming once and be done with it—but to have to face it day after day——I don't blame anybody. I was precious little better than the rest. Only—I was an officer of that old coal-waggon, anyhow——"

"I quite understand," I conveyed that sincere assurance into his ear. He was out of breath with whispering; I could hear him pant slightly. It was all very simple. The same strung-up force which had given twenty-four men a chance, at least, for their lives had, in a sort of recoil, crushed an unworthy mutinous existence.

But I had no leisure to weigh the merits of the matter—footsteps in the saloon, a heavy knock. "There's enough wind to get under way with, sir." Here was the call of a new claim upon my thoughts and even upon my feelings.

"Turn the hands up," I cried through the door. "I'll be on deck directly."

I was going out to make the acquaintance of my ship. Before I left

[3] Boatswain.

the cabin our eyes met—the eyes of the only two strangers on board. I pointed to the recessed part where the little camp-stool awaited him, and laid my finger on my lips. He made a gesture—somewhat vague—a little mysterious, accompanied by a faint smile, as if of regret.

This is not the place to enlarge upon the sensations of a man who feels for the first time a ship move under his feet to his own independent word. In my case they were not unalloyed. I was not wholly alone with my command; for there was that stranger in my cabin. Or, rather, I was not completely and wholly with her. Part of me was absent. That mental feeling of being in two places at once affected me physically as if the mood of secrecy had penetrated my very soul. Before an hour had elapsed since the ship had begun to move, having occasion to ask the mate (he stood by my side) to take a compass bearing of the Pagoda, I caught myself reaching up to his ear in whispers. I say I caught myself, but enough had escaped to startle the man. I can't describe it otherwise than by saying that he shied. A grave, preoccupied manner, as though he were in possession of some perplexing intelligence, did not leave him henceforth. A little later I moved away from the rail to look at the compass with such a stealthy gait that the helmsman noticed it—and I could not help noticing the unusual roundness of his eyes. These are trifling instances, though it's to no commander's advantage to be suspected of ludicrous eccentricities. But I was also more seriously affected. There are to a seaman certain words, gestures, that should in given conditions come as naturally, as instinctively, as the winking of a menaced eye. A certain order should spring on to his lips without thinking; a certain sign should get itself made, so to speak, without reflection. But all unconscious alertness had abandoned me. I had to make an effort of will to recall myself back (from the cabin) to the conditions of the moment. I felt that I was appearing an irresolute commander to those people who were watching me more or less critically.

And, besides, there were the scares. On the second day out, for instance, coming off the deck in the afternoon (I had straw slippers on my bare feet) I stopped at the open pantry door and spoke to the steward. He was doing something there with his back to me. At the sound of my voice he nearly jumped out of his skin, as the saying is, and incidentally broke a cup.

"What on earth's the matter with you?" I asked, astonished.

He was extremely confused. "Beg your pardon, sir. I made sure you were in your cabin."

"You see I wasn't."

"No, sir. I could have sworn I had heard you moving in there not a moment ago. It's most extraordinary . . . very sorry, sir."

I passed on with an inward shudder. I was so identified with my secret double that I did not even mention the fact in those scanty, fearful whispers we exchanged. I suppose he had made some slight noise of some kind or other. It would have been miraculous if he hadn't at one time or another. And yet, haggard as he appeared, he looked always perfectly self-controlled, more than calm—almost invulnerable. On my suggestion he remained almost entirely in the bathroom, which, upon the whole, was the safest place. There could be really no shadow of an excuse for any one ever wanting to go in there, once the steward had done with it. It was a very tiny place. Sometimes he reclined on the floor, his legs bent, his head sustained on one elbow. At others I would find him on the camp-stool, sitting in his grey sleeping-suit and with his cropped dark hair like a patient, unmoved convict. At night I would smuggle him into my bed-place, and we would whisper together, with the regular footfalls of the officer of the watch passing and repassing over our heads. It was an infinitely miserable time. It was lucky that some tins of fine preserves were stowed in a locker in my state-room; hard bread I could always get hold of; and so he lived on stewed chicken, paté de foie gras, asparagus, cooked oysters, sardines—on all sorts of abominable sham delicacies out of tins. My early morning coffee he always drank; and it was all I dared do for him in that respect.

Every day there was the horrible manœuvring to go through so that my room and then the bathroom should be done in the usual way. I came to hate the sight of the steward, to abhor the voice of that harmless man. I felt that it was he who would bring on the disaster of discovery. It hung like a sword over our heads.

The fourth day out, I think (we were then working down the east side of the Gulf of Siam, tack for tack, in light winds and smooth water)—the fourth day, I say, of this miserable juggling with the unavoidable, as we sat at our evening meal, that man, whose slightest movement I dreaded, after putting down the dishes ran up on deck busily. This could not be dangerous. Presently he came down again; and then it appeared that he had remembered a coat of mine which I had thrown over a rail to dry after having been wetted in a shower which had passed over the ship in the afternoon. Sitting stolidly at the head of the table I became terrified at the sight of the garment on his arm. Of course he made for my door. There was no time to lose.

"Steward!" I thundered. My nerves were so shaken that I could not govern my voice and conceal my agitation. This was the sort of thing that made my terrifically whiskered mate tap his forehead with his forefinger. I had detected him using that gesture while talking on deck with a confidential air to the carpenter. It was too far to hear a word, but I had no doubt that this pantomime could only refer to the strange new captain.

"Yes, sir," the pale-faced steward turned resignedly to me. It was this maddening course of being shouted at, checked without rhyme or reason, arbitrarily chased out of my cabin, suddenly called into it, sent flying out of his pantry on incomprehensible errands, that accounted for the growing wretchedness of his expression.

"Where are you going with that coat?"

"To your room, sir."

"Is there another shower coming?"

"I'm sure I don't know, sir. Shall I go up again and see, sir?"

"No, never mind."

My object was attained, as of course my other self in there would have heard everything that passed. During this interlude my two officers never raised their eyes off their respective plates; but the lip of that confounded cub, the second mate, quivered visibly.

I expected the steward to hook my coat on and come out at once. He was very slow about it; but I dominated my nervousness sufficiently not to shout after him. Suddenly I became aware (it could be heard plainly enough) that the fellow for some reason or other was opening the door of the bathroom. It was the end. The place was literally not big enough to swing a cat in. My voice died in my throat, and I went stony all over. I expected to hear a yell of surprise and terror, and made a movement, but had not the strength to get on my legs. Everything remained still. Had my second self taken the poor wretch by the throat? I don't know what I would have done next moment if I had not seen the steward come out of my room, close the door, and then stand quietly by the sideboard.

"Saved," I thought. "But, no! Lost! Gone! He was gone!"

I laid my knife and fork down and leaned back in my chair. My head swam. After a while, when sufficiently recovered to speak in a steady voice, I instructed my mate to put the ship round at eight o'clock himself.

"I won't come on deck," I went on. "I think I'll turn in, and unless the wind shifts I don't want to be disturbed before midnight. I feel a bit seedy."

"You did look middling bad a little while ago," the chief mate remarked without showing any great concern.

They both went out, and I stared at the steward clearing the table. There was nothing to be read on that wretched man's face. But why did he avoid my eyes, I asked myself. Then I thought I should like to hear the sound of his voice.

"Steward!"

"Sir!" Startled as usual.

"Where did you hang up that coat?"

"In the bathroom, sir." The usual anxious tone. "It's not quite dry yet, sir."

For some time longer I sat in the cuddy. Had my double vanished as he had come? But of his coming there was an explanation, whereas his disappearance would be inexplicable. . . . I went slowly into my dark room, shut the door, lighted the lamp, and for a time dared not turn round. When at last I did I saw him standing bolt-upright in the narrow recessed part. It would not be true to say I had a shock, but an irresistible doubt of his bodily existence flitted through my mind. Can it be, I asked myself, that he is not visible to other eyes than mine? It was like being haunted. Motionless, with a grave face, he raised his hands slightly at me in a gesture which meant clearly, "Heavens! what a narrow escape!" Narrow indeed. I think I had come creeping quietly as near insanity as any man who has not actually gone over the border. That gesture restrained me, so to speak.

The mate with the terrific whiskers was now putting the ship on the other tack. In the moment of profound silence which follows upon the hands going to their stations I heard on the poop his raised voice, "Hard alee!" and the distant shout of the order repeated on the main-deck. The sails, in that light breeze, made but a faint fluttering noise. It ceased. The ship was coming round slowly; I held my breath in the renewed stillness of expectation; one wouldn't have thought that there was a single living soul on her decks. A sudden brisk shout, "Mainsail haul!" broke the spell, and in the noisy cries and rush overhead of the men running away with the main-brace we two, down in my cabin, came together in our usual position by the bed-place.

He did not wait for my question. "I heard him fumbling here and just managed to squat myself down in the bath," he whispered to me. "The fellow only opened the door and put his arm in to hang the coat up. All the same——"

"I never thought of that," I whispered back, even more appalled than before at the closeness of the shave, and marvelling at that something unyielding in his character which was carrying him through so finely. There was no agitation in his whisper. Whoever was being driven distracted, it was not he. He was sane. And the proof of his sanity was continued when he took up the whispering again.

"It would never do for me to come to life again."

It was something that a ghost might have said. But what he was alluding to was his old captain's reluctant admission of the theory of suicide. It would obviously serve his turn—if I had understood at all the view which seemed to govern the unalterable purpose of his action.

"You must maroon me as soon as ever you can get amongst these islands off the Cambodje shore," he went on.

"Maroon you! We are not living in a boy's adventure tale," I protested. His scornful whispering took me up.

"We aren't indeed! There's nothing of a boy's tale in this. But there's nothing else for it. I want no more. You don't suppose I am afraid of what can be done to me? Prison or gallows or whatever they may please. But you don't see me coming back to explain such things to an old fellow in a wig and twelve respectable tradesmen, do you? What can they know whether I am guilty or not—or of *what* I am guilty, either? That's my affair. What does the Bible say? 'Driven off the face of the earth.'[4] Very well. I am off the face of the earth now. As I came at night so I shall go."

"Impossible!" I murmured. "You can't."

"Can't? . . . Not naked like a soul on the Day of Judgment. I shall freeze on to this sleeping-suit. The Last Day is not yet—and . . . you have understood thoroughly. Didn't you?"

I felt suddenly ashamed of myself. I may say truly that I understood—and my hesitation in letting that man swim away from my ship's side had been a mere sham sentiment, a sort of cowardice.

"It can't be done now till next night," I breathed out. "The ship is on the off-shore tack and the wind may fail us."

"As long as I know that you understand," he whispered. "But of course you do. It's a great satisfaction to have got somebody to understand. You seem to have been there on purpose." And in the same whisper, as if we two whenever we talked had to say things to each other which were not fit for the world to hear, he added, "It's very wonderful."

We remained side by side talking in our secret way—but sometimes silent or just exchanging a whispered word or two at long intervals. And as usual he stared through the port. A breath of wind came now

[4] After God has punished Cain for killing his brother Abel, Cain addresses God: "Behold, thou hast driven me out this day from the face of the earth" (Gen. 4:14).

and again into our faces. The ship might have been moored in dock, so gently and on an even keel she slipped through the water, that did not murmur even at our passage, shadowy and silent like a phantom sea.

At midnight I went on deck, and to my mate's great surprise put the ship round on the other tack. His terrible whiskers flitted round me in silent criticism. I certainly should not have done it if it had been only a question of getting out of that sleepy gulf as quickly as possible. I believe he told the second mate, who relieved him, that it was a great want of judgment. The other only yawned. That intolerable cub shuffled about so sleepily and lolled against the rails in such a slack, improper fashion that I came down on him sharply.

"Aren't you properly awake yet?"

"Yes, sir! I am awake."

"Well, then, be good enough to hold yourself as if you were. And keep a look out. If there's any current we'll be closing with some islands before daylight."

The east side of the gulf is fringed with islands, some solitary, others in groups. On the blue background of the high coast they seem to float on silvery patches of calm water, arid and grey, or dark green and rounded like clumps of evergreen bushes, with the larger ones, a mile or two long, showing the outlines of ridges, ribs of grey rock under the dank mantle of matted leafage. Unknown to trade, to travel, almost to geography, the manner of life they harbour is an unsolved secret. There must be villages—settlements of fishermen at least—on the largest of them, and some communication with the world is probably kept up by native craft. But all that forenoon, as we headed for them, fanned along by the faintest of breezes, I saw no sign of man or canoe in the field of the telescope. I kept on pointing at the scattered group.

At noon I gave no orders for a change of course, and the mate's whiskers became much concerned and seemed to be offering themselves unduly to my notice. At last I said:

"I am going to stand right in. Quite in—as far as I can take her."

The stare of extreme surprise imparted an air of ferocity also to his eyes, and he looked truly terrific for a moment.

"We're not doing well in the middle of the gulf," I continued casually. "I am going to look for the land breezes to-night."

"Bless my soul! Do you mean, sir, in the dark amongst the lot of all them islands and reefs and shoals?"

"Well, if there are any regular land breezes at all on this coast one must get close inshore to find them, mustn't one?"

"Bless my soul!" he exclaimed again under his breath. All that afternoon he wore a dreamy, contemplative appearance which in him was a mark of perplexity. After dinner I went into my state-room as if I meant to take some rest. There we two bent our dark heads over a half-unrolled chart lying on my bed.

"There," I said. "It's got to be Koh-ring. I've been looking at it ever since sunrise. It has got two hills and a low point. It must be inhabited. And on the coast opposite there is what looks like the mouth of a biggish river—with some town, no doubt, not far up. It's the best chance for you that I can see."

"Anything. Koh-ring let it be."

He looked thoughtfully at the chart as if surveying chances and distances from a lofty height—and following with his eyes his own figure wandering on the blank land of Cochin-China, and then passing off that piece of paper clean out of sight into uncharted regions. And it was as if the ship had two captains to plan her course for her. I had been so worried and restless running up and down that I had not had the patience to dress that day. I had remained in my sleeping-suit, with straw slippers and a soft floppy hat. The closeness of the heat in the gulf had been most oppressive, and the crew were used to see me wandering in that airy attire.

"She will clear the south point as she heads now," I whispered into his ear. "Goodness only knows when, though, but certainly after dark. I'll edge her in to half a mile, as far as I may be able to judge in the dark——"

"Be careful," he murmured warningly—and I realised suddenly that all my future, the only future for which I was fit, would perhaps go irretrievably to pieces in any mishap to my first command.

I could not stop a moment longer in the room. I motioned him to get out of sight and made my way on to the poop. That unplayful cub had the watch. I walked up and down for a while thinking things out, then beckoned him over.

"Send a couple of hands to open the two quarter-deck ports," I said mildly.

He actually had the impudence, or else so forgot himself in his wonder at such an incomprehensible order, as to repeat:

"Open the quarter-deck ports! What for, sir?"

"The only reason you need concern yourself about is because I tell you to do so. Have them opened wide and fastened properly."

He reddened and went off, but I believe made some jeering remark to the carpenter as to the sensible practice of ventilating a ship's quarter-deck. I know he popped into the mate's cabin to impart the fact to him, because the whiskers came on deck, as it were by chance, and stole glances at me from below—for signs of lunacy or drunkenness, I suppose.

A little before supper, feeling more restless than ever, I rejoined, for a moment, my second self. And to find him sitting so quietly was surprising, like something against nature, inhuman.

I developed my plan in a hurried whisper.

"I shall stand in as close as I dare and then put her round. I shall presently find means to smuggle you out of here into the sail-locker, which communicates with the lobby. But there is an opening, a sort of square for hauling the sails out, which gives straight on the quarter-deck and which is never closed in fine weather, so as to give air to the sails. When the ship's way is deadened in stays and all the hands are aft at the main-braces you shall have a clear road to slip out and get overboard through the open quarter-deck port. I've had them both fastened up. Use a rope's end to lower yourself into the water so as to avoid a splash—you know. It could be heard and cause some beastly complication."

He kept silent for a while, then whispered, "I understand."

"I won't be there to see you go," I began with an effort. "The rest . . . I only hope I have understood too."

"You have. From first to last"—and for the first time there seemed to be a faltering, something strained in his whisper. He caught hold of my arm, but the ringing of the supper bell made me start. He didn't, though; he only released his grip.

After supper I didn't come below again till well past eight o'clock. The faint, steady breeze was loaded with dew; and the wet, darkened sails held all there was of propelling power in it. The night, clear and starry, sparkled darkly, and the opaque, lightless patches shifting slowly against the low stars were the drifting islets. On the port bow there was a big one more distant and shadowily imposing by the great space of sky it eclipsed.

On opening the door I had a back view of my very own self looking at a chart. He had come out of the recess and was standing near the table.

"Quite dark enough," I whispered.

He stepped back and leaned against my bed with a level, quiet glance. I sat on the couch. We had nothing to say to each other. Over our heads the officer of the watch moved here and there. Then I heard him move quickly. I knew what that meant. He was making for the companion; and presently his voice was outside my door.

"We are drawing in pretty fast, sir. Land looks rather close."

"Very well," I answered. "I am coming on deck directly."

I waited till he was gone out of the cuddy, then rose. My double moved too. The time had come to exchange our last whispers, for neither of us was ever to hear each other's natural voice.

"Look here!" I opened a drawer and took out three sovereigns. "Take this, anyhow. I've got six and I'd give you the lot, only I must keep a little money to buy some fruit and vegetables for the crew from native boats as we go through Sunda Straits."

He shook his head.

"Take it," I urged him, whispering desperately. "No one can tell what——"

He smiled and slapped meaningly the only pocket of the sleeping-jacket. It was not safe, certainly. But I produced a large old silk handkerchief of mine, and tying the three pieces of gold in a corner, pressed it on him. He was touched, I suppose, because he took it at last and tied it quickly round his waist under the jacket, on his bare skin.

Our eyes met; several seconds elapsed, till, our glances still mingled, I extended my hand and turned the lamp out. Then I passed through the cuddy, leaving the door of my room wide open.... "Steward!"

He was still lingering in the pantry in the greatness of his zeal, giving a rub-up to a plated cruet-stand the last thing before going to bed. Being careful not to wake up the mate, whose room was opposite, I spoke in an undertone.

He looked round anxiously. "Sir!"

"Can you get me a little hot water from the galley?"

"I am afraid, sir, the galley fire's been out for some time now."

"Go and see."

He fled up the stairs.

"Now," I whispered loudly into the saloon—too loudly, perhaps, but I was afraid I couldn't make a sound. He was by my side in an instant—the double captain slipped past the stairs—through a tiny dark passage... a sliding door. We were in the sail-locker, scrambling on our knees over the sails. A sudden thought struck me. I saw myself wandering barefooted, bareheaded, the sun beating on my dark poll. I snatched off my floppy hat and tried hurriedly in the dark to ram it on my other self. He dodged and fended off silently. I wonder what he thought had come to me before he understood and suddenly desisted. Our hands met gropingly, lingered united in a steady, motionless clasp for a second.... No word was breathed by either of us when they separated.

I was standing quietly by the pantry door when the steward returned.

"Sorry, sir. Kettle barely warm. Shall I light the spirit-lamp?"

"Never mind."

I came out on deck slowly. It was now a matter of conscience to shave the land as close as possible—for now he must go overboard whenever the ship was put in stays. Must! There could be no going back for him. After a moment I walked over to leeward and my heart flew into my mouth at the nearness of the land on the bow. Under any other circumstances I would not have held on a minute longer. The second mate had followed me anxiously.

I looked on till I felt I could command my voice.

"She will weather," I said then in a quiet tone.

"Are you going to try that, sir?" he stammered out incredulously.

I took no notice of him and raised my tone just enough to be heard by the helmsman.

"Keep her good full."

"Good full, sir."

The wind fanned my cheek, the sails slept, the world was silent. The strain of watching the dark loom of the land grow bigger and denser was too much for me. I had shut my eyes—because the ship must go closer. She must! The stillness was intolerable. Were we standing still?

When I opened my eyes the second view started my heart with a thump. The black southern hill of Koh-ring seemed to hang right over the ship like a towering fragment of the everlasting night. On that enormous mass of blackness there was not a gleam to be seen, not a sound to be heard. It was gliding irresistibly toward us and yet seemed already within reach of the hand. I saw the vague figures of the watch grouped in the waist, gazing in awed silence.

"Are you going on, sir?" inquired an unsteady voice at my elbow.

I ignored it. I had to go on.

"Keep her full. Don't check her way. That won't do now," I said warningly.

"I can't see the sails very well," the helmsman answered me, in strange, quavering tones.

Was she close enough? Already she was, I won't say in the shadow of the land, but in the very blackness of it, already swallowed up as it were, gone too close to be recalled, gone from me altogether.

"Give the mate a call," I said to the young man who stood at my elbow as still as death. "And turn all hands up."

My tone had a borrowed loudness reverberated from the height of the land. Several voices cried out together, "We are all on deck, sir."

Then stillness again, with the great shadow gliding closer, towering higher, without a light, without a sound. Such a hush had fallen on the ship that she might have been a barque of the dead floating in slowly under the very gate of Erebus.

"My God! Where are we?"

It was the mate moaning at my elbow. He was thunderstruck, and as it were deprived of the moral support of his whiskers. He clapped his hands and absolutely cried out, "Lost!"

"Be quiet," I said sternly.

He lowered his tone, but I saw the shadowy gesture of his despair. "What are we doing here?"

"Looking for the land wind."

He made as if to tear his hair, and addressed me recklessly.

"She will never get out. You have done it, sir. I knew it'd end in something like this. She will never weather, and you are too close now to stay. She'll drift ashore before she's round. O my God!"

I caught his arm as he was raising it to batter his poor devoted head, and shook it violently.

"She's ashore already," he wailed, trying to tear himself away.

"Is she? . . . Keep good full there!"

"Good full, sir," cried the helmsman in a frightened, thin, child-like voice.

I hadn't let go the mate's arm, and went on shaking it. "Ready about, do you hear? You go forward"—shake—"and stop there"—shake—"and hold your noise"—shake—"and see these head-sheets properly overhauled"—shake, shake—shake.

And all the time I dared not look toward the land lest my heart should fail me. I released my grip at last and he ran forward as if fleeing for dear life.

I wondered what my double there in the sail-locker thought of this commotion. He was able to hear everything—and perhaps he was able to understand why, on my conscience, it had to be thus close—no less. My first order "Hard alee!" re-echoed ominously under the towering shadow of Koh-ring as if I had shouted in a mountain gorge. And then I watched the land intently. In that smooth water and light wind it was impossible to feel the ship coming-to. No! I could not feel her. And my second self was making now ready to slip out and lower himself overboard. Perhaps he was gone already . . . ?

The great black mass brooding over our very mastheads began to pivot away from the ship's side silently. And now I forgot the secret stranger ready to depart, and remembered only that I was a total stranger to the ship. I did not know her. Would she do it? How was she to be handled?

I swung the mainyard and waited helplessly. She was perhaps stopped, and her very fate hung in the balance, with the black mass of Koh-ring like the gate of the everlasting night towering over her taffrail. What would she do now? Had she way on her yet? I stepped to the side swiftly, and on the shadowy water I could see nothing except a faint phosphorescent flash revealing the glassy smoothness of the sleeping surface. It was impossible to tell—and I had not learned yet the feel of my ship. Was she moving? What I needed was something easily seen, a piece of paper, which I could throw overboard and watch. I had nothing on me. To run down for it I didn't dare. There was no time. All at once my strained, yearning stare distinguished a white object floating within a yard of the ship's side—white, on the black water. A phosphorescent flash passed under it. What was that thing? . . . I recognised my own floppy hat. It must have fallen off his head . . . and he didn't bother. Now I had what I wanted—the saving mark for my eyes. But I hardly thought of my other self, now gone from the ship, to be hidden for ever from all friendly faces, to be a fugitive and a vagabond on the earth, with no brand of the curse on his sane forehead to stay a slaying hand[5] . . . too proud to explain.

And I watched the hat—the expression of my sudden pity for his mere flesh. It had been meant to save his homeless head from the dangers of the sun. And now—behold—it was saving the ship, by serving me for a mark to help out the ignorance of my strangeness. Ha! It was drifting forward, warning me just in time that the ship had gathered sternway.

"Shift the helm," I said in a low voice to the seaman standing still like a statue.

The man's eyes glistened wildly in the binnacle light as he jumped round to the other side and spun round the wheel.

I walked to the break of the poop. On the overshadowed deck all hands stood by the forebraces waiting for my order. The stars ahead seemed to be gliding from right to left. And all was so still in the world that I heard the quiet remark, "She's round," passed in a tone of intense relief between two seamen.

"Let go and haul."

[5] God sets a mark on Cain "lest any finding him should kill him" (Gen. 4:15).

The foreyards ran round with a great noise, amidst cheery cries. And now the frightful whiskers made themselves heard giving various orders. Already the ship was drawing ahead. And I was alone with her. Nothing! no one in the world should stand now between us, throwing a shadow on the way of silent knowledge and mute affection, the perfect communion of a seaman with his first command.

Walking to the taffrail, I was in time to make out, on the very edge of a darkness thrown by a towering black mass like the very gateway of Erebus—yes, I was in time to catch an evanescent glimpse of my white hat left behind to mark the spot where the secret sharer of my cabin and of my thoughts, as though he were my second self, had lowered himself into the water to take his punishment: a free man, a proud swimmer striking out for a new destiny.

1910

DISCUSSION QUESTIONS

1. Why does the captain immediately feel sympathy, even empathy, for Leggatt? What does he admire in Leggatt and what does that tell us about him? What do the two men have in common? How do they differ?

2. Is the captain justified in aiding and sheltering an escaped, self-confessed murderer? Explain. What made Leggatt strangle the sailor? Are there any extenuating circumstances to mitigate his act? Is the narrator right when he claims that "The same strung-up force which had given twenty-four men a chance, at least, for their lives had, in a sort of recoil, crushed an unworthy mutinous existence" (page 496)? Explain.

3. In what sense, if any, is Leggatt the captain's "other self" (page 487)? Why does Leggatt's presence impair the narrator's capacities as commander of the ship? Why has he lost all "unconscious alertness" (page 497)? When and why does he regain it?

4. Who set the "reefed foresail" and thus saved the *Sephora:* Leggatt or Archbold? Give evidence. Can you be certain? Describe the narrator's attitude toward Archbold. Give examples. How *reliable* are his descriptions of Archbold? Explain through examples.

5. How does the captain plan to allow Leggatt to slip into the water without anyone seeing or hearing him? Why is it "now a matter of conscience to shave the land as close as possible" (page 506)? What risk does such a maneuver involve? Is it justifiable?

6. What significance do you attach to the fact that the "floppy hat" that the captain had given to Leggatt serves to save the ship?

THE EYES

EDITH WHARTON

WE HAD been put in the mood for ghosts, that evening, after an excellent dinner at our old friend Culwin's, by a tale of Fred Murchard's—the narrative of a strange personal visitation.

Seen through the haze of our cigars, and by the drowsy gleam of a coal fire, Culwin's library, with its oak walls and dark old bindings, made a good setting for such evocations; and ghostly experiences at first hand being, after Murchard's opening, the only kind acceptable to us, we proceeded to take stock of our group and tax each member for a contribution. There were eight of us, and seven contrived, in a manner more or less adequate, to fulfill the condition imposed. It surprised us all to find that we could muster such a show of supernatural impressions, for none of us, excepting Murchard himself and young Phil Frenham—whose story was the slightest of the lot—had the habit of sending our souls into the invisible. So that, on the whole, we had every reason to be proud of our seven "exhibits," and none of us would have dreamed of expecting an eighth from our host.

Our old friend, Mr. Andrew Culwin, who had sat back in his armchair, listening and blinking through the smoke circles with the cheerful tolerance of a wise old idol, was not the kind of man likely to be favored with such contacts, though he had imagination enough to enjoy, without envying, the superior privileges of his guests. By age and by education he belonged to the stout Positivist tradition, and his habit of thought had been formed in the days of the epic struggle between physics and metaphysics. But he had been, then and always, essentially a spectator, a humorous detached observer of the immense muddled variety show of life, slipping out of his seat now and then for a brief dip into the convivialities at the back of the house, but never, as far as one knew, showing the least desire to jump on the stage and do a "turn."

Among his contemporaries there lingered a vague tradition of his having, at a remote period, and in a romantic clime, been wounded in a duel; but this legend no more tallied with what we younger men knew of his character than my mother's assertion that he had once been "a charming little man with nice eyes" corresponded to any possible reconstitution of his physiognomy.

"He never can have looked like anything but a bundle of sticks," Murchard had once said of him. "Or a phosphorescent log, rather," some one else amended; and we recognized the happiness of this description of his small squat trunk, with the red blink of the eyes in a face like mottled bark. He had always been possessed of a leisure which he had nursed and protected, instead of squandering it in vain activities. His carefully guarded hours had been devoted to the cultivation of a fine intelligence and a few judiciously chosen habits; and none of the disturbances common to human experience seemed to have crossed his sky. Nevertheless, his dispassionate survey of the universe had not raised his opinion of that costly experiment, and his study of the human race seemed to have resulted in the conclusion that all men were superfluous, and women necessary only because someone had to do the cooking. On the importance of this point his convictions were absolute, and gastronomy was the only science which he revered as a dogma. It must be owned that his little dinners were a strong argument in favor of this view, besides being a reason—though not the main one—for the fidelity of his friends.

Mentally he exercised a hospitality less seductive but no less stimulating. His mind was like a forum, or some open meeting place for the exchange of ideas: somewhat cold and drafty, but light, spacious and orderly—a kind of academic grove from which all the leaves have fallen. In this privileged area a dozen of us were wont to stretch our muscles and expand our lungs; and, as if to prolong as much as possible the tradition of what we felt to be a vanishing institution, one or two neophytes were now and then added to our band.

Young Phil Frenham was the last, and the most interesting, of these recruits, and a good example of Murchard's somewhat morbid assertion that our old friend "liked 'em juicy." It was indeed a fact that Culwin, for all his dryness, specially tasted the lyric qualities in youth. As he was far too good an Epicurean to nip the flowers of soul which he gathered for his garden, his friendship was not a disintegrating influence: on the contrary, it forced the young idea to robuster bloom. And in Phil Frenham he had a good subject for experimentation. The boy was really intelligent, and the soundness of his nature was like the pure paste under a fine glaze. Culwin had fished him out of a fog of family dullness, and pulled him up to a peak in Darien;[1] and the adventure hadn't hurt him a bit. Indeed, the skill with which Culwin had contrived to stimulate his curiosities without robbing them of their bloom of awe seemed to me a sufficient answer to Murchard's ogreish metaphor. There was nothing hectic in Frenham's efflorescence, and his old friend had not laid even a finger tip on the sacred stupidities. One wanted no better proof of that than the fact that Frenham still reverenced them in Culwin.

"There's a side of him you fellows don't see. *I* believe that story about the duel!" he declared; and it was of the very essence of this belief that it should impel him—just as our little party was dispersing—to turn back to our host with the joking demand: "And now you've got to tell us about *your* ghost!"

The outer door had closed on Murchard and the others; only Frenham and I remained; and the devoted servant who presided over Culwin's destinies, having brought a fresh supply of soda water, had been laconically ordered to bed.

[1] See John Keats's "On First Looking into Chapman's Homer": "Then felt I . . . like stout Cortez when with eagle eyes/He stared at the Pacific—and all his men/Looked at each other with a wild surmise—/Silent, upon a peak in Darien."

Culwin's sociability was a night-blooming flower, and we knew that he expected the nucleus of his group to tighten around him after midnight. But Frenham's appeal seemed to disconcert him comically, and he rose from the chair in which he had just reseated himself after his farewells in the hall.

"*My* ghost? Do you suppose I'm fool enough to go to the expense of keeping one of my own, when there are so many charming ones in my friends' closets? Take another cigar," he said, revolving toward me with a laugh.

Frenham laughed too, pulling up his slender height before the chimney piece as he turned to face his short bristling friend.

"Oh," he said, "you'd never be content to share if you met one you really liked."

Culwin had dropped back into his armchair, his shock head embedded in the hollow of worn leather, his little eyes glimmering over a fresh cigar.

"Liked—*liked?* Good Lord!" he growled.

"Ah, you *have,* then!" Frenham pounced on him in the same instant, with a side glance of victory at me; but Culwin cowered gnomelike among his cushions, dissembling himself in a protective cloud of smoke.

"What's the use of denying it? You've seen everything, so of course you've seen a ghost!" his young friend persisted, talking intrepidly into the cloud. "Or, if you haven't seen one, it's only because you've seen two!"

The form of the challenge seemed to strike our host. He shot his head out of the mist with a queer tortoise-like motion he sometimes had, and blinked approvingly at Frenham.

"That's it," he flung at us on a shrill jerk of laughter; "it's only because I've seen two!"

The words were so unexpected that they dropped down and down into a deep silence, while we continued to stare at each other over Culwin's head, and Culwin stared at his ghosts. At length Frenham, without speaking, threw himself into the chair on the other side of the hearth, and leaned forward with his listening smile. . . .

II

"Oh, of course they're not show ghosts—a collector wouldn't think anything of them. . . . Don't let me raise your hopes . . . their one merit is their numerical strength: the exceptional fact of their being *two.* But, as against this, I'm bound to admit that at any moment I could probably have exorcised them both by asking my doctor for a prescription, or my oculist for a pair of spectacles. Only, as I never could make up my mind whether to go to the doctor or the oculist—whether I was afflicted by an optical or a digestive delusion—I left them to pursue their interesting double life, though at times they made mine exceedingly uncomfortable. . . .

"Yes—uncomfortable; and you know how I hate to be uncomfortable! But it was part of my stupid pride, when the thing began, not to admit that I could be disturbed by the trifling matter of seeing two.

"And then I'd no reason, really, to suppose I was ill. As far as I knew I was simply bored—horribly bored. But it was part of my boredom—I remember—that I was feeling so uncommonly well, and didn't know how on earth to work off my surplus energy. I had come back from a long journey—down in South America and Mexico—and had settled down for the winter near New York with an old aunt who had known Washington Irving[2] and corresponded with N. P. Willis.[3] She lived, not far from Irvington, in a damp Gothic villa overhung by Norway spruces and looking exactly like a memorial emblem done in hair. Her personal appearance was in keeping with this image, and her own hair—of which there was little left—might have been sacrificed to the manufacture of the emblem.

"I had just reached the end of an agitated year, with considerable arrears to make up in money and emotion; and theoretically it seemed as though my aunt's mild hospitality would be as beneficial to my nerves as to my purse. But the deuce of it was that as soon as I felt myself safe and sheltered my energy began to revive; and how was I to work it off inside of a memorial emblem? I had, at that time, the illusion that sustained intellectual effort could engage a man's whole activity; and I decided to write a great book—I forget about what. My aunt, impressed by my plan, gave up to me her Gothic library, filled with classics bound in black cloth and daguerreotypes of faded celebrities; and I sat down at my desk to win myself a place among their number. And to facilitate my task she lent me a cousin to copy my manuscript.

"The cousin was a nice girl, and I had an idea that a nice girl was just what I needed to restore my faith in human nature, and principally in myself. She was neither beautiful nor intelligent—poor Alice Nowell!—but it interested me to see any woman content to be so

[2] Well-known American writer (1783–1859).

[3] Nathaniel Parker Willis (1806–1867), American writer and editor.

uninteresting, and I wanted to find out the secret of her content. In doing this I handled it rather rashly, and put it out of joint—oh, just for a moment! There's no fatuity in telling you this, for the poor girl had never seen anyone but cousins. . . .

"Well, I was sorry for what I'd done, of course, and confoundedly bothered as to how I should put it straight. She was staying in the house, and one evening, after my aunt had gone to bed, she came down to the library to fetch a book she'd mislaid, like any artless heroine, on the shelves behind us. She was pink-nosed and flustered, and it suddenly occurred to me that her hair, though it was fairly thick and pretty, would look exactly like my aunt's when she grew older. I was glad I had noticed this, for it made it easier for me to decide to do what was right; and when I had found the book she hadn't lost I told her I was leaving for Europe that week.

"Europe was terribly far off in those days, and Alice knew at once what I meant. She didn't take it in the least as I'd expected—it would have been easier if she had. She held her book very tight, and turned away a moment to wind up the lamp on my desk—it had a ground-glass shade with vine leaves, and glass drops around the edge, I remember. Then she came back, held out her hand, and said: 'Good-bye.' And as she said it she looked straight at me and kissed me. I had never felt anything as fresh and shy and brave as her kiss. It was worse than any reproach, and it made me ashamed to deserve a reproach from her. I said to myself: 'I'll marry her, and when my aunt dies she'll leave us this house, and I'll sit here at the desk and go on with my book; and Alice will sit over there with her embroidery and look at me as she's looking now. And life will go on like that for any number of years.' The prospect frightened me a little, but at the time it didn't frighten me as much as doing anything to hurt her; and ten minutes later she had my seal ring on her finger, and my promise that when I went abroad she should go with me.

"You'll wonder why I'm enlarging on this incident. It's because the evening on which it took place was the very evening on which I first saw the queer sight I've spoken of. Being at that time an ardent believer in a necessary sequence between cause and effect, I naturally tried to trace some kind of link between what had just happened to me in my aunt's library, and what was to happen a few hours later on the same night; and so the coincidence between the two events always remained in my mind.

"I went up to bed with rather a heavy heart, for I was bowed under the weight of the first good action I had ever consciously committed;

and young as I was, I saw the gravity of my situation. Don't imagine from this that I had hitherto been an instrument of destruction. I had been merely a harmless young man, who had followed his bent and declined all collaboration with Providence. Now I had suddenly undertaken to promote the moral order of the world, and I felt a good deal like the trustful spectator who has given his gold watch to the conjurer, and doesn't know in what shape he'll get it back when the trick is over. ... Still, a glow of self-righteousness tempered my fears, and I said to myself as I undressed that when I'd got used to being good it probably wouldn't make me as nervous as it did at the start. And by the time I was in bed, and had blown out my candle, I felt that I really *was* getting used to it, and that, as far as I'd got, it was not unlike sinking down into one of my aunt's very softest wool mattresses.

"I closed my eyes on this image, and when I opened them it must have been a good deal later, for my room had grown cold, and intensely still. I was waked by the queer feeling we all know—the feeling that there was something in the room that hadn't been there when I fell asleep. I sat up and strained my eyes into the darkness. The room was pitch black, and at first I saw nothing; but gradually a vague glimmer at the foot of the bed turned into two eyes staring back at me. I couldn't distinguish the features attached to them, but as I looked the eyes grew more and more distinct: they gave out a light of their own.

"The sensation of being thus gazed at was far from pleasant, and you might suppose that my first impulse would have been to jump out of bed and hurl myself on the invisible figure attached to the eyes. But it wasn't—my impulse was simply to lie still.... I can't say whether this was due to an immediate sense of the uncanny nature of the apparition—to the certainty that if I did jump out of bed I should hurl myself on nothing—or merely to the benumbing effect of the eyes themselves. They were the very worst eyes I've ever seen: a man's eyes—but what a man! My first thought was that he must be frightfully old. The orbits were sunk, and the thick red-lined lids hung over the eyeballs like blinds of which the cords are broken. One lid drooped a little lower than the other, with the effect of a crooked leer; and between these folds of flesh, with their scant bristle of lashes, the eyes themselves, small glassy disks with an agate-like rim, looked like sea pebbles in the grip of a starfish.

"But the age of the eyes was not the most unpleasant thing about them. What turned me sick was their expression of vicious security. I don't know how else to describe the fact that they seemed to belong to a man who had done a lot of harm in his life, but had always kept just inside the danger lines. They were not the eyes of a coward, but of someone much too clever to take risks; and my gorge rose at their look of base astuteness. Yet even that wasn't the worst; for as we continued to scan each other I saw in them a tinge of derision, and felt myself to be its object.

"At that I was seized by an impulse of rage that jerked me to my feet and pitched me straight at the unseen figure. But of course there wasn't any figure there, and my fists struck at emptiness. Ashamed and cold, I groped about for a match and lit the candles. The room looked just as usual—as I had known it would; and I crawled back to bed, and blew out the lights.

"As soon as the room was dark again the eyes reappeared; and I now applied myself to explaining them on scientific principles. At first I thought the illusion might have been caused by the glow of the last embers in the chimney; but the fireplace was on the other side of my bed, and so placed that the fire could not be reflected in my toilet glass, which was the only mirror in the room. Then it struck me that I might have been tricked by the reflection of the embers in some polished bit of wood or metal; and though I couldn't discover any object of the sort in my line of vision, I got up again, groped my way to the hearth, and covered what was left of the fire. But as soon as I was back in bed the eyes were back at its foot.

"They were an hallucination, then: that was plain. But the fact that they were not due to any external dupery didn't make them a bit pleasanter. For if they were a projection of my inner consciousness, what the deuce was the matter with that organ? I had gone deeply enough into the mystery of morbid pathological states to picture the conditions under which an exploring mind might lay itself open to such a midnight admonition; but I couldn't fit it to my present case. I had never felt more normal, mentally and physically; and the only unusual fact in my situation—that of having assured the happiness of an amiable girl—did not seem of a kind to summon unclean spirits about my pillow. But there were the eyes still looking at me.

"I shut mine, and tried to evoke a vision of Alice Nowell's. They were not remarkable eyes, but they were as wholesome as fresh water, and if she had had more imagination—or longer lashes—their expression might have been interesting. As it was, they did not prove very efficacious, and in a few moments I perceived that they had mysteriously changed into the eyes at the foot of the bed. It exasperated me more to feel these glaring at me through my shut lids than to see them, and I opened my eyes again and looked straight into their hateful stare....

"And so it went on all night. I can't tell you what that night was like, nor how long it lasted. Have you ever lain in bed, hopelessly wide awake, and tried to keep your eyes shut, knowing that if you opened 'em you'd see something you dreaded and loathed? It sounds easy, but it's devilishly hard. Those eyes hung there and drew me. I had the *vertige de l'abîme,*[4] and their red lids were the edge of my abyss. . . . I had known nervous hours before: hours when I'd felt the wind of danger in my neck; but never this kind of strain. It wasn't that the eyes were awful; they hadn't the majesty of the powers of darkness. But they had—how shall I say?—a physical effect that was the equivalent of a bad smell: their look left a smear like a snail's. And I didn't see what business they had with me, anyhow—and I stared and stared, trying to find out.

"I don't know what effect they were trying to produce; but the effect they *did* produce was that of making me pack my portmanteau and bolt to town early the next morning. I left a note for my aunt, explaining that I was ill and had gone to see my doctor; and as a matter of fact I did feel uncommonly ill—the night seemed to have pumped all the blood out of me. But when I reached town I didn't go to the doctor's. I went to a friend's rooms, and threw myself on a bed, and slept for ten heavenly hours. When I woke it was the middle of the night, and I turned cold at the thought of what might be waiting for me. I sat up, shaking, and stared into the darkness; but there wasn't a break in its blessed surface, and when I saw that the eyes were not there I dropped back into another long sleep.

"I had left no word for Alice when I fled, because I meant to go back the next morning. But the next morning I was too exhausted to stir. As the day went on the exhaustion increased, instead of wearing off like the fatigue left by an ordinary night of insomnia: the effect of the eyes seemed to be cumulative, and the thought of seeing them again grew intolerable. For two days I fought my dread; and on the third evening I pulled myself together and decided to go back the next morning. I felt a good deal happier as soon as I'd decided, for I knew that my abrupt disappearance, and the strangeness of my not writing, must have been very distressing to poor Alice. I went to bed with an easy mind, and fell asleep at once; but in the middle of the night I woke, and there were the eyes. . . .

"Well, I simply couldn't face them; and instead of going back to my aunt's I bundled a few things into a trunk and jumped aboard the first steamer for England. I was so dead tired when I got on board that I

[4] Vertigo of the abyss.

crawled straight into my berth, and slept most of the way over; and I can't tell you the bliss it was to wake from those long dreamless stretches and look fearlessly into the dark, *knowing* that I shouldn't see the eyes....

"I stayed abroad for a year, and then I stayed for another; and during that time I never had a glimpse of them. That was enough reason for prolonging my stay if I'd been on a desert island. Another was, of course, that I had perfectly come to see, on the voyage over, the complete impossibility of my marrying Alice Nowell. The fact that I had been so slow in making this discovery annoyed me, and made we want to avoid explanations. The bliss of escaping at one stroke from the eyes, and from this other embarrassment, gave my freedom an extraordinary zest; and the longer I savored it the better I liked its taste.

"The eyes had burned such a hole in my consciousness that for a long time I went on puzzling over the nature of the apparition, and wondering if it would ever come back. But as time passed I lost this dread, and retained only the precision of the image. Then that faded in its turn.

"The second year found me settled in Rome, where I was planning, I believe, to write another great book—a definitive work on Etruscan influences in Italian art. At any rate, I'd found some pretext of the kind for taking a sunny apartment in the Piazza di Spagna and dabbling about in the Forum; and there, one morning, a charming youth came to me. As he stood there in the warm light, slender and smooth and hyacinthine,[5] he might have stepped from a ruined altar—one to Antinous,[6] say; but he'd come instead from New York, with a letter from (of all people) Alice Nowell. The letter—the first I'd had from her since our break—was simply a line introducing her young cousin, Gilbert Noyes, and appealing to me to befriend him. It appeared, poor lad, that he 'had talent,' and 'wanted to write'; and, an obdurate family having insisted that his calligraphy should take the form of double entry, Alice had intervened to win him six months' respite, during which he was to travel abroad on a meager pittance, and somehow prove his ability to increase it by his pen. The quaint conditions of the test struck me first: it seemed about as conclusive as a medieval 'ordeal.' Then I was touched by her having sent him to me. I had always wanted to do her some service, to justify myself in my own eyes rather than hers; and here was a beautiful occasion.

[5] Like the youth Hyacinthus, loved but accidentally killed by Apollo.

[6] A youth of matchless beauty who was the favorite of the Emperor Hadrian and drowned in the Nile in A.D. 122.

"I imagine it's safe to lay down the general principle that predestined geniuses don't, as a rule, appear before one in the spring sunshine of the Forum looking like one of its banished gods. At any rate, poor Noyes wasn't a predestined genius. But he *was* beautiful to see, and charming as a comrade. It was only when he began to talk literature that my heart failed me. I knew all the symptoms so well—the things he had 'in him,' and the things outside him that impinged! There's the real test, after all. It was always—punctually, inevitably, with the inexorableness of a mechanical law—it was *always* the wrong thing that struck him. I grew to find a certain fascination in deciding in advance exactly which wrong thing he'd select; and I acquired an astonishing skill at the game. . . .

"The worst of it was that his *bêtise*[7] wasn't of the too obvious sort. Ladies who met him at picnics thought him intellectual; and even at dinners he passed for clever. I, who had him under the microscope, fancied now and then that he might develop some kind of a slim talent, something that he could make 'do' and be happy on; and wasn't that, after all, what I was concerned with? He was so charming—he continued to be so charming—that he called forth all my charity in support of this argument; and for the first few months I really believed there was a chance for him. . . .

"Those months were delightful. Noyes was constantly with me, and the more I saw of him the better I liked him. His stupidity was a natural grace—it was as beautiful, really, as his eyelashes. And he was so gay, so affectionate, and so happy with me, that telling him the truth would have been about as pleasant as slitting the throat of some gentle animal. At first I used to wonder what had put into that radiant head the detestable delusion that it held a brain. Then I began to see that it was simply protective mimicry—an instinctive ruse to get away from family life and an office desk. Not that Gilbert didn't—dear lad!—believe in himself. There wasn't a trace of hypocrisy in him. He was sure that his 'call' was irresistible, while to me it was the saving grace of his situation that it *wasn't,* and that a little money, a little leisure, a little pleasure would have turned him into an inoffensive idler. Unluckily, however, there was no hope of money, and with the alternative of the office desk before him he couldn't postpone his attempt at literature. The stuff he turned out was deplorable, and I see now that I knew it from the first. Still, the absurdity of deciding a man's whole future on a first trial seemed to justify me in withholding my verdict,

[7] Absurdity.

and perhaps even in encouraging him a little, on the ground that the human plant generally needs warmth to flower.

"At any rate, I proceeded on that principle, and carried it to the point of getting his term of probation extended. When I left Rome he went with me, and we idled away a delicious summer between Capri and Venice. I said to myself: 'If he has anything in him, it will come out now,' and it *did*. He was never more enchanting and enchanted. There were moments of our pilgrimage when beauty born of murmuring sound seemed actually to pass into his face—but only to issue forth in a flood of the palest ink....

"Well, the time came to turn off the tap; and I knew there was no hand but mine to do it. We were back in Rome, and I had taken him to stay with me, not wanting him to be alone in his *pension* when he had to face the necessity of renouncing his ambition. I hadn't, of course, relied solely on my own judgment in deciding to advise him to drop literature. I had sent his stuff to various people—editors and critics—and they had always sent it back with the same chilling lack of comment. Really there was nothing on earth to say.

"I confess I never felt more shabby than I did on the day when I decided to have it out with Gilbert. It was well enough to tell myself that it was my duty to knock the poor boy's hopes into splinters—but I'd like to know what act of gratuitous cruelty hasn't been justified on that plea? I've always shrunk from usurping the functions of Providence, and when I have to exercise them I decidedly prefer that it shouldn't be on an errand of destruction. Besides, in the last issue, who was I to decide, even after a year's trial, if poor Gilbert had it in him or not?

"The more I looked at the part I'd resolved to play, the less I liked it; and I liked it still less when Gilbert sat opposite me, with his head thrown back in the lamplight, just as Phil's is now.... I'd been going over his last manuscript, and he knew it, and he knew that his future hung on my verdict—we'd tacitly agreed to that. The manuscript lay between us, on my table—a novel, his first novel, if you please!—and he reached over and laid his hand on it, and looked up at me with all his life in the look.

"I stood up and cleared my throat, trying to keep my eyes away from his face and on the manuscript.

" 'The fact is, my dear Gilbert,' I began—

"I saw him turn pale, but he was up and facing me in an instant.

" 'Oh, look here, don't take on so, my dear fellow! I'm not so awfully cut up as all that!' His hands were on my shoulders, and he was laughing down on me from his full height, with a kind of mortally stricken gaiety that drove the knife into my side.

"He was too beautifully brave for me to keep up any humbug about my duty. And it came over me suddenly how I should hurt others in hurting him: myself first, since sending him home meant losing him; but more particularly poor Alice Nowell, to whom I had so longed to prove my good faith and my desire to serve her. It really seemed like failing her twice to fail Gilbert.

"But my intuition was like one of those lightning flashes that encircle the whole horizon, and in the same instant I saw what I might be letting myself in for if I didn't tell the truth. I said to myself: 'I shall have him for life'—and I'd never yet seen anyone, man or woman, whom I was quite sure of wanting on those terms. Well, this impulse of egotism decided me. I was ashamed of it, and to get away from it I took a leap that landed me straight in Gilbert's arms.

" 'The thing's all right, and you're all wrong!' I shouted up at him; and as he hugged me, and I laughed and shook in his clutch, I had for a minute the sense of self-complacency that is supposed to attend the footsteps of the just. Hang it all, making people happy *has* its charms.

"Gilbert, of course, was for celebrating his emancipation in some spectacular manner; but I sent him away alone to explode his emotions, and went to bed to sleep off mine. As I undressed I began to wonder what their aftertaste would be—so many of the finest don't keep! Still, I wasn't sorry, and I meant to empty the bottle, even if it *did* turn a trifle flat.

"After I got into bed I lay for a long time smiling at the memory of his eyes—his blissful eyes. . . . Then I fell asleep, and when I woke the room was deathly cold, and I sat up with a jerk—and there were *the other eyes. . . .*

"It was three years since I'd seen them, but I'd thought of them so often that I fancied they could never take me unawares again. Now, with their red sneer on me, I knew that I had never really believed they would come back, and that I was as defenceless as ever against them. . . . As before, it was the insane irrelevance of their coming that made it so horrible. What the deuce were they after, to leap out at me at such a time? I had lived more or less carelessly in the years since I'd seen them, though my worst indiscretions were not dark enough to invite the searchings of their infernal glare; but at this particular moment I was really in what might have been called a state of grace; and I can't tell you how the fact added to their horror. . . .

"But it's not enough to say they were as bad as before: they were worse. Worse by just so much as I'd learned of life in the interval; by all the damnable implications my wider experience read into them. I saw now what I hadn't seen before: that they were eyes which had grown hideous gradually, which had built up their baseness coral-wise, bit by bit, out of a series of small turpitudes slowly accumulated through the industrious years. Yes—it came to me that what made them so bad was that they'd grown bad so slowly. . . .

"There they hung in the darkness, their swollen lids dropped across the little watery bulbs rolling loose in the orbits, and the puff of flesh making a muddy shadow underneath—and as their stare moved with my movements, there came over me a sense of their tacit complicity, of a deep hidden understanding between us that was worse than the first shock of their strangeness. Not that I understood them; but that they made it so clear that someday I should. . . . Yes, that was the worst part of it, decidedly; and it was the feeling that became stronger each time they came back. . . .

"For they got into the damnable habit of coming back. They reminded me of vampires with a taste for young flesh, they seemed so to gloat over the taste of a good conscience. Every night for a month they came to claim their morsel of mine: since I'd made Gilbert happy they simply wouldn't loosen their fangs. The coincidence almost made me hate him, poor lad, fortuitous as I felt it to be. I puzzled over it a good deal, but couldn't find any hint of an explanation except in the chance of his association with Alice Nowell. But then the eyes had let up on me the moment I had abandoned her, so they could hardly be the emissaries of a woman scorned, even if one could have pictured poor Alice charging such spirits to avenge her. That set me thinking, and I began to wonder if they would let up on me if I abandoned Gilbert. The temptation was insidious, and I had to stiffen myself against it; but really, dear boy! he was too charming to be sacrificed to such demons. And so, after all, I never found out what they wanted. . . ."

III

The fire crumbled, sending up a flash which threw into relief the narrator's gnarled face under its grey-black stubble. Pressed into the hollow of the chair back, it stood out an instant like an intaglio of yellowish red-veined stone, with spots of enamel for the eyes; then the fire sank and it became once more a dim Rembrandtish blur.

Phil Frenham, sitting in a low chair on the opposite side of the hearth, one long arm propped on the table behind him, one hand supporting his thrown-back head, and his eyes fixed on his old friend's face, had not moved since the tale began. He continued to maintain his silent immobility after Culwin had ceased to speak, and it was I who, with a vague sense of disappointment at the sudden drop of the story, finally asked: "But how long did you keep on seeing them?"

Culwin, so sunk into his chair that he seemed like a heap of his own empty clothes, stirred a little, as if in surprise at my question. He appeared to have half-forgotten what he had been telling us.

"How long? Oh, off and on all that winter. It was infernal. I never got used to them. I grew really ill."

Frenham shifted his attitude, and as he did so his elbow struck against a small mirror in a bronze frame standing on the table behind him. He turned and changed its angle slightly; then he resumed his former attitude, his dark head thrown back on his lifted palm, his eyes intent on Culwin's face. Something in his silent gaze embarrassed me, and as if to divert attention from it I pressed on with another question:

"And you never tried sacrificing Noyes?"

"Oh, no. The fact is I didn't have to. He did it for me, poor boy!"

"Did it for you? How do you mean?"

"He wore me out—wore everybody out. He kept on pouring out his lamentable twaddle, and hawking it up and down the place till he became a thing of terror. I tried to wean him from writing—oh, ever so gently, you understand, by throwing him with agreeable people, giving him a chance to make himself felt, to come to a sense of what he *really* had to give. I'd foreseen this solution from the beginning—felt sure that, once the first ardor of authorship was quenched, he'd drop into his place as a charming parasitic thing, the kind of chronic Cherubino[8] for whom, in old societies, there's always a seat at table, and a shelter behind the ladies' skirts. I saw him take his place as 'the poet': the poet who doesn't write. One knows the type in every drawing room. Living in that way doesn't cost much—I'd worked it all out in my mind, and felt sure that, with a little help, he could manage it for the next few years; and meanwhile he'd be sure to marry. I saw him married to a widow, rather older, with a good cook and a well-run house. And I actually had my eye on the widow.... Meanwhile I did everything to help the transition—lent him money to ease his conscience, introduced him to pretty

[8] Generalized description of a social type based on Cherubino, the page in Mozart's opera *The Marriage of Figaro* (1786).

women to make him forget his vows. But nothing would do him: he had but one idea in his beautiful obstinate head. He wanted the laurel and not the rose, and he kept on repeating Gautier's[9] axiom, and battering and filing at his limp prose till he'd spread it out over Lord knows how many hundred pages. Now and then he would send a barrelful to a publisher, and of course it would always come back.

"At first it didn't matter—he thought he was 'misunderstood.' He took the attitudes of genius, and whenever an opus came home he wrote another to keep it company. Then he had a reaction of despair, and accused me of deceiving him, and Lord knows what. I got angry at that, and told him it was he who had deceived himself. He'd come to me determined to write, and I'd done my best to help him. That was the extent of my offence, and I'd done it for his cousin's sake, not his.

"That seemed to strike home, and he didn't answer for a minute. Then he said: 'My time's up and my money's up. What do you think I'd better do?'

" 'I think you'd better not be an ass,' I said.

" 'What do you mean by being an ass?' he asked.

"I took a letter from my desk and held it out to him.

" 'I mean refusing this offer of Mrs. Ellinger's: to be her secretary at a salary of five thousand dollars. There may be a lot more in it than that.'

"He flung out his hand with a violence that struck the letter from mine. 'Oh, I know well enough what's in it!' he said, red to the roots of his hair.

" 'And what's the answer, if you know?' I asked.

"He made none at the minute, but turned away slowly to the door. There, with his hand on the threshold, he stopped to say, almost under his breath: 'Then you really think my stuff's no good?'

"I was tired and exasperated, and I laughed. I don't defend my laugh—it was in wretched taste. But I must plead in extenuation that the boy was a fool, and that I'd done my best for him—I really had.

"He went out of the room, shutting the door quietly after him. That afternoon I left for Frascati, where I'd promised to spend the Sunday with some friends. I was glad to escape from Gilbert, and by the same token, as I learned that night, I had also escaped from the eyes. I dropped into the same lethargic sleep that had come to me before when I left off seeing them; and when I woke the next morning in my peaceful room above the ilexes, I felt the utter weariness and deep relief that

[9] Théophile Gautier (1811–1872), French poet and novelist.

always followed on that sleep. I put in two blessed nights at Frascati, and when I got back to my rooms in Rome I found that Gilbert had gone.... Oh, nothing tragic had happened—the episode never rose to *that*. He'd simply packed his manuscripts and left for America—for his family and the Wall Street desk. He left a decent enough note to tell me of his decision, and behaved altogether, in the circumstances, as little like a fool as it's possible for a fool to behave...."

IV

Culwin paused again, and Frenham still sat motionless, the dusky contour of his young head reflected in the mirror at his back.

"And what became of Noyes afterward?" I finally asked, still disquieted by a sense of incompleteness, by the need of some connecting thread between the parallel lines of the tale.

Culwin twitched his shoulders. "Oh, nothing became of him—because he became nothing. There could be no question of 'becoming' about it. He vegetated in an office, I believe, and finally got a clerkship in a consulate, and married drearily in China. I saw him once in Hong Kong, years afterward. He was fat and hadn't shaved. I was told he drank. He didn't recognize me."

"And the eyes?" I asked, after another pause which Frenham's continued silence made oppressive.

Culwin, stroking his chin, blinked at me meditatively through the shadows. "I never saw them after my last talk with Gilbert. Put two and two together if you can. For my part, I haven't found the link."

He rose, his hands in his pockets, and walked stiffly over to the table on which reviving drinks had been set out.

"You must be parched after this dry tale. Here, help yourself, my dear fellow. Here, Phil—" He turned back to the hearth.

Frenham made no response to his host's hospitable summons. He still sat in his low chair without moving, but as Culwin advanced toward him, their eyes met in a long look; after which the young man, turning suddenly, flung his arms across the table behind him, and dropped his face upon them.

Culwin, at the unexpected gesture, stopped short, a flush on his face.

"Phil—what the deuce? Why, have the eyes scared *you?* My dear boy—my dear fellow—I never had such a tribute to my literary ability, never!"

He broke into a chuckle at the thought, and halted on the hearth-rug, his hands still in his pockets, gazing down at the youth's bowed head. Then, as Frenham still made no answer, he moved a step or two nearer.

"Cheer up, my dear Phil! It's years since I've seen them—apparently I've done nothing lately bad enough to call them out of chaos. Unless my present evocation of them has made *you* see them; which would be their worst stroke yet!"

His bantering appeal quivered off into an uneasy laugh, and he moved still nearer, bending over Frenham, and laying his gouty hands on the lad's shoulders.

"Phil, my dear boy, really—what's the matter? Why don't you answer? *Have* you seen the eyes?"

Frenham's face was still hidden, and from where I stood behind Culwin I saw the latter, as if under the rebuff of this unaccountable attitude, draw back slowly from his friend. As he did so, the light of the lamp on the table fell full on his congested face, and I caught its reflection in the mirror behind Frenham's head.

Culwin saw the reflection also. He paused, his face level with the mirror, as if scarcely recognizing the countenance in it as his own. But as he looked his expression gradually changed, and for an appreciable space of time he and the image in the glass confronted each other with a glare of slowly gathering hate. Then Culwin let go on Frenham's shoulders, and drew back a step. . . .

Frenham, his face still hidden, did not stir.

1910

DISCUSSION QUESTIONS

1. Why do the narrator and his companions find it hard to believe that Culwin had once been "a charming little man with nice eyes" (page 512)? Has he been "merely a harmless young man" (page 517), as he claims? If you agree, give supporting evidence. If you disagree, explain and give supporting evidence.

2. What affinities exist between the apparitional eyes and Culwin's eyes and personality? Focus particular attention on such metaphorical descriptions as "sea pebbles in the grip of a starfish" (page 517).

3. Why does Frenham, in part IV, suddenly bury his face in his outstretched arms? Why does the gesture mystify Culwin at first? What

specifically brings about Culwin's enlightenment? Who is unwittingly responsible for it?

4. Why does Culwin, at the end of the story, confront his own reflected image "with a glare of slowly gathering hate"? Why has it taken him so long to understand the meaning of the apparition?

5. Culwin blames his inability to understand the apparitional eyes on "the insane irrelevance of their coming" (page 523). Why does their appearance seem irrelevant to him? Why do the eyes seem to him "to gloat over the taste of a good conscience" (page 524). Whose conscience?

6. Explain the *irony* in the following two passages:

"I had always wanted to do her [Alice] some service to justify myself in my own eyes rather than hers." (page 520).

"Why don't you [Phil] answer? *Have* you seen the eyes?" (page 528).

Find at least two more ironic passages and explain the source of the irony in each case.

1. "Can it be," Conrad's narrator asks himself, "that he is not visible to other eyes than mine?" (page 500). What evidence, if any, exists to prove Leggatt's physical presence on board the narrator's ship? Likewise, what proof, apart from each protagonist's testimony, do we have for William Wilson's double or the eyes that haunt Culwin? Which, if any, of the three stories contains definite supernatural elements? Describe them. Do they improve or weaken this kind of story? Why?

2. How and for what purpose are mirrors utilized (literally or figuratively) in each of the three stories?

3. Just as William Wilson gazes at his double asleep in a curtained bed, so does Conrad's captain. Compare the two scenes and account for differences in reaction.

4. If you placed the three protagonists on a moral scale, whom would you judge to be the best of the three and whom the worst? Why? Which of the three seems the most complex character and which the least? Why? Which do you think is the best of the three stories and which is the weakest? Why?

ANALYSIS AND APPLICATION

1. "Not from compunction certainly, but, as it were mechanically, I proceeded to get the ladder in myself" (page 477). Rearrange this sentence in the more customary word order (subject–verb–object). Examine Conrad's sentence within the context of his story and explain why he departed from the normal sentence pattern.

2. "That the school, indeed, did not *feel his design, perceive its accomplishment, and participate in his sneer,* was, for many anxious months, a riddle I could not resolve" (page 460). Examine Poe's sentence within the context of his story and explain why he departed from the normal sentence pattern. How are the three elements of the italicized series related to each other and organized within the sentence?

3. Compare the following two versions:

"To run down for it I didn't dare. There was no time." (page 508)
I didn't dare to run down for it, for there was no time.

Within the context of "The Secret Sharer," which is more effective: Conrad's version or the modified version? Why?

4. Analyze the following extended comparison; then try to restate Wharton's description of Culwin's mind in nonmetaphorical language: "His mind was like a forum, or some open meeting place for the exchange of ideas: somewhat cold and drafty, but light, spacious and orderly—a kind of academic grove from which all the leaves have fallen" (page 513).

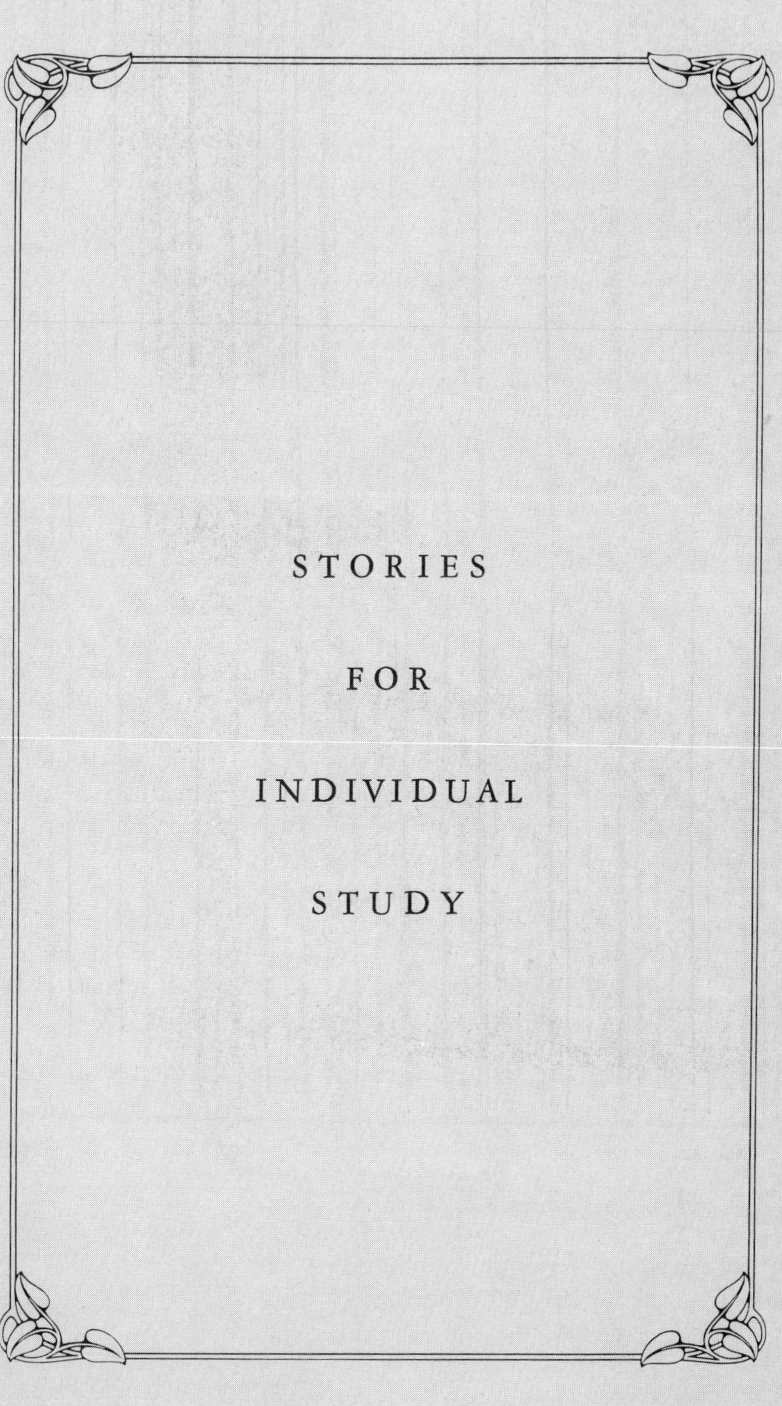

STORIES FOR INDIVIDUAL STUDY

LIFE ISN'T A SHORT STORY

CONRAD AIKEN

THE SHORT story writer had run out of ideas; he had used them all; he was feeling as empty as a bathtub and as blue as an oyster. He stirred his coffee without gusto and looked at his newspaper without reading it, only noting (but with a lackluster eye) that Prohibition was finally dead.[1] He was having his breakfast at one of those white-tiled restaurants which are so symbolic of America—with an air of carbolic purity at the entrance, but steamy purlieus at the rear which imagination trembles to investigate. His breakfast was always the same: two two-minute eggs, a little glass of chilled tomato juice, dry toast, and coffee. The only change, this morning, lay in the fact that he was having

[1] December 1933.

these simple things in a new place—it was a somewhat humbler restaurant than the one he usually entered at eight-thirty. He had looked in through the window appraisingly, and had a little hesitantly entered. But the ritual turned out to be exactly the same as at the others—a ticket at the entrance, where the cashier sat behind a glass case which was filled with cigarettes, chewing gum, and silver-papered cakes of chocolate; a tray at the counter; the precise intonation of "*Two twos, with.*" The only difference, in fact, was that the china was of a pale smoke-blue, a soft and dim blue which, had it been green, would have been pistachio. This gave his coffee a new appearance.

He sat at the marble-topped table near the window, and looked out at the crowded square. A light soft drizzle was falling on the morning rush of cars, wagons, pedestrians, newsboys; before the window bobbed a continuous procession of men and women; and he watched them over the half-seen headlines of his newspaper. A middle-aged woman, walking quickly, her umbrella pulled low over her head, so that the whiteness of her profile was sharp and immediate against the purple shadow. She vanished past the range of his vision before he had had time to see her properly—and for a moment after she had gone he went on thinking about her. She might do for the physical model of his story; but she wasn't fat enough, nor was she blonde, and for some obscure reason he had decided that the heroine must be fat and blonde. Just the same, she was real, she had come from somewhere and was going somewhere, and she was doing it with obvious concentration and energy. The rhythm of her gait was unusually pronounced, each shoulder swayed slightly but emphatically sideways, as if in a series of quick and aggressive but cheerful greetings—the effect, if not quite graceful, was individual and charming. He stopped thinking about her, and recovered his powers of observation, just in time to see a gray Irish face, middle-aged, hook-nosed, under a dirty felt hat, a hand quickly removing the pipe from the mouth, and the lips pouting to eject a long bright arc of spit, which fell heavily out of sight, the pipe then replaced. Such a quantity of spit he could not have imagined—his mouth felt dry at the mere thought of it. Where had it been stored and for how long? and with increasing pleasure, or increasing annoyance? The act itself had been unmistakably a pleasure, and had probably had its origins in pride; one could imagine him having competed, as a boy, in spitting through a knot-hole in a fence. He had trained himself, all his life, in the power of retention; his mouth had become a kind of reservoir.

II

But the "story" came back to him. It had waked him up as a feeling of obscure weight at the back of his head or on the back of his tongue; it had seemed also to be in one corner of the shadowy ceiling above the bookcase, like a cobweb to be removed with a long brush. He had lain in bed looking at it, now and then turning his head to right or left on the pillow as if precisely to turn it away from the idea. It might be Elmira, it might be Akron, it might be Fitchburg—it was a small provincial city, at any rate, the sort of small town that looks its most characteristic in a brick-red postcard of hard straight streets and ugly red houses. But she wouldn't be living in one of these—she would be living in an apartment house of shabby stucco, and the entrance would be through a door of grained varnish and plate glass. It would have an air of jaded superiority. And as for her apartment itself, on the second floor, with a little curly brass number on the door——

The idea had first occurred to him in the lobby of the Orpheum. He had paused to light a cigarette in the passage that led past the lounge, where parrots squawked in cages, and canaries trilled, and goldfish swam in an ornate aquarium, at the bottom of which, dimly seen through the heavy green water, was a kind of crumbling Gothic castle. He was standing there, looking at this, when the two groups of people had suddenly encountered each other with such hearty and heavy surprise. He had caught merely the phrases *"as I live and breathe!"* and *"in the flesh!"* The two men and the two women he had scarcely looked at—the phrases themselves had so immediately assumed an extraordinary importance. They would both, he at once saw, make good titles—it was only later that he had seen that they both had the same meaning. They both simply meant—*alive.*

Alive. And that was the difference between life, as one conceived it in a story, and life as it was, for example, in the restaurant in which he was sitting, or in the noisy square at which he was looking. As I live and breathe—I am standing here living and breathing, you are standing there living and breathing, and it's a surprise and a delight to both of us. In the flesh, too—death hasn't yet stripped our bones, or the crematory tried out our fats. We haven't seen each other for a long while, we didn't know whether we were dead or not, but here we are.

At the same time, there was the awful commonplaceness of the two phrases, the cheapness of them, the vulgarity—they were as old as the hills, and as worn; æons of weather and æons of handshake lay upon them; one witnessed, in the mere hearing of them, innumerable surprised greetings, innumerable mutual congratulations on the mere fact of being still alive. The human race seemed to extend itself backwards through them, in time, as along a road—if one pursued the thought one came eventually to a vision of two small apes peering at each other round the cheeks of a cocoanut and making a startled noise that sounded like *"yoicks!"* Or else, one simply saw, in the void, one star passing another, with no vocal interchange at all, nothing but a mutual exacerbation of heat.... It was very puzzling.

He stirred his coffee, wondered if he had sweetened it, reassured himself by tasting it. Yes. But in this very commonplaceness lay perhaps the idea, he had begun to see, as he lay in bed in the morning, watching the rain: and as he wondered about the large blonde lady in Fitchburg, he had begun to see that Gladys (for that was her name) was just the sort of hopelessly vulgar and commonplace person who would pride herself on her superiority in such matters. She would dislike such phrases, they would disgust her. After the first two or three years of her marriage to Sidney, when the romance had worn off and the glamor had fallen like a mask from his lean Yankee trader's face, when the sense of time had begun to be obtrusive, and the deadly round of the merely quotidian had replaced the era of faint orchids and bright bracelets and expensive theater tickets, it was then that she became conscious of certain tedious phrases he was in the habit of using. There was no concealing the fact any longer that they really came of separate and different worlds; Sidney had had little more than a high-school education, he had no "culture," he had never read a book in his life. He had walked straight from school into his father's hardware shop. What there was to know about cutlery, tools, grass seed, lawn mowers, washing machines, wire nails, white lead paint, and sandpaper, he knew. He was a loyal Elk,[2] a shrewd and honest business man, a man of no vices (unless one counted as a vice a kind of Hoosier aridity) and few pleasures. Occasionally he went to the bowling alleys, a pastime which she had always considered a little vulgar; he enjoyed a good hockey match; he liked a good thriller in the talkies (one of the few tastes they actually shared); and now and then he wanted to sit in the front row at a musical comedy. On these occasions, there was a definite sparkle or gleam about him, a lighting up of his sharp gray eyes, which reminded her of the Sidney to whom she had become engaged. This both puzzled and annoyed her; she felt, as she looked at him, a vague wave of

[2] Member of one of the major benevolent and fraternal orders.

jealousy and hatred. It must have been this gleam which, when focused intently on herself, had misled her into thinking him something that he wasn't and never would be.

III

As I live and breathe.

The story might even be called that.

A horse and wagon drew up at the curbstone outside the window. On the side of the wagon was inscribed, "Acme Towel Supply Company." Of course; it was one of those companies which supply towels and napkins and dishcloths to hotels and restaurants. The driver had jumped down, dropping his reins, and was opening the little pair of shabby wooden doors at the back of the wagon. The brown horse, his head down, his eyes invisible behind blinkers, stood perfectly still, as if deep in thought. His back and sides were shiny with rain, the worn harness dripped, now and then he twitched his shoulder muscles, as if in a slight shiver. Why did towel-supply companies always deliver towels in horse-drawn wagons? It was one of the minor mysteries; a queer sort of survival, for which one saw no possible reason. Beyond the wagon and the horse, the traffic was beginning to move forward again in response to a shrill birdcall from the policeman's whistle. A man in a black slicker had come close to the window and was reading the "specials" which were placarded in cinnamon-colored paper on the glass. When this had been done, he peered into the restaurant between two squares of paper; the quick sharp eyes looked straight at him and then past him and were as quickly gone. This meeting of his eyes had very likely prevented him from coming in; it was precisely such unexpected encounters with one's own image, as seen in the returned glance of another, that changed the course of one's life. And the restaurant had perhaps lost the sale of a couple of doughnuts and a "cup of coffee, half cream."

The way to get at Gladys's character, perhaps, was through her environment, the kind of place she lived in, her street, her apartment, her rooms. First of all, the stucco apartment house, the glass door, on which the name "Saguenay" was written obliquely in large gilt script, with a flourish of broad gilt underneath. Inside the door, a flight of shallow stairs, made of imitation marble, superficially clean, but deeply ingrained with dirt. Her apartment, now that she lived alone, was small, of course—it consisted of a bedroom, a sitting room, a bathroom, and a kitchenette.

One's immediate feeling, on entering the sitting room from the varnished hallway, was that the occupant must be a silly woman. It was plushy, it was perfumed, there was a bead curtain trembling between the sitting room and the kitchenette, at either side of the lace-curtained window hung a golden-wired birdcage, in which rustled a canary, and on the window-sill was a large bowl of goldfish. The ornaments were very ornamental and very numerous; the mantel groaned with souvenirs and photographs; the pictures were uniformly sentimental—several were religious. It was clear that she doted, simply doted, on birds and flowers—talked baby-talk to the canaries and the goldfish, even to the azalea, and always of course in that offensive, little, high-pitched fat-woman's coo. She would come in to them in the morning, wearing a pink flannel wrapper, brushing her hair, and would talk to them or wag a coy finger at them. And how's my sweet little dicky bird this morning? and have they slept well and been good in the night? and have they kept their little eyes shut tight to keep out the naughty bogey-man? And then at once she would forget them entirely, begin singing softly, walk with her head tilted on one side to the bathroom to turn on the bath, return to the kitchen to filch a cookie from the bread-box, and then go languidly to the front door for the milk and the newspaper.

The newspaper was the *Christian Science Monitor;* she took it, not because she was a Scientist, though she had an open mind, but because it was so "cultured." She liked to read about books and music and foreign affairs, and it frequently gave her ideas for little talks to the Women's Club. She had talked about the dole in England, and its distressing effect on the morals of the young men, and she had made a sensation by saying that she thought one should not too hastily condemn the nudist cult in Germany. Everyone knew that the human body craved sunlight, that the ultra-violet rays, or was it the infra-red, were most beneficial, so the idea was at least a healthy one, wasn't it? And the beautiful purity of Greek life was surely an answer to those who thought the human body in itself impure. It raised the whole question of what was purity, anyway! Everyone knew that purity was in the heart, in the attitude, and not really in the body. She thought the idea of playing croquet in the nude, queer as it might seem to us in Fitchburg, most interesting. One ought to think less about the body and more about the mind.

IV

The towel-supply man seemed to have disappeared; perhaps he was getting a cup of coffee at the Waldorf next door. Or making a round of several of the adjacent restaurants all at once. The horse waited patiently, was absolutely still, didn't even stamp a foot. He looked as if he were thinking about the rain. Or perhaps, dismayed by the senseless noise of all the traffic about him, he was simply thinking about his stall, wherever it was. Or more likely, not thinking anything at all. He just stood.

To her friends, of course, and to her sister Emma (who was her chief reason for living in Fitchburg) she posed as a woman with a broken heart, a woman tragically disillusioned, a beautiful romantic who had found that love was dust and ashes and that men were—well, creatures of a lower order. It was all very sad, very pitiful. One ought to have foreseen it, perhaps, or one ought not to have been born so sensitive, but there it was. If you had a soul, if you had perceptions, and loved beautiful things, and if you fell in love while you were still inexperienced and trusting, while you still looked at a world of violets through violet eyes, this was what happened. You gave your heart to someone who didn't deserve it. But what man ever *did* deserve it? Only the poets, perhaps, or the composers, Chopin[3] for instance, those rare creatures, half angel and half man (or was it half bird?), who had great and deep and tender souls. And how many such men could one find in Massachusetts? It was all so impossible, it was all so dreadful. Everyone knew that in America the women were infinitely more refined and sensitive than the men, you had only to look about you. What man ever wanted to talk about poetry with you, or listen to an evening of the Preludes, or to a lecture about the love affair of George Sand[4] and Alfred de Musset?[5] They wouldn't know what you meant; they wanted to go to the bowling alley or talk about the stock market; or else to sit in the front row of the Follies and look at the legs. They were vulgar, they had no imaginations. And she remembered that time at Emma's when Sidney had got so angry and gone on so in that common and vulgar way and made such a scene—whenever she thought of it she got hot all over. Absolutely,

[3] Frédérick Chopin (1810–1849), Polish composer and pianist; his works include *Twenty-Four Preludes,* op. 28.

[4] Pen name of Amandine Aurore Lucie Dupin, Baroness Dudevant (1804–1876), French novelist.

[5] French Romantic poet and dramatist (1810–1857).

it was the most vulgar scene! And done deliberately, too, just because he was so jealous about their having a refined conversation. And when she tried to stop him talking about it, he just went on, getting stubborner and stubborner, and all simply to make her feel ashamed. As if any of them had wanted to hear about those cheap drinking parties of his in Ohio. And that dreadful word, burgoo, that was it, which they had all laughed at, and tried to shame him out of, why what do you mean, burgoo, why Sidney what are you talking about, who ever heard such a word as *burgoo, burgoo!* And even that hadn't been enough, he got red and angry and went on saying it, burgoo, what's wrong with burgoo, of course there is such a word, and damned fine parties they were, too, and if they only had burgoos in Massachusetts life here would be a damned sight better. The idea! It served him right that she got mad and jumped up and said what she did. If you can't talk politely like a gentleman, or let others talk, then I think you had better leave those who will. Why don't you go back to your hardware shop, or back to Ohio, it doesn't seem this is the right environment for you. Or *anywhere* where you can have your precious burgoo.

But of course that was only one incident among so many, it was happening all the time; anybody could see that Sidney was not the man to ever appreciate her. What she always said was that nobody outside a marriage could ever possibly have any *real* idea of the things that went on there, could they. It was just impossible for them even to conceive of it. All those little things that you wouldn't think of—like Sidney's always leaving the dirty lather and little black hairs in the wash-basin after he shaved. Or the way he never noticed when she had on a new hat or ever said anything nice about the meals she got for him, just simply not noticing anything at all. That was a part of it, but much more was his simply not ever being able to talk to her, or to take any interest in intellectual things. And his vulgarity, the commonness of his speech, his manners! Every time she introduced him to somebody he would put his head down and take that ridiculous little confidential step toward them and say, "What was the name? I didn't get the name?" The idea! And if you told him about it he got mad. And as for the number of times every day that he said "as I live and breathe"—!

V

It had begun to rain harder. The sound of it rushed through the opening door as a small man, very dark, a Syrian perhaps, came in shaking his sodden hat so that the drops fell in a curve on the floor. A bright spray was dancing on the roof of the towel wagon, and a heavy stream fell splattering from one corner of an awning. People had begun to run, to scurry, in one's and two's and three's, exactly like one of those movies of the Russian Revolution, when invisible machine guns were turned on the crowds. One would not be surprised to see them fall down, or crawl away on their bellies.

Or to see the whole square emptied of human beings in the twinkling of an eye. Nor would one be surprised to see a lightning flash, either, for it had suddenly become astonishingly dark—the whole dismal scene had that ominous look which seems to wait, in a melodrama, for a peal of thunder. The light was sulphur-colored; it was terrifying; and he watched with fascination all the little windshield wipers wagging agitatedly on the fronts of cars—it gave one the feeling that the poor things were actually frightened, and were breathing faster. As for the horse, he stood unmoving, unmoved. His head was down, and he seemed to be studying with an extraordinary concentration the torrent of muddy water which rushed past his feet. Perhaps he was enjoying it; perhaps he even liked to feel all that tropic weight of rain on his back, experiencing in it a renewal of contact with the real, the elemental. Or perhaps he merely enjoyed standing still. Or perhaps he simply *was*.

But the question arose, ought one now to switch the point of view in the story, and do something more about Sidney? What about Sidney? Where on earth was Sidney all this while? and doing what? Presumably, running his hardware shop—and presumably again in Boston—but this was a little meager, one wanted to know something more than that. One ought to give him a special sort of appearance—a pencil behind his ear, a tuft of white hair over his sallow forehead, sharply pointed brown shoes. Perhaps he was something of a dandy, with a vivid corner of striped handkerchief pointing from his breast pocket; and perhaps he was by no means such a dull fellow as Gladys thought. But this *would* involve a shift in point of view, which was a mistake; it was no doubt better to stick to Gladys, in Fitchburg, and to see Sidney wholly as *she* saw him, to think of him only as *she* thought of him. She would almost certainly, from time to time (self-absorbed as she was, and vain, and vulgar, and with her silly small-town pretensions to culture), she would almost certainly, nevertheless, give him credit for a few virtues. He was generous: he had offered her a divorce, as soon as he knew how she felt about it; and he had behaved like a lamb, really, if she did say so, like a lamb, about the separation. He had done everything he could think of to make it easier for her.

In fact, one thing you *could* say for Sidney was, that he was generous—generous to a fault. She often thought of that. She always thought of it especially on the first of the month, when the check for the separation allowance turned up, as punctually as the calendar—sometimes he even sent her something extra. On these days, when she bustled to the bank with the check tucked into her glove to deposit it and pay the rent, she always felt so secure and happy that she had a very special state of mind about Sidney, something that was almost affection. Of course, it couldn't *be* affection, but it was *like* it—and it was just that feeling, with perhaps the loneliness which had upset her to begin with, which had misled her at last into writing him. It was easy enough now, as she had so often said to Emma, to see what had made her do it; she was sorry for him; but it only went to show how right she had been in the whole idea.

Just the same, it had been natural enough to write to him in that affectionate and grateful way; and when he had answered by so pathetically asking her to let him come to see her she had certainly thought it might be worth trying; even Emma had thought so; perhaps they would find after all that the differences between them were superficial; they could patch things up, maybe she would go back to Boston to live with him. The idea actually excited her—she remembered how she had found herself looking forward to having him come. Emma had offered to put him up for the night, so as to prevent embarrassment. And the thought of having him see her new apartment for the first time, with the canaries and the goldfish and the oriental rugs, and the Encyclopædia Britannica, had given her a very funny feeling, almost like being unfaithful. The day before he came she could hardly sit still. She kept walking to and fro round the apartment, moving the rugs and the chairs, and patting the cushions—and all the time wondering if two years would have changed him much, and what they would say. Naturally, she hadn't held out any real hope to him in her letter, she had only told him she would be willing to talk with him, that was all. He had no right to expect anything else, she had made that clear. However, there was no sense in not being friendly about these things, was there? Even if you were separated you could behave like a civilized human being; Emma agreed with her about that. It was the only decent thing to do. But when the day came, and when finally that afternoon she heard him breeze into Emma's front hall, stamping his feet, and went out to meet him, and saw him wearing the wing collar and the stringy little white tie, and the rubbers, and his little gray eyes shining behind the glasses with the cord, and when the very first thing he said was, just as if nothing at all had ever happened, "Well, as I live and breathe, if it isn't

Gladys!"—and then stood there, not knowing whether to kiss her or shake hands—it was just a misdeal, that was all, just another misdeal.

The whole thing went down, smack, like a house of cards. She could hardly bring herself to shake hands with him, or look at him—she suddenly wanted to cry. She rushed into Emma's room and stayed there on the bed for an hour, crying—Emma kept running in and saying for God's sake pull yourself together, at least go out and talk to him for a while, he's hurt, you can't treat him like this; the poor man doesn't know whether he's going or coming; come on now, Gladys, and be a good sport. He's sitting on the sofa in there with his head down like a horse, not knowing what to say; you simply can't treat him like that. The least you can do is go out and tell him you're sorry and that it was a mistake, and that he'd better not stay, or take him round to your apartment and talk it over with him quietly and then send him back to Boston. Come on now.

But of course she couldn't do it—she couldn't even go with him to the station. Emma went with him, and told him on the platform while they were waiting for the train that it was no use, it had all been a terrible mistake, and she was sorry, they were both sorry, Gladys sent word that she was very sorry. And afterwards, she had said it was so pathetic seeing him with his brand-new suitcase there beside him on the platform, his suitcase which he hadn't even opened, just taking it back to Boston where he came from. . . . When the train finally came, he almost forgot his suitcase; she thought he would have liked to leave it behind.

The towel-supply man came running back with a basket, flung it into the wagon, banged the dripping doors shut, and then jumped nimbly up to his seat, unhooking the reins. Automatically, but as if still deep in thought, the horse leaned slowly forward, lowered his head a little, and began to move. A long day was still ahead of him, a day of crowded and noisy streets, streets full of surprises and terrors and rain, muddy uneven cobbles and greasy smooth asphalt. The wagon and the man would be always there behind him; an incalculable sequence of accidents and adventures was before him. What did he think about, as he plodded from one dirty restaurant to another, one hotel to another, carrying towels? Probably nothing at all; certainly no such sentimental thing as a green meadow, nor anything so ridiculous as a story about living and breathing. It was enough, even if one was a slave, to live and breathe. For life, after all, isn't a short story.

1934

THE POTATO ELF

VLADIMIR NABOKOV

ACTUALLY HIS name was Frederic Dobson. To his friend the conjuror, he talked about himself thus:

"There was no one in Bristol who didn't know Dobson the tailor for children's clothes. I am his son—and am proud of it out of sheer stubbornness. You should know that he drank like an old whale. Some time around 1900, a few months before I was born, my gin-soaked dad rigged up one of those wax-work cherubs, you know—sailor suit, with a lad's first long trousers—and put it in my mother's bed. It's a wonder the poor thing did not have a miscarriage. As you can well understand, I know all this only by hearsay—yet, if my kind informers were not liars, this is, apparently, the secret reason I am—"

And Fred Dobson, in a sad and good-natured gesture, would spread out his little hands. The conjuror, with his usual dreamy smile, would bend down, pick up Fred like a baby, and, sighing, place him on the top of a wardrobe, where the Potato Elf would meekly roll up and start to sneeze softly and whimper.

He was twenty, and weighed less than fifty pounds, being only a couple of inches taller than the famous Swiss dwarf, Zimmermann (dubbed "Prince Balthazar"). Like friend Zimmermann, Fred was extremely well built, and had there not been those wrinkles on his round forehead and at the corners of his narrowed eyes, as well as a rather eerie air of tension (as if he were resisting growth), our dwarf would have easily passed for a gentle eight-year-old boy. His hair, the hue of damp straw, was sleeked down and evenly parted by a line which ran up the exact middle of his head to conclude a cunning agreement with its crown. Fred walked lightly, had an easy demeanor, and danced rather well, but his very first manager deemed it wise to weight the notion of "elf" with a comic epithet upon noticing the fat nose inherited by the dwarf from his plethoric and naughty father.

The Potato Elf, by his sole aspect, aroused a storm of applause and laughter throughout England, and then in the main cities of the Continent. He differed from most dwarfs in being of a mild and friendly nature. He became greatly attached to the miniature pony Snowdrop on which he trotted diligently around the arena of a Dutch circus; and, in Vienna, he conquered the heart of a stupid and glum giant hailing from Omsk by stretching up to him the first time he saw him and pleading like an infant to be taken up in Nurse's arms.

He usually performed not alone. In Vienna, for example, he appeared with the Russian giant and minced around him, neatly attired in striped trousers and a smart jacket, with a voluminous roll of music under his arm. He brought the giant's guitar. The giant stood like a tremendous statue and took the instrument with the motions of an automaton. A long frock coat that looked carved out of ebony, elevated heels, and a top hat with a sheen of columnar reflections increased the height of the stately three-hundred-and-fifty-pound Siberian. Thrusting out his powerful jaw, he beat the strings with one finger. Backstage, in womanish tones, he complained of giddiness. Fred grew very fond of him and even shed a few tears at the moment of separation, for he rapidly became accustomed to people. His life, like a circus horse's, went round and round with smooth monotony. One day in the dark of the wings he tripped over a bucket of house paint and mellowly plopped into it—an occurrence he kept recalling for quite a long while as something out of the ordinary.

In this way the dwarf traveled around most of Europe, and saved money, and sang with a *castrato*-like silvery voice, and in German variety theaters the audience ate thick sandwiches and candied nuts on sticks, and in Spanish ones, sugared violets and also nuts on sticks. The world was invisible to him. There remained in his memory the same faceless abyss laughing at him, and afterwards, when the performance was over, the soft, dreamy echo of a cool night that seems of such a deep blue when you leave the theater.

Upon returning to London he found a new partner in the person of Shock, the conjuror. Shock had a tuneful delivery, slender, pale, virtually ethereal hands, and a lick of chestnut brown hair that came down on one eyebrow. He resembled a poet more than a stage magician, and demonstrated his skill with a sort of tender and graceful melancholy, without the fussy patter characteristic of his profession. The Potato Elf assisted him amusingly, and, at the end of the act, would turn up in the gallery with a cooing exclamation of joy, although a minute before everyone had seen Shock lock him up in a black box right in the middle of the stage.

All this happened in one of those London theaters where there are acrobats soaring in the tinkle and shiver of the trapezes, and a foreign tenor (a failure in his own country) singing barcaroles, and a ventriloquist in naval uniform, and bicyclists, and the inevitable clown-eccentric shuffling about in a minuscule hat and a waistcoat coming down to his knees.

II

Latterly Fred had been growing gloomy, and sneezing a lot, soundlessly and sadly, like a little Japanese spaniel. While not experiencing for months any hankering after a woman, the virginal dwarf would be beset now and then by sharp pangs of lone amorous anguish which went as suddenly as they came, and again, for a while, he would ignore the bare shoulders showing white beyond the velvet boundary of loges, as well as the little girl acrobats, or the Spanish dancer whose sleek thighs were revealed for a moment when the orange-red curly fluff of her nether flounces would whip up in the course of a rapid swirl.

"What you need is a female dwarf," said pensively Shock, producing with a familiar flick of finger and thumb a silver coin from the ear of the dwarf whose little arm went up in a brushing-away curve as if chasing a fly.

That same night, as Fred, after his number, snuffling and grumbling, in bowler and tiny topcoat, was toddling along a dim backstage passage, a door came ajar with a sudden splash of gay light and two voices called him in. It was Zita and Arabella, sister acrobats, both half-undressed, sun-tanned, black-haired, with elongated blue eyes. A shimmer of theatrical disorder and the fragrance of lotions filled the room. The dressing table was littered with powder puffs, combs, cut-glass atomizers, hairpins in an ex-chocolate box, and rouge sticks.

The two girls instantly deafened Fred with their chatter. They tickled and squeezed the dwarf, who, glowering, and empurpled with lust, rolled like a ball in the embrace of the bare-armed teases. Finally, when frolicsome Arabella drew him to her and fell backward upon the couch, Fred lost his head and began to wriggle against her, snorting and clasping her neck. In attempting to push him away, she raised her arm and, slipping under it, he lunged and glued his lips to the hot pricklish hollow of her shaven axilla. The other girl, weak with laughter, tried in vain to drag him off by his legs. At that moment the door banged open, and the French partner of the two aerialists came into the room wearing marble-white tights. Silently, without any resentment, he grabbed the dwarf by the scruff of the neck (all you heard was the snap of Fred's wing collar as one side broke loose from the stud), lifted him in the air and threw him out like a monkey. The door slammed. Shock, who happened to be wandering past, managed to catch a glimpse of the marble-bright arm and of a black little figure with feet retracted in flight.

Fred hurt himself in falling and now lay motionless in the corridor. He was not really stunned, but had gone all limp with eyes fixed on one point, and fast chattering teeth.

"Bad luck, old boy," sighed the conjuror, picking him up from the floor. He palpated with translucent fingers the dwarf's round forehead and added, "I told you not to butt in. Now you got it. A dwarf woman is what you need."

Fred, his eyes bulging, said nothing.

"You'll sleep at my place to-night," decided Shock and carried the Potato Elf toward the exit.

III

There existed also a Mrs. Shock.

She was a lady of uncertain age, with dark eyes which had a yellowish tinge around the iris. Her skinny frame, parchment complexion, lifeless black hair, a habit of strongly exhaling tobacco smoke through her nostrils, the studied untidiness of her attire and hairdo—all this could hardly attract many men, but, no doubt, was to Mr. Shock's liking, though actually he never seemed to notice his wife, as he was always engaged in imagining secret devices for his show, always appeared unreal and shifty, thinking of something else when talking about trivialities, but keenly observing everything around him when immersed in astral fancies. Nora had to be constantly on the lookout since he never missed the occasion to contrive some small, inutile, yet subtly artful deception. There had been, for instance, that time when he amazed her by his unusual gluttony: he smacked his lips juicily, sucked chicken bones clean, again and again heaped up food on his plate; then he departed after giving his wife a sorrowful glance; and a little later the maid, giggling into her apron, informed Nora that Mr. Shock had not touched one scrap of his dinner, and had left all of it in three brand-new pans under the table.

She was the daughter of a respectable artist who painted only horses, spotty hounds, and huntsmen in pink coats. She had lived in Chelsea before her marriage, had admired the hazy Thames sunsets, taken drawing lessons, gone to ridiculous meetings attended by the local Bohemian crowd—and it was there that the ghost-gray eyes of a quiet slim man had singled her out. He talked little about himself, and was still unknown. Some people believed him to be a composer of lyrical poems. She fell headlong in love with him. The poet absentmindedly became engaged to her, and on the very first day of matrimony explained, with a sad smile, that he did not know how to write poetry, and there and then, in the middle of the conversation, he transformed an old alarm-clock into a nickel-plated chronometer, and the chronometer into a miniature gold watch, which Nora had worn ever since on her wrist. She understood that nevertheless conjuror Shock was, in his own way, a poet; only she could not get used to his demonstrating his art every minute, in all circumstances. It is hard to be happy when one's husband is a mirage, a peripatetic legerdemain of a man, a deception of all five senses.

IV

She was idly tapping a fingernail against the glass of a bowl in which several goldfish that looked cut out of orange peel breathed and fin-flashed when the door opened noiselessly, and Shock appeared (silk hat askew, strand of brown hair on his brow) with a little creature all screwed up in his arms.

"Brought him," said the conjuror with a sigh.

Nora thought fleetingly: child. Lost. Found. Her dark eyes grew moist.

"Must be adopted," softly added Shock, lingering in the doorway.

The small thing suddenly came alive, mumbled something and started to scrabble shyly against the conjuror's starched shirtfront. Nora glanced at the tiny boots in chamois spats, at the little bowler.

"I'm not so easy to fool," she sneered.

The conjuror looked at her reproachfully. Then he laid Fred on a plush couch and covered him with a lap-robe.

"Blondinet roughed him up," explained Shock, and could not help adding, "Bashed him with a dumbbell. Right in the tummy."

And Nora, kind-hearted as childless women frequently are, felt such an especial pity that she almost broke into tears. She proceeded to mother the dwarf, she fed him, gave him a glass of port, rubbed his forehead with eau-de-cologne, moistened with it his temples and the infantine hollows behind his ears.

Next morning Fred woke up early, inspected the unfamiliar room, talked to the goldfish, and after a quiet sneeze or two, settled on the ledge of the bay-window like a little boy.

A melting, enchanting mist washed London's gray roofs. Somewhere in the distance an attic window was thrown open, and its pane caught a glint of sunshine. The horn of an automobile sang out in the freshness and tenderness of dawn.

Fred's thoughts dwelt on the previous day. The laughing accents of the girl tumblers got oddly mixed up with the touch of Mrs. Shock's cold fragrant hands. At first he had been ill-treated, then he had been caressed; and, mind you, he was a very affectionate, very ardent dwarf. He dwelt in fancy on the possibility of his rescuing Nora some day from a strong, brutal man resembling that Frenchman in white tights. Incongruously, there floated up the memory of a fifteen-year-old female dwarf with whom he appeared together at one time. She was a bad-tempered, sick, sharp-nosed little thing. The two were presented to the spectators as an engaged couple, and, shivering with disgust, he had to dance an intimate tango with her.

Again a lone klaxon sang out and swept by. Sunlight was beginning to infuse the mist over London's soft wilderness.

Around half-past seven the flat came to life. With an abstract smile Mr. Shock left for an unknown destination. From the dining room came the delicious smell of bacon and eggs. With her hair done anyhow, wearing a kimono embroidered with sunflowers, appeared Mrs. Shock.

After breakfast she offered Fred a perfumed cigarette with a red-petaled tip and half-closing her eyes had him tell her about his existence. At such narrative moments Fred's little voice deepened slightly: he spoke slowly, choosing his words, and, strange to say, that unforeseen dignity of diction became him. Bent-headed, solemn, and elastically tense, he sat sideways at Nora's feet. She reclined on the plush divan, her arms thrown back, revealing her sharp bare elbows. The dwarf, having finished his tale, lapsed into silence but still kept turning this way and that the palm of his tiny hand, as if softly continuing to speak. His black jacket, inclined face, fleshy little nose, tawny hair, and that middle parting reaching the back of his head vaguely moved Nora's heart. As she looked at him through her lashes she tried to imagine that it was not an adult dwarf sitting there, but her non-existing little son in the act of telling her how his schoolmates bullied him. Nora stretched her hand and stroked his head lightly—and, at that moment, by an enigmatic association of thought, she called forth something else, a curious, vindictive vision.

Upon feeling those light fingers in his hair, Fred at first sat motionless, then began to lick his lips in feverish silence. His eyes, turned askance, could not detach their gaze from the green pompon on Mrs. Shock's slipper. And all at once, in some absurd and intoxicating way, everything came into motion.

V

On that smoke-blue day, in the August sun, London was particularly lovely. The tender and festive sky was reflected in the smooth spread of the asphalt, the glossy pillar boxes glowed crimson at the street corners, through the Gobelin green of the Park cars flashed and rolled with a low hum—the entire city shimmered and breathed in the mellow warmth, and only underground, on the platforms of the Tube,[1] could one find a region of coolness.

Every separate day in the year is a gift presented to only one man—the happiest one; all other people use his day, to enjoy the sunshine or berate the rain, never knowing, however, to whom that day really

[1] Subway.

belongs; and its fortunate owner is pleased and amused by their ignorance. A person cannot foreknow which day exactly will fall to his lot, what trifle he will remember forever: the ripple of reflected sunlight on a wall bordering water or the revolving fall of a maple leaf; and it often happens that he recognizes *his* day only in retrospection, long after he has plucked, and crumpled, and chucked under his desk the calendar leaf with the forgotten figure.

Providence granted Fred Dobson, a dwarf in mouse-gray spats, the merry August day in 1920 which began with the melodious hoot of a motor horn and the flash of a casement swung open in the distance. Children coming back from a walk told their parents, with gasps of wonder, that they had met a dwarf in a bowler hat and striped trousers, with a cane in one hand and a pair of tan gloves in the other.

After ardently kissing Nora good-bye (she was expecting visitors), the Potato Elf came out on the broad smooth street, flooded with sunlight, and instantly knew that the whole city had been created for him and only for him. A cheerful taxi driver turned down with a resounding blow the iron flag of his meter; the street started to flow past, and Fred kept slipping off the leathern seat, while chuckling and cooing under his breath.

He got out at the Hyde Park entrance, and without noticing the looks of curiosity, minced along, by the green folding chairs, by the pond, by the great rhododendron bushes, darkling under the shelter of elms and lindens, above a turf as bright and bland as billiard cloth. Riders sped past, lightly going up and down on their saddles, the yellow leather of their leggings creaking, the slender faces of their steeds springing up, their bits clinking; and expensive black motor cars, with a dazzling glitter of wheel spokes, progressed sedately over the ample lacework of violet shade.

The dwarf walked, inhaling the warm whiffs of benzine, the smell of foliage that seemed to rot with the over-abundance of green sap, and twirled his cane, and pursed his lips as if about to whistle, so great was the sense of liberation and lightness overwhelming him. His mistress had seen him off with such hurried tenderness, had laughed so nervously, that he realized how much she feared that her old father, who always came to lunch, would begin to suspect something if he found a strange gentleman in the house.

That day he was seen everywhere: in the park where a rosy nurse in a starched bonnet offered him for some reason a ride in the pram she was pushing; and in the halls of a great museum; and on the escalator that slowly crept out of rumbling depths where electric winds blew among brilliant posters; and in an elegant shop where only men's handkerchiefs were sold; and on the crest of a bus where he was hoisted by someone's kind hands.

And after a while he became tired—all that motion and glitter dazed him, the laughing eyes staring at him got on his nerves, and he felt he must ponder carefully the ample sensation of freedom, pride, and happiness which kept accompanying him.

When finally a hungry Fred entered the familiar restaurant where all kinds of performers gathered and where his presence could not surprise anyone, and when he looked around at those people, at the old dull clown who was already drunk, at the Frenchman, a former enemy, who now gave him a friendly nod, Mr. Dobson realized with perfect clarity that never again would he appear on the stage.

The place was darkish, with not enough lamps lit inside and not enough outside day filtering in. The dull clown resembling a ruined banker, and the acrobat who looked oddly uncouth in mufti, were playing a silent game of dominoes. The Spanish dancing girl, wearing a cartwheel hat that cast a blue shadow on her eyes, sat with crossed legs all alone at a corner table. There were half-a-dozen people whom Fred did not know; he examined their features which years of make-up had bleached; meanwhile the waiter brought a cushion to prop him up, changed the tablecloth, nimbly laid the cover.

All at once, in the dim depths of the restaurant, Fred distinguished the delicate profile of the conjuror, who was talking in undertone to an obese old man of an American type. Fred had not expected to run here into Shock—who never frequented taverns—and in point of fact had totally forgotten about his existence. He now felt so sorry for the poor magician that, at first, he decided to conceal everything; but then it occurred to him that Nora could not cheat anyway and would probably tell her husband that very evening ("I've fallen in love with Mr. Dobson. . . . I'm leaving you")—and that she should be spared a difficult, disagreeable confession, for was he not her knight, did he not feel proud of her love, should he not, therefore, be justified in causing her husband pain, no matter the pity?

The waiter brought him a piece of kidney pie and a bottle of ginger beer. He also switched on more light. Here and there, above the dusty plush, crystal flowers glowed forth, and the dwarf saw from afar a golden gleam bring out the conjuror's chestnut forelock and the light and shade shuttle over his tender transparent fingers. His interlocutor rose, clawing at the belt of his pants and obsequiously grinning, and Shock accompanied him to the cloakroom. The fat American donned a wide-brimmed hat, shook Shock's ethereal hand, and, still hitching up his pants, made for the exit. Momentarily one discerned a chink of lingering daylight, while the restaurant lamps glowed yellower. The door closed with a thud.

"Shock!" called the Potato Elf, wiggling his short feet under the table.

Shock came over. On his way, he pensively took a lighted cigar out of his breast pocket, inhaled, let out a puff of smoke, and put the cigar back. Nobody knew how he did it.

"Shock," said the dwarf, whose nose had reddened from the ginger beer, "I must speak to you. It is most important."

The conjuror sat down at Fred's table and leaned his elbow upon it.

"How's your head—doesn't hurt?" he inquired indifferently.

Fred wiped his lips with the napkin; he did not know how to start, still fearing to cause his friend too much anguish.

"By the way," said Shock, "tonight I appear together with you for the last time. That chap is taking me to America. Things look pretty good."

"I say, Shock—" and the dwarf, crumbling bread, groped for adequate words. "The fact is. . . . Be brave, Shock. I love your wife. This morning, after you left, she and I, we two, I mean, she—"

"Only I'm a bad sailor," mused the conjuror, "and it's a week to Boston. I once sailed to India. Afterwards I felt as a leg does when it goes to sleep."

Fred, flushing purple, rubbed the tablecloth with his tiny fist. The conjuror chuckled softly at his own thoughts, and then asked, "You were about to tell me something, my little friend?"

The dwarf looked into his ghostly eyes and shook his head in confusion.

"No, no, nothing. . . . One can't talk to you."

Shock's hand stretched out—no doubt he intended to snip out a coin from Fred's ear—but for the first time in years of masterly magic, the coin, not grasped by the palm muscles firmly enough, fell out the wrong way. He caught it up and rose.

"I'm not going to eat here," said he, examining curiously the crown of the dwarf's head. "I don't care for this place."

Sulky and silent, Fred was eating a baked apple.

The conjuror quietly left. The restaurant emptied. The languorous Spanish dancer in the large hat was led off by a shy, exquisitely dressed young man with blue eyes.

"Well, if he doesn't want to listen, that settles it," reflected the dwarf;

he sighed with relief and decided that after all Nora would explain things better. Then he asked for notepaper and proceeded to write her a letter. It closed as follows:

Now you understand why I cannot continue to live as before. What feelings would you experience knowing that every evening the common herd rocks with laughter at the sight of your chosen one? I am breaking my contract, and tomorrow I shall be leaving. You will receive another letter from me as soon as I find a peaceful nook where after your divorce we shall be able to love one another, my Nora.

Thus ended the swift day given to a dwarf in mouse-colored spats.

VI

London was cautiously darkening. Street sounds blended in a soft hollow note, as if someone had stopped playing but still kept his foot on the piano pedal. The black leaves of the limes in the park were patterned against the transparent sky like aces of spades. At this or that turning, or between the funereal silhouettes of twin towers, a burning sunset was revealed like a vision.

It was Shock's custom to go home for dinner and change into professional tails so as to drive afterwards straight to the theater. That evening Nora awaited him most impatiently, quivering with evil glee. How glad she was to have now her own private secret! The image of the dwarf himself she dismissed. The dwarf was a nasty little worm.

She heard the lock of the entrance door emit its delicate click. As so often happens when one has betrayed a person, Shock's face struck her as new, as almost that of a stranger. He gave her a nod, and shamefully, sadly lowered his long-lashed eyes. He took his place opposite her at the table without a word. Nora considered his light gray suit that made him seem still more slender, still more elusive. Her eyes lit up with warm triumph; one corner of her mouth twitched malevolently.

"How's your dwarf?" she inquired, relishing the casualness of her question. "I thought you'd bring him along."

"Haven't seen him today," answered Shock, beginning to eat. All at once he thought better of it—took out a vial, uncorked it with a careful squeak, and tipped it over a glassful of wine.

Nora expected with irritation that the wine would turn a bright blue, or become as translucent as water, but the claret did not change its hue. Shock caught his wife's glance and smiled dimly.

"For the digestion—just drops," he murmured. A shadow rippled across his face.

"Lying as usual," said Nora. "You've got an excellent stomach."

The conjuror laughed softly. Then he cleared his throat in a business-like way, and drained his glass in one gulp.

"Get on with your food," said Nora. "It will be cold."

With grim pleasure she thought, "Ah, if you only knew. You'll never find out. That's my power!"

The conjuror ate in silence. Suddenly he made a grimace, pushed his plate away, and started to speak. As usual, he kept looking not directly at her, but a little above her, and his voice was melodious and soft. He described his day, telling her he had visited the King at Windsor where he had been invited to amuse the little dukes who wore velvet jackets and lace collars. He related all this with light vivid touches, mimicking the people he had seen, twinkling, cocking his head slightly.

"I produced a whole flock of white doves from my gibus,[2]" said Shock.

"And the dwarf's little palms were clammy, and you're making it all up," reflected Nora in brackets.

"Those pigeons, you know, went flying around the Queen. She shoo-flied them but kept smiling out of politeness."

Shock got up, swayed, lightly leaned on the table edge with two fingers, and said, as if completing his story:

"I'm not feeling well, Nora. That was poison I drank. You shouldn't have been unfaithful to me."

His throat swelled convulsively, and, pressing a handkerchief to his lips, he left the dining room. Nora sprang up; the amber beads of her long necklace caught at the fruit knife upon her plate and brushed it off.

"It's all an act," she thought bitterly. "Wants to scare me, to torment me. No, my good man, it's no use. You shall see!"

How vexing that Shock had somehow discovered her secret! But at least she would now have the opportunity to reveal all her feelings to him, to shout that she hated him, that she despised him furiously, that he was not a person, but a phantom of rubber, that she could not bear to live with him any longer, that—

The conjuror sat on the bed, all huddled up and gritting his teeth in anguish, but he managed a faint smile when Nora stormed into the bedroom.

"So you thought I'd believe you," she said, gasping. "Oh no, that's

[2] Collapsible top hat.

the end! I, too, know how to cheat. You repel me, oh, you're a laughingstock with your unsuccessful tricks—"

Shock, still smiling helplessly, attempted to get off the bed. His foot scraped against the carpet. Nora paused in an effort to think what else she could yell in the way of insult.

"Don't," uttered Shock with difficulty. "If there was something that I . . . please, forgive. . . ."

The vein in his forehead was tensed. He hunched up still more, his throat rattled, the moist lock on his brow shook, and the handkerchief at his mouth got all soaked with bile and blood.

"Stop playing the fool!" cried Nora and stamped her foot.

He managed to straighten up. His face was wax pale. He threw the balled rag into a corner.

"Wait, Nora. . . . You don't understand. . . . This is my very last trick. . . . I won't do any other. . . ."

Again a spasm distorted his terrible, shiny face. He staggered, fell on the bed, threw back his head on the pillow.

She came near, she looked, knitting her brows. Shock lay with closed eyes and his clenched teeth creaked. When she bent over him, his eyelids quivered, he glanced at her vaguely, not recognizing his wife, but suddenly he did recognize her and his eyes flickered with a humid light of tenderness and pain.

At that instant Nora knew that she loved him more than anything in the world. Horror and pity overwhelmed her. She whirled about the room, poured out some water, left the glass on the washstand, dashed back to her husband, who had raised his head and was pressing the edge of the sheet to his lips, his whole body shuddering as he retched heavily, staring with unseeing eyes which Death had already veiled. Then Nora with a wild gesture dashed into the next room, where there was a telephone, and there, for a long time, she joggled the holder, repeated the wrong number, rang again, sobbing for breath and hammering the telephone table with her fist; and finally when the doctor's voice responded, Nora cried that her husband had poisoned himself, that he was dying; upon which she flooded the receiver with a storm of tears, and cradling it crookedly, ran back into the bedroom.

The conjuror, bright-faced and sleek, in white waistcoat and impeccably pressed black trousers, stood before the pier glass and, elbows parted, was meticulously working upon his tie. He saw Nora in the mirror, and without turning gave her an absentminded twinkle while whistling softly and continuing to knead with transparent fingertips the black ends of his silk bow.

VII

Drowse, a tiny town in the north of England, looked, indeed, so somnolent that one suspected it might have been somehow mislaid among those misty, gentle-sloped fields where it had fallen asleep forever. It had a post office, a bicycle shop, two or three tobacconists with red and blue signs, an ancient gray church surrounded by tombstones over which stretched sleepily the shade of an enormous chestnut tree. The main street was lined with hedges, small gardens, and brick cottages diagonally girt with ivy. One of these had been rented to a certain F. R. Dobson whom nobody knew except his housekeeper and the local doctor, and he was no gossiper. Mr. Dobson, apparently, never went out. The housekeeper, a large stern woman, who had formerly been employed in an insane asylum, would answer the casual questions of neighbors by explaining that Mr. Dobson was an aged paralytic, doomed to vegetate in curtained silence. No wonder the inhabitants forgot him the same year that he arrived in Drowse: he became an unnoticeable presence whom people took for granted as they did the unknown bishop whose stone effigy had been standing so long in its niche above the church portal. The mysterious old man was thought to have a grandchild—a quiet fair-haired little boy who sometimes, at dusk, used to come out of the Dobson cottage with small, timid steps. This happened, however, so seldom that nobody could say for sure that it was always the same child, and, of course, twilight at Drowse was particularly blurry and blue, softening every outline. Thus the uncurious and sluggish Drowsians missed the fact that the supposed grandson of the supposed paralytic did not grow as the years went by and that his flaxen hair was nothing but an admirably made wig; for the Potato Elf started to go bald at the very beginning of his new existence, and his head was soon so smooth and glossy that Ann, his housekeeper, thought at times what fun it would be to fit one's palm over that globe. Otherwise, he had not much changed: his tummy, perhaps, had grown plumper, and purple veins showed through on his dingier, fleshier nose which he powdered when dressed up as a little boy. Furthermore, Ann and his doctor knew that the heart attacks besetting the dwarf would come to no good.

He lived peacefully and inconspicuously in his three rooms, subscribed to a circulating library at the rate of three or four books (mostly novels) per week, acquired a black yellow-eyed cat because he mortally feared mice (which bumped about somewhere behind the wardrobe as if rolling minute balls of wood), ate a lot, especially sweetmeats (sometimes jumping up in the middle of the night and pattering along the chilly floor, eerily small and shivery in his long nightshirt, to get, like a little boy, at the chocolate-coated biscuits in the pantry), and recalled less and less frequently his love affair and the first dreadful days he had spent in Drowse.

Nevertheless, in his desk, among wispy, neatly folded playbills, he still preserved a sheet of peach-colored notepaper with a dragon-shaped watermark, scribbled over in an angular, barely legible hand. Here is what it said:

DEAR MR. DOBSON

I received your first letter, as well as your second one, in which you ask me to come to D. All this, I am afraid, is an awful misunderstanding. Please try to forget and forgive me. Tomorrow my husband and I are leaving for the States and shall probably not be back for quite some time. I simply do not know what more I can write you, my poor Fred.

It was then that the first attack of angina pectoris occurred. A meek look of astonishment remained since then in his eyes. And during a number of days afterwards he would walk from room to room, swallowing his tears and gesturing in front of his face with one trembling tiny hand.

Presently, though, Fred began to forget. He grew fond of the coziness he had never known before—of the blue film of flame over the coals in the fireplace, of the dusty small vases on their own rounded small shelves, of the print between two casements: a St. Bernard dog, complete with barrelet, reviving a mountaineer on his bleak rock. Rarely did he recollect his past life. Only in dream did he sometimes see a starry sky come alive with the tremor of many trapezes while he was being clapped into a black trunk: through its walls he distinguished Shock's bland singsong voice but could not find the trap in the floor of the stage and suffocated in sticky darkness, while the conjuror's voice grew sadder and more remote and melted away, and Fred would wake up with a groan on his spacious bed, in his snug, dark room, with its faint fragrance of lavender, and would stare for a long time, gasping for breath and pressing his child's fist to his stumbling heart, at the pale blur of the window blind.

As the years passed, the yearning for a woman's love sighed in him fainter and fainter, as if Nora had drained him of all the ardor that had tormented him once. True, there were certain times, certain vague spring evenings, when the dwarf, having shyly put on short pants and the blond wig, left the house to plunge into crepuscular dimness, and there, stealing along some path in the fields, would suddenly stop as he looked with anguish at a dim pair of lovers locked in each other's arms near a hedge, under the protection of brambles in blossom. Presently that too passed, and he ceased seeing the world altogether. Only once in a while the doctor, a white-haired man with piercing black eyes, would come for a game of chess and, across the board, would consider with scientific delight those tiny soft hands, that little bulldoggish face, whose prominent brow would wrinkle as the dwarf pondered a move.

VIII

Eight years elapsed. It was Sunday morning. A jug of cocoa under a cozy in the guise of a parrot's head was awaiting Fred on the breakfast table. The sunny greenery of apple trees streamed through the window. Stout Ann was in the act of dusting the little pianola on which the dwarf occasionally played wobbly waltzes. Flies settled on the jar of orange marmalade and rubbed their front feet.

Fred came in, slightly sleep-rumpled, wearing carpet slippers and a little black dressing gown with yellow frogs. He sat down slitting his eyes and stroking his bald head. Ann left for church. Fred pulled open the illustrated section of a Sunday paper and, alternately drawing in and pouting his lips, examined at length prize pups, a Russian ballerina folding up in a swan's languishing agony, the top hat and mug of a financier who had bamboozled everyone.... Under the table the cat, curving her back, rubbed herself against his bare ankle. He finished his breakfast; rose, yawning: he had had a very bad night, never yet had his heart caused him such pain, and now he felt too lazy to dress, although his feet were freezing. He transferred himself to the window-nook armchair and curled up in it. He sat there without a thought in his head, and near him the black cat stretched, opening tiny pink jaws.

The doorbell tinkled.

"Doctor Knight," reflected Fred indifferently, and remembering that Ann was out, went to open the door himself.

Sunlight poured in. A tall lady all in black stood on the threshold. Fred recoiled, muttering and fumbling at his dressing gown. He dashed back into the inner rooms, losing one slipper on the way but ignoring it, his only concern being that whoever had come must not notice he was a dwarf. He stopped, panting, in the middle of the parlor. Oh, why hadn't he simply slammed shut the entrance door! And who on earth could be calling on him? A mistake, no doubt.

And then he heard distinctly the sound of approaching steps. He retreated to the bedroom; wanted to lock himself up, but there was no key. The second slipper remained on the rug in the parlor.

"This is dreadful," said Fred under his breath and listened.

The steps had entered the parlor. The dwarf emitted a little moan and made for the wardrobe, looking for a hiding place.

A voice that he certainly knew pronounced his name, and the door of the room opened:

"Fred, why are you afraid of me?"

The dwarf, bare-footed, black-robed, his pate beaded with sweat, stood by the wardrobe, still holding on to the ring of its lock. He recalled with the utmost clarity the orange-gold fish in their glass bowl.

She had aged unhealthily. There were olive-brown shadows under her eyes. The little dark hairs above her upper lip had become more distinct than before; and from her black hat, from the severe folds of her black dress, there wafted something dusty and woeful.

"I never expected—" Fred slowly began, looking up at her warily.

Nora took him by the shoulders, turned him to the light, and with eager, sad eyes examined his features. The embarrassed dwarf blinked, deploring his wiglessness and marveling at Nora's excitement. He had ceased thinking of her so long ago that now he felt nothing except sadness and surprise. Nora, still holding him, shut her eyes, and then, lightly pushing the dwarf away, turned toward the window.

Fred cleared his throat and said:

"I lost sight of you entirely. Tell me, how's Shock?"

"Still performing his tricks," replied Nora absently. "We returned to England only a short while ago."

Without removing her hat she sat down near the window and kept staring at him with odd intensity.

"It means that Shock—" hastily resumed the dwarf, feeling uneasy under her gaze.

"—Is the same as ever," said Nora, and, still not taking her glistening eyes from the dwarf, quickly peeled off and crumpled her glossy black gloves which were white inside.

"Can it be that she again—?" abruptly wondered the dwarf. There rushed through his mind the fish bowl, the smell of eau de cologne, the green pompoms on her slippers.

Nora got up. The black balls of her gloves rolled on the floor.

"It's not a big garden but it has apple trees," said Fred, and continued to wonder inwardly: had there really been a moment when I—? Her skin is quite sallow. She has a mustache. And why is she so silent?

"I seldom go out, though," said he, rocking slightly back and forth in his seat and massaging his knees.

"Fred, do you know why I'm here?" asked Nora.

She rose and came up to him quite close. Fred with an apologetic grin tried to escape by slipping off his chair.

It was then that she told him in a very soft voice:

"The fact is I had a son from you."

The dwarf froze, his gaze fixing a minuscule casement burning on the side of a dark blue cup. A timid smile of amazement flashed at the corners of his lips, then it spread, and lit up his cheeks with a purplish flush.

"My . . . son. . . ."

And all at once he understood everything, all the meaning of life, of his long anguish, of the little bright window upon the cup.

He slowly raised his eyes. Nora sat sideways on a chair and was shaking with violent sobs. The glass head of her hat-pin glittered like a teardrop. The cat, purring tenderly, rubbed itself against her legs.

He dashed up to her, he remembered a novel read a short while ago: "You have no cause," said Mr. Dobson, "no cause whatever for fearing that I may take him away from you. I am so happy!"

She glanced at him through a mist of tears. She was about to explain something, but gulped—saw the tender and joyful radiance with which the dwarf's countenance breathed—and explained nothing.

She hastened to pick up her crumpled gloves.

"Well, now you know. Nothing more is necessary. I must be going."

A sudden thought stabbed Fred. Acute shame joined the quivering joy. He inquired, fingering the tassel of his dressing gown.

"And . . . and what is he like? He is not—"

"Oh, on the contrary," replied Nora rapidly. "A big boy, like all boys." And again she burst into tears.

Fred lowered his eyes.

"I would like to see him."

Joyously he corrected himself:

"Oh, I understand! He must not know that I am like this. But perhaps you might arrange—"

"Yes, by all means," said Nora, hurriedly, and almost sharply, as she stepped through the hall. "Yes, we'll arrange something. I must be on my way. It's a twenty-minute walk to the railway station."

She turned her head in the doorway and for the last time, avidly and mournfully, she examined Fred's features. Sunlight trembled on his bald head, his ears were of a translucent pink. He understood nothing in his amazement and bliss. And after she had gone, Fred remained standing for a long time in the hallway, as if afraid to spill his full heart with an imprudent movement. He kept trying to imagine his son, and all he could do was to imagine his own self dressed as a schoolboy and wearing a little blond wig. And by the act of transferring his own aspect onto his boy, he ceased to feel that he was a dwarf.

He saw himself entering a house, a hotel, a restaurant, to meet his son. In fancy, he stroked the boy's fair hair with poignant parental pride.... And then, with his son and Nora (silly goose—to fear he would snatch him away!), he saw himself walking down a street, and there—

Fred clapped his thighs. He had forgotten to ask Nora where and how he could reach her!

Here commenced a crazy, absurd sort of phase. He rushed to his bedroom, began to dress in a wild hurry. He put on the best things he had, an expensive starched shirt, practically new, striped trousers, a jacket made by Resartre of Paris years ago—and as he dressed, he kept chuckling, and breaking his fingernails in the chinks of tight commode drawers, and had to sit down once or twice to let his swelling and knocking heart rest; and again he went skipping about the room looking for the bowler he had not worn for years, and at last, on consulting a mirror in passing, he glimpsed the image of a stately elderly gentleman, in smart formal dress, and ran down the steps of the porch, dazzled by a new idea: to travel back with Nora—whom he would certainly manage to overtake—and to see his son that very evening!

A broad dusty road led straight to the station. It was more or less deserted on Sundays—but unexpectedly a boy with a cricket bat appeared at a corner. He was the first to notice the dwarf. In gleeful surprise he slapped himself on the top of his bright-colored cap as he watched Fred's receding back and the flicking of his mouse-gray spats.

And instantly, from God knows where, more boys appeared, and with gaping stealthiness started to follow the dwarf. He walked faster and faster, now and then looking at his watch, and chuckling excitedly. The sun made him feel a little queasy. Meanwhile, the number of boys increased, and chance passers-by stopped to look in wonder. Somewhere afar church chimes rang forth: the drowsy town was coming to life—and all of a sudden it burst into uncontrollable, long-restrained laughter.

The Potato Elf, unable to master his eagerness, switched to a jog.

One of the lads darted in front of him to have a look at his face; another yelled something in a rude hoarse voice. Fred, grimacing because of the dust, ran on, and abruptly it seemed to him that all those boys crowding in his wake were his sons, merry, rosy, well-built sons—and he smiled a bewildered smile as he trotted along, puffing and trying to forget the heart breaking his chest with a burning ram.

A cyclist, riding beside the dwarf on glittering wheels, pressed his fist to his mouth like a megaphone and urged the sprinter along as they do at a race. Women came out on their porches and, shading their eyes and laughing loudly, pointed out the running dwarf to one another. All the dogs of the town woke up. The parishioners in the stuffy church could not help listening to the barking, to the inciting halloos. And the crowd that kept up with the dwarf continued to grow around him. People thought it was all a capital stunt, circus publicity, or the shooting of a picture.

Fred was beginning to stumble, there was a singing in his ears, the front stud of his collar dug into his throat, he could not breathe. Moans of mirth, shouts, the tramping of feet deafened him. Then through the fog of sweat he saw at last her black dress. She was slowly walking along a brick wall in a torrent of sun. She looked back, she stopped. The dwarf reached her and clutched at the folds of her skirt.

With a smile of happiness he glanced up at her, attempted to speak, but instead raised his eyebrows in surprise and collapsed in slow motion on the sidewalk. All around people noisily swarmed. Someone, realizing that this was no joke, bent over the dwarf, then whistled softly and bared his head. Nora looked listlessly at Fred's tiny body resembling a crumpled black glove. She was jostled. A hand grasped her elbow.

"Leave me alone," said Nora in a toneless voice. "I don't know anything. My son died a few days ago."

1929

Translated by Dmitri Nabokov in collaboration with the author.

A PAINFUL CASE

JAMES JOYCE

MR JAMES Duffy lived in Chapelizod because he wished to live as far as possible from the city of which he was a citizen and because he found all the other suburbs of Dublin mean, modern and pretentious. He lived in an old sombre house and from his windows he could look into the disused distillery or upwards along the shallow river on which Dublin is built. The lofty walls of his uncarpeted room were free from pictures. He had himself bought every article of furniture in the room: a black iron bedstead, an iron washstand, four cane chairs, a clothes-rack, a coal-scuttle, a fender and irons and a square table on which lay a double desk. A bookcase had been made in an alcove by means of shelves of white wood. The bed was clothed with white bed-clothes and a black and scarlet rug covered the foot. A little hand-mirror hung above the washstand and during the day a white-shaded lamp stood as the sole ornament of the mantelpiece. The books on the white wooden shelves were arranged from below upwards according to bulk. A complete Wordsworth[1] stood at one end of the lowest shelf and a copy of the *Maynooth Catechism,*[2] sewn into the cloth cover of a note-book, stood at one end of the top shelf. Writing materials were always on the desk. In the desk lay a manuscript translation of Hauptmann's *Michael Kramer,*[3] the stage directions of which were written in purple ink, and a little sheaf of papers held together by a brass pin. In these sheets a sentence was inscribed from time to time and, in an ironical moment, the headline of an advertisement for *Bile Beans* had been pasted on to the first sheet. On lifting the lid of the desk a faint fragrance escaped—the fragrance of new cedarwood pencils or of a bottle of gum or of an over-ripe apple which might have been left there and forgotten.

Mr Duffy abhorred anything which betokened physical or mental disorder. A mediæval doctor would have called him saturnine. His face, which carried the entire tale of his years, was of the brown tint of Dublin streets. On his long and rather large head grew dry black hair and a tawny moustache did not quite cover an unamiable mouth. His cheekbones also gave his face a harsh character; but there was no harshness in the eyes which, looking at the world from under their tawny eyebrows, gave the impression of a man ever alert to greet a redeeming instinct in others but often disappointed. He lived at a little distance from his body, regarding his own acts with doubtful side-glances. He had an odd autobiographical habit which led him to compose in his mind from time to time a short sentence about himself containing a subject in the third person and a predicate in the past tense. He never gave alms to beggars and walked firmly, carrying a stout hazel.

He had been for many years cashier of a private bank in Baggot Street. Every morning he came in from Chapelizod by tram. At mid-day he went to Dan Burke's and took his lunch—a bottle of lager beer and a small trayful of arrowroot biscuits.[4] At four o'clock he was set

[1] William Wordsworth (1770–1850), major English Romantic poet.

[2] Catechism (1885) authorized by the National Synod of Maynooth for "General Use throughout the Irish Church."

[3] Drama (1900) by Gerhardt Hauptmann (1862–1946), German playwright.

[4] Crackers made with an easily digested starch obtained from the tubers of certain tropical plants.

free. He dined in an eatinghouse in George's Street where he felt himself safe from the society of Dublin's gilded youth and where there was a certain plain honesty in the bill of fare. His evenings were spent either before his landlady's piano or roaming about the outskirts of the city. His liking for Mozart's music brought him sometimes to an opera or a concert: these were the only dissipations of his life.

He had neither companions nor friends, church nor creed. He lived his spiritual life without any communion with others, visiting his relatives at Christmas and escorting them to the cemetery when they died. He performed these two social duties for old dignity' sake but conceded nothing further to the conventions which regulate the civic life. He allowed himself to think that in certain circumstances he would rob his bank but, as these circumstances never arose, his life rolled out evenly—an adventureless tale.

One evening he found himself sitting beside two ladies in the Rotunda. The house, thinly peopled and silent, gave distressing prophecy of failure. The lady who sat next him looked round at the deserted house once or twice and then said:

—What a pity there is such a poor house to-night! It's so hard on people to have to sing to empty benches.

He took the remark as an invitation to talk. He was surprised that she seemed so little awkward. While they talked he tried to fix her permanently in his memory. When he learned that the young girl beside her was her daughter he judged her to be a year or so younger than himself. Her face, which must have been handsome, had remained intelligent. It was an oval face with strongly marked features. The eyes were very dark blue and steady. Their gaze began with a defiant note but was confused by what seemed a deliberate swoon of the pupil into the iris, revealing for an instant a temperament of great sensibility. The pupil reasserted itself quickly, this half-disclosed nature fell again under the reign of prudence, and her astrakhan jacket, moulding a bosom of a certain fulness, struck the note of defiance more definitely.

He met her again a few weeks afterwards at a concert in Earlsfort Terrace and seized the moments when her daughter's attention was diverted to become intimate. She alluded once or twice to her husband but her tone was not such as to make the allusion a warning. Her name was Mrs Sinico. Her husband's great-great-grandfather had come from Leghorn. Her husband was captain of a mercantile boat plying between Dublin and Holland; and they had one child.

Meeting her a third time by accident he found courage to make an appointment. She came. This was the first of many meetings; they met always in the evening and chose the most quiet quarters for their walks together. Mr Duffy, however, had a distaste for underhand ways and, finding that they were compelled to meet stealthily, he forced her to ask him to her house. Captain Sinico encouraged his visits, thinking that his daughter's hand was in question. He had dismissed his wife so sincerely from his gallery of pleasures that he did not suspect that anyone else would take an interest in her. As the husband was often away and the daughter out giving music lessons Mr Duffy had many opportunities of enjoying the lady's society. Neither he nor she had had any such adventure before and neither was conscious of any incongruity. Little by little he entangled his thoughts with hers. He lent her books, provided her with ideas, shared his intellectual life with her. She listened to all.

Sometimes in return for his theories she gave out some fact of her own life. With almost maternal solicitude she urged him to let his nature open to the full; she became his confessor. He told her that for some time he had assisted at the meetings of an Irish Socialist Party where he had felt himself a unique figure amidst a score of sober workmen in a garret lit by an inefficient oil-lamp. When the party had divided into three sections, each under its own leader and in its own garret, he had discontinued his attendances. The workmen's discussions, he said, were too timorous; the interest they took in the question of wages was inordinate. He felt that they were hard-featured realists and that they resented an exactitude which was the product of a leisure not within their reach. No social revolution, he told her, would be likely to strike Dublin for some centuries.

She asked him why did he not write out his thoughts. For what, he asked her, with careful scorn. To compete with phrasemongers, incapable of thinking consecutively for sixty seconds? To submit himself to the criticisms of an obtuse middle class which entrusted its morality to policemen and its fine arts to impresarios?

He went often to her little cottage outside Dublin; often they spent their evenings alone. Little by little, as their thoughts entangled, they spoke of subjects less remote. Her companionship was like a warm soil about an exotic. Many times she allowed the dark to fall upon them, refraining from lighting the lamp. The dark discreet room, their isolation, the music that still vibrated in their ears united them. This union exalted him, wore away the rough edges of his character, emotionalised his mental life. Sometimes he caught himself listening to the sound of his own voice. He thought that in her eyes he would ascend to an angelical stature; and, as he attached the fervent nature of his companion more and more closely to him, he heard the strange impersonal voice which he recognised as his own, insisting on the soul's incurable loneliness. We cannot give ourselves, it said: we are our own. The end of these discourses was that one night during which she had shown every sign of unusual excitement, Mrs Sinico caught up his hand passionately and pressed it to her cheek.

Mr Duffy was very much surprised. Her interpretation of his words disillusioned him. He did not visit her for a week; then he wrote to her asking her to meet him. As he did not wish their last interview to be troubled by the influence of their ruined confessional they met in a little cakeshop near the Parkgate. It was cold autumn weather but in spite of the cold they wandered up and down the roads of the Park for nearly three hours. They agreed to break off their intercourse: every bond, he said, is a bond to sorrow. When they came out of the Park they walked in silence towards the tram; but here she began to tremble so violently that, fearing another collapse on her part, he bade her good-bye quickly and left her. A few days later he received a parcel containing his books and music.

Four years passed. Mr Duffy returned to his even way of life. His room still bore witness of the orderliness of his mind. Some new pieces of music encumbered the music-stand in the lower room and on his shelves stood two volumes by Nietzsche:[5] *Thus Spake Zarathustra* and *The Gay Science.* He wrote seldom in the sheaf of papers which lay in his desk. One of his sentences, written two months after his last interview with Mrs Sinico, read: Love between man and man is impossible because there must not be sexual intercourse and friendship between man and woman is impossible because there must be sexual intercourse. He kept away from concerts lest he should meet her. His father died; the junior partner of the bank retired. And still every morning he went into the city by tram and every evening walked home from the city after having dined moderately in George's Street and read the evening paper for dessert.

One evening as he was about to put a morsel of corned beef and cabbage into his mouth his hand stopped. His eyes fixed themselves on a paragraph in the evening paper which he had propped against the water-carafe. He replaced the morsel of food on his plate and read the paragraph attentively. Then he drank a glass of water, pushed his plate to one side, doubled the paper down before him between his elbows

[5] Friedrich Wilhelm Nietzsche (1844–1900), German philosopher, critic, and poet.

and read the paragraph over and over again. The cabbage began to deposit a cold white grease on his plate. The girl came over to him to ask was his dinner not properly cooked. He said it was very good and ate a few mouthfuls of it with difficulty. Then he paid his bill and went out.

He walked along quickly through the November twilight, his stout hazel stick striking the ground regularly, the fringe of the buff *Mail* peeping out of a side-pocket of his tight reefer over-coat. On the lonely road which leads from the Parkgate to Chapelizod he slackened his pace. His stick struck the ground less emphatically and his breath, issuing irregularly, almost with a sighing sound, condensed in the wintry air. When he reached his house he went up at once to his bedroom and, taking the paper from his pocket, read the paragraph again by the failing light of the window. He read it not aloud, but moving his lips as a priest does when he reads the prayers *Secreto*.[6] This was the paragraph:

DEATH OF A LADY AT SYDNEY PARADE

A PAINFUL CASE

To-day at the City of Dublin Hospital the Deputy Coroner (in the absence of Mr Leverett) held an inquest on the body of Mrs Emily Sinico, aged forty-three years, who was killed at Sydney Parade Station yesterday evening. The evidence showed that the deceased lady, while attempting to cross the line, was knocked down by the engine of the ten o'clock slow train from Kingstown, thereby sustaining injuries of the head and right side which led to her death.

James Lennon, driver of the engine, stated that he had been in the employment of the railway company for fifteen years. On hearing the guard's whistle he set the train in motion and a second or two afterwards brought it to rest in response to loud cries. The train was going slowly.

P. Dunne, railway porter, stated that as the train was about to start he observed a woman attempting to cross the lines. He ran towards her and shouted but, before he could reach her, she was caught by the buffer of the engine and fell to the ground.

A juror—You saw the lady fall?

Witness—Yes.

[6] Secret: prayer said in a low or inaudible voice by the celebrant at the end of the Offertory in the Catholic liturgy.

Police Sergeant Croly deposed that when he arrived he found the deceased lying on the platform apparently dead. He had the body taken to the waiting-room pending the arrival of the ambulance.

Constable 57E corroborated.

Dr Halpin, assistant house surgeon of the City of Dublin Hospital, stated that the deceased had two lower ribs fractured and had sustained severe contusions of the right shoulder. The right side of the head had been injured in the fall. The injuries were not sufficient to have caused death in a normal person. Death, in his opinion, had been probably due to shock and sudden failure of the heart's action.

Mr H. B. Patterson Finlay, on behalf of the railway company, expressed his deep regret at the accident. The company had always taken every precaution to prevent people crossing the lines except by the bridges, both by placing notices in every station and by the use of patent spring gates at level crossings. The deceased had been in the habit of crossing the lines late at night from platform to platform and, in view of certain other circumstances of the case, he did not think the railway officials were to blame.

Captain Sinico, of Leoville, Sydney Parade, husband of the deceased, also gave evidence. He stated that the deceased was his wife. He was not in Dublin at the time of the accident as he had arrived only that morning from Rotterdam. They had been married for twenty-two years and had lived happily until about two years ago when his wife began to be rather intemperate in her habits.

Miss Mary Sinico said that of late her mother had been in the habit of going out at night to buy spirits. She, witness, had often tried to reason with her mother and had induced her to join a league. She was not at home until an hour after the accident.

The jury returned a verdict in accordance with the medical evidence and exonerated Lennon from all blame.

The Deputy Coroner said it was a most painful case, and expressed great sympathy with Captain Sinico and his daughter. He urged on the railway company to take strong measures to prevent the possibility of similar accidents in the future. No blame attached to anyone.

Mr Duffy raised his eyes from the paper and gazed out of his window on the cheerless evening landscape. The river lay quiet beside the empty distillery and from time to time a light appeared in some house on the Lucan road. What an end! The whole narrative of her death revolted him and it revolted him to think that he had ever spoken to her of what he held sacred. The threadbare phrases, the inane expressions of sympathy, the cautious words of a reporter won over to conceal the details of a commonplace vulgar death attacked his stomach. Not merely had she degraded herself; she had degraded him. He saw the squalid tract of her vice, miserable and malodorous. His soul's companion! He thought of the hobbling wretches whom he had seen carrying cans and bottles to be filled by the barman. Just God, what an end! Evidently she had been unfit to live, without any strength of purpose, an easy prey to habits, one of the wrecks on which civilisation has been reared. But that she could have sunk so low! Was it possible he had deceived himself so utterly about her? He remembered her outburst of that night and interpreted it in a harsher sense than he had ever done. He had no difficulty now in approving of the course he had taken.

As the light failed and his memory began to wander he thought her hand touched his. The shock which had first attacked his stomach was now attacking his nerves. He put on his overcoat and hat quickly and went out. The cold air met him on the threshold; it crept into the sleeves of his coat. When he came to the public-house at Chapelizod Bridge he went in and ordered a hot punch.

The proprietor served him obsequiously but did not venture to talk. There were five or six working-men in the shop discussing the value of a gentleman's estate in County Kildare. They drank at intervals from their huge pint tumblers and smoked, spitting often on the floor and sometimes dragging the sawdust over their spits with their heavy boots. Mr Duffy sat on his stool and gazed at them, without seeing or hearing them. After a while they went out and he called for another punch. He sat a long time over it. The shop was very quiet. The proprietor sprawled on the counter reading the *Herald* and yawning. Now and again a tram was heard swishing along the lonely road outside.

As he sat there, living over his life with her and evoking alternately the two images in which he now conceived her, he realised that she was dead, that she had ceased to exist, that she had become a memory. He began to feel ill at ease. He asked himself what else could he have done. He could not have carried on a comedy of deception with her; he could not have lived with her openly. He had done what seemed to him best. How was he to blame? Now that she was gone he understood how lonely her life must have been, sitting night after night alone in that room. His life would be lonely too until he, too, died, ceased to exist, became a memory—if anyone remembered him.

It was after nine o'clock when he left the shop. The night was cold and gloomy. He entered the Park by the first gate and walked along under the gaunt trees. He walked through the bleak alleys where they had walked four years before. She seemed to be near him in the darkness. At moments he seemed to feel her voice touch his ear, her hand touch his. He stood still to listen. Why had he withheld life from her? Why had he sentenced her to death? He felt his moral nature falling to pieces.

When he gained the crest of the Magazine Hill he halted and looked along the river towards Dublin, the lights of which burned redly and hospitably in the cold night. He looked down the slope and, at the base, in the shadow of the wall of the Park, he saw some human figures lying. Those venal and furtive loves filled him with despair. He gnawed the rectitude of his life; he felt that he had been outcast from life's feast. One human being had seemed to love him and he had denied her life and happiness: he had sentenced her to ignominy, a death of shame. He knew that the prostrate creatures down by the wall were watching him and wished him gone. No one wanted him; he was outcast from life's feast. He turned his eyes to the grey gleaming river, winding along towards Dublin. Beyond the river he saw a goods train winding out of Kingsbridge Station, like a worm with a fiery head winding through the darkness, obstinately and laboriously. It passed slowly out of sight; but still he heard in his ears the laborious drone of the engine reiterating the syllables of her name.

He turned back the way he had come, the rhythm of the engine pounding in his ears. He began to doubt the reality of what memory told him. He halted under a tree and allowed the rhythm to die away. He could not feel her near him in the darkness nor her voice touch his ear. He waited for some minutes listening. He could hear nothing: the night was perfectly silent. He listened again: perfectly silent. He felt that he was alone.

1914

BARBADOS

PAULE MARSHALL

DAWN, LIKE the night which had preceded it, came from the sea. In a white mist tumbling like spume over the fishing boats leaving the island and the hunched, ghost shapes of the fishermen. In a white, wet wind breathing over the villages scattered amid the tall canes. The cabbage palms roused, their high headdresses solemnly saluting the wind, and along the white beach which ringed the island the casuarina trees began their moaning—a sound of women lamenting their dead within a cave.

The wind, smarting of the sea, threaded a wet skein through Mr. Watford's five hundred dwarf coconut trees and around his house at

From *Soul Clap Hands and Sing* by Paule Marshall. Reprinted with the permission of the author.

the edge of the grove. The house, Colonial American in design, seemed created by the mist—as if out of the dawn's formlessness had come, magically, the solid stone walls, the blind, broad windows and the portico of fat columns which embraced the main story. When the mist cleared, the house remained—pure, proud, a pristine white—disdaining the crude wooden houses in the village outside its high gate.

It was not the dawn settling around his house which awakened Mr. Watford, but the call of his Barbary doves from their hutch in the yard. And it was more the feel of that sound than the sound itself. His hands had retained, from the many times a day he held the doves, the feel of their throats swelling with that murmurous, mournful note. He lay abed now, his hands—as cracked and calloused as a cane cutter's—filled with the sound, and against the white sheet which flowed out to the white walls he appeared profoundly alone, yet secure in loneliness, contained. His face was fleshless and severe, his black skin sucked deep into the hollow of his jaw, while under a high brow, which was like a bastion raised against the world, his eyes were indrawn and pure. It was as if during all his seventy years, Mr. Watford had permitted nothing to sight which could have affected him.

He stood up, and his body, muscular but stripped of flesh, appeared to be absolved from time, still young. Yet each clenched gesture of his arms, of his lean shank as he dressed in a faded shirt and work pants, each vigilant, snapping motion of his head betrayed tension. Ruthlessly he spurred his body to perform like a younger man's. Savagely he denied the accumulated fatigue of the years. Only sometimes when he paused in his grove of coconut trees during the day, his eyes tearing and the breath torn from his lungs, did it seem that if he could find a place hidden from the world and himself he would give way to exhaustion and weep from weariness.

Dressed, he strode through the house, his step tense, his rough hand touching the furniture from Grand Rapids which crowded each room. For some reason, Mr. Watford had never completed the house. Everywhere the walls were raw and unpainted, the furniture unarranged. In the drawing room with its coffered ceiling, he stood before his favorite piece, an old mantel clock which eked out the time. Reluctantly it whirred five and Mr. Watford nodded. His day had begun.

It was no different from all the days which made up the five years since his return to Barbados. Downstairs in the unfinished kitchen, he prepared his morning tea—tea with canned milk and fried bakes[1]—

[1] Flattish, round cakes made of flour, sugar, salt, and baking powder.

and ate standing at the stove while lizards skittered over the unplastered walls. Then, belching and snuffling the way a child would, he put on a pith helmet, secured his pants legs with bicycle clasps and stepped into the yard. There he fed the doves, holding them so that their sound poured into his hands and laughing gently—but the laugh gave way to an irritable grunt as he saw the mongoose tracks under the hutch. He set the trap again.

The first heat had swept the island like a huge tidal wave when Mr. Watford, with that tense, headlong stride, entered the grove. He had planted the dwarf coconut trees because of their quick yield and because, with their stunted trunks, they always appeared young. Now as he worked, rearranging the complex of pipes which irrigated the land, stripping off the dead leaves, the trees were like cool, moving presences; the stiletto fronds wove a protective dome above him and slowly, as the day soared toward noon, his mind filled with the slivers of sunlight through the trees and the feel of earth in his hands, as it might have been filled with thoughts.

Except for a meal at noon, he remained in the grove until dusk surged up from the sea; then returning to the house, he bathed and dressed in a medical doctor's white uniform, turned on the lights in the parlor and opened the tall doors to the portico. Then the old women of the village on their way to church, the last hawkers caroling, "Fish, flying fish, a penny, my lady," the roistering saga-boys[2] lugging their heavy steel drums to the crossroad where they would rehearse under the street lamp—all passing could glimpse Mr. Watford, stiff in his white uniform and with his head bent heavily over a Boston newspaper. The papers reached him weeks late but he read them anyway, giving a little savage chuckle at the thought that beyond his world that other world went its senseless way. As he read, the night sounds of the village welled into a joyous chorale against the sea's muffled cadence and the hollow, haunting music of the steel band. Soon the moths, lured in by the light, fought to die on the lamp, the beetles crashed drunkenly against the walls and the night—like a woman offering herself to him—became fragrant with the night-blooming cactus.

Even in America Mr. Watford had spent his evenings this way. Coming home from the hospital, where he worked in the boiler room, he would dress in his white uniform and read in the basement of the large rooming house he owned. He had lived closeted like this,

[2] Gay and pleasure-loving fellows, not given to working and popular with the ladies.

detached, because America—despite the money and property he had slowly accumulated—had meant nothing to him. Each morning, walking to the hospital along the rutted Boston streets, through the smoky dawn light, he had known—although it had never been a thought—that his allegiance, his place, lay elsewhere. Neither had the few acquaintances he had made mattered. Nor the women he had occasionally kept as a younger man. After the first months their bodies would grow coarse to his hand and he would begin edging away.... So that he had felt no regret when, the year before his retirement, he resigned his job, liquidated his properties and, his fifty-year exile over, returned home.

The clock doled out eight and Mr. Watford folded the newspaper and brushed the burnt moths from the lamp base. His lips still shaped the last words he had read as he moved through the rooms, fastening the windows against the night air, which he had dreaded even as a boy. Something palpable but unseen was always, he believed, crouched in the night's dim recess, waiting to snare him.... Once in bed in his sealed room, Mr. Watford fell asleep quickly.

The next day was no different except that Mr. Goodman, the local shopkeeper, sent the boy for coconuts to sell at the race track and then came that evening to pay for them and to herald—although Mr. Watford did not know this—the coming of the girl.

That morning, taking his tea, Mr. Watford heard the careful tap of the mule's hoofs and looking out saw the wagon jolting through the dawn and the boy, still lax with sleep, swaying on the seat. He was perhaps eighteen and the muscles packed tightly beneath his lustrous black skin gave him a brooding strength. He came and stood outside the back door, his hands and lowered head performing the small, subtle rites of deference.

Mr. Watford's pleasure was full, for the gestures were those given only to a white man in his time. Yet the boy always nettled him. He sensed a natural arrogance like a pinpoint of light within his dark stare. The boy's stance exhumed a memory buried under the years. He remembered, staring at him, the time when he had worked as a yard boy for a white family, and had had to assume the same respectful pose while their flat, raw, Barbadian voices assailed him with orders. He remembered the muscles in his neck straining as he nodded deeply and a taste like alum on his tongue as he repeated the "Yes, please," as in a litany. But, because of their whiteness and wealth, he had never dared hate them. Instead his rancor, like a boomerang, had rebounded, glancing past him to strike all the dark ones like himself, even his mother with her spindled arms and her stomach sagging with a child who was, invariably, dead at birth. He had been the only one of ten to live, the only one to escape. But he had never lost the sense of being pursued by the same dread presence which had claimed them. He had never lost the fear that if he lived too fully he would tire and death would quickly close the gap. His only defense had been a cautious life and work. He had been almost broken by work at the age of twenty when his parents died, leaving him enough money for the passage to America. Gladly had he fled the island. But nothing had mattered after his flight.

The boy's foot stirred the dust. He murmured, "Please, sir, Mr. Watford, Mr. Goodman at the shop send me to pick the coconuts."

Mr. Watford's head snapped up. A caustic word flared, but died as he noticed a political button pinned to the boy's patched shirt with "Vote for the Barbados People's Party" printed boldly on it, and below that the motto of the party: "The Old Order Shall Pass." At this ludicrous touch (for what could this boy, with his splayed and shigoed feet[3] and blunted mind, understand about politics?) he became suddenly nervous, angry. The button and its motto seemed, somehow, directed at him. He said roughly, "Well, come then. You can't pick any coconuts standing there looking foolish!"—and he led the way to the grove.

The coconuts, he knew, would sell well at the booths in the center of the track, where the poor were penned in like cattle. As the heat thickened and the betting grew desperate, they would clamor: "Man, how you selling the water coconuts?" and hacking off the tops they would pour rum into the water within the hollow centers, then tilt the coconuts to their heads so that the rum-sweetened water skimmed their tongues and trickled bright down their dark chins. Mr. Watford had stood among them at the track as a young man, as poor as they were, but proud. And he had always found something unutterably graceful and free in their gestures, something which had roused contradictory feelings in him: admiration, but just as strong, impatience at their easy ways, and shame . . .

That night, as he sat in his white uniform reading, he heard Mr. Goodman's heavy step and went out and stood at the head of the stairs in a formal, proprietory pose. Mr. Goodman's face floated up into the light—the loose folds of flesh, the skin slick with sweat as if oiled, the eyes scribbled with veins and mottled, bold—as if each blemish there was a sin he proudly displayed or a scar which proved he had met life

[3] Refers to the shiga, or *Bacillus shigella,* which causes dysentery and in the West Indies is believed to enter the body by lodging under the toenails.

head-on. His body, unlike Mr. Watford's, was corpulent and, with the trousers caught up around his full crotch, openly concupiscent. He owned the one shop in the village which gave credit and a booth which sold coconuts at the race track, kept a wife and two outside women, drank a rum with each customer at his bar, regularly caned his fourteen children, who still followed him everywhere (even now they were waiting for him in the darkness beyond Mr. Watford's gate) and bet heavily at the races, and when he lost gave a loud hacking laugh which squeezed his body like a pain and left him gasping.

The laugh clutched him now as he flung his pendulous flesh into a chair and wheezed, "Watford, how? Man, I near lose house, shop, shirt and all at races today. I tell you, they got some horses from Trinidad in this meet that's making ours look like they running backwards. Be-Jese, I wouldn't bet on a Bajan[4] horse tomorrow if Christ heself was to give me the tip. Those bitches might look good but they's nothing 'pon a track."

Mr. Watford, his back straight as the pillar he leaned against, his eyes unstained, his gaunt face planed by contempt, gave Mr. Goodman his cold, measured smile, thinking that the man would be dead soon, bloated with rice and rum—and somehow this made his own life more certain.

Sputtering with his amiable laughter, Mr. Goodman paid for the coconuts, but instead of leaving then as he usually did, he lingered, his eyes probing for a glimpse inside the house. Mr. Watford waited, his head snapping warily; then, impatient, he started toward the door and Mr. Goodman said, "I tell you, your coconut trees bearing fast enough even for dwarfs. You's lucky, man."

Ordinarily Mr. Watford would have waved both the man and his remark aside, but repelled more than usual tonight by Mr. Goodman's gross form and immodest laugh, he said—glad of the cold edge his slight American accent gave the words—"What luck got to do with it? I does care the trees properly and they bear, that's all. Luck! People, especially this bunch around here, is always looking to luck when the only answer is a little brains and plenty of hard work. . . ." Suddenly remembering the boy that morning and the political button, he added in loud disgust, "Look that half-foolish boy you does send here to pick the coconuts. Instead of him learning a trade and going to England where he might find work he's walking about with a political button. He and all in politics now! But that's the way with these down in here.

[4] Barbadian.

They'll do some of everything but work. They don't want work!" He gestured violently, almost dancing in anger. "They too busy spreeing."

The chair creaked as Mr. Goodman sketched a pained and gentle denial. "No, man," he said, "you wrong. Things is different to before. I mean to say, the young people nowadays is different to how we was. They not just sitting back and taking things no more. They not so frighten for the white people as we was. No man. Now take that said same boy, for an example. I don't say he don't like a spree, but he's serious, you see him there. He's a member of this new Barbados People's Party. He wants to see his own color running the government. He wants to be able to make a living right here in Barbados instead of going to any cold England. And he's right!" Mr. Goodman paused at a vehement pitch, then shrugged heavily. "What the young people must do, nuh? They got to look to something...."

"Look to work!" And Mr. Watford thrust out a hand so that the horned knuckles caught the light.

"Yes, that's true—and it's up to we that got little something to give them work," Mr. Goodman said, and a sadness filtered among the dissipations in his eyes. "I mean to say we that got little something got to help out. In a manner of speaking, we's responsible..."

"Responsible!" The word circled Mr. Watford's head like a gnat and he wanted to reach up and haul it down, to squash it underfoot.

Mr. Goodman spread his hands; his breathing rumbled with a sigh. "Yes, in a manner of speaking. That's why, Watford man, you got to provide little work for some poor person down in here. Hire a servant at least! 'Cause I gon tell you something..." And he hitched forward his chair, his voice dropped to a wheeze. "People talking. Here you come back rich from big America and build a swell house and plant 'nough coconut trees and you still cleaning and cooking and thing like some woman? Man, it don't look good!" His face screwed in emphasis and he sat back. "Now there's this girl, the daughter of a friend that just dead, and she need work bad enough. But I wouldn't like to see she working for these white people 'cause you know how those men will take advantage of she. And she'd make a good servant, man. Quiet and quick so, and nothing a-tall to feed and she can sleep anywhere about the place. And she don't have no boys always around her either. ..." Still talking, Mr. Goodman eased from his chair and reached the stairs with surprising agility. "You need a servant," he whispered, leaning close to Mr. Watford as he passed. "It don't look good, man. People talking. I gon send she."

Mr. Watford was overcome by nausea. Not only from Mr. Goodman's smell—a stench of salt fish, rum and sweat, but from an outrage which was like a sediment in his stomach. For a long time he stood there almost kecking from disgust, until his clock struck eight, reminding him of the sanctuary within—and suddenly his cold laugh dismissed Mr. Goodman and his proposal. Hurrying in, he locked the doors and windows against the night air and still laughing, he slept.

The next day, coming from the grove to prepare his noon meal, he saw her. She was standing in his driveway, her bare feet like strong dark roots amid the jagged stones, her face tilted toward the sun—and she might have been standing there always waiting for him. She seemed of the sun, of the earth. The folktale of creation might have been true with her: that along a river bank a god had scooped up the earth—rich and black and warmed by the sun—and molded her poised head with its tufted braids and then with a whimsical touch crowned it with a sober brown felt hat which should have been worn by some stout English matron in a London suburb, had sculptured the passionless face and drawn a screen of gossamer across her eyes to hide the void behind. Beneath her bodice her small breasts were smooth at the crest. Below her waist, her hips branched wide, the place prepared for its load of life. But it was the bold and sensual strength of her legs which completely unstrung Mr. Watford. He wanted to grab a hoe and drive her off.

"What it 'tis you want?" he called sharply.

"Mr. Goodman send me."

"Send you for what?" His voice was shrill in the glare.

She moved. Holding a caved-in valise and a pair of white sandals, her head weaving slightly as though she bore a pail of water there or a tray of mangoes, she glided over the stones as if they were smooth ground. Her bland expression did not change, but her eyes, meeting his, held a vague trust. Pausing a few feet away, she curtsied deeply. "I's the new servant."

Only Mr. Watford's cold laugh saved him from anger. As always it raised him to a height where everything below appeared senseless and insignificant—especially his people, whom the girl embodied. From this height, he could even be charitable. And thinking suddenly of how she had waited in the brutal sun since morning without taking shelter under the nearby tamarind tree, he said, not unkindly, "Well, girl, go back and tell Mr. Goodman for me that I don't need no servant."

"I can't go back."

"How you mean can't?" His head gave its angry snap.

"I'll get lashes," she said simply. "My mother say I must work the day and then if you don't wish me, I can come back. But I's not to leave till night falling, if not I get lashes."

He was shaken by her dispassion. So much so that his head dropped from its disdaining angle and his hands twitched with helplessness. Despite anything he might say or do, her fear of the whipping would keep her there until nightfall, the valise and shoes in hand. He felt his day with its order and quiet rhythms threatened by her intrusion—and suddenly waving her off as if she were an evil visitation, he hurried into the kitchen to prepare his meal.

But he paused, confused, in front of the stove, knowing that he could not cook and leave her hungry at the door, nor could he cook and serve her as though he were the servant.

"You know anything about cooking?" he shouted finally.

"Yes, please."

They said nothing more. She entered the room with a firm step and an air almost of familiarity, placed her valise and shoes in a corner and went directly to the larder. For a time Mr. Watford stood by, his muscles flexing with anger and his eyes bounding ahead of her every move, until feeling foolish and frighteningly useless, he went out to feed his doves.

The meal was quickly done and as he ate he heard the dry slap of her feet behind him—a pleasant sound—and then silence. When he glanced back she was squatting in the doorway, the sunlight aslant the absurd hat and her face bent to a bowl she held in one palm. She ate slowly, thoughtfully, as if fixing the taste of each spoonful in her mind.

It was then that he decided to let her work the day and at nightfall to pay her a dollar and dismiss her. His decision held when he returned later from the grove and found tea awaiting him, and then through the supper she prepared Afterward, dressed in his white uniform, he patiently waited out the day's end on the portico, his face setting into a grim mold. Then just as dusk etched the first dark line between the sea and sky, he took out a dollar and went downstairs.

She was not in the kitchen, but the table was set for his morning tea. Muttering at her persistence, he charged down the corridor, which ran the length of the basement, flinging open the doors to the damp, empty rooms on either side, and sending the lizards and the shadows long entrenched there scuttling to safety.

He found her in the small slanted room under the stoop, asleep on an old cot he kept there, her suitcase turned down beside the bed, and the shoes, dress and the ridiculous hat piled on top. A loose night shift muted the outline of her body and hid her legs, so that she appeared suddenly defenseless, innocent, with a child's trust in her curled hand and in her deep breathing. Standing in the doorway, with his own breathing snarled and his eyes averted, Mr. Watford felt like an intruder. She had claimed the room. Quivering with frustration, he slowly turned away, vowing that in the morning he would shove the dollar at her and lead her like a cow out of his house. . . .

Dawn brought rain and a hot wind which set the leaves rattling and swiping at the air like distraught arms. Dressing in the dawn darkness, Mr. Watford again armed himself with the dollar and, with his shoulders at an uncompromising set, plunged downstairs. He descended into the warm smell of bakes and this smell, along with the thought that she had been up before him, made his hand knot with exasperation on the banister. The knot tightened as he saw her, dust swirling at her feet as she swept the corridor, her face bent solemn to the task. Shutting her out with a lifted hand, he shouted, "Don't bother sweeping. Here's a dollar. G'long back."

The broom paused and although she did not raise her head, he sensed her groping through the shadowy maze of her mind toward his voice. Behind the dollar which he waved in her face, her eyes slowly cleared. And, surprisingly, they held no fear. Only anticipation and a tenuous trust. It was as if she expected him to say something kind.

"G'long back!" His angry cry was a plea.

Like a small, starved flame, her trust and expectancy died and she said, almost with reproof, "The rain falling."

To confirm this, the wind set the rain stinging across the windows and he could say nothing, even though the words sputtered at his lips. It was useless. There was nothing inside her to comprehend that she was not wanted. His shoulders sagged under the weight of her ignorance, and with a futile gesture he swung away, the dollar hanging from his hand like a small sword gone limp.

She became as fixed and familiar a part of the house as the stones—and as silent. He paid her five dollars a week, gave her Mondays off and in the evenings, after a time, even allowed her to sit in the alcove off the parlor, while he read with his back to her, taking no more notice of her than he did the moths on the lamp.

But once, after many silent evenings together, he detected a sound apart from the night murmurs of the sea and village and the metallic tuning of the steel band, a low, almost inhuman cry of loneliness which chilled him. Frightened, he turned to find her leaning hesitantly toward him, her eyes dark with urgency, and her face tight with bewilderment and a growing anger. He started, not understanding, and her arm lifted to stay him. Eagerly she bent closer. But as she uttered the low cry again, as her fingers described her wish to talk, he jerked around, afraid that she would be foolish enough to speak and that once she did they would be brought close. He would be forced then to acknowledge something about her which he refused to grant; above all, he would be called upon to share a little of himself. Quickly he returned to his newspaper, rustling it to settle the air, and after a time he felt her slowly, bitterly, return to her silence. . . .

Like sand poured in a careful measure from the hand, the weeks flowed down to August and on the first Monday, August Bank holiday, Mr. Watford awoke to the sound of the excursion buses leaving the village for the annual outing, their backfire pelleting the dawn calm and the ancient motors protesting the overcrowding. Lying there, listening, he saw with disturbing clarity his mother dressed for an excursion—the white head tie wound above her dark face and her head poised like a dancer's under the heavy outing basket of food. That set of her head had haunted his years, reappearing in the girl as she walked toward him the first day. Aching with the memory, yet annoyed with himself for remembering, he went downstairs.

The girl had already left for the excursion, and although it was her day off, he felt vaguely betrayed by her eagerness to leave him. Somehow it suggested ingratitude. It was as if his doves were suddenly to refuse him their song or his trees their fruit, despite the care he gave them. Some vital part which shaped the simple mosaic of his life seemed suddenly missing. An alien silence curled like coal gas throughout the house. To escape it he remained in the grove all day and, upon his return to the house, dressed with more care than usual, putting on a fresh, starched uniform, and solemnly brushing his hair until it lay in a smooth bush above his brow. Leaning close to the mirror, but avoiding his eyes, he cleaned the white rheum at their corners, and afterward pried loose the dirt under his nails.

Unable to read his papers, he went out on the portico to escape the unnatural silence in the house, and stood with his hands clenched on the balustrade and his taut body straining forward. After a long wait he heard the buses return and voices in gay shreds upon the wind. Slowly his hands relaxed, as did his shoulders under the white uniform; for the first time that day his breathing was regular. She would soon come.

But she did not come and dusk bloomed into night, with a fragrant heat and a full moon which made the leaves glint as though touched with frost. The steel band at the crossroads began the lilting songs of sadness and seduction, and suddenly—like shades roused by the night and the music—images of the girl flitted before Mr. Watford's eyes. He saw her lost amid the carousings in the village, despoiled; he imagined someone like Mr. Goodman clasping her lewdly or tumbling her in the canebrake. His hand rose, trembling, to rid the air of her; he tried to summon his cold laugh. But, somehow, he could not dismiss her as he had always done with everyone else. Instead, he wanted to punish and protect her, to find and lead her back to the house.

As he leaned there, trying not to give way to the desire to go and find her, his fist striking the balustrade to deny his longing, he saw them. The girl first, with the moonlight like a silver patina on her skin, then the boy whom Mr. Goodman sent for the coconuts, whose easy strength and the political button—"The Old Order Shall Pass"—had always mocked and challenged Mr. Watford. They were joined in a tender battle: the boy in a sport shirt riotous with color was reaching for the girl as he leaped and spun, weightless, to the music, while she fended him off with a gesture which was lovely in its promise of surrender. Her protests were little scattered bursts: "But, man, why you don't stop, nuh . . . ? But, you know, you getting on like a real-real idiot. . . ."

Each time she chided him he leaped higher and landed closer, until finally he eluded her arm and caught her by the waist. Boldly he pressed a leg between her tightly closed legs until they opened under his pressure. Their bodies cleaved into one whirling form and while he sang she laughed like a wanton with her hat cocked over her ear. Dancing, the stones moiling underfoot, they claimed the night. More than the night. The steel band played for them alone. The trees were their frivolous companions, swaying as they swayed. The moon rode the sky because of them.

Mr. Watford, hidden by a dense shadow, felt the tendons which strung him together suddenly go limp; above all, an obscure belief which, like rare china, he had stored on a high shelf in his mind began to tilt. He sensed the familiar specter which hovered in the night reaching out to embrace him, just as the two in the yard were embracing. Utterly unstrung, incapable of either speech or action, he stumbled into the house, only to meet there an accusing silence from the clock, which had missed its eight o'clock winding, and his newspapers lying like ruined leaves over the floor.

He lay in bed in the white uniform, waiting for sleep to rescue him, his hands seeking the comforting sound of his doves. But sleep eluded him and instead of the doves, their throats tremulous with sound, his scarred hands filled with the shape of a woman he had once kept: her skin, which had been almost bruising in its softness; the buttocks and breasts spread under his hands to inspire both cruelty and tenderness. His hands closed to softly crush those forms, and the searing thrust of passion, which he had not felt for years, stabbed his dry groin. He imagined the two outside, their passion at a pitch by now, lying together behind the tamarind tree, or perhaps—and he sat up sharply—they had been bold enough to bring their lust into the house. Did he not smell their taint on the air? Restored suddenly, he rushed downstairs. As he reached the corridor, a thread of light beckoned him from her room and he dashed furiously toward it, rehearsing the angry words which would jar their bodies apart. He neared the door, glimpsed her through the small opening, and his step faltered; the words collapsed.

She was seated alone on the cot, tenderly holding the absurd felt hat in her lap, one leg tucked under her while the other trailed down. A white sandal, its strap broken, dangled from the foot and gently knocked the floor as she absently swung her leg. Her dress was twisted around her body—and pinned to the bodice, so that it gathered the cloth between her small breasts, was the political button the boy always wore. She was dreamily fingering it, her mouth shaped by a gentle, ironic smile and her eyes strangely acute and critical. What had transpired on the cot had not only, it seemed, twisted the dress around her, tumbled her hat and broken her sandal, but had also defined her and brought the blurred forms of life into focus for her. There was a woman's force in her aspect now, a tragic knowing and acceptance in her bent head, a hint about her of Cassandra[5] watching the future wheel before her eyes.

Before those eyes which looked to another world, Mr. Watford's anger and strength failed him and he held to the wall for support. Unreasonably, he felt that he should assume some hushed and reverent pose, to bow as she had the day she had come. If he had known their names, he would have pleaded forgiveness for the sins he had committed against her and the others all his life, against himself. If he could have borne the thought, he would have confessed that it had been love, terrible in its demand, which he had always fled. And that love had been the reason for his return. If he had been honest he would have whispered—his head bent and a hand shading his eyes—that unlike Mr.

[5] Daughter of Priam, King of Troy, endowed by Apollo with prophetic power that was never to be believed.

Goodman (whom he suddenly envied for his full life) and the boy with his political button (to whom he had lost the girl), he had not been willing to bear the weight of his own responsibility.... But all Mr. Watford could admit, clinging there to the wall, was, simply, that he wanted to live—and that the girl held life within her as surely as she held the hat in her hands. If he could prove himself better than the boy, he could win it. Only then, he dimly knew, would he shake off the pursuer which had given him no rest since birth. Hopefully, he staggered forward, his step cautious and contrite, his hands quivering along the wall.

She did not see or hear him as he pushed the door wider. And for some time he stood there, his shoulders hunched in humility, his skin stripped away to reveal each flaw, his whole self offered in one outstretched hand. Still unaware of him, she swung her leg, and the dangling shoe struck a derisive note. Then, just as he had turned away that evening in the parlor when she had uttered her low call, she turned away now, refusing him.

Mr. Watford's body went slack and then stiffened ominously. He knew that he would have to wrest from her the strength needed to sustain him. Slamming the door, he cried, his voice cracked and strangled, "What you and him was doing in here? Tell me! I'll not have you bringing nastiness round here. Tell me!"

She did not start. Perhaps she had been aware of him all along and had expected his outburst. Or perhaps his demented eye and the desperation rising from him like a musk filled her with pity instead of fear. Whatever, her benign smile held and her eyes remained abstracted until his hand reached out to fling her back on the cot. Then, frowning, she stood up, wobbling a little on the broken shoe and holding the political button as if it was a new power which would steady and protect her. With a cruel flick of her arm she struck aside his hand and, in a voice as cruel, halted him. "But you best move and don't come holding on to me, you nasty, pissy old man. That's all you is, despite yuh big house and fancy furnitures and yuh newspapers from America. You ain't people, Mr. Watford, you ain't people!" And with a look and a lift of her head which made her condemnation final, she placed the hat atop her braids, and turning aside picked up the valise which had always lain, packed, beside the cot—as if even on the first day she had known that this night would come and had been prepared against it....

Mr. Watford did not see her leave, for a pain squeezed his heart dry and the driven blood was a bright, blinding cataract over his eyes. But his inner eye was suddenly clear. For the first time it gazed mutely upon the waste and pretense which had spanned his years. Flung there against the door by the girl's small blow, his body slowly crumpled under the weariness he had long denied. He sensed that dark but unsubstantial figure which roamed the nights searching for him wind him in its chill embrace. He struggled against it, his hands clutching the air with the spastic eloquence of a drowning man. He moaned—and the anguished sound reached beyond the room to fill the house. It escaped to the yard and his doves swelled their throats, moaning with him.

1961

DEATH OF A TRAVELING SALESMAN

EUDORA WELTY

R. J. BOWMAN, who for fourteen years had traveled for a shoe company through Mississippi, drove his Ford along a rutted dirt path. It was a long day! The time did not seem to clear the noon hurdle and settle into soft afternoon. The sun, keeping its strength here even in winter, stayed at the top of the sky, and every time Bowman stuck his head out of the dusty car to stare up the road, it seemed to reach a long arm down and push against the top of his head, right through his hat—like the practical joke of an old drummer, long on the road. It made him feel all the more angry and helpless. He was feverish, and he was not quite sure of the way.

This was his first day back on the road after a long siege of influenza. He had had very high fever, and dreams, and had become weakened and pale, enough to tell the difference in the mirror, and he could not think clearly.... All afternoon, in the midst of his anger, and for no reason, he had thought of his dead grandmother. She had been a comfortable soul. Once more Bowman wished he could fall into the big feather bed that had been in her room.... Then he forgot her again.

This desolate hill country! And he seemed to be going the wrong way—it was as if he were going back, far back. There was not a house in sight.... There was no use wishing he were back in bed, though. By paying the hotel doctor his bill he had proved his recovery. He had not even been sorry when the pretty trained nurse said good-bye. He did not like illness, he distrusted it, as he distrusted the road without signposts. It angered him. He had given the nurse a really expensive bracelet, just because she was packing up her bag and leaving.

But now—what if in fourteen years on the road he had never been ill before and never had an accident? His record was broken, and he had even begun almost to question it.... He had gradually put up at better hotels, in the bigger towns, but weren't they all, eternally, stuffy in summer and drafty in winter? Women? He could only remember little rooms within little rooms, like a nest of Chinese paper boxes, and if he thought of one woman he saw the worn loneliness that the furniture of that room seemed built of. And he himself—he was a man who always wore rather wide-brimmed black hats, and in the wavy hotel mirrors had looked something like a bullfighter, as he paused for that inevitable instant on the landing, walking downstairs to supper.... He leaned out of the car again, and once more the sun pushed at his head.

Bowman had wanted to reach Beulah[1] by dark, to go to bed and sleep off his fatigue. As he remembered, Beulah was fifty miles away from the last town, on a graveled road. This was only a cow trail. How had he ever come to such a place? One hand wiped the sweat from his face, and he drove on.

He had made the Beulah trip before. But he had never seen this hill or this petering-out path before—or that cloud, he thought shyly, looking up and then down quickly—any more than he had seen this day before. Why did he not admit he was simply lost and had been for miles? ... He was not in the habit of asking the way of strangers, and these people

[1] Town in Bolivar County, northwestern Mississippi, on Lake Beulah; symbolic name denoting the future prosperity of Israel (Isa. 62:4); land of peace and rest, near the end of life's journey, described in John Bunyan's *Pilgrim's Progress* (1678).

never knew where the very roads they lived on went to; but then he had not even been close enough to anyone to call out. People standing in the fields now and then, or on top of the haystacks, had been too far away, looking like leaning sticks or weeds, turning a little at the solitary rattle of his car across their countryside, watching the pale sobered winter dust where it chunked out behind like big squashes down the road. The stares of these distant people had followed him solidly like a wall, impenetrable, behind which they turned back after he had passed.

The cloud floated there to one side like the bolster on his grandmother's bed. It went over a cabin on the edge of a hill, where two bare chinaberry trees clutched at the sky. He drove through a heap of dead oak leaves, his wheels stirring their weightless sides to make a silvery melancholy whistle as the car passed through their bed. No car had been along this way ahead of him. Then he saw that he was on the edge of a ravine that fell away, a red erosion, and that this was indeed the road's end.

He pulled the brake. But it did not hold, though he put all his strength into it. The car, tipped toward the edge, rolled a little. Without doubt, it was going over the bank.

He got out quietly, as though some mischief had been done him and he had his dignity to remember. He lifted his bag and sample case out, set them down, and stood back and watched the car roll over the edge. He heard something—not the crash he was listening for, but a slow, un-uproarious crackle. Rather distastefully he went to look over, and he saw that his car had fallen into a tangle of immense grapevines as thick as his arm, which caught it and held it, rocked it like a grotesque child in a dark cradle, and then, as he watched, concerned somehow that he was not still inside it, released it gently to the ground.

He sighed.

Where am I? he wondered with a shock. Why didn't I do something? All his anger seemed to have drifted away from him. There was the house back on the hill. He took a bag in each hand and with almost childlike willingness went toward it. But his breathing came with difficulty, and he had to stop to rest.

It was a shotgun house,[2] two rooms and an open passage between, perched on the hill. The whole cabin slanted a little under the heavy heaped-up vine that covered the roof, light and green, as though forgotten from summer. A woman stood in the passage.

[2] House in which all the rooms are in a direct line to each other.

He stopped still. Then all of a sudden his heart began to behave strangely. Like a rocket set off, it began to leap and expand into uneven patterns of beats which showered into his brain, and he could not think. But in scattering and falling it made no noise. It shot up with great power, almost elation, and fell gently, like acrobats into nets. It began to pound profoundly, then waited irresponsibly, hitting in some sort of inward mockery first at his ribs, then against his eyes, then under his shoulder blades, and against the roof of his mouth when he tried to say, "Good afternoon, madam." But he could not hear his heart—it was as quiet as ashes falling. This was rather comforting; still, it was shocking to Bowman to feel his heart beating at all.

Stock-still in his confusion, he dropped his bags, which seemed to drift in slow bulks gracefully through the air and to cushion themselves on the gray prostrate grass near the doorstep.

As for the woman standing there, he saw at once that she was old. Since she could not possibly hear his heart, he ignored the pounding and now looked at her carefully, and yet in his distraction dreamily, with his mouth open.

She had been cleaning the lamp, and held it, half blackened, half clear, in front of her. He saw her with the dark passage behind her. She was a big woman with a weather-beaten but unwrinkled face; her lips were held tightly together, and her eyes looked with a curious dulled brightness into his. He looked at her shoes, which were like bundles. If it were summer she would be barefoot.... Bowman, who automatically judged a woman's age on sight, set her age at fifty. She wore a formless garment of some gray coarse material, rough-dried from a washing, from which her arms appeared pink and unexpectedly round. When she never said a word, and sustained her quiet pose of holding the lamp, he was convinced of the strength in her body.

"Good afternoon, madam," he said.

She stared on, whether at him or at the air around him he could not tell, but after a moment she lowered her eyes to show that she would listen to whatever he had to say.

"I wonder if you would be interested—" He tried once more. "An accident—my car..."

Her voice emerged low and remote, like a sound across a lake. "Sonny he ain't here."

"Sonny?"

"Sonny ain't here now."

Her son—a fellow able to bring my car up, he decided in blurred relief. He pointed down the hill. "My car's in the bottom of the ditch. I'll need help."

"Sonny ain't here, but he'll be here."

She was becoming clearer to him and her voice stronger, and Bowman saw that she was stupid.

He was hardly surprised at the deepening postponement and tedium of his journey. He took a breath, and heard his voice speaking over the silent blows of his heart. "I was sick. I am not strong yet. . . . May I come in?"

He stooped and laid his big black hat over the handle on his bag. It was a humble motion, almost a bow, that instantly struck him as absurd and betraying of all his weakness. He looked up at the woman, the wind blowing his hair. He might have continued for a long time in this unfamiliar attitude; he had never been a patient man, but when he was sick he had learned to sink submissively into the pillows, to wait for his medicine. He waited on the woman.

Then she, looking at him with blue eyes, turned and held open the door, and after a moment Bowman, as if convinced in his action, stood erect and followed her in.

Inside, the darkness of the house touched him like a professional hand, the doctor's. The woman set the half-cleaned lamp on a table in the center of the room and pointed, also like a professional person, a guide, to a chair with a yellow cowhide seat. She herself crouched on the hearth, drawing her knees up under the shapeless dress.

At first he felt hopefully secure. His heart was quieter. The room was enclosed in the gloom of yellow pine boards. He could see the other room, with the foot of an iron bed showing, across the passage. The bed had been made up with a red-and-yellow pieced quilt that looked like a map or a picture, a little like his grandmother's girlhood painting of Rome burning.

He had ached for coolness, but in this room it was cold. He stared at the hearth with dead coals lying on it and iron pots in the corners. The hearth and smoked chimney were of the stone he had seen ribbing the hills, mostly slate. Why is there no fire? he wondered.

And it was so still. The silence of the fields seemed to enter and move familiarly through the house. The wind used the open hall. He felt that he was in a mysterious, quiet, cool danger. It was necessary to do what? . . . To talk.

"I have a nice line of women's low-priced shoes . . ." he said.

But the woman answered, "Sonny 'll be here. He's strong. Sonny 'll move your car."

"Where is he now?"

"Farms for Mr. Redmond."

Mr. Redmond. Mr. Redmond. That was someone he would never have to encounter, and he was glad. Somehow the name did not appeal to him.... In a flare of touchiness and anxiety, Bowman wished to avoid even mention of unknown men and their unknown farms.

"Do you two live here alone?" He was surprised to hear his old voice, chatty, confidential, inflected for selling shoes, asking a question like that—a thing he did not even want to know.

"Yes. We are alone."

He was surprised at the way she answered. She had taken a long time to say that. She had nodded her head in a deep way too. Had she wished to affect him with some sort of premonition? he wondered unhappily. Or was it only that she would not help him, after all, by talking with him? For he was not strong enough to receive the impact of unfamiliar things without a little talk to break their fall. He had lived a month in which nothing had happened except in his head and his body—an almost inaudible life of heartbeats and dreams that came back, a life of fever and privacy, a delicate life which had left him weak to the point of—what? Of begging. The pulse in his palm leapt like a trout in a brook.

He wondered over and over why the woman did not go ahead with cleaning the lamp. What prompted her to stay there across the room, silently bestowing her presence upon him? He saw that with her it was not a time for doing little tasks. Her face was grave; she was feeling how right she was. Perhaps it was only politeness. In docility he held his eyes stiffly wide; they fixed themselves on the woman's clasped hands as though she held the cord they were strung on.

Then, "Sonny's coming," she said.

He himself had not heard anything, but there came a man passing the window and then plunging in at the door, with two hounds beside him. Sonny was a big enough man, with his belt slung low about his hips. He looked at least thirty. He had a hot, red face that was yet full of silence. He wore muddy blue pants and an old military coat stained and patched. World War? Bowman wondered. Great God, it was a Confederate coat. On the back of his light hair he had a wide filthy black hat which seemed to insult Bowman's own. He pushed down the dogs from his chest. He was strong, with dignity and heaviness in his way of moving.... There was the resemblance to his mother.

They stood side by side.... He must account again for his presence here.

"Sonny, this man, he had his car to run off over the prec'pice an' wants to know if you will git it out for him," the woman said after a few minutes.

Bowman could not even state his case.

Sonny's eyes lay upon him.

He knew he should offer explanations and show money—at least appear either penitent or authoritative. But all he could do was to shrug slightly.

Sonny brushed by him going to the window, followed by the eager dogs, and looked out. There was effort even in the way he was looking, as if he could throw his sight out like a rope. Without turning Bowman felt that his own eyes could have seen nothing: it was too far.

"Got me a mule out there an' got me a block an' tackle," said Sonny meaningfully. "I *could* catch me my mule an' git me my ropes, an' before long I'd git your car out the ravine."

He looked completely around the room, as if in meditation, his eyes roving in their own distance. Then he pressed his lips firmly and yet shyly together, and with the dogs ahead of him this time, he lowered his head and strode out. The hard earth sounded, cupping to his powerful way of walking—almost a stagger.

Mischievously, at the suggestion of those sounds, Bowman's heart leapt again. It seemed to walk about inside him.

"Sonny's goin' to do it," the woman said. She said it again, singing it almost, like a song. She was sitting in her place by the hearth.

Without looking out, he heard some shouts and the dogs barking and the pounding of hoofs in short runs on the hill. In a few minutes Sonny passed under the window with a rope, and there was a brown mule with quivering, shining, purple-looking ears. The mule actually looked in the window. Under its eyelashes it turned target-like eyes into his. Bowman averted his head and saw the woman looking serenely back at the mule, with only satisfaction in her face.

She sang a little more, under her breath. It occurred to him, and it seemed quite marvelous, that she was not really talking to him, but rather following the thing that came about with words that were unconscious and part of her looking.

So he said nothing, and this time when he did not reply he felt a curious and strong emotion, not fear, rise up in him.

This time, when his heart leapt, something—his soul—seemed to leap too, like a little colt invited out of a pen. He stared at the woman while the frantic nimbleness of his feeling made his head sway. He could not move; there was nothing he could do, unless perhaps he might embrace this woman who sat there growing old and shapeless before him.

But he wanted to leap up, to say to her, I have been sick and I found out then, only then, how lonely I am. Is it too late? My heart puts up a struggle inside me, and you may have heard it, protesting against emptiness.... It should be full, he would rush on to tell her, thinking of his heart now as a deep lake, it should be holding love like other hearts. It should be flooded with love. There would be a warm spring day... Come and stand in my heart, whoever you are, and a whole river would cover your feet and rise higher and take your knees in whirlpools, and draw you down to itself, your whole body, your heart too.

But he moved a trembling hand across his eyes, and looked at the placid crouching woman across the room. She was still as a statue. He felt ashamed and exhausted by the thought that he might, in one more moment, have tried by simple words and embraces to communicate some strange thing—something which seemed always to have just escaped him...

Sunlight touched the furthest pot on the hearth. It was late afternoon. This time tomorrow he would be somewhere on a good graveled road, driving his car past things that happened to people, quicker than their happening. Seeing ahead to the next day, he was glad, and knew that this was no time to embrace an old woman. He could feel in his pounding temples the readying of his blood for motion and for hurrying away.

"Sonny's hitched up your car by now," said the woman. "He'll git it out the ravine right shortly."

"Fine!" he cried with his customary enthusiasm.

Yet it seemed a long time that they waited. It began to get dark. Bowman was cramped in his chair. Any man should know enough to get up and walk around while he waited. There was something like guilt in such stillness and silence.

But instead of getting up, he listened.... His breathing restrained, his eyes powerless in the growing dark, he listened uneasily for a warning sound, forgetting in wariness what it would be. Before long he heard something—soft, continuous, insinuating.

"What's that noise?" he asked, his voice jumping into the dark. Then wildly he was afraid it would be his heart beating so plainly in the quiet room, and she would tell him so.

"You might hear the stream," she said grudgingly.

Her voice was closer. She was standing by the table. He wondered why she did not light the lamp. She stood there in the dark and did not light it.

Bowman would never speak to her now, for the time was past. I'll sleep in the dark, he thought, in his bewilderment pitying himself.

Heavily she moved on to the window. Her arm, vaguely white, rose straight from her full side and she pointed out into the darkness.

"That white speck's Sonny," she said, talking to herself.

He turned unwillingly and peered over her shoulder; he hesitated to rise and stand beside her. His eyes searched the dusky air. The white speck floated smoothly toward her finger, like a leaf on a river, growing whiter in the dark. It was as if she had shown him something secret, part of her life, but had offered no explanation. He looked away. He was moved almost to tears, feeling for no reason that she had made a silent declaration equivalent to his own. His hand waited upon his chest.

Then a step shook the house, and Sonny was in the room. Bowman felt how the woman left him there and went to the other man's side.

"I done got your car out, mister," said Sonny's voice in the dark. "She's settin' a-waitin' in the road, turned to go back where she come from."

"Fine!" said Bowman, projecting his own voice to loudness. "I'm surely much obliged—I could never have done it myself—I was sick. . . ."

"I could do it easy," said Sonny.

Bowman could feel them both waiting in the dark, and he could hear the dogs panting out in the yard, waiting to bark when he should go. He felt strangely helpless and resentful. Now that he could go, he longed to stay. From what was he being deprived? His chest was rudely shaken by the violence of his heart. These people cherished something here that he could not see, they withheld some ancient promise of food and warmth and light. Between them they had a conspiracy. He thought of the way she had moved away from him and gone to Sonny, she had flowed toward him. He was shaking with cold, he was tired, and it was not fair. Humbly and yet angrily he stuck his hand into his pocket.

"Of course I'm going to pay you for everything—"

"We don't take money for such," said Sonny's voice belligerently.

"I want to pay. But do something more . . . Let me stay—tonight. . . ." He took another step toward them. If only they could see him, they would know his sincerity, his real need! His voice went on, "I'm not very strong yet, I'm not able to walk far, even back to my car, maybe, I don't know—I don't know exactly where I am—"

He stopped. He felt as if he might burst into tears. What would they think of him!

Sonny came over and put his hands on him. Bowman felt them pass (they were professional too) across his chest, over his hips. He could feel Sonny's eyes upon him in the dark.

"You ain't no revenuer[3] come sneakin' here, mister, ain't got no gun?"

To this end of nowhere! And yet *he* had come. He made a grave answer. "No."

"You can stay."

"Sonny," said the woman, "you'll have to borry some fire."

"I'll go git it from Redmond's," said Sonny.

"What?" Bowman strained to hear their words to each other.

"Our fire, it's out, and Sonny's got to borry some, because it's dark an' cold," she said.

"But matches—I have matches—"

"We don't have no need for 'em," she said proudly. "Sonny's goin' after his own fire."

"I'm goin' to Redmond's," said Sonny with an air of importance, and he went out.

After they had waited a while, Bowman looked out the window and saw a light moving over the hill. It spread itself out like a little fan. It zigzagged along the field, darting and swift, not like Sonny at all. . . . Soon enough, Sonny staggered in, holding a burning stick behind him in tongs, fire flowing in his wake, blazing light into the corners of the room.

"We'll make a fire now," the woman said, taking the brand.

When that was done she lit the lamp. It showed its dark and light. The whole room turned golden-yellow like some sort of flower, and the walls smelled of it and seemed to tremble with the quiet rushing of the fire and the waving of the burning lampwick in its funnel of light.

The woman moved among the iron pots. With the tongs she dropped hot coals on top of the iron lids. They made a set of soft vibrations, like the sound of a bell far away.

[3] Revenue officer, in this case looking for illegal distillers of whiskey.

She looked up and over at Bowman, but he could not answer. He was trembling....

"Have a drink, mister?" Sonny asked. He had brought in a chair from the other room and sat astride it with his folded arms across the back. Now we are all visible to one another, Bowman thought, and cried, "Yes sir, you bet, thanks!"

"Come after me and do just what I do," said Sonny.

It was another excursion into the dark. They went through the hall, out to the back of the house, past a shed and a hooded well. They came to a wilderness of thicket.

"Down on your knees," said Sonny.

"What?" Sweat broke out on his forehead.

He understood when Sonny began to crawl through a sort of tunnel that the bushes made over the ground. He followed, startled in spite of himself when a twig or a thorn touched him gently without making a sound, clinging to him and finally letting him go.

Sonny stopped crawling and, crouched on his knees, began to dig with both his hands into the dirt. Bowman shyly struck matches and made a light. In a few minutes Sonny pulled up a jug. He poured out some of the whisky into a bottle from his coat pocket, and buried the jug again. "You never know who's liable to knock at your door," he said, and laughed. "Start back," he said, almost formally. "Ain't no need for us to drink outdoors, like hogs."

At the table by the fire, sitting opposite each other in their chairs, Sonny and Bowman took drinks out of the bottle, passing it across. The dogs slept; one of them was having a dream.

"This is good," said Bowman. "This is what I needed." It was just as though he were drinking the fire off the hearth.

"He makes it," said the woman with quiet pride.

She was pushing the coals off the pots, and the smells of corn bread and coffee circled the room. She set everything on the table before the men, with a bone-handled knife stuck into one of the potatoes, splitting out its golden fiber. Then she stood for a minute looking at them, tall and full above them where they sat. She leaned a little toward them.

"You all can eat now," she said, and suddenly smiled.

Bowman had just happened to be looking at her. He set his cup back on the table in unbelieving protest. A pain pressed at his eyes. He saw that she was not an old woman. She was young, still young. He could think of no number of years for her. She was the same age as Sonny, and she belonged to him. She stood with the deep dark corner of the room behind her, the shifting yellow light scattering over her head and her gray formless dress, trembling over her tall body when it bent over them in its sudden communication. She was young. Her teeth were shining and her eyes glowed. She turned and walked slowly and heavily out of the room, and he heard her sit down on the cot and then lie down. The pattern on the quilt moved.

"She's goin' to have a baby," said Sonny, popping a bite into his mouth.

Bowman could not speak. He was shocked with knowing what was really in this house. A marriage, a fruitful marriage. That simple thing. Anyone could have had that.

Somehow he felt unable to be indignant or protest, although some sort of joke had certainly been played upon him. There was nothing remote or mysterious here—only something private. The only secret was the ancient communication between two people. But the memory of the woman's waiting silently by the cold hearth, of the man's stubborn journey a mile away to get fire, and how they finally brought out their food and drink and filled the room proudly with all they had to show, was suddenly too clear and too enormous within him for response. . . .

"You ain't as hungry as you look," said Sonny.

The woman came out of the bedroom as soon as the men had finished, and ate her supper while her husband stared peacefully into the fire.

Then they put the dogs out, with the food that was left.

"I think I'd better sleep here by the fire, on the floor," said Bowman.

He felt that he had been cheated, and that he could afford now to be generous. Ill though he was, he was not going to ask them for their bed. He was through with asking favors in this house, now that he understood what was there.

"Sure, mister."

But he had not known yet how slowly he understood. They had not meant to give him their bed. After a little interval they both rose and looking at him gravely went into the other room.

He lay stretched by the fire until it grew low and dying. He watched every tongue of blaze lick out and vanish. "There will be special reduced prices on all footwear during the month of January," he found himself repeating quietly, and then he lay with his lips tight shut.

How many noises the night had! He heard the stream running, the fire dying, and he was sure now that he heard his heart beating, too, the sound it made under his ribs. He heard breathing, round and deep, of the man and his wife in the room across the passage. And that was all.

But emotion swelled patiently within him, and he wished that the child were his.

He must get back to where he had been before. He stood weakly before the red coals and put on his overcoat. It felt too heavy on his shoulders. As he started out he looked and saw that the woman had never got through with cleaning the lamp. On some impulse he put all the money from his billfold under its fluted glass base, almost ostentatiously.

Ashamed, shrugging a little, and then shivering, he took his bags and went out. The cold of the air seemed to lift him bodily. The moon was in the sky.

On the slope he began to run, he could not help it. Just as he reached the road, where his car seemed to sit in the moonlight like a boat, his heart began to give off tremendous explosions like a rifle, bang bang bang.

He sank in fright onto the road, his bags falling about him. He felt as if all this had happened before. He covered his heart with both hands to keep anyone from hearing the noise it made.

But nobody heard it.

1936

BEGGAR MY NEIGHBOR

DAN JACOBSON

MICHAEL SAW them for the first time when he was coming home from school one day. One moment the street had been empty, glittering in the light from the sun behind Michael's back, with no traffic on the roadway and apparently no pedestrians on the broad sandy pavement; the next moment these two were before him, their faces raised to his. They seemed to emerge directly in front of him, as if the light and shade of the glaring street had suddenly condensed itself into two little piccanins[1] with large eyes set in their round, black faces.

"*Stukkie brood?*" the elder, a boy, said in a plaintive voice. A piece of bread. At Michael's school the slang term for any African child was

[1] Short for *pickaninny,* a small Negro child.

just that: *stukkie brood.* That was what African children were always begging for.

"Stukkie brood?" the little girl said. She was wearing a soiled white dress that was so short it barely covered her loins; there seemed to be nothing at all beneath the dress. She wore no socks, no shoes, no cardigan, no cap or hat. She must have been about ten years old. The boy, who wore a torn khaki shirt and a pair of gray shorts much too large for him, was about Michael's age, about twelve, though he was a little smaller than the white boy. Like the girl, the African boy had no shoes or socks. Their limbs were painfully thin; their wrists and ankles stood out in knobs, and the skin over these protruding bones was rougher than elsewhere. The dirt on their skin showed up as a faint grayness against the black.

"I've got no bread," the white boy said. He had halted in his surprise at the suddenness of their appearance before him. They must have been hiding behind one of the trees that were planted at intervals along the pavement. "I don't bring bread from school."

They did not move. Michael shifted his school case from one hand to the other and took a pace forward. Silently, the African children stood aside. As he passed them, Michael was conscious of the movement of their eyes; when he turned to look back he saw that they were standing still to watch him go. The boy was holding one of the girl's hands in his.

It was this that made the white child pause. He was touched by their dependence on one another, and disturbed by it too, as he had been by the way they had suddenly come before him, and by their watchfulness and silence after they had uttered their customary, begging request. Michael saw again how ragged and dirty they were, and thought of how hungry they must be. Surely he could give them a piece of bread. He was only three blocks from home.

He said, "I haven't got any bread here. But if you come home with me, I'll see that you get some bread. Do you understand?"

They made no reply; but they obviously understood what he had said. The three children moved down the pavement, their shadows sliding over the rough sand ahead of them. The Africans walked a little behind Michael, and to one side of him. Once Michael asked them if they went to school, and the boy shook his head; when Michael asked them if they were brother and sister, the boy nodded.

When they reached Michael's house, he went inside and told Dora, the cook-girl, that there were two piccanins in the lane outside, and that he wanted her to cut some bread and jam for them. Dora grumbled that she was not supposed to look after every little beggar in town, and Michael answered her angrily, "We've got lots of bread. Why shouldn't we give them some?" He was particularly indignant because he felt that Dora, being of the same race as the two outside, should have been even readier than he was to help them. When Dora was about to take the bread out to the back gate, where the piccanins waited, Michael stopped her. "It's all right, Dora," he said in a tone of reproof, "I'll take it," and he went out into the sunlight, carrying the plate in his hand.

"Stukkie brood," he called out to them. "Here's your *stukkie brood."*

The two children stretched their hands out eagerly, and Michael let them take the inch-thick slices from the plate. He was pleased to see that Dora had put a scraping of apricot jam on the bread. Each of the piccanins held the bread in both hands, as if afraid of dropping it. The girl's mouth worked a little, but she kept her eyes fixed on the white boy.

"What do you say?" Michael asked.

They replied in high, clear voices, "Thank you, baas."[2]

"That's better. Now you can eat." He wanted to see them eat it; he wanted to share their pleasure in satisfying their strained appetites. But without saying a word to him, they began to back away, side by side. They took a few paces, and then they turned and ran along the lane toward the main road they had walked down earlier. The little girl's dress fluttered behind her, white against her black body. At the corner they halted, looked back once, and then ran on, out of sight.

A few days later, at the same time and in the same place, Michael saw them again, on his way home from school. They were standing in the middle of the pavement, and he saw them from a long way off. They were obviously waiting for him to come. Michael was the first to speak, as he approached them.

"What? Another piece of bread?" he called out from a few yards away.

"Yes, baas," they answered together. They turned immediately to join him as he walked by. Yet they kept a respectful pace or two behind.

"How did you know I was coming?"

"We know the baas is coming from school."

"And how do you know that I'm going to give you bread?"

There was no reply; not even a smile from the boy, in response

[2] Boss, or master.

to Michael's. They seemed to Michael, as he glanced casually at them, identical in appearance to a hundred, a thousand, other piccanins, from the peppercorns[3] on top of their heads to their wide, callused, sand-gray feet.

When they reached the house, Michael told Dora, "Those *stukkie broods* are waiting outside again. Give them something, and then they can go."

Dora grumbled once again, but did as she was told. Michael did not go out with the bread himself; he was in a hurry to get back to work on a model car he was making, and was satisfied to see, out of his bedroom window, Dora coming from the back gate a few minutes later with an empty plate in her hand. Soon he had forgotten all about the two children. He did not go out of the house until a couple of hours had passed; by then it was dusk, and he took a torch[4] with him to help him find a piece of wire for his model in the darkness of the lumber shed. Handling the torch gave Michael a feeling of power and importance, and he stepped into the lane with it, intending to shine it about like a policeman on his beat. Immediately he opened the gate, he saw the two little children standing in the half-light, just a few paces away from him.

"What are you doing here?" Michael exclaimed in surprise.

The boy answered, holding his hand up, as if warning Michael to be silent. "We were waiting to say thank you to the baas."

"What!" Michael took a step toward them both, and they stood their ground, only shrinking together slightly.

For all the glare and glitter there was in the streets of Lyndhurst[5] by day, it was winter, midwinter; and once the sun had set, a bitter chill came into the air, as swiftly as the darkness. The cold at night wrung deep notes from the contracting iron roofs of the houses and froze the fish ponds in all the fine gardens of the white suburbs. Already Michael could feel its sharp touch on the tips of his ears and fingers. And the two African children stood there barefoot, in a flimsy dress and torn shirt, waiting to thank him for the bread he had had sent out to them.

"You mustn't wait," Michael said. In the half-darkness he saw the white dress on the girl more clearly than the boy's clothing; and he remembered the nakedness and puniness of her black thighs. He stretched his hand out, with the torch in it. "Take it," he said. The

[3] Little tight knots of hair.

[4] Flashlight.

[5] Suburb of Johannesburg, South Africa.

torch was in his hand, and there was nothing else that he could give to them. "It's nice," he said. "It's a torch. Look." He switched it on and saw in its beam of light a pair of startled eyes, darting desperately from side to side. "You see how nice it is," Michael said, turning the beam upward, where it lost itself against the light that lingered in the sky. "If you don't want it, you can sell it. Go on, take it."

A hand came up and took the torch from him. Then the two children ran off, in the same direction they had taken on the first afternoon. When they reached the corner all the street lights came on, as if at a single touch, and the children stopped and stared at them, before running on. Michael saw the torch glinting in the boy's hand, and only then did it occur to him that despite their zeal to thank him for the bread they hadn't thanked him for the torch. The size of the gift must have surprised them into silence, Michael decided; and the thought of his own generosity helped to console him for the regret he couldn't help feeling when he saw the torch being carried away from him.

Michael was a lonely child. He had neither brothers nor sisters; both his parents worked during the day, and he had made few friends at school. But he was not by any means unhappy in his loneliness. He was used to it, in the first place; and then, because he was lonely, he was all the better able to indulge himself in his own fantasies. He played for hours, by himself, games of his own invention—games of war, of exploration, of seafaring, of scientific invention, of crime, of espionage, of living in a house beneath or above his real one. It was not long before the two African children, who were now accosting him regularly, appeared in some of his games, for their weakness, poverty, and dependence gave Michael ample scope to display in fantasy his kindness, generosity, courage and decisiveness. Sometimes in his games Michael saved the boy's life, and was thanked for it in broken English. Sometimes he saved the girl's, and then she humbly begged his pardon for having caused him so much trouble. Sometimes he was just too late to save the life of either, though he tried his best, and then there were affecting scenes of farewell.

But in real life, Michael did not play with the children at all: they were too dirty, too ragged, too strange, too persistent. Their persistence eventually drove Dora to tell Michael's mother about them; and his mother did her duty by telling Michael that on no account should he play with the children, nor should he give them anything of value.

"Play with them!" Michael laughed at the idea. And apart from bread and the torch he had given them nothing but a few old toys, a singlet or two, a pair of old canvas shoes. No one could begrudge them those gifts. The truth was that Michael's mother begrudged the piccanins neither the old toys and clothes nor the bread. What she was anxious to do was simply to prevent her son playing with the piccanins, fearing that he would pick up germs, bad language, and "kaffir[6] ways" generally from them, if he did. Hearing both from Michael and Dora that he did not play with them at all, and that he had never even asked them into the backyard, let alone the house, Michael's mother was satisfied.

They came to Michael about once a week, meeting him as he walked back from school, or simply waiting for him outside the back gate. The spring winds had already blown the cold weather away, almost overnight, and still the children came. Their words of thanks varied neither in tone nor length, whatever Michael gave them; but they had revealed, in response to his questions, that the boy's name was Frans and the girl's name was Annie, that they lived in Green Point Location, and that their mother and father were both dead. During all this time Michael had not touched them, except for the fleeting contact of their hands when he passed a gift to them. Yet sometimes Michael wished that they were more demonstrative in their expressions of gratitude to him; he thought that they could, for instance, seize his hand and embrace it; or go down on their knees and weep, just once. As it was, he had to content himself with fantasies of how they spoke of him among their friends, when they returned to the tumbled squalor of Green Point Location; of how incredulous their friends must be to hear their stories about the kind white *kleinbaas*[7] who gave them food and toys and clothing.

One day Michael came out to them carrying a possession he particularly prized—an elaborate pen and pencil set which had been given to him for a recent birthday. He had no intention of giving the outfit to the African children, and he did not think that he would be showing off with it in front of them. He merely wanted to share his pleasure in it with someone who had not already seen it. But as soon as he noticed the way the children were looking at the open box, Michael knew the mistake he had made. "This isn't for you," he said abruptly. The children blinked soundlessly, staring from the box to Michael and back to the box again. "You can just look at it," Michael said. He held the box

[6] Member of the Bantu-speaking tribes of South Africa; used disparagingly, originally an Arabic Moslem term for infidel.

[7] Little boss or master.

tightly in his hand, stretching it forward, the pen and the propelling[8] pencils shining inside the velvet-lined case. The two heads of the children came together over the box; they stared deeply into it.

At last the boy lifted his head. "It's beautiful," he breathed out. As he spoke, his hand slowly came up toward the box.

"No," Michael said, and snatched the box away.

"Baas?"

"No." Michael retreated a little, away from the beseeching eyes, and the uplifted hand.

"Please, baas, for me?"

And his sister said, "For me also, baas."

"No, you can't have this." Michael attempted to laugh, as if at the absurdity of the idea. He was annoyed with himself for having shown them the box, and at the same time shocked at them for having asked for it. It was the first time they had asked for anything but bread.

"Please, baas. It's nice." The boy's voice trailed away on the last word, in longing; and then his sister repeated the word, like an echo, her own voice trailing away too. "Ni-ice."

"No! I won't give it to you! I won't give you anything if you ask for this. Do you hear?"

Their eyes dropped, their hands came together, they lowered their heads. Being sure now that they would not again ask for the box, Michael relented. He said, "I'm going in now, and I'll tell Dora to bring you some bread."

But Dora came to him in his room a few minutes later. "The little kaffirs are gone." She was holding the plate of bread in her hand. Dora hated the two children, and Michael thought there was some kind of triumph in her voice and manner as she made the announcement.

He went outside to see if she was telling the truth. The lane was empty. He went to the street, and looked up and down its length, but there was no sign of them there either. They were gone. He had driven them away. Michael expected to feel guilty; but to his own intense surprise he felt nothing of the kind. He was relieved that they were gone, and that was all.

When they reappeared a few days later, Michael felt scorn toward them for coming back after what had happened on the last occasion. He felt they were in his power. "So you've come back?" he greeted

[8] Mechanical

them. "You like your *stukkies brood,* hey? You're hungry, so today you'll wait, you won't run away."

"Yes, baas," they said, in their low voices.

Michael brought the bread out to them; when they reached for it he jokingly pulled the plate back and laughed at their surprise. Then only did he give them the bread.

"Thank you, baas."

"Thank you, baas."

They ate the bread in Michael's presence; watching them, he felt a little more kindly disposed toward them. "All right, you can come another day, and there'll be some more bread for you."

"Thank you, baas."

"Thank you, baas."

They came back sooner than Michael had expected them to. He gave them their bread and told them to go. They went off, but again did not wait for the usual five or six days to pass before approaching him once more. Only two days had passed, yet here they were with their eternal request—"*Stukkie brood*, baas?"

Michael said, "Why do you get hungry so quickly now?" But he gave them their bread.

When they appeared in his games and fantasies, Michael no longer rescued them, healed them, casually presented them with kingdoms and motor cars. Now he ordered them about, sent them away on disastrous missions, picked them out to be shot for cowardice in the face of the enemy. And because something similar to these fantasies was easier to enact in the real world than his earlier fantasies, Michael soon was ordering them about unreasonably in fact. He deliberately left them waiting; he sent them away and told them to come back on days when he knew he would be in town; he told them there was no bread in the house. And when he did give them anything, it was bread only now; never old toys or articles of clothing.

So, as the weeks passed, Michael's scorn gave way to impatience and irritation, irritation to anger. What angered him most was that the two piccanins seemed too stupid to realize what he now felt about them, and instead of coming less frequently, continued to appear more often than ever before. Soon they were coming almost every day, though Michael shouted at them and teased them, left them waiting for hours, and made them do tricks and sing songs for their bread. They did everything he told them to do; but they altogether ignored his instructions as to which days they should come. Invariably, they would be waiting for him, in the shade of one of the trees that grew alongside the main road from school, or standing at the gate behind the house with sand scuffed up about their bare toes. They were as silent as before; but more persistent, inexorably persistent. Michael took to walking home by different routes, but they were not to be so easily discouraged. They simply waited at the back gate, and whether he went into the house by the front or the back gate he could not avoid seeing their upright, unmoving figures.

Finally, he told them to go and never come back at all. Often he had been tempted to do this, but some shame or pride had always prevented him from doing it; he had always weakened previously, and named a date, a week or two weeks ahead, when they could come again. But now he shouted at them, "It's finished! No more bread—nothing! Come on, *voetsak!*[9] If you come back I'll tell the garden boy to chase you away."

From then on they came every day. They no longer waited right at the back gate, but squatted in the sand across the lane. Michael was aware of their eyes following him when he went by, but they did not approach him at all. They did not even get up from the ground when he passed. A few times he shouted at them to go, and stamped his foot, but he shrank from hitting them. He did not want to touch them. Once he sent out Jan, the garden boy, to drive them away; but Jan, who had hitherto always shared Dora's views on the piccanins, came back muttering angrily and incomprehensibly to himself; and when Michael peeped into the lane he saw that they were still there. Michael tried to ignore them, to pretend he did not see them. He hated them now; even more, he began to dread them.

But he did not know how much he hated and feared the two children until he fell ill with a cold, and lay feverish in bed for a few days. During those days the two children were constantly in his dreams, or in his half-dreams, for even as he dreamed he knew he was turning on his bed; he was conscious of the sun shining outside by day, and at night of the passage light that had been left on inside the house. In these dreams he struck and struck again at the children with weapons he found in his hands; he fled in fear from them down lanes so thick with sand his feet could barely move through it; he committed lewd, cruel acts upon the bare-thighed girl, and her brother shrieked to tell the empty street of what he was doing. Michael struck out at him with a piece of heavy cast-iron guttering. Its edge dug sharply into Michael's hands as the blow fell, and when he lifted the weapon he

[9] Be gone!

saw the horror he had made of the side of the boy's head, and how the one remaining eyeball still stared unwinkingly at him.

Michael thought he was awake, and suddenly calm. The fever seemed to have left him. It was as though he had slept deeply, for days, after that last dream of violence; yet his impression was that he had woken directly from it. The bedclothes felt heavy on him, and he threw them off. The house was silent. He got out of bed and went to look at the clock in the kitchen: it was early afternoon. Dora and Jan were resting in their rooms across the yard, as they always did after lunch. Outside, the light of the sun was unremitting, a single golden glare. He walked back to his bedroom; there, he put on his dressing gown and slippers, feeling the coolness inside his slippers on his bare feet. He went through the kitchen again, quietly, and onto the back stoep,[10] and then across the backyard. The sun seemed to seize his neck as firmly as a hand grasping, and its light was so bright he was aware of it only as a darkness beyond the little stretch of ground he looked down upon. He opened the back gate. Inevitably, as he had known they would be, the two were waiting.

He did not want to go beyond the gate in his pajamas and dressing gown, so, shielding his eyes from the glare with one hand, he beckoned them to him with the other. Together, in silence, they rose and crossed the lane. It seemed to take them a long time to come to him, but at last they stood in front of him, with their hands interlinked. Michael stared into their dark faces, and they stared into his.

"What are you waiting for?" he asked.

"For you." First the boy answered; then the girl repeated, "For you."

Michael looked from the one to the other; and he remembered what he had been doing to them in his dreams. Their eyes were black to look into. Staring forward, Michael understood what he should have understood long before: that they came to him not in hope or appeal or even in reproach, but in hatred. What he felt toward them, they felt toward him; what he had done to them in his dreams, they did to him in theirs.

The sun, their staring eyes, his own fear came together in a sound that seemed to hang in the air of the lane—a cry, the sound of someone weeping. Then Michael knew that it was he who was crying. He felt the heat of the tears in his eyes, he felt the moisture running down his cheeks. With the same fixity of decision that had been his in his dreams of violence and torture, Michael knew what he must do. He beckoned them forward, closer. They came. He stretched out his hands, he felt

[10] Verandah or porch.

under his fingers the springy hair he had looked at so often before from the distance between himself and them; he felt the smooth skin of their faces; their frail, rounded shoulders, their hands. Their hands were in his, and he led them inside the gate.

He led them into the house, through the kitchen, down the passage, into his room, where they had never been before. They looked about at the pictures on the walls, the toys on top of the low cupboard, the twisted white sheets and tumbled blankets on the bed. They stood on both sides of him, and for the first time since he had met them, their lips parted into slow, grave smiles. Michael knew that what he had to give them was not toys or clothes or bread, but something more difficult. Yet it was not difficult at all, for there was nothing else he could give them. He took the girl's face in his hands and pressed his lips to hers. He was aware of the darkness of her skin, and of the smell of it, and of the faint movement of her lips, a single pulse that beat momentarily against his own. Then it was gone. He kissed the boy, too, and let them go. They came together, and grasped each other by the hand, staring at him.

"What do you want now?" he asked.

A last anxiety flickered in Michael and left him, as the boy slowly shook his head. He began to step back, pulling his sister with him; when he was through the door he turned his back on Michael and they walked away down the passage. Michael watched them go. At the door of the kitchen, on their way out of the house, they paused, turned once more, and lifted their hands, the girl copying the boy, in a silent, tentative gesture of farewell.

Michael did not follow them. He heard the back gate swing open and then bang when it closed. He went wearily back to his bed, and as he fell upon it, his relief and gratitude that the bed should be there to receive him, changed suddenly into grief at the knowledge that he was already lying upon it—that he had never left it.

His cold grew worse, turned into bronchitis, kept him in bed for several weeks. But his dreams were no longer of violence; they were calm, spacious, and empty of people. As empty as the lane was, when he was at last allowed out of the house, and made his way there immediately, to see if the children were waiting for him.

He never saw them again, though he looked for them in the streets and lanes of the town. He saw a hundred, a thousand, children like them; but not the two he hoped to find.

1962

AWAKENING

ISAAC BABEL

ALL THE folks in our circle—brokers, shopkeepers, clerks in banks and steamship offices—used to have their children taught music. Our fathers, seeing no other escape from their lot, had thought up a lottery, building it on the bones of little children. Odessa more than other towns was seized by the craze. And in fact, in the course of ten years or so our town supplied the concert platforms of the world with infant prodigies. From Odessa came Mischa Elman,[1] Zimbalist,[2] Gabrilowitsch.[3] Odessa witnessed the first steps of Jascha Heifetz.[4]

When a lad was four or five, his mother took the puny creature to Zagursky's. Mr. Zagursky ran a factory of infant prodigies, a factory of Jewish dwarfs in lace collars and patent-leather pumps. He hunted

[1] Russian violinist (1891–1967).

[2] Efrem Zimbalist (1899–   ), Russian-born American violinist.

[3] Ossip Solomonovitch Gabrilowitsch (1878–1936), Russian pianist and conductor.

[4] Russian-born American violinist (1901–   ).

them out in the slums of the Moldavanka, in the evil-smelling courtyards of the Old Market. Mr. Zagursky charted the first course, then the children were shipped off to Professor Auer[5] in St. Petersburg. A wonderful harmony dwelt in the souls of those wizened creatures with their swollen blue hands. They became famous virtuosi. My father decided that I should emulate them. Though I had, as a matter of fact, passed the age limit set for infant prodigies, being now in my fourteenth year, my shortness and lack of strength made it possible to pass me off as an eight-year-old. Herein lay father's hope.

I was taken to Zagursky's. Out of respect for my grandfather, Mr. Zagursky agreed to take me on at the cut rate of a rouble a lesson. My grandfather Leivi-Itzkhok was the laughingstock of the town, and its chief adornment. He used to walk about the streets in a top hat and old boots, dissipating doubt in the darkest of cases. He would be asked what a Gobelin was, why the Jacobins[6] betrayed Robespierre,[7] how you made artificial silk, what a Caesarean section was. And my grandfather could answer these questions. Out of respect for his learning and craziness, Mr. Zagursky only charged us a rouble a lesson. And he had the devil of a time with me, fearing my grandfather, for with me there was nothing to be done. The sounds dripped from my fiddle like iron filings, causing even me excruciating agony, but father wouldn't give in. At home there was no talk save of Mischa Elman, exempted by the Tsar himself from military service. Zimbalist, father would have us know, had been presented to the King of England and had played at Buckingham Palace. The parents of Gabrilowitsch had bought two houses in St. Petersburg. Infant prodigies brought wealth to their parents, but though my father could have reconciled himself to poverty, fame he must have.

"It's not possible," people feeding at his expense would insinuate, "it's just not possible that the grandson of such a grandfather..."

But what went on in my head was quite different. Scraping my way through the violin exercises, I would have books by Turgenev[8] or Dumas[9] on my music stand. Page after page I devoured as I deedled

[5] Leopold Auer (1845–1930), Hungarian violinist and teacher.

[6] Radical Republicans during the French Revolution (1789–1799).

[7] Maximilien François Marie Isodore de Robespierre (1758–1794), revolutionist and Jacobin leader.

[8] Ivan Sergeyevich Turgenev (1818–1883), major Russian novelist and short story writer.

[9] Alexandre Dumas (1802–1870), known as Dumas père, French novelist and playwright.

away. In the daytime I would relate impossible happenings to the kids next door; at night I would commit them to paper. In our family, composition was a hereditary occupation. Grandfather Leivi-Itzkhok, who went cracked as he grew old, spent his whole life writing a tale entitled "The Headless Man." I took after him.

Three times a week, laden with violin case and music, I made my reluctant way to Zagursky's place on Witte (formerly Dvoryanskaya) Street. There Jewish girls aflame with hysteria sat along the wall awaiting their turn, pressing to their feeble knees violins exceeding in dimensions the exalted persons they were to play to at Buckingham Palace.

The door to the sanctum would open, and from Mr. Zagursky's study there would stagger big-headed, freckled children with necks as thin as flower stalks and an epileptic flush on their cheeks. The door would bang to, swallowing up the next dwarf. Behind the wall, straining his throat, the teacher sang and waved his baton. He had ginger curls and frail legs, and sported a big bow tie. Manager of a monstrous lottery, he populated the Moldavanka and the dark culs-de-sac of the Old Market with the ghosts of pizzicato and cantilena.[10] Afterward old Professor Auer lent these strains a diabolical brilliance.

In this crew I was quite out of place. Though like them in my dwarfishness, in the voice of my forebears I perceived inspiration of another sort.

The first step was difficult. One day I left home laden like a beast of burden with violin case, violin, music, and twelve roubles in cash—payment for a month's tuition. I was going along Nezhin Street; to get to Zagursky's I should have turned into Dvoryanskaya, but instead of that I went up Tiraspolskaya and found myself at the harbor. The allotted time flew past in the part of the port where ships went after quarantine. So began my liberation. Zagursky's saw me no more: affairs of greater moment occupied my thoughts. My pal Nemanov and I got into the habit of slipping aboard the S. S. *Kensington* to see an old salt named Trottyburn. Nemanov was a year younger than I. From the age of eight onward he had been doing the most ingenious business deals you can imagine. He had a wonderful head for that kind of thing, and later on amply fulfilled his youthful promise. Now he is a New York millionaire, director of General Motors, a company no less powerful than Ford. Nemanov took me along with him because I silently obeyed all his orders. He used to buy pipes smuggled in by Mr. Trottyburn. They were made in Lincoln by the old sailor's brother.

[10] Simple or sustained melody.

"Gen'lemen," Mr. Trottyburn would say to us, "take my word, the pets must be made with your own hands. Smoking a factory-made pipe—might as well shove an enema in your mouth. D'you know who Benvenuto Cellini[11] was? He was a grand lad. My brother in Lincoln could tell you about him. Live and let live is my brother's motto. He's got it into his head that you just has to make the pets with your own hands, and not with no one else's. And who are we to say him no, gen'lemen?"

Nemanov used to sell Trottyburn's pipes to bank-managers, foreign consuls, well-to-do Greeks. He made a hundred percent on them.

The pipes of the Lincolnshire master breathed poetry. In each one of them thought was invested, a drop of eternity. A little yellow eye gleamed in their mouthpieces, and their cases were lined with satin. I tried to picture the life in Old England of Matthew Trottyburn, the last master-pipemaker, who refused to swim with the tide.

"We can't but agree, gen'lemen, that the pets has to be made with your own hands."

The heavy waves by the sea wall swept me further and further away from our house, impregnated with the smell of leeks and Jewish destiny. From the harbor I migrated to the other side of the breakwater. There on a scrap of sandspit dwelt the boys from Primorskaya Street. Trouserless from morn till eve, they dived under wherries, sneaked coconuts for dinner, and awaited the time when boats would arrive from Kherson and Kamenka laden with watermelons, which melons it would be possible to break open against moorings.

To learn to swim was my dream. I was ashamed to confess to those bronzed lads that, born in Odessa, I had not seen the sea till I was ten, and at fourteen didn't know how to swim.

How slow was my acquisition of the things one needs to know! In my childhood, chained to the Gemara,[12] I had led the life of a sage. When I grew up I started climbing trees.

But swimming proved beyond me. The hydrophobia of my ancestors —Spanish rabbis and Frankfurt money-changers—dragged me to the bottom. The waves refused to support me. I would struggle to the shore pumped full of salt water and feeling as though I had been flayed, and return to where my fiddle and music lay. I was fettered to the

[11] Italian sculptor and goldsmith (1500–1571), and author of a famous autobiography.

[12] Second part of the Talmud, providing a commentary on the first.

instruments of my torture, and dragged them about with me. The struggle of rabbis versus Neptune continued till such time as the local water-god took pity on me. This was Yefim Nikitich Smolich, proofreader of the *Odessa News*. In his athletic breast there dwelt compassion for Jewish children, and he was the god of a rabble of rickety starvelings. He used to collect them from the bug-infested joints on the Moldavanka, take them down to the sea, bury them in the sand, do gym with them, dive with them, teach them songs. Roasting in the perpendicular sunrays, he would tell them tales about fishermen and wild beasts. To grownups Nikitich would explain that he was a natural philosopher. The Jewish kids used to roar with laughter at his tales, squealing and snuggling up to him like so many puppies. The sun would sprinkle them with creeping freckles, freckles of the same color as lizards.

Silently, out of the corner of his eye, the old man had been watching my duel with the waves. Seeing that the thing was hopeless, that I should simply never learn to swim, he included me among the permanent occupants of his heart. That cheerful heart of his was with us there all the time; it never went careering off anywhere else, never knew covetousness and never grew disturbed. With his sunburned shoulders, his superannuated gladiator's head, his bronzed and slightly bandy legs, he would lie among us on the other side of the mole, lord and master of those melon-sprinkled, paraffin-stained waters. I came to love that man, with the love that only a lad suffering from hysteria and headaches can feel for a real man. I was always at his side, always trying to be of service to him.

He said to me:

"Don't you get all worked up. You just strengthen your nerves. The swimming will come of itself. How d'you mean, the water won't hold you? Why shouldn't it hold you?"

Seeing how drawn I was to him, Nikitich made an exception of me alone of all his disciples. He invited me to visit the clean and spacious attic where he lived in an ambience of straw mats, showed me his dogs, his hedgehog, his tortoise, and his pigeons. In return for this wealth I showed him a tragedy I had written the day before.

"I was sure you did a bit of scribbling," said Nikitich. "You've the look. You're looking in *that* direction all the time; no eyes for anywhere else."

He read my writings, shrugged a shoulder, passed a hand through his stiff gray curls, paced up and down the attic.

"One must suppose," he said slowly, pausing after each word, "one must suppose that there's a spark of the divine fire in you."

We went out into the street. The old man halted, struck the pavement with his stick, and fastened his gaze upon me.

"Now what is it you lack? Youth's no matter—it'll pass with the years. What you lack is a feeling for nature."

He pointed with his stick at a tree with a reddish trunk and a low crown.

"What's that tree?"

I didn't know.

"What's growing on that bush?"

I didn't know this either. We walked together across the little square on the Alexandrovsky Prospect. The old man kept poking his stick at trees; he would seize me by the shoulder when a bird flew past, and he made me listen to the various kinds of singing.

"What bird is that singing?"

I knew none of the answers. The names of trees and birds, their division into species, where birds fly away to, on which side the sun rises, when the dew falls thickest—all these things were unknown to me.

"And you dare to write! A man who doesn't live in nature, as a stone does or an animal, will never in all his life write two worthwhile lines. Your landscapes are like descriptions of stage props. In heaven's name, what have your parents been thinking of for fourteen years?"

What *had* they been thinking of? Of protested bills of exchange, of Mischa Elman's mansions. I didn't say anything to Nikitich about that, but just kept mum.

At home, over dinner, I couldn't touch my food. It just wouldn't go down.

"A feeling for nature," I thought to myself. "Goodness, why did that never enter my head? Where am I to find someone who will tell me about the way birds sing and what trees are called? What do *I* know about such things? I might perhaps recognize lilac, at any rate when it's in bloom. Lilac and acacia—there are acacias along De Ribas and Greek Streets."

At dinner father told a new story about Jascha Heifetz. Just before he got to Robinat's he had met Mendelssohn, Jascha's uncle. It appeared that the lad was getting eight hundred roubles a performance. Just work out how much that comes to at fifteen concerts a month!

I did, and the answer was twelve thousand a month. Multiplying and carrying four in my head, I glanced out of the window. Across the cement courtyard, his cloak swaying in the breeze, his ginger curls poking out from under his soft hat, leaning on his cane, Mr. Zagursky, my music teacher, was advancing. It must be admitted he had taken his time in spotting my truancy. More than three months had elapsed since the day when my violin had grounded on the sand by the breakwater.

Mr. Zagursky was approaching the main entrance. I dashed to the back door, but the day before it had been nailed up for fear of burglars. Then I locked myself in the privy. In half an hour the whole family had assembled outside the door. The women were weeping. Aunt Bobka, exploding with sobs, was rubbing her fat shoulder against the door. Father was silent. Finally he started speaking, quietly and distinctly as he had never before spoken in his life.

"I am an officer," said my father. "I own real estate. I go hunting. Peasants pay me rent. I have entered my son in the Cadet Corps. I have no need to worry about my son."

He was silent again. The women were sniffling. Then a terrible blow descended on the privy door. My father was hurling his whole body against it, stepping back and then throwing himself forward.

"I am an officer," he kept wailing. "I go hunting. I'll kill him. This is the end."

The hook sprang from the door, but there was still a bolt hanging onto a single nail. The women were rolling about on the floor, grasping father by the legs. Crazy, he was trying to break loose. Father's mother came over, alerted by the hubbub.

"My child," she said to him in Hebrew, "our grief is great. It has no bounds. Only blood was lacking in our house. I do not wish to see blood in our house."

Father gave a groan. I heard his footsteps retreating. The bolt still hung by its last nail.

I sat it out in my fortress till nightfall. When all had gone to bed, Aunt Bobka took me to grandmother's. We had a long way to go. The moonlight congealed on bushes unknown to me, on trees that had no name. Some anonymous bird emitted a whistle and was extinguished, perhaps by sleep. What bird was it? What was it called? Does dew fall in the evening? Where is the constellation of the Great Bear? On what side does the sun rise?

We were going along Post Office Street. Aunt Bobka held me firmly by the hand so that I shouldn't run away. She was right to. I was thinking of running away.

1930

Translated by Walter Morison

YOUNG GOODMAN BROWN

NATHANIEL HAWTHORNE

YOUNG GOODMAN Brown came forth at sunset into the street at Salem village; but put his head back, after crossing the threshold, to exchange a parting kiss with his young wife. And Faith, as the wife was aptly named, thrust her own pretty head into the street, letting the wind play with the pink ribbons of her cap while she called to Goodman Brown.

"Dearest heart," whispered she, softly and rather sadly, when her lips were close to his ear, "prithee put off your journey until sunrise and sleep in your own bed to-night. A lone woman is troubled with such dreams and such thoughts that she's afeard of herself sometimes. Pray tarry with me this night, dear husband, of all nights in the year."

"My love and my Faith," replied young Goodman Brown, "of all nights in the year, this one night must I tarry away from thee. My journey, as thou callest it, forth and back again, must needs be done 'twixt now and sunrise. What, my sweet, pretty wife, dost thou doubt me already, and we but three months married?"

"Then God bless you!" said Faith, with the pink ribbons; "and may you find all well when you come back."

"Amen!" cried Goodman Brown. "Say thy prayers, dear Faith, and go to bed at dusk, and no harm will come to thee."

So they parted; and the young man pursued his way until, being about to turn the corner by the meeting-house, he looked back and saw the head of Faith still peeping after him with a melancholy air, in spite of her pink ribbons.

"Poor little Faith!" thought he, for his heart smote him. "What a wretch am I to leave her on such an errand! She talks of dreams, too. Methought as she spoke there was trouble in her face, as if a dream had warned her what work is to be done to-night. But no, no; 't would kill her to think it. Well, she's a blessed angel on earth; and after this one night I'll cling to her skirts and follow her to heaven."

With this excellent resolve for the future, Goodman Brown felt himself justified in making more haste on his present evil purpose. He had taken a dreary road, darkened by all the gloomiest trees of the forest, which barely stood aside to let the narrow path creep through, and closed immediately behind. It was all as lonely as could be; and there is this peculiarity in such a solitude, that the traveller knows not who may be concealed by the innumerable trunks and the thick boughs overhead; so that with lonely footsteps he may yet be passing through an unseen multitude.

"There may be a devilish Indian behind every tree," said Goodman Brown to himself; and he glanced fearfully behind him as he added, "What if the devil himself should be at my very elbow!"

His head being turned back, he passed a crook of the road, and, looking forward again, beheld the figure of a man, in grave and decent attire, seated at the foot of an old tree. He arose at Goodman Brown's approach and walked onward side by side with him.

"You are late, Goodman Brown," said he. "The clock of the Old South was striking as I came through Boston, and that is full fifteen minutes agone."

"Faith kept me back a while," replied the young man, with a tremor in his voice, caused by the sudden appearance of his companion, though not wholly unexpected.

It was now deep dusk in the forest, and deepest in that part of it where these two were journeying. As nearly as could be discerned, the second traveller was about fifty years old, apparently in the same rank of life as Goodman Brown, and bearing a considerable resemblance to him, though perhaps more in expression than features. Still they might have been taken for father and son. And yet, though the elder person was as simply clad as the younger, and as simple in manner too, he had an indescribable air of one who knew the world, and who would not have felt abashed at the governor's dinner table or in King William's[1] court, were it possible that his affairs should call him thither. But the only thing about him that could be fixed upon as remarkable was his staff, which bore the likeness of a great black snake, so curiously wrought that it might almost be seen to twist and wriggle itself like a living serpent. This, of course, must have been an ocular deception, assisted by the uncertain light.

"Come, Goodman Brown," cried his fellow-traveller, "this is a dull pace for the beginning of a journey. Take my staff, if you are so soon weary."

"Friend," said the other, exchanging his slow pace for a full stop, "having kept covenant by meeting thee here, it is my purpose now to return whence I came. I have scruples touching the matter thou wot'st[2] of."

"Sayest thou so?" replied he of the serpent, smiling apart. "Let us walk on, nevertheless, reasoning as we go; and if I convince thee not thou shalt turn back. We are but a little way in the forest yet."

"Too far! too far!" exclaimed the goodman, unconsciously resuming his walk. "My father never went into the woods on such an errand, nor his father before him. We have been a race of honest men and good Christians since the days of the martyrs; and shall I be the first of the name of Brown that ever took this path and kept"—

"Such company, thou wouldst say," observed the elder person, interpreting his pause. "Well said, Goodman Brown! I have been as well acquainted with your family as with ever a one among the Puritans; and that's no trifle to say. I helped your grandfather, the constable, when he lashed the Quaker woman so smartly through the streets of Salem; and it was I that brought your father a pitch-pine knot, kindled at my own hearth, to set fire to an Indian village, in King Philip's

[1] William III, King of England (1689–1702) as joint sovereign with Mary II.

[2] Knows.

war.[3] They were my good friends, both; and many a pleasant walk have we had along this path, and returned merrily after midnight. I would fain be friends with you for their sake."

"If it be as thou sayest," replied Goodman Brown, "I marvel they never spoke of these matters; or, verily, I marvel not, seeing that the least rumor of the sort would have driven them from New England. We are a people of prayer, and good works to boot, and abide no such wickedness."

"Wickedness or not," said the traveller with the twisted staff, "I have a very general acquaintance here in New England. The deacons of many a church have drunk the communion wine with me; the selectmen of divers towns make me their chairman; and a majority of the Great and General Court[4] are firm supporters of my interest. The governor and I, too—But these are state secrets."

"Can this be so?" cried Goodman Brown, with a stare of amazement at his undisturbed companion. "Howbeit, I have nothing to do with the governor and council; they have their own ways, and are no rule for a simple husbandman like me. But, were I to go on with thee, how should I meet the eye of that good old man, our minister, at Salem village? Oh, his voice would make me tremble both Sabbath day and lecture day.[5]"

Thus far the elder traveller had listened with due gravity; but now burst into a fit of irrepressible mirth, shaking himself so violently that his snake-like staff actually seemed to wriggle in sympathy.

"Ha! ha! ha!" shouted he again and again; then composing himself, "Well, go on, Goodman Brown, go on; but, prithee, don't kill me with laughing."

"Well, then, to end the matter at once," said Goodman Brown, considerably nettled, "there is my wife, Faith. It would break her dear little heart; and I'd rather break my own."

"Nay, if that be the case," answered the other, "e'en go thy ways, Goodman Brown. I would not for twenty old women like the one hobbling before us that Faith should come to any harm."

As he spoke he pointed his staff at a female figure on the path, in whom Goodman Brown recognized a very pious and exemplary dame, who had taught him his catechism in youth, and was still his moral

[3] Led by Metacomet (King Philip), chief of the Wampanoag tribe against the New England colonists (1675–1676).

[4] Colonial legislative body with judicial powers.

[5] In colonial New England, the day set aside for public lectures, usually Thursday.

and spiritual adviser, jointly with the minister and Deacon Gookin.

"A marvel, truly, that Goody Cloyse[6] should be so far in the wilderness at nightfall," said he. "But with your leave, friend, I shall take a cut through the woods until we have left this Christian woman behind. Being a stranger to you, she might ask whom I was consorting with and whither I was going."

"Be it so," said his fellow-traveller. "Betake you to the woods, and let me keep the path."

Accordingly the young man turned aside, but took care to watch his companion, who advanced softly along the road until he had come within a staff's length of the old dame. She, meanwhile, was making the best of her way, with singular speed for so aged a woman, and mumbling some indistinct words—a prayer, doubtless—as she went. The traveller put forth his staff and touched her withered neck with what seemed the serpent's tail.

"The devil!" screamed the pious old lady.

"Then Goody Cloyse knows her old friend?" observed the traveller, confronting her and leaning on his writhing stick.

"Ah, forsooth, and is it your worship indeed?" cried the good dame. "Yea, truly is it, and in the very image of my old gossip, Goodman Brown, the grandfather of the silly fellow that now is. But—would your worship believe it?—my broomstick hath strangely disappeared, stolen, as I suspect, by that unhanged witch, Goody Cory, and that, too, when I was all anointed with the juice of smallage,[7] and cinquefoil, and wolf's bane"—

"Mingled with fine wheat and the fat of a new-born babe," said the shape of old Goodman Brown.

"Ah, your worship knows the recipe," cried the old lady, cackling aloud. "So, as I was saying, being all ready for the meeting, and no horse to ride on, I made up my mind to foot it; for they tell me there is a nice young man to be taken into communion to-night. But now your good worship will lend me your arm, and we shall be there in a twinkling."

"That can hardly be," answered her friend. "I may not spare you my arm, Goody Cloyse; but here is my staff, if you will."

[6] Sarah Cloyse, as well as Martha Cory and Martha Carrier, was an actual person tried during the 1692 Salem witchcraft trials, at which Hawthorne's ancestor John Hathorne may have been one of the judges. Martha Cory and Martha Carrier were hanged, whereas Sarah Cloyse was still in prison when the witchcraft persecution ended.

[7] Parsley or wild celery.

So saying, he threw it down at her feet, where, perhaps, it assumed life, being one of the rods which its owner had formerly lent to the Egyptian magi. Of this fact, however, Goodman Brown could not take cognizance. He had cast up his eyes in astonishment, and, looking down again, beheld neither Goody Cloyse nor the serpentine staff, but his fellow-traveller alone, who waited for him as calmly as if nothing had happened.

"That old woman taught me my catechism," said the young man; and there was a world of meaning in this simple comment.

They continued to walk onward, while the elder traveller exhorted his companion to make good speed and persevere in the path, discoursing so aptly that his arguments seemed rather to spring up in the bosom of his auditor than to be suggested by himself. As they went, he plucked a branch of maple to serve for a walking stick, and began to strip it of the twigs and little boughs, which were wet with evening dew. The moment his fingers touched them they became strangely withered and dried up as with a week's sunshine. Thus the pair proceeded, at a good free pace, until suddenly, in a gloomy hollow of the road, Goodman Brown sat himself down on the stump of a tree and refused to go any farther.

"Friend," said he, stubbornly, "my mind is made up. Not another step will I budge on this errand. What if a wretched old woman do choose to go to the devil when I thought she was going to heaven: is that any reason why I should quit my dear Faith and go after her?"

"You will think better of this by and by," said his acquaintance, composedly. "Sit here and rest yourself a while; and when you feel like moving again, there is my staff to help you along."

Without more words, he threw his companion the maple stick, and was as speedily out of sight as if he had vanished into the deepening gloom. The young man sat a few moments by the roadside, applauding himself greatly, and thinking with how clear a conscience he should meet the minister in his morning walk, nor shrink from the eye of good old Deacon Gookin. And what calm sleep would be his that very night, which was to have been spent so wickedly, but so purely and sweetly now, in the arms of Faith! Amidst these pleasant and praiseworthy meditations, Goodman Brown heard the tramp of horses along the road, and deemed it advisable to conceal himself within the verge of the forest, conscious of the guilty purpose that had brought him thither, though now so happily turned from it.

On came the hoof tramps and the voices of the riders, two grave old voices, conversing soberly as they drew near. These mingled sounds appeared to pass along the road, within a few yards of the young man's hiding-place; but, owing doubtless to the depth of the gloom at that particular spot, neither the travellers nor their steeds were visible. Though their figures brushed the small boughs by the wayside, it could not be seen that they intercepted, even for a moment, the faint gleam from the strip of bright sky athwart which they must have passed. Goodman Brown alternately crouched and stood on tiptoe, pulling aside the branches and thrusting forth his head as far as he durst without discerning so much as a shadow. It vexed him the more, because he could have sworn, were such a thing possible, that he recognized the voices of the minister and Deacon Gookin, jogging along quietly, as they were wont to do, when bound to some ordination or ecclesiastical council. While yet within hearing, one of the riders stopped to pluck a switch.

"Of the two, reverend sir," said the voice like the deacon's, "I had rather miss an ordination dinner than to-night's meeting. They tell me that some of our community are to be here from Falmouth and beyond, and others from Connecticut and Rhode Island, besides several of the Indian powwows, who, after their fashion, know almost as much deviltry as the best of us. Moreover, there is a goodly young woman to be taken into communion."

"Mighty well, Deacon Gookin!" replied the solemn old tones of the minister. "Spur up, or we shall be late. Nothing can be done, you know, until I get on the ground."

The hoofs clattered again; and the voices, talking so strangely in the empty air, passed on through the forest, where no church had ever been gathered or solitary Christian prayed. Whither, then, could these holy men be journeying so deep into the heathen wilderness? Young Goodman Brown caught hold of a tree for support, being ready to sink down on the ground, faint and overburdened with the heavy sickness of his heart. He looked up to the sky, doubting whether there really was a heaven above him. Yet there was the blue arch, and the stars brightening in it.

"With heaven above and Faith below, I will yet stand firm against the devil!" cried Goodman Brown.

While he still gazed upward into the deep arch of the firmament and had lifted his hands to pray, a cloud, though no wind was stirring, hurried across the zenith and hid the brightening stars. The blue sky was still visible, except directly overhead, where this black mass of cloud was sweeping swiftly northward. Aloft in the air, as if from the depths of the cloud, came a confused and doubtful sound of voices.

Once the listener fancied that he could distinguish the accents of townspeople of his own, men and women, both pious and ungodly, many of whom he had met at the communion table, and had seen others rioting at the tavern. The next moment, so indistinct were the sounds, he doubted whether he had heard aught but the murmur of the old forest, whispering without a wind. Then came a stronger swell of those familiar tones, heard daily in the sunshine at Salem village, but never until now from a cloud of night. There was one voice, of a young woman, uttering lamentations, yet with an uncertain sorrow, and entreating for some favor, which, perhaps, it would grieve her to obtain; and all the unseen multitude, both saints and sinners, seemed to encourage her onward.

"Faith!" shouted Goodman Brown, in a voice of agony and desperation; and the echoes of the forest mocked him, crying, "Faith! Faith!" as if bewildered wretches were seeking her all through the wilderness.

The cry of grief, rage, and terror was yet piercing the night, when the unhappy husband held his breath for a response. There was a scream, drowned immediately in a louder murmur of voices, fading into far-off laughter, as the dark cloud swept away, leaving the clear and silent sky above Goodman Brown. But something fluttered lightly down through the air and caught on the branch of a tree. The young man seized it, and beheld a pink ribbon.

"My Faith is gone!" cried he, after one stupefied moment. "There is no good on earth; and sin is but a name. Come, devil; for to thee is this world given."

And, maddened with despair, so that he laughed loud and long, did Goodman Brown grasp his staff and set forth again, at such a rate that he seemed to fly along the forest path rather than to walk or run. The road grew wilder and drearier and more faintly traced, and vanished at length, leaving him in the heart of the dark wilderness, still rushing onward with the instinct that guides mortal man to evil. The whole forest was peopled with frightful sounds—the creaking of the trees, the howling of wild beasts, and the yell of Indians; while sometimes the wind tolled like a distant church bell, and sometimes gave a broad roar around the traveller, as if all Nature were laughing him to scorn. But he was himself the chief horror of the scene, and shrank not from its other horrors.

"Ha! ha! ha!" roared Goodman Brown when the wind laughed at him. "Let us hear which will laugh loudest. Think not to frighten me with your deviltry. Come witch, come wizard, come Indian powwow, come devil himself, and here comes Goodman Brown. You may as well fear him as he fear you."

In truth, all through the haunted forest there could be nothing more frightful than the figure of Goodman Brown. On he flew among the black pines, brandishing his staff with frenzied gestures, now giving vent to an inspiration of horrid blasphemy, and now shouting forth such laughter as set all the echoes of the forest laughing like demons around him. The fiend in his own shape is less hideous than when he rages in the breast of man. Thus sped the demoniac on his course, until, quivering among the trees, he saw a red light before him, as when the felled trunks and branches of a clearing have been set on fire, and throw up their lurid blaze against the sky, at the hour of midnight. He paused, in a lull of the tempest that had driven him onward, and heard the swell of what seemed a hymn, rolling solemnly from a distance with the weight of many voices. He knew the tune; it was a familiar one in the choir of the village meeting-house. The verse died heavily away, and was lengthened by a chorus, not of human voices, but of all the sounds of the benighted wilderness pealing in awful harmony together. Goodman Brown cried out, and his cry was lost to his own ear by its unison with the cry of the desert.

In the interval of silence he stole forward until the light glared full upon his eyes. At one extremity of an open space, hemmed in by the dark wall of the forest, arose a rock, bearing some rude, natural resemblance either to an altar or a pulpit, and surrounded by four blazing pines, their tops aflame, their stems untouched, like candles at an evening meeting. The mass of foliage that had overgrown the summit of the rock was all on fire, blazing high into the night and fitfully illuminating the whole field. Each pendent twig and leafy festoon was in a blaze. As the red light arose and fell, a numerous congregation alternately shone forth, then disappeared in shadow, and again grew, as it were, out of the darkness, peopling the heart of the solitary woods at once.

"A grave and dark-clad company," quoth Goodman Brown.

In truth they were such. Among them, quivering to and fro between gloom and splendor, appeared faces that would be seen next day at the council board of the province, and others which, Sabbath after Sabbath, looked devoutly heavenward, and benignantly over the crowded pews, from the holiest pulpits in the land. Some affirm that the lady of the governor was there. At least there were high dames well known to her, and wives of honored husbands, and widows, a great multitude, and ancient maidens, all of excellent repute, and fair young girls, who trembled lest their mothers should espy them. Either the sudden gleams of light flashing over the obscure field bedazzled Goodman Brown, or he recognized a score of the church members of Salem village famous for their especial sanctity. Good old Deacon Gookin had arrived, and waited at the skirts of that venerable saint, his revered pastor. But, irreverently consorting with these grave, reputable, and pious people, these elders of the church, these chaste dames and dewy virgins, there were men of dissolute lives and women of spotted fame, wretches given over to all mean and filthy vice, and suspected even of horrid crimes. It was strange to see that the good shrank not from the wicked, nor were the sinners abashed by the saints. Scattered also among their pale-faced enemies were the Indian priests, or powwows, who had often scared their native forest with more hideous incantations than any known to English witchcraft.

"But where is Faith?" thought Goodman Brown; and, as hope came into his heart, he trembled.

Another verse of the hymn arose, a slow and mournful strain, such as the pious love, but joined to words which expressed all that our nature can conceive of sin, and darkly hinted at far more. Unfathomable to mere mortals is the lore of fiends. Verse after verse was sung; and still the chorus of the desert swelled between like the deepest tone of a mighty organ; and with the final peal of that dreadful anthem there came a sound, as if the roaring wind, the rushing streams, the howling beasts, and every other voice of the unconcerted wilderness were mingling and according with the voice of guilty man in homage to the prince of all. The four blazing pines threw up a loftier flame, and obscurely discovered shapes and visages of horror on the smoke wreaths above the impious assembly. At the same moment the fire on the rock shot redly forth and formed a glowing arch above its base, where now appeared a figure. With reverence be it spoken, the figure bore no slight similitude, both in garb and manner, to some grave divine of the New England churches.

"Bring forth the converts!" cried a voice that echoed through the field and rolled into the forest.

At the word, Goodman Brown stepped forth from the shadow of the trees and approached the congregation, with whom he felt a loathful brotherhood by the sympathy of all that was wicked in his heart. He could have well-nigh sworn that the shape of his own dead father beckoned him to advance, looking downward from a smoke wreath, while a woman, with dim features of despair, threw out her hand to warn him back. Was it his mother? But he had no power to retreat one step, nor to resist, even in thought, when the minister and good old Deacon Gookin seized his arms and led him to the blazing rock. Thither came also the slender form of a veiled female, led between Goody Cloyse, that pious teacher of the catechism, and Martha Carrier,[8] who had received the devil's promise to be queen of hell. A rampant hag was she. And there stood the proselytes beneath the canopy of fire.

"Welcome, my children," said the dark figure, "to the communion of your race. Ye have found thus young your nature and your destiny. My children, look behind you!"

They turned; and flashing forth, as it were, in a sheet of flame, the fiend worshippers were seen; the smile of welcome gleamed darkly on every visage.

"There," resumed the sable form, "are all whom ye have reverenced from youth. Ye deemed them holier than yourselves, and shrank from your own sin, contrasting it with their lives of righteousness and prayerful aspirations heavenward. Yet here are they all in my worshipping assembly. This night it shall be granted you to know their secret deeds: how hoary-bearded elders of the church have whispered wanton words to the young maids of their households; how many a woman, eager for widows' weeds, has given her husband a drink at bedtime and let him sleep his last sleep in her bosom; how beardless youths have made haste to inherit their fathers' wealth; and how fair damsels—blush not, sweet ones—have dug little graves in the garden, and bidden me, the sole guest, to an infant's funeral. By the sympathy of your human hearts for sin ye shall scent out all the places—whether in church, bed-chamber, street, field, or forest—where crime has been committed, and shall exult to behold the whole earth one stain of guilt, one mighty blood spot. Far more than this. It shall be yours to penetrate, in every bosom, the deep mystery of sin, the fountain of all wicked arts, and which inexhaustibly supplies more evil impulses than human power—than my power at its utmost—can make manifest in deeds. And now, my children, look upon each other."

They did so; and, by the blaze of the hell-kindled torches, the wretched man beheld his Faith, and the wife her husband, trembling before that unhallowed altar.

"Lo, there ye stand, my children," said the figure, in a deep and solemn tone, almost sad with its despairing awfulness, as if his once angelic nature could yet mourn for our miserable race. "Depending

[8] See footnote 6.

upon one another's hearts, ye had still hoped that virtue were not all a dream. Now are ye undeceived. Evil is the nature of mankind. Evil must be your only happiness. Welcome again, my children, to the communion of your race."

"Welcome," repeated the fiend worshippers, in one cry of despair and triumph.

And there they stood, the only pair, as it seemed, who were yet hesitating on the verge of wickedness in this dark world. A basin was hollowed, naturally, in the rock. Did it contain water, reddened by the lurid light? or was it blood? or, perchance, a liquid flame? Herein did the shape of evil dip his hand and prepare to lay the mark of baptism upon their foreheads, that they might be partakers of the mystery of sin, more conscious of the secret guilt of others, both in deed and thought, than they could now be of their own. The husband cast one look at his pale wife, and Faith at him. What polluted wretches would the next glance show them to each other, shuddering alike at what they disclosed and what they saw!

"Faith! Faith!" cried the husband, "look up to heaven, and resist the wicked one."

Whether Faith obeyed he knew not. Hardly had he spoken when he found himself amid calm night and solitude, listening to a roar of the wind which died heavily away through the forest. He staggered against the rock, and felt it chill and damp; while a hanging twig, that had been all on fire, besprinkled his cheek with the coldest dew.

The next morning young Goodman Brown came slowly into the street of Salem village, staring around him like a bewildered man. The good old minister was taking a walk along the graveyard to get an appetite for breakfast and meditate his sermon, and bestowed a blessing, as he passed, on Goodman Brown. He shrank from the venerable saint as if to avoid an anathema. Old Deacon Gookin was at domestic worship, and the holy words of his prayer were heard through the open window. "What God doth the wizard pray to?" quoth Goodman Brown. Goody Cloyse, that excellent old Christian, stood in the early sunshine at her own lattice, catechizing a little girl who had brought her a pint of morning's milk. Goodman Brown snatched away the child as from the grasp of the fiend himself. Turning the corner by the meeting-house, he spied the head of Faith, with the pink ribbons, gazing anxiously forth, and bursting into such joy at sight of him that she skipped along the street and almost kissed her husband before the whole village. But Goodman Brown looked sternly and sadly into her face, and passed on without a greeting.

Had Goodman Brown fallen asleep in the forest and only dreamed a wild dream of a witch-meeting?

Be it so if you will; but, alas! it was a dream of evil omen for young Goodman Brown. A stern, a sad, a darkly meditative, a distrustful, if not a desperate man did he become from the night of that fearful dream. On the Sabbath day, when the congregation were singing a holy psalm, he could not listen because an anthem of sin rushed loudly upon his ear and drowned all the blessed strain. When the minister spoke from the pulpit with power and fervid eloquence, and, with his hand on the open Bible, of the sacred truths of our religion, and of saint-like lives and triumphant deaths, and of future bliss or misery unutterable, then did Goodman Brown turn pale, dreading lest the roof should thunder down upon the gray blasphemer and his hearers. Often, awaking suddenly at midnight, he shrank from the bosom of Faith; and at morning or eventide, when the family knelt down at prayer, he scowled and muttered to himself, and gazed sternly at his wife, and turned away. And when he had lived long, and was borne to his grave a hoary corpse, followed by Faith, an aged woman, and children and grandchildren, a goodly procession, besides neighbors not a few, they carved no hopeful verse upon his tombstone, for his dying hour was gloom.

1835

THE JUDGMENT

FRANZ KAFKA

It was a Sunday morning in the very height of spring. Georg Bendemann, a young merchant, was sitting in his own room on the first floor of one of a long row of small, ramshackle houses stretching beside the river which were scarcely distinguishable from each other except in height and coloring. He had just finished a letter to an old friend of his who was now living abroad, had put it into its envelope in a slow and dreamy fashion, and with his elbows propped on the writing table was gazing out of the window at the river, the bridge and the hills on the farther bank with their tender green.

He was thinking about his friend, who had actually run away to

Russia some years before, being dissatisfied with his prospects at home. Now he was carrying on a business in St. Petersburg, which had flourished to begin with but had long been going downhill, as he always complained on his increasingly rare visits. So he was wearing himself out to no purpose in a foreign country, the unfamiliar full beard he wore did not quite conceal the face Georg had known so well since childhood, and his skin was growing so yellow as to indicate some latent disease. By his own account he had no regular connection with the colony of his fellow countrymen out there and almost no social intercourse with Russian families, so that he was resigning himself to becoming a permanent bachelor.

What could one write to such a man, who had obviously run off the rails, a man one could be sorry for but could not help. Should one advise him to come home, to transplant himself and take up his old friendships again—there was nothing to hinder him—and in general to rely on the help of his friends? But that was as good as telling him, and the more kindly the more offensively, that all his efforts hitherto had miscarried, that he should finally give up, come back home, and be gaped at by everyone as a returned prodigal, that only his friends knew what was what and that he himself was just a big child who should do what his successful and home-keeping friends prescribed. And was it certain, besides, that all the pain one would have to inflict on him would achieve its object? Perhaps it would not even be possible to get him to come home at all—he said himself that he was now out of touch with commerce in his native country—and then he would still be left an alien in a foreign land embittered by his friends' advice and more than ever estranged from them. But if he did follow their advice and then didn't fit in at home—not out of malice, of course, but through force of circumstances—couldn't get on with his friends or without them, felt humiliated, couldn't be said to have either friends or a country of his own any longer, wouldn't it have been better for him to stay abroad just as he was? Taking all this into account, how could one be sure that he would make a success of life at home?

For such reasons, supposing one wanted to keep up correspondence with him, one could not send him any real news such as could frankly be told to the most distant acquaintance. It was more than three years since his last visit, and for this he offered the lame excuse that the political situation in Russia was too uncertain, which apparently would not permit even the briefest absence of a small business man while it allowed hundreds of thousands of Russians to travel peacefully abroad. But during these three years Georg's own position in life had changed a lot. Two years ago his mother had died, since when he and his father had shared the household together, and his friend had of course been informed of that and had expressed his sympathy in a letter phrased so dryly that the grief caused by such an event, one had to conclude, could not be realized in a distant country. Since that time, however, Georg had applied himself with greater determination to the business as well as to everything else.

Perhaps during his mother's lifetime his father's insistence on having everything his own way in the business had hindered him from developing any real activity of his own, perhaps since her death his father had become less aggressive, although he was still active in the business, perhaps it was mostly due to an accidental run of good fortune—which was very probable indeed—but at any rate during those two years the business had developed in a most unexpected way, the staff had had to be doubled, the turnover was five times as great, no doubt about it, farther progress lay just ahead.

But Georg's friend had no inkling of this improvement. In earlier years, perhaps for the last time in that letter of condolence, he had tried to persuade Georg to emigrate to Russia and had enlarged upon the prospects of success for precisely Georg's branch of trade. The figures quoted were microscopic by comparison with the range of Georg's present operations. Yet he shrank from letting his friend know about his business success, and if he were to do it now retrospectively that certainly would look peculiar.

So Georg confined himself to giving his friend unimportant items of gossip such as rise at random in the memory when one is idly thinking things over on a quiet Sunday. All he desired was to leave undisturbed the idea of the home town which his friend must have built up to his own content during the long interval. And so it happened to Georg that three times in three fairly widely separated letters he had told his friend about the engagement of an unimportant man to an equally unimportant girl, until indeed, quite contrary to his intentions, his friend began to show some interest in this notable event.

Yet Georg preferred to write about things like these rather than to confess that he himself had got engaged a month ago to a Fräulein Frieda Brandenfeld, a girl from a well-to-do family. He often discussed this friend of his with his fiancée and the peculiar relationship that had developed between them in their correspondence. "So he won't be coming to our wedding," said she, "and yet I have a right to get to know all your friends." "I don't want to trouble him," answered Georg, "don't misunderstand me, he would probably come, at least I think so, but he would feel that his hand had been forced and he would be hurt, perhaps he would envy me and certainly he'd be discontented and without being able to do anything about his discontent he'd have to go away again alone. Alone—do you know what that means?" "Yes, but may he not hear about our wedding in some other fashion?" "I can't prevent that, of course, but it's unlikely, considering the way he lives." "Since your friends are like that, Georg, you shouldn't ever have got engaged at all." "Well, we're both to blame for that; but I wouldn't have it any other way now." And when, breathing quickly under his kisses, she still brought out: "All the same, I do feel upset," he thought it could not really involve him in trouble were he to send the news to his friend. "That's the kind of man I am and he'll just have to take me as I am," he said to himself, "I can't cut myself to another pattern that might make a more suitable friend for him."

And in fact he did inform his friend, in the long letter he had been writing that Sunday morning, about his engagement, with these words: "I have saved my best news to the end. I have got engaged to a Fräulein Frieda Brandenfeld, a girl from a well-to-do family, who only came to live here a long time after you went away, so that you're hardly likely to know her. There will be time to tell you more about her later, for today let me just say that I am very happy and as between you and me the only difference in our relationship is that instead of a quite ordinary kind of friend you will now have in me a happy friend. Besides that, you will acquire in my fiancée, who sends her warm greetings and will soon write you herself, a genuine friend of the opposite sex, which is not without importance to a bachelor. I know that there are many reasons why you can't come to see us, but would not my wedding be precisely the right occasion for giving all obstacles the go-by? Still, however that may be, do just as seems good to you without regarding any interests but your own."

With this letter in his hand Georg had been sitting a long time at the writing table, his face turned towards the window. He had barely acknowledged, with an absent smile, a greeting waved to him from the street by a passing acquaintance.

At last he put the letter in his pocket and went out of his room across a small lobby into his father's room, which he had not entered for months. There was in fact no need for him to enter it, since he saw his father daily at business and they took their midday meal together at an eating house; in the evening, it was true, each did as he pleased, yet even then, unless Georg—as mostly happened—went out with friends or, more recently, visited his fiancée, they always sat for a while, each with his newspaper, in their common sitting room.

It surprised Georg how dark his father's room was even on this sunny morning. So it was overshadowed as much as that by the high wall on the other side of the narrow courtyard. His father was sitting by the window in a corner hung with various mementoes of Georg's dead mother, reading a newspaper which he held to one side before his eyes in an attempt to overcome a defect of vision. On the table stood the remains of his breakfast, not much of which seemed to have been eaten.

"Ah, Georg," said his father, rising at once to meet him. His heavy dressing gown swung open as he walked and the skirts of it fluttered round him.—"My father is still a giant of a man," said Georg to himself.

"It's unbearably dark here," he said aloud.

"Yes, it's dark enough," answered his father.

"And you've shut the window, too?"

"I prefer it like that."

"Well, it's quite warm outside," said Georg, as if continuing his previous remark, and sat down.

His father cleared away the breakfast dishes and set them on a chest.

"I really only wanted to tell you," went on Georg, who had been vacantly following the old man's movements, "that I am now sending the news of my engagement to St. Petersburg." He drew the letter a little way from his pocket and let it drop back again.

"To St. Petersburg?" asked his father.

"To my friend there," said Georg, trying to meet his father's eye.—In business hours he's quite different, he was thinking, how solidly he sits here with his arms crossed.

"Oh yes. To your friend," said his father, with peculiar emphasis.

"Well, you know, Father, that I wanted not to tell him about my engagement at first. Out of consideration for him, that was the only reason. You know yourself he's a difficult man. I said to myself that someone else might tell him about my engagement, although he's such a solitary creature that that was hardly likely—I couldn't prevent that—but I wasn't ever going to tell him myself."

"And now you've changed your mind?" asked his father, laying his enormous newspaper on the window sill and on top of it his spectacles, which he covered with one hand.

"Yes, I've been thinking it over. If he's a good friend of mine, I said to myself, my being happily engaged should make him happy too. And so I wouldn't put off telling him any longer. But before I posted the letter I wanted to let you know."

"Georg," said his father, lengthening his toothless mouth, "listen to me! You've come to me about this business, to talk it over with me. No doubt that does you honor. But it's nothing, it's worse than nothing, if you don't tell me the whole truth. I don't want to stir up matters that shouldn't be mentioned here. Since the death of our dear mother certain things have been done that aren't right. Maybe the time will come for mentioning them, and maybe sooner than we think. There's many a thing in the business I'm not aware of, maybe it's not done behind my back—I'm not going to say that it's done behind my back—I'm not equal to things any longer, my memory's failing, I haven't an eye for so many things any longer. That's the course of nature in the first place, and in the second place the death of our dear mother hit me harder than it did you.—But since we're talking about it, about this letter, I beg you, Georg, don't deceive me. It's a trivial affair, it's hardly worth mentioning, so don't deceive me. Do you really have this friend in St. Petersburg?"

Georg rose in embarrassment. "Never mind my friends. A thousand friends wouldn't make up to me for my father. Do you know what I think? You're not taking enough care of yourself. But old age must be taken care of. I can't do without you in the business, you know that very well, but if the business is going to undermine your health, I'm ready to close it down tomorrow forever. And that won't do. We'll have to make a change in your way of living. But a radical change. You sit here in the dark, and in the sitting room you would have plenty of light. You just take a bite of breakfast instead of properly keeping up your strength. You sit by a closed window, and the air would be so good for you. No, Father! I'll get the doctor to come, and we'll follow his orders. We'll change your room, you can move into the front room and I'll move in here. You won't notice the change, all your things will be moved with you. But there's time for all that later, I'll put you to bed now for a little, I'm sure you need to rest. Come, I'll help you to take off your things, you'll see I can do it. Or if you would rather go into the front room at once, you can lie down in my bed for the present. That would be the most sensible thing."

Georg stood close beside his father, who had let his head with its unkempt white hair sink on his chest.

"Georg," said his father in a low voice, without moving.

George knelt down at once beside his father, in the old man's weary face he saw the pupils, over-large, fixedly looking at him from the corners of the eyes.

"You have no friend in St. Petersburg. You've always been a leg-puller and you haven't even shrunk from pulling my leg. How could you have a friend out there! I can't believe it."

"Just think back a bit, Father," said Georg, lifting his father from the chair and slipping off his dressing gown as he stood feebly enough, "it'll soon be three years since my friend came to see us last. I remember that you used not to like him very much. At least twice I kept you from seeing him, although he was actually sitting with me in my room. I could quite well understand your dislike of him, my friend has his peculiarities. But then, later, you got on with him very well. I was proud because you listened to him and nodded and asked him questions. If you think back you're bound to remember. He used to tell us the most incredible stories of the Russian Revolution.[1] For instance, when he was on a business trip to Kiev and ran into a riot, and saw a priest on a balcony who cut a broad cross in blood on the palm of his hand and held the hand up and appealed to the mob. You've told that story yourself once or twice since."

Meanwhile Georg had succeeded in lowering his father down again and carefully taking off the woollen drawers he wore over his linen underpants and his socks. The not particularly clean appearance of this underwear made him reproach himself for having been neglectful. It should have certainly been his duty to see that his father had clean changes of underwear. He had not yet explicitly discussed with his bride-to-be what arrangements should be made for his father in the future, for they had both of them silently taken it for granted that the old man would go on living alone in the old house. But now he made a quick, firm decision to take him into his own future establishment. It almost looked, on closer inspection, as if the care he meant to lavish there on his father might come too late.

He carried his father to bed in his arms. It gave him a dreadful feeling to notice that while he took the few steps towards the bed the old man on his breast was playing with his watch chain. He could not lay him down on the bed for a moment, so firmly did he hang on to the watch chain.

But as soon as he was laid in bed, all seemed well. He covered himself up and even drew the blankets farther than usual over his shoulders. He looked up at Georg with a not unfriendly eye.

"You begin to remember my friend, don't you?" asked Georg, giving him an encouraging nod.

"Am I well covered up now?" asked his father, as if he were not able to see whether his feet were properly tucked in or not.

"So you find it snug in bed already," said Georg, and tucked the blankets more closely round him.

[1] Probably refers to the revolutionary disturbances of 1905.

"Am I well covered up?" asked the father once more, seeming to be strangely intent upon the answer.

"Don't worry, you're well covered up."

"No!" cried his father, cutting short the answer, threw the blankets off with a strength that sent them all flying in a moment and sprang erect in bed. Only one hand lightly touched the ceiling to steady him.

"You wanted to cover me up, I know, my young sprig, but I'm far from being covered up yet. And even if this is the last strength I have, it's enough for you, too much for you. Of course I know your friend. He would have been a son after my own heart. That's why you've been playing him false all these years. Why else? Do you think I haven't been sorry for him? And that's why you had to lock yourself up in your office—the Chief is busy, mustn't be disturbed—just so that you could write your lying little letters to Russia. But thank goodness a father doesn't need to be taught how to see through his son. And now that you thought you'd got him down, so far down that you could set your bottom on him and sit on him and he wouldn't move, then my fine son makes up his mind to get married!"

Georg stared at the bogey conjured up by his father. His friend in St. Petersburg, whom his father suddenly knew too well, touched his imagination as never before. Lost in the vastness of Russia he saw him. At the door of an empty, plundered warehouse he saw him. Among the wreckage of his showcases, the slashed remnants of his wares, the falling gas brackets, he was just standing up. Why did he have to go so far away!

"But attend to me!" cried his father, and Georg, almost distracted, ran towards the bed to take everything in, yet came to a stop halfway.

"Because she lifted up her skirts," his father began to flute, "because she lifted her skirts like this, the nasty creature," and mimicking her he lifted his shirt so high that one could see the scar on his thigh from his war wound, "because she lifted her skirts like this and this you made up to her, and in order to make free with her undisturbed you have disgraced your mother's memory, betrayed your friend and stuck your father into bed so that he can't move. But he can move, or can't he?"

And he stood up quite unsupported and kicked his legs out. His insight made him radiant.

Georg shrank into a corner, as far away from his father as possible. A long time ago he had firmly made up his mind to watch closely every least movement so that he should not be surprised by any indirect attack, a pounce from behind or above. At this moment he recalled this long-forgotten resolve and forgot it again, like a man drawing a short thread through the eye of a needle.

"But your friend hasn't been betrayed after all!" cried his father, emphasizing the point with stabs of his forefinger. "I've been representing him here on the spot."

"You comedian!" Georg could not resist the retort, realized at once the harm done and, his eyes starting in his head, bit his tongue back, only too late, till the pain made his knees give.

"Yes, of course I've been playing a comedy! A comedy! That's a good expression! What other comfort was left to a poor old widower? Tell me—and while you're answering me be you still my living son—what else was left to me, in my back room, plagued by a disloyal staff, old to the marrow of my bones? And my son strutting through the world, finishing off deals that I had prepared for him, bursting with triumphant glee and stalking away from his father with the closed face of a respectable business man! Do you think I didn't love you, I, from whom you are sprung?"

Now he'll lean forward, thought Georg, what if he topples and smashes himself! These words went hissing through his mind.

His father leaned forward but did not topple. Since Georg did not come any nearer, as he had expected, he straightened himself again.

"Stay where you are, I don't need you! You think you have strength enough to come over here and that you're only hanging back of your own accord. Don't be too sure! I am still much the stronger of us two. All by myself I might have had to give way, but your mother has given me so much of her strength that I've established a fine connection with your friend and I have your customers here in my pocket!"

"He has pockets even in his shirt!" said Georg to himself, and believed that with this remark he could make him an impossible figure for all the world. Only for a moment did he think so, since he kept on forgetting everything.

"Just take your bride on your arm and try getting in my way! I'll sweep her from your very side, you don't know how!"

Georg made a grimace of disbelief. His father only nodded, confirming the truth of his words, towards Georg's corner.

"How you amused me today, coming to ask me if you should tell your friend about your engagement. He knows it already, you stupid boy, he knows it all! I've been writing to him, for you forgot to take my writing things away from me. That's why he hasn't been here for years, he knows everything a hundred times better than you do yourself, in his left hand he crumples your letters unopened while in his right hand he holds up my letters to read through!"

In his enthusiasm he waved his arm over his head. "He knows everything a thousand times better!" he cried.

"Ten thousand times!" said Georg, to make fun of his father, but in his very mouth the words turned into deadly earnest.

"For years I've been waiting for you to come with some such question! Do you think I concern myself with anything else? Do you think I read my newspapers? Look!" and he threw Georg a newspaper sheet which he had somehow taken to bed with him. An old newspaper, with a name entirely unknown to Georg.

"How long a time you've taken to grow up! Your mother had to die, she couldn't see the happy day, your friend is going to pieces in Russia, even three years ago he was yellow enough to be thrown away, and as for me, you see what condition I'm in. You have eyes in your head for that!"

"So you've been lying in wait for me!" cried Georg.

His father said pityingly, in an offhand manner: "I suppose you wanted to say that sooner. But now it doesn't matter." And in a louder voice: "So now you know what else there was in the world besides yourself, till now you've known only about yourself! An innocent child, yes, that you were, truly, but still more truly have you been a devilish human being!—And therefore take note: I sentence you now to death by drowning!"

Georg felt himself urged from the room, the crash with which his father fell on the bed behind him was still in his ears as he fled. On the staircase, which he rushed down as if its steps were an inclined plane, he ran into his charwoman on her way up to do the morning cleaning of the room. "Jesus!" she cried, and covered her face with her apron, but he was already gone. Out of the front door he rushed, across the roadway, driven towards the water. Already he was grasping at the railings as a starving man clutches food. He swung himself over, like the distinguished gymnast he had once been in his youth, to his parents' pride. With weakening grip he was still holding on when he spied between the railings a motor-bus coming which would easily cover the noise of his fall, called in a low voice: "Dear parents, I have always loved you, all the same," and let himself drop.

At this moment an unending stream of traffic was just going over the bridge.

1913

Translated by Willa and Edwin Muir

KING OF THE BINGO GAME

RALPH ELLISON

THE WOMAN in front of him was eating roasted peanuts that smelled so good that he could barely contain his hunger. He could not even sleep and wished they'd hurry and begin the bingo game. There, on his right, two fellows were drinking wine out of a bottle wrapped in a paper bag, and he could hear soft gurgling in the dark. His stomach gave a low, gnawing growl. "If this was down South," he thought, "all I'd have to do is lean over and say, 'Lady, gimme a few of those peanuts, please ma'm,' and she'd pass me the bag and never think nothing of it." Or he could ask the fellows for a drink in the same way. Folks down South stuck together that way; they didn't even have to know you.

But up here it was different. Ask somebody for something, and they'd think you were crazy. Well, I ain't crazy. I'm just broke, 'cause I got no birth certificate to get a job, and Laura 'bout to die 'cause we got no money for a doctor. But I ain't crazy. And yet a pinpoint of doubt was focused in his mind as he glanced toward the screen and saw the hero stealthily entering a dark room and sending the beam of a flashlight along a wall of bookcases. This is where he finds the trapdoor, he remembered. The man would pass abruptly through the wall and find the girl tied to a bed, her legs and arms spread wide, and her clothing torn to rags. He laughed softly to himself. He had seen the picture three times, and this was one of the best scenes.

On his right the fellow whispered wide-eyed to his companion. "Man, look a-yonder!"

"Damn!"

"Wouldn't I like to have her tied up like that . . ."

"Hey! That fool's letting her loose!"

"Aw, man, he loves her."

"Love or no love!"

The man moved impatiently beside him, and he tried to involve himself in the scene. But Laura was on his mind. Tiring quickly of watching the picture he looked back to where the white beam filtered from the projection room above the balcony. It started small and grew large, specks of dust dancing in its whiteness as it reached the screen. It was strange how the beam always landed right on the screen and didn't mess up and fall somewhere else. But they had it all fixed. Everything was fixed. Now suppose when they showed that girl with her dress torn the girl started taking off the rest of her clothes, and when the guy came in he didn't untie her but kept her there and went to taking off his own clothes? *That* would be something to see. If a picture got out of hand like that those guys up there would go nuts. Yeah, and there'd be so many folks in here you couldn't find a seat for nine months! A strange sensation played over his skin. He shuddered. Yesterday he'd seen a bedbug on a woman's neck as they walked out into the bright street. But exploring his thigh through a hole in his pocket he found only goose pimples and old scars.

The bottle gurgled again. He closed his eyes. Now a dreamy music was accompanying the film and train whistles were sounding in the distance, and he was a boy again walking along a railroad trestle down South, and seeing the train coming, and running back as fast as he could go, and hearing the whistle blowing, and getting off the trestle to solid ground just in time, with the earth trembling beneath his feet, and feeling relieved as he ran down the cinder-strewn embankment onto the highway, and looking back and seeing with terror that the train had left the track and was following him right down the middle of the street, and all the white people laughing as he ran screaming . . .

"Wake up there, buddy! What the hell do you mean hollering like that! Can't you see we trying to enjoy this here picture?"

He stared at the man with gratitude.

"I'm sorry, old man," he said. "I musta been dreaming."

"Well, here, have a drink. And don't be making no noise like that, damn!"

His hands trembled as he tilted his head. It was not wine, but whiskey. Cold rye whiskey. He took a deep swoller, decided it was better not to take another, and handed the bottle back to its owner.

"Thanks, old man," he said.

Now he felt the cold whiskey breaking a warm path straight through the middle of him, growing hotter and sharper as it moved. He had not eaten all day, and it made him light-headed. The smell of the peanuts stabbed him like a knife, and he got up and found a seat in the middle aisle. But no sooner did he sit than he saw a row of intense-faced young girls, and got up again, thinking, "You chicks musta been Lindy-hopping[1] somewhere." He found a seat several rows ahead as the lights came on, and he saw the screen disappear behind a heavy red and gold curtain; then the curtain rising, and the man with the microphone and a uniformed attendant coming on the stage.

He felt for his bingo cards, smiling. The guy at the door wouldn't like it if he knew about his having *five* cards. Well, not everyone played the bingo game; and even with five cards he didn't have much of a chance. For Laura, though, he had to have faith. He studied the cards, each with its different numerals, punching the free center hole in each and spreading them neatly across his lap; and when the lights faded he sat slouched in his seat so that he could look from his cards to the bingo wheel with but a quick shifting of his eyes.

Ahead, at the end of the darkness, the man with the microphone was pressing a button attached to a long cord and spinning the bingo wheel and calling out the number each time the wheel came to rest. And each time the voice rang out his finger raced over the cards for the number. With five cards he had to move fast. He became nervous; there were too many cards, and the man went too fast with his grating voice. Perhaps he should just select one and throw the others away.

[1] Jitterbug dance that originated in Harlem.

But he was afraid. He became warm. Wonder how much Laura's doctor would cost? Damn that, watch the cards! And with despair he heard the man call three in a row which he missed on all five cards. This way he'd never win . . .

When he saw the row of holes punched across the third card, he sat paralyzed and heard the man call three more numbers before he stumbled forward, screaming.

"Bingo! Bingo!"

"Let that fool up there," someone called.

"Get up there, man!"

He stumbled down the aisle and up the steps to the stage into a light so sharp and bright that for a moment it blinded him, and he felt that he had moved into the spell of some strange, mysterious power. Yet it was as familiar as the sun, and he knew it was the perfectly familiar bingo.

The man with the microphone was saying something to the audience as he held out his card. A cold light flashed from the man's finger as the card left his hand. His knees trembled. The man stepped closer, checking the card against the numbers chalked on the board. Suppose he had made a mistake? The pomade on the man's hair made him feel faint, and he backed away. But the man was checking the card over the microphone now, and he had to stay. He stood tense, listening.

"Under the O, forty-four," the man chanted. "Under the I, seven. Under the G, three. Under the B, ninety-six. Under the N, thirteen!"

His breath came easier as the man smiled at the audience.

"Yessir, ladies and gentlemen, he's one of the chosen people!"

The audience rippled with laughter and applause.

"Step right up to the front of the stage."

He moved slowly forward, wishing that the light was not so bright.

"To win tonight's jackpot of $36.90 the wheel must stop between the double zero, understand?"

He nodded, knowing the ritual from the many days and nights he had watched the winners march across the stage to press the button that controlled the spinning wheel and receive the prizes. And now he followed the instructions as though he'd crossed the slippery stage a million prize-winning times.

The man was making some kind of a joke, and he nodded vacantly. So tense had he become that he felt a sudden desire to cry and shook it away. He felt vaguely that his whole life was determined by the bingo wheel; not only that which would happen now that he was at last before it, but all that had gone before, since his birth, and his mother's birth and the birth of his father. It had always been there, even though he had not been aware of it, handing out the unlucky cards and numbers of his days. The feeling persisted, and he started quickly away. I better get down from here before I make a fool of myself, he thought.

"Here, boy," the man called. "You haven't started yet."

Someone laughed as he went hesitantly back.

"Are you all reet?"

He grinned at the man's jive talk, but no words would come, and he knew it was not a convincing grin. For suddenly he knew that he stood on the slippery brink of some terrible embarrassment.

"Where are you from, boy?" the man asked.

"Down South."

"He's from down South, ladies and gentlemen," the man said. "Where from? Speak right into the mike."

"Rocky Mont," he said. "Rock' Mont, North Car'lina."

"So you decided to come down off that mountain to the U.S.," the man laughed. He felt that the man was making a fool of him, but then something cold was placed in his hand, and the lights were no longer behind him.

Standing before the wheel he felt alone, but that was somehow right, and he remembered his plan. He would give the wheel a short quick twirl. Just a touch of the button. He had watched it many times, and always it came close to double zero when it was short and quick. He steeled himself; the fear had left, and he felt a profound sense of promise, as though he were about to be repaid for all the things he'd suffered all his life. Trembling, he pressed the button. There was a whirl of lights, and in a second he realized with finality that though he wanted to, he could not stop. It was as though he held a high-powered line in his naked hand. His nerves tightened. As the wheel increased its speed it seemed to draw him more and more into its power, as though it held his fate; and with it came a deep need to submit, to whirl, to lose himself in its swirl of color. He could not stop it now, he knew. So let it be.

The button rested snugly in his palm where the man had placed it. And now he became aware of the man beside him, advising him through the microphone, while behind the shadowy audience hummed with noisy voices. He shifted his feet. There was still that feeling of helplessness within him, making part of him desire to turn back, even now that the jackpot was right in his hand. He squeezed the button until his fist ached. Then, like the sudden shriek of a subway whistle, a doubt tore through his head. Suppose he did not spin the wheel long enough?

What could he do, and how could he tell? And then he knew, even as he wondered, that as long as he pressed the button, he could control the jackpot. He and only he could determine whether or not it was to be his. Not even the man with the microphone could do anything about it now. He felt drunk. Then, as though he had come down from a high hill into a valley of people, he heard the audience yelling.

"Come down from there, you jerk!"

"Let somebody else have a chance . . ."

"Ole Jack thinks he done found the end of the rainbow . . ."

The last voice was not unfriendly, and he turned and smiled dreamily into the yelling mouths. Then he turned his back squarely on them.

"Don't take too long, boy," a voice said.

He nodded. They were yelling behind him. Those folks did not understand what had happened to him. They had been playing the bingo game day in and night out for years, trying to win rent money or hamburger change. But not one of those wise guys had discovered this wonderful thing. He watched the wheel whirling past the numbers and experienced a burst of exaltation: This is God! This is the really truly God! He said it aloud, "This is God!"

He said it with such absolute conviction that he feared he would fall fainting into the footlights. But the crowd yelled so loud that they could not hear. Those fools, he thought. I'm here trying to tell them the most wonderful secret in the world, and they're yelling like they gone crazy. A hand fell upon his shoulder.

"You'll have to make a choice now, boy. You've taken too long."

He brushed the hand violently away.

"Leave me alone, man. I know what I'm doing!"

The man looked surprised and held on to the microphone for support. And because he did not wish to hurt the man's feelings he smiled, realizing with a sudden pang that there was no way of explaining to the man just why he had to stand there pressing the button forever.

"Come here," he called tiredly.

The man approached, rolling the heavy microphone across the stage.

"Anybody can play this bingo game, right?" he said.

"Sure, but . . ."

He smiled, feeling inclined to be patient with this slick looking white man with his blue sport shirt and his sharp gabardine suit.

"That's what I thought," he said. "Anybody can win the jackpot as long as they get the lucky number, right?"

"That's the rule, but after all . . ."

"That's what I thought," he said. "And the big prize goes to the man who knows how to win it?"

The man nodded speechlessly.

"Well then, go on over there and watch me win like I want to. I ain't going to hurt nobody," he said, "and I'll show you how to win. I mean to show the whole world how it's got to be done."

And because he understood, he smiled again to let the man know that he held nothing against him for being white and impatient. Then he refused to see the man any longer and stood pressing the button, the voices of the crowd reaching him like sounds in distant streets. Let them yell. All the Negroes down there were just ashamed because he was black like them. He smiled inwardly, knowing how it was. Most of the time he was ashamed of what Negroes did himself. Well, let them be ashamed for something this time. Like him. He was like a long thin black wire that was being stretched and wound upon the bingo wheel; wound until he wanted to scream; wound, but this time himself controlling the winding and the sadness and the shame, and because he did, Laura would be all right. Suddenly the lights flickered. He staggered backwards. Had something gone wrong? All this noise. Didn't they know that although he controlled the wheel, it also controlled him, and unless he pressed the button forever and forever and ever it would stop, leaving him high and dry, dry and high on this hard high slippery hill and Laura dead? There was only one chance; he had to do whatever the wheel demanded. And gripping the button in despair, he discovered with surprise that it imparted a nervous energy. His spine tingled. He felt a certain power.

Now he faced the raging crowd with defiance, its screams penetrating his eardrums like trumpets shrieking from a jukebox. The vague faces glowing in the bingo lights gave him a sense of himself that he had never known before. He was running the show, by God! They had to react to him, for he was their luck. This is *me,* he thought. Let the bastards yell. Then someone was laughing inside him, and he realized that somehow he had forgotten his own name. It was a sad, lost feeling to lose your name, and a crazy thing to do. That name had been given him by the white man who had owned his grandfather a long lost time ago down South. But maybe those wise guys knew his name.

"Who am I?" he screamed.

"Hurry up and bingo, you jerk!"

They didn't know either, he thought sadly. They didn't even know their own names, they were all poor nameless bastards. Well, he didn't need that old name; he was reborn. For as long as he pressed the button he was The-man-who-pressed-the-button-who-held-the-prize-who-was-the-King-of-Bingo. That was the way it. was, and he'd have to press the button even if nobody understood, even though Laura did not understand.

"Live!" he shouted.

The audience quieted like the dying of a huge fan.

"Live, Laura, baby. I got holt of it now, sugar. Live!"

He screamed it, tears streaming down his face. "I got nobody but YOU!"

The screams tore from his very guts. He felt as though the rush of blood to his head would burst out in baseball seams of small red droplets, like a head beaten by police clubs. Bending over he saw a trickle of blood splashing the toe of his shoe. With his free hand he searched his head. It was his nose. God, suppose something has gone wrong? He felt that the whole audience had somehow entered him and was stamping its feet in his stomach, and he was unable to throw them out. They wanted the prize, that was it. They wanted the secret for themselves. But they'd never get it; he would keep the bingo wheel whirling forever, and Laura would be safe in the wheel. But would she? It had to be, because if she were not safe the wheel would cease to turn; it could not go on. He had to get away, *vomit* all, and his mind formed an image of himself running with Laura in his arms down the tracks of the subway just ahead of an A train, running desperately *vomit* with people screaming for him to come out but knowing no way of leaving the tracks because to stop would bring the train crushing down upon him and to attempt to leave across the other tracks would mean to run into a hot third rail as high as his waist which threw blue sparks that blinded his eyes until he could hardly see.

He heard singing and the audience was clapping its hands.

> Shoot the liquor to him, Jim, boy!
> Clap-clap-clap
> Well a-calla the cop
> He's blowing his top!
> Shoot the liquor to him, Jim, boy!

Bitter anger grew within him at the singing. They think I'm crazy. Well let 'em laugh. I'll do what I got to do.

He was standing in an attitude of intense listening when he saw that they were watching something on the stage behind him. He felt weak. But when he turned he saw no one. If only his thumb did not ache so. Now they were applauding. And for a moment he thought that the wheel had stopped. But that was impossible, his thumb still pressed the button. Then he saw them. Two men in uniform beckoned from the end of the stage. They were coming toward him, walking in step, slowly, like a tap-dance team returning for a third encore. But their shoulders shot forward, and he backed away, looking wildly about. There was nothing to fight them with. He had only the long black cord which led to a plug somewhere back stage, and he couldn't use that because it operated the bingo wheel. He backed slowly, fixing the men with his eyes as his lips stretched over his teeth in a tight, fixed grin; moved toward the end of the stage and realizing that he couldn't go much further, for suddenly the cord became taut and he couldn't afford to break the cord. But he had to do something. The audience was howling. Suddenly he stopped dead, seeing the men halt, their legs lifted as in an interrupted step of a slow-motion dance. There was nothing to do but run in the other direction and he dashed forward, slipping and sliding. The men fell back, surprised. He struck out violently going past.

"Grab him!"

He ran, but all too quickly the cord tightened, resistingly, and he turned and ran back again. This time he slipped them, and discovered by running in a circle before the wheel he could keep the cord from tightening. But this way he had to flail his arms to keep the men away. Why couldn't they leave a man alone? He ran, circling.

"Ring down the curtain," someone yelled. But they couldn't do that. If they did the wheel flashing from the projection room would be cut off. But they had him before he could tell them so, trying to pry open his fist, and he was wrestling and trying to bring his knees into the fight and holding on to the button, for it was his life. And now he was down, seeing a foot coming down, crushing his wrist cruelly, down, as he saw the wheel whirling serenely above.

"I can't give it up," he screamed. Then quietly, in a confidential tone, "Boys, I really can't give it up."

It landed hard against his head. And in the blank moment they had it away from him, completely now. He fought them trying to pull him up from the stage as he watched the wheel spin slowly to a stop. Without surprise he saw it rest at double zero.

"You see," he pointed bitterly.

"Sure, boy, sure, it's O.K.," one of the men said smiling.

And seeing the man bow his head to someone he could not see, he felt very, very happy; he would receive what all the winners received.

But as he warmed in the justice of the man's tight smile he did not see the man's slow wink, nor see the bow-legged man behind him step clear of the swiftly descending curtain and set himself for a blow. He only felt the dull pain exploding in his skull, and he knew even as it slipped out of him that his luck had run out on the stage.

1944

NIGHT-SEA JOURNEY

JOHN BARTH

"ONE WAY or another, no matter which theory of our journey is correct, it's myself I address; to whom I rehearse as to a stranger our history and condition, and will disclose my secret hope though I sink for it.

"Is the journey my invention? Do the night, the sea, exist at all, I ask myself, apart from my experience of them? Do I myself exist, or is this a dream? Sometimes I wonder. And if I am, who am I? The Heritage I supposedly transport? But how can I be both vessel and contents? Such are the questions that beset my intervals of rest.

"My trouble is, I lack conviction. Many accounts of our situation seem plausible to me—where and what we are, why we swim and whither. But implausible ones as well, perhaps especially those, I must admit as possibly correct. Even likely. If at times, in certain humors—stroking in unison, say, with my neighbors and chanting with them 'Onward! Upward'—I have supposed that we have after all a common Maker, Whose nature and motives we may not know, but Who engendered us in some mysterious wise and launched us forth toward some end known but to Him—if (for a moodslength only) I have been able to entertain such notions, very popular in certain quarters, it is because our night-sea journey partakes of their absurdity. One might even say: I can believe them *because* they are absurd.

"Has that been said before?

"Another paradox: it appears to be these recesses from swimming that sustain me in the swim. Two measures onward and upward, flailing with the rest, then I float exhausted and dispirited, brood upon the night, the sea, the journey, while the flood bears me a measure back and down: slow progress, but I live, I live, and make my way, aye, past many a drowned comrade in the end, stronger, worthier than I, victims of their unremitting *joie de nager.*[1] I have seen the best swimmers of my generation go under. Numberless the number of the dead! Thousands drown as I think this thought, millions as I rest before returning to the swim. And scores, hundreds of millions have expired since we surged forth, brave in our innocence, upon our dreadful way. 'Love! Love!' we sang then, a quarter-billion strong, and churned the warm sea white with joy of swimming! Now all are gone down—the buoyant, the sodden, leaders and followers, all gone under, while wretched I swim on. Yet these same reflective intervals that keep me afloat have led me into wonder, doubt, despair—strange emotions for a swimmer!—have led me, even, to suspect . . . that our night-sea journey is without meaning.

"Indeed, if I have yet to join the hosts of the suicides, it is because (fatigue apart) I find it no meaningfuller to drown myself than to go on swimming.

"I know that there are those who seem actually to enjoy the night-sea; who claim to love swimming for its own sake, or sincerely believe that 'reaching the Shore,' 'transmitting the Heritage' (*Whose* Heritage, I'd like to know? And to whom?) is worth the staggering cost. I do not. Swimming itself I find at best not actively unpleasant, more often tiresome, not infrequently a torment. Arguments from function and design

[1] Joy of swimming.

don't impress me: granted that we can and do swim, that in a manner of speaking our long tails and streamlined heads are 'meant for' swimming; it by no means follows—for me, at least—that we *should* swim, or otherwise endeavor to 'fulfill our destiny.' Which is to say, Someone Else's destiny, since ours, so far as I can see, is merely to perish, one way or another, soon or late. The heartless zeal of our (departed) leaders, like the blind ambition and good cheer of my own youth, appalls me now; for the death of my comrades I am inconsolable. If the night-sea journey has justification, it is not for us swimmers ever to discover it.

"Oh, to be sure, 'Love!' one heard on every side: 'Love it is that drives and sustains us!' I translate: we don't know *what* drives and sustains us, only that we are most miserably driven and, imperfectly, sustained. *Love* is how we call our ignorance of what whips us. 'To reach the Shore,' then: but what if the Shore exists in the fancies of us swimmers merely, who dream it to account for the dreadful fact that we swim, have always and only swum, and continue swimming without respite (myself excepted) until we die? Supposing even that there *were* a Shore—that, as a cynical companion of mine once imagined, we rise from the drowned to discover all those vulgar superstitions and exalted metaphors to be literal truth: the giant Maker of us all, the Shores of Light beyond our night-sea journey!—whatever would a swimmer do there? The fact is, when we imagine the Shore, what comes to mind is just the opposite of our condition: no more night, no more sea, no more journeying. In short, the blissful estate of the drowned.

" 'Ours not to stop and think; ours but to swim and sink. . . .' Because a moment's thought reveals the pointlessness of swimming. 'No matter,' I've heard some say, even as they gulped their last: 'The night-sea journey may be absurd, but here we swim, will-we nill-we, against the flood, onward and upward, toward a Shore that may not exist and couldn't be reached if it did.' The thoughtful swimmer's choices, then, they say, are two: give over thrashing and go under for good, or embrace the absurdity; affirm in and for itself the night-sea journey; swim on with neither motive nor destination, for the sake of swimming, and compassionate moreover with your fellow swimmer, we being all at sea and equally in the dark. I find neither course acceptable. If not even the hypothetical Shore can justify a sea-full of drownèd comrades, to speak of the swim-in-itself as somehow doing so strikes me as obscene. I continue to swim—but only because blind habit, blind instinct, blind fear of drowning are still more strong than the horror of our journey. And if on occasion I have assisted a fellowthrasher, joined in the cheers and songs, even passed along to others strokes of genius from the drownèd great, it's that I shrink by temperament from making myself conspicuous. To paddle off in one's own direction, assert one's independent right-of-way, overrun one's fellows without compunction, or dedicate oneself entirely to pleasures and diversions without regard for conscience—I can't finally condemn those who journey in this wise; in half my moods I envy them and despise the weak vitality that keeps me from following their example. But in reasonabler moments I remind myself that it's their very freedom and self-responsibility I reject, as more dramatically absurd, in our senseless circumstances, than tailing along in conventional fashion. Suicides, rebels, affirmers of the paradox —nay-sayers and yea-sayers alike to our fatal journey—I finally shake my head at them. And splash sighing past their corpses, one by one, as past a hundred sorts of others: friends, enemies, brothers; fools, sages, brutes—and nobodies, million upon million. I envy them all.

"A poor irony: that I, who find abhorrent and tautological the doctrine of survival of the fittest (*fitness* meaning, in my experience, nothing more than survival-ability, a talent whose only demonstration is the fact of survival, but whose chief ingredients seem to be strength, guile, callousness), may be the sole remaining swimmer! But the doctrine is false as well as repellent: Chance drowns the worthy with the unworthy, bears up the unfit with the fit by whatever definition, and makes the night-sea journey essentially *haphazard* as well as murderous and unjustified.

" 'You only swim once.' Why bother, then?

" 'Except ye drown, ye shall not reach the Shore of Life.' Poppycock.

"One of my late companions—that same cynic with the curious fancy, among the first to drown—entertained us with odd conjectures while we waited to begin our journey. A favorite theory of his was that the Father does exist, and did indeed make us and the sea we swim—but not a-purpose or even consciously; He made us, as it were, despite Himself, as we make waves with every tail-thrash, and may be unaware of our existence. Another was that He knows we're here but doesn't care what happens to us, inasmuch as He creates (voluntarily or not) other seas and swimmers at more or less regular intervals. In bitterer moments, such as just before he drowned, my friend even supposed that our Maker wished us unmade; there was indeed a Shore, he'd argue, which could save at least some of us from drowning and toward which it was our function to struggle—but for reasons unknowable to us He wanted desperately to prevent our reaching that happy place and fulfilling our destiny. Our 'Father,' in short, was our adversary and would-be killer! No less outrageous, and offensive to traditional opinion, were the fellow's speculations on the nature of our Maker: that He might well be no swimmer Himself at all, but some sort of monstrosity, perhaps even tailless; that He might be stupid, malicious, insensible, perverse, or asleep and dreaming; that the end for which He created and launched us forth, and which we flagellate ourselves to fathom, was perhaps immoral, even obscene. Et cetera, et cetera: there was no end to the chap's conjectures, or the impoliteness of his fancy; I have reason to suspect that his early demise, whether planned by 'our Maker' or not, was expedited by certain fellow-swimmers indignant at his blasphemies.

"In other moods, however (he was as given to moods as I), his theorizing would become half-serious, so it seemed to me, especially upon the subjects of Fate and Immortality, to which our youthful conversations often turned. Then his harangues, if no less fantastical, grew solemn and obscure, and if he was still baiting us, his passion undid the joke. His objection to popular opinions of the hereafter, he would declare, was their claim to general validity. Why need believers hold that *all* the drownèd rise to be judged at journey's end, and non-believers that drowning is final without exception? In *his* opinion (so he'd vow at least), nearly everyone's fate was permanent death; indeed he took a sour pleasure in supposing that every 'Maker' made thousands of separate seas in His creative lifetime, each populated like ours with millions of swimmers, and that in almost every instance both sea and swimmers were utterly annihilated, whether accidentally or by malevolent design. (Nothing if not pluralistical, he imagined there might be millions and billions of 'Fathers,' perhaps in some 'night-sea' of their own!) However—and here he turned infidels against him with the faithful—he professed to believe that in possibly a single night-sea per thousand, say, one of its quarter-billion swimmers (that is, one swimmer in two hundred fifty billions) achieved a qualified immortality. In some cases the rate might be slightly higher; in others it was vastly lower, for just as there are swimmers of every degree of proficiency, including some who drown before the journey starts, unable to swim at all, and others created drowned, as it were, so he imagined what can only be termed impotent Creators, Makers unable to Make, as well as uncommonly fertile ones and all grades between. And it pleased him to deny any necessary relation between a Maker's productivity and His other virtues—including, even, the quality of His creatures.

"I could go on (*he* surely did) with his elaboration of these mad notions—such as that swimmers in other night-seas needn't be of our kind; that Makers themselves might belong to different *species,* so to speak; that our particular Maker mightn't Himself be immortal, or that we might be not only His emissaries but His 'immortality,' continuing His life and our own, transmogrified, beyond our individual deaths. Even this modified immortality (meaningless to me) he conceived as relative and contingent, subject to accidental or deliberate termination: his pet hypothesis was that Makers and swimmers *each generate the other*—against all odds, their number being so great—and that any given 'immortality-chain' could terminate after any number of cycles, so that what was 'immortal' (still speaking relatively) was only the cyclic process of incarnation, which itself might have a beginning and an end. Alternatively he liked to imagine cycles within cycles, either finite or infinite: for example, the 'night-sea,' as it were, in which Makers 'swam' and created night-seas and swimmers like ourselves, might be the creation of a larger Maker, Himself one of many, Who in turn et cetera. Time itself he regarded as relative to our experience, like magnitude: who knew but what, with each thrash of our tails, minuscule seas and swimmers, whole eternities, came to pass—as ours, perhaps, and our Maker's Maker's, was elapsing between the strokes of some supertail, in a slower order of time?

"Naturally I hooted with the others at this nonsense. We were young then, and had only the dimmest notion of what lay ahead; in our ignorance we imagined night-sea journeying to be a positively heroic enterprise. Its meaning and value we never questioned; to be sure, some must go down by the way, a pity no doubt, but to win a race requires that others lose, and like all my fellows I took for granted that I would be the winner. We milled and swarmed, impatient to be off, never mind where or why, only to try our youth against the realities of night and sea; if we indulged the skeptic at all, it was as a droll, half-contemptible mascot. When he died in the initial slaughter, no one cared.

"And even now I don't subscribe to all his views—but I no longer scoff. The horror of our history has purged me of opinions, as of vanity, confidence, spirit, charity, hope, vitality, everything—except dull dread and a kind of melancholy, stunned persistence. What leads me to recall his fancies is my growing suspicion that I, of all swimmers, may be the sole survivor of this fell journey, tale-bearer of a generation. This suspicion, together with the recent sea-change, suggests to me now that nothing is impossible, not even my late companion's wildest visions, and brings me to a certain desperate resolve, the point of my chronicling.

"Very likely I have lost my senses. The carnage at our setting out; our decimation by whirlpool, poisoned cataract, sea-convulsion; the panic stampedes, mutinies, slaughters, mass suicides; the mounting evidence that none will survive the journey—add to these anguish and fatigue; it were a miracle if sanity stayed afloat. Thus I admit, with the other possibilities, that the present sweetening and calming of the sea, and what seems to be a kind of vasty presence, song, or summons from the near upstream, may be hallucinations of disordered sensibility....

"Perhaps, even, I am drowned already. Surely I was never meant for the rough-and-tumble of the swim; not impossibly I perished at the outset and have only imaged the night-sea journey from some final deep. In any case, I'm no longer young, and it is we spent old swimmers, disabused of every illusion, who are most vulnerable to dreams.

"Sometimes I think I am my drownèd friend.

"Out with it: I've begun to believe, not only that *She* exists, but that She lies not far ahead, and stills the sea, and draws me Herward! Aghast, I recollect his maddest notion: that our destination (which existed, mind, in but one night-sea out of hundreds and thousands) was no Shore, as commonly conceived, but a mysterious being, indescribable except by paradox and vaguest figure: wholly different from us swimmers, yet our complement; the death of us, yet our salvation and resurrection; simultaneously our journey's end, mid-point, and commencement; not membered and thrashing like us, but a motionless or hugely gliding sphere of unimaginable dimension; self-contained, yet dependent absolutely, in some wise, upon the chance (always monstrously improbable) that one of us will survive the night-sea journey and reach... Her! *Her,* he called it, or *She,* which is to say, Other-than-a-he. I shake my head; the thing is too preposterous; it is myself I talk to, to keep my reason in this awful darkness. There is no She! There is no You! I rave to myself; it's Death alone that hears and summons. To the drowned, all seas are calm....

"Listen: my friend maintained that in every order of creation there are two sorts of creators, contrary yet complementary, one of which gives rise to seas and swimmers, the other to the Night-which-contains-the-sea and to What-waits-at-the-journey's-end: the former, in short, to destiny, the latter to destination (and both profligately, involuntarily, perhaps indifferently or unwittingly). The 'purpose' of the night-sea journey—but not necessarily of the journeyer or of either Maker!—my friend could describe only in abstractions: *consummation, transfiguration, union of contraries, transcension of categories.* When we laughed, he would shrug and admit that he understood the business no better than we, and thought it ridiculous, dreary, possibly obscene. 'But one of you,' he'd add with his wry smile, 'may be the Hero destined to complete the night-sea journey and be one with Her. Chances are, of course, you won't make it.' He himself, he declared, was not even going to try; the whole idea repelled him; if we chose to dismiss it as an ugly fiction, so much the better for us; thrash, splash, and be merry, we were soon enough drowned. But there it was, he could not say how he knew or why he bothered to tell us, any more than he could say what would happen after She and Hero, Shore and Swimmer, 'merged identities' to become something both and neither. He quite agreed with me that if the issue of that magical union had no memory of the night-sea journey, for example, it enjoyed a poor sort of immortality; even poorer if, as he rather imagined, a swimmer-hero plus a She equaled or became merely another Maker of future night-seas and the rest, at such incredible expense of life. This being the case—he was persuaded it was—the merciful thing to do was refuse to participate; the genuine heroes, in his opinion, were the suicides, and the hero of heroes would be the swimmer who, in the very presence of the Other, refused Her proffered 'immortality' and thus put an end to at least one cycle of catastrophes.

"How we mocked him! Our moment came, we hurtled forth, pretending to glory in the adventure, thrashing, singing, cursing, strangling, rationalizing, rescuing, killing, inventing rules and stories and relationships, giving up, struggling on, but dying all, and still in darkness, until only a battered remnant was left to croak 'Onward, upward,' like a bitter echo. Then they too fell silent—victims, I can only presume, of the last frightful wave—and the moment came when I also, utterly desolate and spent, thrashed my last and gave myself over to the current, to sink or float as might be, but swim no more. Whereupon, marvelous to tell, in an instant the sea grew still! Then warmly, gently, the great tide turned, began to bear me, as it does now, onward and upward will-I nill-I, like a flood of joy—and I recalled with dismay my dead friend's teaching.

"I am not deceived. This new emotion is Her doing; the desire that possesses me is Her bewitchment. Lucidity passes from me; in a moment I'll cry 'Love!' bury myself in Her side, and be 'transfigured.' Which is to say, I die already; this fellow transported by passion is not I; *I am he who abjures and rejects the night-sea journey!* I. . . .

"I am all love. 'Come!' She whispers, and I have no will.

"You who I may be about to become, whatever You are: with the last twitch of my real self I beg You to listen. It is *not* love that sustains me! No; though Her magic makes me burn to sing the contrary, and though I drown even now for the blasphemy, I will say truth. What has fetched me across this dreadful sea is a single hope, gift of my poor dead comrade: that You may be stronger-willed than I, and that by sheer force of concentration I may transmit to You, along with Your official Heritage, a private legacy of awful recollection and negative resolve. Mad as it may be, my dream is that some unimaginable embodiment of myself (or myself plus Her if that's how it must be) will come to find itself expressing, in however garbled or radical a translation, some reflection of these reflections. If against all odds this comes to pass, may You to whom, through whom I speak, do what I cannot: terminate this aimless, brutal business! Stop Your hearing against Her song! Hate love!

"Still alive, afloat, afire. Farewell then my penultimate hope: that one may be sunk for direst blasphemy on the very shore of the Shore. Can it be (my old friend would smile) that only utterest nay-sayers survive the night? But even that were Sense, and there is no sense, only senseless love, senseless death. Whoever echoes these reflections: be more courageous than their author! An end to night-sea journeys! Make no more! And forswear me when I shall forswear myself, deny myself, plunge into Her who summons, singing . . .

" 'Love! Love! Love!' "

1966

BIOGRAPHICAL NOTES

AIKEN

Conrad Aiken (1889–1973), born in Savannah, Georgia, was educated at the Middlesex School, Concord, Massachusetts, and at Harvard University. Although he is known primarily as a poet, his fiction, much of it psychological, often complements his poetry. He wrote five novels, beginning with *Blue Voyage* (1927). His short stories appeared in three volumes between 1925 and 1934, and were collected in *Short Stories of Conrad Aiken* (1950) and his *Collected Short Stories* (1960).

ANDERSON

Sherwood Anderson (1876–1941) was born in Camden, Ohio, the son of an itinerant harness maker and house painter. After relatively little formal education and a number of odd jobs, he served in Cuba during the Spanish-American War. On his return in 1899, he became an advertising writer in Chicago and later managed a paint factory near Cleveland, Ohio. In 1912, he gave up the world of business to begin a writing career in Chicago. With the publication of *Winesburg, Ohio* in 1919, Anderson's reputation as a major short story writer was established and continued to grow with later volumes of stories: *The Triumph of the Egg* (1921), *Horses and Men* (1923), and *Death in the Woods* (1933). His writings also include three autobiographical works and a number of novels.

BABEL

Isaac Babel (1894–1941) was born in the Moldavanka district of Odessa, Russia, the son of a Jewish businessman, who made the boy study "Yiddish, the Bible, and the Talmud." After attending commercial school, he moved in 1915 to St. Petersburg, where in the following year Maxim Gorki published Babel's first two stories. In 1917, he enlisted in the imperial Russian army, but soon joined the Bolshevik forces. His *Odessa Tales* appeared in 1924, followed two years later by the highly acclaimed *Red Cavalry* stories. Because the stark realism of his stories was soon criticized as defaming Russian heroes, Babel was arrested in 1939, tried by a military court, and imprisoned in Siberia, where he died on 17 March 1941. Works available in English include *Red Cavalry* (1929), *Collected Stories* (1955), *Lyubka the Cossack, and Other Stories* (1963), and *You Must Know Everything* (1969).

BALDWIN

James Baldwin (1924–) was born in New York City, where he graduated from De Witt Clinton High School in 1942. From the age of fourteen until he lost his faith three years later, Baldwin was an evangelical preacher in Harlem. Aside from some essays and reviews, he published little until his first novel, *Go Tell It on the Mountain,* written over ten years, appeared in 1952, followed by *Giovanni's Room* (1956), *Another Country* (1962), *Tell Me How Long the Train's Been Gone* (1968), and *If Beale Street Could Talk* (1974). Besides several plays and a collection of stories, *Going to Meet the Man* (1965), he has also produced five volumes of essays, including *Nobody Knows My Name* (1961) and *The Fire Next Time* (1963).

BARTH

John Barth (1930–) was born in Cambridge, Maryland, and educated at the Juilliard School of Music and Johns Hopkins University. His first novel, *The Floating Opera,* appeared in 1956, followed two years later by *The End of the Road.* His penchant for experimentation and parody is most apparent in *The Sot-Weed Factor* (1960) and *Giles Goat Boy* (1966), as well as in his two collections of stories, *Lost in the Funhouse: Fiction for Print, Tape, Live Voices* (1968) and *Chimera* (1972).

BIERCE

Ambrose Bierce (1842–1914?), born in Meigs County, Ohio, received little formal education other than a year at the Kentucky Military Institute. Joining the Union army at nineteen, he saw service throughout the Civil War, an experience that later became the inspiration for many of his best stories. After the war, Bierce began a journalistic and literary career in San Francisco, soon becoming an editor, an influential columnist, and, by the 1880s, virtually the literary dictator of the West coast. Although his first volume of sketches, *The Friend's Delight,* was published in 1873, his best stories were not collected until twenty years later: *Tales of Soldiers and Civilians* (1891) and *Can Such Things Be?* (1893). Bierce disappeared on a trip to Mexico in 1913; he is believed to have died there in 1914.

BORGES

Jorge Luis Borges (1899–) was born in Buenos Aires, Argentina, and educated at the Collège de Genève, Switzerland. A prolific poet and essayist in the 1920s, Borges slowly turned to fiction in the following decade. Encouraged by the success of "Pierre Menard, Author of the *Quijote*" (1938), he produced over the next eleven years three volumes of stories that established his fame: *The Garden of the Forking Paths* (1941), *Ficciónes* (1944), and *El Aleph* (1949). After the fall of Perón in 1955, Borges was named director of the national library and professor of English literature at the University of Buenos Aires. Works available in English include *Labyrinths* (1962), *Ficciónes* (1962), *A Personal Anthology* (1967), and *The Book of Sand* (1977).

BOWEN

Elizabeth Bowen (1899–1973) was born in Dublin of Anglo-Irish descent and was taken to Kent, England, at the age of seven. Completing her formal education in 1916, she spent the remainder of the First World War in Dublin working in a hospital for shell-shocked veterans. A volume of her short stories, *Encounters,* was published in 1923, followed by *The Hotel* (1927), her first novel. Her principal works of fiction include *The House in Paris* (1935), *The Death of the Heart* (1938), and *The Heat of the Day* (1949), as well as seven collections of short stories.

CAPOTE

Truman Capote (1924–) was born in New Orleans and educated in New York City at Trinity School and St. John's Academy. In 1948, he won the O. Henry Award for "Shut a Final Door." His early stories were collected in *A Tree of Night and Other Stories* (1949), and his first novel, *Other Voices, Other Rooms,* appeared in 1948, followed by *The Grass Harp* (1951), *Breakfast at Tiffany's* (1958), and *In Cold Blood* (1966).

CHEKHOV

Anton Chekhov (1860–1904), Russian playwright and short story writer, was born in Taganrog on the Sea of Azov. The grandson of a serf who had bought his own freedom, Chekhov attended the classical Gymnasium and in 1879 entered the medical school of Moscow University. While a medical student, he supported himself and his family through contributions to humor magazines, using the pseudonym Antosha Chekhonte. By 1885, three hundred of his stories had been published, though the majority of them were superficial, even hack work. The important stories on which his reputation rests began to be published in 1886 and were collected in three volumes: *Motley Stories* (1886), *At Twilight* (1887), and *Stories* (1888). His greatest plays began to appear in the next decade: *The Sea Gull* (1896), *Uncle Vanya* (1899), *The Three Sisters* (1901), and *The Cherry Orchard* (1904).

CONRAD

Joseph Conrad (1857–1924) was born Józef Teodor Konrad Nalecz Korzeniowski at Berdyczew, Poland, then under Russian control. The son of a Polish revolutionary and poet, he was orphaned at eleven and brought up by his uncle. At seventeen he became a sailor in the merchant marine, a career he followed for twenty years, moving up to his first command in the British merchant navy in 1888. Although he had arrived in England in 1878 knowing little English, he began his writing career in his adopted language only a decade later with *Almayer's Folly,* a novel published in 1895. With the appearance of *Outcast of the Island* (1896), his career as a sailor gradually ended, although his writings did not make him financially secure until 1910. Conrad's best novels include *Lord Jim* (1900), *Nostromo* (1904), *The Secret Agent* (1907), *Under Western Eyes* (1911), *Chance* (1913), and *Victory* (1915).

DINESEN

Isak Dinesen (1885–1962), the pseudonym of Karen Blixen, was born in Rungstedlund, Denmark. She studied English at Oxford University and painting in Copenhagen, Paris, and Rome. In 1914, she went with her husband to British East Africa (now Kenya) to live on a large coffee plantation. After a divorce in 1921, she managed the plantation alone for ten years. Writing in English, which she herself translated into Danish, she first came to prominence with *Seven Gothic Tales* (1934), followed by *Winter's Tales* (1942), *Last Tales* (1957), *Anecdotes of Destiny* (1958), and the posthumous collection, *Carnival* (1977).

ELLISON

Ralph Ellison (1914–) was born in Oklahoma City and educated at the Tuskegee Institute in Alabama. He has lectured and taught in Europe and at many American universities. His literary reputation rests primarily on *The Invisible Man* (1952), an extraordinary first novel that was chosen by a poll of two hundred writers and critics as the most important work of American fiction to appear between 1945 and 1965. Besides a collection of essays, *Shadow and Act* (1964), Ellison has published eleven short stories, as yet uncollected, as well as six excerpts from a novel-in-progress.

FAULKNER

William Faulkner (1897–1962), born in New Albany, Mississippi, spent most of his life in nearby Oxford. After serving in the Canadian air force during the First World War, Faulkner attended the University of Mississippi at Oxford from 1919 to 1921. Encouraged and helped by the writer Sherwood Anderson, whom he met in New Orleans in 1924, Faulkner wrote his first novel, *Soldier's Pay* (1926). With the publication in 1929 of *Sartoris* and the masterful *The Sound and the Fury,* the saga of Yoknapatawpha, Faulkner's fictional Mississippi county, began to evolve. Although most of the novels and stories that he wrote over the next thirty years elaborated on that saga, it is his three great novels of the thirties—*As I Lay Dying* (1930), *Light in August* (1932), and *Absalom, Absalom!* (1936)—together with *The Sound and the Fury* that probably constitute Faulkner's greatest achievement, and led to his receiving the 1950 Nobel Prize for literature.

GREENE

Graham Greene (1904–), born in Berkhamsted, Hertfordshire, England, was educated at the Berkhamsted School, where his father was headmaster, and later at Balliol College, Oxford. From 1926 to 1930, he was sub-editor of the London *Times,* and between 1935 and 1939, film critic of the *Spectator,* later becoming its literary editor. His first novel, *The Man Within,* was published in 1929. His principal novels, strongly colored by his Catholicism, include *Brighton Rock* (1938), *The Power and the Glory* (1940), *The Heart of the Matter* (1948), and *The End of the Affair* (1951). Greene's short fiction has been collected in *Twenty-One Stories* (1947) and in his *Collected Stories* (1973).

HAWTHORNE

Nathaniel Hawthorne (1804–1864) was born in Salem, Massachusetts, and graduated from Bowdoin College, Maine, in 1825, the classmate of Longfellow and Franklin Pierce. After a literary apprenticeship of twelve years, which he spent secluded in Salem, he published his first volume of short stories, *Twice-Told Tales,* in 1837. Married in 1842, he lived four years in the Old Manse at Concord, the neighbor of Thoreau and Emerson, before being appointed surveyor at the Salem custom house in 1846, the year *Mosses from an Old Manse,* another collection of stories, appeared. With the publication of *The Scarlet Letter* in 1850, his reputation as a major American writer was established, and he moved to Lenox, Massachusetts, to begin his most prolific period: *The House of Seven Gables* (1851), *The Blithedale Romance* (1852), and *The Marble Faun* (1860).

HEMINGWAY

Ernest Hemingway (1898–1961) was born in Oak Park, Illinois, and spent much of his boyhood in Michigan. After graduating from high school and working for a short period as a reporter on the Kansas City *Star,* he went to Europe during the First World War, serving in an American ambulance unit and later in an Italian combat force. Severely wounded, he later returned to Europe as correspondent for the Toronto *Star.* Joining such other expatriates as Gertrude Stein, F. Scott Fitzgerald, and Ezra Pound in Paris in the early twenties, Hemingway began his literary career with *Three Stories and Ten Poems* (1923) and *In Our Time* (1924), a collection of stories and sketches. His best novels, *The Sun Also Rises* (1926) and *A Farewell to Arms* (1929), soon followed. Other important works of fiction include *To Have and Have Not* (1937), *For Whom the Bell Tolls* (1940), and *The Old Man and the Sea* (1952), as well as two memorable books of nonfiction: *Death in the Afternoon* (1932) and *The Green Hills of Africa* (1935). Hemingway was awarded the Nobel Prize for literature in 1954. He died of a self-inflicted gunshot wound in 1961.

JACKSON

Shirley Jackson (1919–1965) was born in San Francisco and educated at Syracuse University, from which she was graduated in 1940, the year of her marriage to literary critic Stanley Edgar Hyman. With the publication of "My Life with R. H. Macy" in *The New Republic* in 1941, her short stories began to appear nationally. They were collected in *The Lottery, or The Adventures of James Harris* (1949) and in two posthumous volumes: *The Magic of Shirley Jackson* (1966) and *Come Along With Me* (1968).

Beginning with *The Road Through the Wall* (1948), she wrote six novels, including *The Bird's Nest* (1954) and *The Haunting of Hill House* (1959).

JACOBSON

Dan Jacobson (1929–) was born in Johannesburg, South Africa, of East European parents and was educated at the University of Witwatersrand. He left South Africa in 1954 and eventually settled in England. His first novel, *The Trap* (1955), like his next four novels, deals with South Africa. In his more recent novels, *The Rape of Tamar* (1970) and *The Wonder-Worker* (1973), he has abandoned this subject. Jacobson has also published three collections of short stories: *Long Way from London* (1958), *The Zulu and the Zeide* (1959), and *Through the Wilderness* (1968).

JAMES

Henry James (1843–1916), younger brother of the Harvard psychologist and philosopher William James, was born in New York City and privately educated, largely in Europe. After briefly attending Harvard Law School, he began his literary career with reviews and short stories. His earliest volume of stories, *A Passionate Pilgrim,* appeared in 1871, followed in 1875 by the serialization of his first important novel, *Roderick Hudson.* By 1876, James had permanently settled in England, where he was to remain through most of his prolific life. His major novels, many dealing with the international theme of Americans in Europe or Europeans in America, include *The American* (1877), *The Europeans* (1878), *The Portrait of a Lady* (1881), *The Princess Casamassima* (1887), and the three great novels of his final creative years: *The Wings of the Dove* (1902), *The Ambassadors* (1903), and *The Golden Bowl* (1904). Among his more than one hundred shorter works of fiction are such remarkable artistic achievements as *Daisy Miller* (1879), *The Spoils of Poynton* (1897), and *The Turn of the Screw* (1898).

JOYCE

James Joyce (1882–1941) was born in Dublin, Ireland, and educated at Jesuit schools and at University College, Dublin. After abandoning his ideas of becoming a physician or trying his hand as a teacher, he began his first novel, *Stephen Hero,* later rewritten as *Portrait of the Artist as a Young Man* (1916). In 1905, he accepted a position at a Berlitz school in Trieste. Attempts to get his collection of short stories, *Dubliners,* published proved futile until 1914. With the outbreak of the First World War,

Joyce moved to Zürich, Switzerland, where he worked on *Ulysses* (1922), the monumental novel depicting one day in the life of its hero, Leopold Bloom. His last novel, *Finnegans Wake* (1939), which he worked on for seventeen years, depicts the subconscious world of dreams.

KAFKA

Franz Kafka (1883–1924) was born in Prague, Czechoslovakia, into a Jewish middle-class family and educated at the German Gymnasium and German University at Prague, receiving his doctorate in law in 1906. Two years later, he joined the semigovernmental Worker's Accident Insurance Institute, where he remained until tuberculosis forced his retirement in 1922. Since only a few of his stories were published during his lifetime, he was little known at the time of his death in 1924, gaining recognition only after Max Brod, his literary executor, in defiance of his friend's wishes, published the extant manuscripts that Kafka had wanted destroyed. These include three unfinished novels, *The Trial* (1925), *The Castle* (1926), and *Amerika* (1927), as well as many short stories, collected in translation in his *Complete Stories* (1971).

LAWRENCE

David Herbert Lawrence (1885–1930), son of a coal miner, was born and raised in Eastwood, a mining town near Nottingham, England. Encouraged by his mother, a former teacher, Lawrence attended Nottingham High School and later Nottingham University. Though he was briefly a schoolteacher, the publication of his first novel, *The White Peacock* (1911), led him to give up teaching for a career as a writer. *Sons and Lovers,* his first major novel, appeared in 1913; others include *The Rainbow* (1915), *Women in Love* (1920), *Aaron's Rod* (1922), *The Plumed Serpent* (1926), *Lady Chatterley's Lover* (1928), and his posthumous novelette, *The Man Who Died* (1930). Lawrence was not only a masterful writer of novels and short stories but also a poet, essayist, and critic of distinction.

LONDON

Jack London (1876–1916) was born in San Francisco, the illegitimate son of an Irish astrologer. He grew up in poverty, doing odd jobs on the Oakland waterfront, and became in his teens an oyster pirate and a hobo. After a year at Oakland High School and one semester at the University of California at Berkeley, he joined in 1894 the Klondike gold rush. Though he found no gold, his experience became the basis for some of his best fiction. In 1900, his first collection of stories, *The Son of Wolf,* appeared, followed in 1903 by *The Call of the Wild,* the novel that made him a best-selling author. By 1913, he was one of the best-paid and most well-known writers in the world. His principal works include *The Sea-Wolf* (1904), *The People of the Abyss* (1903), *The Road* (1907), and *Martin Eden* (1909).

MANSFIELD

Katherine Mansfield (1888–1923), the pseudonym of Kathleen Mansfield Beauchamp, was born near Wellington, New Zealand. In 1902, she went to London to study music at Queen's College, but her interest soon turned to literature. Her first collection of stories, *In a German Pension,* appeared in 1911, when she was only twenty-three. In 1918, she married John Middleton Murry, the well-known critic, whom she had met seven years earlier. Recognition as a major practitioner of the short story came only during the last years of her life with the publication of *Bliss* (1920), *The Garden Party* (1922), and *The Dove's Nest* (1923).

MARSHALL

Paule Marshall (1929–) was born in Brooklyn, New York, of Barbadian parents. After graduating from Brooklyn College, she worked as a librarian, wrote articles for the magazine *Our World,* and began her first novel, *Brown Girl, Brownstone,* published in 1959. *Soul Clap Hands and Sing* (1961) consists of four stories set in Barbados, Brooklyn, British Guiana, and Brazil. A second novel, *The Chosen Place, The Timeless People,* appeared in 1969. She is presently working on a third novel, tentatively entitled *Ibo Landing.*

MAUPASSANT

Guy de Maupassant (1850–1893) was born near Dieppe, in Normandy, France. Educated at a small seminary in Yvetôt, he later attended the *lycée* at Le Havre before going to Paris in 1869 to study law. After service during the Franco-Prussian War (1870–1871), he worked ten years as a government clerk in Paris. During this period, Maupassant's writing skills were developed and perfected under the guidance and exacting discipline of Gustave Flaubert, the great French novelist. With the publication of his first story, "Boule de Suif" (1880), which was a huge success, his stories began to appear regularly in French newspapers. Between 1880 and 1890, he published some three hundred stories besides six novels and three travel books. In 1892, after a mental breakdown during which he tried to commit suicide, he was placed for the remainder of his life in a private asylum.

NABOKOV

Vladimir Nabokov (1899–1977) was born in St. Petersburg, Russia, the son of a distinguished jurist and member of the First Duma. He attended the Tenishev School and published two books of verse before emigrating from Russia with his family in 1919. After studying French and Russian literature at Trinity College, Cambridge, and graduating with honors in 1923, Nabokov resided in Berlin, publishing his first novel, *Mashenka,* in 1926. Arriving in the United States in 1940, he decided to write henceforth in English. *Lolita* (1955) and *Pnim* (1957) were both written while he was teaching at Cornell University, whereas *Pale Fire* (1962) and *Ada* (1969) appeared after the success of *Lolita* had made him wealthy enough to give up teaching. Beginning with *Nine Stories* (1947), five volumes of his stories have appeared in English. His complete writings, if published together, would number about thirty-five volumes.

O'CONNOR, FLANNERY

Flannery O'Connor (1925–1964) was born in Savannah, Georgia, and was graduated from the Georgia State College for Women in 1945. Awarded a fellowship to attend the Writer's Workshop of the University of Iowa, she published her first story, "The Geranium," in *Accent* in 1946. *Wise Blood,* her first novel, appeared in 1952, followed by a volume of stories, *A Good Man Is Hard to Find* in 1955. Before her death from lupus in 1964, she completed a second novel, *The Violent Bear It Away* (1960), and her last collection of stories, *Everything That Rises Must Converge* (1965).

O'CONNOR, FRANK

Frank O'Connor (1903–1966), the pseudonym of Michael O'Donovan, was born and raised in Cork, Ireland, where he attended the Christian Brothers school. After fighting with the Irish Republicans and serving a year in a British prison, O'Connor worked as a librarian in Cork before being appointed to the municipal librarianship of Dublin. In the 1950s much of his time was devoted to teaching at American universities. His early stories appeared in the *Irish Statesman,* and in 1931, *Guests of the Nation,* his first volume of stories, was published. Although he served as a director of the Abbey Theatre from 1935 to 1939 and wrote two significant critical studies, *The Mirror in the Roadway: A Study of the Modern Novel* (1956) and *The Lonely Voice: A Study of the Short Story* (1962), it is in his ten volumes of short stories that he achieved his greatest artistic success.

POE

Edgar Allan Poe (1809–1849) was born in Boston and raised in Richmond, Virginia. After his father's desertion and his mother's death, John Allan became his unofficial guardian in 1811. Educated in England and privately in Richmond, he entered the University of Virginia in 1826, but was soon forced to withdraw because of gambling debts. After the anonymous publication of his *Tamerlane and Other Poems* in 1827, he enlisted for two years in the army, followed by a brief period at West Point. Completely estranged from Allan by 1832, Poe struggled to support himself by his writing, working in a number of editorial positions, notably on the *Southern Literary Messenger.* Although he was beset by poverty, the last decade of his life saw the publication of much of his best work in *Tales of the Grotesque and Arabesque* (1839), *Tales* (1845), and *The Raven and Other Poems* (1845).

SEABOUGH

Samuel Seabough (d. 1883) took over the editorship of the San Andreas *Independent* in 1858. He transferred the newspaper to Stockton, California, in 1861, where it became the Stockton *Independent.* In 1867, Seabough moved to Sacramento to edit the *Union* and later became the chief editorial writer for the San Francisco *Chronicle.*

TWAIN

Mark Twain (1835–1910), pen name of Samuel Clemens, was born in Florida, Missouri, and grew up in the river town of Hannibal, Missouri, which was later portrayed in *Tom Sawyer* (1876) and in his masterpiece, *Huckleberry Finn* (1884). Apprenticed as a printer after the death of his father in 1847, he left Hannibal in 1853 to become a journeyman printer, wandering journalist, and river pilot on the Mississippi. His mastery of humorous writing owes much to his experiences in the far West, particularly as a reporter for the Virginia City (Nevada) *Enterprise* from 1862 to 1863. With the publication of *Innocents Abroad* in 1869, his fame as a humorist was established. Important later works include *Roughing It* (1871), *Life on the Mississippi* (1883), *A Connecticut Yankee in the Court of King Arthur* (1889), *Pudd'nhead Wilson* (1894), and *The Mysterious Stranger,* published posthumously in 1916.

VONNEGUT

Kurt Vonnegut (1922–) was born in Indianapolis, Indiana, and educated at Cornell University, Carnegie Institute of Technology, and, after service in the Second World War, the University of Chicago. In 1947, he became a police reporter and later worked for General Electric, which he satirized in his first novel, *Player Piano* (1951). Since 1950, he has been a freelance writer, whose short stories have been collected in *Canary in a Cathouse* (1961) and *Welcome to the Monkey House* (1968). His novels include *The Sirens of Titan* (1959), *Cat's Cradle* (1963), and *Slaughterhouse-Five* (1969).

WELTY

Eudora Welty (1909–) was born in Jackson, Mississippi, and educated at the Mississippi State College for Women in Columbus, the University of Wisconsin, and the Columbia University School of Advertising. Her literary career began in 1936 with the publication of "Death of a Traveling Salesman." *A Curtain of Green* (1941), her first volume of stories, was followed by three more collections of short fiction plus five novels: *The Robber Bridegroom* (1942), *Delta Wedding* (1946), *The Ponder Heart* (1954), *Losing Battles* (1970), and *The Optimist's Daughter* (1972).

WHARTON

Edith Wharton (1862–1937) was born in New York City into a wealthy, socially prominent family and was privately educated. Her marriage in 1885 to Edward Wharton proved tragic because of his infidelity and recurrent mental illness. In the 1890s, she began to contribute stories and poems to *Scribner's Magazine.* Her earliest volume of stories, *The Greater Inclination,* appeared in 1899, followed by the novelette *Touchstone* (1900) and her first novel, *The Valley of Decision* (1902). By 1911, she had permanently moved to Paris, where she was divorced in 1913. Her principal works include *The House of Mirth* (1905), *Ethan Frome* (1911), *The Custom of the Country* (1913), and *Age of Innocence* (1920).

WILSON

Angus Wilson (1913–), born in Bexhill, Sussex, England, was educated at Westminster School, London, and Merton College, Oxford. He served in the Foreign Office from 1942 to 1946, and was a staff member of the British Museum from 1937 to 1955 and deputy superintendent of its reading room from 1949 to 1955. Since 1963, he has been teaching English literature at the University of East Anglia. Beginning as a short story writer, he published his first volume, *The Wrong Set,* in 1949, followed in 1950 by *Such Darling Dodos.* His earliest novel, *Hemlock and After,* appeared in 1952, followed by six others, including *Anglo-Saxon Attitudes* (1956) and *Late Call* (1964).

A GLOSSARY OF LITERARY TERMS

Action: The event or sequence of events making up a story. An action may be external or internal (taking place within a character's mind).

Allegory: See Figurative Language.

Allusion: An implicit reference to a person, place, event, or object, real or fictitious, outside of the story.

Ambiguity: A word or group of words having several possible meanings. Utilized effectively, such multiple meanings can enrich a writer's means of expression.

Ambivalence: Conflicting feelings, held simultaneously, toward some person or object. William Wilson, for example, both admires and hates his namesake.

Antagonist: The principal opponent of the main character (the *protagonist*). In "The Basement Room," for example, Mrs. Baines is the antagonist.

Atmosphere: The predominant mood (cheerful, foreboding, tense, calm, etc.) that a story evokes.

Cliché: An expression that is no longer fresh or forceful because it has been overworked. Such stale phrases suggest imprecision and insensitivity in a writer, though they may be used deliberately for an *ironic* effect. Note Charlotte's expressions in "Next Door." Trite ideas and situations may also be considered clichés.

Connotation: See Denotation.

Denotation: The explicit or specific meaning of a word. *Connotation,* on the contrary, refers to the implicit or suggestive meanings that have come to be attached to some words through particular usage or circumstances. The word *baby,* for example, *denotes* a very young child, but it also *connotes* such suggestive meanings as innocence and helplessness, which the more formal word *infant* would not evoke.

Denouement: The final resolution, clarification, or unraveling of the plot.

Dialogue: Those parts of a story that directly present conversation between characters. In such works as "Paste" and "The Eyes," dialogue is a crucial means of enlightening both characters and reader.

Diction: A writer's choice of words, wording. Not to be confused with clarity of enunciation, an alternate meaning of *diction* that refers to oral expression rather than written language.

Didactic: Designed to be clearly instructive.

Dramatized Narrator: See Point of View.

Episode: An incident or event that is part of the plot but has a unity of its own. An *episodic* work of fiction is made up of loosely joined episodes having little causal connection.

Exposition: The presentation of essential background information about what occurred before the action of the story commenced.

Figurative Language: Explicit or implicit comparisons in which one thing is likened to another. The most explicit comparison is a *simile,* in which two objects are connected by *as* or *like:* Internal commerce continually moves through the romantic pass of the Notch like through a great artery. Without the connective *like,* the statement becomes a *metaphor:* The romantic pass of the Notch is a great artery through which internal commerce continually moves. In both these comparisons, the literal object *pass* is being likened to a figurative counterpart *artery.* Adopting I. A. Richard's terminology, we may call the object (pass) the *tenor* and its figurative counterpart (artery) the *vehicle.* Because this metaphor has only one point of resemblance, it is a *simple metaphor.* When correspondences are increased to several areas, an *extended metaphor* results: "The romantic pass of the Notch is a great artery, through which the life-blood of internal commerce is continually throbbing" ("The Ambitious Guest"). Thus far the metaphor has remained explicit since tenor and vehicle are both present. However, once the tenor (pass) is left out, an *implicit* or *implied metaphor* is formed: The life blood of internal commerce continually throbs through the great artery of the Notch. A *symbol* can also be regarded as an implicit comparison, since here too the tenor is left to be inferred by the reader rather than stated. However, although the vehicle (artery) is used only figuratively and represents a single, simple tenor (pass), a vehicle that is a symbol (such as Flannery O'Connor's geranium or D. H. Lawrence's chrysanthemums) has an objective reality, may have several levels of meaning not easily paraphrased, and may be used and developed extensively throughout a work. Any concrete part of a story (object, action, or feeling) may thus have wider and more abstract significance than its literal meaning would suggest. An *allegory* is a work dominated by symbols that are interrelated to form an elaborate system of equivalencies designed to convert an abstract doctrine or thesis into a concrete narrative, such as Bunyan's *Pilgrim's Progress.*

Flashback: To interrupt a story's chronology by having an earlier scene or incident relived in a character's memory. Flashbacks may offer an unobtrusive means of conveying exposition. Note, for example, Flannery O'Connor's complex handling of flashbacks in "Judgement Day."

Foreshadowing: Giving a hint to the reader that anticipates future events or developments. Foreshadowing may create suspense or foreboding, as in "The Ambitious Guest."

Image, Imagery (images taken collectively): Any expression that appeals to one of the five senses, particularly through *similes* and *metaphors.* A story's *atmosphere* often depends on such sensory detail. See, for example, the second paragraph of "Sleepy."

Irony: Always involves a degree of incongruity or discrepancy between appearance and reality or expectation and realization. *Irony of statement,* or *verbal irony,* usually signifies saying the opposite of what one means or less than one feels (understatement). Verbal irony that is openly taunting or caustic is called *sarcasm.* However, sarcasm should not be loosely used in place of the much broader term irony. *Irony of situation* stems from an incongruity between what we expect to happen and what actually does happen, often the very reversal of our expectations. For example, in "The Ambitious Guest," the victims' attempt to escape the slide becomes the very act that dooms them. *Dramatic irony* occurs when the reader possesses particular knowledge of which one or more characters is ignorant. A second reading of a story may also create such dramatic irony, since foreknowledge often enables us to see the discrepancy between a character's expectations and the actual outcome of events.

Metaphor: See Figurative Language.

Motif: A recurrent word, phrase, *image,* object, or situation that through frequent repetition helps to develop and support the *theme* of a work of fiction.

Narrative Frame: A story within which one or more other stories is presented. Such a frame may merely serve as a perfunctory introduction or, as in "The Notorious Jumping Frog of Calaveras County," it may function as an integral part of the whole, as significant as the tale that it introduces.

Narrator-Agent: See Point of View.

Observer: See Point of View.

Plot: An author's selection and arrangement of events to form a meaningful causal pattern. "Sleepy" and "The Child-Who-Was-Tired," for example, tell the same basic story but by means of different plots.

Point of View: In fiction, point of view does not refer to an author's or a character's opinions but literally denotes the point or angle from which events are viewed: the focus of narration. All works of fiction are told by someone, a narrator who influences our responses either through his or her interpretation of events, selection of details, or style of presentation. A narrator without personal traits, such as in "The Ambitious Guest" or "Jewelry," is an *undramatized narrator,* often little more than a mask for the author. On the other hand, a *dramatized narrator* has a recognizable personal character and is called a *narrator-agent* if participating in the story (Jackie in "First Confession," Quentin in "That Evening Sun") or an *observer* if remaining outside the story. In either case, a dramatized narrator uses a *first-person point of view* that usually restricts the reader to what the narrator may naturally know. A *third-person-limited point of view* also confines the reader's understanding to what one character may know or feel, although such a *reflector* is not the narrator. In "Paste" we are restricted to Charlotte's thoughts and impressions, since the narrator will not give away any information outside the reflector's knowledge. James has simply imposed Charlotte's subjectivity on us so that our moment of recognition may coincide with hers. A *third-person omniscient point of view,* in contrast, may open any number of characters to inner scrutiny. In "The Basement Room," we are given revealing glimpses into the minds of most of the characters, as well as direct comments by the narrator. An *objective point of view,* on the other hand, such as that used in "The Killers," offers no inner view of characters or comments by the narrator but merely records what happens. See also *unreliable narrator.*

Protagonist: The main, or central, character of a work of fiction or drama. Compare with *antagonist.*

Pun: An ironic or humorous play on two meanings of the same word or two distinct words pronounced alike (homonyms) or similar in sound.

Reflector: See Point of View.

Reliable: See Unreliable Narrator.

Scene: Those parts of a work of fiction that depict a concrete action set in a specific time and place, which could conceivably be enacted on a stage. *Summary,* in contrast, is a more compressed and economical means of narration that may rapidly traverse great distances in space and time. Which parts of a story to present as scenery and which as summary is a crucial artistic choice. Compare, for example, Mansfield's and Chekhov's means of depicting the girl's workday in "The Child-Who-Was-Tired" and "Sleepy," respectively.

Sentimental: The evocation of emotions in excess of what the occasion justifies.

Setting: The place (locale) and/or time (historical period) in which the action of the story occurs.

Simile: See Figurative Language.

Structure: The arrangement of component parts that shape a work of fiction. See "Dry September," discussion question 1.

Style: The manner or mode in which writers express themselves or use language. Style involves such linguistic elements as *diction, figurative language,* rhythm, and sentence structure.

Summary: See Scene.

Symbol: See Figurative Language.

Theme: The dominant idea or thesis of a work of fiction that finds concrete expression in the plot.

Tone: The author's attitude toward his or her subject, reflected in and inferred from the story. Just as a speaker may use tone of voice to suggest an attitude of sympathy or contempt, so may a writer employ such elements as *diction, imagery,* and syntax to convey his or her feelings. Mistaking or ignoring an author's tone is one of the principal causes for misinterpreting works of fiction. Not to be confused with *atmosphere.*

Undramatized Narrator: See Point of View.

Unreliable Narrator: A *dramatized first-person narrator* or a *reflector* (see *point of view*) who, because of innocence, ignorance, self-deception, or delusion, misinterprets an experience or misjudges a character. *Reliability* does not usually refer to a character's honesty but to power of judgment. In such stories as "The Secret Sharer," determining whether or not the narrator is reliable is of paramount importance in arriving at a reasonable interpretation.

AUTHOR~TITLE INDEX

ABCDEFGHIJ–H–798